THE DILEMMA

Also by Penny Vincenzi

Old Sins
Wicked Pleasures
An Outrageous Affair
Another Woman
Forbidden Places

The Glimpses (short stories)

Penny
Vincenzi

The Dilemma

ORION

Copyright © 1996 Penny Vincenzi

The right of Penny Vincenzi to be identified as the author of this work
has been asserted by her in accordance with the
Copyright, Designs and Patents Act 1988.

First published in Great Britain in 1996 by
Orion
An imprint of Orion Books Ltd
Orion House, 5 Upper St Martin's Lane, London WC2H 9EA

A CIP catalogue record for this book is available
from the British Library

Typeset by Deltatype Ltd, Birkenhead, Merseyside
Printed in Great Britain by
Clays Ltd, St Ives plc

For Paul, with love. And even
more gratitude than usual . . .

Acknowledgments

I could not possibly have written this book without the expertise, patience and advice of a great many people; I would like to tell them how genuinely and deeply grateful I am.

Some of them wished to remain anonymous, but I hope will still be aware of my gratitude; could I thank publicly, please: Robert Young, Douglas Piller, Roger Holland, Alistair Sarre, Huw Jones and Lorraine and Roger Hill. And Sue Stapely who once again imparted not only much legal wisdom but a wealth of more far ranging information besides.

I also owe huge thanks to Carol Osborne, who keeps the home fires burning brightly and warmly; without her they would go out very quickly and creativity would grind to a halt.

I owe every kind of gratitude to my publishers: to Cathy Douglas and Sarah Binnersley, who sorted out the nuts and bolts; to Louise Page who publicised the book (as always) so tirelessly; to Claire Hegarty who dressed it up (as always) so beautifully; to Richard Hussey who supervised its production (as always) so calmly; and of course to Rosie Cheetham, who edited it (as always) so brilliantly, and somehow remained so soothingly and cheerfully unreproachful as a succession of delivery dates came and went. Essential and rare qualities!

And of course to Desmond Elliott, my Agent, who managed (as always) to make me laugh and to keep a sense of perspective through the very darkest, before-the-dawn hours; and last, but of course not least, to my daughters Polly, Sophie, Emily and Claudia who listened to my frequent wails of woe and continued to express a patient certainty that it would all be all right in the end.

Penny Vincenzi
Llangennith, Wales, July 1996

Prologue

July 1994

'All I want you to do,' said Bard with a kind of deadly patience, 'is say I wasn't in London that day. That I was with you. In the country. Or somewhere, anywhere. It's hardly a major lie. That surely isn't so very much to ask?'

Francesca looked at him for a long time, at this man she had thought she knew so well and loved so much, and felt panic rising so hard within her she felt physically near to choking on it.

Knowing that if she refused it would not only mean that Bard might go to prison, would certainly be convicted as a crook (albeit of the more socially acceptable variety), that her children would be branded for the rest of their lives as the children of a crook, that the entire family, including her own mother, would turn against her, that many other people would face disgrace and disillusion, that some other scapegoat would have to be found for what Bard had undoubtedly done; but it would also mean that she would be free of him, free of the fear, the pressure, the nightmare, the lies. And free to go where she really wanted to go, with whom she really wanted to be.

And she sat there in silence, staring at him, and she could see the desperation growing in his eyes, desperation and increasing antagonism, and fear added to her panic and she thought she could not imagine a dilemma more deadly, more dangerous, than the one she was in now.

Chapter One

Journalists writing about the Isambard Channings (and indeed Francesca Channing herself in semi-serious conversation) liked to say that Bard had proposed to her on television. This was not strictly true of course, but it made a nice story; what had actually happened was that she had been sitting in her pyjamas watching breakfast television and nursing a streaming cold one dark morning early in 1982, and there he had been sitting on a sofa with Anne Diamond, his brilliant dark eyes fixed intently on her (in the way Francesca was to come to know so well), talking about the rather high-profile deal he had just made, buying a small chain of cinemas via which he planned, as he put it, to get into movies ('Do you think Kevin Costner has a chance against me?'), and Anne Diamond had said in her artfully artless way 'And are you thinking of getting married again, Mr Channing?' and he had said no he wasn't, because he hadn't found the right person, but he wanted her to know he was always looking for the right person and if anyone watching might care to apply for the job, he would be delighted to hear from them. 'And that includes you, of course,' he said to Anne, who looked at him from under her eyelashes and said she would certainly consider it, but she was very busy at the moment, and Francesca had promptly switched off the television and sat down and written a letter to Mr Isambard Channing, c/o TVAM, Camden Lock, and said she would like to submit her application for the position he had outlined on the television that morning and was enclosing a CV (Name Francesca Duncan-Brown, Age 21, Marital status single, Educ. Heathfield and St James's Secretarial College, Current employer Gilmour, Hanks Gilmour, Advertising Agency, Personal Assistant to the Creative Director).

She did not receive a reply and forgot all about it.

A year later she was sitting in Reception at the agency (the receptionist having been struck down with what she called a stomach bug and what everyone else knew was the result of mixing vodka and coke – in the powdered rather than the liquid version, as Francesca's boss, Mark Smithies, rather neatly expressed it), when one of the smoked glass doors was pushed rather impatiently open and Bard Channing walked in. She was later to discover that he did everything impatiently, that the normal pace of life frustrated him; her first encounter with the quality made her edgy, almost anxious, as if she must be in some way falling short of his requirements.

He had an extraordinarily powerful presence; looking up at him, smiling her careful receptionist smile, Francesca felt as if she had received a mild slug in the stomach. He was quite short, probably no more than five foot eight or nine, heavily built, with a bullet-shaped head, the dark hair cut quite short. He was, she thought, almost ugly, and thought in the same moment that he was obviously hugely photogenic because on the television, flirting with Anne Diamond, he had looked quite good. Then he smiled and she realised that was the difference; the heavy features lightened, even in some strange way the big hawklike nose, and the dark, heavily lidded eyes became brilliant and alive.

'I've an appointment with Mike Gilmour,' he said. 'Channing is the name, Isambard Channing.'

His voice was lighter than she remembered, with an accent she couldn't quite place: almost London but almost something else as well, something softer, something slow and flat. Later she was to discover it was Suffolk, a legacy from three years as an evacuee in the war.

'Yes of course,' she said, and then, unable to resist it, added, 'I did recognise you. Please take a seat over there and I'll call Mr Gilmour.'

He did not respond to her remark, to her friendliness, simply moved over to one of the leather sofas, pulling out a sheaf of papers and ignoring the copies of *Country Life* that GHG kept in Reception to imply that their clients were country gentlemen rather than the City wideboys that most of them actually were. Francesca felt mildly relieved that he had never answered the letter, never mind interviewed her about the position.

He had come to see Mike Gilmour about possibly placing some of his business with the agency; the initial meeting went well. Two days later he was back.

Francesca was still in Reception. 'Good morning, Mr Channing,' she said, 'I'll call Mr Gilmour.'

'Thank you,' he said, and then, without moving, added, 'You seem much too bright to be doing that job. Why aren't you with all those other smart girls upstairs?'

Francesca felt an illogical sense of loyalty to the humble calling of receptionist.

'It's important,' she said, only just polite, 'this job. Giving a first impression of the agency. I like it.'

'Quite right,' he said unexpectedly. 'Quite right. If you're ever looking for a change of job, you can come and work for me.'

'That's very good of you,' said Francesca, feeling herself patronised and hugely irritated by him, 'but I did actually apply to you for a job once and you didn't even answer my letter.'

'Oh really?' said Bard Channing, and his voice was instantly alert. 'I'm extremely sorry. If you'd like to tell me when that was and the post you applied for, I shall take it up with Personnel. I don't like that kind of inefficiency.'

'It was a year ago,' said Francesca, 'and the post was that of your wife.'

'Oh,' he said and the eyes softened, sparkled into humour. 'Oh, that one. I got quite a lot of letters. I'm afraid it was rather a rash offer. I ignored them. It seemed the safest thing to do. I should have asked for photographs, then I would have known at least to interview you.'

'I wouldn't have thought personal appearance would be a prime requirement for your prospective wife,' said Francesca tartly. 'I'm disappointed in you, Mr Channing.'

'And what prime requirement would you think I'd be looking for?'

'Resilience,' said Francesca (God, this is going to get me fired).

'Possibly. Yes. Anything else?'

The brilliant eyes were fixed on her now, hardly smiling; oh well, she thought recklessly, it can't get any worse.

'A brain. Obviously. A good one. Possibly not too good.'

'Oh really? Why would you think that?'

'I – think you'd both find it rather trying. If she was cleverer than you.'

He glared at her, then suddenly laughed. 'Quite right,' he said. 'Absolutely spot on. Anyway, better get Gilmour at the double. I'm running late as it is.'

Francesca felt slightly sick when he had finally gone up in the lift, half expecting a summons from Mike Gilmour or at the very least Personnel. But nothing happened; she was just beginning to look forward to telling everyone else about it at lunch, when Bard Channing walked through Reception with Gilmour. He winked at her as he passed the desk, said goodbye to Gilmour and disappeared though the swing doors opening onto Brook Street. Francesca smiled sweetly at Gilmour, who nodded at her briefly and went back into the lift; she was in the middle of a complicated call from a photographic studio who had sent over the wrong prints and needed them back urgently when she looked up and saw Bard Channing standing in front of her desk. Some deeply perverse instinct made her finish the call before responding to him; then: 'Yes Mr Channing?'

'I enjoyed our conversation this morning,' he said. 'I'd rather like to continue with it. How would the Connaught suit you? This evening, six o'clock. In the American Bar.'

Francesca was so shocked she knocked a pile of envelopes off the desk. Shit, she thought, now he'll think he's made me nervous. Which he hadn't. Of course he hadn't.

'Well – yes – that would be – thank you,' she said, hating herself for her lack of cool, and then determinedly redeeming herself and the situation. 'Six is a little early. Could it be half past?'

'No,' he said, 'I have another meeting at seven. Six or nothing.'

'Six then,' said Francesca, 'thank you.'

And so it was that, having won the first, she lost the second round to Bard Channing.

'So tell me about yourself, Miss — what is your name?' he said to her, smiling over the champagne cocktail he had ordered for her. ('They make the best in the world here, and I mean the world'). 'How absurd that I don't even know your name.'

'Duncan-Brown. Francesca Duncan-Brown.'

'Miss Duncan-Brown. What a very upmarket name. Are you an upmarket girl altogether?'

'I don't know quite what you mean,' said Francesca coolly.

'Of course you do. I mean are you posh? Did you grow up in a big house and have a pony and go to an expensive boarding school? I, as no doubt you can see, am not posh at all, and I have a great fascination with the subject.'

'Yes, yes and yes,' said Francesca, laughing.

'How very nice for you. And do you have a boyfriend?'

'Yes, I do.'

'Is he posh also?'

'Quite, I suppose. I've never really thought about it.'

'I don't suppose you have. What's his name?'

'Patrick. Patrick Forster. And he works for Christie's. In the research department.'

'And did you know him when you applied for the job with me?'

'No I didn't,' said Francesca.

6

'I'm pleased to hear it. I don't like two timing. Not in a wife, future or otherwise.'

'Are you really looking for a wife?' said Francesca.

'I am. Are you really interested?'

'No, of course not!'

'Why of course? Could be interesting. Lots of perks.'

'Well – for a start –'

'Don't say it. I'm much too old for you. Quite right. I'm forty-three and you must be at least twenty years younger than that. Am I right?'

'Close. I'm twenty-two.'

'Greater obstacles have been overcome. Of which there are two very considerable ones, I have to say.'

'And what are they?'

'My daughters, for a start,' he said and there was genuine sadness now on his face, real pain in his voice. 'They're very young, Kirsten is eleven and Victoria only seven, and they have been very damaged, I fear, by an extremely unpleasant divorce. Kirsten in particular is intensely hostile to me, their mother is fast becoming an alcoholic, and the girls have to live with that on a daily basis. I hate it, but I don't know what I can do.'

'No,' said Francesca, 'no, I can see that.'

'How extraordinary I should be telling you this,' he said suddenly. 'When I've hardly met you, hardly know your name. You invite confidences, Miss Duncan-Brown.'

'Thank you,' said Francesca, unable to think of anything more interesting to say.

'Now then,' he said, his voice suddenly and deliberately lighter again, 'perhaps you'd like to tell me what you would do, if you found yourself hired for this position we were discussing earlier. How would you deal with my daughters? My difficult daughters?'

'Oh – I don't really know,' said Francesca. 'Try to leave them be, I should think, not pressure them, not try to take them over. They'd be bound to hate me. For a long time.'

'They would indeed. More than one putative Mrs Channing has withdrawn her application in the face of that hatred. The quality of resilience you put top of your list was certainly absolutely correct. What an extremely wise head you have on your very young shoulders.'

'Well,' said Francesca, 'it's easy to be wise in theory. Isn't it?'

'More wisdom. Yes, it is.' He looked at her thoughtfully. 'How do you like that silly job of yours? I still don't think it's worthy of you.'

'I don't really work in Reception,' said Francesca, smiling, relieved to be on slightly safer ground, 'but I wasn't going to tell you that.'

'Why not?' he said, waving impatiently at the waiter, ordering two more cocktails.

'Because it really annoyed me. You making assumptions.'

'I'm afraid,' he said, 'I make rather a lot of assumptions. It goes with my style of doing things. So what do you do, then?'

She told him.

'And you like that?'

'Yes, I do. One day I want my own agency.'

'Very ambitious. Why don't you start right away?'

'Well, because I don't know enough,' she said, laughing, 'and also there's the little matter of money. You need capital, to get going. We don't have any, me and my mother.'

'Or your father?'

'My father's dead,' she said briefly. 'He killed himself. Eight years ago. After losing an awful lot of money.'

He stared at her. 'He wasn't Dick Duncan-Brown, was he?'

'Yes, he was.'

'Good Lord. I knew him. Or rather I met him. A long time ago. I actually went to him for a loan. He turned me down.'

'Really?' she said. 'I must tell my mother. It would amuse her.'

'Why?'

'Because he knew so many people. And always backed the wrong ones.'

There was a silence. Then: 'Is there just you? Or do you have brothers and sisters?'

'Just me. My mother said I was so nice she didn't want to risk spoiling things. She's very good at saying the right thing,' she added, laughing.

'I like her already. Tell me more,' he said.

'She's great. My best friend. Corny I know, but she is. She's very stylish and very funny, and she's never let any of it get her down. She picked up all the pieces when he died, and went out and got herself a job selling dresses in Harrods, and was running the department in no time. We had a really nice house in Wiltshire and she sold it, just like that, no fuss, and bought a flat in Battersea, and she has a wild social life, better than mine, actually, and – well, that's her. She's called Rachel,' she added.

'She sounds very interesting. I'd like to meet her.'

'Why? I'm sure it could be arranged.'

'Well you know what they say.'

8

'No,' she laughed. 'What do they say?'

'They say first look at the mother,' he said, his eyes half serious, probing into hers, and then in a gesture that was almost shocking in its unexpectedness reached out and very briefly touched her cheek. 'And now I must go.'

She sat staring after him, feeling quite extraordinarily disturbed.

Next day, a phone call announced some flowers for her in Reception; she went down to two dozen red roses. Pinned to them, in his own writing, was a card from Bard Channing. 'I'd like to proceed to a second interview.'

Francesca crushed an impulse to phone immediately, hung on until the end of the day. Then: 'The flowers are lovely,' she said, 'but I really am suited. I told you. Thank you anyway.'

'I have another job for you,' he said.

'I know, but I don't want it.'

'Not that one. In my company, in the advertising department. We could talk about it. Over lunch perhaps. Tomorrow?'

'I'm busy for lunch. I'm sorry.'

'All right. Some other time, then.'

'Perhaps.'

He was hugely dangerous. She thought of his hand on her cheek and longed to see him again; she said goodbye and put the phone down quickly.

Two weeks went past, then: 'Francesca? This is Bard Channing.'

'Oh – hallo, Mr Channing. I don't really –'

'Please call me Bard. You calling me Mr Channing makes me feel old. Which you no doubt think I am.'

'Of course not.'

'Of course you do. Now I was only going to suggest that I took you to lunch. And that you brought your mother. I would really like to meet her.'

'Oh,' said Francesca. His power to discomfit her was impressive. Perversely she quite liked it. Patrick Forster spent his life doing the reverse, and it irritated the hell out of her. 'Oh, well I –'

'Good. Now I can do Wednesday this week, or Thursday or Friday next with a bit of juggling. I'm sure your mother is worth juggling for. Does she still work at Harrods?'

'No, she came into a bit of money and now she's a lady who lunches economically. Her description, not mine.'

'I like her more and more. And we can talk some more about your job at the same time.'

'Which one?' said Francesca.

'Either,' he said. 'They're both still available.'

Rachel and Bard ignored her through most of the lunch (the Ritz – he had told her to ask her mother where she would like to go). Rachel turned up looking dazzling in an ivory slub silk suit, an absurd red feathered hat set on her silvery fair hair, red high-heeled shoes, all new, Francesca thought, silly woman, bought to impress him. Her love for her mother did not blind her to her faults. She watched Bard Channing being most willingly charmed, delighted even, by her still considerable beauty, by her determined flirtatious flattery, her transparent efforts to please him, the superior being, the male, her large blue eyes fixed on his face, her small hand every so often touching his, and she sat, at first amused and then irritated, drinking rather too fast, feeling like a foolish schoolgirl, while they gossiped about rather remote mutual acquaintances, discussed times past, laughed at jokes she didn't understand and generally made her feel just slightly less important than the waiters. Towards the end of the meal she began to sulk, then finally (tears stinging behind her eyes) excused herself, saying she had to get back to work; they smiled at her briefly and returned to their conversation, scarcely seeming to notice her departure.

She was hurling things around her desk later that afternoon, nursing a very nasty headache, when Reception rang to say Mr Channing was downstairs. 'Tell him I'm in a meeting,' said Francesca, and rang off. Two minutes later the phone rang again; it was Bard Channing.

'I just wanted to say I could see that wasn't very nice for you and I'm sorry. It was just that I liked your mother so very much, and –'

'That's quite all right,' said Francesca coolly. 'You obviously have a great deal in common. Next time you can just go out on your own. Now you must excuse me, I'm very busy.'

'Francesca,' said Bard, and there was just the slightest touch of menace in his voice, 'Francesca, I really don't have time for this sort of thing. I get quite enough of it at home.' And he put the phone down.

It was five years before she met him again: he did not after all place his business with GHG, and Francesca left there after six months to go to another agency called Manners Bullingford as a trainee account executive. She was happy there, absorbed, felt she was actually getting somewhere; she became engaged with just the merest shadow of misgiving to Patrick Forster and married him on a sparkly April day in 1988 at Battersea Old Church, to which occasion her mother wore the white slub silk suit she had bought for lunch with Bard Channing. As a result Francesca thought of Bard rather more than she might otherwise have done; and she continued to do so from time to time right through the first three years of her marriage, which was perfectly happy but somehow not totally and properly satisfying. She and Patrick had a pretty little house in Fulham, two cats, a Shogun, gave dinner parties once a week and had sex rather less frequently.

At the beginning of 1988, Patrick announced that it was time they started to think about having a family; Francesca thought of her burgeoning career (she was now an account director at a highly successful, high-profile agency called Fellowes Barkworth); of the occasional doubts she still had about her relationship with Patrick; and slightly to her surprise of Bard Channing, and told Patrick she thought it was too soon. Patrick was clearly disappointed, but said he was prepared to wait a little longer.

It was a dark, heavy November afternoon when she was called into a meeting to discuss a new business pitch; the project was to raise the profile of and develop a corporate image for a property company which owned several of the new Amercian-style shopping malls; the budget was large, the creative work challenging. The company was the Channing Corporation.

The entire group was to go to Channing House the following week for a presentation; Bard Channing himself would not be there. 'Far too high powered,' said Mike Fellowes, the account director, 'but we're seeing a couple of his henchmen. Just as well, I imagine. From all accounts, Channing's a bit of a brute.'

'Not true,' said Francesca.

'You've met him?'

'I've met him.'

'Good Lord.'

She smiled round the group, and made it clear that was the end of the discussion.

She found herself dressing with particular care for the presentation at Channing House, in a new black crepe suit from Nicole Farhi. As she sat at the dressing table, doing her make-up, she looked at the picture of herself and her mother taken on some hotel terrace when she had been twenty-one, a lifetime ago it seemed, the untidily lovely person she had been then, the wild permed curls tumbled on her shoulders, the sunfreckled just-slightly-plump face grinning over the huge cocktail in her hand, and compared it with the sleek, glossy creature in the mirror, with her sharply etched cheekbones, her perfect creamy skin, her sleekly carved dark hair, and sighed just briefly, wondered exactly how happy she was and why indeed she should be wondering that today.

Bard was not there, as they had been told; the presentation went well. They were given a boardroom lunch; after it, Francesca excused herself and went in search of the Ladies'. And walking back along the corridor, found herself face to face with Bard Channing.

'Well,' he said, smiling at her with patent and extraordinary pleasure. 'Can it be true? Francesca! How very nice to see you. You look –'

'Older?' said Francesca, smiling.

'Grown up, I would say. And even more beautiful. I like the hair. Almost as much as I did before,' he said, and grinned at her.

'Thank you,' said Francesca carefully. It seemed the only safe thing to say.

'Why are you here?'

'I – my agency and I – are doing a presentation. To your publicity people.'

'Oh yes, of course. I knew I should have come. And are you now very important and high-powered?'

'Very,' she said, laughing.

'Good. The vacancy for that other job is still open by the way.'

'Oh really? I'm pretty well suited now. Thank you,' she added carefully.

'Does that mean you're married?' he said.

'Yes it does.'

'To the posh young man?'

'To the posh young man.'

'And are you happy?'

'Oh yes. Very happy.'

'Well,' he said, and there was a flicker of something behind the dark eyes, not as strong as pain, shock perhaps, distaste, 'well, that's extremely unfortunate. My fault entirely, I shouldn't have left it so long.'

'Perhaps not,' said Francesca. 'How are your daughters?'

'Oh – difficult. Particularly Kirsten. The battles increase. She's dying to be a model, and I've told her she has to go to university.'

'She could do both,' said Francesca, 'lots of girls do. You should let her try. It's a horrible life, unless you're incredibly successful, she'll probably be most grateful to get back to her studies. I'd have thought that would be much better than forbidding it.'

'Still wise,' he said, 'even though the shoulders are slightly older. I would never have thought of that. Could you recommend an agency she should go to?'

'Yes of course. Ring me at my office, here's my card, I'll give you a couple of names and numbers.'

'Thank you. I will. Nice to see you again.'

He smiled at her, and then looked at her, the dark eyes suddenly serious, and reached and touched her face, very briefly, as he had that night in the Connaught. It had the same profound effect on her.

He phoned her two days later for the numbers and then a week after that to tell her Kirsten had been signed up by Models One. 'And she's being almost polite to me. Can I buy you lunch to say thank you?'

She hesitated briefly, knowing full well what might happen if she said yes. She said yes, and it did.

She learnt much of him over that first lunch: how life had been at once kind and unkind to him, had given him a wonderful mother and a dreadful father ('Like me,' she said, smiling at him: 'Yes, but your father didn't knock you about,' he said, not smiling at all); had given him a brilliantly fast, deductive brain and a dyslexia so severe that everyone except his mother had thought he was ineducable until he was at least nine; had sent his father off to Germany where he had been most mercifully killed; had rained bombs down on the little house in Dalston where he had lived with his mother and grandparents, had killed the grandparents and put his mother in hospital and had then sent him off, an evacuee, to the wilds of Suffolk to some kind and gentle countryfolk, who cared for him until the war was over and had put some stability into his turbulent little history; had failed to provide him with a job, even in the surging boom years of the 'fifties, for who would take on a boy without a single examination to his name, and whose handwriting on letters was a laboured ungainly sprawl when so many grammar-school boys were filling in application forms in perfectly formed, neat handwriting; and had then finally set him down in a pub one night next to a rather pushy young estate agent who told him his firm was looking for a junior negotiator, and he had been taken on by them at an appallingly low salary, but on a fair bit of commission of which he had, to his own great surprise, earned rather a lot; and that he had then proceeded to the just-beginning-to-boom commercial sector. At this point the story became a little vague, but he had proceeded to junior partner there, and gone finally into business with one of his own clients (having found, through another chance meeting in another pub, a derelict building in the City for which he had been able to negotiate an absurdly good price), and from then on (he told her with a charming blend of arrogance and self-deprecation) it was all absurdly well-documented and she could read about it for herself. And of course she had read about it long ago and had had it revised for her before the presentation: the runaway success in the first property boom, when there had been so great a dearth of commercial property – largely due to the Socialist government that had tried and failed to stop speculative development with a rash of new planning regulations – his survival of the first big crash of 1973, his swift move into the Middle East, his going public in the 1980s, his continuing steady growth, and his situation now, settled comfortably around the middle of the *Sunday Times* list of the 250 richest people in the country, with a publicly quoted company worth £100m, 35% of which was still held by him and his partners in the company.

Fate had been equally quixotic with his personal life; had sent him first a wife who had been loving and lovely and had died after bearing him a still-born son, when their only other child Liam had been just seven years old, and a second who was as unstable and faithless as she was charismatic and beautiful; had endowed him with considerable charm and a magnetic sexuality, but really very little in the way of looks, and a height that could only optimistically be described as five foot ten inches and was actually nearer five-eight and a half.

He was (she also discovered that first lunch, and indeed consequently), while being without doubt the most arrogant, the most egocentric, man she had ever met (and, he told her, almost certainly the worst-tempered), also funny, intensely charming, and had a curiously old-fashioned chivalry about him; he walked on the outside of pavements, held open doors for her, saw her into the car if he was driving it himself, pulled out and pushed in chairs with great thoroughness.

'I've been well brought up,' he told her almost indignantly when she remarked on this. 'My mother, like yours, is wonderful. Although rather different,' he added, smiling, 'and I want you to meet her. She has to approve all my wives.'

'I'm not going to be your wife, Bard.'

'Francesca, you are.'

'I love you,' he said after a second, rather unseemly lunch (also at the Connaught) where he had spent much of the time with one hand on her thigh (evoking, with that simple act, a more frantic desire than Patrick had ever managed in the whole of their sexual lives), and the

14

other alternately holding hers or gently massaging the nape of her neck. 'I really love you.'

'Bard, don't be absurd, of course you don't love me,' said Francesca, clinging with some difficulty to the remnants of common sense, 'you don't even know me. And I don't know you,' she added, 'which some people would consider at least faintly relevant.'

'Oh,' he said, and there was a distant expression in his eyes, a darkness, a brooding that she had not seen before (but was often, increasingly, to see again), 'I am best not known too well. But I'm sure that doesn't apply to you. Come and live with me, and then I can get to know you.'

'Bard, I'm married.'

'So am I.'

'You're not. You're divorced. That's totally different.'

'I don't see why.'

'Of course you see why. You're being ridiculous.'

'I am not being ridiculous,' he said and he bent over and kissed her hand, one finger at a time, and then, his eyes very serious, very tender; 'I love you. Come to bed with me.'

'Now?'

'Why not?'

'Here?'

'Well, upstairs. I have a room.'

'Of course you don't,' said Francesca.

'Well, I could get one.'

'Bard no. Really. I can't.'

'Don't you want to?'

'No.'

'You're lying.'

'I'm lying,' she said, and laughed. 'But I'm not going to.'

It was another week before he finally talked her into bed; a week during which he bombarded her with flowers, with phone calls, with letters, with faxes, all declaring overwhelming, undeniable love; finally she heard herself on the phone to Patrick, telling him she had to attend an out-of-town meeting, and wouldn't be back till the morning.

'I'm sorry, darling,' she said, hating herself as she spoke what was nearly the simple truth, 'new client. You know what that means.'

And she lay in bed with Bard, in a four-poster bed in a hotel somewhere in Oxfordshire, discovering sex as if for the first time, discovering passion, discovering herself, hearing her own voice crying out, greedy, primitive, joyous, and knew she was properly in love.

★

It took a while to accept the fact, longer to tell Patrick. Guilt and affection for him consumed her; she struggled, toiled over her marriage for months, told Bard she must forget him and he her, left him three times and went back four. It was only when she was more by careless design than actual accident, pregnant with Bard's child, pregnant with Jack, that finally she knew she had to give in, bow to the inevitable.

The first year with Bard was extraordinary: a long, exalting exhausting series of dramas; of moving out of her small house, and into Bard's huge one (an absurd, excessive mansion St John's Wood which she initially hated and grew slowly fond of as she made it hers); of leaving her easy, undemanding life with Patrick and entering Bard's difficult, overwhelming one; of the change from being in command of her life to being out of control of it, from knowing where she was and what she was doing to having no idea at all; the change from affection to love, from sexual pleasure to physical passion; and perhaps most shattering of all of it, from woman to mother. Her own mother had told her, but had not been able (of course) to prepare her for the overwhelming, unexpected force of the love she would feel, the fierce and total commitment to this small being, who first took over her body and changed it beyond all recognition, subjected her to much discomfort and indeed considerable pain, and who then lay in her arms and gazed squintily up at her through dark eyes that were exactly like his father's, and proceeded from then to enslave her entirely, to disturb her sleep, invade her days, distort her emotions, and recentre her universe. Bard, who had seen it all before, was amused by her besottedness, at her surprise at it indeed, and even as he warned her that he was not to be moved too much aside, was still charmed by it. He was a most exemplary father to small children (while being a fairly disastrous one as they grew up), surprisingly patient, tender, insistent upon (once the birth was well over) being involved, oddly competent at such basic tasks as nappy-changing and winding, enormously proud not only of Francesca but at the change he had wrought in her.

'This time I'm going to get it right,' he said, bending over the crib, studying Jack's small, fierce profile, so like his own. And studying the larger one, thinking how wrong he had got it before, his fatherhood, how bad and how ongoing an effect it had on her life, Francesca hoped most fervently that he would.

Liam had been the greatest of the shadows over the new brightness of her life: Liam who had lost first his mother when he had been just a little boy of seven, and then his father who had rejected him, hated

16

him almost, for being alive when his mother was dead; Liam who had been sent first to stay with his grandmother and then away to school; who had hated the stepmother who had arrived quickly, far too quickly, after his mother had died; hated the new small siblings who had seemed to have so much more of their father's love; Liam who had grown to regard that father with a hard, unforgiving hatred.

He had many gifts, had Liam, a brilliant mind, romantically dark, brooding looks, and a most mellifluously beautiful voice, all infinitely suited to his chosen career at the Bar, but success had eluded him, for which he blamed fate, difficult clients, hostile judges, ruthless rivals and above all his father; 'He sponges off his wife,' Bard had said briefly, 'farts about waiting for his big break. She'd throw him out if she had any sense.' The hostility between the two of them was ferocious, and in that first year of her marriage Francesca met him only twice, once at the family party Bard had given to introduce her to the rest of his family, and once after Jack's birth when he had come, tautly polite, to the hospital with his wife to visit her. They had not come to the wedding; had made an excuse that they had to be away, and it was perfectly clear to Francesca that they had only come to the hospital because Naomi Channing (who clearly knew on which side her bread was buttered and who was doing the spreading) had seen it was in both of their interests to do so. Naomi was a high-flier, a banker, already in her own world famously successful; she seemed, Francesca thought, to regard Liam with a kind of proprietory distaste.

'Sweet,' she had said, looking briefly into the crib, 'a bit like Jasper, don't you think, Liam?'

Liam had said shortly he didn't think the baby looked in the least like Jasper, their own small boy, and excused himself, saying he wanted to have a cigarette; afterwards Francesca couldn't remember his addressing a single word to her directly.

The other children had come to visit her too: Barnaby charmingly pleased, little Victoria hugely excited, Kirsten with her already daunting beauty sullenly, silently hostile. Francesca had looked at her, tried and failed to make her smile, to respond, tried and failed not to mind, and wondered how long it would be before she managed to win Kirsten round. It seemed almost as impossible a task as befriending Liam.

The second year of her marriage was very different from her first. The changes, the dramas were accomplished; it only remained for her to adjust to them. Unlike her mother, Francesca found adjustment hard.

The first change was her own status, as Bard Channing's wife.

Nothing could have prepared her for it, for what she had become. Rachel had tried to warn her of that too, of the quite extraordinary transition from equal partner to trophy wife, and had failed entirely. Her function before had been to run her house, do her job, earn her salary, see to her husband's well-being. Of those, only the last still properly remained to her: and even that she was forced to share with a battery of staff, efficient, competent, familiar with the task as she was not, both at home and at Channing House. She had, to assist her in the running of the house in Hamilton Terrace, a housekeeper, a daily woman, a gardener, a nanny, and Bard's driver Horton who, whenever Bard was away, was available to drive her or Nanny about as well. There were, in permanent residence at Stylings, the house in Sussex, another housekeeper, another daily woman, two gardeners, one of whom doubled as groom for Bard's and the children's horses. All these people were in theory there to help and support her, to do what she asked them, to make her life easy; all of them in practice, troubled her, worried her, made her life more difficult. Nanny Crossman was a particularly unwelcome presence: middle-aged, uniformed, rigid in her views, she had looked after all Pattie's children and Bard had insisted she came back after Jack's birth, to take over where she had left off, as Nanny herself put it. Francesca had protested she didn't want a nanny, Jack was her baby and she was going to look after him herself and if she did have any help, she would prefer it not to come in a form like Nanny Crossman's, rather something younger, more fun, less daunting. But Bard had told her (correctly) that she had no idea how much she was going to have to do and how tired and disorientated she was going to feel, that Nanny could at least see her through the first few weeks and then they could review the whole thing. At the end of the first few weeks, she was still tired, still feeling disorientated, and caught in a Catch-22 situation, in which Nanny's competence emphasised her own lack of it and her ability to handle Jack grew horribly slowly. She continued to tell herself that it was a temporary situation, that as soon as she felt just a little more in command she would get rid of Nanny, hire some cheerful mother's help, and continued to feel not in command at all. This feeling was increased by Bard's making it very clear that from his point of view Nanny's departure would not only be unwelcome but highly unwise; and despite a few spirited exchanges on the subject, Francesca finally settled into an uneasy truce with him, the terms being that she would set the rest of her life in order and then they would review this particular aspect again. They never had.

She didn't feel much happier about the housekeeper at Hamilton

Terrace; Sandie Jerome had arrived soon after Pattie Channing's departure, had seen Pattie's children grow up, regarded them with a proprietory affection, and the house as almost her own. She knew Liam, had worked with Nanny, and admired Bard; she was totally familiar with every aspect of running the house, knew what the children and their father liked to eat and when, organised the rest of the staff, paid the bills, liaised with Bard's secretary over his arrivals and departures. She was thirty-something, blonde, well dressed, attractive in a hard way; she had been her own boss for years, was extremely well paid (like all Bard's staff), she had a flat in the basement of the house, a car, generous time off. She was polite, co-operative and helpful to Francesca while making it very clear indeed that Sandie knew precisely how important to her she was.

Francesca didn't like her, but she needed her; that Sandie knew she needed her, and in the early days could not have managed without her, made her uncomfortable, increased her own lack of self-confidence. The combination of Nanny and Sandie and what she knew to be their joint view of her was formidably unsettling. The actual day-to-day running of her new life was not too difficult; the woman who had run a big department in her advertising agency, who had charmed and entertained clients, manipulated colleagues, administered budgets, hired and organised staff, was scarcely going to be thrown by the organisation of even a couple of households. What did throw her was her new situation in life. She had lost, in the moment she became Mrs Isambard Channing, personal status, independence, and in her darker moments, self-respect. Skills, learnt and developed over years of professional life, were no longer relevant, talents, once recognised and fostered and highly valued, no longer required. Personal ambition had had to be buried along with financial independence; her purpose now, her function in life, was to support Bard, to be what he required, to do what he asked. Initially there was much to enjoy, it was fun: stocking the large wardrobe necessary to her role, redecorating the houses, being photographed and interviewed by the glossy magazines (their editors delighted to have a beautiful and intelligent new recruit to the ranks of page-filling wives), planning and giving parties. And she was genuinely, seriously, passionately in love with Bard, difficult as he was, arrogant, bad tempered, demanding; and even as their relationship moved from novelty to familiarity, from exploration to discovery, from questioning to certainty, she knew, intellectually, physically, emotionally that he was what she wanted, he was what she loved.

But as time passed, as Jack passed from infant to baby to small child, as the houses were completed, the clothes bought, the practical problems solved, she discovered the darker side to it all. She confronted frustration, boredom even, a sense of wasting herself, a terrible realisation that she was filling time rather than using it; she watched dismayed as people found her interesting only inasmuch as she was Bard's wife, her views only worth consideration insofar as they concurred with his. She resented being a possession, hated the view that she had won a great prize, was angered by the clear assumption that she had lost nothing. She found Bard's male colleagues and clients and associates patronising, their wives dispiriting (being quite happy to be trophies, clothes horses, spenders); she missed problems, struggles, challenge, except in relation to Bard; she loathed his dismissal of all she had been, his patent certainty that what she had become must be more than enough for her.

They fought over that, angrily; she would not give in, she said, would not become a lady who lunches, a devotee of the gym, a charity queen. She wanted to work again, she told him, to use her brain, her skills, be useful, independent. She went through all the arguments: that she was bored frequently, frustrated constantly, that she missed using her brain and her wits; that it was a high-powered, successful woman he had fallen in love with and surely he'd like that person kept alive; and then everybody worked these days, it was different from when he had married Pattie, even the most dazzlingly wealthy, well-connected wives had their own lives, sold jewellery, did up houses, ran antique businesses, why not she. And he would appear at times to be listening to her quite carefully, reasonably even, and then suddenly would start shouting at her, his face heavy with rage; would tell her he found it incomprehensible and more than that, insulting, that she should find being his wife, the mother of his children, frustrating and boring; that he had no interest in what other women, other wives did; that her job was to be his wife, that he'd spent too many years without support, without total commitment, that it was his most crucial need to have that. 'You want to cheat on the deal, is that it?' he said to her once at the height of a row. 'It's got a bit tough, so you're looking to change the terms. I'm sorry, Francesca, we have an agreement. If you want to renege on it, it's up to you. But I will not be a party to it.'

'Bard, what you're talking about is not a partnership,' said Francesca, her voice rising in an angry despair, 'it's prostitution.'

He had looked at her with what she could only describe as loathing, and then stormed up to his dressing room and slept there, leaving her as angry as he, but also shaken and to an extent ashamed, such was his power to manipulate her emotions and her thinking.

She did not suggest that she should work for anyone else, or even for herself in some freelance capacity again, but she did ask him once if she could not work in some way for him (thinking this would please him), have some role in his company, and was so angry when he found that laughable she left him, moved out with Jack into her mother's flat.

She did that twice; went back the first time because he came as near to an apology as he was capable of (which was not very near, but she could see what it cost him), and the second because she discovered she was pregnant again. She lost that baby painfully and sadly a few weeks later but his tenderness and sweetness over it made her forgive him.

Gradually, sorrowfully, she watched herself give in, become the wife he wanted, the one she knew she had to be if she loved him, as she knew she did.

She became involved in charity work, which was half satisfying at least, giving her causes the passionate commitment she had once given her job. She organised balls, auctions, lunches, gave interviews to journalists only if they would mention her causes. Her profile grew; she was, in her own way, her own world, extremely well known. People fought to have her on their committees, to get onto hers; she was ruthless in her pursuit of their names, their reputations, their money. Bard teased her about it in his good moods, complained about it in his bad, but recognised it was important to her, and struggled to make the compromise and at least accept it.

She even started to go, half amused at herself, half shocked, to the gym early every day, finding (reluctantly) in the physical exhaustion further release from her mental frustrations. She hated all the other physical recreations of her new circle, the tennis, the golf, particularly the sailing which Bard so loved; she had always loathed the water, was almost phobic about it. It disappointed him, and he showed it; he had several boats – a motor yacht moored at the villa he owned in Greece, a high-speed power boat in which he raced several times a year, a couple of sailing boats moored at Chichester – and adored them all; Francesca refused to go in any of them. 'You can't share much of what's important to me,' she said one weekend at Stylings when he was reproaching her for refusing yet again even to try sailing, 'and I can't share everything that's important to you. It's called marriage, Bard.'

'I suppose you mean your fucking career,' he said, and stormed out of the house for twenty-four hours, returning slightly shamefaced with an antique gold watch chain he knew she had wanted and a rare promise to attend her next charity dinner.

They fought a lot in the early years, both of them swiftly angry, awkwardly stubborn; gradually Francesca at least learnt to stay silent, to see a day, an occasion, a happiness in danger and to recognise it was not worth it, that she would not in any case win anything except her own self-respect, and that seemed increasingly unimportant.

He never apologised to her, for anything; he seemed incapable of it, the words physically refusing to emerge. The nearest he came to it was telling her he loved her, and that he could not even consider living without her; in time she came to recognise this for what it was and to find it almost acceptable.

He also had, she discovered with some dismay, an immense capacity for secrecy; it was almost pathological and she hated it. He would tell her he was going away, or that he was working late, or attending some dinner, and that would be the end of it; more information as to his destination, the subject of the meeting, the purpose of the .dinner, would not be forthcoming. It seemed to be born not of a desire to conceal, to confuse. His life and affairs were like some vast jigsaw puzzle, and pieces were handed out judiciously to people to put in place as best they could. She complained about it, struggled with it, fought against it, questioned him, demanded to know; only to be met by the blank look she had come to recognise, the crushing phrase 'you don't need to know that'.

'I will decide what I need to know,' she would cry, and he would look at her in silence and still say nothing; when she pressed him, he would tell her again that she didn't need to know, and he had no interest in telling her, it was tedious for him to have to go over it all interminably and not relevant for her.

'But I want to understand your business,' she would say, 'I want to share it with you,' and he would then say she couldn't possibly, it was too complex and in any case there was no point, he had no interest in her sharing it, and sometimes they would fight over it, and sometimes she would accept it, but either way, the information never came.

But the hardest thing of all was that she felt she was not actually the person he wanted; he had fallen in love with her when she had been someone else, someone competent, independent, successful, and now he wanted someone very different, was struggling to change her into that person. And that was very difficult to bear.

Physically, she found their relationship infinitely, endlessly joyful; Bard was a lover of great tenderness as well as passion, surprisingly and sweetly inventive, thoughtful, responsive. He could arouse her violently, almost painfully, could take her with him to depths and heights that the very memory of, days later, made her body throb and lurch with delight, but he could also draw her into sex, into love, slowly, gently, easing her into new territories, new discoveries of herself. In bed, at least, they were perfectly happy.

Her two great allies in those years were her mother, whose blithe pragmatism saw her through many dark and bloody battles, and her mother-in-law, whom she came to regard with a deep and grateful love. Jess Channing was seventy-eight, and Bard was her only child. She regarded him with a mixture of profound love and severe disapproval, treated him exactly as she had when he was a small boy, and was the only person in the world who could tell him what to do. She was a brilliant woman, self-educated, widely read, ferociously proud of her working-class roots, and ashamed of Bard's abandonment of them.

She lived alone in a small house in Kennington, wore unrelieved black, and was teetotal apart from Christmas when she sank, unaided, at least two bottles of port; she attributed her iron constitution to this fact, her ability at seventy-eight to walk, as she did, at least two miles a day, to clean her house single-handed from top to bottom every week (including laundering her own sheets, which she had done by hand until finally accepting a washing machine from Bard as a seventieth birthday present, and which she still regarded with some suspicion as second best), and working virtually full time as secretary in her local Labour constituency party in Vauxhall.

Bard had taken Francesca to meet her as soon as she had given in and agreed to marry him; Jess had liked and accepted her immediately for what she was, rather than viewing her as an adulteress and usurper of Pattie, as she might well have done.

'I don't approve of any of it,' she said, 'but you're clearly what Isambard needs, and I think you'll do him good. And those poor children of his,' she added.

After the wedding, when they were all back at the house, she had taken Francesca aside and asked if she was happy; Francesca had said she was, and Jess had taken her to her large, black-encased bosom and kissed her rather sternly.

'Good,' she said, 'that's as it should be. Now it isn't going to be easy, but you know that, I imagine.'

Francesca said she did.

Jess looked at her and smiled her sudden sweet smile. 'You must continue to be firm with him,' she said. 'He's horribly spoilt, and I don't seem to be able to do much with him any more. And any nonsense, come to me.'

She had not gone to Jess with any nonsense from Bard, feeling she would in fact be straining her maternal loyalty considerably, but she had on occasions gone to her with nonsense from the children, notably Kirsten. She knew it was admitting defeat, but she felt defeated; Kirsten's coldness, her ongoing silent insolence (open rudeness was more rare and punished severely by her father), was always unpleasant and often intolerable. Term times at least had been bearable when she had been away at school, but she had been removed from Benenden by Bard only just in time to prevent expulsion and had then been sent to St Paul's, and was unrelievedly at home. Francesca could see she was unhappy, that she had had a dreadful time indeed, but she felt powerless to help. Kirsten adored Jess, and confided in her, and Jess in turn eased a little of her hatred away from Francesca, and comforted Francesca over the hatred. It would have been much worse without her.

The other two were comparatively easy; Tory was sweet and malleable, and Barnaby had been charmingly manipulative from the cradle; by the time Francesca and Bard were married he was seventeen, and an unarguable, if unreliable, delight in her life.

Of Liam she saw nothing, heard nothing; felt only the weight of his hostility to Bard and she supposed to her; and thought of him hardly at all.

Chapter Two

It always amused Francesca when she heard women debating when and where their children had been conceived: the vagueness, the could-have-beens and might-not-have-beens. She had known precisely when Jack had been conceived and when she lay, released finally and mercifully from pain, holding the small Kitty Channing, she could look back nine months almost to the hour and say when had been her beginning.

They had been, she and Bard, in the house in Greece, just for a few days; he had been away on endless business trips – another of the things she had not envisaged when she had agreed to marry him, the loneliness of the long-distance wife – and they had been quarrelling a lot when he had been around. He had told her he wanted her all to himself again so that he could remember how much and why he loved her. It was the afternoon of their last day; they had been lying on the beach in the late afternoon, she half asleep on her stomach, sated with warmth, with sun, with new happiness, he reading, and he had reached out for her, she had felt his hand, his demanding, skilful hand, on her back, moving, smoothing down her, had turned, met his eyes, smiled at him, and without a word, stood up and walked into the house, into the cool, up to their room.

'Oh God,' he had said, as he came in, looked at her lying there, waiting for him, and moved across, lay beside her, turned her face to look into his.

'I love you,' he had said, 'so much, so very very much,' and she had leant forward and kissed him, slowly, carefully at first, then as his hands began to move on her again, harder; had felt the yearning, the longing, the hunger for him deep within herself, and as he met her hunger with his own, entered her, moved slowly towards her centre, she had felt the longing and the hunger at once increase and ease, had felt the lovely, flowing, unfolding of herself towards him, greeting him, had felt herself, with him, within a great arc of pleasure, bright, brilliant pleasure, and as she moved to him, with him, fiercer, harder now, she reached out and pushed herself higher, sharper, and the arc broke, shattered into dazzling fragments, fragments that she felt in every cell, every vessel, every particle of her, leaping, probing at her, and for a very long time afterwards, she lay afraid to move, feeling the pleasure so slowly, so sweetly, ebbing from her.

And felt, knew indeed, what had happened to her.

The pregnancy was not easy, though; she was faint, nauseous as she had never been with Jack, she had migraines, for the first time in her life, her back hurt, her legs ached, she bled a great deal, had to spend many weeks in bed, was sleepless, fretful, terrified of another miscarriage, with none of the joyful serenity she had looked forward to. Labour was short, but savage; she stayed at the house too long, remembering the endless tedium of Jack's birth (while forgetting the pain, which had in any case been very skilfully controlled), and then arrived too late for an epidural, was carried from the ambulance straight into the delivery room, was pushing the baby out, feeling she would break, tear into shreds, frightened by the pain, the harshness of it, unblunted by any drugs, for she hated the gas and air, it made her dizzy, sick, turned it away; heard herself groan, again and again, call out, try to be brave, push again, heard someone scream, a long, loud call of agony, and before she could realise it was herself, beg for relief, Kitty was there, slithering out, tiny, red faced, her little Grecian spring baby, born in London at Christmas time.

Kitty was a difficult baby, and Jack, a demanding, hugely naughty four-year-old, was difficult about her; for the first time Francesca was grateful for Nanny. Kitty fed reluctantly and did not take much at a time; she was small and gained weight very slowly. She slept in periods of what seemed more like minutes rather than hours, and she was restless and miserable even when she had just been fed. There was nothing wrong, both the paediatrician and the GP assured Francesca, she had passed all her tests, she was absolutely fine; she was just a difficult baby, it happened sometimes. Francesca took none of this reassuring information in, and fretted over her until even Rachel lost patience.

'You're just being ridiculous, darling, and you're doing her no good at all, never mind everybody else. She's a difficult baby, lots of them are. Do try to relax and enjoy her a bit at least.'

'It's all right for you,' said Francesca, 'she's not your baby, you've never had a difficult baby, a baby that worries you, you don't know how I feel.'

She looked at her mother over Kitty's head and frowned at her, and was astonished to see Rachel's eyes filled with tears. She had obviously been harsher than she meant.

'Sorry, Mummy,' she said, 'I didn't mean to be cross, I made Jack cry this morning as well.'

'It's all right,' said Rachel, brushing the tears slightly impatiently away. 'Sorry, so silly to over-react like that. I'm a bit tired myself I expect. What does Bard say about it? He's had enough children to be able to compare her.'

'Bard says if Nanny and Dr Hemmings and the paediatrician all say she's all right, she's all right. He said Tory was quite a bad baby and look at her now. And then he told me he was going away for a week. Bloody man.'

'Where to this time?' said Rachel.

'Oh, I don't know,' said Francesca vaguely. 'Sweden, I think.'

'Sweden! Doesn't sound like Bard.'

'No, I know. Maybe I've got it wrong. I find it very difficult to distinguish his trips one from another.'

'You should go with him more,' said Rachel briskly.

'Oh Mummy, don't start that please. I don't want to, and he doesn't want me too. All right?'

'Yes all right, darling. I'm sorry. Now then, are you going to have this little creature christened soon?'

'Yes, I am. End of March, I thought. She should have settled down a bit by then and the weather'll be nicer. I'm going to ask Tory to be godmother, she's been so sweet lately, I thought she might be pleased.'

'Good idea,' said Rachel.

She decided to hold the christening at Stylings.

'More suitable somehow to a christening, the country, I think, don't you, Bard?' said Francesca. 'And it's not as if it's a long way for everyone, only just over an hour from London. And the garden will be coming at least a bit alive. Is that all right?'

'Yes, if it's what you want,' said Bard. He sounded very distracted; he looked tired. Francesca debated asking him if something was wrong, if he was worried about something, and then rejected the idea. He wouldn't tell her anyway.

'I'd like to ask Pete Barbour to be Kitty's godfather,' he said a few days later. 'All right?'

Peter Barbour was the financial director of Channings; stiff, pompous with a slightly distant smile, a tendency to over-dress

(Rachel had once described Pete as wearing an eight-piece suit), and a complete inability to make any kind of light conversation.

'No, not really,' said Francesca. 'Why Pete, for heaven's sake? He's not even a proper friend.'

'He is to me,' said Bard shortly, 'and I would like it. And so would he.'

'But –'

'Francesca, please. It's not a lot to ask. I want him to be Kitty's godfather. And ideally I'd like Vivienne Barbour to be a godmother.'

'Oh, no,' said Francesca. She was prepared to fight very hard on this one. 'Not Vivienne. Not with that ghastly arch manner of hers, and her refined little ways – I'm sorry, Bard, but no. Pete if we must, but –'

'Well, who were you thinking of?'

'Tory.'

'Tory?' He was clearly pleasantly surprised. 'Oh, well, yes, that would be nice.'

'I thought so. She's been so sweet lately, and she's very fond of Kitty. And I just don't think anyone needs more than two godparents, one of each sex, any more than they need three parents. So – yes, we'll have Pete, if you really insist, but no, we won't have Vivienne.'

Bard scowled at her, but didn't say any more, and she knew that she had won.

Nanny was very disapproving of her decision to have the christening at Stylings. 'None of the other children were baptised in the country, Mrs Channing, I don't see why –'

'Well, a change is nice, Nanny, I think,' said Francesca briskly, 'and the drawing room at Stylings is beautiful in the afternoon sun. And we can have a huge fire and –'

'It will be very difficult to get the children down there,' said Nanny, as if Stylings were set in some remote equatorial region rather than at a point just off the A24. 'It will need a great deal of planning.'

'I think we can manage that,' said Francesca, 'just,' and went to discuss catering with Sandie.

Sandie was also rather unwilling to accept Stylings as a venue; it meant a lot more complication, she said, and she raised similar objections to Nanny about getting the food organised at a distance.

'Sandie, we're going to Sussex, not Outer Mongolia,' said Francesca briskly. 'There is the occasional shop down there, I believe. Now I'd like you to come down to help, if you don't mind, Mrs Dawkins isn't up to that sort of party, and –'

'Well, I suppose it can be arranged. As long as I can have another day off in lieu,' said Sandie, her rather hard blue eyes meeting Francesca's. Don't try cutting into my free time, that look said, I don't like you enough to make any concessions to you.

'Yes, Sandie, of course you can. And Horton will be coming of course, to see to the drink. He's very happy about it,' she added firmly.

Later when she walked into the nursery she found Sandie in there talking to Nanny: they both looked at her awkwardly, suddenly silent, and Sandie hurried out of the room. Discussing the christening, no doubt, and her inconvenient plans for it, she thought, and wished she didn't mind, could brush it aside or confront it. At least Horton had been helpful and positive. She sometimes didn't think she'd know what she'd do without Horton. He pervaded every area of the family; he was not only a driver, but he helped with the gardening in Sussex, waited at table at London dinner parties, and had even been known to baby-sit in a crisis. He was in his late fifties, small and extremely thin, and oddly good looking; he never laughed, seldom smiled, but had a wonderful sense of fun, a seemingly bottomless fund of bedtime stories for the children, and a nature of extraordinary sweetness. Jess frequently remarked that he was too good for this world, whereupon Bard would reply that if Horton left it he would follow him as fast as he possibly could. Horton had applied for the job of chauffeur twenty years earlier when Bard was just beginning to make enough money to pay for some props, as he put it; had worked rather trustingly for shares in Channing Holdings when things took a dive in the mid-'seventies and was now reportedly rather rich, but he steadfastly refused to consider retiring or even doing less work.

Tory was, as Francesca had hoped, very pleased to be invited to be godmother.

'I'd love it,' she said. 'I love Kitty, she's so sweet, thank you, Francesca.'

'That's all right. I'm so pleased. I'm afraid the godfather's a bit out of your age range, but never mind.'

'Pity Barnaby's away,' said Tory thoughtfully. 'He'd have been ideal.'

'Er – yes,' said Francesca, flinching slightly from the thought of the unreliable, feckless Barnaby, so badly behaved, even while so infinitely agreeable, entrusted with the spiritual wellbeing of her innocent baby. He was currently roaming the world, rucksacked, his in-between-university-courses trip. (Or rather until some other place of further education could be persuaded to take him on, the Universities of both East Anglia and Plymouth having told him regretfully that they didn't feel a great deal was to be gained from their further association.)

She was missing Barnaby; he might be lazy, unreliable and manipulative, but he was charming, and genuinely sweet natured. She sometimes wondered how Bard's genes had managed to produce him at all. He was also very sexy, of course, and very good looking; Rachel had more than once told Francesca that given a straight choice between Bard and Barnaby, she would not have known which way to turn. Francesca, while insisting she did not see him quite in that light (having been over the past five years rather too intimately involved in keeping the details of his hugely active love life, various other over-indulgences, some of them illegal, and his disastrous scholastic record, from his father), still admitted that when Barnaby was around, life was undoubtedly more interesting and a lot more fun. But he wasn't around and certainly wouldn't be on 27 March, the day of the christening, and perhaps it was all to the good; he would only have drunk far too much, or started chatting up their friends' wives, or encouraged little Jack in some terrible naughtiness. Jack adored Barnaby; he said he wanted to be him when he grew up.

'Tory,' she said now, 'could you ask Kirsten for me? She might be more likely to come if you did. Your father would be so pleased.'

'Yes, of course I will,' said Tory, flushing slightly. They both knew that Kirsten would be too busy, would be unable to make the long journey from London, even in the new Golf GTi her father had given her for her twenty-first birthday, but she had to be asked. And she just might say yes.

Kirsten didn't say yes.

Francesca also sent an invitation to Liam and Naomi; a stilted, third-person refusal came back, in Liam's rather flamboyant handwriting. Just to impress on us that it's him who doesn't want to come, rather than Naomi, thought Francesca, throwing it in the bin before Bard could see it and become angry or alternatively upset. She was never sure how mutual the dislike between Bard and Liam was; Bard would never discuss it.

'So I ask you all to raise your glasses to my new daughter. And of course her beautiful mother. Kitty. Francesca and Kitty.'

Bard's voice was rich, heavy with emotion; his eyes, the brilliant dark eyes, fixed on her and Kitty were thoughtful, tender. Francesca smiled back at him, and thought that in spite of everything, if you

30

could see and feel happiness it would be this moment in this room, a bright, warm, smiling thing, set down in the long, light drawing room, with the quirky spring sunshine dappling the walls, great vases and bowls of flowers everywhere, all yellow and white, lilies and daffodils and narcissi and freesias, and the roomful of friends, smiling with such truly genuine pleasure and affection at the three of them, herself and Bard and the tiny Kitty, her small face relaxed most determinedly in sleep, lying peacefully (for once) in her mother's arms, dressed in the myriad layers of ivory satin and lace that had adorned Francesca and her mother and her mother's mother and so on back for almost a hundred and fifty years of christenings.

There were shadows over the brightness of course; Kirsten's absence, Liam's absence; but Tory had behaved so beautifully all day, been charming to everyone, and now was sitting cuddling Jack on her knee, careless of the effect his already filthy sailor suit was having on her extremely pale pink silk dress.

She was so lovely, Tory, Francesca thought, looking at her, smiling, with her father's dark eyes and her mother's fair hair – and there was another shadow; they had heard only that morning that Pattie was once again in the clinic, after a bad lapse into her alcoholism. Bard, as always on hearing this news, had flown into a violent rage, said why couldn't Pattie get a grip on herself, it was outrageous, hard on him, impossible for the children, and had gone out to the stables and saddled up his horse and gone for a long ride. He came back hot, exhausted but calmer. What upset him, in truth, Francesca knew, was that a goodly proportion of Pattie's problems had been brought upon her by himself and his behaviour and he knew it; she sometimes wondered if she might not in time become an alcoholic too.

She caught her mother's eye on the other side of the room, where she stood working womanfully at flirting with Peter Barbour. Her mother saw her and winked almost imperceptibly at her. Jess, almost colourful today with a white shirt under her black suit and a red feather in her black hat, raised her tankard of water to her and smiled.

'Right then,' said Bard, as the glasses were lowered again, and the room smiled expectantly. 'Cake, I think now ... ah Horton, yes, put it there.'

The cake was cut, was passed round; people moved back into cocktail party mode. Francesca headed for her mother, to relieve her of Pete Barbour, but Bard had got there first.

'Rachel, have some cake. And some more champagne. You look absolutely gorgeous. As always.'

'Oh Bard, for heaven's sake. Don't waste good flattery on me. You know I don't need it. Francesca my darling, the baby's just puked down that heavenly robe. Shall I go and change her, or at least find Nanny?'

'No, Mummy, it's all right. I'll do it. You stay here and charm people. And keep Jack from doing anything too awful and upsetting his father, if you can. He's on a short fuse, even if he is full of fatherly pride.'

'And husbandly. You're a clever girl. Give me a kiss.'

Francesca obediently offered her face, breathing in the cloud of Chanel No.5 that always so determinedly surrounded her mother, smiling into the drift of osprey fathers from her absurdly excessive pink hat. It was so like Rachel to say that, to say exactly the right thing at exactly the right time, to tell her she was clever. Not lucky, as most people would, and frequently did, just clever. Anyone could be lucky. But actually, she supposed, moving through the crowd of guests, smiling, excusing herself with the now wailing Kitty, she was lucky. By any standards. And happy? Yes, of course she was. 'All right, Kitty,' she said, planting a kiss on the indignantly scarlet little face, 'we're going to find some food straight away.'

As she passed Bard's study, she heard the phone ringing insistently. That was funny; he must have forgotten to put the answering machine on. Or maybe someone – no prizes for guessing who – had taken it off. Tory had said repeatedly that she was expecting a very important and highly confidential call. She had made it sound as if it would be from a member of the Royal Family or the Cabinet at the very least. A new boyfriend, no doubt. Or maybe it was Barnaby; he might be calling from some beach or other … It was part of his highly dangerous charm that he managed to remember special occasions and to mark them with phone calls, letters, flowers for Francesca, for his grandmother, for Rachel even; Jess, who disapproved of him totally, was nonetheless always won over by his unfailing remembrance of her birthday, even from the middle of the Himalayas or the heart of the rainforest.

Francesca went in, juggling with Kitty and her frills, frowning slightly as she tucked the receiver under her chin. She looked round as she did so, and saw Jack in the doorway, a piece of cake in each hand, blowing her a kiss, and her heart contracted with love.

'Hallo?' she said. 'Hallo. Four-nine-one.' There was a long silence: it sounded a bit like an intercontinental connection. 'Barnaby?' she said. 'Barnaby, is that you?'

It wasn't Barnaby, but it was a voice she recognised; recognised with a pang of distaste, a carefully elocuted voice, slightly loud: 'Oh, is that Francesca? Francesca, this is Teresa Booth here. I wonder if I could speak to your husband?'

Teresa Booth, thought Francesca: of all people, at all times. Damn, why did she have to call now? Teresa Booth who was newly married to Douglas Booth, Bard's partner, founding partner of Channings, Teresa Booth whom Bard loathed, who put him in a foul mood within minutes, Teresa Booth whom Bard had absolutely refused to ask to the christening.

'I'm sorry,' she said, 'he's awfully busy at the moment. Can I get him to call you back? We've – well, there are a few people here.'

'No, I'd really like to speak to him now,' said Teresa Booth. Her voice was polite, but very firm; it carried an unmistakable, slightly odd determination.

'Well,' said Francesca, equally determined, 'I really can't get him just yet. I'm so sorry. But I will get him to call you as soon as possible. Or can I take a message?'

'No, dear, no message. And I would like to speak to him before – well, let's see, before seven. Duggie and I are going out then.'

'Yes, all right,' said Francesca, feeling irritation rise up, gently but unmistakably, deep within her. 'I'll see what I can do.'

'Please do, dear. He'll know what it's about. I suppose it's the christening party going on, is it? I hope it's been a success.'

'Yes – yes it has. Thank you. Not really a party, of course, just a family gathering. Well, goodbye, Teresa.'

'Goodbye. I'll expect to hear from Bard shortly.'

Awful woman, thought Francesca; and then thought anxiously she should have insisted on inviting them, gone against Bard's wishes, Douglas had been with Bard for so long, and of course if he'd still been married to dear Suzanne, she would have done. Suzanne, Douglas's beloved wife of twenty years, had died suddenly of cancer, and he had married Teresa shockingly swiftly, within six months. 'He's lonely,' Bard had said, in an endeavour to explain it to himself as much as anyone else and failing; they had all loved Suzanne, gentle, sweet Suzanne, and she too had been infinitely kind and welcoming to Francesca. And Teresa was so totally the opposite, harsh and brash and making it plain she disliked Bard as much as he did her. And so they had agreed not to invite either of them today. Since it was very much family. Well, almost. Family and godparents. And very old friends. That did just about make it all right. Just.

All the same, it was unfortunate Teresa should have phoned today, this afternoon. Francesca put the phone down, and something very faint, like a tendril of cloud in a clear sky, drifted across her happiness, the brightness of the day. She went on up the stairs slowly, holding Kitty to her, wondering what it was, what thought or memory, that was troubling her. And then she realised and smiled at the absurdity of it: it was the bad fairy, the wicked uninvited fairy, intruding on the guests at the christening of the Sleeping Beauty, causing trouble, making threats...

Francesca slid off her red jacket, unbuttoned her cream silk shirt while Kitty roared; they had got off very lightly in the church, only the merest whimper, the non-stop feeding of the morning had paid off. She was still an exceptionally demanding little baby: miserable, she could fairly be called, only it did not seem an adjective appropriate to something so precious, so much beloved. And in spite of the endless feeding, she was still gaining weight so very slowly. Jack had demanded his food as noisily, eaten as greedily, but in between times he had slept and grown. Obviously there was nothing really wrong, but maybe if Kitty didn't start gaining weight soon, she really would take her to see another paediatrician; she knew they all thought she was simply neurotic – the GP, Nanny, Bard – but nonetheless she wanted the faceless, shadowy fears that haunted her sleep (or such sleep as Kitty allowed her) and even sometimes her days, banished properly, efficiently, knowledgeably. She could handle a difficult baby, as long as difficult was all she was; but she wanted the pronouncement 'difficult' to be official. Looking down at her small daughter now, her heart contracting with love, enjoying the sensation of the little mouth working at her breast, she felt her small hands, so cold as always, and pulled up the frills to check her feet, but they were warm for once; for the hundredth, the thousandth time, she told herself Bard was right, she was indeed being neurotic, and set her mind to more practical matters such as how many people might wish to stay on for supper, and who might drive Jess home if she wished to be among them. Jess had a phobia about sleeping anywhere but her own high, hard, horribly uncomfortable bed; it was a souvenir of her work for the Red Cross canteen at St Thomas's Hospital during the war, and she resisted totally any attempt to acquire anything newer or more comfortable. Well, if no-one else would take her, Horton would, and then he could go to the house in St John's Wood.

She heard footsteps on the stairs, looked up to see Bard in the doorway. He was looking at her as he always did, very intent, unsmiling, his dark eyes fixed on her in total attention.

'Are you all right?' he said, moving over, kissing the top of her head.

'Yes, I'm fine. Thank you. Kitty was getting tired of the party. She's been very good.'

'It's a very nice party.'

Francesca smiled at him. 'I know.'

'I love you,' he said.

He bent down lower, kissed her briefly but hard on the mouth. Francesca responded to him, to the kiss, felt it not only on her mouth but echoing through her, sweet, disturbing, strong. After six years of Bard, of the difficulties of him, she was still helplessly moved by him sexually.

Kitty, sensing a distraction from the job in hand, in her mother squirmed, lost the breast, started to wail; Francesca laughed.

'Now look what you've done. Poor baby. Oh, Bard, there was a call for you, I'm afraid. From Teresa Booth. She was very insistent. She said she'd like to speak to you before seven.'

'Oh God,' he said, 'bloody woman.'

'But you will ring her?'

'Of course I'm not going to ring her. Well, in my own good time, possibly. Certainly not now.' And he turned away and walked over to the window, stood with his back to her, looking out.

'We should have asked them, really, Bard.'

'No we shouldn't,' he said.

'Well, she's obviously put out.'

'I don't give a fuck if she's put out,' he said and he turned round and looked at her, and it wasn't just irritation on his face, in his dark eyes, it was anger, raw, hardly suppressed. Francesca looked at him thoughtfully.

'You don't know what it was about? She said you would.'

'No I don't,' he said, 'of course I don't. How should I?'

'I don't know,' said Francesca. 'I don't know anything about your business affairs. Do I?'

'What makes you think it's business?'

'Well, Bard, I certainly hope it's business. I don't want you developing some intimate relationship with Teresa Booth.' She laughed, was looking down at Kitty as she spoke, but he didn't laugh and when she looked up, he wasn't smiling, was glaring at her.

'Don't be so bloody ridiculous,' he said.

'Sorry!' said Francesca. 'Bad joke.'

'Yes it was.'

'Sorry,' she said again, anxious to defuse his wrath, to placate him, restore his earlier mood; this was no time, no occasion for a row. 'But I do think you should ring her. She really was very pressing.'

'Yes all right, Francesca, I'll ring her. When I have a moment. We do have a houseful of guests. You going to be long?'

'No, I don't think so.'

'Good.' He hauled himself back into good humour with a visible effort. 'Well, no doubt she'll call again, if I don't manage to obey her summons. I'd better get back to the party.'

'Yes. I'll be down in a minute.'

Francesca looked after his broad back thoughtfully. It wasn't possible to know Bard as intimately as she did without having a very shrewd idea when he was lying.

Rachel was greatly enjoying the christening. She enjoyed most of the social occasions Bard Channing involved her in. She enjoyed Bard himself and his presence in her life rather more than she knew she should. She was at sixty-one still highly attractive, and she knew Bard recognised that fact and even at times responded to it: there had been one unfortunate occasion when Francesca had been very pregnant with Jack, and Rachel had been staying with her in Sussex. Bard had come home unexpectedly from a trip abroad, and after Francesca had gone up to bed he had got out the brandy bottle, and they had started talking. Rachel thought, Bard told her, like a man, which clearly he saw as a huge compliment and indeed she took as one; but she realised things were getting a little out of hand when she suddenly felt his hand caressing the nape of her neck, and felt herself light with longing to respond. 'Time for bed, I think,' she said briskly, 'alone,' and went very quickly up to her room where she lay awake for a very long time, half longing for and half dreading his hand on the doorhandle. In the morning they were both suffering from bad hangovers and remorse, but something had remained from the encounter, an intimacy, a sense that they had become closer than they actually had, and a very warm, joky, sexy friendship. Rachel knew that at times, in her lower moments, Francesca found this at best irritating and at worst depressing.

And Francesca did have lower moments. Rachel, whose philosophy of life was rather more robust than her daughter's, found them as much irksome as worrying, given what most people would have regarded as Francesca's outstanding good fortune, but she did her best to help her out of them without becoming too involved. She had a horror of being an interfering mother-in-law. She had actually had a horror of being a mother-in-law altogether, with all that it implied; she watched her youth moving relentlessly away from her with genuine pain, mixed at times with sheer panic, but Bard was as near to an ideal son-in-law as was possible, not least because he was her junior by only a few years and they could both make jokes about the whole thing, and in much the same way, and while becoming a grandmother had been truly appalling in theory, it was surprisingly all right in practice, since people spent their whole time expressing charming astonishment that she could possibly be old enough to be one at all.

And the children were so lovely, both of them, especially little Jack – Rachel had an innate preference for males of any age – and it was certainly a delicious relationship, with its inbuilt facility for her to withdraw when the going began to get a bit too tough, and she and Francesca had certainly become closer as a result of it.

She looked rather nervously round for the Barbours; she really didn't want to get involved with the terrible Vivienne, Pete was bad enough. But they had moved over to Jess and were talking to her; Rachel saw Victoria standing near her, and decided even she would be an improvement conversationally on the Barbours. She was really very sweet, Victoria, and she had behaved beautifully that day, looking after Jack and chatting prettily to everyone. She was a lot nicer than her sister. Now there was a nasty piece of work. Tough as they came. What possible harm could it have done her, even given her loyalty to her wretched mother, to have come today for a couple of hours to make her father happy? He was so good to her: what she really needed was her bottom smacking. Exceptional to look at though: even Rachel, usually determinedly unimpressed by female beauty, found Kirsten quite dazzling. Where Victoria was simply and charmingly pretty, Kirsten was beautiful. She had somehow in her fine, fair, classically perfect features, her large green eyes, her wealth of rich, ripe gold hair, something of her father's strength and individuality. Her nose might be straight and perfect, but it was strong, chiselled, her mouth curvily perfect but heavily sensuous too, her jaw fine but remarkable in shape, almost square, her head set proudly on her long, white neck. She was tall, half an inch off six feet, her hips narrow, her legs ultra long, but her bosom fine and full; she had lovely hands and, more unusually, beautiful feet, narrow and long; and she had a most memorable voice, deep and throaty, almost rough in its texture. Rachel had always considered, quite detachedly, that Francesca was beautiful, but beside Kirsten she looked almost ordinary.

The room was thinning out now. Rachel looked at her watch: almost five-fifteen, it would soon be down to family only and the opportunity for a casual, careful word with Bard would be lost, he would be moving away now, his relentless mind leaving the party, moving back onto the only thing that properly engaged it, his company, and all its interminably attendant problems and pressures, and quite unapproachable. She would have to be quick. She moved forward to where he was saying goodbye to Peter Barbour, and tapped him gently on the arm.

'Bard darling. Could we have the quickest word?'

'Yes, of course we could,' he said swiftly, as always courteous and charming with her. 'Business or pleasure?'

'Both. Of course,' said Rachel. 'But I don't want to get into details, not now. I have a little proposition, and I'd like your opinion on it.'

'All right,' he said after a moment's silence. 'Let's have breakfast one morning next week. That suit you? Ring Marcia in the morning, no use me trying to think of a day now, but I'll tell her you're calling and to fix it. That all right for you?'

'Yes of course. Thank you, Bard. I'd be so grateful.'

That was perfect: ringing Marcia Grainger, Bard's appallingly efficient secretary, without warning was fatal, she always gave an icy-smooth brush off, conveying the clear impression that anyone lower than the Prime Minister, the governor of the Bank of England or just possibly the heir to the throne, had no real business even dialling Bard's number, and certainly absolutely no chance of gaining any kind of access to him. But Bard would tell Marcia to expect her call, he never forgot anything like that, and then something could be fixed. Rachel gave Bard the briefest pat on his arm, the lightest kiss on the cheek, and went off in search of a piece of christening cake, thinking how extraordinarily charming and considerate Bard could be when he chose. He was actually, she knew, acutely sensitive, beneath the arrogance; and she wondered not for the first time that afternoon how much it had hurt him that Liam had not been there. Kirsten was just a spoilt, silly child; Liam was thirty-four years old and really should have at least begun to grow up.

'Liam,' said Naomi, 'you're thirty-four years old. You really should begin to grow up.'

Liam looked up at her from his desk. She was standing in the doorway of his study, holding a tray with two large whiskies on it and a newspaper tucked under her arm, and she had a very determined look on her face.

'And in what precise way did you think this growing up should be manifested?' he said coldly.

'Getting a job,' she said, setting down the tray on his desk, picking up one of the glasses. 'Earning some money. Supporting me a bit for a change.'

'Naomi, do we really have to go over all this again? We agreed that until I established myself you would –'

'Yes, well everything's just changed, Liam. That agreement isn't very relevant any longer.'

'I'm sorry?'

'I've been made redundant.'

'What?' said Liam. He picked up the other glass, took a large slug of the whisky, waited for the room to steady. It didn't. 'What on earth do you mean?'

'I mean what I say. I've lost my job. As of – well, three months from tomorrow. Well, actually, tomorrow.'

'But Naomi, nobody loses their job on a Sunday.'

'I have. Dick just called, it was really good of him, he just got back from New York and said he didn't want me to have to cope with the shock in the office. Rationalisation, it's called. The Americans. You know? That old chestnut. Six of us are out. Including Dick actually.' She smiled at him, slightly awkwardly, looked down at her own glass. He realised it was shaking, and managed to feel a touch of sympathy mixed with his own panic.

'Naomi, I'm so sorry,' he said carefully. 'How awful for you. But –'

'Yes? But what?'

'Well, I was going to say I'm sure you can get something else.'

'Well, Liam, I'm not so sure, I'm afraid. It's bloody tough out there. And anyway –'

'Anyway what?'

'Liam, we're in a mess already. Aren't we? Even with my salary.'

'I wouldn't say that,' said Liam heavily.

'Of course we are. We have negative equity on this house, the children's school fees are roaring up, you want Jasper to board next year, the overdraft is looking hideous, the bank are getting extremely edgy, you earned – what, about nine grand last year –'

'Naomi, I do know all this. You remind me of it quite often. Could I remind you, as we're running through this rather familiar script, that when I establish myself –'

'Liam, you've been establishing yourself for almost ten years. I think it's time you faced the fact it isn't going to happen.'

'Well, thank you for that vote of confidence.'

She ignored him. 'And anyway, if I'm going to be out of a job, something drastic has to be done. And I think it's your turn and it's time you did it.'

'Oh really? And what would you like me to do? Give up the Bar, go and work in McDonald's perhaps –'

'I think you should go to your father.'

'No, Naomi,' said Liam. 'I will not to go my father.'

'Why not?'

'You know why not. It is absolutely out of the question.'

'Well, I'm sorry,' said Naomi, 'but I don't see why you shouldn't. Have you seen this piece in the paper today?'

'No,' said Liam.

He had, of course; had read it over and over again, tasting the old bitterness almost physically, filled with hatred towards them all.

'Well, I'll read it to you. "Kitty Channing, born last December to Francesca, 'Bard' Channing's stunning third wife, will be christened in Sussex today, in the church near Stylings, Channing's magnificent Queen Anne country retreat. Kitty represents the latest jewel in his already glittering crown, born as she was in a year that saw him move into the top third of the elite *Sunday Times* Richest People in Britain list. To mark Kitty's birth, Francesca was given –" oh I can't go on, it makes me feel sick. You must get the drift. And meanwhile we have to cancel our summer holiday and I have to go crawling round again with my CV. It's ridiculous, Liam, and I've been sitting up there thinking and there really there is absolutely no reason why he shouldn't at least lend us some money to tide us over. Now are you going to go and see him, ask him for help, or shall I? That might be better, at least I won't start hurling insults at him halfway through the conversation.'

She sat down on the sofa opposite his desk, her grey eyes very steely as she looked at him. She was wearing jeans and a denim shirt; her long red hair trailed over her shoulder in a plait. She had no make-up on. She didn't look like a high-flying, international banker, Liam thought, and then with a lurch of his guts, realised she wasn't one any longer.

'Look,' he said carefully, 'look, let's think about this a bit longer.'

'Liam, we don't have time to think a bit longer. I've been doing sums down there, even before Dick called. Carla has to go, immediately, whatever happens. It's ridiculous, shelling out nearly two hundred pounds a week for a nanny when even Hattie is at school half the day. But if the bank get wind of this they'll make us sell the house.'

'Oh stop this,' he said wearily. 'I get so extremely tired of it, of having my nose rubbed in how totally dependent we are on your income, your dazzling success. I've been doing my best, for God's sake.'

'Well, your best isn't good enough, and my success seems to have dimmed a bit. Unfortunately for all of us. I'm sorry, Liam, and I know how much you hate him, or say you do, but I think you owe it to me and the children to go and ask him for at least a loan. And I warn you, if you don't do it, I certainly shall. I'm going to read to Hattie now. I'll see you later.'

Liam watched her go out of the door and then picked up the paper, looked at the picture of Francesca holding Jack at the last christening, looked at his father standing there with her, his arm round her, champagne glass in his hand, smiling at the camera, looked at the caption to the picture: 'Channing and the jewels in his crown', threw it suddenly, viciously across the room.

'I hate you,' he said, quite quietly, staring at where it had fallen. 'Christ, how I hate you.'

Chapter Three

Francesca watched the Booths' silver XJS coming round the corner of the drive with some foreboding. It wasn't just the thought of the next few hours which depressed her, it was the effect that four hours of Teresa Booth's company would have on Bard's temper for the next twenty-four. For which much of the blame would be laid at her door, because it had been her bloody idea (as he had already told her three times that morning) to invite them. Which it had; but it wasn't exactly something she was yearning to do. Easter Sunday would have been much nicer if they could have remained on their own. She had just felt that things were becoming potentially difficult, rather than merely awkward, with the Booths; that their lack of hospitality was verging on the rude, and that something had to be done about it. 'They probably won't be able to come anyway,' she said, when she announced to Bard she thought they ought to ask them, and 'Please God,' he had said, but they were able to come, Duggie had accepted immediately, his voice rich with pleasure and something else – relief? – had said he knew they were free all weekend. Maybe they really were lonely; if so, she thought with a pang of guilt, Duggie at least didn't deserve it.

Thank goodness her mother was there; not only to tease Bard out of the filthy mood, which she was extremely good at, but to take the edge off any awkwardness at the lunch table, to flirt with Duggie, which he always enjoyed. And there would be awkwardness; Teresa Booth would make sure of that. It was her speciality, the loaded remark, the barbed joke. Francesca tried very hard to be charitable about her, to tell herself it must be difficult to come into a family – well, extended family anyway, which is what Channings was – where everyone had adored her predecessor and not feel excluded, compared, criticised: but just the same they had all tried very hard – at first anyway. Except for Bard. Nobody could say Bard had tried at all.

But she certainly had, had given a party for them when they had first been married, so that Teresa could meet all the company people and the family – of course, Kirsten leaving after an hour rather pointedly had been unfortunate – and some of their closer friends. And she had asked Teresa if she would perhaps like to be on one of her charity committees – Teresa had smiled sweetly at that one and said she was a working woman and didn't really have time for such things. 'I'm afraid I see doing charity work as therapy, Francesca dear,' was one of her particularly well-chosen phrases – had even (most determinedly turning the other cheek) invited her and Duggie for the weekend at Stylings, but it had all been in vain, and she might as well not have bothered, Teresa remained – what? Not hostile exactly, but the opposite of friendly. And treated her, moreover, as if she was not only her junior (which of course she was), but her inferior. And after a few months, Francesca had simply given up.

But now, guilty at not asking them to the christening, remorseful at the thought that she might have distressed Duggie, she was trying again, and was, she told Bard, determined to make a fuss of them. Well, a fuss of Duggie.

And Bard, who loved Duggie, who had shared every trauma of his life, both personal and professional, for almost twenty-five years (but who really could not quite forgive him for marrying Teresa), had agreed.

They always spent Easter at Stylings; it was a tradition almost as sacred as Christmas, which was always spent in London. Bard got up extremely early on Easter day and spent at least two hours laying the course for the Easter egg hunt; this was always far too difficult and complex for little Jack (who had that morning been found retired happily munching after the first half-hour and his only find), and fairly well beyond Francesca as well. Tory, who had been down for twenty-four hours, had left just after breakfast, saying she could remember the miseries of the hunt very clearly and didn't want them revived. But Rachel, dressed in Barbour and wellies, had been still staunchly tramping through the vegetable garden in the middle of the morning, three shiny-ribboned eggs from Harrods clutched to her bosom. It was not only her pleasure in the hunt, Francesca knew (perfectly genuine, Rachel loved challenges of any kind); she did it to please Bard, and they would then sit in the study after lunch, picking over her finds, checking off clues, and he would lead her in triumph to any she had missed. Rachel always came for Easter Sunday; she said it was her favourite day in the year, even more so than Christmas, and she personally cooked a turkey and brought her lemon Pavlova, Bard's favourite pudding, and an Easter cake from Fortnum's for the children. All of which should give Duggie some pleasure at least, thought Francesca, as she took Jack's hand and walked, smiling determinedly, towards the car.

'Teresa, hallo,' she said now, going forward, taking the small, plump beringed hand, kissing the air somewhere in the vicinity of Teresa's well-powdered face, 'it's so nice to see you.'

'Yes, it's been a bit of a long time,' said Teresa. 'Hallo Jack, I've got a present for you.'

Jack surrendered his face (smeared with an interesting mixture of chocolate, mud and grass clippings from sitting on the mower with Horton while he mowed the lawn) for her kiss, before saying, 'What is it?' and then after a fairly brief pause and a nudge from Francesca, 'Thank you.'

'It's a car,' said Teresa, 'and you drive it by remote control. Douglas, get it out of the boot, will you, darling?'

She always called him 'darling' in public, and she always went in for a great deal of overt physical affection towards him, taking his arm, kissing him, holding his hand when they were sitting together. Francesca had often wondered if it was different in private; she felt a great deal of it was cosmetic, designed to be noticed, designed even to embarrass, such as when she reached for his hand across the table, demanded a cuddle, made arch references to their needing an early night. It irritated Bard almost beyond endurance; he behaved in the totally opposite way, scarcely touching Francesca when people were around, passionately demonstrative when they were on their own.

Teresa moved on now, towards the house, clearly looking for Bard; Francesca went up to Duggie, who had his arms full of parcels, flowers, a bottle of champagne, and gave him a hug.

'Darling Duggie, how are you? It's so nice to see you.'

'Bless you, darling, it's nice to be here. Now these are for you, and this is for the old fella. Where is he, by the way?'

His voice, his expression even, were wistful; in the old days, Bard had always been out to greet him and Suzanne even before Francesca.

'Oh, he's in the shower,' said Francesca hastily. 'He's been playing landowner all morning, planting some trees or something. He won't be a minute.'

'Good. Now here you are, young chap. Here's something to keep you quiet.'

He handed Jack a huge, elaborately wrapped parcel; 'Cool,' said Jack, who had just learnt the word from watching *Neighbours* (which Nanny disapproved of and Francesca therefore let him watch with her whenever she could) and used it all the time. He started ripping off bows, shiny paper, shedding them on the drive. 'This is really cool.'

'Jack darling, don't do that, pick up the paper and bring it inside. I'm sure Duggie and Teresa would like to see you open it.'

'OK,' he said, and started running inside, holding one very small piece of paper.

Francesca picked the rest up, laughing, and said to Duggie, 'He's absolutely so naughty, so strong willed. But so charming, as well, I find it terribly hard to get cross with him.'

'He's Bard all over again then,' said Duggie, smiling at her. 'You all right, darling?'

'Yes, I'm fine. Really. And you? You look well.'

He did; he looked tanned and slimmer than the last time she had seen him. He was an extremely good-looking man, tall and very erect, with thick silver hair, brilliant blue eyes and a heavy white moustache, always impeccably dressed; he looked like the popular conception of a retired brigadier.

'Yes, well, we've just been to some health farm in Portugal, played a lot of golf, well, I did, Teresa lay by the pool. She said I had to get some weight off. Worried about my health, bless her.'

Ironic, thought Francesca, when Teresa herself was unarguably plump; good looking, in her flashy way, sexy even – the plumpness somehow contributing to that – but it was she who carried excess flesh, not Duggie. Well, maybe she really did want to look after him, was concerned for his health.

'You look pretty good to me,' she said, taking his arm with difficulty, round the parcels.

'Sweet of you, darling, but I'm fifty-nine, you know. Five years older than that whipper-snapper of a husband of yours. Have to be careful.'

'I think you look five years younger,' said Francesca.

'So how are things at Channing House?' said Teresa, putting down her knife and fork after toying with a plate of mozzarella and tomato salad and pushing it aside. 'I'm sorry, Francesca dear, I really can't eat this. I'm not really allowed cheese.'

'Oh, I'm sorry,' said Francesca, 'very sorry. Shall I –'

'No, no, dear, you couldn't have known. It's not as if we often eat together. Yes Bard, how are things? You let that place in Docklands yet?'

As if she didn't know he hadn't, thought Francesca; bloody woman.

'No,' he said shortly, 'not yet.'

'It's been a long time, hasn't it? The interest must be rolling up nicely.'

'Teresa, I really don't want my lunch ruined by being told unpalatable things I already know,' said Bard. Francesca kicked him under the table; he forced his heavy features into what she knew was supposed to be a smile.

'Nothing could ruin this lunch,' said Rachel blithely. 'Teresa, why is it you're not allowed cheese? Is it a reducing diet, or –'

'No, I have gallstones,' said Teresa. 'Extremely painful, if you irritate them. And any fat does that.'

'Gallstones?' said Jack. 'What are they?'

'Small deposits which form in your gall bladder,' said Teresa.

'In your bladder? So do they come out when you do a –'

'Jack, that will do,' said Rachel. 'Why don't you help Mrs Dawkins by taking out the dish? No, not the china one, darling, the big silver one. And tell her we're ready for the next course.'

'OK,' said Jack.

'And the Newcastle development, what about that? Proving up to your expectations?' said Teresa.

'Yes, thank you. Very profitable.'

'Well, that's something.'

'Teresa, we are not on the breadline,' said Bard. Francesca looked at him; the muscle at the side of his forehead that twitched when he was about to lose his temper stabbed warningly. She smiled at Teresa quickly.

'Tell us about your trip to Portugal. That sounds fun.'

'It was fun,' she said, 'great fun. Although Douglas spent a bit more time on the golf course than I might have hoped. Playing and networking as usual. I thought the idea was for us to spend some time together. He's such a workaholic. Like you, Bard, of course. I sometimes feel I could cite Channings as co-respondent.'

'Surely there's no likelihood of a divorce?' said Rachel, smiling radiantly at her.

'No, of course not,' said Teresa. She was sitting next to Duggie; she reached for his hand, and kissed it. 'Couple of kids on honeymoon, aren't we, sweetheart?'

He smiled back at her, clearly embarrassed, but equally clearly pleased. He really does love her, thought Francesca; he really does look happy. Remembering the raw grief on his face for weeks after Suzanne had died, the worry over his excessive drinking, she felt pleased, even grateful to Teresa.

'Good,' said Rachel briskly, 'how very nice. And Teresa, you have a company of your own, don't you?'

'I do indeed. My timeshare company. We have some lovely properties.'

'How interesting!' said Rachel. 'Where are they?'

'Oh, the usual places. Majorca, Marbella, I've just bought a couple in Portugal.'

'How exciting. It's going well, then?' said Rachel.

'Oh, extremely well. A very nice little earner. Although since the recession slightly less nice. But we've all had to lower our sights rather, haven't we, Bard? All of us in the property business?'

'Yes,' said Bard shortly. He looked as if he'd like to ram a couple of pieces of mozzarella down Teresa's fat neck, thought Francesca. She tried to catch Bard's eye and failed totally.

'Tell me, Teresa, how are your children?'

'Oh – very well. Thank you. My daughter lives in Florida, as you know, and I see very little of her' – estranged, thought Francesca and no wonder – 'but my son is based in Spain, runs my company out there. He's a very bright boy; in fact, Bard, I was thinking you really should –'

There was a loud crash from the hall: Jack had clearly dropped the serving dish. Francesca offered a large prayer of thanks that it was the silver one, and pushed her chair back.

'Oh dear. The butler's done it. I'd better go and sort it out. Excuse me.'

'I'll come with you,' said Bard. She looked at him in astonishment; he never proffered assistance of any kind. In the kitchen he glared at her. 'Why the fuck did you have to invite them? Bloody woman. I'm going to have to disappear for a bit. Can't stand it any longer. Make some excuse, will you?'

And he was gone

'Well,' she said smiling, going back into the dining room, carrying a dish piled high with gloriously buttery, golden roasted potatoes, 'no great harm done. I'm terribly sorry, Bard's had to take a call from New York. Won't be too long, he hopes. And Teresa, I'm afraid you may not be able to eat these potatoes, but Mrs Dawkins is just mashing you some quickly.'

'How kind,' said Teresa.

They stayed for tea; Teresa consumed two very buttery crumpets and two slices of the Fortnum cake.

'How lucky that butter doesn't upset your gallstones,' said Rachel sweetly.

'Isn't it?' said Teresa equally sweetly back. 'I'd like to see these trees you've planted, Bard, I'm thinking of putting some in myself, beeches you said, can you show them to me before we leave?'

'Well – I don't think –' said Bard. He looked at Francesca and scowled; she said hurriedly, 'Teresa, it's a bit dark now and very cold. Maybe next time …'

'Oh, I don't want to risk them being a tall forest,' said Teresa briskly. 'No, I'd like to see them now.'

'Well, then I shall come with you,' said Rachel, 'and Jack, darling, you come too, I have an idea there might be an Easter egg somewhere around there.'

'OK,' said Jack.

The tree inspection took quite a long time; when they came back, Bard disappeared into his study. Francesca went in after twenty minutes.

'You are to come back this minute,' she said, her voice low with rage. 'I will not have you being rude to her.'

'She's rude to me.'

'That's not the point.'

'Of course it's the point.'

He looked at her, and she stared back at him, absolutely determined that he should do what she asked. Such tiny victories were important to her, reassured her that she had at least some influence in his life. Suddenly he smiled.

'Oh – all right. As long as –' He stood up, put his arm round her waist suddenly, moved his hand down onto her bottom, caressed it, moulding its small, taut shape. 'As long as we can go to bed early tonight. Very early. All right?'

'All right,' said Francesca. She smiled at him, savouring the thought already, her senses surging sweetly, pleasurably. 'I promise. Very early.'

Teresa accepted a sherry, then a second. Duggie drank ginger ale, saying he had to drive.

'Come along, darling,' he said finally, patting her knee. 'We've completely outstayed our welcome.'

'Of course you haven't,' said Francesca. 'Why not stay for –'

'Goodness,' said Rachel, 'is that the time? Darlings, I must go. I have a terribly important date with my television at nine. Sorry to break up the party, but –'

48

She stood up, started bustling round the room, picking up things; the activity, as such activity always is, was infectious, and the Booths got up too, started moving towards the front door. Duggie disappeared upstairs – 'got to see a man about a dog' – and Teresa suddenly turned to Bard.

'Bard,' she said, 'I was saying to Duggie, if that golf complex of yours up in Scotland ever came to anything, I'd be interested in joining forces with you. With my company. Getting a couple of timeshares up there.'

Francesca looked at Bard.

'I didn't know you had anything up in Scotland,' she said, genuinely interested. 'I love Scotland, I'd like to go.'

'Oh, yes,' said Teresa, 'a lovely area apparently. Isn't it, Bard? Just waiting to be – well, given the Channing touch. As far as I can make out.'

Francesca looked at Bard, and tried to analyse his expression. It was no longer irritation, nor rage either; it was a dead-eyed careful blank. And she felt something herself then: a drift of unease, a darkening of the day. She had felt it before, and couldn't think where or when: silly, she thought, probably almost every day, living with Bard was one long sense of unease.

'Oh – there's nothing to see yet,' he was saying, 'much better things to show you. And not remotely suited to your purpose, Teresa, and anyway, I certainly wouldn't want to get into something like that.' His tone made his views of the timeshare business very plain.

'Oh, well,' she said, 'just an idea.'

She smiled at him. It was a particularly sweet smile.

They finally left at six-thirty; Bard stood on the steps of the house, glaring after their car.

'Bloody woman,' he said. 'God, I loathe her. Rachel, bless you. I'd have topped myself if you hadn't been here.'

'Well, thanks,' said Francesca. 'No, Mummy, you were wonderful. Do you really have to go? You could stay if you like.'

'No, darling, I have to be up and doing very early tomorrow. Bless you. Jack, give me a kiss. And we'll go to McDonald's together very soon.'

'Cool,' said Jack.

'Jack, you are filthy. I'm going to take you up and bath you now, this minute.'

'Yes, you go,' said Bard. 'I'll see your mother off.'

Francesca went upstairs with Jack to find Nanny. She was

extremely glad the lunch was over; but she had found it nonetheless interesting. Teresa's determination to needle Bard, to ask awkward questions, seemed to her above and beyond any petty social vendetta, and his dislike of her seemed to border on the pathological. Not that such emotions were exactly rare in him, and for very little reason.

Later, as they lay in bed, had talked, after Bard had agreed he had behaved less than perfectly, Francesca had agreed he had been unusually provoked, after he had reached for her, roused her, after she had experienced the piercing, greedy, grateful pleasure of making love with him, after he had told her he loved her, he said, quite suddenly, staring at the ceiling, his hand tangling in her hair: 'How much do you love me, do you think, Francesca?'

His voice was light, almost teasing; she turned, leaned on her elbow.

'Very very much,' she said, 'you know I do, why, why do you ask?'

He turned and looked at her, his eyes travelling over her face, exploring hers; then he said, 'Let's try and put a measure on it.' He loved these games; designed to confuse, to unsettle her. She had once asked him if he did it in the office. He looked at her in total astonishment, and said yes, of course he did.

'Oh Bard,' she said now. 'You mean if you lost all your money?'

'We could start with that.'

'Well, I wouldn't care, you know I wouldn't. I don't give a toss about your money.'

'You'd go out scrubbing floors, would you? To keep a crust in our mouths?'

'Don't be stupid, I could do better than that. I'd just get my job back, I'd enjoy it.'

'Yes, I know you could,' he said shortly. 'All right then, suppose I had another woman.'

'I'd be very sorry for her,' she said, laughing. 'That's easy.'

'No, really. Would you love me through that?'

'No,' she said slowly, 'I couldn't possibly.'

'Ah, so we have one boundary post already.'

Francesca suddenly felt a touch of genuine fear, the game seeming more serious. 'Bard, are you trying to tell me something?'

'No, of course not,' he said, kissing her. 'I couldn't. It's unthinkable, unimaginable.'

'Good,' she said briskly. 'Next?'

He was silent for a minute, then: 'Just suppose,' he said, 'just suppose I asked you to do something. Something you disapproved of?'

She looked at him, genuinely intrigued by this one. 'What sort of thing?'

'Oh – I don't know. Forge a signature on a cheque, help me falsify some documents, something like that.'

'Oh, no,' she said at once, 'I couldn't do that. Not something dishonest. Not even for you.'

'Whatever the situation?'

'Whatever the situation.'

'Very disloyal of you.'

'No,' she said slowly, 'no, I don't think so. But you wouldn't ask, would you? I know you wouldn't, so it isn't even a question I can properly consider.'

'I'll try not to,' he said, smiling, kissing her, pulling her to him, 'and I'm afraid you don't love me very much at all. Now let's go to sleep.'

He was asleep in minutes, clearly untroubled; but she lay awake for a while, thinking more seriously now about love and its limits and how they should be set. And remembered too when she had felt the drift of unease before: at Kitty's christening when Teresa Booth had telephoned. She thrust it, as she had then, deep into her head, and fell finally asleep.

Kirsten almost wished she had gone down to Stylings for the Easter egg hunt with Tory, so awful had been her Sunday. Kirsten was quite used to unhappiness, her life was measured in it, episodes of it: from being sent briefly away to school at nine (and seeing her beloved small brother dispatched, sobbing, even younger); to sitting on the landing late one night and watching through the banisters as her adored father left the family home in Hampstead with nothing but an overnight bag; thence to watching her mother becoming an increasingly helpless alcoholic in a series of ever more horrifying, relentlessly predictable episodes, culminating in her falling down the stairs and concussing herself, lying in a pool of blood (where the twelve-year-old Kirsten found her, coming in from school one afternoon), she could not remember many periods of calm and none of stability. There had been personal unhappiness too, mostly connected with men and all contributing to her sense of personal failure; several disastrous love affairs, two pregnancies (one of which at least had, she acknowledged if only to herself, not been an accident), and two subsequent abortions; and getting a Third in Law at Bristol when she knew perfectly well she could and should have got at least a 2:1. And since then unemployment, on a fairly impressive scale. Life generally, she thought, as she drove much too fast down the Old Brompton Road early that Sunday evening, was a bitch, but today it had surpassed itself; she was hardly even surprised when a flashing blue light appeared in her rear-view mirror (although the snidely just-polite policemen reduced her to tears as nothing else had yet been able to do), and she arrived at her flat in a state of near-hysteria to find Tory singing happily and covering her pristine white kitchen with black breadcrumbs as she scraped the toast she had just burnt.

'Tory, you silly cow, look what you're doing. I spent hours cleaning that all up this morning. What are you doing here anyway, why aren't you still down in Sussex toadying to fucking Francesca and her fucking children? Get out, go on, get out – oh Tory, I'm sorry, don't you cry too, I'm really sorry, here, take my hanky and I'll pour us both a glass of wine ...'

'Not wine,' said Tory, in a small, tear-stained voice, 'I've had too much already, I've got a headache, let's have some tea, I've boiled the kettle –'

Kirsten sat looking at her sister, nursing a large mug of tea and rubbing her eyes like a small child, and felt a terrible remorse. Tory was the one person in the whole world Kirsten felt truly loved her – with the possible exception of Granny Jess – and she treated her like shit. Poor Tory; she tried so hard to please her, hero-worshipped her almost, asked her advice over everything, and what did she get in return? Abuse. She put her hand out now and covered Tory's with it; Tory smiled at her rather shakily.

'I'm sorry, Tory. I really am. I'm a bitch. You don't deserve me.'

'That's true,' said Tory, but she managed a wobbly smile.

'I had such a foul awful day, really total shit, I lost all my credit cards, left them in the Seven Eleven I think, anyway they've gone, and then I had an argument with a lamppost and took the skin off the side of my car and then coming home tonight I got done for speeding. Sixty in the Old Brompton Road. I may even lose my licence. God, Tory, why am I such a mess?'

'Where's Toby? I thought you were staying there tonight.'

'Oh,' said Kirsten. 'Oh, Toby,' and promptly burst into tears again.

'What is it?' said Tory. 'What's happened now?'

'He's – well, it's all over.'

'Over? But I thought there was talk of you moving in.'

'There was. But I told him to take a running jump. Today.'

'Why?'

'Tory stop asking questions. I just did, that's all. Leave me alone.'

'All right,' said Victoria, her small face hurt again. 'More tea?'

'Oh Tory, I'm sorry. Sorry sorry sorry. All right, I'll tell you. I didn't tell him anything of the sort, he told me. We had a huge mega-row and he – well, he said it was all over. Finito. That – well –' Kirsten took a deep breath, feeling, hoping that telling the truth might somehow purge her, make her feel better, like going to Confession. God, she hadn't been to Confession for years, maybe she should –

'Well what?' said Victoria, putting a second mug of tea down. 'What did he say?'

'That I was a brat. A spoilt, ridiculous brat. That I could come back when I'd grown up. Those were his very words. If you want to know.' She rummaged in her bag for her cigarettes and lit one, smiled rather thinly at Tory through the smoke. 'Maybe he's right. I don't know.'

'Well,' said Tory carefully, 'I suppose you are spoilt. I mean we all are. But –'

'Yes, but there's spoilt and spoilt. Isn't there? Oh, I don't know. I feel such a mess. I hardly know what my name is any more. Pass me those letters, will you, Tory, I've hardly been home for days.'

'Yes,' said Tory, looking at them idly, 'they're mostly bills, from the look of them.'

'Oh well. I'm so overdrawn already, a bit more won't make any difference. Let me see. Oh God. The letter from Hawkins Myerling. God, dear God, please let them want me. Please please please.' There was a silence while she tore open the envelope: then: 'Oh well. Another slice of failure.' She sat staring at the white piece of paper, with its severe letter heading, the ultra-neat word-processed letter making a mockery of its 'With reference to your letter ... we very much regret ... wish you well in the future ...' Hawkins Myerling had been her last hope, the very last respectable firm who were likely to take her on to do her articles; it was either out into the provinces, or giving up law altogether. Well, she could hardly blame them, who on earth would take on someone with a Third? It had been hopeless from the beginning. Christ, she'd made a mess of everything, everything – the page blurred in front of her and she burst into tears again.

'Oh Tory, I'm such a disaster, such a total disaster. I can't handle life at all, I'm just not fit to be around this fucking planet. Everything I do I make a hash of. What am I going to do, Tory? Just what am I going to do?' The door bell shrilled. 'If that's Toby, I'm not here, I've gone out with a horny bloke who –'

'It won't be Toby,' said Tory, 'it'll be Johnny and Arabella. I'm sorry, Kirsten, I'll get rid of them. We'll go to the pub.'

'No, no, it doesn't matter. I'll just disappear into my room with a bottle of vodka and a bottle of pills. Sorry, Tory, joke, bad joke. Didn't mean it.'

'I know,' said Victoria, getting up, her face a confused mixture of concern and relief (She really is too little to handle all this, thought Kirsten remorsefully, I shouldn't do it to her, I won't again), 'but I'll tell you what I think you should do. I think you should go and work for Dad, for a bit at least. It's crazy, you not getting anywhere, not doing anything, when he's waiting there with open arms, dying to help. He's so proud of you, he wants to have you in the firm so much. It would at least be a start, better than sitting around here all day and shopping, or temping for those awful people.'

'You know I'd rather die,' said Kirsten wearily, 'and just think of all the times I've told him to stuff his bloody jobs in his bloody company. I can't go crawling to him now.'

'Yes, well, thank your lucky stars he'd still take you on if you did,' said Tory. 'Most fathers wouldn't. He was telling Rachel Duncan-Brown even today how proud of you he was, and how clever you were and how he was just waiting for you to come and take over Channings so he could retire. He adores you, Kirsten, he asked me to give you his love, to tell you to ring him, I really think you should think about it.' The doorbell rang again. 'Look, I must go, I'll see you later.'

'OK,' said Kirsten listlessly, 'and seriously, don't worry about going out, I'm going to have a bath and then go to bed early. And yes, all right, before you say it all again I will think about it. Thank you. You're a star, Tory, you really are.'

She lay in the bath for a long time, thinking about it: about the relief of having a real job, not just something to do, but a purpose in life, a sense she was going somewhere, getting something, the knowledge that she was using her talents, her brain, and (not to be sniffed at, this one) that she would be earning some money; her allowance from her father was generous, but it didn't really begin to meet her considerable extravagances. And she also thought of the humiliation she would have to face, not only of apologising to her father for her behaviour at their past few meetings but of implicitly promising the behaviour would be good for the foreseeable future; of having to be at least polite to Francesca (and that terrible mother of hers should their paths cross, which she supposed would be fairly unlikely); of being made to exist in a state of permanent gratitude and dependence, inevitable she knew, however hard she worked; and – worst of all, much much the worst – of knowing that everyone would be saying she could only get a job because she was her father's daughter. She had made such a huge issue of making her own way in life, of not taking the easy option (while taking such minor eases, of course, as the flat and the car), it would be extremely hard to be seen to be taking it after a period that had not been outstanding for its success.

And then she thought about Toby, and how much his words had hurt; she wasn't at all sure how much she cared about Toby, but he was – he had been – a most important factor in her life, not only a source of huge pleasure in her bed, but a stylish accessory, an amusing companion, and, perhaps most important of all, for she didn't have many, a good and reliable friend. And a truthful one. She forced herself to remember, to listen again to what he had said: that she was spoilt, self-indulgent, lazy, hysterical, and wondered if he would think more or less of her if she went crawling humbly to her father, eating large portions of humble pie in his presence, and asked him after all to take her on.

The bath was cold by the time she had made her decision; she dressed again, and wrote a letter to her father. It wasn't a very long letter but it took her a long time; when she had finished she decided it was too important to entrust to the Royal Mail and that she might in any case change her mind if she waited until the morning to post it; she would drive to St James's Square and deliver it herself.

It was quite late when she got there, almost midnight, and she was sitting in the car, finding even the simple fact of getting out of the car and pushing the envelope through the door painful when she saw Hugh, the night porter, let someone out of the front door of the large and rather beautiful building that was Channing House and salute briefly. Whoever it was got into the car parked immediately outside, and started it up; someone working late, thought Kirsten, and as the car came towards her she switched her interior light off in case she was recognised. She wondered if it was someone she knew: Charlie Prentice, the company lawyer or Peter Barbour perhaps, but as the car (Jaguar XJS, silver, flashy) passed her she saw it was a female face, which made it doubly intriguing. A middle-aged (but very well preserved) female face, heavily made up, under a bouffant cloud of silver blonde hair: a face she recognised. Je-sus, thought Kirsten, what have we here: the terrible Teresa Booth. She had only met her twice, at parties at the London house; had thought she was a nightmare with her hard, brilliant blue eyes, her jutting bosom, her husky, ginny voice, pushing Duggie around, telling him what to do. She had got the impression her father loathed her, yet here she was, apparently quite a familiar visitor to Channing House, able to come and go so late, and with Hugh saluting her. How extraordinary, she thought, getting out of her car, walking slowly across to push her letter through the door of Channing House. Well, maybe her enforced spell there might be just slightly more interesting than she had expected.

Rachel wasn't used to feeling nervous. She sailed through life on a raft of self-confidence, never doubting that people would be pleased to see her, would be amused by her, if they were men would be attracted to her; even at her lowest hours, when her husband had quite clearly been heading his company and indeed his family straight into the bankruptcy court, when he had gone out into the barn of their house and shot himself, when she had been showing people round that same beautiful house she loved so much and was forced to sell, when she had to go out and work in a series of humiliating jobs with girls half her age and with a quarter of her brain, she had retained her innate courage, her high spirits, her ability to find in everything at least an element of entertainment, of fun. Her daughter was not, she feared, quite like her in this; Francesca was less intrinsically optimistic, more naturally fearful, than she. She possessed courage, great courage, but it was of a less joyous nature; it met demands and was found equal to them, but it did not go out to find them, standards flying.

For more than one reason she had found it impossible to tell Francesca she was having her twice-postponed breakfast meeting with Bard next morning. It was one thing to flirt with Bard, to play the perfect mother-in-law, to sparkle at his dinner parties, to support his wife as and when necessary, and quite another to go behind that wife's back and ask him for money. However excellent her motives.

'Well now, Rachel,' he said, settling at the table over a bowl of muesli piled high with apricots and prunes, a plate of croissants at his side, tucking a napkin into his neck, 'what can I do for you?'

'Go on a diet,' said Rachel briskly. 'I don't want my daughter widowed.'

'I had a health check only last week,' said Bard. 'All clear.'

'You must be overweight.'

'Not really,' said Bard cheerfully. He never minded such comments; his self-confidence was such that personal criticism left him entirely unmoved. 'Depends how you look at me. And I can't stand people who are mimsy over their food. Like the dreadful Booth woman. Of course I weigh too much, but it's mostly muscle. I'm very fit, you know, Rachel. Go to the gym at least three times a week, and sailing's very good exercise. Not that I've done much of that, lately. I wish I could persuade Francesca to sail.'

'She hates the water,' said Rachel. 'It frightens her.'

'I know. But if she'd only –'

'Bard, she has tried. Believe me.'

'I know, I know. Now let's get back to you. What is it you want from me? Money?'

'Yes,' said Rachel, startled into directness herself. 'Money. But not for me, of course. For something very – well, something very important to me.'

'And why did we have to have a meeting to discuss it? Why not just ask me, if you want a donation?'

'It's – it's more than a donation,' said Rachel. She felt the palms of her hand growing moist; she picked up a glass of orange juice, noticed it shook as she held it. Damn. She'd meant to appear so cool, so detached. If she wasn't careful he'd start really quizzing her. Then she'd find herself in very deep water.

'Well, what is it, then?'

'I'm – well, I've got very involved in a charity.'

'What sort of charity?'

'A – well, I suppose in the loosest possible terms, it's in the area of mental handicap,' said Rachel carefully.

'Really? Not the kind of thing I'd have expected you to be involved in, Rachel.'

'Why?' said Rachel. She hadn't meant to sound so challenging, but the assumption he was clearly making irritated her. 'Because I don't appear to you the do-gooding sort? Because you'd imagined if it was a charity, it would be something rather more socially acceptable? Like Poppy Day? Or the Red Cross. Is that it?'

'Yes,' he said simply, 'that's exactly it. There's no need to look quite so indignant, Rachel, I can't help my misconceptions. I see you as a highly sophisticated, highly amusing woman, very warm, very attractive if we are going to get personal; I don't see you as a person who is going to show more than the most ephemeral concern for those less fortunate than herself. Except if it happened to be her own family. I'm sorry. I obviously malign you.'

Rachel took a deep breath, forced herself to smile, to look relaxed. 'Well, I'm pleased you find me attractive and amusing, Bard,' she said. 'I could even return the compliment. But yes, you do misjudge me. A little anyway. Can I tell you about it? About my – this charity?' The words 'her own family' echoed round her head; she tried to dismiss them.

'Please do. There's obviously a lot to talk about. Could you just hang on a minute?'

'Of course.'

He got up, went over to the buffet, came back with a plateful of black pudding, mushrooms, tomatoes and bacon. 'Sorry,' he said, grinning, seeing her face. 'But I didn't want to be distracted by hunger. I'm all yours.'

'Well,' said Rachel, 'perhaps I'd better start with some background ... There's a Home, which I've been aware of for some time –'

'How?' said Bard.

'I'm sorry?'

'How have you been aware of it?'

'A friend of mine had a daughter there. She's – well, she's died now. The friend, that is. But I went there a couple of times. To visit the daughter. And –'

'Where is it?'

'Devon. North Devon–Cornish borders. It's run by some nuns, affiliated to a convent. It's absolutely wonderful.'

'Ye-es?'

'Well, the thing is they are under huge financial pressure. For many years they were supported by legacies, and of course the Church itself used to be much richer.'

'I thought the Catholic Church was still pretty rich,' said Bard drily. Rachel looked at him; she had forgotten that Pattie had been, no doubt still was, a staunch Catholic.

'The Church may be. This convent certainly isn't. Of course it's very hard for these places to pay their way anyway, and with a whole lot of terribly expensive regulations coming through from the EEC the house just isn't suitable any more, and it soaks up money in a way you wouldn't believe ...'

'I probably would,' said Bard. 'I know about money being soaked up.'

'Well, anyway, a very big house, an old priory ironically enough, has come up for sale, about three miles away. If we – if they bought it, it would be marvellous. It has quite a bit of land and so they could have a market garden there, keep chickens, perhaps a goat, that sort of thing, and generally be a lot more self-sufficient. Best of all it has a lot of outbuildings, including a pair of wonderful greenhouses. And there's another place that could be a bakery. So –'

'And who would fund the purchase of this place?' said Bard. His eyes were very bright, very fierce, as he looked at her; Rachel returned the look steadily.

'A charity. A new charity. We've – they've applied for Charitable status. The thing is, if we can show that what we are doing incorporates some kind of rehabilitation, we might very well get that. And it would be so very much better for the – the residents. I mean the nuns are wonderfully kind, but – well, with the right people in charge, and some backing, it could become a sort of small community. Not completely self-sufficient perhaps, but certainly helping to pay its own way.'

'I see,' said Bard, 'and where do I come in?'

'Well,' said Rachel, 'well, you see, one of the requirements for a charity is trustees. Three, actually. Three trustees.'

'And what do these three trustees have to do?'

'Well – they have to – that is, the requirement is – as you probably know –'

'Come on, Rachel,' said Bard. He sounded impatient. 'As presentations go, I've seen a lot better. I'm disappointed in you.'

'They have to underwrite all the losses,' said Rachel quickly. She drained her coffee cup, signalled to the waiter to refill it. 'I mean, that's the main thing.'

'Yes indeed. And manage the land, run the bank accounts, see to the annual reports. I know, Rachel, I know very well. I've been involved in charities before.'

'Ah,' said Rachel. She looked at him and her eyes were much harder suddenly. 'So why did you ask me, then?'

'Because I wanted to make you say it. I didn't see why I should make it easy for you,' said Bard lightly. 'You're asking a very great deal. And perhaps now you'd like to tell me why I should do this. Why I should expose myself to possibly huge financial risk, get involved in something with which I have no connection whatsoever...'

'There shouldn't be a financial risk,' said Rachel, 'I wouldn't have asked you if there was. The house alone is worth a great deal of money. It's simply a matter of – well, providing guarantees, I suppose.'

'And do you have the other two trustees?'

'No, not yet. We have approached a couple of people, but so far no-one has actually agreed.'

'I wonder why. And I suppose there's a degree of urgency?'

'Well – well, yes, there is. Quite a big degree actually.' Damn, she wasn't handling this at all well. 'There's a developer after the priory, he wants to split it into units, sell them off and –'

'Very sensible,' said Bard. 'He should make a lot of money. That sounds a much more attractive proposition to me.'

'Oh Bard, don't,' said Rachel. 'Let's for heaven's sake keep to the subject.'

'I thought the priory was the subject.'

'Not really, no. The subject is the community, and the need to establish the charity.'

'And how is it exactly you're so very involved in all this?' said Bard. 'The connection seems quite tenuous to me. I don't understand.'

Rachel looked at him, struggling to keep her gaze steady. 'Not really. I told you, I went there –'

'With your friend?'

'Yes.'

'Have I met this friend? Was she at the wedding, perhaps, or –'

'No, no you haven't. I told you. She's died.'

'I see. How sad. Go on.'

'Well, I was just so impressed with it, that's all. I saw how much the nuns were doing for these people, how hard they worked, I – well, I hate to see anything like that go under. For lack of funds. When they're all prepared to work their butts off, not just the nuns, but the residents as well, that's so important, to keep going, to remain at least to a degree independent. I would have thought that would appeal to you, Bard. It's one of the reasons I thought of asking you.'

'Oh really?' he said. He had finished his plate of black pudding now, was piling honey onto a croissant; he took a large bite, then sat back in his chair looking at her. His eyes were very hard. He's going to refuse, she thought, and it will all be my fault for handling it badly. She should never have even tried; now she had exposed herself to a lot of worry for nothing. Fool, stupid stupid fool ...

'Well,' he said cutting into her thoughts, 'well, it does sound – interesting. Very interesting indeed, actually, Rachel. I might very well be persuaded to help.'

Rachel didn't even take in his words at first, so sure had she been he was going to refuse; then she stood up, knocking over the sugar bowl, leant across and kissed his cheek.

'Bard, you are wonderful. I do promise you you'd never regret it. I –'

'Rachel, hold your fire. I didn't say I would. I said I might. But I'd want to know a lot more about it.'

'Of course. Of course you would.'

'And the first thing I'd want to do is forget the cock-and-bull story about your friend and her daughter and hear the real reason you're so involved with the place.'

Careful, Rachel, don't let him panic you; she sat down again and looked at him very steadily.

'It's not a cock-and-bull story, Bard, it's –'

'Oh come off it, Rachel. You're up against a veteran here, when it comes to lying. Takes one to know one. If I'm going to take on what is a very considerable risk, despite what you say, I think I deserve to know the truth.'

'Bard, I've told you –'

'OK.' He shrugged. 'Let's forget the whole thing, shall we? I've got quite sufficient claims on my charity budget. And I'm already extremely late for my nine-thirty meeting. So –'

'Bard, let me just show you the place. The convent and the Help House, as the nuns call it, and the priory. I'm sure I can change your mind. Absolutely sure.'

He looked at her, drained his cup and then stood up and smiled his sudden, brilliant smile.

'All right. If I can possibly find the time, I'll come on an odyssey to Devon with you. It'll be a fun day anyway. Ring Marcia and fix it.'

Rachel sat staring at his broad back, lit the cigarette she had been longing for (Bard was an obsessive anti-smoker) with shaking hands. She should never have started this. She must have been mad to think she could get away with it. But the alternative was just too awful to think about.

Marcia Grainger was waiting for Bard when he got in, her back particularly rigid. Most people's disapproval could be read from their eyes or the set of their mouths, Marcia's from the set of her back. And she was a tall woman, tall and statuesque; there was no ignoring that back.

'Ah, Mr Channing,' she said now, rather unnecessarily, 'you're here. Your nine-thirty appointment has been waiting for some time.'

'Won't do him any harm,' said Bard cheerfully.

'Alas no. It has, however, done me a little,' said Marcia. 'He has been extremely ungracious and says he can only be here until eleven. Which he assures me he made plain to you yesterday when you spoke.'

'Oh, Christ,' said Bard. 'Where is he?'

'In the boardroom. I have naturally made him coffee. Perhaps you should go straight along there now.'

'Yes, perhaps I should. Any messages? Urgent ones?'

'Only two. One from the Swedish people, can you phone them, and one from a Mr Townsend. A journalist. He says you are seeing him at two-thirty this afternoon, and he wanted to confirm it.'

'Tell him I can't see him,' said Bard. 'He'll have to re-schedule.'

He was halfway out of the room when he turned back to Marcia. 'On second thoughts, I want the whole thing cancelled. Tell Sam to do it. And tell her I want any interviews cancelled. For the foreseeable future. All right?'

'Quite all right,' said Marcia. She did not like the press, and she deeply disapproved of Bard's easy relationship with them.

'Fuck,' said Gray Townsend. 'Fuck it, Sam, why? That was all settled, I thought, I've even got the piece scheduled, it was one of a series about the property guys –'

'Gray, I'm sorry,' said Sam Illingworth. 'I just work here, I just got this directive. Mr Channing is terribly busy and doesn't have any time at the moment.'

'Well, it's very sudden,' said Gray, 'his busy-ness. And I mean he's obviously in bullish mood, I've just been reading about Channing North in *The Times*; I can make a lot of that, if it would help – and obviously it would –'

'Gray, I'm sure you would. But Mr Channing just says no. No interviews at the moment. And I'm sorry it's such short notice, I really am.'

'Is it the Docklands business? Is he feeling sensitive about that? I know he's had quite a lot of adverse publicity about it –'

'No. Honestly, it's not that. I told you, he's just too busy.'

'Oh shit,' said Gray. 'Well, look, I'll just have to shunt everything round a bit. I'm doing a whole load of these things, so if he changes his mind –'

'Yes of course. I'll be right in touch. I'm sorry, Gray. For myself as well; it would have been great.'

'Yes, it would. Never mind. Cheers, Sam.'

'Bye, Gray.'

'What are you on about?' said Tricia Thorpe, Gray's assistant, hearing the expletives. 'Gray, could you please either OK that headline or come up with another one, I've already had one bollocking from Dave because we, as he puts it, have been sitting on it, and ...'

'Yeah, just give me a few more minutes. I just think it looks a bit tabloid, now that it's right across three columns.'

'I'll give you five more minutes,' said Tricia briskly, 'and then I'm setting Dave on you. Anyway, what are you cursing about?'

'Oh, Bard Channing's pulled out of that series I'm doing. Bloody shame. He's much the most interesting person in it. Or would have been.'

'Why?' said Tricia. 'I thought he loved publicity.'

'He does. Usually. Says he's too busy. That's like Branson saying he's too shy. I don't get it.'

'Maybe he's in trouble. Doesn't want to broadcast the fact.'

'Oh, I don't think so. The last figures were very good. Although if he doesn't let that building in Docklands soon, he will be.'

'Really? Do you mean he'll go bust? Well then, that's the reason —'

'No, it's not that bad. He's more soundly based than that. I think ... But that place is a positive black hole for swallowing up money.'

'Well, I'm disappointed too,' said Tricia. 'I was looking forward to meeting Mr Channing.'

'Why did you think you were going to?'

'Oh, I'd have made some excuse. Hidden your tape recorder and come rushing in with it. I think he's terribly sexy.'

'Do you really?' said Gray. 'How extraordinary. He looks like a gorilla to me.'

'Very nice-looking gorilla. Anyway, he's got that lovely wife. She really is all over the papers. There was a picture of her greeting some minor royal to a charity do in the *Mail on Sunday*. What's her name, Frances or something —'

'Francesca. You are well informed. Yeah, I wonder if I could get at him through her? Write a feature about her and her charity work or something —'

'You could try,' said Tricia. The phone rang; she picked it up. 'Financial Editor. Oh, Dave. Yes, just a —' Gray shook his head violently at her, gestured at the door, mouthing 'not here', started tapping furiously into his computer; Tricia looked at him, grinned. 'Dave, he's sitting here making strange faces at me. I hope he's all right. He looks a bit as if he's having a fit. Or — what was that, Gray? Oh, sorry, Dave, apparently I was meant to tell you he's gone out ...'

Having rejigged his headline for his lead article for Sunday's paper ('Major's Minus'; he was very pleased with that one), Gray sat and thought again about Bard Channing pulling out of the interview and his series. It intrigued him and he wasn't sure quite why. It was so totally out of character, he had been extremely enthusiastic before, offered him almost limitless access, through Sam Illingworth. The whole thing was a mystery. But there had to be an explanation, and it was worth trying to get it. He picked up the phone, called Sam, asked her to meet him for a drink one evening that week.

'Gray, if it's to try and twist Mr Channing's arm, through me, it won't work. He's made up his mind.'

'Oh no,' said Gray untruthfully, 'nothing like that. I'd just like to see you, Sam, buy you a drink, and maybe find out more about this northern thing. OK?'

'OK,' said Sam, 'but I hope you won't feel you're wasting your time.'

'I'm sure I won't,' said Gray, 'now how about next Monday? You free?'

'Next Monday'd be fine.'

'Good. See you then. American Bar at six.'

Graydon Townsend considered himself a very fortunate man. He was often heard to say that he had a job, a house, a lifestyle and girlfriend all of which he loved 'and not in that order, either'. The job was that of Financial Editor of the *News on Sunday* (which he famously described as the 'best of the broadsheets, *Sunday Times* excepted', which pleased the editor of the *Sunday Times* and ensured Gray the possibility of a job there one day and infuriated all the rest); the house was a very pretty Victorian semi near Clapham Common; the lifestyle was stylish, expensive and interesting; and the girlfriend was pretty, talented and (he was frequently also heard modestly to say) as much in love with him as he was with her. She was called Briony and she was a photographic stylist, quite a bit younger than him; indeed, he liked to call her his child-bride. Gray was thirty-seven, tall, slim with rather streaky, floppy brown hair and (appropriately) grey eyes. He was not good looking in the classical sense; his face was just too long, his nose slightly hawklike, but it managed to convey exactly what he was: intelligent, amusing and charming. He dressed extremely well (and expensively), knew a lot of interesting people, and was very good indeed at his job. He was also rather engagingly good natured; it was unusual enough for him to be out of sorts for Briony to notice it immediately. Which she did that night.

He was sitting in the conservatory reading the *Evening Standard* when she came in; he looked up at her and only just smiled.

'Hi, Gray. You're home early.'

'Nothing to stay in the office for,' said Gray gloomily.

'What's the matter?'

'Oh – just a bit pissed off. Had an interview with Bard Channing, you know, property guy, all lined up for today, and the bugger cancelled it at the last minute.'

'I'm sure he'll re-schedule.'

'Hope so.'

'I'll get you a cup of tea. Or are you ready for something stronger?'

'No, tea'd be good. Thanks.'

Briony came back into the conservatory with a large cup of extremely weak tea. That was how Gray liked it made: with a teabag barely waved across it, and hardly any milk. The greatest trial he had to endure in his working life was the tea machine at the *News*, spewing out as it did rich, almost bright brown liquid with blobs of barely dissolved powdered milk in it. Since the paper had moved into the high-tech world and the days of the kettle in the secretary's office were merely a sweet memory, Gray had tried a great many remedies for the tea machine, including a large Thermos which he made up every morning, but even that developed a stewed taste after about midday; he acknowledged that there were worse things in life to be endured, but he nevertheless suffered from it. Gray's love of alcohol – especially of Australian wine – was considerable, but he had frequently gone on record as saying that given a straight choice between the wine and the tea, the tea would have to win; that he could not live, and certainly could not work, without it. He chain-drank through the day, from a jumbo-size teacup, refilling it as soon as it emptied.

'Thanks, darling. That's perfect. Listen to this, what do you think about this, it's in one of these invention catalogues. It's a kind of plug-in wand you immerse in a cup of cold water to make it hot. Could be the answer to my tea problem. Shall I get one?'

'You could try,' said Briony. 'I don't know why you don't just take a kettle into the office and be done with it.'

'I tried twice, and it really wasn't worth it. It's against the rules, so every secretary in the floor was borrowing it, and it was never there when I wanted it.'

'What a tragedy your life is, Graydon,' said Briony briskly. 'Shall we go to the cinema tonight?'

'If you want to,' said Gray, 'but I thought we agreed we'd stay home, and I'd cook something. In fact I've already mixed the pasta dough, and I've bought that eye-wateringly expensive wild asparagus, it won't be nearly so nice tomorrow. And ...'

'Yeah, yeah, I know, and there's a bottle of Hardy's in the fridge,' said Briony easily. 'It's all right, Gray, I won't disturb your little plans.'

'They're not plans,' said Gray, smiling at her. 'Just – well, plans. Doesn't matter.'

'Yes it does,' said Briony, 'to you. Don't worry about it. We'll stay in. We can see the film tomorrow.'

Her voice, light and even tempered, her smile, quick and friendly, made Gray feel guilty. Much more guilty than if she had made a fuss. Just the same she was right; he didn't want to go out, having decided to stay in, he hated having his plans changed. He liked to look at an evening, or a day, its arrangements neatly in place, usually with one of his favourite activities contained within it, cooking or reading, or indeed – if it had been planned – a cinema or a concert, and then to proceed through it, in an orderly, pleasing manner. His professional life was so chaotic that in his own time he craved order; it was another expression of his acute tidiness, his love of method, of systems.

'Honestly Bri,' he said, not really meaning it, knowing he was safe, 'it doesn't matter. We can go out.'

'No, no really. I'd love to eat in, as long as you cook. And I've got an early start anyway. Huge session for *Ideal Home*.'

'All right, darling. If that's really all right.'

'It is.'

He picked up the paper again, then put it down, studied her, thinking how pretty she was, how lucky he was to have her. She was small and thin, almost skinny, with a heart-shaped, rather serious face, long brown hair and very beautiful dark blue eyes. Gray got up suddenly and went over and kissed her.

'I love you,' he said.

'Good,' said Briony, just slightly briskly. 'Can I borrow the *Standard*?'

'Sure.'

'I saw Francesca Channing last week,' she said suddenly. 'I was working for *Vogue*, and they'd been photographing her along with some other high-profile women in the charity business. She's awfully pretty. And she seemed nice as well.'

'She is,' said Gray, 'and extremely bright and very charming. A touch neurotic though.'

'You seem to know a lot about her.'

'I don't actually. I only met her once, at some dinner. It was fairly early in the marriage, she's probably hardened up a bit now.'

'Why should she have?'

'Because she'll need to, that's why. Bard Channing is not very good to his women. Shit.'

'What's the matter?'

'Bloody Shields has done that piece in *The Times* that I've been talking about for ages, about over-gullible investors. Fuck. I'm an idiot, Bri.'

'That's true,' said Briony agreeably.

'That's not what you're meant to say,' said Gray.

'I know,' said Briony, 'but it's true.' She looked at him thoughtfully for a moment and then she said, 'Gray?'

'Yes, darling?'

'Gray, I want to ask you something.'

'Yes, darling.'

'Gray, how would you feel about us having a baby?'

Panic ripped through Gray, hot, bright panic; it took him by surprise how bad it was. He sat quite still, staring at her, trying to appear calm, trying to establish how serious she was, how much she really meant it, not trusting himself to react in any way.

'Well,' he said finally, relieved to hear his own voice sounding level and reasonable, 'well, I don't know. I mean I really hadn't thought about it.'

'Not at all? Not ever? I can't believe that.'

'I don't know why not,' he said. 'Why should I have? It's not the sort of thing I would think about. Is it?'

'I don't see why not,' said Briony. 'You're thirty-seven. Past the sort of age people normally start to think about such things. Well past it, actually. I'm twenty-eight. The sort of age you begin to hear the clock ticking. The biological one, you know.'

'Yes,' said Gray, and he could hear his own voice sounding dull, 'yes, I do know.'

'And we've been together for almost four years. The sort of time that – well, it's quite a long time. You keep saying you love me. I love you. We have a lot going for us. We're very happy together. Surely you must think there's more to life than making the right sauce for the right pasta and going to the right restaurant and going to the right off-the-beaten-track place twice a year with the right clothes in the right luggage.'

'Oh I don't know,' said Gray lightly. It was what he actually meant, but he was trying to make it sound like a joke; he could tell by her face he had failed.

'Darling Briony,' he said quickly, 'darling, darling Briony, of course there's more to life than that. But our life is so perfect just now; why not enjoy it for a while? And you're doing so well with your career, the best stylist in London according to *Arena*, do you really want to give all that up yet? And if I take my three-month sabbatical this autumn, we can go to India, like we always said, surely you don't want to –'

'Oh no,' said Briony, and her voice was heavy suddenly, 'of course I don't want to. That's why I mentioned it. I didn't mean it. Who could want a baby more than all that crap? No-one in their right minds, Gray, could they? So how long do we have to go on with all this perfection? Five years? Seven? Till it's too late for me to have a baby at all? Gray, I don't want to –'

'Bri, it wouldn't be too late. You'd still only be thirty-three. Loads of time.'

'Not necessarily. The fertility clinics are full of people who thought just that, who waited and waited and said right now, and then suddenly it wasn't quite so easy. It worries me, Gray, it really really does.'

'Look,' said Gray, going over to her, taking her hand. She pulled it away, sat staring out at the darkening garden. 'Look, darling, I can understand you're worried. But we really do have lots of time. I do think it's a terrible mistake to rush it ... A terrible mistake. I mean, surely you'd want to be married first: you know I do, and you don't, or say you don't ...'

'It's a much smaller decision,' said Briony, her blue eyes very large in her small pale face. She looked not much more than a child herself, thought Gray, sitting there in her leggings and her big jumper, her light brown hair caught back in a ribbon. 'You know it is. It doesn't really matter. You just want it because it's romantic –'

'No I don't,' said Gray, mildly indignant, 'I want it because I love you. I want it very much.'

'Yes, all right,' said Briony, 'sorry. It just doesn't seem very important to me. But a baby, that is important.'

'Well, I agree with you there,' said Gray, and he could hear something close to panic in his own voice. 'Very, very important. To both of us. Life-transforming. And we both have to feel – well, absolutely ready for it.'

'And you don't?'

'No,' he said, 'no, I'm sorry, I don't. I – well, I can't even begin to imagine it.'

'But why not? I don't understand why not.'

'I suppose,' he said, simply, 'if you really want to know, because I don't like children. I can't help it, I just don't. It's nothing to do with you, with us. But I will think about it. Think about getting to like them. Carefully. I promise.'

Briony sat looking at him. She looked more herself suddenly, calmer, He felt a slight easing of the panic: maybe it's just talk, he thought, maybe she just wanted to see how I felt.

'Darling,' he said tentatively, 'darling, shall we –'

'No, Gray,' said Briony, 'we won't. Whatever it was, whatever diversionary tactic you think you might embark on, don't. I just wanted to see how you felt, that's all, and now I know. I have to assimilate it, that's all, think what I'm going to do.'

'What do you mean, do?' said Gray sharply. 'What can you do? I don't understand –'

'Oh, don't worry, Gray. I'm not going to flush my pills down the loo without telling you, nothing like that. But you must be able to see that if you feel this way, it affects how I feel about you. You must. And –'

The phone on the table rang sharply; Briony picked it up. 'Seven-four-three-nine,' she said, and her voice was colder than he had ever heard it, even more than when they had had one of their blazing, epic, bi-annual rows. 'Yes, he's here. Can I say who's calling? Right. Hold on.' She turned to Gray, her face absolutely blank. 'It's for you. A woman. Teresa Booth. Mean anything to you?'

Gray shook his head violently; the last thing he could face now was a conversation with some stranger.

'I'm sorry,' said Briony into the phone, 'I was wrong, he's actually just gone out. Could you call him tomorrow at the office? Yes, fine, any time after eleven. Goodbye.'

She put the phone down and looked at Gray, still cold, still hurt. 'She'll call in the morning. I think I'll go and have a bath. OK?'

'OK,' said Gray. He felt as if he had been saved, albeit briefly, from some great, almost unimaginable, danger.

He looked at his watch. It was just after seven. Time to start making the sauce.

Chapter Four

Bard Channing was in a rage. The news cut a swathe through Channing House. There was Bard as he normally was, volatile, awkward, overbearing and bad tempered, and then there was Bard in a rage. The two conditions did not bear comparison.

Oliver Clarke had witnessed the dawn of the rage, and it was he indeed who had conveyed the news of it beyond the confines of his own small office adjacent to Pete Barbour's.

He had watched Bard walk into Pete's office in the way he did when he was really angry, less heavily than usual and very fast, his face taut and set, looking straight ahead of him, and slam the door behind him so hard that the windows reverberated. Jean Rivers, Pete's secretary, who had just brought Oliver's post in, looked up startled at the noise, and made a face at Oliver.

'One of those days,' she said quietly, and disappeared again.

Oliver started sorting through his post and pretended he wasn't trying to hear what was going on next door; he could hear voices, Bard's voice rising, roaring, and the occasional choice phrase – 'bring the whole fucking pack of cards down'; 'lunatic incompetence', were two that came through particularly clearly – alternating with the lower, level hum of Pete's voice and then Bard's again, louder still. 'I don't care where it fucking comes from, Pete, just find it.'

The phone rang on Oliver's desk suddenly; it was Sue in Reception with a package for him: 'Those disks you wanted, I think,' and he went out, grateful to have a genuine reason to escape from the line of fire in which he sat. Channing never saw him on the way into Pete's office but as he came out he looked directly at him, and if he was in a rage, or even a bad temper, he was quite capable of shouting at Oliver for some infinitesimal thing, like having a window open in winter, or for simply looking up at him as he went past.

'Haven't you got anything to do?' he had said one morning, as Oliver glanced up and smiled nervously at him. 'Better find it, or get out. This is not a charitable concern I'm running here, you know.'

'Into the bunkers,' Oliver said now to Sue, picking up the package. 'Heavy artillery attack coming in.'

'Sir?'

'Yup.'

'What's it about?'

'No idea.'

'Thanks for the warning,' she said, and grinned at him.

As Oliver went back into his office, Bard came out; he glared at Oliver but didn't say anything. His face was ashen, his eyes very dark. He walked into Jean's office; Oliver could see through her open door, watched as he literally threw a heavy envelope onto her desk. 'Get that round to Methuens fast,' he said, and stalked out again.

Oliver waited a few moments, then went in. 'What on earth's happened?'

'I've no idea,' said Jean, who was desperately trying to get through to the messengers, 'except that he asked Pete for some bank statements earlier, and I took them along to Marcia's office. You know the rest.'

'Wow,' said Oliver.

Oliver had worked at Channings for just over six months, as assistant to Pete Barbour. He didn't like it and indeed it wasn't at all what he wanted to do; he had got a 2:1 degree in economics from University College, London, and then been taken on by a very good firm to do his articles. He had been there a year or so, and passed his first set of exams, when the very good firm had struck the rocks and laid forty of its staff off at all levels – including its articled clerks.

Oliver might have stuck it out and found another firm had he not just taken out a mortgage that was fractionally higher than he could actually afford on a small house in Ealing, and bought a new car; he might still have stuck it out, but his sister, Melinda, had panicked, told their mother, and she had phoned Bard Channing as she had done on every serious crisis in the past twenty years and asked him if he could help. And Bard Channing, as always, had helped, and arranged for him to see Pete, who needed an assistant. It was impossible for Oliver to refuse. Pete Barbour had been extremely nice, said he understood it wasn't quite what Oliver wanted, and even said he could go for interviews if he wanted to; so far there hadn't been any. Articles in good accountancy firms, especially for people who were halfway through, were hard to come by.

The whole thing had hit Oliver very hard, especially as he had begun to feel he could at last stand on his own feet and stop being beholden to Bard Channing. He knew he was very lucky to have him

71

as his mentor, he knew how grateful he should be for all Mr Channing had done for him – giving him work experience, topping up his grant at university, helping out with buying clothes and even his first car, getting him holiday jobs – and he actually was grateful, but he still was looking forward to it stopping. Stopping being grateful, stopping being the poor relation.

He didn't mind so much all that Channing did for his mother: making sure she really was in the best nursing home, visiting her regularly, and sending her flowers and books and baskets of fruit and an endless supply of the rather pop classical CDs she loved, and lavish presents on her birthday (like a player for the CDs); or even what he did for Melinda, paying for her French exchange when she'd been doing her GCSEs and for her piano lessons, but none of it felt right. His mother told him not to be silly, that it was wonderful that Mr Channing was so good to them, an awful lot of people wouldn't have been, would just have lost interest, and he had never for a moment rubbed their noses in it, made them feel grateful; and Melinda had a crush on the whole bloody family, had spent weeks making a dress for the new baby for instance, in the hope they'd be asked to the christening (of course they weren't), and as for her passion for Barnaby, her conviction that he liked her too, that really was pathetic.

It was almost exactly twenty years now since their father had died, Oliver thought, staring at the date in his diary: 14 April, and his father had been killed on the 17th. That was always a bad day; his mother still got very upset and he and Melinda always went to see her, took her to his grave in the churchyard and laid some flowers on it, and talked about him. Neither Oliver nor Melinda could remember their father: Melinda had been a tiny baby, and Oliver three when it had happened; when he had crashed the car, wrapped it round a tree that awful foggy, unseasonal April night. He had been driving home from the office, not Channing House then of course, nothing so grand, he and Bard and Douglas Booth were operating from a building in Bayswater, but they had still been doing well, riding the first recession, 'the real one', Channing always called it, building their empire. And Nigel Clarke had never seen the real rewards, reaped the big bucks; and neither had his wife or children. But Bard Channing had been very good to them. Very good indeed.

In a funny way, Oliver felt he was paying for it now.

Things had quietened considerably by lunchtime. Bard had calmed down (the news of this spread almost as fast as that of the rage had) and had in any case gone out, Pete Barbour had emerged from his own office, looking still slightly shaken but almost cheerful, and Oliver was just thinking that he might after all be able to go and meet one of his former colleagues for a drink when the phone rang.

'Oliver? Oliver, this is Teresa Booth.'

He couldn't think for a moment who she was; then remembered going to her wedding, having to dance with her even, briefly ('Come along, Oliver, I'm intent on stepping out with every male in the family'), being not quite sure if he liked her or not. He hadn't met her since.

'Oh, Mrs Booth. Yes, hallo. How are you?'

'I'm absolutely fine, Oliver, thank you. How are you? And how is your poor mother? I liked her so much, and one of the things I'm determined to do, now my house is finally finished and my business affairs properly under control, is go and visit her. Could you give me the telephone number and address of her nursing home?'

'Yes, of course. It's —'

She interrupted him. 'No, you can give it me when I see you. Which is the other reason I'm phoning. I want to buy you lunch, Oliver. I'd like to get to know you a bit better, and I've discovered a link with your family, a cousin of mine used to work with your father. Small world, isn't it? Long before Channings, when he was at McIntyres, you know, they were all really young, of course. She was asking me if I knew anything about him, and about you two youngsters, and your mother, and I promised I'd try and get some news for her.'

'Oh,' said Oliver, 'oh, I see. Well —'

'So I thought what a wonderful excuse to have lunch with an attractive young man. Would you do that for me, Oliver? Come and meet me one day?'

'Well — yes,' said Oliver, hoping he didn't sound too unenthusiastic. 'Yes, that would be very nice.'

'Good,' said Teresa Booth. She sounded as if she'd just clinched some business deal. 'Well now, I'm sure you're much busier than I am, so you say a day. One day next week, I thought. How about Thursday? Thursday at the Café Pelican, in St Martin's Lane? That suit you?'

Oliver found himself saying it would suit him very well, and thanking her. He put the phone down, wondering why it was quite such an unattractive prospect, and wondering also what on earth she really wanted.

Kirsten woke up early on Sunday morning and decided she was going to do three things before the day was over: have some really good sex, go to Mass, and see her mother. The first two were comparatively easy: Toby (who had thrown her so thoroughly out of bed a few weeks earlier) had phoned her the day before and said he'd like to see her; the church was just around the corner. But it was a long drive to Somerset, and although she hadn't lost her licence, she had got a hefty fine and six points on it, and staying within the speed limit would make a very long day of it. Then she felt ashamed of begrudging her mother that, and picked up the phone and called the nursing home.

Yes, they said, that would be very nice, Mrs Channing would like to see her, she was very much better, probably home in another fortnight – oh God, thought Kirsten, so soon, at least when Pattie was being dried out no-one had to worry about her, and then promptly felt guilty again. She was a cow; it was time she went to church. She said she'd be down soon after lunch and then called Toby; his answering machine was on. Where was he, at nine in the morning on a Sunday? Bastard. She slammed the phone down again without leaving a message, had a shower, got dressed and drove herself to St Augustine's in the Fulham Palace Road.

She sat in the church, watching intently as the priest offered up the bread and the wine for consecration and thus transubstantiation, trying to recapture the total, blinding, dazzling faith of her childhood that Christ was there, for her, in the bread and the wine, helping her to manage, helping her to be good. She went up to the altar rail, knelt, received the host, waited, waited actually praying for the peace, the comfort, the knowledge: but it did not come. She went back to her seat, and knelt again, prayed again, but still in vain, as always these days; hot tears of frustration, of misery, of disappointment rose behind her eyes, made a fierce ache in her heart. What had happened, she wondered, to the little girl who had believed so passionately, so deeply she had wanted to be a nun, and who even when that had passed had known with a sweet surety that God was in Heaven, and that He loved her? Lost, that little girl was, lost for ever, left behind while Kirsten had had to learn to care for a mother who had often been so drunk she could not even get herself to bed but had fallen asleep on the stairs; to struggle with mourning for a father who had walked away and refused to take her; to care for and lie to a sister who was still too small to understand; to battle with the taunts at school about a mother who was always late for everything, if indeed she came at all, and a father who was always in the papers with a long succession of pretty girls at his side; who had wanted to be loved so much she was climbing into bed with boys before her fifteenth birthday; and who had done something so wicked at sixteen in having an abortion she was destined straight for Hell; and who had now to live with the knowledge that there was in her father's home another family, all much beloved, with a mother who would always be there for them. No wonder she was gone, that good, hopeful little girl; and how stupid, how appallingly stupid to think that the God who had cared for her would come back for a moment to the person she had become.

Angry suddenly, with herself as much as the Church, with her own failure as much as God's, Kirsten stood up, strode out, her high heels beating out a retreat on the flagged floor. People stared at her, half shocked, half reproving; she stared back, praying there would be no more tears. God answered that one at least. Outside, it was bright, sunny, the sky brilliant, dappled with white; she walked down the street towards her car, fast at first, angrily fast, then more slowly, as she forced common sense into herself. How stupid, how unutterably foolish to look for easy answers, instant comfort; what was the matter with her that she expected so much for so little, from one hour, less, in her bigoted, superstitious Church?

'Time to grow up, Kirsten,' she said aloud, as she turned into her own street, and felt her spirits lift at the sight of Toby's car parked in front of her flat.

'You look cheerful,' he said, getting out, coming to meet her, giving her a hug. 'What did I do?'

'More than God could,' said Kirsten, hugging him back. 'I think I'm going to give Him up.' And then felt so horrified at herself, at her own blasphemy, that she crossed herself.

'You and that Church of yours,' said Toby. 'Did you ever think of being a nun?'

'Yes I did,' said Kirsten, looking at him very seriously, and then seeing the incredulity on his face, unable to bear the ridicule, she forced herself to laugh.

'I've missed you,' he said, and bent to kiss her; his mouth was very hard, very hungry, and her own meeting it felt the same. Five minutes later they were in bed.

Kirsten was very good at sex: she was imaginative, tireless, uninhibited, noisy. Most of her boyfriends liked it; a few didn't, complaining she was too dominant, too greedy. Toby seemed to like it very much.

'You make love like a man,' he said, released finally from her demanding, almost frantic body, falling away from her, smoothing her stomach tenderly, kissing her hand, her hair.

'How do you know?' said Kirsten, laughing, She reached out, touched him, bent and kissed his penis, licking it tenderly, thoughtfully; she was still excited, the throbbing of her final orgasm only just easing, leaving her; she knew she could do with more.

'It's no use, Kirsten,' he said, smiling, pulling her head up by her mane of hair, 'no use at all. I'm done for. Now what did you say? Oh yes, how do I know. Because I am one, you fool.'

'So how do girls make love?' said Kirsten. 'No, don't tell me, I might get jealous.'

'They don't take over,' said Toby, 'but that's fine, I like being taken over. It's good.' He lay back and looked at her. 'I've missed you,' he said, 'really missed you. I'm sorry about – well, I'm sorry.'

'No, I deserved it,' said Kirsten. 'You were right. I am a brat. Everyone says so. Even my sister.'

She heard the sadness in her own voice, was startled by it. She looked at Toby and saw he had heard it too.

'Well,' he said, 'maybe I like brats. I'm a pretty fine example of one myself.'

'That's true,' said Kirsten, smiling. Toby had been born with several silver spoons in his mouth, the only child of rich and doting parents; he had arrived at his present employment, in a firm of City brokers, by way of Eton and Oxford; was tall, athletic (he'd got a half blue for rugby), good looking and charming; had been given a flat in Kensington for his twenty-fifth birthday, and amongst his other talents was a very good lover. He also had a fairly healthy ego.

'How would you like to do something really seriously unbrattish for the rest of the day?' she said.

'What?'

'Drive me to Somerset. I want to see my mother.'

'Sure. On one condition.'

'What?'

'You take up tonight where you just left off,' he said. 'I can see I might very well have recovered by then.'

'My pleasure,' said Kirsten.

Toby didn't like talking while he drove; he said it wrecked his concentration. As he drove his BMW at a steady eighty-five, even on the single-carriageway stretches of the A303, Kirsten was happy to be silent. They stopped at a pub just north of Taunton, for a late lunch; Kirsten, feeling sick, ordered a Perrier and a salad.

'I'd forgotten how exciting it is, driving with you,' she said, slightly weakly.

'It's exciting doing most things with me. So what are you doing with yourself?' he said, falling on a plateful of pork pie and pickle. 'I should have asked, sorry. So busy telling you about me. Is it true you're working for your dad?'

'Good Lord,' said Kirsten, 'how did you know?'

'The Square Mile is a pretty small place. Tell me what happened. Did Hell actually freeze over?'

'What?'

'You once told me that Hell would have to freeze over before you'd do that. I thought you were a girl of your word.'

'Oh – well. Not quite, obviously.' She felt embarrassed suddenly, ashamed of her hostility to the father who had taken her on so generously, so unconditionally (apart from that she should work her arse off and ask for no favours), ashamed too that she had no intention of staying, and that he had no idea of that; and then sharply remembering the childhood she had relived that morning in church, she said, 'Toby, I just got sick of being a loser. And I thought he owed me one.'

'No doubt he did. So what are you doing? Cleaning the toilets? Licking his boots before meetings?'

'No,' said Kirsten, angry suddenly, 'no, not at all. I'm working in the PR department.'

'Wow,' said Toby, and his eyes danced with malice, 'a proper job. What a clever girl you are.'

'Oh fuck off,' said Kirsten.

'Sorry, darling. But why PR? Why not the legal department at least?'

'I don't know, Toby,' said Kirsten, and her voice was suddenly weary. 'He said publicity would suit me best, and that I'd learn most about the company there. I just do what I'm told.'

'Uh-huh. Well, he's a brilliant man, your dad, from all accounts. You'll learn a lot wherever you are. Nice boss?'

'Yes, very nice, actually,' said Kirsten. 'I really like her. She's called Sam. Sam Illingworth. Quite young, pretty. She's very nice to me, anyway.'

'How young is young?'

'Oh – thirty-something. Not really young.'

'She is for that job. Not like your dad to promote young women, is it? He got his leg over her, do you think?'

'No I don't,' said Kirsten irritably. 'It's so gross, that kind of question, Toby. My father may be a monster, but he doesn't play games in the office. Well, not those kinds of games. And Sam certainly wouldn't.'

She was surprised at her own indignation; clearly she had absorbed more of the company ethos than she had thought.

'Quite the little company mouthpiece, aren't you?' said Toby amused, cutting into her thoughts. 'You'll be giving me a quick rundown on the share price movement next.'

'Oh Toby, do shut up,' said Kirsten.

'No I won't. You look so sexy when you're cross. Now let's get this good work over, and then head for home again. I'm looking forward to my reward already.'

'I'll be a bit late tonight, darling,' said Gray to Briony over breakfast (brioches from Harvey Nichols, orange juice he'd squeezed on the state-of-the-art juicer Briony had given him last Christmas), 'got a meeting.'

'Gray, who with? You promised we could see *Schindler's List* tonight.'

'Oh, hell. I'm sorry, darling,' said Gray, just slightly wary of explaining that the meeting was with an attractive woman, and at the Savoy Hotel. 'Could we go to the late show instead?'

'No, I'm sorry,' said Briony, in the cool, slightly detached tones she'd adopted recently, 'I really don't want to be late tonight, Gray. I have a big job on tomorrow. Judy wants to see it, I'll go with her.'

'But Bri, I want to see it with you,' said Gray plaintively, 'I really really do.'

'Well, that's a great shame, Gray,' said Briony. 'But you could cancel your meeting. I don't suppose you'd thought of that ...'

'Can't we go tomorrow?'

'No, Gray, I'm going to be late tomorrow. We said tonight. I'll go with Judy, that's fine. Really. I'll see you at home.'

She went out and shut the door just too firmly; Gray sat staring after her, feeling the gnawing mixture of remorse and resentment that had become increasingly familiar to him ever since Briony had first broached the Big B subject (as he referred to it in an effort at lightheartedness).

'Bloody hormones,' he said to what was left of the brioches.

Even for someone who made an art form of being unforthcoming when necessary, Sam Illingworth was giving a bravura performance. Bard Channing was simply terribly busy, and he didn't want to give up any time to something like a profile. 'And don't tell me you'd only be an hour, Gray, because you know you wouldn't. You've already told him you want to shadow him for a day or two, interview other key people, he just won't do it. At the moment.'

Gray sighed, then threw up his hands. 'OK. I know when I'm beaten. Want to tell me about the northern thing?'

'Only if you really want to know,' said Sam, 'which I suspect you don't.'

'Try me,' said Gray.

He sat and watched her while she went into her carefully smooth PR spiel; about how Bard Channing wanted to expand the northern office, wanted to put up at least two more shopping malls, how he felt they were the only way forward for shopping, including fashion shopping –

'But you're really not interested, are you?' she said with her sudden brilliant smile (she really was very attractive, Gray thought, looking at her, not his type really, too glossy, and she rather wore her competence on the sleeves of her power suits, but still ...). He wrenched his mind back to what she was saying.

'Of course I am.'

'Gray! Let me buy you another drink. And we can discuss the weather or something. I really am sorry about this, I feel a bit of an idiot myself –'

She's as baffled as I am, thought Gray; I wonder what this is really all about. He sat looking at Sam, not saying anything and becoming slowly aware of a sensation that he knew very well. It was absolutely unique, that sensation, a stirring somewhere deep within him, unfailingly exciting, and totally reliable, part physical, part emotional. 'It's like –' he had said to Briony once, trying to explain it, 'it's actually rather like sex.' He didn't experience it very often, but when he did, he knew to trust it implicitly: it had never failed him. It told him he was onto a story.

'Well, let's see what happens,' he said. 'Now tell me, how is the real business doing? Is he still hanging onto the Docklands scheme? That really is a slow turnaround. The place is still a desert. I went down the other week, to have lunch with a chum at the *Telegraph*. It's all this bloody government's fault, not getting on with that railway, that's the key.'

'Yes, I know it's very slow. And that the recovery still exists largely in the minds of politicians, as we all know. The thing about Channings is, of course, it's such a broad base it can carry a loss for a long time. And Bard has a strong predilection for bucking trends.'

'Yeah, it's one of the things I wanted to talk to him about,' said

Gray, and sighed. 'Well, keep in touch. Let me know if there are any new developments, won't you? I must go. Got a piece to rework.'

'OK, fine,' said Sam.

She signed the check; they walked together to the foyer.

'Thanks again,' said Gray. 'Great martinis. I don't usually like them, but –' He stopped. Coming in through the doors was one of the most beautiful girls he had ever seen. She was extremely tall, with a mane of red-gold hair, and extraordinarily brilliant blue-green eyes, the colour of the sea. She was wearing a leather jacket, and something which required more than a little imagination to translate it into a skirt. She looked harassed; paused, caught sight of Sam and smiled a brief, careful smile.

'Hi,' she said, and rushed on.

'Hallo,' said Sam.

'Who on earth was that?' said Gray. He felt rather odd, disorientated; as if he had suddenly found himself in a country where everyone spoke a different language.

'My new assistant,' said Sam.

'Interesting,' said Gray. He couldn't think of anything more intelligent to say.

'Indeed,' said Sam, and Gray could see by the amusement in her eyes that his reaction to the girl was extremely obvious, 'and moreover she's Bard Channing's daughter. The eldest,' she added, 'and the tallest,' and smiled again.

'Good God,' said Gray.

He looked after the eldest Miss Channing, but she had disappeared down the long corridor that led to the River Room. He contemplated making some excuse to follow her, then looked at Sam Illingworth's face and smiled, slightly embarrassed. 'Maybe I could profile her. Channing and Daughter, it would make a very good peg.'

'Indeed it would,' said Sam. 'Well, just let me know.'

Gray went home to a solitary supper which he ate in front of his word processor. He didn't make a lot of progress on his piece; most of his brain seemed to be inextricably engaged elsewhere. He went to bed early, and woke to find Briony climbing rather carefully in beside him. He turned over and pulled her against him, suddenly wanting her rather badly; to his surprise she started kissing him, feeling for him, winding her long legs round him.

'It's all right,' she said, and he could hear the smile in her voice, 'I've taken my pill.'

Gray was torn between relief and a feeling of guilt that the reassurance was necessary; in the morning, he felt strangely remorseful and especially tender towards Briony. It was only when he was parking his motorbike – his beloved Harley Davidson, referred to by Tricia as 'the wife' – in his space beneath the *News* offices, that he realised why. He had fallen asleep (after some extremely good sex) and then dreamed, not of Briony at all, but of a girl half a foot taller than she, with a great mass of golden hair and eyes the colour of the sea.

'So Francesca, you'll be in charge of the raffle, will you, and the tombola?'

Diana Martin-Wright flashed Francesca the smile that Bard Channing had once described as a guillotine with lips; the committee of the Grasshopper Ball (in aid of research into allergy-based diseases) were meeting at her house in Campden Hill Square.

'*And* the tombola? Diana, that's a bit tough,' said Francesca.

'Not really, darling. I did them both last time, it's actually much more efficient, the thing is while you're asking people for big things, it's easy to ask them for little ones too. I mean sweet Jane Packer, for instance, she donated two wonderful dried-flower arrangements for my raffle and then popped in a two-hour lesson at her school into the tombola. Honestly, it's easy. Just use your contacts. You of all people should know about that, Francesca.'

'What on earth do you mean, Diana?'

'Well, your commercial background of course. You're a profession-al woman, or were. The rest of us are just poor struggling amateurs. Which reminds me, do you think Nicky would give a free hairdo? For the raffle? You go there, don't you? Or don't you any more?'

'Well, thanks for the compliment,' said Francesca, laughing. 'I'm obviously looking very scruffy.'

'Oh, of course I didn't mean that. Just that I hadn't seen you in there lately.'

Diana was famous for her lack of tact; she probably had meant it.

'No, well, I must have missed you. If you're there so much, Diana, why don't you ask him?'

'Oh, I don't think wires should cross like that. The right hand simply has to know what the left is doing.'

'Oh I see,' said Francesca.

'Good, that's all marvellous. Honestly, when people know it's charity they'll do anything, anything at all.'

Which was a lie, Francesca thought; these days people would do very little for charity. It had been so easy, a few years ago, in the dear old lush, flash 'eighties when there had been wall-to-wall money everywhere, when giving it away was not only a nice tasteful way of showing what a lot you'd got, but tax-efficient as well. Now people not only had a lot less, but they wanted to hang on to what they had. And if you were running a business on a sliver-thin margin, when the slightest thing could upset the balance of the books, the thought of giving away a two- or three-hundred-pound jacket or a flight to Paris, or even two hours of a hair stylist's time, made people nervous. It wasn't actually going to tip them over into insolvency, but they just weren't prepared to take any chances.

'Oh and also, Francesca, I do need help with selling space in the programme,' said Diana, reaching for her glass of mineral water. 'Now that would be right up your street, wouldn't it, easy for you I should think, could you let me have a hit list within the week? How many pages do you think you could personally sell, ten, fifteen —'

'I really don't know,' said Francesca. 'Times are hard, Diana, and there are so many calls for this sort of thing —'

'Oh I get so tired of being told times are hard,' said Diana. 'It is absolutely no excuse at all, just a ridiculous cop-out. We all have to make sacrifices these days, I certainly do, it's just a question of adjustment. Now if you —'

Francesca looked at her, sitting in her first-floor drawing room (newly styled by Jane Churchill) in one of the most expensive pieces of real estate in London, dressed by Jasper Conran, thought of her new BMW parked outside the door, her three children parked in one of England's major public schools, and wondered precisely what sacrifices she considered she had made. These women never failed to fascinate her.

Diana dispatched her committee with the regretful explanation that she had to go and see her dressmaker; Francesca walked down the hill towards her car, drawing up a mental hit list of the people she could sell pages in the ball's programme to, at £2,000 a time. It was rather short: nothing like the fifteen Diana had clearly indicated, and as she negotiated the heavy traffic in between Notting Hill Gate and St John's Wood, and she tried to lengthen it, the name Teresa Booth came into her head. She had her own company, the timeshare operation, which she never stopped talking about; she might like to advertise. And she could possibly sell her a couple of tickets to the ball as well. It was worth a try; she could only say no.

She phoned Teresa in her office, and was told she was at home: obviously not quite the tycoon she led them all to believe. Her housekeeper answered the phone, said she would go and ask if Mrs

Booth was available; a long pause then followed, before Teresa's husky voice came down the line.

'Francesca dear! To what do I owe this honour?'

'Hallo Teresa,' said Francesca, ignoring this, 'how are you?'

'Very well, thank you. Very busy, my company is expanding considerably and there is a great deal to do. Of course you ladies of leisure would find that hard to appreciate –'

'I have worked, Teresa,' said Francesca, keeping her voice level with an effort of considerable will, 'and I can just about remember being under pressure. Anyway, it's about your company I'm phoning.'

'Oh yes? Don't tell me you want a job?'

'No, I don't. Well, I would like a job, actually, but the children and Bard keep me pretty busy.'

'Yes, dear, I'm sure.'

Francesca counted up to five almost audibly, and then said, 'But I wondered if I could twist your arm, and persuade you, or rather your company, to buy a page in the programme of a ball I'm helping with. In November, it's the Grasshopper Ball, medical research, terribly good cause and –'

'How much?'

'Two thousand pounds a page,' said Francesca.

'Good God. That's a great deal of money.'

'Yes I know. But think of the target audience, Teresa. These are people with real money ...'

'Francesca dear, people with real money aren't very interested in timeshares, are they? Certainly not in places like Marjorca and even Marbella.'

'Oh I don't know,' said Francesca. She realised she was rather enjoying herself; it was like being back at the agency. 'I don't think you can assume anything. I know several people who have a timeshare in ski-resorts –'

'Bit different, dear, but do go on.'

'And there are a lot of hangers-on at these things, people anxious to be seen to be doing the right thing –'

'So they haven't all got real money?'

'It depends what you mean by real,' said Francesca, carefully patient. 'If they've got enough to buy the tickets, they've got enough to buy a timeshare. Or at least consider one. And then it's a very impressive showcase, Teresa. You'd be alongside the very best. Tiffanys, Aspreys, Gucci, they were all there last time, and Kuoni came in; the sort of class acts that could well enhance your image.'

'Does that mean you don't think Home Time is a class act?'

Damn, she'd asked for that one. 'No, of course not. But a good ambience never did anyone any harm. You might consider a half page.'

'No, I don't want to look cheapskate. I'll take a page.' The swiftness of this startled Fancesca; she had expected a much longer battle.

'Oh. Wonderful! Well, that is just marvellous. Thank you. I'm delighted. You're very kind. Now I wonder if you'd like to join us, you and Duggie, buy a couple of tickets, you could be on our table naturally –'

'No thank you, dear. Not my scene. As I told you. I don't get along with those kind of people too well. I don't have much to say to them.'

'I'm sure you would –' Francesca's voice tailed off slightly.

'No, Francesca, really. And I might say too much. Anyway, you let me know nearer the time, and I'll send a cheque. And I'd like to know precisely whose ad I'm alongside.'

'Oh – well, that could be difficult.'

'I don't see why. Sorry, Francesca, that's a precondition. I don't want to be slung in alongside Sainsbury's.'

'Well, obviously they don't advertise. But – yes, all right. I'll confirm that. Thank you. Er – how's Duggie?'

'Oh, pretty well. Up in Scotland for a few days. Playing golf. And making money for your husband.'

'Ah,' said Francesca. It seemed a strange remark, since anything Duggie made for Bard he also made for himself; they had an equal shareholding. Or so she had always understood.

'How is your husband?'

'Oh, he's fine. Thank you.' There was a silence, then she said, 'Well, Teresa, I must –'

'Do you see much of young Oliver Clarke?' said Teresa suddenly.

'Oliver? Er – no. Why?'

'He seems a delightful young man. Not at all spoilt. What a difficult life he's had. They've all had.'

'Yes. Yes indeed. Um – how do you know him?'

'Oh, I make it my business to know anyone I find interesting. And I find him very interesting.'

'Really?' Francesca didn't know what else to say. What on earth was the woman going on about?

'But your husband has been very good to them all, hasn't he? Extraordinarily good, some might say.'

'Well – he has been good, yes. But Nigel Clarke was his partner. Their partner. And I think he felt responsible when he was killed.'

'Oh really! Responsible! How interesting you should say that.'

'I don't see why. Anyone would have. A young woman, with two small children, widowed like that. Duggie must have told you.'

'Oh – yes. Yes, he told me the story. Of course.'

There was an odd emphasis on the word 'story'. Francesca suddenly felt uncomfortable, defensive on Bard's behalf.

'But he was hardly killed on company business, was he? I mean he was in a car crash, simply driving home to his family, I understood.'

'Yes, of course he was. But Bard is a very – conscientious – person. And he felt he had a duty to look after Nigel's family. Well, to keep an eye on them.'

'Yes, I see. Well, that is very nice. Very nice indeed. And for such a long time. And so very generously –'

'Teresa, I'm sorry, but I really must go.' She couldn't take much more of this. 'I have to collect Jack from a party. He loves his car, by the way. Thank you again. And thank you for today, for your generosity. If you change your mind about the tickets, just let me know. Love to Duggie.'

'Yes, of course. Goodbye, Francesca.'

Without quite knowing why, she wanted to speak to Bard; she dialled his private number. Marcia answered it, sounding, as always, smugly unhelpful.

'I'm afraid he's not here, Mrs Channing.'

'Well, when will he be back?'

'I really have no idea; I'm sorry.'

'But isn't it in his diary?'

'Mrs Channing, he's in a meeting at the Bank of England.'

'Ah. How long is this meeting sceduled to last?'

'Meetings with Mr George are rather open-ended affairs, Mrs Channing,' said Marcia patiently, as if talking to a small child. A not very bright child, Francesca thought.

'Yes, I see. And has he been at the Bank of England all day?'

'He has been out of the office all day.'

'But not at the bank?'

'No. He's been out of town. I'm sorry, I would have thought he'd have told you that.'

'Sadly not. Well, ask him to ring me when he gets back, would you, Marcia? I must say, if my husband ever committed a serious crime, you'd be a very good witness for the defence.'

'I'm sorry?'

'It's all right, Marcia, just a joke. Goodbye.'

'Good afternoon, Mrs Channing.'

At the same time as Bard Channing was attending his meeting at the Bank of England, Desmond North, a senior divisional manager of Methuens merchant bank (situated only a few streets away) was studying, just a little uneasily, a report of the continuing failure of the Docklands development in general, and the Channing Corporation's stake in it in particular, to show any signs of achieving its much vaunted potential. He put in a request to one of his managers to supply him with a statement of the Channing account with the bank. Looking at it over his Earl Grey tea and shortbread biscuits (the latter forbidden to him by Mrs North, in the interests of his health), he was reassured to see that the figures looked, under the circumstances, perfectly healthy.

He did, however, ask the manager in question, an earnest and ambitious young man who had his eye on a job even bigger than Mr North's own, if he thought it might be prudent to bring a firm of accountants into Channings and do a full report. The earnest young man, whose name was Michael Jackson (a fact which caused him some anguish), said he thought it would be very prudent and that he would get on the case first thing in the morning.

Bard finally came in at half-past eight.

'Hi.'

'Hallo, Bard. How was your day?'

'Oh – pretty much the same as always. I'm going up to change,' he said. 'I'll be with you in a minute.'

He came back ten minutes later, a large whisky in his hand. He bent and kissed her head, caressed the nape of her neck. 'You all right?'

'Oh – yes, thank you. So tell me about your day, Bard? What did you do?'

'I'm sorry?'

'I want to know what you did today. I want to hear all about it, your conversation with the Governor this afternoon, what deals you made, what his outlook is for the financial health of the country in the foreseeable future, where you went this morning, out of town –'

'I really cannot tell you all that,' he said scowling at her. 'Certainly not about my meeting, it was highly complex, it would be very tedious for you.'

'No it wouldn't. I really want to know.'

'We were just discussing financial trends,' he said after a pause. 'Falling inflation, that sort of thing.'

'Oh really? Just you and him?'

'No of course not, there were a dozen of us.'

'All in property? Or different industries?'

'Different ones,' he said. 'What is all this, Francesca? I'd rather hear about Jack's schooling than rehearse the tedious details of my day.'

'It can't be much more tedious than mine. I'm just trying to do what you told me to do, Bard, make you my career. Take an interest, all that sort of thing. Only it's difficult if you won't tell me. All right then, what about this morning? Where did you go, what was that about?'

He looked at her for a moment, his eyes blank, then he said, 'I went to look at a possible site.'

'Where?'

'I'm sorry?'

'I said where was it?'

'Oh – in the west of England. Near Bristol.'

'Big site?'

'What?'

'I said was it a big site?'

'Pretty big, yes.'

'Bard honestly,' said Francesca, losing her temper suddenly, 'you ought to set up an espionage agency with Marcia Grainger. You'd be a brilliant pair. Never crack under interrogation. Well, would you like to hear what I did today?'

'Yes. Yes, all right. What did you do today?'

'Went to a lunch, to discuss the Grasshopper Ball. Got landed with selling advertising space in the programme. You'll take a page, won't you?'

'What?'

'Bard, please listen to me. I said would you take space in –'

'Talk to Sam about it,' he said.

'All right. Oh, and I had the most extraordinary conversation with Teresa Booth.'

He was with her then: sharply and totally. 'What on earth were you talking to her about?'

'Well, I sold her a page in the programme. A whole page, two thousand quid's worth. I was really surprised. That company of hers must be doing quite well.'

'Yes.'

'And then she started talking about the Clarkes.'

'The Clarkes?'

She watched him closely; he was lying back, taking another slug of whisky, ostensibly relaxed. But the muscle was twitching on the side of his head.

'Yes, the Clarkes. And making sort of – oh, I don't know. Innuendoes.'

'What the hell do you mean?'

'There's no need to sound so cross.'

'I'm not cross,' said Bard, scowling, 'I was surprised, that's all. It sounded an odd thing to say. What sort of innuendoes?'

'Well, maybe not innuendoes. Hints. About how very responsible you seem to feel about Nigel's death, how very very underlined generous you'd been to them all.'

'I haven't been especially generous,' he said.

'Well, she seems to think you have. She was quite – odd about it. What exactly did happen about that, Bard, he wasn't killed while he was on company business, was he?'

'No of course he wasn't,' he said. 'Why on earth did you think that?'

'Because she seems to think so.'

'Bloody woman. She's a pain in the arse.'

'That's true. But Bard, what exactly did happen? I thought he was just driving home, late at night, and –'

'Francesca,' he said, and his voice was heavy with irritation, 'that *is* exactly what happened. Can we stop this, please? I've come home for a bit of peace and relaxation and it's been one bloody inquisition after the other.'

'Well, I'm very sorry, Bard,' she said, the irony icily heavy in her voice, 'I'll just creep back into my little hole and get on with some nice quiet embroidery. Or perhaps I should go and check on the kitchen floor, in case it's not quite shiny enough. Would you like that better? Anyway, I won't talk to you or bother you any more.'

'Oh for God's sake,' he said, and went out of the room. She heard him go into his study and slam the door.

'Bastard,' she said ferociously, and tried to concentrate on an article she was reading in *The Times*. She was too cross to think about their conversation for a while; but later, as her thoughts settled, she found herself increasingly troubled by it. Not his bad temper, but his unease. About her talking to Teresa Booth in general and about the Clarkes in particular. She felt yet again the drift of unease – more than a drift now, a stab almost, sharp, insistent – and then it was gone. No reason for it really; no reason at all.

Chapter Five

Rachel wondered if she should, if she could, jump. End it all. Anything, anything would be preferable to this, this awful rising and plunging and dipping and circling, and the terrible noise, and the fear that any moment now she was going to be sick. She must be mad to have agreed to this, totally mad; nothing else in the world would have persuaded her, not bridge with Omar Sharif, not lunch with Paul Newman — such old heroes, Rachel mused, trying to distract herself, old men, how depressing — to this long helicopter ride on a windy day — not that she'd known it was going to be windy, of course, who could? But Bard had said he was short of time, and if they were going to go, it would have to be in the helicopter. Knowing he was aware of her terror of flying, even in a large, liner-style jumbo, even on Concorde with its built-in five-star pampering, she wondered if he had done it on purpose, to test her. If he had, then it was all the more important to say yes, to go. And she was so terrified already, of what he might think, say, ask, a mere death-trap of a helicopter ride seemed only a little worse. A dozen times since their breakfast she had lifted the phone to cancel, to tell him she'd found someone else, simply to say she was ducking out. But then she'd remember the priory and what it could be, and the nuns and their faith in her and – well, and everyone there, dependent on her – and she'd put it down again, known she had to go on. The alternative for all of them was too hideous.

Christ, this was awful. The vibrations of the thing seemed to have entered her body; her stomach itself had become detached from its moorings, was shaking wildly within her, heaving along with the helicopter. She desperately wanted to pee, but that was obviously impossible. God, why had she had that tea at the heliport? Rachel looked out, trying to distract herself by the scenery, but the scenery rose and fell at her, making her feel worse. 'How much longer?' she shouted at Bard, and he raised his eyes briefly from the papers he was scribbling all over and said, 'Only about forty-five minutes,' and shut

90

off from her again. She closed her eyes and, for want of anything else to do, prayed.

It was actually less than that, a little over half an hour, when the northern coast of Devon came into sight, and they were swooping down over Exmoor, towards Hartland Point; she had arranged for them to land in the field next to the convent, had warned the nuns (who were all hugely excited at the prospect); as the helicopter suddenly dropped dead into the centre of the field and her tortured stomach leapt painfully into her chest, she saw some of them with the residents, leaning on the gate, watching. Mary, as she had known she would be, was with them.

She climbed out finally, gratefully, and really thought she was going to black out; Bard had to steady her.

'You OK?'

'No,' said Rachel, 'I'm not. I'm not getting back in that thing. I'll go back on the train.'

'Rachel!' he said. 'Toughest woman I know. I'm surprised at you. Right, let's go and case the joint.' He grinned at her cheerfully; she looked back at him thoughtfully and fondly. She knew he was tired, he had had a gruelling trip to Stockholm, there was some problem with a new development, and yet when she had phoned, half fearful that he would cancel, to ask him if the arrangement stood, he had said almost indignantly that of course it did. He was as famous for never cancelling arrangements – except with the Press – never reneging on agreements, as he was for his rages and his ruthlessness.

'This is very good of you, Bard,' she said simply. 'I do appreciate it.'

'I haven't yet said I'd do any more than look,' he said. 'Remember that, please.'

'I'll remember.'

Reverend Mother greeted them very sweetly; she said she had coffee waiting in her room. 'Or would you like something more substantial, we have some delicious fresh rolls in the oven?'

'Sounds good,' said Bard, 'thank you. My mother-in-law tells me I overeat, I don't want to risk my reputation by refusing anything.'

'Perhaps, Mary, you would go and fetch some rolls,' said Reverend Mother.

Mary came back, the rolls carefully piled in a basket, honey, butter and plates on a tray. Her tongue stuck out just slightly with the effort of concentration; she set them down, smiled at Bard, then went over to Rachel and took her hand.

'Mary is my special friend here,' said Rachel carefully.

'So I see.'

'The honey is from our own bees,' said Reverend Mother. 'Our latest achievement.'

'It's quite an achievement,' said Bard. He looked over at Rachel and grinned at her. 'You should market it properly. Worldwide.'

'This is very good of you, Mr Channing,' said Reverend Mother. 'We are so grateful.'

'I've already said, and I hope you realise,' he said, wiping his mouth and his fingers, 'I'm only examining the project. At this stage.'

'Of course. I understand. But for a man as busy as yourself, finding the time to do even that is difficult, I imagine.'

'Well,' said Brad, 'I should think you are quite busy here.'

'We are. That is why we understand busy-ness.' She smiled at him, a sweet, sudden, conspiratorial smile: Good God, thought Rachel, if she wasn't a nun I would think she was flirting with him.

They finished their coffee: Reverend Mother stood up.

'Well now, you will want to do our tour here, and then we can go over to the priory. Rachel my dear, you can show Mr Channing round here. And Mary, I think perhaps you had better not go with them. They have important business to discuss.'

'She can come with us,' said Bard. He winked at Mary, who had been gazing at him, following the progress of each bite of roll and honey into his mouth with patent pleasure; she smiled back. She was looking very sweet, Rachel thought, pink faced and well; she was wearing a new sweater she had brought with her last time, and some new trainers that she most assuredly had not. It always upset her, the clothes that Mary wore, even while she knew their role was to be hard wearing, practical and – most important – easy to put on, so that maximum independence could be achieved. Jumpers, not blouses, pull-on trousers or skirts without buttons or zips, trainers with Velcro fastenings. Surely, she had said to Reverend Mother once, surely some ordinary slip-on shoes would do; and Reverend Mother had said yes, of course they would do, but they would not be so comfortable, or so hard wearing, and besides Mary loved her trainers. She always chose them herself on expeditions to Bideford.

She had expected the tour of the Help House to be quick, but Bard constantly delayed it, talking to the residents, peering into pots and ovens in the kitchen, asking how the knitting machine worked that dear Brenda, who could hardly manage to dress herself, manipulated with such skill, insisting on a visit to the henhouse with Richard, who took his hand and led him on an egg-finding expedition.

'I should instigate an Easter egg hunt here,' he said to Rachel, with a grin. 'I fancy they'd do a lot better than my lot.'

All this time, Mary walked with them, quietly, studying Bard carefully; suddenly she whispered something to Rachel, who laughed.

'What did she say?'

'She said you had a good face.'

'Oh really?' said Bard shortly. 'Well, she doesn't know me very well.'

'No, she doesn't,' said Rachel, 'but her judgment is usually pretty reliable.'

They got into Reverend Mother's mud-spattered Ford Fiesta after an hour and drove to the priory. Mary and Richard, who had taken a great fancy to Bard, were told gently but firmly they could not come.

'I don't see why not,' said Bard, 'if it's going to be their home.'

'It might not be,' said Reverend Mother, 'so they would be very disappointed. And besides, the others might be resentful. It doesn't do to show favouritism.'

'I see,' said Bard.

The priory was in its own small valley, just in from the coast; a huge, grey sheltered house, it had been used most recently as a prep school which had been forced to close in the wake of the recession and the slow ending of the British upper classes' tradition of estrangement from their children at a hideously early age. It was freezing cold inside, but dry and clean; rooms were filled with piled-up desks, with maps and globes and blackboards, with games paraphernalia, the upstairs ones with bunks and iron beds.

'We inherit those if we want them,' said Reverend Mother. 'They would probably be of some use.'

Outside, there were still rugby posts, football goal nets, a hideous empty swimming pool filled with leaves, and several dead field mice.

'It would be wonderful to have a pool,' said Rachel. 'They love swimming, and at the moment they have to go to Exmouth.'

'What about the sea?' said Bard.

'Too dangerous for them usually. This is a very treacherous coast, the surf is heavy.'

But the most wonderful thing about the whole place was the outbuildings, seven altogether, that the school had neglected, but which had clearly been, in the days of the priory's true occupancy, used for what they would be again: henhouses, bakeries, a laundry.

'It would be a dream come true,' said Reverend Mother, leading them from one to the next. 'We could make the place if not pay its way, then certainly make a big contribution towards its keep.'

'I would doubt that,' said Bard briefly.

She looked at him, gave him her quick smile again. 'I've done some cash flows, Mr Channing, some projections. They are quite conservative and they still show considerable room for optimism.'

'Have you indeed. And where did you learn to do such things?'

'I taught myself. We have a computer, at the convent. It's important, you know, in this modern world, to have a grasp of financial reality. God alone does not provide.'

'But He helps those who help themselves, does He?'

'He seems to. If we are lucky.'

There was a vast walled vegetable garden, several large greenhouses, albeit with most of the glass missing, and several meadows. 'For the bees.'

They walked back to the car; Bard looked at Reverend Mother.

'OK. The asking price is four hundred thousand pounds. What do you reckon you need over and above that to put the place in order?'

'We need a million altogether,' she said, 'and then of course money to keep us going. Everything has to be paid for. We can't produce all our food, nor of course our clothes. We try to grow enough wood for the house fires, but we need proper central heating. The residents generally are not very robust, several of our Down's Syndrome people are prone to chest problems. It is terribly expensive, and we simply can't manage any longer.'

'So what would your annual outgoings be? What does your cash flow say?'

'Sixty thousand a year, for the twelve residents we have now. If we had the priory, we could take more, maybe up to twenty. That would reduce the per capita cost. And with the increased input from the smallholding as I see it, I don't see why we should need any more than that even at first, diminishing as time went on. We plan to have a pick-your-own fruit farm, to run the laundry as a commercial concern –'

'Not much call for that, I'd have thought,' said Bard.

'You'd be surprised. There is a local hospital for instance, their laundry contract is up for tender. Then the bakery would possibly service the village shops; the honey, eggs of course, and I thought if we could keep a few cows, we'd need advice on that, we could make cheeses to sell, yoghurt –'

He looked at her and smiled. 'You're a real businesswoman, aren't you?' he said. 'I could use you in my company.'

'I don't think I could find the time,' she said, smiling back. 'But I think I would enjoy working with you.'

94

'And would you run this Utopia yourself?'

'I fear not. It would be too big a project, I would need to get some kind of a manager. I thought perhaps a man and his wife, who could do some of the pastoral care for the residents. I have neglected the more spiritual side of my work recently, I need to do more of that –'

'Like what?'

'Like our Sunday schools, our charity work, we have services in our chapel of course, we do a lot of visiting and counselling, you'd be surprised how much of the work of the Mother Church goes on –'

'Oh no,' said Bard, 'I wouldn't. My second wife was – is a Catholic.'

'Oh really?' She was clearly interested, but no more, asked no questions; how clever she is, thought Rachel, how good a diplomat.

They reached the convent again at midday. 'We can offer you lunch,' said Reverend Mother, 'but I understand you are short of time.'

'Yes, we are. I have to get back. But I'd like to see those cash flows of yours, and I'd like to be able to ring you and talk to you about them. Is there any time that's better than any other?'

'Oh no,' she smiled. 'I can usually be found. And I am not often on my knees in a stone cell. Unfortunately. Thank you again for coming, Mr Channing. It is wonderfully good of you.'

They walked back to the helicopter; Rachel looked at it with resigned misery and total dread. Mary and Richard and Reverend Mother walked with them.

When they reached the helicopter, Mary and Richard shook Bard's hand, with perfect, formal politeness, and Mary reached up and hugged Rachel.

'Love you lots,' she said.

'I love you lots,' too,' said Rachel, hugging her back. Her eyes met Bard's over Mary's head; they were determinedly and absolutely blank.

'Right,' he said as the helicopter rose, circled, swooped, 'we'd better talk, I think.'

'Well, perhaps not till you've looked at the figures and everything.'

'Oh Rachel, fuck the figures,' said Bard. 'I'll do this if I think it's right. But what I want to know is exactly what your interest in it all is. Don't lie to me, because I don't like it.'

Rachel looked at him, and then out of the window. The horizon was hurtling up towards her again; her own stomach seemed to be following suit.

She raised agonised eyes to Bard, grabbed the paper bag the

unbearably cheerful pilot had given her – 'in case, but you won't need it' – and said, 'All right. I'll tell you. It might help to take my mind off this torture. But if you tell Francesca I will kill you. I really mean it, Bard.'

'I won't tell her,' he said, 'whatever it is. I promise.'

It was always unbelievable, death, Gray thought. Especially sudden death. You felt it must be a mistake, that everyone had got it wrong, that any moment someone would say no of course not, he isn't really, whatever made you think that? He'd been sitting at his desk when the news came in: Tricia had put her head round the door and said have you heard about John Smith? and he'd said no, what, has he joined the Tories and she'd said no, the angels. And he'd said what on earth do you mean, and she'd said, 'Gray, he's died.'

Older people always said they knew exactly what they were doing when they heard about President Kennedy's assassination; this was less dramatic, but still an appalling shock. He knew he would remember this, remember sitting there, staring at Tricia for a long time. Later, other friends said the same thing. It was a parallel to Kennedy's death in some ways: a charismatic, charming man, his promise unfulfilled, robbed of much of his life.

'Shit,' said Gray. 'Holy shit!'

He asked Tricia to get him some tea and drank it, hardly noticing how strong it was.

The editorial conference was all about Smith, who would do what and how on the Sunday. Gray was briefed, predictably, to write about the massive inroads he had made on corporate and City consciousness; mindful of another piece he had been working rather intermittently on, he decided to get a quote from Bard Channing. He dialled Sam Illingworth's line; her secretary told him she'd gone away for a few days. 'In Greece,' she added helpfully.

'How nice for her.'

'Yes. But Miss Channing's here,' said the secretary brightly. 'Could she help?'

Gray had been about to say he didn't think so, when he had a rather forceful vision of Miss Channing (the eldest) and said maybe she could. She came on the line.

'Mr Townsend? Can I help you?'

Her voice suited her, damn her; it was husky, reeked of sex.

'I'm not sure,' he said. 'I actually wanted to speak to your –' no, wrong move, she was probably touchy about working for him – 'to Mr Channing –'

'About – ?' The voice was quite brisk.

'About John Smith.'

'What about John Smith?'

'He's dead, Miss Channing. I thought you would have heard.'

'I had heard, Mr Townsend. Thank you.'

'Well, I'm doing a piece for the *News on Sunday* about Smith's great success in the City. Persuading the Establishment to be less frightened of a Labour government. You know the sort of thing.'

'Mr Channing doesn't work in the City,' said Kirsten.

Christ, she had a lot to learn about PR, Gray thought. He hung onto his temper with an effort.

'His work reverberates in the City, Miss Channing. It seems deeply relevant to me. And there's all this talk of a leadership challenge to Major. I'd like to get his reaction. If it wouldn't be too much of an imposition – I'm sure Sam would have –' He let his voice trail away, hoping to worry her into co-operation.

He heard her digesting his irritation, trying to second-guess Sam, to think what she would have done. Then she said, 'Well – maybe. I'll see what I can do. He's away this week.'

'Not, I hope, in Greece with Sam Illingworth.'

Christ, that was unforgivable. Crass, vulgar, totally out of order. What on earth had made him say that?

There was a long silence. Then Kirsten said, 'No, Mr Townsend, actually. He's in Stockholm, if you really want to know.'

'Look,' he said, 'look, I'm terribly sorry. I didn't mean – that is – oh Christ. I really shouldn't have said that.'

'No. No you shouldn't.'

There was a silence. Then: 'Look,' he said again, 'I'm sure you won't want to help me now. But if you can, if you can get a quote, I'd be extremely grateful.'

'Yes, all right,' said Kirsten Channing. 'I'll call you back if I have anything.' She put the phone down.

Stupid fucking bastard, said Gray Townsend conversationally to himself. It didn't seem to be his day.

At about three-thirty his phone rang.

'Mr Townsend? This is Kirsten Channing. I have a quote for you. I couldn't get it before because Mr Channing was in a meeting.'

He was so surprised he knocked his cup of tea (hopelessly cold anyway, and too weak even for him, made with his new gadget) all over his desk. Certainly not his day.

'Fuck,' he said.

'I beg your pardon?'

'Oh, I'm sorry,' he said. 'I'm so sorry. I knocked my tea over. That's all.'

'I see. Well, do you want to mop it up or shall I give you this quote?'

'No, I'll take it. Oh, dear God, everything's soaked. Can I call you back? In a minute?'

'Sure. Only don't be too long, because I have to go and meet someone at five.'

'I don't think it's going to take me an hour and a half to mop up half a cup of tea.'

'I hope not.'

God, she needed her bottom smacked. Hard. Frequently.

He rang back after ten minutes. 'Right. Let's get this over with. I don't want to keep you.'

'Oh,' she said, and her voice was suddenly slightly bleak. 'You're not. Meeting cancelled.'

'Ah. Well, anyway, quote. Please?'

'Mr Channing said to tell you that John Smith was a great socialist, a brilliant politician and a true friend, that he had had a profound effect on the crucially changing attitude of the City to the Labour party. And that he would have welcomed him onto the board of Channing Holdings and had he done so, he – that is my – Mr Channing – would probably have had to resign within the year. Is that all right? If it's not enough, he said to give you his number in Stockholm and you could call it between six and eight tonight.'

'That's brilliant. Thank you.'

'My pleasure.'

'Look,' said Gray suddenly. 'You obviously went to quite a lot of trouble to get that for me. And I was very offensive about your – Mr Channing. And you've had your meeting cancelled; would you let me buy you a drink this evening? Just to make amends.'

'Oh no, I don't think –' she started: then there was a sudden silence, and she said, 'Well, that would be very nice. Maybe I can think of something offensive to say back.'

'Maybe you can. I deserve it. Look, the Groucho at six suit you? I'm quite tall and dark, and I've got –'

'It's all right, Mr Townsend,' said Kirsten Channing, 'I know what you look like. I've just found your picture at the top of your last Sunday's column.'

He supposed it would be arrogant to assume that she had changed her mind and agreed to meet him because she liked the look of him.

★

She was waiting for him when he arrived, on the leather sofa just inside the door of the Groucho; looking more demure than when he had last seen her, wearing a pale pink suit, the skirt of which extended at least halfway down her thighs, a cream silk shirt and a pair of high-heeled beige ankle boots, a fashion which Gray hated, but which every girl in London seemed determined to wear. Her hair was piled up, tidily untidy, onto the top of her head, and cascaded down in a series of long, corn-coloured fronds onto her shoulders. Gray felt a slug of response to her and her beauty somewhere deep in his guts, and tried to ignore it.

'Sorry I'm late. My taxi seemed to know every clogged-up street between Holborn and here. Let's go in.'

She stood up; in her heels she was as tall as him. She led him up the steps into the bar. He was very aware that a great many people were looking at them and cursed himself for bringing her somewhere so public. Briony would hear of this, in no time at all. Fortunately everyone was obsessed with Smith; three people greeted him and all three said how dreadful it was.

'What would you like?' he said to Kirsten. 'They do a very nice house champagne.'

'Cool,' said Kirsten.

'I hope so,' said Gray, wondering if she'd get the rather schoolboy joke; if she did, she clearly didn't think it worth responding to. They sat down at a table in the window and Kirsten looked at him rather complacently.

'I have another quote for you. From Mr Channing.'

'You do? That's great.'

'Yes. He rang back and I said I was meeting you and he said to tell you that in his opinion, the death of John Smith had robbed the Labour party of at least fifty per cent of its brains.'

'Good Lord,' said Gray. 'That's a great quote.'

'I thought you'd like it.' She smiled, sipped her champagne, looked around the room. She must think I'm a thousand years old, thought Gray, and struggled to find something to talk about that would interest her. Herself was probably a fairly good bet.

'Are you enjoying it there?' he said. 'At Channings?'

'Not much.'

'No,' he said, 'I wouldn't have thought you were.'

'Why not?'

'Well – am I allowed to refer to the faint connection between you and the proprietor?'

'You are,' said Kirsten. For the first time she smiled at him, properly smiled, a warm, conspiratorial smile; Gray looked at her, astonished, without smiling back. It invaded every corner or her face, that smile, lightened it, transformed it, gave it charm, warmth; she looked less remarkably beautiful for a moment, and infinitely more desirable.

'What did I say?' she said eventually.

'Nothing. You didn't say anything. I – well, never mind.'

'Why didn't you think I'd like being at Channings?'

'Well – I'd have thought it must be a bit of a hard row to hoe. Everyone thinking how you were only there because of your dad. Not knowing what everyone really thinks of you. Knowing also they probably all think you're a spoilt brat. Not being able to let your guard down there. Watching everyone else not letting their guard down. Pretty horrible.'

'Yeah,' she said, sipping her champagne, looking into the glass thoughtfully, 'pretty horrible.'

'So why are you there?'

'Because,' she said after a moment's pause, clearly trying to decide whether to be truthful or not, 'because I couldn't get any other job.'

'I can't believe that.'

'It's true. I got a lousy degree. Not one law firm in the country wanted me to do my articles with them. I'm a hopeless secretary, got fired three times. I walked out of Miss Selfridge and The Gap. Even McDonald's didn't want me. Hobson's choice, really.' She sighed.

'I'm sure I'm not the first person to say this and I don't want it to come out sounding wrong, but did you think of being a model?'

'No, not really,' she said, smiling at him again. 'I tried it once, when I was much younger. It's a dog's life. Or rather a bitch's. Even if you do well. Boring, Christ it's boring.'

'I see,' he said. 'Well, I suppose you're –'

'Don't say it. I can't bear people saying it.'

'Saying what?'

'That I'm lucky really.'

'I wasn't going to say that. I was going to say I suppose you're not going to stay very long.'

'No,' she said, 'not very long. Although I didn't really say that, did I?' The smile again: sudden, conspiratorial.

'No. No, you didn't.'

'You know, I'm really enjoying this conversation.'

'Good. So am I.'

'Are you married?'

'Well, not exactly,' said Gray carefully.

'Permanent partner?'

'Pretty permanent.' Now why did he say that, why not just 'Yes'?

'What does she do?'

'She's a photographic stylist. She's called Briony and we live in a very nice house in Clapham.'

'So it is permanent?'

'Well – yes. I suppose so. Yes.'

'You don't sound very sure. What's rocking the boat?'

'Oh – nothing. Nothing really.' This was getting out of hand. 'How about you?'

'Well, I have a boyfriend. He's very good-looking and he earns lots of money, and he's a good laugh,' she added cheerfully.

'But you're not in love with him?'

'No,' she said, and he might have asked her if she was a transvestite, so amused was the expression on her face. 'No, of course not. I don't believe in love.'

'Oh really? And what's made you so cynical about love at such a young age?'

'My father,' she said.

By seven they had drunk the entire bottle of champagne and two glasses more each; Kirsten stood up slightly unsteadily, took his hand and pulled him up, laughing.

'I have to go. I've got to mug up on some stuff before tomorrow.'

'What happens tomorrow?'

'Oh, I'm actually being allowed to draft a press release all on my own.'

'About?'

'Oh, some new shops in the Manchester shopping mall. Nothing very exciting.'

'I see. Well, everyone has to start somewhere. Anyway,' he said, carefully casual, remembering sharply his instinct that there was a story somewhere here, 'it was very nice of your father to give me those quotes. Since he seems to have taken against publicity rather.'

'He has?'

'Yes, I was going to do a big profile on him, but he pulled out.'

'Oh,' she said. 'Well, he's like that. Irrational. Awkward. I should know. Only I didn't say that. Oh God, I've had too much champagne. Sam would kill me if she'd heard me.'

'Kirsten,' said Gray, 'I swear I didn't hear you say that. And I certainly won't tell Sam.'

'I hope not.'

'And is it really true he's given out a directive about interviews recently? Not giving them.'

'Yeah, he has. I was surprised he gave you that quote today, actually. And he is on an even shorter fuse than usual. Lot of serious shouting going on in the office. Oh God, I shouldn't have said that either. You did mean it, didn't you? About not telling anyone what I said?' It was rather touching, the first sign he had seen that she had any insecurities. Or any sense of loyalty to her job.

'I did indeed. God's honour.'

'I don't suppose you believe in God.'

'Well – I'm not sure. Probably not. I won't tell anyway. What about you?'

'You mean do I believe in God? Yes,' she said, suddenly and surprisingly sober. 'Oh yes, I'm afraid I do.'

'So God yes, love no.'

'That's about right.'

Interesting; she was altogether much more interesting than he would have imagined. 'Well, anyway, I do promise. This is all off the record.'

'Sam says nothing you say to any journalist is ever off the record.'

'Sam's right. Usually. But in this case, she's wrong. Promise.'

'Well, thank you. And for the drink. It's been fun.'

'My pleasure. I hope I'm forgiven too. For what I said. About Sam and your dad.'

'Of course. It was a pretty jerky thing to say, but I won't tell anyone.'

And she was gone.

'How's your mother, Oliver?'

It was obviously one of Bard Channing's days for being nice to the human race, thought Oliver; he had already told Sue in Reception she looked very pretty, and instructed Pete Barbour to take a long weekend.

'She's not very well, Mr Channing. She's had an awful bout of her arthritis, so her hands are really bad, and her back hurts her a lot. The consultant says she could benefit from some warmth, so –'

'What sort of warmth?'

'Well, you know, sunshine. That sort of warmth.'

'I see. Well, she must have it. If it's going to do a lot for her. Now if you need any help –'

'It's very kind of you, Mr Channing,' said Oliver, enjoying for once not having to ask, to take, to be grateful, 'but Mrs Booth, you know, has offered us one of her timeshare places and –'

'Mrs Booth?' said Bard. 'Mrs Booth! What the hell has it got to do with Mrs Booth?'

'Well, I was telling her about Mum,' said Oliver, 'and what the doctor had said, and –'

'When were you talking to Mrs Booth, for God's sake?' said Bard, his voice quieter suddenly, very intense, and his eyes were very dark, probing on Oliver's face. Oliver met them steadily. It wasn't easy.

'Last week, Mr Channing. When I had lunch with her.'

'You had lunch with Teresa Booth? What the hell for?'

'She asked me,' said Oliver.

'I hardly imagined you asked yourself. What did she want?'

'She didn't want anything, much. She just wanted to talk to me.'

'About?'

Oliver began to get irritated by this. It was nothing to do with Bard Channing whom he had lunch with. The irritation gave him courage. 'About all sorts of things,' he said, his voice very level. 'She was interested in our family, about my dad –'

'Your father? What in God's name interested her about your father?'

'Mr Channing,' said Oliver, ignoring with an effort the twitching muscle in Bard's forehead, the underlying throb of temper in his voice, 'I don't want to be rude, but I don't see why she shouldn't be interested in my father. Mr Booth worked with him, you both did, he helped found the company and –'

'And what were you able to tell her about your father?' said Bard, levelling his voice with almost visible effort.

'Well, not a lot, obviously. But she wants to go and see Mum, talk to her about him, she's got a cousin who knew him apparently, and –'

'Teresa Booth is going to visit your mother?'

'Yes. I've got to arrange a Sunday.'

'I see.' There was a silence. A further effort at restoring normality to the voice, the face. 'Well, I'm sure that will be very nice for them both. I hope she doesn't upset your mother.'

'I'm sure she won't, Mr Channing. She seems very kind indeed to me.'

'I'm delighted to hear it,' said Bard, 'and I hope you're right. I can only urge you to think about it quite carefully, Oliver. Your mother is a very sensitive woman. Sensitive and frail. It might not be the best idea for her to start reliving the past with a total stranger.'

'Well, I'll be there,' said Oliver, 'and anyway, Mrs Booth isn't quite a total stranger. And Mr Booth has always been terribly kind to Mum.'

'Is he joining in this visit?'

'No, I don't think he is,' said Oliver.

'Well, remember what I said. Please. And meanwhile, I don't want you going off to some strange place of Mrs Booth's that none of us knows anything about. You borrow my house in Greece, all of you. I have staff there, they can look after you, it will be far less stressful for your mother. I'll arrange transport the other end. All right?'

'Well, I –'

'Oliver, please don't argue. Your mother's health is too important. I'll get on to her personally this morning, tell her what we've agreed. And you'd better get on with your work. You've wasted enough time this morning already.'

He disappeared into his office, slamming the door, shouting for Marcia. The good mood was obviously over.

Oliver looked after him. He'd hated every minute of that conversation. Channing had been completely out of order. What the hell did it have to do with him who he talked to? And now they'd all have to be grateful again. Because he knew perfectly well what his mother would want to do.

He turned to go back to his own office, and saw Kirsten Channing striding along the corridor behind him; she smiled at him rather distantly, didn't speak. The arrogance of that reinforced Oliver's misery, his hostility to the whole Channing clan.

'Shit,' he said aloud, shutting his own door behind him, 'shit, shit, shit.'

Babies were meant to grow. That much Francesca knew for sure. Some grew faster than others, of course, and Jack had grown very fast, so it was not really a fair comparison. But Kitty just wasn't growing at all. She had put on just half a pound in the past month: less than two ounces a week. It just wasn't enough; it was scary. She didn't care what Nanny said, what the GP said, what Bard said; she was going to take her to see a specialist.

She dialled her mother's number: Rachel sounded distracted.

'Yes darling, what is it? Is it important, because if not could I ring you back? I'm just going out –'

'It is important, yes. But if you're in a hurry I'd rather wait. I don't want you not concentrating.'

There was a silence, then Rachel said, 'Yes, if you don't mind. I'll only be an hour. I've got to go and see someone.'

'Who?'

'Oh – only my solicitor.'

Her tone was just too casual; Francesca was suspicious.

'What about? Anything serious?'

'Oh, good heavens no. Just some tax things.'

'Tax? Are you sure you mean your solicitor?'

'What? No, of course you're right, I mean my accountant. Anyway, darling, I'll call you back. If it really can wait.'

'It can.'

She was up to something. No doubt about it.

It was two hours before she rang back: 'Sorry, darling. Took longer than I thought.'

Francesca, who was by now engrossed in working the brochure for a big charity auction she was involved in, was irritated by the delay. 'Doesn't really matter. Fortunately. You're getting awfully hard to get hold of, Mummy. Last week I tried all day, Wednesday it was. Where were you then?'

'Oh – goodness knows. I can't remember. I'm very busy with my charity at the moment, Francesca. The one down in Devon, you know? The convent.'

'Oh – yes. Yes of course.' She tried to sound interested, knew she'd failed, in her mother's charities. 'Anyway, I want to talk to you about Kitty. She's just not very well, she keeps on and on not being very well, and I think I'm going to take her to a paediatrician.'

'That sounds sensible. What sort of not very well?'

'Oh, I don't know. She's always got a cold, and she's fretful, she doesn't feed very well, she still doesn't. And she's not gaining weight, that's what's really worrying me.'

'She wouldn't be if she isn't feeding.'

'No I know, but –'

'She *is* very small. What does your doctor say?'

'Oh, he says she's fine. And Nanny says she's fine, but I just know she's not. So if you were me, would you get another opinion? I mean how does she seem to you?'

'She's very small, as I said. And not very happy. On the other hand, she looks all right. But if you're worried, darling, I should get another opinion. Just don't hesitate.'

'That's what I thought you'd say. I just wanted to know you didn't think I was being neurotic.'

'Francesca, when it comes to children and their health, you can't be neurotic enough. In my not very humble opinion.'

'Thank you. I will, then.'

Francesca didn't tell Bard she was taking Kitty to a paediatrician; she didn't tell anyone except her mother. She couldn't face the fuss. Nanny continued to be emphatic there was nothing whatsoever wrong with Kitty, whenever she asked her; pointed out that Dr Hemmings, who had looked after all the children, pronounced her perfectly healthy, as had the paediatrician at the Princess Diana hospital where Kitty had been born (although Nanny clearly set rather less store by that judgment, the paediatrician in question being under forty and female), and she was in any case altogether opposed to what she called meddling medics: all a healthy baby needed, she said extremely frequently, was plenty of fresh air and sleep, and a good routine. Since taking Kitty to Harley Street would interrupt the routine, expose her to some rather unfresh air and keep her from sleeping, she would certainly not endorse the idea; and moreover in the event of such an event taking place, she would insist not only on accompanying Francesca but on giving the consultant her own view of the situation, at some length. It seemed best therefore not to tell her.

As for Bard, he found anything to do with illness deeply distasteful; it disturbed him horribly. Francesca had learned very early in their relationship to keep extremely quiet about any minor ailments, and in the case of anything more major to retire to bed and instruct Bard to stay away. He was, for a creature of rampant and uninhibited sexuality, interestingly wary of the normal female functions, and hated any reference even to something as sanitised as PMT; he had been in a permanent state of tension as the births of the children approached lest he might find himself in some way involved, and insisted on Rachel sleeping at the house for the final few weeks of each pregnancy so that she and not he could be with Francesca up to the time she was safely in her room at the hospital. He found the notion of a father being present at the birth not merely disagreeable, but repellent; 'I'm sorry, Francesca, but I'd rather die,' he said simply, and she had laughed and said that would be counter-productive and she really didn't mind at all.

Whether this attitude was produced, as Francesca thought, by the traumas of Marion's death and the more distasteful aspects of Pattie's alcoholism, or as Rachel opined, by over-zealous potty training by Jess – 'Very Freudian, Mummy, I'm surprised at you' – it did not greatly trouble her.

And so she told Nanny that she was going to the hairdresser and leaving Kitty with her mother while she did so before joining her for lunch; Nanny, her face taut with disapproval, said she would take Jack to Kensington Gardens and then out to lunch. 'It's so important in my view he isn't made to feel jealous of his sister,' she said, as if Francesca could not have been expected to think of such a thing of her own accord. 'Although I really think Kitty would be a lot better staying here with me. She's getting another cold, and she's been crying a lot this morning.'

'I know, Nanny,' said Francesca humbly, 'but my mother does like to see her, and she's in today, so it seemed –'

'Well, I suppose you know best, but I hope your mother won't be taking her anywhere unsuitable,' said Nanny. She had a deep mistrust of Rachel.

'Nanny, I do assure you my mother won't take Kitty anywhere at all, never mind unsuitable,' said Francesca briskly (wondering precisely what kind of place Nanny had in mind: Raymond's Revue Bar perhaps, or a quick drive round the red-light district at King's Cross?). 'I'll be back at teatime. Could you see if you could get Jack's hair cut if you're going to be near Harrods? It's a bit long.'

'Mrs Channing? Mr Lauder will see you now. If you go down the corridor, first door on the right –'

'Thank you,' said Francesca. Her legs felt suddenly weak as she stood up, and the pseudo-drawing room that was Harley Street's version of a waiting room seemed a huge space to cross.

She was with Mr Lauder a long time; he was cheerfully pompous, began by making her feel foolish as she outlined the baby's problems, her slowness to gain weight, her general fretfulness, her tendency to be cold, and then became more gentle, told her to undress the baby so that he could examine her, whereupon Kitty promptly started to scream and Francesca had to feed her to quieten her, particularly so he could listen to her chest.

He was an especially long time doing that; Francesca stood watching him, looking at the stethoscope, so big and cold and somehow threatening on the tiny, white chest, holding Kitty's little hands, trying to keep her mind blank, herself under control, trying not to ask foolish questions, to pester him, to break the chill silence in which he listened so carefully to what must be in any case the tiniest, faintest sound, watching his face for clues, for anxiety, for tension, for a reassuring smile, and finding none of them.

'Mrs Channing, if you would like to dress Kitty again, we can have another chat.'

He was very gentle, very sweet. He said there was a slight, very very slight, almost undetectable, murmur in Kitty's heart. 'Terribly easy to miss, especially in a new-born. It's a sound like rushing water. I'm a bit surprised your GP didn't – but still. Never mind. You did the right thing in coming to me. Don't look so frightened, Mrs Channing, it really isn't very serious.'

'But what does it mean?'

'Well it could indicate something trivial. Or more serious. That's all I can tell you at the moment. And it very probably isn't anything in the least serious. Not seriously serious, I mean. It's quite common in babies, far more common than most people realise, and I would advise you to –'

The voice went on. Francesca sat listening to it, hardly aware of it as a voice, hearing only the words, words which confirmed what she had always known, always feared, that Kitty was ill, was damaged, was not a strong, perfect baby at all. What would have happened, she thought in a great surge of fierce protective rage, what would have happened if she had believed them all, had shut up? If she had left her, had abandoned her to them and their foolish, ridiculous reassurances, her little frail, tender, trusting creature, not quite whole, not strong enough for the world, for life. How bad would things have had to be before anyone had listened to her? Would the little heart have begun really to stumble, unequal to its daunting task? If Bard or Nanny Crossman or Dr Hemmings had walked in at that moment, she would have flown at them, attacked them physically, wanted to hurt them, damage them, as her daughter was hurt and damaged –

'So I think the next step, just to be quite sure we're onto the right thing, is to do some tests. An ECG and some X-rays, and something called an echo cardiogram.'

'What's that?' said Francesca, tryng to speak normally, to fight the panic out of her voice.

'Well, it's another type of X-ray. A bit like an ultrasound. It will tell us a lot more about her heart and how it's working. In the meantime, try not to worry too much. It almost certainly isn't anything very serious. Now if you'll just bear with me a moment, I'll arrange all that –'

Chapter Six

'Right,' said Bard, 'let's run over this again, shall we? You want me to buy your house?'

'Yes,' said Liam, 'that's right.'

'Of which more than its value belongs to the building society.'

'Yes.'

'And then you'll pay me rent?'

'Yes.'

Bard sat back in his chair and looked at him, an expression of acute distaste on his face. Liam wondered if his own was as apparent. He hoped it was. He had agreed finally to go through with this, to perform the actions, say the words, had been forced into it by the sheer force of Naomi's will; but that was all. He would not go further, profess humility, express remorse. He knew, had he done so, he might have succeeded; but in his own estimation he would have failed. His hatred for his father was too important to deny, even in self-interest; like love, it must not be betrayed.

He sat back himself, and waited; waited for the anwer, waited for it to be over, waited to be able to leave, to report back, to say to Naomi, there you see, I told you, no good, no point, no help, no humanity.

'Well, I don't know,' said Bard, pushing himself away from his desk, tipping up his chair, looking at Liam with brilliant, thoughtful eyes. 'I can't see anything in that for me. Can you?'

'Oh, I don't know,' said Liam. 'It's an extremely nice house.'

'But I already have two extremely nice houses. Three, if you include the one in Greece. I really don't need another. And anyway, I'm not going to be able to live in yours. Am I?'

'I would imagine not. No.'

'How did you get into this mess, Liam?'

Oh Christ; he was going to do it, demand his due, tighten the screws, squeeze the blood from the stone.

'Well,' he said, 'well, the recession. And –'

'Ah, yes, the recession. Such an excellent scapegoat. Such a splendid excuse. Do you know anyone who has not been affected by the recession, Liam?'

'Yes of course I do.' There was no escape; it had to be gone through.

'Well then. I rest my case.'

There was a silence, then Bard leant forward again. 'I'll tell you how you got into it. Bad judgment. Overspending. Letting your wife keep you, while you carried on with that absurd wank of a profession of yours. How much did you earn last year, Liam? Twenty thousand? Fifteen, maybe? Or even less than that? Yes, I rather thought so. Have you considered getting a proper job, rather than coming to me?'

'Yes,' said Liam, 'actually, I've applied for several. But it's not easy. As you really should know.'

'Yes,' said Bard, 'I do know. On the other hand, neither is it easy for me, Liam. As you in your turn should know. Whatever your misapprehensions. It isn't easy for anyone at all. Making money, making your way, is never easy, and keeping it is even less so. As you have, rather suddenly it seems, discovered.'

Another silence; Liam waited.

'So it's your turn, is it, now? Your wife's failed you, and you've actually got to deliver. Only instead of doing it yourself, getting out there, working your own scrawny arse off, you come whining to me, with your hand out. God help me.'

'I don't exactly have my hand out,' said Liam (don't lose your temper, Liam, don't give him that satisfaction). 'You seem to have failed to appreciate the fact that I'm offering you a business deal.'

'Oh for Christ's sake,' said Bard, 'spare me that, please. A deal! A house I don't want, at a price I wouldn't pay. No thank you. I've done a lot for you, Liam, given you a great many advantages. You always manage most conveniently to forget them. Now it's your turn. Get off your backside, and sort your own life out. I'm not going to do it for you. If I did, I'd be failing you.'

'Fine,' said Liam, standing up. 'I'd hate you to fail me. You never have, of course, have you?'

'Meaning?'

'Meaning, as you perfectly well know, that you've failed me all my life.' Shit, he hadn't meant to start on this. Stop it, Liam, stop it. Not a good idea, not clever.

'Oh Jesus help me,' said Bard, 'are we to hear all this again? The rejection, the wicked stepmothers, the rival siblings ...'

He managed to make it all sound so trivial, of so little importance.

That was, as it always had been, the most painful thing. Liam turned his back on him and walked out of the room without another word.

On the way downstairs, Liam felt violently ill: he thought he was going to pass out, throw up. He made for a chair and put his head between his knees; he was sitting there, praying no-one would come, when he felt a hand on his shoulders.

'Are you all right? Can I help?'

Liam looked up and through the swirling fog of nausea, saw Francesca. She was wearing a black coat, she had no make-up on, and she looked very pale, very drawn; even in his misery he could see she was upset.

'Yes. Yes thank you,' he said shortly, embarrassed that she should see him like this, embarrassed still more that she should be so clearly concerned. 'I'm fine. Sorry.'

'I didn't realise it was you,' she said, embarrassed herself now, unsure of his reaction as much as her own. 'What are you doing here?'

'I came to see my father.'

'Oh really?' She half smiled. 'Well, he can be very upsetting. I should know.'

'Yes. Well.' He couldn't think what else to say. He slumped back in his chair, still feeling sick.

'Are you sure you're all right?' she said. 'You look terrible. Look, let me get you a glass of water. Or a cup of tea, would that be better?'

'No, really, Francesca, I'm fine. Just – well, I'm fine.'

He sat staring at her, wishing she would go away; and then there was a great gale of Obsession perfume and Marcia Grainger swept towards them, smiling slightly grimly, her severe suit and rigid hairstyle oddly at variance with the rich, strong perfume.

'Mrs Channing! Were we expecting you?'

'I don't know, Marcia,' said Francesca, a touch of a smile on her mouth, 'were you?'

'Well, Mr Channing certainly didn't tell me,' said Marcia severely.

'Didn't tell you what, Marcia?'

'That you were coming.'

'No, he couldn't have done that, because he didn't know,' said Francesca briskly. 'But I was – passing, and I felt – well, I wondered – if he was terribly busy or if I could see him.'

'I will go and enquire,' said Marcia. 'Perhaps you'd like to come up to my office in a moment.' The Obsession moved up the staircase.

'I must go now,' said Liam, grateful for the excuse. 'I hope you see him. If that's what you want.'

She smiled. 'It is. Believe it or not. Thank you. I hope you feel better.'

He was standing at the bus stop in Lower Regent Street, in a sudden downpour of rain, still feeling ghastly, wondering what on earth he was going to say to Naomi, the bank, everyone, when a large beige Mercedes driven by Francesca pulled up beside it, and she signalled for him to get in. Reluctantly grateful, afraid of looking churlish in front of the rest of the queue, he did so.

'I couldn't drive past you,' she said, 'you don't look at all well. Where are you going?'

'Islington.'

'Ah. Well, I can take you some of the way. I'm going to St John's Wood.'

'Thank you. That's very kind.' He felt intensely uncomfortable, unwilling to appear friendly, be polite to her, unable not to be. 'Did you – did you get to see my father?'

'No,' she said, and her voice was very bleak and dead. 'No, he couldn't stop.'

'Ah.'

'It was on the off-chance,' she said determinedly. 'I don't usually do that. But – you see – well, Kitty – that's the new baby, you know –'

'Yes, I know of course.' He felt a stab of guilt run through him that she should have felt he might not know. She had tried very hard to be friendly and he had rejected her at every turn. For absolutely no logical reason whatsoever. And now she was being extremely kind to him. And was clearly very upset.

'Is something wrong with her?' he said finally.

'Quite wrong. She – they think – she has – might have – oh shit, I've got in the bus lane and now that cop's coming over. What do I do?'

'Cry,' said Liam without hesitation.

Francesca burst into tears. The policeman, who looked like a rather young fifteen, gave her a sharp warning, directed her into the middle lane, waved her on. Liam handed her a handkerchief and she blew her nose, wiped her eyes and drove up Regent Street rather erratically.

'That was very good,' he said, looking at her in amusement. 'Can you always cry to order?'

'No,' said Francesca, 'I can't. Oh God, I'm going to start again. Fatal with me, letting it begin. Liam, if I pull over, could you drive? I'm going to kill us both, at this rate.'

'Yes, of course. Look, just pull over there, by the Beeb, and we can swop.'

'Thank you,' said Francesca. He got out; she eased herself over into the passenger seat and caught her skirt on the brake. It pulled up, revealing the whole of one thigh and, as she struggled to free it, the crotch of her pants. Liam tried not to look but couldn't help it; she saw his eyes as she tugged it down and laughed rather shakily.

'Indecent exposure,' she said. 'Sorry.'

'My pleasure,' said Liam, re-starting the car.

She looked at him and half smiled back, then blew her nose hard, and relaxed into the seat. 'I'm sorry,' she said, 'about all this. Really sorry.'

'Want to tell me about it?' Sitting in her car, sheltered from the rain, it seemed the least he could do.

'I might cry again.'

'Don't worry about it.'

'It's Kitty. She's not very well. She – she might have – probably does have, a heart problem.'

'What sort of a heart problem?'

'We don't quite know yet. I just took her to see a consultant this morning, for the very first time. He heard a murmur and she has to have something called an echo cardiogram done. Next week actually. On Tuesday. Oh God, I'm sorry, why should you care which day it's got to be, why should you be interested?'

'Don't be silly,' he said, and meant it. 'Of course I'm interested. But you say you don't know how bad it is yet?'

'No. Nor even if it's bad at all. But it's just been such a terrifying, awful day. And she's not a healthy baby, you see, she's tiny and she cries a lot and it's so frightening –'

'Yes, of course it is.'

'And the thing is I just wanted to tell Bard, to be with him. And he – well, he was busy, and he really isn't very good at sympathy. Certainly wasn't just then. And that makes it worse.'

'You don't need to tell me,' he said. 'I know.'

She turned to look at him.

He was silent for a moment, then said, the memories rawly revived by the interview with his father, 'When my mother died, you know. I was quite small. He – well, he wasn't very good then, either.'

'Oh God,' said Francesca. 'Oh Liam, I –'

He went on talking, surprised that he should be doing so to her, unable to stop. 'First he was so totally engrossed in his own misery he had nothing to spare for me, and then he worked himself out of it and I never saw him. And then – well, you know what happened next.'

'Yes. Yes of course I do.'

'Oh I'm sorry,' he said. 'It really has nothing to do with you. Nothing at all.'

'Of course it does. I'm married to your father. It has a lot to do with me.'

'Well,' he said, 'I don't quite see it that way. But anyway, I do know about – well, how difficult he can be.'

'Yes. Yes, I suppose you do.' She was obviously embarrassed now, felt she had gone too far, been disloyal about Bard to the one person she should not have been. She was silent, staring out at the park. They had stopped at some traffic lights, and he was able to study her; she really was very pretty, he thought, more than pretty, although not quite beautiful, with her neatly sculpted nose and perfectly pointed chin, and the die-straight dark brown hair. She felt him looking at her, turned to him and smiled.

'I'm sure you don't care,' she said, 'but you've made me feel better.'

'Of course I care,' he said, guilty again at this reminder of his bad behaviour, his hostility. The lights had changed; he moved forward. There was a silence; then: 'Look,' he said, carefully, 'look, I really think you should try very hard not to worry about Kitty. I know it's easy to for me to talk, but if it was really bad, they'd have had her in for further tests straight away. Not waited until next week. What you have to do is take one hour at a time. Not even a day. Keep telling yourself it'll be all right.'

'Yes,' she said, 'yes, you're right, I know. But it's hard. Anyway, I do feel better. Thank you. Well enough to drive home. Now where shall I drop you? We're not in a very good place for getting to Islington, I've brought you too far. Do you want to try and get a cab? We could go up to Swiss Cottage.'

'No,' he said, 'I'll get the Tube.'

'But –'

'Honestly. It's fine.'

'All right then. I think this time I'll change places in a more seemly manner.'

She got out and stood looking at him, then held out her hand. She looked just slightly awkward.

'I haven't asked you what you were seeing Bard about because I thought you'd prefer it if I didn't. But whatever it was I hope it went well.'

'It didn't.'

'Oh. Well, I'm sorry.' She got back into the car and smiled up at him; a quick, conspiratorial smile. 'He's not really so bad, you know,' she said, and was gone.

Liam stood looking after her, trying to decide which of a series of emotions was uppermost: anger at his situation, an increased loathing of his father, or a sense of acute surprise that someone he had always made himself regard as tough and hostile and dislikeable, could be so gentle, so friendly and even so extremely desirable.

'I'll sue,' said Bard, his face dark with rage. 'I'll sue the lot of them.'

'Bard, don't be ridiculous, who are you going to sue and what good would that do?'

'It would do me a lot of good. And them a lot of harm. How dare they miss something like this, how dare they?'

'So who are you going to sue?' said Francesca. It was so absurd it was funny, but it was distracting her just slightly from her misery. 'The hospital? The obstetrician? Dr Hemmings? Nanny?'

'I'm sorry?'

'She said she was quite sure Kitty was all right as well. And she's meant to be an expert, isn't she? So where are you going to stop? It's ridiculous.'

Bard looked at her and scowled. 'Well, who is this chap Lauder, anyway? Are we sure he's the best man for the job? How did you find him, maybe we should get a second opionion even now –'

'He was recommended by Jimmy Browne. I really think he knows what he's doing.'

'Oh,' said Bard. He was silent for a moment. Jimmy Browne was a friend of theirs; he was also one of the foremost surgeons in the country, a pioneer of certain micro-surgery techniques and a major voice on the British Medical Council. 'I still don't see why we can't get a second opinion.'

'Bard, we'll get one. When they do the echo cardiogram. And if you're not satisfied then, we can find someone else. But I really don't think we should rock the boat now. It will just enrage Mr Lauder and cause a delay.'

'I cannot imagine why you didn't talk to me about this in the first place,' he said. 'I'd obviously have wanted to come with you, heard what the chap said for myself.'

'Oh, Bard, really! In the first place, you'd have probably told me not to make a fuss about nothing, to talk to Nanny about her, and in the second you probably wouldn't have come with me, you'd have told me you had meetings, that you didn't know when you'd be back, or where you'd be, that you didn't have time. Or more likely Marcia would have told me all those things.'

He looked at her, and the expression on his face was shocked: shocked and just slightly ashamed. 'Don't be absurd,' he said, but she had seen the shock and the shame and it was comforting, almost reassuring.

She was silent.

'Well, I shall certainly come when you go next week,' he said finally. 'What day is it? Tuesday. Yes. And if there is any doubt, any doubt at all, about the diagnosis, then I think we should take her to the States. Their medicine is far in advance of ours and –'

'Bard, I have never heard such nonsense,' said Francesca, laughing in spite of her anguish. 'Of course it isn't, I don't know who you've been talking to. And the last thing that Kitty needs just now is a transatlantic flight. Whatever would Nanny say?'

'Oh God!' shouted Kirsten. 'God. Shit. Toby. Oh, my God, oh Toby, now now now –'

Her body arched, spasmed; released from it, from the long, wild, glorious sweating struggle, she soared, she flew, free, wild, triumphant, into her orgasm. On and on she travelled, riding it, riding the great undulating peaks of pleasure; for a moment, several moments, she thought, feared, it was over, and she lay, relaxing onto Toby, waiting, longing for its return and then it came again, sharper, stronger, purer, and then finally, finally she tumbled off it, and knew it was the end, and she lay, panting, still moaning gently, but smiling now, the head that had been raised to shout, to roar, relaxed onto the pillow, the arms that had clenched and clung so frantically to Toby's body softening round him, the legs that had twined and tensed and thrashed about them both relaxed and easy, dangling over the edge of the bed they had so nearly fallen off.

Toby eased himself carefully back into its centre, rolled her tenderly off him, lay looking at her, playing with her hair.

'Kirsten,' he said simply, 'you are one hell of a lay.'

'What a revolting expression,' said Kirsten.

'Why?'

'It's sexist and insulting. And old-fashioned. That's what men used to do to girls, lay them down and do them. And the girls just lay there.'

'Yeah well, nobody's going to get very far trying to do that to you. I'm sorry, darling, I didn't mean to offend you. I just wanted to let you know how great it was. Jesus, look at the time, I'm going to be so late. Wish I worked for my daddy and could keep any old hours that suited me.'

'Oh shut up,' said Kirsten irritably. 'I don't. I keep telling you, Toby, it isn't like that. I'm never late in — well, hardly ever, and I work hard and I don't pull rank.'

'Sorry, sorry, sorry. In that case I won't suggest what I was going to suggest.'

'What?'

'That you ask for next week off. I'm going to New York, heard yesterday, some hiccup over there. I'd really love you to come.'

'Oh Toby, I'd really love me to come too. But I can't, it's too short notice and anyway, I — oh shit, I could ask. Couldn't I? Or could I? Oh God, I'd love to go to New York, I haven't been for at least a year.'

'Poor little soul,' said Toby, 'my heart bleeds. Sorry, Kirsten, sorry.'

He climbed out of bed, walked towards the bathroom. She lay and looked at him, at the body that gave her so much pleasure, that she wanted so much, was so jealous about; then got up, put on a robe and went into the kitchen and poured them each a huge glass of orange juice. Toby reappeared in his towel, kissed her rather absently and drained the glass.

'I needed that. Thirsty work, sex. Especially with you. Now listen, darling, forget the insults, just see if you can't get a week off. Or even do something over there for your dad. He has an office there, doesn't he?'

'Well, not a real one. The bulk of his business is most definitely here. But yeah, OK. I will ask. It would be so wonderful. I'd love it. Thank you for asking me.'

'Darling,' said Toby, 'the pleasure will be entirely mine. Or at any rate, a great deal of it. I assure you.'

Kirsten arrived at Channing House in a good mood. It was a combination of the sex, the fact that the sky was blue (she was deeply affected by the weather) and the sun beginning to feel warm, and the thought that this time next week she might be in New York. The best time in the whole year for it too: you could keep Paris, Florence, London even; spring belonged in New York, with the sun playing on the fountains and the wide streets great warm avenues of light, and the park filled with blossom and bright new green, and the shop windows absurdly over-stacked with flowers and flowery clothes and even the cab drivers better tempered. Oh, it would be lovely. She had to go.

'I'm not sure,' said Sam, carefully. 'We're quite busy at the moment, with the purchase of that new site in Glasgow and all this nonsense about Docklands –'

Kirsten looked at her; she knew exactly what Sam was thinking: that there was no more reason why she should not go than that she should, they were not especially busy, it was only for a week, previous holiday arrangements were always honoured (and who was to know this was not previous, after all): except, except that she was the boss's daughter, and carried explicit instructions with her that there should be no privileges, no special deals, no special treatment of any kind. Positive discrimination, that's what it is, she thought; indeed had she been a new recruit fresh from typing school there would have been no question but that she should go. She saw Sam's eyes waver for a moment and drove hard home.

'Oh Sam, please! I'll work twice as hard today and twice as hard when I get back. I promise. And I'd so like to go. And maybe I could do something useful over there, I don't know what –'

'I don't know either,' said Sam, and laughed. 'Oh hell, why not,' she said suddenly. 'But it will mean you working your tail off when you get back.'

'I will, I will,' said Kirsten fervently, thinking that it would be worked off in rather more pleasant fashion next week. 'Thank you, Sam, thank you so much.'

She called Toby. 'I can come, I can come.'

'I know that,' he said, laughing. 'I'll fix your ticket,' and put the phone down again.

She worked right through her lunch hour to show her gratitude, wrote a lot of letters about the Manchester shopping mall – quasi releases really, but each one a bit different, Sam said it always helped – to the provincial press that she had been putting off for days, even did a load of photocopying that the temporary junior had done all wrong, even rang Granny Jess and invited herself to dinner for when she got back. Then at four, Sam came in looking uneasy.

'I'm sorry, Kirsten. You have to go and see Mr Channing. Right away.'

She knew what it meant, and so did Sam; she sighed and walked slowly down the stairs to the first floor, her heart heavy.

Bard was sitting behind his great desk, scowling; he looked like some great heavy pugnacious bird, thought Kirsten, a crow or a vulture. God, she disliked him sometimes. Most of the time.

'Shut the door,' he said without even greeting her.

Kirsten shut the door, then walked slowly back and faced him. She knew what was coming, and she knew the form it would come in.

'You disgust me,' he said quietly. 'You really do.'

'Why?'

'You come in here, begging for a job, promising the moon, telling me you'll work your arse off, that you won't ask for favours, or special treatment, that you'll behave yourself, do what you're told –'

'I have done all those things. I have worked my arse off, I have behaved, I have done what I was told, and I haven't –'

'Oh, is that so. You haven't what? Asked for favours? What do you think asking for a week off at a day's notice is, after working here for precisely, what – just over a month? It's a bloody big favour, Kirsten, by any standards, and if you had any experience of the real world, you'd know it. And if you didn't happen to work for someone as nice, as good natured, as reasonable as Sam it would never have been granted at all. What do you think everyone will be saying, how do you think this makes me look? They'll be saying I'm allowing you to use me and abuse this company, so that you can pass your time however you like and get paid into the bargain. I'm ashamed of you, Kirsten, deeply ashamed. Of course you can't go.'

'That's all you care about, isn't it?' said Kirsten. 'How it makes you look. You don't give a fuck –'

'Don't swear.'

'You swear. You don't give a fuck whether I'm actually working, actually being useful, actually learning anything, as long as from where you're sitting on your lousy, over-large throne it all looks all right.'

'Oh for God's sake,' he said, 'get out of here. You're beginning to sound like a small spoilt child rather than a large one. Just get out. You are not going to New York and that's the end of it. If Sam hadn't said a lot of very nice things about you, I'd kick you right out of the front door.'

'I might prefer that.'

He shrugged. 'Suit yourself.'

She was about to tell him what to do with his job when she had a rather vivid picture of her week's mail – demands for money from Harrods, Harvey Nichols, Barclaycard, Amex, Christ knew who else. She needed the money he paid her: it was generous. And he certainly wouldn't reinstate her allowance. Which had been pathetic anyway. And besides, she also knew it would afford him more satisfaction if she left, if she stalked out of his office and told him she was never coming back. He'd say he always knew she hadn't got the guts to stick it out, that she was lazy as well as spoilt, that – oh God, it made her want to spew just thinking about it. No, she'd stay, and work, and prove him wrong, and get her own back some other way.

She nodded at him rather formally. 'Very well. I do hope you have a nice weekend.'

'Thank you,' he said, his mood suddenly changing as it so easily did, becoming communicative and almost friendly. 'Francesca is very tired, she's had a lot of worries lately. We're going down to Stylings. We've just bought Jack a pony ...'

'How very nice for him,' said Kirsten. 'Do give Francesca my best wishes. I'm sorry she's worried.'

She couldn't help it; there was an edge to her voice. Bard looked at her.

'Don't be so bloody childish,' he said. 'One day, when you've grown up a bit and have some genuine worries of your own, not just where you're going to get your next frock from, I hope you'll remember that remark and feel ashamed of yourself.'

'Sorry.'

She was so blinded by her own tears that she walked into Marcia on her way out and trod on her foot. She apologised briefly, hoping fervently that she had managed to hurt the old bag.

She went back to her own small office and sat down; she was still crying. She was crying for many reasons, and not being able to go to New York was not the major one.

Her phone rang; she sniffed loudly and picked it up.

'Kirsten?' It was her mother; she sounded low.

'Oh, hi Mum. You OK?' said Kirsten, putting as much sympathy into her voice as she could.

'I suppose so. A bit – tired. Depressed. This is always a bad time, you know. When I've got used to being home, and I feel rather alone. Not quite picked up the pieces. Father Bryant has been round and he's been marvellous but – what I really need is a little holiday, of course. But I can't really afford it and anyway I've no-one really to go with. You couldn't ... ?'

'No,' said Kirsten sharply. 'I know I couldn't. I just asked Dad for – well, some time off.'

'And?'

'He said no. In his own inimitable way.'

'Oh dear. What a pity.'

'What about your nice friend Anne? Couldn't she go with you? Or even Gerald?'

'Anne doesn't have the money, dear, and Gerald is so busy with his new company. I hardly seem to see him these days either.'

'What's he doing?' said Kirsten, nudged out of her self-centred misery for a while.

'Oh, just working with some new people. They really appreciate him, have him under contract. But they're based in Guildford, so he's always down there.'

Gerald was her mother's boyfriend, a rather under-employed lighting consultant. Kirsten couldn't stand him, but at least he was kind to her mother and kept her company. The first time she had met him, he had told her how impressed he was by Pattie, and what a wonderfully brave woman she was. 'She really does meet this thing head on, doesn't she?'

Kirsten, who mostly observed her mother meeting this thing by running away from it, managed a slightly frosty smile and held out her hand to say goodbye; but he said (rather shaming her), 'I think she's very lonely. I've heard her story and it's very sad. I would like to be her friend, if that's all right with you.'

Kirsten had said briskly that it was perfectly all right by her and then felt ashamed of her hostility; it had been nice of him to ask her, and he clearly did feel a genuine concern for her mother. That had been two years ago, and he had remained constant to Pattie even through the one very nasty lapse (as she called it) that had put her back in the nursing home; he tried to see she went to her AA meetings, that she ate, that she didn't get too low.

Kirsten's attitude towards her mother generally remained what it had been right through her childhood: a mixture of sympathy, exasperated despair, and a degree of guilt that she was unable to help her more, did not do more for her, give her more time; but tonight she felt simply sorry for her, her life seemed so particularly lonely and difficult. Not only was there the constant battle against her alcoholism, but she had to endure being kept on a fairly tight spending budget by Bard (although most generously provided for in other ways: flat in Fulham, car run on the company, accounts for her clothes at Harrods and Peter Jones, anything in fact she could not easily convert into alcohol). But Kirsten contrasted her that evening, in her sadness, with bloody Francesca, sitting in that pair of mansions, with those two little brats, and Bard dancing attendance on her, and fussing because she was tired. Tired! What had she got to be tired about, with her nanny and her housekeepers and Horton to take her everywhere? And endless holidays – no way Francesca wasn't going to get to New York if she fancied it – eternally photographed and written about as if she were something special, someone important, when all she'd done was snap up her father in a weak moment. Stupid bitch.

Kirsten lit a cigarette: she was trying to give it up but this was one of the times when even another moment without one looked like bloody torture. Toby had been vile as well, told her she shouldn't have told him she was coming without checking properly, now he'd got to unbook the ticket and it had been done through his firm, there'd be hell to pay.

'I'm really sorry, Mum,' she said. 'Sorry you're down, sorry I can't go away with you. Listen, I'll come over some time this weekend. When are you free?'

'Oh will you, darling?' Pattie's voice was suddenly less tired, genuinely warm with pleasure. 'That would be so lovely. Come on Sunday morning. Maybe we could even go to Mass together.'

'Maybe,' said Kirsten. 'Anyway, I'll be over. I'll ring you. Bye, Mum.'

Her phone rang again almost at once. 'Miss Channing? Kirsten Channing?'

'Yes.'

'Kirsten, I don't know if you'll remember me. Judy Wyatt, *Daily Graphic*. We met at that super reception Sam Illingworth organised to tell us all about the exciting new venture of your father's. In the North of England.'

'Oh – yes, of course,' said Kirsten warily. She had no idea who Judy Wyatt was; just one of the female journalist clones with ginny pseudo-posh voices and flashy clothes reeking of cigarette smoke (she must give it up, she must, she must), and drinking hard at eleven in the morning. Or perhaps one of the older, cosier, more pathetic ones, with gushy faces and cloying handshakes, drinking even harder, even earlier.

'I certainly remember you. What an intriguing project that is, isn't it? Of your father's?'

'Er – which one?' said Kirsten cautiously. 'He has so many –'

'Yes, of course he does. But it was that new complex in Newcastle I was thinking of. Such an interesting field. But maybe there are others you could tell us about.'

'Well – maybe. Yes.'

'Look, I don't know what you'd think about this. But my editor thinks it's so interesting that you are working alongside your father. It really is a very good story. It must be wonderful for you. To get in on the ground floor, so to speak.'

'Oh it is,' said Kirsten fervently. 'Absolutely wonderful.'

'Are you the heir apparent, Kirsten? No brothers?'

'Oh – yes, a couple,' said Kirsten lightly.

'Two brothers! My goodness. What a prolific man your father is. Of course one of them must be in his latest family. What beautiful children they are, I saw a picture of them with their mother in the *Tatler* the other day. You must be so fond of them, almost like a second mum to them in some ways I expect.'

'Almost.' She had gone into auto-mode now.

'Do you see a lot of Francesca Channing? She's so beautiful, isn't she? Of course it can't be an easy life, I imagine, being married to a high-profile businessman like your father. She must have to work very hard –'

Something snapped inside Kirsten. It was the combination of hearing her mother's tiredly quiet voice, alone and lonely, and Toby's telling her she was a stupid little cow, and her father's telling her she was spoilt and lazy and that he was taking Francesca away for the weekend with the children, and remembering all the weekends she had had to care for her mother, trying to keep her from finding the bottles she had hidden herself and now wanted and couldn't find, or facing her wrath because she, Kirsten, had thrown them away, and trying to look after little Victoria too, and sometimes giving in and ringing her father who was often, so often, just not there: and realising that hardly anyone knew any of that, any of it at all and how unfair it was.

'Oh I don't know,' she said to Judy Wyatt, 'I don't know that she works very hard. She has quite an easy time of it really. Compared to what my mother had. She did have a hard time, you know. Really hard. Bringing us three up all on her own ...'

There was a short but potent silence on the other end of the line, and then Judy Wyatt said, 'That does sound very tough. Poor woman. She was obviously lucky to have you. Kirsten, this sounds like such an interesting story. Perhaps we could talk. It would be a very good piece for our readers. What we call a touchpoint. Something they could identify with. Could you perhaps have a drink with me so we could talk some more?'

'Well – yes,' said Kirsten. 'Yes, perhaps. I'd have to ask. I'm very junior here,' she added, trying to sound light-hearted.

'I can't believe that. Anyway, this isn't official Channing business PR, is it? Just a little background for our women readers. Anyway, of course you must ask. I'll – look, now I come to think about it, what are you doing right now? After work?'

'Oh – well – not a lot, actually.'

Not packing to go to New York, not going out to dinner with Toby. Not going off for a restorative country weekend. Just stewing in her own juice, reflecting on her own inadequacies as a person. Thanks to her father.

'What about now? I could meet you in no time, if you could spare half an hour. You're in St James's Square, aren't you? What about the bar at the Ritz? In – what, twenty minutes?'

'The Ritz?' said Kirsten, surprised. She hadn't expected that; women journalists were obviously on bigger expenses than she thought.

'Well, it's nice and quiet there,' said Judy Wyatt. 'Better for talking, I always think. But if you'd rather go somewhere trendy, Soho Soho for instance, that would be fine. Of course I am a member of the Groucho, but the world and his newspaper will be there tonight.'

'No, the Ritz'd be fine. But I mustn't be long. And I don't know what I can tell you that will be interesting.'

'Oh Kirsten, I do assure you I'm not asking you for an in-depth sob story,' said Judy Wyatt soothingly, 'just a little background. For our women readers. As I said.'

Chapter Seven

So it was official: no longer a fear, no longer a shadowy neurosis, but official, a long – or rather several long – words. Kitty had some long words, she had a ventricular septal defect, which meant she had a hole in that part of her heart that sent the blood circulating round her small body. And so it wasn't very effective, and the blood wasn't being circulated very well. And it would possibly – 'only possibly, I must stress that' – need surgery to correct it.

Francesca stood there, holding her baby when she came back from the X-ray department, holding the small body that was not getting all the blood it needed when it needed it, that was so often cold, that didn't gain weight, that clearly endured discomfort and perhaps endured pain, and that would have to endure more, would have to be cut into and probed and clipped and stitched, the tiny white chest mutilated with a great red gash, and she gripped Bard's hand and looked at Mr Lauder in an agony of fear and said (while thinking how mundane the words were, how foolishly inadequate), 'What happens now?'

'Well,' he said, 'well, what happens now is that I should refer her to a cardio-thoracic surgeon. Who will decide exactly when and if she should have surgery. I cannot stress enough that this is not a serious case, and neither is it urgent. It may well be that Kitty would be better served if we waited a while, until she is a little older and stronger.'

'But suppose –' said Francesca, and it took all her courage even to ask, and there was agony in her voice as she said it, 'suppose it gets worse, suppose she – she doesn't get the chance to be older and stronger.'

'That will be for the surgeon to decide.' Mr Lauder smiled his blandest, most reassuring smile. 'I have to tell you I think it is extremely unlikely that he won't agree with me. However, of course we don't want to risk anything, nor waste any time at all. Now if you can just bear with me, I will –'

And he was off on his medical routine, the one they all went into so swiftly and easily, lifting phones, making notes, raising eyebrows, smiling, nodding, running through the script, the well-rehearsed lines about nothing to worry about and excellent people and superb units and best possible care and earliest possible dates and that he would send her tracings and notes over to Mr Moreton-Smith, a consultant cardiovascular surgeon at St Andrew's, immediately, and if he thought she should be seen sooner, then that could be arranged too.

'That's almost a week,' said Francesca. 'Why not before?'

'Mrs Channing, as I have said, there is really no great urgency with this. She is not a severe case and most surgeons prefer to wait until the child is older. I don't want to raise your hopes, but in some, many cases even, the hearts repair themselves and surgery is not actually necessary. This is a very tiny hole, your baby is not seriously ill. You told me, I think, that she had gained almost a pound since I first saw her; that is excellent, most encouraging – you must try not to worry, Mrs Channing, Mr Channing. Of course it's upsetting, but –'

On and on the voice went, the detached voice, talking sense, talking knowledge, and of course it would, Francesca thought, it had no connection, that voice, with the owner of the heart that had been brought to him, the hurting, inefficient heart, she was just a patient to him, a small patient, not a part of him, that had been nourished and cherished by him, not something so dear, so important that he would feel his own heart hurting beyond endurance. She looked down at the baby, unusually peaceful, uncharacteristically asleep, and she cradled her close, shutting the world out from her, the hard world that had bestowed such injustice, such outrage on her, rested her cheek on the tiny, silky head, and tried to be calm.

'And what's the prognosis?' said Bard suddenly.

'I'm sorry?'

'How much danger is she actually in? What are her chances of a total recovery, with or without surgery? What are the risks of the surgery itself?'

Mr Lauder smiled at him and paused before he spoke, making it clear he had given the questions proper and careful consideration. 'She is not, so far as it is possible to make such a statement, and in my opinion, in any immediate danger. The chances of a total recovery are obviously dependent on a great many factors, which I would prefer you to discuss with Mr Moreton-Smith. The risks inherent in any surgery are of course there, and it would be wrong of me to dismiss them, and again would be affected by the length of the operation, the degree of anaesthesia required, the child's general health, but again, Mr Moreton-Smith would be better able to tell you –'

'Well, this is all pretty bloody useless, isn't it?' said Bard.

'I'm sorry?'

'All these ifs and buts and maybes. What I want are some facts, and I want to know how we get them, get something more satisfactory than all this nonsense.'

'Mr Channing,' said Mr Lauder, all reasonable calm, indicating most clearly that he understood Bard's distress, even as he must, as a man of medicine, dismiss it, and speaking as if to a moderately intelligent child, 'I do assure you this is as definite a diagnosis as you will get at this stage. Medicine is not an exact science, as of course you know, especially in a situation like this one. Your daughter is very young, very tiny; one is inevitably dealing in ifs and buts, as you put it, in uncertainties –'

'Well, I'd like to check that out for myself, I'm afraid,' said Bard, 'I cannot believe it's impossible to get a more definite diagnosis, as you put it, than the one we've had this morning.'

'Bard –' said Francesca. 'Bard, I don't –'

'Mr Channing, of course you may get a second opinion. That is your absolute right. But I would be very –' He hesitated, then smiled again, the smile yet more gracious, more chillingly confident, '– very surprised if you were told anything more definite. However, if it is your wish, then I suggest you see another paediatrician and perhaps you would then feel you would like to come back to me and discuss your daughter's case more fully.'

'Fine,' said Bard. 'That's what we will do. Because –'

'Mr Lauder,' said Francesca, taking a deep breath, not looking at Bard, 'I'm not quite sure about this. Would it delay matters if we did that? Would it mean you wouldn't send the tracings to Mr Moreton-Smith immediately –'

'No, no, I should still do that, of course. And report back to you. But I would not ask him then to see her, as the matter would be in abeyance while you sought a second opinion –'

'Well, we will discuss this between ourselves,' said Francesca, still not looking at Bard, her voice very clear, 'and then phone you. If we may.'

'Of course. And, as I say, this is not a serious case, and I would urge you again to try not to worry too much.' He stood up, smiling, holding out his hand to Francesca and then to Bard, tickled Kitty gently under her small chin. 'Beautiful,' he said, 'quite beautiful. I'm sure she'll be fine.'

'How could you do that?' said Francesca, as soon as they were outside in the street. 'How could you be so rude, so arrogant?'

'He was rude and arrogant,' said Bard, 'not to mention incompetent, talking to us as if we were halfwits, not giving us any proper answers –'

'Bard, there aren't any proper answers, as you put it. Well, we've had quite a lot already. He can't say any more yet, he can't do a prognosis about whether or not surgery will be required, how much danger she might or might not be in. I'm not in the least surprised he talked to you as if you were a halfwit, you were behaving like one.'

'Oh for God's sake,' he said. 'I've had enough to put up with this morning without listening to this.'

'Oh really?' said Francesca. Rage swept over her, so strong, so blinding it was almost pleasurable. 'You've had a lot to put up with? Bard, how can you talk like that, while Kitty is ill, really ill and possibly in pain, certainly suffering, we don't know how much, while I feel like just picking her up and running away with her, while Mr Lauder, having put his considerable expertise at our disposal, has to listen your insults. I feel sick, Bard, sick to the bottom of my heart, and that performance of yours has certainly contributed to it. I'm going to take Kitty home, and I am not going to seek any second opinions until we've seen Mr Moreton-Smith. Then if we're not happy, we can think again.'

'Francesca, we will do what I think best.'

'No, we won't. Because it isn't best for Kitty. Not at this stage. We're only talking a few days. She's been ill all her little life.' She held Kitty closer to her suddenly, as if to protect her. 'And I might say, if I hadn't taken matters into my own hands, seen Mr Lauder in the first place, she would have gone on being ill, possibly until it was too late. So don't start telling me what's best for her, please. Anyway, I'm going home now. I don't know what you're going to do.'

'Obviously I'm going to the office. I've got a lot on.'

'Obviously.'

'I'll call you. Later. When I've had time to think about this.'

She shrugged. 'Fine.' She turned away from him, unlocked her car door, started buckling Kitty into the complex straps of her little seat.

'Francesca –'

'Yes, Bard?' She could hear her own voice, ice cold.

'Francesca, I – I'm only concerned with what's best for Kitty. That's all I want.'

'Is it? Is it really?'

'Yes, of course it bloody well is.'

'Good,' she said coolly and got into the car.

★

128

He didn't phone, not all afternoon; but he arrived home, most extraordinarily, at six, his arms full of flowers, his dark eyes full of remorse.

'I love you,' he said, kissing her, 'and we have to get through this thing somehow. We'll see this Moreton-Smith man and then we'll see someone else.'

It was the nearest he was going to get to apologising; knowing what it had cost him, she smiled, took the flowers, kissed him back. 'Thank you. I love you too. And yes, we will get through it. And we can see Mr Moreton-Smith next Tuesday. Quite soon really.'

'You've fixed it, then?'

She met his eyes steadily. 'Yes. Yes, I spoke to Mr Lauder this afternoon.'

She thought he might lose his temper then, tell her she had no right to go ahead until he had agreed; but there was a pause and then he said, clearly with great difficulty, 'Fine. I'll come with you.'

Of all humiliations, Liam thought this must surely be the worst. To sit in some crummy office, opposite some little nerd in a shiny suit and a flashy tie with slicked-back hair and a framed photograph of some bimbo with streaked blonde hair and huge boobs bursting out of her bikini, and beg. It was even worse than begging from his father. At least he had some sort of respect for his father.

'Right, Mr Channing,' said Des Carter (that was the name painted proudly on the small plaque that stood on his desk), 'let's just go over this once more. Now you bought Forty-seven Marquis for – what was it – four hundred and twenty thousand in 1988. It's now worth – what shall we say, on the open market? Three-fifty? Terrible, isn't it? Really terrible. I said to my wife only last night, thank God we didn't get into that. We could have done, only too easily, believe me. But her father's a builder, he saw it coming of course, and we waited to buy. Saw the prices tumbling down. We were lucky. Anyway, you don't want to hear my story, do you?'

'Oh – I don't know,' said Liam carefully. 'Be nice to the buggers,' had been the last advice his solicitor had given him, 'let them throw the book at you, don't argue. They're all little Hitlers, love the sense of power. Just stay humble. You'll do better that way.'

'So now you can't keep up your payments. Dear oh dear. You have my sympathy, Mr Channing, you really do. We see so much of this and really it doesn't get any easier for us.'

For us neither, thought Liam gritting his teeth.

'Now your monthly repayments are – let's see – three thousand seven hundred. Quite a lot, isn't it? I can see it could represent quite a drain. Now what is the combined family income?'

'About – about a hundred and fifty thousand.'

'That doesn't sound too bad. Still, a big hunk out of it though. What do you do, Mr Channing? Ah yes, barrister I see. Well, you guys make loads of dosh don't you? Coining it in?'

'Not all of us, no. Unfortunately. It's quite tough actually.'

'Really?' He looked blankly surprised. 'And your wife, she's a banker?'

'Yes.'

'So hers is the primary income?'

'Yes. That is, it was.' He felt himself beginning to sweat. 'But she's been made redundant. Usual story, you know, takeover. The Americans. Of course I'm sure it's only a temporary hitch. She has a very good track record. But in the meantime –'

'Yes, of course. The meantime. Which is what we're looking at, isn't it? What about your own income, are you able to increase or even supplement that, Mr Channing? In the meantime?'

Slimy little shit, thought Liam. 'I'm not – sure. Naturally I'm trying.'

'Well, good for you, Mr Channing. Lots of people aren't prepared to try even. So full marks to you.'

A quarter of an hour later, Liam left, with a reprieve of sorts: six months without making any further mortgage repayments ('Of course you realise these would be added on to the capital sum at the end?'). At least they would continue to have a roof over their heads. A roof probably not worth the best quality slates it was made of, but at least the bed and breakfast didn't beckon. On the other hand there wasn't going to be much more breakfast if he didn't get anything out of the bank. The overdraft still stood at £9,000, and the charges on it were hideous. Naomi's redundancy money had simply taken the top off it; the manager had told them if it did not at least stop rising, he would simply start returning cheques.

'This is not a charity, Mr Channing. I can't go on supporting you indefinitely.'

The problem was, anything at all he did manage to earn simply got lost in the overdraft; Naomi had suggested they open a Post Office Giro account for anything they could salvage, and that had helped a bit; they had sold a few of their beloved pieces of Staffordshire and some silver and put the money in there, but it was almost run through now, and he was terrified of overdrawing on it, with the inevitable checks on his credit rating, and the antagonism of their own manager. Something had to be done; he had to get something out of the buggers.

Naomi had told him he should go straight on to the bank from the building society that morning, but that seemed to Liam the equivalent of washing down bitter pills with gall: he decided to go home, call the bank and speak to the manager, and maybe he would have something positive to tell him, maybe there would be a reply to one of the innumerable letters he had written applying for jobs as in-house barrister. It was a favourite route for those for whom private practice had not proved sufficiently profitable: less glamorous, less prestigious, but more secure. So far he had not had a great deal of luck.

He walked down Marquis Terrace towards their house; once it had seemed to him Arcadia, a beautiful street, the finest example of Islington Georgian, shutters all intact, fireplaces all present, furniture all stylish, every single one filled with successful, moneyed, ambitious people – Type A Terrace it ought to be called, Naomi had once said; he hadn't known what she'd meant and she had said, 'Really Liam, surely even you must know about Type A personalities, they're the pushy, driven lot. The ones who are statistically most prone to heart attacks,' she added briskly.

A couple of the Terrace nannies were pushing small, trendily clothed children along it in large gleaming pushchairs; they both smiled at him slightly awkwardly, began talking rather too busily (knowing his own nanny had been told to leave, knowing full well why). He looked blankly back at them, not really caring; he had more important things to worry about than the nanny mafia.

Liam pushed open the door, looked at the hall table; the usual pile of bills and envelopes telling him their contents were not circulars, mostly chase-up letters on credit and charge cards, and two officious-looking white envelopes. Replies, thought Liam, feeling sick, and walked into the kitchen, sat down heavily.

'Dear Mr Channing (they both said, uncompromisingly), Thank you for your letter. Although we were impressed by ...'

He didn't read on; stood up again, plugged in the kettle. The kitchen was a mess, he thought, looking round it distastefully – Naomi certainly had no talent for the domestic life. Crumbs and tea stains all over the white tiled surface, a milk bottle and a margarine tub on the black marble table, and two unfinished cups of tea on the draining board. Surely she could at least tidy up after herself. Where was she anyway, the children were both at school, she should be here, working on job applications. That was the pact. They would both make a job of getting a job.

She had been very good when he had first got back that day, supportive and cool; had cursed and reviled his father for some time, and then said quite cheerfully (pre-empting his own speech, somewhat to his surprise) that actually it would have been terrible to be under any kind of obligation to him, far better make their own way: they had even gone to bed and had some rather amazing sex. Liam had lain (slightly detachedly) as her body tensed and throbbed and eased, and wondered how long her positive mood would last.

A very short time it turned out: as the days had gone by, they were patently failing to make their own way. All Naomi's contacts had said of course, normally they would be thrilled to have her on board, but with things still being, if not bad not good – well, they would get back to her the minute they had anything for her; and he had spent long miserable days applying for jobs far below his capabilities, as he had ventured outside the legal framework, had applied for (and failed to get) consultancies, jobs in marketing, in sales (sales, for God's sake!), and their spirits had been sucked inevitably into a downward spiral, and they had become first loudly quarrelsome and then silently hostile.

Everything, thought Liam, staring out at the small walled garden (and even that looked neglected now and there really was no excuse for that, except that when the nanny had looked after the children and Mrs Barker had done the housework there had been more time and energy for trimming and pruning and going off to the Garden Centre for shrubs and tubs and terracottas), everything conspired to remind him how unsatisfactory their life had become. All the things that had once seemed unremarkable – the pile of clean sheets and duvet covers in the airing cupboard, the great heaps of thick fluffy towels, the rows of perfectly ironed shirts in his wardrobe, the immaculately filled fridge, the cosy hour before the children's bedtime when he and they sat and cuddled on the sofa, they in their clean pyjamas, their hair washed and shining, and he read them stories, the fresh flowers in the hall and the drawing room, the fun of shopping together on Saturday morning, all of them, hurling things into the trolley in Waitrose, anything anyone fancied, going for a walk with one or two other families in the Terrace and then having tea together, which invariably became drinks and then sometimes supper – all those things had assumed huge importance by their absence. Especially to Liam. He craved, he required, domestic order. Without it he felt a kind of outrage, a sense of neglect, of being unattended to. Naomi never ironed anything, certainly not his shirts; the hour before bedtime was now the one where he had to bath and feed the children, and story time had become a lot shorter. Flowers were expensive, shopping a worrying chore (was their payment card going to be accepted, had they overspent?), and the other families best avoided, as hospitality could no longer be returned, drinks no longer offered, and tactful questions had become increasingly difficult to answer cheerfully.

He made his coffee and sat down at the table meaning to go through last Sunday's papers for jobs; but he could hear a baby crying in the garden next door and he suddenly thought of Francesca and the tiny, sickly Kitty. At least their children were healthy, his and Naomi's, they had that to be thankful for. Liam was, if nothing else, a devoted father. The removal of the buffer of the nanny between himself and Jasper and Hattie had made them seem at once more exasperating and exhausting and troubling and more precious and important to him. He loved them as he had never loved anyone, with a fierce, possessive passion; he watched them sometimes as they played, or ate or even fought, their small beings intent on their task, and would feel quite overwhelmed with amazement that they were his: and with concern for the responsibility of them. It was not a tedious responsibility, rather a pleasurable one, coming from the sense of importance that they gave him, true importance, necessity even. He would like to know how Kitty was, he decided; and besides, Francesca had been so kind to him that day, so thoughtful, had been so patently willing to forgive his past rudeness and hostility. He owed it to her at least to make a phone call.

He picked up the phone, quickly, before he could change his mind, and dialled the house in Hamilton Terrace; Sandie, the housekeeper, answered. He had always rather liked Sandie; more importantly she had liked him.

'Is Mrs Channing there, please, Sandie? This is Liam Channing.'

'Liam!' She didn't quite say 'Good God', but the words hung in the air. 'How are you?'

'Oh, pretty well, Sandie, thank you. And you?'

'I'm fine, Liam, yes. But Mrs Channing is out at the – oh, no, here she is now. Just a moment, Liam, I'll tell her you're on the line.'

There was a pause; he heard Sandie say, 'It's Liam Channing,' heard Francesca pause before taking the phone, heard her large earring go down on the hall table as she picked it up.

'Liam! Hallo. This is a pleasant surprise.'

'I'm pleased it's pleasant,' he said, and meant it.

'Yes,' she said, slightly awkwardly, 'it – well yes, it is pleasant.'

'I realised I'd never thanked you for the other day. You were very kind.'

'I think the benefit was mutual actually,' she said. 'I'd have been arrested otherwise. Or at best crashed the car.'

'I don't think so. Anyway, thank you. And also, I wanted to ask you how Kitty was.'

'Oh. How very nice of you.'

Her voice was lower, suddenly, disproportionately emotional. 'Yes, well, we still don't really know. We saw the paediatrician today, she has had tests. She's – not too good. Although not too bad. She does have a hole in her heart, but it's very small. We have to see the surgeon next week. That's all we know.'

'I'm so sorry,' he said.

'Yes. Yes, thank you.'

'It must be a great worry for you both,' he said carefully.

'Yes. Yes, of course it is. Bard is – well, terribly upset. We both are.'

She sounded awkward; well, it was an awkward conversation. Then she said, 'And how are things with you?'

'Oh – filthy,' he said, without thinking.

'I'm sorry. What sort of filthy?'

'Oh – you know.'

'No, I don't know.'

He'd have to tell her now, he supposed; or if he didn't have to, he found he wanted to.

'Naomi's lost her job. We're in a bit of a mess. Her being the major breadwinner and all that. Classic 'nineties problems, you know. Negative equity on the house. That sort of thing.'

'Liam, I'm so sorry. Is that what you were seeing Bard about the other day?'

'Yes.'

'And he was helpful? I hope he was.'

'Not very,' said Liam, and found he was enjoying it, enjoying telling, showing her what a bastard she was married to. 'Not at all, actually, I'm afraid.'

'I see.' Another long pause; what could she say? 'Oh, dear. I wish I could help. I don't think I can. But surely Naomi can get another –'

'She's working on it. It isn't easy.'

'No, I'm sure it isn't. How is Naomi?'

'Fine,' he said briefly.

'Good.' There was a silence, then she said, 'Well, thank you for ringing, Liam. It was very kind. And – I can't think what I can do, but I'm always here if you want to talk.'

'Yes. Thank you.'

'How odd,' she said suddenly, 'that we should be having this conversation. How very odd. I must go. Goodbye, Liam.'

'Goodbye, Francesca.'

Yes, he thought, how very odd.

'So very kind,' said Heather Clarke, looking up from a letter from Bard. 'What a dear man he is. And even a private plane to take us to the island. And his staff to wait on us. How can we even begin to show him how grateful we are? It worries me sometimes.'

'I shouldn't let it,' said Oliver. He was finding his mother's attitude to Bard Channing increasingly irritating. 'The house is there, the staff is there, why shouldn't he lend it to us? Well, to you.'

'Oliver, dear, that's a very harsh attitude,' said Heather disapprovingly. 'None of that is the point, it's thinking of it all, and of us, that makes it so kind.'

'I don't know,' said Oliver. 'I think he ought to think of you, I think he owes you a lot.'

'Oliver, what does Mr Channing owe me?' said Heather. 'Don't be silly.'

'I agree with Mum,' said Melinda. 'I think Mr Channing's really sweet.'

'You should work with him,' said Oliver, 'then you wouldn't think he was so sweet.'

'Your father worked with him. He never complained.'

'Didn't he?' said Oliver, looking at her with interest. 'Didn't he ever?'

'They had their differences, of course. But –'

'What sort of differences?'

'Oliver dear, being in business is like a marriage. You father always said that too. It has its ups and downs, you have to give and take. There were things I'm sure that they didn't see eye to eye on, but –'

'Yeah, and I bet Dad didn't ever get his way. Old man Channing overrides everybody and everything. If you don't do what he wants, God help you. Do you know he even wanted to stop you seeing Mrs Booth?'

'He did? How do you know?' said Heather.

'Because he said so. Tried to pretend it might upset you, be bad for you.'

'I think that's quite sweet,' said Heather. She went rather pink. 'I suppose he thinks talking about the old days ... Did he seem very bothered by it, Oliver?'

'Well – not bothered. He just didn't want you to. Don't worry about it.'

There was a silence. Then: 'I shall worry about it,' said Heather decisively. 'If it bothers Mr Channing that much, I won't see her. I didn't like her particularly anyway, so there's really no point. I'll ring her, Oliver, and tell her I don't feel up to it. Mr Channing is much more important.'

'All right,' said Oliver. 'Fine.' He was very weary of the whole subject; it had got him into trouble with Channing, and now he could see there might well be trouble from Teresa Booth. 'Now look, I think your passport's expired, I'll have to get you a new one. Or do you think you could do that, Melinda?'

'I don't think I can,' said Melinda. 'We're awfully busy at the office at the moment.'

'You always are,' said Oliver shortly. 'Unlike me, of course. OK, I'll see to it.' He was finding his womenfolk rather tiresome at the moment. Time he got another girlfriend. Only it was quite a while since he'd met anyone he really fancied. Really fancied, in the sense of liked as well. Maybe on the Greek island ...

'Oh Christ. Oh shit. Holy fucking shit,' said Kirsten.

Her stomach heaved; she felt icy cold, then very hot, as if she were going to faint. She closed her eyes, then opened them again, praying that she had imagined it, that what she had just read had been a delusion, the result of drinking too much red wine the night before.

It hadn't.

'Fuck,' she said, and then again. 'Fuck.'

'Kirsten, what on earth is the matter?' said Toby. 'Or are you making some kind of a suggestion? Because I don't think I could – not just yet.' He looked at her, grinning over the breakfast table and his copy of the *News of the World*, his own favourite Sunday reading.

'Shut up,' said Kirsten. 'Just shut up, Toby, will you.' She forced her eyes back to the page, made herself go on reading it. She was going to spew, she really was.

'Babe, are you all right? You look awful.'

'No. No, I'm not. Look, Toby, read this.' The paper, as she held it out to him, shook; she felt hot and cold at the same time. Toby took it, smiling at her slightly anxiously; a smile that slowly left his face as he read.

'Jesus,' he said. 'Holy shit. Where did this load of bollocks come from?'

'Me,' said Kirsten. Her voice was faint, shaky.

'You? Don't be insane. It can't have done.'

'It did.'

He read on, then: 'You mean you talked to this woman?'

'Yup. I did.'

He stared at her, then shook his head, smiling slightly doubtfully. 'You're an idiot,' he said finally.

'Thanks.'

'Sorry. But it's true. When, for fuck's sake?'

'Last Friday. Well, the one before last. When you went to New York and I couldn't come. You know – ten days ago.'

'But why?'

'Oh Toby, I don't know. Well, I suppose I do. He'll kill me, Toby. Absolutely kill me. Shit, what am I going to do?' Tears of fright, of panic, welled in her eyes, started rolling down her cheeks. She looked at it again, lying there, in all its horror, irredeemable, inescapable. 'Tycoon's family's hidden heartbreak,' read the teaser flash on the front page of the *Sunday Graphic*. Women's section, page 42. Page 42 showed a large colour photograph of Kirsten taken several years earlier in her Benenden school uniform; God knew where they'd got it. She looked very pretty, but rather strained. It was obviously a lucky photograph, thought Kirsten, dredged out of the cuttings library. The picture was underneath a headline which ran right across the two pages, and said 'Kirsten Channing tells of her childhood hell', Judy Wyatt Exclusive.

Next to it was a smaller picture of Kirsten, Barnaby and Victoria, taken at about the same time, with Pattie, sitting on a beach, captioned 'The family Bard Channing left to sink or swim', and on the opposite page, a very recent one of Francesca with Jack and Kitty taken for the christening in the drawing room at Stylings, Kitty in myriad frills, Jack in his sailor suit. 'The new young family with everything.'

' "It was not unusual," Kirsten Channing told me, her husky voice shaky with the memory, "for me to come home and find my mother sobbing helplessly. Life on her own, after my father had left, when I was only eleven, was a terrible struggle for her. She was lonely and very hurt, and she was trying to bring us up single-handed. As the eldest, I felt I had to do everything I could to help, and as my younger brother had been sent away to school at my father's insistence, I found the burden very heavy. My mother depended on me totally, not only emotionally, but also in a practical way. She couldn't afford much help, and she was often unwell."

'Kirsten loyally did not expand on the nature of her mother's "unwellness": Pattie Channing was in fact an alcoholic, and her small daughter had to bear the burden and the shame of that fact as well. An old school friend told me that more than once Kirsten came home to find her mother lying unconscious, once at the foot of the stairs, having fallen from top to bottom.

'Was her father not available if Kirsten needed him? "He was always working. He's one of the great workaholics of all time. He was never there, not even at weekends, although he used to come and take us out sometimes. But if my mother was in a very bad way, I never wanted to leave her. Then my father would get upset. I suppose that was understandable, but it was very difficult for me. I would stand listening to him shouting while my mother cried, trying to decide which of them I should spend the day with."

'Bard Channing undoubtedly had to work long and hard; he is a self-made millionaire in the property field. As well as a mansion in St John's Wood, and a vast estate in Sussex, he owns a house in Greece, and a luxury yacht moored in the South of France, *Lay Lady Lay*, named after a Bob Dylan song.

'He met the third Mrs Channing fifteen years ago; he has another son, by his first wife, Liam, from whom he is estranged. Liam, who is struggling to find work as a barrister, lives in a small house in North London.

'Bard Channing proposed to Francesca on television, in front of millions. She in fact married another man and then divorced him before finally yielding to his charms. And of course, the luxury lifestyle.

'She never speaks to Pattie Channing, has never been near her small Fulham home ...'

'You really are an idiot,' said Toby again.

'Toby, for Christ's sake stop saying that. It doesn't help.'

'Sorry. Er – is there any chance he won't see it? I mean surely he wouldn't subscribe to this rag?'

'Oh don't be so stupid, of course he'll see it,' said Kirsten, her voice rising in agony. 'He sees everything. Everything that's written about him. If not today, tomorrow. Anyway, people will be ringing him by now, I'm sure. Oh God. Oh God, Toby, what shall I do?'

'Don't know. I really don't know, darling.' He was very serious now, obviously shaken by what had happened.

'She promised me,' said Kirsten, 'she promised –'

'Promised you what?'

'Not to write anything without showing me.'

'Kirsten, when were you born? Really!'

'I know, I know. But I was so angry, so upset with my father. He'd been foul to me, really bawled me out. Told me I was lazy, and taking him and everyone else for a ride, and that –'

'Yes?'

'Disgusted him.'

'Sounds a bit strong,' said Toby.

'Oh, that's quite mild for him. Honestly, Toby, you have no idea. And then he said he was going to take Francesca to the country for a few days, that she was tired, and I wasn't to start creating over the weekend. I know why now, their baby's ill, something wrong with her heart, that makes it worse. Oh, God. But I didn't then, I thought it was a fuss about nothing, And then Mum rang, and she sounded really really low, and I kept thinking of the difference between us and them. And then that slag phoned –'

'Which slag?' said Toby. 'I'm getting confused.'

'The journalist slag. And she said how wonderful it must be for me to be working for my father and how lovely Francesca was and something – snapped. And I went for a drink with her, and – well, you've read the rest. I have been a bit worried, but the thing is, Toby, I didn't say all this. Well, not as much as it sounds. I never said about Mum being an alcoholic –'

'No, it says you didn't,' said Toby, who was half-reading the article again as she talked.

'And I did try to be – well, truthful, I said how he bought her the house and came at weekends and everything. But – well anyway,' she said, her voice wobbling, 'what do you think I should do?'

'I'm not sure,' said Toby. 'I'm really not sure. How about you ring your boss? Sam thingy. See if she's got any ideas.'

'Oh,' said Kirsten, 'oh Toby, that's a good idea. The press is her area. She may be able to get this woman to tell my father I didn't say all this, print a retraction, something –' Her voice, tearful, choky, was neverthless suddenly hopeful. 'Yes, I'll ring her now. Toby, you are clever.'

She rang Sam; Sam said she hadn't seen the *Graphic*, but she'd read the piece and ring her back. Five minutes later she was on the phone;

Kirsten could tell by her voice, heavy, struggling against panic, that there wasn't a lot of hope of a retraction.

'Kirsten, this is awful. Terrible. Why on earth did you talk to that woman?'

'I don't know,' wailed Kirsten, 'I just don't know. I was upset. I was drunk. Oh Sam, what am I going to do? What's he going to do?'

'Fire us both, I should think,' said Sam, with an attempt at cheerfulness.

'You! Why you?'

'Because the press is my area. He thinks I can control it. He'll say I should have known you'd talked to her, that I should have impressed upon you not to do so, that I should have got wind of it and stopped it ...'

'Sam, that's just not fair. Of course you –'

'Whether it's fair, Kirsten, is irrelevant. As you very well know. He'll say it. Look, I think the best thing we can do is talk to him together. What are you doing today?'

'Well – supposed to be going to see my mother.'

'Call it off. Oh I don't know. She won't be feeling too good if she sees it, will she?'

'No,' said Kirsten. 'Oh God, why am I so dumb? If only, if only I hadn't talked to her –'

'Kirsten, if you knew how many times that's been said over stories in the Sunday papers. Or any papers, come to that –'

'Look, I'd better see Mum. I'll try and make sure she's OK. Maybe get her boyfriend round –'

'Her boyfriend! You're lucky they didn't get that one in.'

'Oh, he's not really. Just a friend. And then maybe we should go down to Stylings this afternoon. They're there. I think you're right. No point running away from it.'

'Kirsten,' said Sam, 'you're a brave girl.'

Graydon Townsend was grazing swiftly through all the papers, as he liked to do before he even got out of bed on Sunday; he read the article about the Channings with horror and a growing incredulity that someone as intelligent and sharp as Kirsten should have poured her heart out to a third-rate journalist like Judy Wyatt. He also felt very sorry for them all: for Kirsten – why on earth hadn't someone warned the silly bitch, he was surprised at Sam Illingworth – for Sam herself, who would no doubt take an enormous amount of flak, for Francesca, who really didn't deserve it, all that crap about how she'd never visited the first wife in her little house, of course she hadn't

140

visited her, what second – no, third – wife would? He felt very sorry for Pattie, having her alcoholism described so vividly, and he even felt faintly sorry for Bard Channing; was rash enough to say so to Briony after reading selected items from the Wyatt garbage aloud to her.

'You're nuts,' she said briefly. 'Why should anyone feel sorry for him? The thing is, Gray, whatever you say, he's done all these things. He did walk out on his wife, and he did therefore subject his children to all that misery, and Pattie was an alcoholic, he knew that. It's her I feel sorriest for. Can't say my heart bleeds too much for the daughter. She's obviously a very tough nut.'

'Yes and no,' said Gray without thinking, and then spent the next ten minutes assuring Briony quite untruthfully that any knowledge he had of Kirsten Channing was based on a very brief encounter at a press lunch to announce the northern development.

'Anyway,' she said, 'we'd better get up because we're going to have lunch with Marianne and Tim.'

'Oh no,' he said, 'not them. Please not them.'

She looked at him, her blue eyes very hard. 'And why not them? Oh, just don't bother answering, Gray, and you needn't bother coming either. I'll go on my own. You stay here and perfect some little sauce or dust down a few linen jackets.'

'Briony, I –'

'Just piss off,' she said, most unusually for her, the mildest of creatures: looking at her as she reached for her robe, he saw tears sparkling at the back of her eyes. He reached out for her hand, but she shook him off, and disappeared into the bathroom.

Marianne and Tim had a baby. This was not the only reason Gray didn't want to go, although the constant unveiling of a huge veined breast, a dripping nipple and a distinctly grubby bra did not seem entirely charming to him, and nor did the enthusiastic accounts of how long after midnight the baby had slept the previous night, as opposed to the one before, or the earnest discussion on the state of the latest nappy. He also found their house (1930s) and garden (small rectangular lawn surrounded with equally geometric flowerbeds) depressing, the interminable tweeting of the two canaries which lived in the kitchen enraging, and Briony and Marianne's reminiscences about their wild days at art school hugely tedious. But he knew, deep down, it was the baby, and Briony knew it too.

She came back half an hour later, looking heartbreakingly pretty in a long white skirt and clinging pink T-shirt, and said, 'Gray, I think I'll go and spend tonight with my sister. I want to talk to her and I don't really want to talk to you.'

'About the – the baby issue.'

'Yes.'

'Look, darling, I –'

'You think it would have to be like Marianne and Tim, I know you do, and it really wouldn't. I'd never ever discuss nappy duty or –'

'Briony, I know that. But you would change. We'd both change. There'd be something wrong if we didn't. And I just don't see why we have to.'

'Because I want to.' She was shouting at him now. 'I want it so much. And you won't even think about it properly.' And then she was gone. The slam of the door echoed in his ears all day.

Francesca found it rather hard to care about the article, as she found it rather hard to care about anything at the moment. She could not imagine how she had ever thought any of the things that had beset her throughout her life – exams, boyfriends, losing her virginity, the odd pregnancy scare, and so on to more serious ones, her first marriage, her dangerous relationship with Bard within it, and the discovery of that, the contemplation of what marriage to him was really going to mean, and then the realisation of what it did – mattered; none of these things could begin to compare with the heavy, ugly weight of this new fear, the fear about Kitty and her frail little heart. She fell asleep with it beside her on the pillow, woke with it snapping instantly onto her consciousness in the morning, carried it about with her all day. She replayed Mr Lauder's words again and again to herself: the hole was small, the risk slight, most children with her condition were fine, and she found them, those words, seriously wanting; she still longed, more than anything in the world, to sit down and scream, very loudly and repeatedly, several times a day. She was focused entirely on the meeting with Mr Moreton-Smith on Tuesday; although she knew that would solve nothing immediately, she felt it was at least some kind of certainty, they would be further down the road, on this nightmare journey, there would be new areas shaded in on the map, new signposts to follow. And until then, nothing, nothing at all, seemed to have any reality. Certainly not an absurd article in a tacky Sunday paper, not even an article that cast herself in a bad light, that had further estranged her from Kirsten, and Kirsten from Bard, that had driven Bard into a rage and horror so violent that she had sent Nanny out for a long walk with both the children until he had calmed and quietened down. It just didn't seem to matter. It wasn't important. It wasn't life and death.

★

Kirsten was in the shower when her father rang: a subdued Toby came to tell her. 'He sounds none too pleased,' he said.

She wrapped herself in her thick robe, hugging it tightly round her for comfort, picked up the phone. 'Dad?'

'Unfortunately yes. I can tell you I would much rather someone else was your father. For God's sake, Kirsten, have you no brains at all? How could you do it? To me? To your mother? To Francesca? To yourself, for that matter? Talk to this – God almighty, Kirsten, I cannot believe it. Even of you.'

'Dad, can I come and see you? With Sam? Maybe explain.'

'Come and see me? You certainly can not. I don't want to see you. I don't want you anywhere near me. Just stay away. Well away. Apart from anything else, I don't want Francesca subjected to any more of this than she has to be. She has enough to cope with at the moment. And tell Sam to stay away as well. I don't want either of you here, do you understand?'

Kirsten was silent.

'What's Sam got to do with it, anyway? Did she have some part in this?'

'No,' said Kirsten quickly, 'absolutely no part at all. I just thought –'

'I didn't know you could think. You've shown very little sign of it so far. On second thoughts, get Sam to ring me, would you?'

'Yes. Yes, all right. Dad, I'm sorry, really sorry –'

'I daresay you are,' he said, and put the phone down.

Kirsten walked back into the kitchen; she felt exhausted, sore all over. 'I think you'd better go,' she said to Toby. 'I really need to be on my own.'

'Well, if you're sure –' he said. He was obviously relieved. He didn't like dramas, Toby didn't. He liked his life comfortable.

She heard his car driving away, with considerable relief; and then had to rush into the bathroom where she was violently and repeatedly sick.

Chapter Eight

Gray rang Channings first thing on Monday morning and asked to speak to Kirsten. A carefully polite voice told him she wasn't there at the moment. 'We're not sure when she will be in.'

I bet you're not, Gray thought. 'Well, could I speak to Sam, please? It's Graydon Townsend.'

Sam came on the phone: she sounded subdued. 'Hi, Gray.'

'Morning, Sam. I just phoned to say I was sorry. About the piece in the *Graphic*. Ghastly woman she is, Judy Wyatt. Should have been put down at birth.'

'Oh I don't know,' said Sam wearily. 'Kirsten was very silly.'

'Kirsten is very silly. But she's also very young and inexperienced.'

'I know. I feel very responsible.'

'Well, you shouldn't. I don't suppose Big Daddy is too pleased, though.'

'He's beside himself. Blames me, of course. Says he can't understand why it can't all be retracted. The usual.'

'Yes ... Bloody shame, the whole thing. Poor old you. Well, if there's anything I can do ...'

'Gray, you're very sweet.'

'That's OK. I don't suppose it'll help my cause though, will it? Getting my interview, I mean?'

Sam almost laughed. 'I'm afraid not. Sorry, Gray.'

'Well, look, tell Kirsten I called, will you? Just to say I was sorry?'

'Yes of course. I gather you and she had a drink the other night.'

'We did, and I don't want any scurrilous rumours about that one. I'm in enough trouble at home as it is.'

'Of course not. Bye, Gray.'

'Bye, Sam.'

Gray liked Mondays. Most Sunday-paper people didn't work on Mondays, but he often did. It was a good time to think, to digest all the other papers, to review everything he had been doing the week before. It was all part of his methodical way of working, his need to be in control, to have things in order. He spent most of the day rehashing a rather heavy piece on the Labour leadership struggle, and then at four o'clock was unable to ignore the tugging inside his head on the subject of Bard Channing any longer, and called him up on his profile database. It still vaguely surprised him, having been a trainee journalist fifteen years earlier, that looking people up no longer entailed going through huge, tattered files in the newspaper library, that it was all there at the press of a button. He wasn't even sure he preferred it; there was an impersonality about the information that skated across the screen, that gave everyone a monochrome uniformity. The old cuttings, with their yellowing pages and fading photographs, were vivid, brought subjects – even financial institutions – to life. Nevertheless the new way was very much more efficient.

He started with a survey of the Channing press coverage in the past year. The references, even in the UK press, were legion; the man certainly had a genius for publicity. There was a lot about the Newcastle development, quite a bit about Docklands and the continuing failure of the place to come alive economically, some suprisingly good year-end figures, some stuff about Francesca and the new baby, even the appointment of Kirsten to the firm. Nothing remotely interesting there.

He decided to go back to basics, called up Channing Holdings; it was capitalised at £100m, the share price hovering at about the £3 mark. Perfectly pukka. He looked at its list of directors. Nothing very unexpected here: he knew most of them by name, had met a couple personally. Dear old Douglas Booth, known to the entire world as Duggie, whose boardroom was the golf course, such an apparent old duffer, but with a nose for a contact like a sniffer dog. Peter Barbour, Finance Director, boring old Pete; caricature of an accountant, with his pompous manner and his Savile Row suits; it was hard to imagine Pete even having sex without his waistcoat on. And then the three non-executives, Henry Withington – nice chap, Henry, good front man for Bard, legal background – Brigadier Gen. Sir Charles Forsyth (retd), also inevitable, he thought with a grin, funny how these sharp guys all loved titles and medals and all that sort of thing, and Michael Samuels, an estate surveyor. A long list of shareholders, individuals and companies: some familiar, some not.

None of which was going to make a story.

They were all directors of the various subsidiary companies, of course: Channing North, Channing European, Channing Leisure. That was one he hadn't been too aware of: leisure centres, he supposed, in some of the big shopping developments. Might be worth investigating.

Gray went slightly thoughtfully through to the news room, tapped into the Jordans database, with its wealth of information on companies, their directors, their shareholdings – and the other companies they were directors of.

Channing held a huge proportion of the shares: 20%. With Douglas Booth's 10% and Barbour's 5%, they had an indubitable controlling interest. Which meant they could do what they liked. Interestingly, Booth had several other directorships: not surprising, he was hardly full-time at Channings. A golfwear company; a chain of health food shops; a timeshare company. Called Travelfax, trading as Home Time. Travelfax. Damn silly name. What was it? He called up Travelfax. Registered company. Address in Birmingham. Sounded innocuous. Two other directors, Teresa Didcot and Angela Phelps. Obviously two bimbos who'd wanted a man's help. And if the timeshares were in Portugal or somewhere like that, a golfing man would be very useful. Amazing, the far-reaching benefits of golf. The picture of business life in Britain would be quite different without it. Even today. He called up the two ladies on his screen: Teresa Didcot was the MD, Angela Phelps the marketing manager. They both had addresses in Birmingham. Nothing else there.

He went back to the other directors: Pete Barbour earned £150,000; now where did he live, oh God, how predictable, Burwood Park, Weybridge, Surrey. Gray could imagine the house, large and lush, probably with a swimming pool, but nothing absurdly expensive. If ever a man was going to live carefully within his means it was Pete. Henry Withington, Brigadier Forsyth and Samuels, all absolutely predictable too, all taking standard non-executive salaries, all with quite modest shareholdings. But nice little earners, all of them – providing Channings held up.

Gray went back to his desk feeling frustrated. Nothing to get his teeth into at all. Maybe his instinct had failed him. Maybe he was getting old, losing his touch. The thought depressed him disproportionately. He supposed it was partly because of Briony. Briony and his non-existent paternal instinct.

He sighed, looked at his watch. It was five-thirty, time to go home. Home to Briony, home to problems. To hormones. Bloody hormones. She'd even gone off sex. He really couldn't face it yet. He'd stay here a bit longer.

He switched his machine on again, looked at it with a mixture of affection and irritation. It always got to him when things weren't going well. It sat there, doing what he told it, telling him things, showing him things, reminding him to save things, pointing out he'd not switched it off, or had called two files the same thing, but it was no bloody use at all, really. Not when your brain had done its best and had been found wanting. He suddenly remembered sharply a piece of advice his first boss had given him, a shrewd old journalist on the *Daily Mail*. 'What you have to rely on, in this game, is your ability to persuade people to tell you things they shouldn't tell you.' Judy Wyatt had been pretty damn good at that, persuading Kirsten Channing to tell her things she shouldn't have. Who could he get to work on? Who was likely to tell him anything? Who knew something they shouldn't pass on? About Channings? About Channing himself? He sat there, drawing circles on a piece of paper with a pencil, forcing his brain to yield things by sheer force of will. It was a trick he had learnt as a student; it was all in there somewhere, you just had to find it and force it out. Kirsten might: just might. Once her wounds had begun to heal a bit. She would be angrier with her father than ever now. Sam was much too wary, much too loyal. Francesca Channing, now she would be interesting to talk to. Wives always were. They tended to know more than they thought they did. He would like to talk to Francesca. He had found her very attractive. Of course Francesca would be extremely wary of the press at the moment. But the *News* was a hugely responsible paper, and he was the financial editor. A chance meeting, a sympathetic chat, a few damning words about the gutter press. You never knew. Duggie might; but Duggie was very good at telling you very little. Gray was never sure if it was deliberate, but anyway, he was masterly at it. Pete Barbour? Surely not Pete. Pete was about as communicative as the Oracle at Delphi. Still, you never knew. It was the quiet ones who just occasionally told you the most. Simply by default. Worth a try at least. Marica Grainger of course, the old dragon, she would have a few stories to tell. Old-style secretaries like her, fiercely defensive, self-important, always did. But getting anything out of her would make the task of squeezing blood from a stone look like very light work. Apart from anything else she was probably half in love with Bard, would go to the stake for him. Booth was probably a better bet. He was worth a try.

Booth. Booth. That meant something, touched at something. Patiently he pursued it, pursued the thread through his brain, pressing on the paper harder and harder, drawing ever darker circles. Booth, Duggie Booth. What was it, where was it, how could he find it? And then he got it: Briony's voice on the day she had first broached the subject of the baby, answering the phone in the conservatory, passing it to him, saying 'It's for you. A woman called Teresa Booth.' Teresa Booth. Was she related to Duggie? It seemed possible. Booth was not exactly a rare name, but still. Bit of a coincidence. And then there was another Teresa, he thought setting his machine to work again, swearing at it as it ground into action, fought its way through the lists, the entries. There it was: Teresa Didcot of Travelfax. There was no phone number for Teresa Didcot, and when he tried to get one he found she was ex-directory. Well, that could be got round, perfectly easily; meanwhile he could call Travelfax. There was no reply to that: there wouldn't be now of course, it was well after six, merely a recorded message, telling him to leave his name and number and that he would be got back to. He decided to try again next day, rather than give himself away too soon. And tomorrow he would find out if Teresa Booth was indeed Mrs Douglas Booth. Of Deepdene, Lord's Crescent, near Abingdon. And what it was she had decided at one point she would like to tell him, and why it was that she had so swiftly changed her mind.

He felt extremely cheerful suddenly, and rather sexy. He phoned Briony, left a message on the answering machine telling her he loved her and that he was very sorry for his behaviour the day before and would like to take her out to dinner, and went to wash out his cup. The gadget that was supposed to warm water just didn't work; he had thrown it away in disgust and tried to take to herb tea. So far, he told Briony, he hadn't found a single one that didn't taste like horse piss. She hadn't seemed very interested. He was just putting on the very chic linen jacket she had given him for his last birthday when the phone rang. It was Kirsten Channing.

'I just rang to say thank you for your message,' she said, and sounded as if she meant it. 'The whole of the rest of the world seems to have sent me to Coventry.'

Her voice wobbled; Gray grinned into the phone and said he was just leaving, but he could manage a quick drink if she'd like to get a lift down from Coventry, and where exactly was she?

'At home. In Fulham.'

'Well, look, I belong to the Harbour Club, why not meet there?'

She came in looking very pale and heavy eyed, wearing jeans and an oversize T-shirt, drank two glasses of wine very quickly and then started to cry.

Gray went to sit next to her and put his arm round her; he gave her his handkerchief.

'This is silk,' she said, looking at it after blowing her nose several times. 'No use at all for tears. Or snot.'

'Well, I'm sorry. Next time I'll try and have a box of double-strength Kleenex about my person.'

'No, no,' she said, the tears starting to flow again, 'you don't understand, I was sorry about spoiling it.'

'Don't worry about my hanky,' said Gray, 'I have dozens of the things. And you mustn't be so upset. You'd be amazed how fast people forget these things. Three weeks, maybe two, the Princess of Wales or Fergie or Madonna will have done something outrageous and no-one will remember anything about you and your undoubtedly difficult family.'

'Not true,' she said. 'Certainly not my father. He never forgets anything. Except what he's done himself. And no-one in my family is speaking to me. Except for Granny Jess. That's my dad's mother. She was really kind, had me to lunch today, and said she'd talk to my father. She's very rigidly moral, you see; she thinks he should never have left my mother, that it's all his fault anyway.'

'I daresay she has a point,' said Gray. 'Honestly, Kirsten, I don't think you should worry too much. Your dad will get over it, and since he's fired you, and since you don't live with him, he can take his time over it.'

'It's all very well,' said Kirsten, 'but I don't have any money. I mean any. I'm a walking negative-equity situation.'

'What do you really want to do?' said Gray.

'Oh I don't know. I still like the idea of law, but –'

'What sort of degree have you got?'

'A Third,' said Kirsten, and started crying again.

'You're a bright girl. Why not better?'

'I fucked about,' she said briefly. 'Didn't work. Drank a lot. Did a lot of drugs. I was lucky to get a Third.'

'Well, I don't think I can help you there, I'm afraid. Here, take my handkerchief again.'

'I didn't expect you could,' she said, blowing her nose.

Gray thought for a minute and then remembered a friend with a PR company. He would give his eye teeth to have Kirsten Channing sitting in his office. 'He was saying only the other day he needed someone who sounded a bit like you.'

'In what way?' said Kirsten, slightly defensively.

'I don't think I want to spell it out, you might get above yourself. Or it might make you cross. Anyway, it would be quite menial, glorified receptionist really. And nothing smart like working for

Channings. The accounts seem to be mostly household goods. But at least a job and a salary. Would that be the sort of thing?'

'Anything would be the sort of thing at the moment,' said Kirsten.

'Well, look, let me see what I can do. It may be very boring and it certainly can't compete with a pupillage in Lincoln's Inn. But –'

'I don't care,' she said, 'I really, really don't care. I don't honestly think I'm up to that anyway.' She looked at him and half smiled. 'You're so nice, Gray,' she said suddenly, 'really nice. A proper friend. I haven't got many.'

'Oh come off it.'

'No really, I haven't. And I behave so badly it's not really surprising.'

'If even half that garbage was true,' he said, 'I'm not surprised you behave badly. Was it?'

'Oh yes,' she said, 'it was much worse than that.'

There was a silence, then she said, 'You've got to go. Thank you again. For everything. The drinks. Listening. Saying you'd call your friend. I wish I could do something in return.'

Gray, disliking himself just slightly, but knowing an opportunity when he saw one, paused briefly and then said, 'You can. Actually. A couple of things.'

'What?'

'You can tell me something. Douglas Booth's new wife, is she called Teresa, do you happen to know?'

'Yes she is. Terrible woman. We all had to go to their wedding, of course. Very flashy, overweight, blonde, too much perfume, you know the sort of thing.'

'Do I get the impression you don't like her very much?' said Gray, laughing.

'Not very much,' said Kirsten, smiling again, sniffing. 'And she doesn't like us either. Not even my dad: well, least of all my dad.'

'Interesting. I wonder why not.'

'Oh well, you know, we've all known Duggie for ever, we were fond of Suzanne, I suppose she's jealous. Or something.'

'Uh-huh. And does she have a timeshare company or something like that?'

'Well, she's got a company. Never stops talking about it. I don't really know what it is. I try not to listen to her. I tell you one quite odd thing. I saw her leaving Channing House really late one night. On her own, without Duggie. Bit odd.'

'Really?' The slug came again, the slug of excitement. 'Is she often in the office?'

'No. I've never seen her there since. I suppose she was picking some papers up for Duggie or something.'

'Well, that's certainly all very interesting.'

'What's the other thing?'

'I'd like to meet your stepmother. The lovely Francesca.'

'I thought you had.'

'I have. But only very formally, at a reception. I want to meet her by accident. Get to know her a little.'

Kirsten looked at him thoughtfully. 'Why?'

'Let's call it research.'

'She'd never talk to you. Not the press. Specially not after my little *faux pas*. And she's very upset at the moment, apparently.'

'Oh really? Any particular reason?'

'Yes, their baby's ill. Something to do with her heart. That's made me feel worse, I didn't know at the time, I meant the time when I talked to Wyatt.'

'Of course you didn't,' he said soothingly, 'but it does sound as if they all have enough on their plates at the moment. Is it very serious? The baby's illness?'

'I'm not sure. Quite serious, I think.'

'How very sad. Well – forget that one. For now anyway.'

'What are you researching?'

'Oh,' he said lightly, 'my big piece on the property market, that's all. Since your dad won't see me, I have to do a profile by remote control, so to speak.'

'Oh, I see.'

'But I'm interested in the Booth ménage. Sounds fascinating.'

'Mmm.' She looked at him thoughtfully. 'You're not up to anything really bad, are you? I've got very nervous about – well, about –'

'The press,' said Gray. 'Of course you have. But no, I'm not up to anything remotely bad. As you put it.' He smiled at her carefully. 'Now don't cry any more. OK?'

He leant forward, kissed her gently on the mouth. He meant it to be friendly, almost fatherly – didn't he? – but her mouth was soft and very fluid, and despite himself his lips moved on hers, parting them just slightly, and then he drew back, looked at her. Her eyes were very dark, the pupils very big; he could see she was as moved, however lightly, as he was.

'I'd like to do that again some time,' he said. 'And now I must go.'

But he didn't go home: he went back to the office for a while and made some phone calls.

★

In Stockholm, Jon Bartok, Senior Director of the Konigstrom Bank, decided, after a long afternoon studying some figures, that the time had come to involve himself rather more closely with one of his major clients.

'I would like to talk to Mr Channing in London,' he said to his secretary. 'Could you get him on the phone, please?'

'Personally?'

'Yes, personally.'

The secretary buzzed through to him five minutes later. 'I'm afraid Mr Channing is not available just at the moment,' she said, 'and Mrs Grainger, his personal secretary, is unable to say exactly when he will be able to call.'

'That woman is a disaster area,' said Bartok. 'Would you be kind enough then to send Mr Channing a fax asking him to call me urgently.'

'On the general number?'

'No, I have a number for his dedicated machine. I fancy that will bring us a result pretty quickly.'

Five minutes later, Bard Channing was on the phone; Bartok listened carefully to what he had to say and then said he would like to hold further discussions with him and Mr Barbour within the next few days.

'It is not so much your account with us I am concerned with,' he said. 'It appears to be in good health, but there are a few things I would like clarification on. Perhaps it would be a good plan if you came over here so we could talk personally.'

Bard Channing said he thought it would be an excellent plan and that he would instruct his secretary to talk to Jon Bartok's secretary to find a suitable date and make the arrangements.

'I think I would like the date to be very soon,' said Jon Bartok mildly. 'I have, for instance, a window in my diary late tomorrow. It would suit me very well if you could possibly make yourselves available then. Failing that, the following morning.'

His secretary was in the office during this conversation, placing letters for signature on his desk. Mr Bartok did not often, she reflected, call a meeting at quite such short notice. Especially not with international clients. He had to be quite concerned to do that; really quite concerned.

'You are still coming tomorrow, aren't you?' said Francesca to Bard. He had come in for a sandwich at nine and now was disappearing upstairs to his study, his arms full of files; he looked distracted, exhausted even.

'Yes, of course I am. Although I have to fly out to Stockholm in the afternoon. Unless of course the news is – well, unless I decide I should stay. Why do you ask?'

'Oh – don't know. I thought perhaps with all this about Kirsten –'

'Kirsten has been dealt with,' he said shortly. 'I don't intend to waste any more time or emotional energy on her.'

'How very orderly of you,' said Francesca. She knew she should have simply accepted what he said, been grateful he was coming, but the remark irritated her disproportionately.

'What's that supposed to mean?'

'It means how clever of you to put your family into compartments and divisions, just like your company.'

'I'm sorry?'

'Oh nothing.'

'Francesca, I'd like to know what you're talking about.'

'Oh God, Bard, I just meant the company is all sliced up, Channing UK, Channing European, the shopping malls, all that sort of thing, all with their percentage share of your attention. And so is the family: Kirsten now exiled, nought per cent, Pattie parked in Fulham, five per cent, Kitty currently allotted quite a large percentage –'

'That's a filthy thing to say.'

'It wasn't meant to be. It just suddenly struck me.'

'Well, you should keep such thoughts to yourself. I'm doing my best, Francesca – for everybody.'

'Yes, Bard, I know. I'm – I'm sorry.'

She was; this was the third violent quarrel they had had since seeing Mr Lauder. Frightening, swift, damaging, all seeming to gather momentum from almost nowhere. Of course it was because they were distressed and very tired; but even so, each seemed to lead to the next with alarming speed.

He nodded at her curtly, disappeared upstairs. She sat, trying to concentrate on what she was reading: an article in the Sunday paper about the Labour leadership race. It seemed monumentally unimportant.

'Gray you're not listening to me.'

'Briony, I am listening to you.'

'You're not.'

'This is a ridiculous conversation,' said Gray irritably. He was sitting in the conservatory, drinking a glass of extremely good white port with which, as he had said to Briony, he was going to wash down the Mozart piano concerto. Well, the Mozart clearly had to go. He switched off the stereo, sighed and said, 'All right, maybe not to every word. Start again. And I'll listen now, whether or not I was before.'

'I'm going away for a few days,' said Briony. 'To stay with my parents actually.'

'Oh. A bit sudden, isn't it?'

'Yes. A bit. But what it's about isn't sudden.'

'I presume,' said Gray, 'it's the baby business?'

'Yes. Yes it is. Only I don't quite see it as business, as you put it.'

'Oh, Bri, you know what I −'

'Yes I know what you mean, Gray. Look, I don't want to get into a long discussion now. But I've been very patient and it's over three months since I told you I wanted − well, what I wanted. I've tried and tried, but it won't go away, Gray. And I think you owe it to me to give me an answer. Not an "oh Bri" answer, but a proper one. I need to know.'

'Need to know exactly what, Briony?' He could hear his voice sounding weary; he struggled to lighten it. He realised the port had all gone from his glass, and had no recollection of drinking it.

'What you think. I mean if you say, yes, OK in a year, even in two maybe, but it's a definite something, then I can wait. If you can't even say that much, then − then I have some very real thinking to do.'

'Briony, can't we discuss it properly? I really don't want to be pressurised like this −'

'Gray, there's nothing more to discuss. And I'm sorry if it feels like pressurising, but I have to know. It's too important to leave unresolved. Just let's not talk about it any more, OK?'

'Yes, Briony. If that's what you want.'

'It's not exactly what I want. But I think it's what we ought to do.'

Gray was silent, his mind churning; he felt sick, cornered. He drained a second glass of port and looked at Briony, as she stood looking down at him; she was wearing black linen shorts and a white T-shirt, her legs were tanned, her face, completely bare of make-up, was lightly freckled. She looked so lovely, and he loved her so much it hurt. Why couldn't she understand that? That he simply loved her, he wanted her, all to himself, he didn't want to share her, to share their life with anyone, anyone at all: certainly not someone small, noisy and demanding who from all the evidence available to him would wreck not only their social and professional life, but their sex life as well.

She came over to him, bent down and kissed him lightly. She smelt gorgeous, sweet and summery; he caught her wrist, tried to pull her down towards him.

'No Gray, I'm late already.'

'You're going tonight?' He felt shocked, already bereft.

'Yes, I think it's best. Having decided. I told Mum I'd be there before eleven, and she worries so much. And I really don't want to have any more to do with you until – well, until. Bye. I'll see you – well, shall we say in a week? That should be long enough.'

And she picked up her big canvas satchel and was gone.

'Shit,' said Gray. 'Shit shit shit.'

'I've been shortlisted for a job in Edinburgh,' said Naomi. 'If I get it, I think I'm going to take it.'

'Oh really? That's extremely interesting. Do I get asked for my opinion?'

'I can't see that it would be relevant.'

'Well, have you decided what the rest of us will do? Do we accompany you to Edinburgh, or stay here, waiting for visits?'

'Well, obviously you'd have to come. We'd all move up there.'

'I see. Suppose I don't want to go and live in Edinburgh?'

She shrugged. 'Frankly, Liam, I don't think you have a lot of choice.'

'What you're saying,' he said, 'and rubbing my nose in it, is that the only person who can support us is you.'

'Yes,' she said, 'that is what I'm saying. Who else is there?'

'You have a very charming way of putting things,' he said, and walked out of the room.

She was right, of course. He didn't have a lot of choice. He continued to apply for jobs, and the jobs continued to go to other people. The whole thing was a bloody nightmare.

The article in the Sunday paper had made him angry and upset. There had been a long paragraph about him, in bold type, headed 'Bard Channing's Son and Heir', informing the *Graphic*'s readers that Liam Channing was a barrister, living in a small house in North London with his wife Naomi and their two children. 'He has not spoken to his father for years; his mother died when he was a small boy and Bard Channing has not had a lot of time for him since. He was sent away to school at eight, just about the time Channing was re-marrying: a foretaste of what Kirsten was to endure. Life has not been easy for Liam Channing; he gets very little work and they are forced to live on what his wife earns.'

It had made his situation official, famous, public. It had been true, yet of course presented an entirely false picture, making him sound like a fool, a no-hoper, some kind of a moron. They had had to go to a lunch party that day; Naomi had refused to cancel, saying there were important contacts for her there, and it was obvious most of the other guests had read the article. There was an embarrassment in the air, a false heartiness, a reluctance to talk to him for more than a few minutes at a time. He got through it somehow, went on smiling politely, being charmingly interested in everyone, their high-profile careers, their glossy lifestyles (because they might of course be useful to him, as well as to Naomi), pretending he was one of them, as secure, as smug as they. And hating them, and hating Naomi who was only temporarily not a success, and hating Kirsten who was resonsible for his misery that day, and most of all hating his father and longing for revenge on them all.

He was lying on the study sofa reading at midday when Naomi came in and looked at him rather coldly. 'I presume you can collect the children after school,' she said. 'I've got a lunch and I'll probably be late back.'

'Yes of course. I'm glad I have my uses,' he said, trying to sound cheerful. 'Who's the lunch with?'

'Dick Marsh.'

'Why on earth are you meeting him?'

Dick Marsh was an erstwhile colleague of Naomi's; noisy, excitable, cheerfully vulgar. He found her very attractive and was fond of telling Liam so. Liam loathed him.

'Because it might be fun.'

'I'm sure it'll be fun. Is that a reason to have lunch with him?'

'I think so. And I want to talk about this job offer with him.'

'I see. So you talk to him about it, but not me.'

'I think his opinion is rather more relevant,' she said coolly.

'Naomi, for fuck's sake —'

'Don't swear, Liam, please.'

'I'll swear if I want to. Why should you talk about your future — our future — to that dickhead?'

'I want his view on the job. And the effect on my career.'

'Jesus bloody Christ,' he said, hurling his book across the room, standing up, 'you are totally out of order, Naomi. Do you realise how you treat me? Like some kind of servant, the paid help, ordering me about, ignoring my views, not just about this but bloody everything. I am sick of it, absolutely sick of it.'

She looked at him in silence for a moment, then said coolly, 'The paid help is a bit more useful, Liam.'

'Thank you for that. Thank you very much. If you wanted to humiliate me further, you could hardly have done a better job.'

'I'm sorry,' she said, 'but it's hardly my fault. What's happened to you.'

'I daresay not. But your attitude is appalling. I feel you have no respect for me whatsoever.'

She was silent.

'Well, do you?' he said, and rage was rising in him now, choking, ugly. 'Do you? Answer me, please.'

'No,' she said slowly, 'no, I don't think I do. I can't respect you, Liam, because there's nothing to respect. It's not that you haven't got a job, that you don't contribute much financially, it's your attitude. You're so terribly sorry for yourself, you feel it's everyone's fault but your own. On and on you go about your miserable childhood, your bastard of a father, your wicked stepmother. Nothing's down to you, is it? The fact of the matter is you're a lousy barrister, you're never going to make it as far as I can see, and it has nothing to do with your bloody father. I'm going out now, and I don't know when I'll be back. And maybe, Liam, we should consider a separation. There doesn't seem much of this marriage left.'

Liam lay down again on the sofa for a while, when she had gone, feeling rather sick, trying not to think about what she had said, hearing it over and over again, hammering against his brain. Not about wanting a separation, but his blaming everyone else, being a lousy barrister. He included her now in his hatred, the source of his misery. The injustice was mind blowing. He was not a lousy barrister, he knew that; he could be, was indeed, a brilliant barrister, lucid, swift thinking, stylish, eloquent. He had lacked much opportunity, but when it did come, he was not found wanting. And Naomi had no idea, nobody did, exactly what he had endured, had to live through, all the time he had been growing up. Of course it had had an effect on him, on every area of his life. The loneliness, the rejection, the loss of love, the dreadful sense of injustice. He had loved his mother so much, and she had gone and taken everything with her: happiness, laughter, tenderness, care, and he had been left, all by himself, just seven years old, alone in the world, sent away by a father who had no time, no love for him, away to a school where he had been mocked, bullied, beaten. And Naomi dared to dismiss that. He looked at his watch; God, he wanted a drink. He hadn't got much money, but enough for a pint. He picked up *The Times*, went into a pub and ordered a pint of bitter, sat drinking it, trying to concentrate on what Bernard Levin was talking about. It was very difficult. He hadn't had any breakfast and he felt slightly dizzy when he stood up. Better clear his head. The walk home – he was up at Highbury – might do him good. But it didn't; when he got back he was completely shattered. He went straight to the drinks cupboard, and got out the whisky bottle – plenty left; they'd carefully saved it in case of unexpected visitors. He poured out a very large slug, added ice, lay down and switched on the television. If they were all so intent on casting him as a layabout, a no-hoper, he might as well start behaving like one.

Mr Moreton-Smith was less easy, more formal, than Mr Lauder: he was tall and very thin, with a rather forbidding expression, and he talked very fast, but with huge energy and intensity. He was altogether most patently filled with energy; even when he was sitting still at his desk, he constantly moved things about on it, doodled vigorously on his pad, shifted in his chair, stood up to answer his phone, sat down again when he had finished. Francesca wasn't at all sure if she liked him, but she could see Bard did.

'Yes, well, I've studied the tracings and so on, and listened very carefully to your baby's heart, and I'm going to tell you exactly what I think. No certainties, mind you, we can't ever go in for those' – Francesca looked at Bard anxiously, but his face was politely blank – 'much as we'd like to, of course. Now this is quite a small hole. *Quite.*'

'Oh,' said Francesca. 'We were told – that is –'

'Yes?'

'Well, that it was very small.' It was a how-long-is-a-piece-of-string observation: how ridiculous, she thought, to be talking in such vague terms about something so crucial.

'It is, of course. But these things are relative. The heart itself is pretty small' – he smiled at them both, and at Kitty – 'like its owner. But it is there, and it is causing her some problems. Although she is holding her own. Very well, under the circumstances. She's a tough little thing. But she is very small, she is failing to thrive, and when she starts moving around, she will quite possibly be short of breath. Now it is possible that the hole will close of its own accord. Very possible.'

'Oh,' said Francesca. She felt rather sick, looked at Bard. He was looking at the floor.

'But in time, it is very – possible that we shall have to operate. However, I wouldn't dream of doing that at the moment, while she is so tiny and while it is not crucial. So I don't want you thinking this is a really urgent situation. It isn't.'

'I see,' said Francesca. This seemed much worse than she had somehow expected. Bard still didn't speak.

'Now what I am going to do is give her some medication. Which will help her a great deal. Number one, we'll put her on some diuretics. The thing about a dicky heart, even a slightly dicky heart, is that fluid tends to be retained in the body, so that should help her a bit for a start. And then we'll give her something called Digoxin. Now what Digoxin does is strengthen the heart. Helps it to do its work.' He smiled at them again, a quick, reassuring smile. 'This will improve her circulation, get rid of the problem of the cold little feet and hands. And I think she will generally improve a lot. What I want you to do is to bring her back in three months' time: we'll do another echo cardiogram, take stock generally, and take it from there. Hopefully no surgery will be necessary for a while, and certainly not until we have a chance to assess her further. Of course if she gets a cold, a chest infection, anything, it must be treated very seriously. I want you to inform your GP immediately and tell him to get in touch with Mr Lauder or with me if he is in the least anxious. Is that clear? It's very important.'

'Yes of course,' said Francesca. She couldn't imagine seeing so much as a frown passing across Kitty's small face without rushing her off to Casualty. Mr Moreton-Smith looked at her and smiled: a kind, if rather distant, smile.

'What is important,' he said, clearly recognising exactly how she felt, 'is that she – and all of you – lead as normal a life as possible. She won't benefit from over-fussing. If she gets a cold we can deal with it, so don't keep her away from other children. Try to enjoy her, try not to make any brothers or sisters feel she has to be treated like fine china. Babies are very, very tough: even slightly poorly ones. The quality of her everyday life is extremely important.'

'Yes, I see,' said Francesca. She smiled at him; his old-fashioned language, words like 'dicky' and 'poorly' were for some reason reassuring, he seemed to be setting Kitty's illness in some kind of normal context; the nightmare quality was just slightly receding.

'Right. Well, good luck. Please try not to worry. She's not done badly for such a tiddler. And I'll see you in three months' time.'

'Yes,' said Francesca. 'Goodbye.'

Bard was still silent.

Back in Reception he smiled at her slightly awkwardly. 'Nice chap. I liked him.'

'Yes. So did I,' she said, trying to believe it.

'And not too bad. What he had to tell us.'

'No,' said Francesca, perversely irritated. 'Not too good, either. It's obviously more serious that Mr Lauder implied. And I hate the thought of all those drugs pumped into her.'

'Yes, I know. But if they do the trick for now, does it matter?'

'Well, I don't know. Who knows what they do, those things? But – well, yes, I suppose it could be much, much worse.'

'Much.'

She looked at him; she knew the signs, he was impatient to be gone. We've had our percentage, she thought; no point asking for more.

'I suppose you'll go, then? On your trip?'

'Yes, if that's all right with you.'

'Yes, of course it is.' Of course it isn't: not at this time, not now.

'I mean, you can cope? On your own, with all this?'

'I'm quite used to coping, Bard. On my own.' She tried to sound less cold; it didn't work. He recognised it, stopped trying so hard.

'Francesca, you heard what he said. She is to lead as normal a life as possible. We all have to do that. I'm as worried as you are, but –'

'I don't think you are. Actually.'

'That's unfair,' he said. 'And I don't like your –' He stopped abruptly, obviously still anxious to make an attempt at conciliation. 'Look, Francesca, our quarrelling isn't going to help.'

'No, of course it isn't.'

He put out his arm, touched hers. 'So –' His mobile rang, shrilly, into the tension, increasing it. 'Yes? Yes, all right. Yes, I know that. Yes of course. I'm on my way.' He looked at her, smiled slightly shamefacedly. 'Sorry. Have to go.'

'Who was that?'

'What?'

'I said who was that?'

'Marcia. Meeting's about to start. I'm already late.'

'Well, that won't do,' she said lightly. 'You'd better go. You'll leave an address? In Stockholm?'

'Yes, of course.'

'And you'll be back – when?'

'Oh – Friday. Early evening.'

'Good. I'll – I'll miss you,' she said, and knew the words sounded slightly false.

'I'll miss you too. Goodbye, Francesca.'

He leant forward to kiss her; she turned her face just a little so that he only caught her cheek, not her lips. She met his eyes and saw the hurt in them and still she couldn't make the emotional move, tell him she didn't mean to be hostile, that she needed him, wanted him with her. Looking at his retreating back, she felt as if something had been physically broken between them.

Gray had driven to the office much too fast on the bike; he knew it was silly, that if he were stopped he would probably not even pass the breath test, he'd drunk so much and so late the night before, when Briony had left. He knew several people who'd been done in the morning recently. He actually felt so miserable, so heartsore, he didn't think he'd care. He wondered who on earth he could talk to about all this; it really wasn't something he felt he could handle on his own. No-one at the office, that was for sure; it would be all over the building by mid-morning. He supposed he couldn't really be the new man because he didn't have any of the sort of friends he could have late-night locker-room chats with over the cocoa; his friends, his confidantes had always been women. And they would all take Briony's side. At least he supposed they would. Anyway, if he couldn't even think who to talk to, there was certainly no-one close enough.

'Bloody hormones,' he said aloud for the hundredth time as he parked the bike.

He walked into his office, shouted at Tricia to get him some tea, and switched on his answering machine. Perhaps Briony would have relented, phoned to say she hadn't really meant it.

She hadn't. Three people had phoned; one was some very persistent PR who wanted to have lunch with him, one was Kirsten Channing, saying his friend had taken her on, and could she buy him a drink to say thank you; and the third was Teresa Booth.

Gray promptly shed his lethargy, his depression, his sense of outrage that life was being so tough on him. Teresa Booth, eh? Or if you liked to think of her that way, Teresa Didcot, MD of Home Time. Previously Teresa Carfax.

He dialled the number; it was picked up immediately. The voice that said 'Teresa Booth' was slightly husky, carefully refined.

'Mrs Booth, it's Graydon Townsend.'

'Ah. Yes. Mr Townsend, what are you playing at?'

He was slightly fazed, and at the same time almost relieved, by the directness of her approach. It was going to save a lot of pussyfooting around.

'I'm sorry?'

'First you call me, under my business name, at home – how did you get that number, by the way?'

'Directory enquiries,' said Gray smoothly.

'Mr Townsend, I'm ex-directory.'

'Really! Well, I do assure you –'

'Private eye, I suppose. Ex-cop. They're always good for a few ex-directory numbers.'

'Mrs Booth, I really –'

'And then you spin my partner some complicated story about an article about timeshares –'

'It's true. I was planning one.'

'I doubt that greatly. But I hope you got the literature the poor girl sent you.'

'Not yet. But no doubt it will arrive. It all sounds very interesting, your company.'

'And then you start pumping her about whether I am or am not actually Teresa Booth – what possible relevance could that have had, Mr Townsend?'

'Quite a bit. Duggie is one of your directors, after all.'

'Will that appear in the article?'

'I'm not sure. It might.'

'If the article appears at all.'

'I'm sorry?'

'Mr Townsend, I really wasn't born yesterday. As you would see if we were to meet. I don't think you have very much intention of writing anything about my company. Actually.'

'Well, you're wrong,' said Gray. 'I am interested in these timeshares. The way the market for them has upped and downed.'

'Oh yes? And that's your only interest in me, is it?'

'No, of course not. I'll tell you why I was interested to know if you were Teresa Booth. You phoned me at home, one Sunday, a couple of months or so ago, and then rang off. Do you remember?'

She hesitated, just too long, then said, 'No. I don't think I do. It must have been someone else. It's not such an unusual name, is it?'

'No, of course it isn't. Well now, look, I really would like to hear more about your company.'

'Oh really?'

'Yes. I think it's interesting.'

'Well,' she said, and he could hear from her voice she had decided quite suddenly to go along with him, to play ball, 'I'm free this evening, for a drink.'

'Great,' said Gray, 'Where would you like to go?'

'No, you say. I'm the old-fashioned type, like to do what men tell me.'

'You sound like a Ritz girl to me,' said Gray. God, he hoped he hadn't got to flirt with her. 'The Terrace Bar at six?'

'That would be fine,' she said. She was clearly unimpressed. Not a pushover, then. Not at all.

Liam had drunk an awful lot of whisky; he hadn't realised how much until he heard the doorbell and saw the bottle was almost empty. One of the other mothers from school was standing on the doorstep with Jasper.

'He said you were supposed to come for him, Liam, but we waited for a while. I hope you don't mind.'

'No, of course not,' said Liam, 'thank you, how dreadful of me, I'm so sorry.'

'Oh God, it's easily done. So much to remember, isn't there? Naomi's working I presume? So clever isn't she, so high powered, we're all quite dazzled by her.'

'Yes, yes she's quite something,' said Liam, articulating with care, and then remembered Hattie; where the hell was she? Christ, not outside her school as well? No, Naomi had said something about her being with her little friend down the road.

'Look,' he said, 'would you excuse me, I have to go and get Hattie.'

'Yes of course,' said the mother, smiling graciously at him over her pie-frill shirt. Her eyes swept the hall, through to the kitchen (could she see the whisky bottle? she could probably smell it).

'Thank you again,' he said, anxious to get rid of her.

'Liam, any time. Any time.'

He ran down to the house where Hattie was. She was playing happily, the nanny said, and told him to leave her.

'She's fine, Mr Channing. Honestly.'

'No,' he said, 'no I'd better take her.'

'He forgot me,' said Jasper cheerfully to Hatttie. 'You're lucky.'

Naomi arrived back at about five-thirty, in a taxi. He was watching *Neighbours* with the children; he had finished the whisky, was trying to sober up with coffee. It didn't seem to be working.

She looked at him coldly. 'Hallo.'

'Hallo.' He got up slightly shakily. 'Good lunch?'

'Yes, thank you. You look terrible,' she said.

'He's been drinking whisky,' said Hattie.

'How responsible of him,' said Naomi icily. 'Did you manage to collect Jasper from school?'

It didn't seem worth lying; she'd hear anyway. 'No. I forgot.'

'You forgot. Dear God. I can't rely on you for anything, can I? You'd better pull yourself together; we're supposed to be going out to dinner this evening.'

'Oh really? Where to?'

'The Macmillans'.'

The Macmillans lived in Hampstead: they were very high powered. She was a translator, he was a surgeon. The very thought of sitting round their table, being waited on by their Philippino maid, made Liam feel worse.

'I'm not coming,' he said.

'Liam, of course you must come. It's far too late to cancel.'

'Naomi, I'm not coming. I don't remember you asking me if I'd like to go, and I just can't face it.'

'All right,' she said. 'Fine. I'll go on my own. At least it'll save on the babysitter. Could you manage at least to phone and cancel her? I'm going up to have a bath and change. I have to be there early, because Mary wants to discuss her investments with me before everyone else arrives.'

'Yes, all right,' he said. He put an arm round each of the children and they settled down luxuriously against him, sucking their thumbs, *Home and Away* now: Naomi didn't usually allow them to watch either. He fell into a confused doze, woke to hear the familiar syrup of the music.

'Come on,' he said, 'teatime. What do you want?'

'Can we have fish and chips?' said Hattie hopefully.

'Well —'

'Oh go on, Daddy, please.'

'Well look.' He smiled down at her, tapped the side of his nose. 'All right. But it'll have to be a secret. Mummy wouldn't like it. We'll go and get them when she's gone.'

'Cool,' said Jasper.

Naomi came in. 'I'm off now,' she said. 'I'll probably be late. Don't wait up.'

'No, I won't,' he said.

They walked down to the fish and chip shop. On the way back, he bought another quarter bottle of whisky, all he could afford; he felt he deserved it. He felt quite different suddenly, oddly in command. In future he was going to do what he liked; there didn't seem any point trying to please anybody else anyway.

They ate the fish and chips, and he put the children to bed; he sat down to watch the seven-thirty news on Channel 4 and to drink some more whisky. He knew everything that had happened in the world that day, had watched and heard innumerable bulletins, but he wanted to see it again. The familiarity was strangely soothing; he fell into a confused sleep.

Gray was sitting waiting for her, carefully early, when she came in. He knew who she was immediately, sat watching her for a moment as she looked round for him. She was tanned, dressed in a brilliant pink silk suit. Just too much brown bosom showed beneath the jacket; just too little skirt covered the admittedly shapely thighs. She had on a great deal of jewellery: several gold chains round her neck and wrists, a couple of diamond rings, a probably genuine Rolex watch; her shoes were black, very high heeled, her bag a large, bechained Chanel. She must be wearing a great many thousands pounds, Gray thought; either Home Time did extremely well (which he knew it didn't, he'd looked it up, it had hardly broken even for the past two years), or Duggie was doing better than he'd thought.

He stood up, gestured to the chair beside him; she came over, smiling, took his hand and then sat down. She was very sexy, he thought, in a flashy way. She'd know how to make a man happy. Lucky old Duggie. Funny she'd gone for him though. He was hardly her style. A bit bumbling, not that rich. Well, she was mid, probably late, forties. Maybe it wasn't so easy.

He'd ordered a bottle of champagne; a deferentially blank-faced waiter poured it for them both. Teresa Booth raised her glass.

'Cheers,' she said. 'And what about telling me what you really want?'

'Oh, you know,' he said, taken aback by the swiftness of her attack, 'this and that.' He suddenly realised he was feeling better; he smiled at her. She smiled back.

'Let's start with this, then. And then we can move onto that.'

'OK.' He decided he should stick to his story; it was as good a starting point as any. 'Tell me about Home Time. How did you start it?'

'All right,' she said, grinning at him conspiratorially, 'we'll play it your way. Started it in the early 'eighties. Did a bomb in '86, '87, made a lot of money. Lost a lot in '89. When I met Duggie, it was failing badly. He put some money into it ...'

'Enough to keep it afloat? Or to make it profitable again?'

'It's floating.'

'Why do you keep on with it? That genuinely intrigues me. Duggie can clearly keep you in the manner to which you've been accustomed. Or better.'

'I like it,' she said, surprising him. 'Money isn't everything. I get bored. My son's got his own life. My daughter doesn't talk to me –'

'Why not?'

'I really don't think we need to go into that, Mr Townsend. Anyway, my mother told me never to talk to strange journalists. Do you mind if I smoke?'

'Of course not,' said Gray, who minded terribly.

She got out a pack, offered him one, lit her own with a gold Cartier lighter.

'Anyway, whatever the reason we fell out, she's living in Florida. I have tried, held out the olive branch, but she's stubborn. Like her mother.' She laughed; she had a very sexy laugh.

'And your son?'

'Ah, now he's different. We're pretty close. Talk a lot. But he's not based in London. He's out in Marbella, looks after my properties out there.'

'You ought to get Bard Channing to give him a job,' said Gray lightly.

'I might,' she said. It was an odd response: she didn't say she was working on it, or she'd like that, simply implied that it was her choice. He found it interesting.

'So it's the old thing?' he said. 'Bored housewife syndrome.'

'You could say that.'

'And golf with Duggie doesn't appeal?'

'No. I loathe golf.'

'How did you meet him?'

'Oh, originally at a party somewhere. I was with my ex.'

'Oh, I'm sorry. I thought you were a widow.'

'No, no, not me. The bastard left me – oh, four years ago. For some twenty-year-old piece of skirt.' So it was Duggie's money all over her, then.

'And you – bumped into Duggie again?'

'Yes, that's right. Just happened to bump into him. His wife had died by then and – are you married, Mr Townsend?'

'What? Oh – no. Well, not exactly. Bit of a long story, that one.'

'Want to tell me about it?'

'No,' he said quickly. 'No, I wouldn't inflict it on you.'

'I'm a good listener,' she said. 'You'd be surprised.'

Gray looked at her, at the brilliant blue eyes, oddly concerned beneath the heavily mascaraed lashes. 'I don't think I would be actually,' he said. 'Surprised, I mean.'

She smiled at him. 'Anyway,' she said, 'back to you and your questions. That's about all I can tell you about Home Time. It's doing OK. It keeps me –'

'Out of mischief?'

'Oh no,' she said, laughing, 'I wouldn't say that. What was the other thing you wanted to know?'

Gray put on his most ingenuous expression. 'I'm researching an article on the whole commercial property business, Channing included. How soon, if ever, it's going to pull out of the recession. How all the big firms are surviving. And the slightly smaller ones, like Channings. And I'm talking to as many people as I can. I was waiting to speak to Duggie and then I stumbled on you. Figuratively speaking of course.'

Teresa Booth looked at him in silence for a moment or two and then she laughed. 'Mr Townsend,' she said, 'you'll have to do better than that. Come on. Try again. What do you want to know?'

'All right,' said Gray with a grin. 'I want to know why you called me that day. It intrigues me. It was you, wasn't it?'

Teresa lit another cigarete, drew on it hard, blew the smoke out again. 'Yes,' she said finally, 'yes it was.'

'And why did you ring?'

'Let's just say,' she said, 'I was thinking of giving you a story. Well, not a story exactly, a lead. And then I decided against it.'

'A story about Channings?'

'You could say that.'

'Do you want to give it to me now?'

'No. No I don't.'

'Why not?'

'Well – things have changed.'

'Mrs Booth, you certainly know how to torment a guy,' said Gray in his best American accent.

'I've been working on that a long time. And please call me Terri. With an i at the end.'

'All right. Thank you. As long as you call me Gray. With an a in the middle.'

The waiter poured some more champagne; the bottle was almost empty. 'We'd better have another,' said Gray, 'or are you in a hurry?'

'No,' she said. 'I'm not in a hurry. I'm enjoying myself.'

She moved imperceptibly nearer to him; her left leg, crossed carelessly over the other, was just touching his. It was not an entirely unpleasant sensation.

'Good,' he said. 'Now tell me, is there any question of your coming back to me with this story? The one you phoned about?'

'Oh,' she said, 'I don't know. Not that precise one, anyway.'

'Right. Well, maybe another one. What does Duggie think about the way Channings is going, do you think? This new development up in the north is a bit rash, isn't it? And there is talk of – well, of problems. The Docklands development is still losing big bucks. That waterfront complex in Cardiff has been a disappointment. And –'

'You'll have to ask him that yourself, Graydon.'

'I'd like to. Very much. Maybe you could ask him to ring me.'

'Oh I'm not doing that for you. You'll have to ring him yourself. Of course Duggie doesn't think too much, anyway,' she added cheerfully, 'which is not to say he's not bloody clever. He has instinct, does Douglas. Goes for money like a pre-programmed missile. But I don't talk business to him that often. Not about Channings anyway. He doesn't like it.'

'Why not?' said Gray.

'Oh per-lease,' said Teresa Booth. 'Because he likes to play his cards close to his chest, that's why. That's how he's been so successful all these years. Right from way back. He's just kept quiet and brought home the bacon.'

'And then Bard Channing fries it up into nice crispy little bits?'

'That's about the size of it. Yes. Very nice little partnership. Big one, rather.'

'Yes indeed. But you reckon Duggie knows where a few bodies are buried? Is that what you're saying?'

She looked at him, the brilliant blue eyes instantly and absolutely blank. 'That's an interesting way of putting it. But you could say that, yes,' she said.

Gray smiled at her, his most engaging smile. 'And have you got a whiff of any bodies?'

'Oh, now that would really be telling, wouldn't it?'

'I suppose it would. But that's what I've got you here for.'

'Yes, and you're not doing very well, are you?' she said, grinning at him, leaning forward for him to refill her glass, displaying more of her brown cleavage.

'I'm afraid not. What do you think of Channing, can you tell me that? Channing the man, that is.'

He expected some bland answer, but: 'I don't like him very much,' she said, 'not very much at all. And actually I don't like his wife either. But we don't want to get into that one at this precise moment. Want to tell me about your – how did you describe her, your "not exactly" wife now?'

Greatly to his surprise, encouraged by rather more than half the second bottle of champagne, Gray found he did. She listened carefully and didn't interrupt him; when he had finished, she sat back in her chair and looked at him. Her eyes were very probing; she had a way of exploring with them, moved reflectively from his eyes to his mouth, up again to his hair, then took in the whole of his body. It was oddly disturbing, even interesting.

'I have to tell you,' she said, 'that I think you should tell your nice girlfriend – who you obviously love very much – the answer's no. My ex-husband didn't want children either, I went ahead and had them, and it was very bad for our relationship. He couldn't stand it. I tried, God I tried, to keep them out of his hair. But it doesn't work. They're there and that's it. They're magic, Graydon, absolute magic, if you like them. If you don't, they're a turn-off. They really are.'

'But,' he said, 'but I'm afraid then I'll lose her.'

'Yes, well,' she said, and her voice was surprisingly gentle, 'and if she has them, I think she'll lose you.'

'Well,' he said, 'thank you for listening. It's been fun.'

'I've liked it too,' she said. She stood up. 'I'd better go now. Places to go, things to do.'

'Me too,' said Gray with a sigh. 'I've got to go to Glasgow tomorrow.'

'Really? You'll pass Duggie on the way. He's been playing golf up there.'

'You know,' he said, 'we should pool our information. We'd do a lot better.'

'Well, maybe. I might consider it. If things get more interesting.' She smiled at him. 'Goodbye, Graydon. Thank you for the drink. It was fun.' She was quite a tall woman; she had to reach up only slightly to kiss him on the cheek. She was very warm, and she smelt of something heady and strong. She might be a million miles away from being his type, thought Graydon confusedly, but she really was extremely sexy. Lucky old Duggie. She deserved all those diamonds.

He got a cab not home (because there was no point really), but to the office. Teresa Booth's words 'right from way back' had intrigued him. That was what he should do: go right back. Right back. He switched on the machine, called up Channings, began patiently trawling through all the old stuff. But they only had ten years' worth on disk. It would mean going through the real files, and he couldn't get at them now. So there was nothing for it but to go home. To an empty house.

He sat in the conservatory for a long time, watching the sky deepen and darken, listening to a blackbird singing importantly in the tree facing him on the common. He wondered if the blackbird's girlfriend had pestered it to let her have babies. Of course the blackbird wouldn't have had a lot of choice. Maybe it was better that way. But he did, and it was an absolute sod. He fell asleep in the chair, hearing Teresa Booth's voice saying he should tell Briony no, and wondering if he had the courage. And alternatively, if he had the courage to tell her yes.

Liam woke up to hear Hattie calling him. He looked at his watch; it was still only ten.

'Daddy, I've got a tummy ache. It's really bad. I want some medicine.'

She suffered from stomach cramps: the doctor had diagnosed infantile migraine, prescribed Calpol.

'I'll get you some. Want some warm milk?'

'Yes please.'

There wasn't any Calpol; he remembered the last time she'd had it, the bottle had been nearly empty. He'd promised Naomi to get some, and forgotten. As usual. He took the milk up to Hattie's room.

'I'm sorry, darling, no medicine. Try just the milk.'

'It won't work. I know it won't.' She started to cry, doubled up. 'It's bad, Daddy, it's really hurting.'

'Well –' He knew he shouldn't drive to the chemist, wasn't safe behind the wheel.

'The Duncans next door will have some,' said Jasper helpfully, appearing in the doorway. 'They always do, for their baby's teeth, Mummy borrowed some once before.'

'Oh. Oh, all right. You look after Hattie, Jas, all right?'

'Yes, course.'

He went next door; he felt terribly confused. The door opened; Martina Duncan, who was an accountant, smiled at him brightly.

'Liam! How nice. Come in, have a drink.'

'No,' he said, 'no really. I won't. Nice idea but – better not. Er – Hattie's not feeling very well, got a bad tummy ache, Jasper thought you'd have some Calpol. Naomi's out, so I can't. Go out I mean. To the – the shops. The chemist –'

She looked at him sharply; she clearly realised he was drunk. 'Yes I think so. Come in.'

He went into their hall, felt a wave of violent nausea; he got outside just in time, threw up on their steps. He looked down at it, and Martina looked down at it, trying to be civilised, trying to be polite.

'Look Liam, don't worry. Dicky will clear it up. You must feel rotten. I'll just get the –' She vanished inside the house, closed the door.

'Sorry,' he shouted at it. 'Sorry, don't worry about the Calpol.' Christ. Christ almighty, he thought, looking at the step, at his shoes, what a fucking awful mess. How on earth was he going to talk himself out of this one? Naomi would be furious. And he had to get the bloody Calpol. Whatever else, Hattie had to have that. He owed her that. But he wasn't going to risk any more neighbourly encounters. He'd drive down to King's Cross, there was a chemist near there open. Now he'd thrown up he'd be quite sober. It was only a five-minute drive anyway. He went back into the house, shouted at Jasper to stay with Hattie, grabbed his keys and a can of Coke and got into the car.

He was fine, he discovered, as he drove carefully down the street. Sober as a judge. He took several swigs of the Coke, opened the window. That was much better. Much better. Christ, what a mess though. What on earth – shit, that car was almost on the wrong side of the road. He swerved violently; the car hooted loudly and angrily. Silly bugger. They were so aggressive, drivers these days. What was it called, it had an official name, like everything else now. Oh yes, road rage.

He was going down the straight wide road towards St Pancras, into the one-way system, when it happened. A car was very close behind him, flashing its lights: bastard, why did they have to do that? He put his foot down, took the big bend just a bit too fast, he didn't have any option, but that was all right, he'd been driving this baby for so long, it was like wearing a pair of running shoes, OK now, shit, the bastard was still flashing and – Jesus Christ, what was that moron doing in the middle of the road? He jammed on his brakes, skidded hard, hit a lamp post, somersaulted twice. His last thought as he lost conscious-ness, his last surprisingly lucid thought, was what the papers would say next day: 'Tycoon's unemployed son tested for alcohol after car crash.'

Chapter Nine

Francesca lay limply, gasping for breath, and hoped she wasn't actually going to faint. She thought she might; she had all the symptoms, the dizziness, the sick clamminess, the ceiling above her was advancing and receding. She concentrated very hard on one of the lights, willing it to steady, breathing as slowly as she could; she felt desperately sick now, and wondered if she could possibly make it to the lavatory. Probably not. God she was stupid; this had happened once before, right there, in the middle of the gym, she had had to call for help, be half carried to one of the side rooms and laid down until she felt better, the nurse had been called and listened to her heart and taken her blood pressure. And then ticked her off, politely but very firmly. And quite right the nurse had been too. She really ought to know better. It was just that when she was really miserable, in that awful fretting, grinding way, pushing her body to its ultimate extreme was wonderfully cathartic. She knew that if she could only hang on now, not pass out, not be sick, and then make the shower and possibly the sauna, a wonderful cool peace would descend on her and she would look back at the frantic creature of an hour ago and scarcely recognise her.

Yes, that was better; she was going to be all right. A few more minutes and she'd be able to make her escape: luckily no-one was there that she knew, no-one to fuss over her, ask her if she was feeling ill – guaranteed to bring the earlier feelings of unbearable stress and tension winging back. Slowly, carefully, she eased herself off the leg press machine, and walked gingerly across the gym; she sat in the changing room for a few minutes, trying not to look at herself in the merciless mirrors – the white face, the sweat-streaked leotard, the hair clinging to her head – and then went into the shower. And then realised she had done it, had managed what she had been working towards all week: a positive frame of mind. Able to tell herself that she loved Bard, that she had missed him, that the jagged rift that was widening so alarmingly between them was therefore unnecessary, a product of her own stubbornness as much as his, that she must begin again, make amends, show him she was sorry. As soon as he arrived home, that evening.

When she got home, it was still only half-past eight: good, she could take Jack to school. She loved doing that, loved seeing his evident popularity, his busy, cheerful little figure disappearing into a crowd of identically dressed small boys. Nanny was giving Kitty her breakfast and nodded to Francesca slightly coolly; she didn't approve of her going off to the gym, called it her physical jerks, in a very distasteful tone.

'I think Kitty's a bit better already, you know,' she said to Nanny now. 'Her colour's improved, and when I looked at her in the night she was sleeping less restlessly.'

'Well, that's possible,' said Nanny, grudgingly, 'but it's very early days yet!'

'Yes, Nanny, I know. But I'm allowed to be hopeful, aren't I?'

'Yes, Mrs Channing, if you say so.'

She went upstairs smiling to change; it was a beautiful day, golden, warm, good tempered; and tomorrow they were going to Stylings, the four of them, and perhaps best of all, Nanny had asked for the weekend off. 'If you can possibly spare me, Mrs Channing, I know with Kitty being unwell it must be very difficult for you, but my sister has particularly asked me to go, it's her birthday, most inconvenient –'

'Nanny, I don't think your parents could actually have been expected to foresee how inconvenient it might be,' said Francesca, smiling at her sweetly.

'I'm sorry, Mrs Channing, I don't quite – oh, well, yes, I see –' Nanny flushed a dark red, clearly deeply embarrassed by this oblique reference to her sister's conception. That was mean, Francesca, she thought, but hard to resist.

Anyway, the omens were all there; it was going to be a good day.

She was driving back from delivering Jack at school when a well-bred voice on LBC News informed her that Liam Channing, the unemployed son of Bard Channing the property tycoon, was in intensive care following a serious car crash, and had been found to have four times the legal limit of alcohol in his system.

'Oh my God,' she said, and stopped the car. She was informed further that Mr Channing had a fractured leg, a punctured lung and had been seriously concussed, but was now out of danger, according to the hospital. His car had hit a lamp post after swerving violently to avoid a pedestrian on a zebra crossing, and then went into another car. That driver was unhurt but a Mr Brian Jessop who was in the car behind him said he had been driving like a madman, far too fast, and at one point appeared to be considering turning and driving back up the one-way system. 'Relations between Mr Channing and his father are said to be strained,' said the voice, before moving on to the weather and the cricket scores.

'Oh God,' said Francesca again. 'Poor, poor Liam. What a nightmare.' She felt very upset; and then thought of Bard and wondered if he knew. She would have to get hold of him, somehow. In spite of everything, she knew he cared about Liam, that he would be upset.

She drove home slowly, wondering what to do; she thought she would like at least to send Liam some flowers, and then realised she didn't even know which hospital he was in. She would have to ring Naomi and find out. Although she would probably be at the hospital.

Naiomi wasn't at the hospital; she was at home, and she sounded remarkably calm.

'He's perfectly all right,' she said in her rather flat voice. 'Out of danger. He's at St Mary's Paddington. In the men's general ward. If you want to phone.'

'Well, I thought I'd send some flowers,' said Francesca.

'I don't suppose his father's shown any interest,' said Naomi.

'His father doesn't know,' said Francesca, 'he's away. But I'm quite sure he would be very concerned, if he did.'

'Yes, I'm sure,' said Naomi. 'Anyway, do send some flowers, that would be nice. And don't worry about him, I've been to see him and he's recovering. So Mr Channing doesn't need to waste any of his valuable time or energy on him.'

'Naomi,' said Francesca, 'I really don't think you should talk like that about Bard.'

'Don't you?' said Naomi. 'I'm afraid I do.' And she put the phone down.

'Silly bitch,' said Francesca, quite shaken by this conversation.

She sent Liam some flowers and then phoned the hospital to see how he was and to tell him she would come and see him, possibly the next day. They told her he was comfortable and out of immediate danger but that he would be there for several days, if not weeks.

Then she phoned Marcia and asked her if she could get hold of Bard, and ask him to ring her. 'His son's been in a car crash. He's all right, but he's in hospital. I think Mr Channing ought to know.'

'I will contact Mr Channing, certainly, yes. And ask him to ring you.'

There was a slight emphasis on the word 'ask'. Silly bitch, thought Francesca again.

Jon Bartok, in an informal report to the other main board directors of the Konigstrom Bank, said that he had had a very satisfactory meeting with Mr Channing and Mr Barbour, and that after a most careful and thorough review of the affairs of the Channing Corporation, he felt that subject to certain restructuring of the loan, it should be continued for a further three months, subject to the usual reviews.

Bard finally phoned at three, from Arlanda airport.

'Bard, hallo. I thought you ought to know Liam's –'

'Yes,' he said sounding impatient, 'Marcia told me. How on earth did it happen?'

She told him, including the fact that Liam had been drunk. There seemed little point hiding it; he would find out sooner or later.

'Stupid bloody irresponsible behaviour, getting behind the wheel in that condition. What's the matter with him?'

'Bard, I don't know,' said Francesca. 'It's not my responsibility what your other children do or what happens to them. He's badly hurt, that's the point, and I have to say you don't seem very concerned about him. Perhaps that's what the matter with him.'

'Oh for God's sake,' he said, 'don't start lecturing me, Francesca. I've had it up to here.'

'Sorry,' she said, shocked at herself that they were quarrelling again. 'I – I didn't mean to lecture you. I was upset, that's all. I've sent him some flowers from us both, anyway.'

'Right. Look, Francesca, I'm afraid I've got to go out this evening, after all.'

'Oh,' said Francesca. Disappointment stung her; she felt cheated, foolish even. She had asked Sandie to cook Bard's favourite meal – nursery food, fish pie and then trifle – and had even planned what to wear: a red silk dress Bard had bought her, with a split up the side, and the scent he liked best, Poison by Christian Dior. All a bit tarty, but then she'd been feeling a bit tarty, had thought herself into savouring being in bed with him. And now – 'Why? I thought –'

'I've got a dinner.'

'What sort of dinner?'

'Oh, the usual. I'd missed it, in my diary, with all the events of the week. Can't be helped.'

'And you really have to go?'

'Yes, I do. George Hardie is speaking, I'm on his table.' Already she could hear the irritation at the question; she took a deep breath. Think positive, Francesca, don't look for problems.

'Oh I see. Well, never mind. There's always the weekend.'

'Ah yes, the weekend.' A silence. Then: 'I'm not sure I'll be able to go to Stylings. After all.'

'Bard, whyever not? You promised –'

'I know I promised. But I – well, I have to a lot to do. As a result of this Stockholm trip.'

'Surely you can work down there.'

'Possibly. I'm not sure.'

She didn't speak: she didn't dare, knew she would say something damaging, something angry.

'Kitty all right?' he said.

'Yes. Yes, she's fine. Slept all night again.'

'Good.' There was a silence; then he said, 'Well look, I'll see you later. If the traffic's not too bad.'

The phone went dead; she sat staring at it, hating it, hating what it had done to her.

He was home before six; holding parcels, flowers. He was always good about presents.

'A pity,' he said, kissing her, stroking her cheek, 'about this evening. Can't be helped, I'm afraid. I'd much rather be here with you.'

'Well, never mind, it doesn't matter,' she said, trying to sound warm, forgiving, knowing she didn't. 'You shouldn't have wasted time coming home, you could have gone straight to the office.'

'I know. But I wanted to see you.'

'Did you?'

'Yes of course I did. Very much.'

'What about Liam?'

'Oh, I've spoken to Marcia, who's rung Naomi. He seems fine. He's just a fool. I realy haven't got the time or energy to worry about Liam.'

'Bard, he's been in intensive care,' she said, shocked at his attitude, in spite of everything.

'Yes, and now he's out of it. Where are the children?'

'In the nursery,' she said, making an effort to sound normal, 'Jack's watching *The Jungle Book*.'

'Again? We watched that the last night I was here.'

'Again.' Jack was addicted to *The Jungle Book*, could recite it word for word along with the characters, sang all the songs with them too, in his loud, tuneless little voice. 'He obviously didn't hear you come in or he'd be all over you. He's been looking forward to you getting back.'

'Glad somebody was.'

'Bard, that's not fair. I was —'

'I know. But I swear I won't be late.'

'I expect you will,' she said lightly, 'but it doesn't matter.'

'Why don't you go to bed early? You look all in.'

'I might. But then you'll wake me up.'

'I'll try. Wouldn't you like that?'

Francesca looked at him. She did like it usually: it was one of her delights, from their earliest days together, to be asleep and to be awoken by him, wanting her; she would surface, sweetly confused, to feel his mouth on her, on her face, her neck, his hands on her breasts then moving down her, and she would turn to him, tumbling into desire, her body softening, moistening for him. She would come quickly on those nights, leaping, curving deep within herself, her arms entwined round his neck, crying out with pleasure, and he would follow her almost immediately: a swift joyful pleasure, stolen from sleep, and then they would lie together, she now wide awake but not caring, he settling heavily into sleep, telling her several times before he was finally lost to her how much he loved her.

But tonight, tonight she could not, would not want him (her earlier mood quite lost); she felt her face close, even as she managed a small smile, said no, she was really so tired, that if she got Kitty settled she would prefer not to be disturbed, would he mind sleeping in his dressing room?

'No, that's fine,' said Bard, turning away from her, 'absolutely fine. Of course. Look, I'll change in the office I think, probably easier, I want to catch Marcia.'

'Fine,' she said. 'Good idea.' He also had a dressing room at Channing House where he kept a complete wardrobe (its care controlled by Marcia): suits, shirts, dinner jacket, shoes, changes of underwear; he had a bed there too, where he slept occasionally, and a shower which he used sometimes twice a day. Marcia kept all that pristine too, saw the sheets and towels were changed, that it was supplied with all his favourite toiletries (Egoïste by Chanel, so appropriate Francesca had said, laughing when she first found it there). She thought again that evening, as she often had before, that he had no need for a real home or indeed a real wife at all.

'I'll just go up and get a couple of things,' he said, 'and then I'll go. I'll see you in the morning.'

'Yes, fine,' she said.

She heard the door slam; sat in her small sitting room for a while thinking, and then went upstairs feeling bleak and physically cold, to the nursery bathroom where Jack was in the bath. His small solid little body (Bard's body, she thought) was clean, but his cheerful face under its thatch of dark hair was still filthy, smeared with tomato sauce, and what Nanny Crossman called good honest dirt from where he and a small friend had been digging in the garden that afternoon (they were making a tunnel, they said, from St John's Wood to Primrose Hill, so that the rabbits could come down it), and something else, some strange flaky substance that looked hideously scab-like.

'Jack, what on earth is that on your face?'

'Goldfish food,' he said.

'What's it doing on your face? Didn't Nanny give you any tea?'

'Yes of course,' said Nanny sternly, appearing in the doorway. 'He had chicken and fruit salad.'

'And tomato sauce, I see,' said Francesca lightly.

'Mrs Channing, I was about to –'

'Nanny, I don't give a fig if he has tomato sauce on his face. He's obviously had a lovely day. How's Kitty? I thought I might –'

'Still asleep, Mrs Channing,' said Nanny, making it very clear that anything Francesca thought she might do would not be welcome. 'She's very tired, and sleeping peacefully. I think she should be left until she wakes.'

'Yes, all right, Nanny. I wasn't going to take her clubbing. Jack, I'm just going to change and then we can have some stories together. All right?'

'Great, Mum.'

'Mummy,' said Nanny automatically. Francesca winked at Jack; his determination not to be an ideal Crossman baby appeared to be growing daily.

'When will Dad be back?'

'Oh – not till late after all. Sorry.'

'That's OK. Did he get my baseball bat, do you think?'

'I don't know, darling. I hope so.'

'Cool.'

'I don't know what that's supposed to mean, Jack,' said Nanny. 'What about the proper word?'

'Cool is the proper word for a baseball bat. That's what they are. Cool.'

Nanny sighed and picked up the bath towel.

*

Francesca went into her bedroom, and sat down on the bed; she felt very tired and her head ached, horribly disappointed at the way the evening had turned out. She had had such good intentions, had felt so strong and confident about everything, and now it seemed they were still heading for the same dangerous abyss – at a terrifying speed. What had gone wrong with them, why had it happened, where had it begun? Not long ago: only three months, maybe less. On the day of the christening, for instance, she knew, she could remember, being perfectly happy. It wasn't just Kitty either; they just seemed to be losing each other. It was all very frightening. And it was, at least in part, her fault. It must be.

She sat there thinking; felt suddenly remorseful at being so hostile to Bard that evening. He would have much preferred to have stayed at home with her, or she was fairly sure he would. He had looked absolutely exhausted; he had clearly had a difficult time, had come back to see her, and she had failed him, rejected him, turned away. 'Bitch,' she said aloud. 'Stupid, stubborn bitch.'

She got up to put her rings away and saw his pearl shirt studs on his bedside table: he had obviously meant to take them with him, for the dinner that night. He loved those studs, hated not having them. She looked at her watch. She would have plenty of time to drive to the office with them before he left; it would be an olive branch and she could say she was sorry, ask him to wake her after all when he came in.

She picked them up, put them loose in her jacket pocket and went up to the nursery bathroom door again.

'Jack darling, I'm really sorry, but Daddy's just phoned, he's left something important behind. I'm going to take them down to the office myself, I'll be back in an hour. OK? All right, Nanny?'

'That will be perfectly all right, Mrs Channing,' Nanny. 'But I can't keep Jack up for very long, he'll get overtired and that isn't –'

'Nanny, I won't be very long. I promise.' She bent and kissed Jack. 'Love you.'

'Love you too.'

It was, despite her optimism, almost seven when she reached Channing House. The traffic was bad, every traffic light was set staunchly against her, and then she couldn't find anywhere to park. She finally dumped the car right outside the door, blocking in a rather flashy little Rover (clearly a visitor, she thought) and ran in; Hugh, the night porter was already at his post in the small office just inside the door.

'Evening, Mrs Channing.'

'Good evening, Hugh. Is my husband still here?'

'He is, yes, Mrs Channing. Shall I –'

'Oh good. No, don't tell him I'm coming, I want it to be a surprise. Oh and Hugh, I've blocked someone in, here's my key in case they come down before me. OK?'

'Right oh, Mrs Channing. But –'

'Thanks, Hugh.'

She pressed the lift button, waited impatiently for twenty seconds or so, and then decided to walk up.

The staircase was an open one, leading to the first two floors; it was marble, with a very nice cast-iron rail, noisy and slippery; countless time and efficiency experts had urged Bard to have it taken out, walled in, carpeted, but he always refused. It was one of his more provocative pronouncements, much beloved by the press, that anyone who was fool enough either to slip on it, or fail to appreciate it, had no business in his building.

Bard's office was on the first floor, off a beautifully curving landing; Marcia's was next to it, with an interconnecting door. As Francesca reached the landing she thought she heard footsteps on the flight of stairs above her; she stood still for a moment, wondering if it might be Bard, but they stopped at once. Obviously an echo.

Bard's door was uncompromisingly closed; better perhaps to go via Marcia. She would probably have left, but at least she could see if Bard had someone with him.

She knocked gently on Marcia's door and went in: she had indeed left, but her presence filled the room, totally daunting still. Not a pencil, not a sheet of paper, not even a leaf of the one rather severe plant on her windowsill stood out of place; the room was a study in straight lines, in order, in silence. Her word processor, her fax machine, her telephone with its answering machine all stood, stolidly mute, on her large black desk, and her chair was set so absolutely dead centre of her desk, she might have measured out its position with ruler and protractor.

Francesca looked slightly nervously at the door that led to Bard's office; it was closed, but she could hear no sound through it. She reached out and switched on the intercom: again silence. He was clearly not there. She pushed open the big door gingerly, still slightly fearful that he might be sitting working, but he was not, and the chair was pushed back from his great desk, as chaotic as Marcia's was tidy. She stood there for a moment, quite still, faintly awed as always by the thought that from this single room was controlled ultimately the complex mass that was Channings: this was the nucleus of it, a huge resource of intellectual and financial power. She had found it from the very beginning as moving as she found it exciting: that the man who said he loved her, who wanted her, who wished to place much of his life with her, who occupied her bed and possessed her senses, could be at the same time this other alien and incomprehensible creature; it excused so much of what he did, how he behaved, the searing rages, the brooding darkness. But sometimes as she watched him at home, as he did something mundane and unremarkable, as he read to Jack or held the baby, or as he reached out for her, held her, as they talked or laughed or argued or fought, she would think of that other creature and find him almost impossible to believe in.

His briefcase was still by the chair, his computer was switched on; a great mass of figures, totally incomprehensible, filled the screen. Amidst the wild sea of papers on his desk, she saw his diary lying open: she went over to it, thinking she could find out when exactly the dinner started, and as she did so the fax machine, the dedicated one on the low table by his desk, with his own personal number on it (she used to send messages to that number, in the early days, loving, raw, raunchy messages) hummed loudly: a single sheet came out.

She jumped, then, unable to resist the temptation, looked at it: it was a completely unheaded piece of paper, no address, no fax number on it, just the message.

'Re revised Letter of Wishes,' it read, 'please re-confirm new percentage allocation to both US dollar and Gib accounts. Also new allotment to WFF.'

There was an illegible squiggle on the bottom and that was all.

What fun they must all have here playing tycoons, thought Francesca, half amused, half wistful; it was like living some TV series. And what a ridiculously obscure message, all initials and codes. Just like Bard; playing games and making things more complicated, more difficult, than they really were.

'What the hell are you doing here?' It was Bard's voice, and he was standing in the doorway wearing his dinner jacket, and he looked immensely angry. And more than angry, something else. He seemed – what? Something she had never seen before, something more frightening than the anger. He looked scared.

Against all the odds, all common sense, Francesca felt awkward, almost scared too; and then as swiftly angry with herself for feeling it.

'Bard, I'm sorry to have disturbed you,' she said, her voice cold, ironic. 'I brought your studs in. Your pearl studs, you know? You'd left them behind and –'

'You came all this way, just to bring me my studs? I find that very hard to believe. Why the hell didn't you ring first? And why didn't Hugh tell me you were here?'

'I wanted to surprise you. I thought you'd be pleased, I wanted to say – oh forget it. For God's sake, Bard, I –'

And then she realised he was not alone, that someone else had come into the room with him, someone quite clearly very much at home, in command, far more so than she was. It was Teresa Booth. Teresa Booth, overdressed as always, in brilliant blue silk, her silver-blonde hair in a tight, bright cloud round her face, smiling graciously, almost condescendingly at her.

Francesca stood quite still for a moment; she felt winded and dazed, as if she had been punched in the stomach and hit over the head at the same time. Then she took a deep breath and said, 'Teresa! What a surprise! What are you doing here?'

'Francesca dear! I could ask you the same thing.'

'I'm sorry, Teresa, but I don't think you could.' She looked at Bard; he was still standing, silent, white faced, staring at her.

'Well, I can see you both have a great deal on your minds. I'll leave you. Have a good evening, Bard. And please don't wake me up when you get in.'

She couldn't remember driving home; afterwards she thought she was lucky not to have had an accident. She ran up the stairs to the nursery; the children were both asleep. She went to her room, lay down on the bed, staring up at the ceiling, shaking, deathly cold, as in the run-up to a fever.

What the hell was going on? Surely, surely Bard couldn't be having an affair with Teresa Booth. That really was unthinkable. It strained every ounce of credulity she had. On the other hand, there was clearly something between them. Teresa had been so in command, so absolutely unfazed by the situation, enjoying it even, so plainly joined with Bard in something. But what? Business? Well, that was possible. But surely they would have told her. An errand for Duggie? In which case surely she would have said so; Bard would have said so. And he had looked so totally shocked by her appearance in the office, had been so angry with her; he had behaved like someone guilty, someone afraid. She turned her mind to his behaviour generally over the past few weeks: no different, really, from usual. He had been alternately distracted, harassed, bad tempered, and then easily relaxed and affectionate; had slept well some nights, others had been at his desk when she had gone to bed or (more rarely) working there when she woke early to find him missing: he had been away a lot, out a lot, but no more than usual. There was nothing, nothing at all, to indicate that the underlying rock-bottom base of their lives had changed in any way. She had been shocked by his attitude to Liam, shocked at the depths of the animosity between them it had revealed, but even that had been at least in character. And yet, yet; this evening, she had arrived in his life unexpectedly, and his reaction had been one of guilt and shock.

'Fuck,' said Francesca aloud, Francesca who never swore, who hated obscene language, 'fuck you, Bard, fuck you.'

She lay there for a long time, just trying to establish how she felt, what she might do, then fell into a confused half sleep.

She woke up hours later, icy cold; went into the bathroom, ran herself a bath.

She was lying in it, still feeling cold and wretched, when she heard the front door open, Bard's footsteps heavy on the stairs, in their room. He pushed open the bathroom door, looked down at her in the water. Francesca looked back at him, filled with distaste, and with a sense of invasion. She crossed her arms across her bare breasts, said, 'Please go out of here.'

'Oh for God's sake,' he said. He still looked white, shocked. 'I'd like to talk to you.'

'All right. I'll be through in a few minutes.'

When she came back into their room, he was sitting on the bed; he was in his dinner jacket, holding a large brandy. He didn't say anything, just sat looking at her.

'Bard, I'm very tired,' said Francesca. 'I'd really like to –'

'Francesca,' he said, 'what the hell are you playing at?'

'Playing at!' said Francesca. 'What am I playing at! What about you, Bard, what are you doing? What were you doing with Terri Booth, and why –'

There was a long silence. Then: 'Jesus!' said Bard, standing up, staring at her, his face dark and heavy with anger. 'Dear sweet Jesus, Francesca, you cannot think that I and Terri Booth are – really could not believe it of you. That you should be that insane, that ...'

'Well, I'm sorry you should be so very surprised,' said Francesca, 'but what do you expect me to think?'

'Francesca for God's sake, she's my partner's wife. She was simply in the office, picking up some papers. Papers to take home to Duggie.'

'In which case why did neither of you say so?'

'Because you were giving a very good impression of Ophelia doing the mad scene. Or Lady Macbeth. Or any other deranged creature. It was embarrassing and it was irritating. I simply wasn't prepared to go to any great efforts to reassure you.'

'Well, I am so sorry,' said Francesca, 'so extremely sorry. I will endeavour not to be embarrassing or irritating in future, Bard. I seem to be like the rest of your family, including your own son, nothing but an embarrassment, a nuisance to you. And I have to say I don't find your explanation very satisfactory. On the other hand I don't think I can face hearing another, equally unlikely one.'

'Oh for Christ's sake –' he said. 'Francesca, please –'

Francesca cut him short. 'Look, I'm very tired. I'd really like to get to sleep. Perhaps you'd like to go into the dressing room. I don't think we're getting very far this way.'

'Francesca –' There was a silence and he looked at her, thoughtfully for a long time, as if weighing up what he should say, what he might do. Then finally he almost visibly shook his head, sat down suddenly on the bed and took her hand. 'I can hardly bear it,' he said, 'that you should think that I could go from you to – well.' His voice tailed off; he sat looking at her, his dark eyes very heavy.

'I love you, Francesca. Very much. I would never cheat on you. I couldn't. I had hoped you would know that.'

'Well, then tell me!' she cried out. 'Tell me what was going on. Please. I need to know. It was – I was scared. I felt shut out. I don't understand why you can't explain.'

'I can only say,' he said, 'that you had no reason to feel that way. And there was nothing to explain. It was a business matter, to do with Duggie and me, and – yes, with her, in a way, and that is all there is to it.'

'But Bard, what? What business matter, why won't you tell me?'

'Because it is nothing to do with you,' he said.

'Then I have no option but to continue to think you're lying.'

'Oh, don't be so absurd.'

'Bard, I am not being absurd.'

'You are being absurd.' His voice had risen now, raw, angry. 'That is arrant nonsense,' he said, 'total arrant nonsense.'

'Bard, tell me. What was she doing there, what were you doing with her?'

He looked at her in silence for a long time, his eyes first angry, then thoughtful. Finally he said, 'I was discussing a business proposition with her. She needed some money put into her company, and I agreed that I would help her.'

'Oh.' The explanation was so simple, so plausible, she was completely taken aback. She had expected a labyrinth of explanation at best, a long involved tale of talks and meetings and discussions. Then she said, 'Why?'

'I'm sorry?'

'I said why did you agree to help her? And why you, why not Duggie? And why couldn't you have told me in the first place, instead of that ridiculous piece of play-acting?'

'Oh for Christ's sake. How much longer is this going on, do I have to tell you how much is involved, the form in which the loan takes, the rate of repayment, the interest rate?'

'It goes on until I am satisfied, Bard.'

'Well, you must remain unsatisfied. I am simply not prepared to be cross-questioned like this. It's insulting, it's horrible.'

'And don't you think it was insulting, horrible for me, finding you there this evening with her, your attitude to me, her attitude?'

'It shouldn't have been, no. Not if you trusted me. Which you obviously don't.'

'And how am I supposed to trust you,' she cried out in agony at his incomprehension, 'if you won't tell me what's going on? If you have all these half secrets, tell me semi-truths. Trust doesn't come from nothing, Bard, from nowhere. It has to be fed and nurtured. Not neglected and abused.'

'Oh stop being so bloody melodramatic. You sound like a Victorian housemaid.'

'Bard, be careful, please –'

'It's you who should be careful,' he said, 'of the damage you are doing. Thinking you can walk into my life, my professional life, and start behaving like this. I warn you, Francesca, you start questioning me as to the way I conduct my business at your peril.'

She sat staring at him in silence, absorbing his rage, his arrogant hostility, his deliberate distortion of the situation in an attempt to divert her; then she got up, went over to her dressing table, rummaging through a drawer for she knew not quite what, her back deliberately turned to him. 'Your business is your own affair, of course,' she said, 'if you want to keep it that way. And your professional life. But your private life is not. That is mine too, Bard, mine and our children's. Please remember that. And what I saw this evening seemed to me not entirely professional.'

'Fuck you,' he said suddenly, 'fuck you. Fuck you for thinking I'd cheat on you. I find it hard to bear.' And he turned away from her, ran down the stairs and she heard the front door bang violently; and then she was alone, alone in the big silent house, wondering what on earth she had done. And knowing at the same time that Bard was most certainly guilty of something, and that he was also very afraid. The unease settled on her again: no longer a drift, something hard, something tangible. It was becoming quite difficult now to push it away.

'Rachel?' It was Reverend Mother's voice. 'Rachel, there is no real need for alarm, but Mary has hurt herself. I thought you should know.'

'Hurt herself? How? How bad is it?'

'She fell down the cellar steps. She was trying to carry too many things down, to the stores, you know how she will do that.'

'And —'

'Well, she's in hospital.'

'In hospital? That must mean it's bad, what's she done, should I come down —'

'She's broken her ankle. Which isn't at all serious. But she had a very nasty bump on her head. She's — she has a hairline fracture, and she's concussed, and they're keeping her in for a couple of days, for observation. Now she really isn't too bad, they have stressed that repeatedly, there is no real danger as long as she can be kept quiet. And they've sedated her mildly, because — well, you know how she is.'

'I do. Oh God. Is she very — upset?'

Mary hated hospitals, always had, ever since she had had to be admitted as a small child with a very deep cut on her foot and been held down by one unsympathetic nurse while another stitched it, rather brutally, without a local anaesthetic.

'A — a little, yes. Yes, I'm afraid she is. I stayed with her for a while, but of course I've had to get back.'

'Should I come down?' said Rachel. 'I could, very easily. Would that help?'

'I think it would help more than anything in the world. She's in Exeter General. Easy from the station.'

'I'll leave at once.'

She had just finished packing an overnight bag, when the phone rang again. It was Francesca; she sounded strained and almost tearful.

'Mummy? Can I come round?'

'Well, darling, I — I was just going out.'

'Can't it wait? Or shall I come when you get back? I need to talk.'

'The thing is, I'm going away for a couple of days.'

'Away? Where to, what for?'

Because it seemed simpler, Rachel lied. 'I'm going to stay with my old friend Joan Duncan. You know? In Leicestershire. She's a bit down, and —'

'Oh. Oh I see,' said Francesca.

'You sound a bit down yourself. It's not Kitty, is it, darling?'

'What? Oh, no, no she's a bit better, I think. But I – Mummy, couldn't you possibly wait just for an hour? I could come straight away.'

Rachel thought fast. It was a considerable dilemma. Mary needed her; there was no doubt about it. She was alone in the world, apart from the nuns who were all too busy to sit at her bedside for more than a few minutes; Rachel was the one person who could help her, the one person available. But Francesca needed her too, and would not understand why she could not have her. There had been a previous similar incident, when Mary had had a very bad attack of gastroenteritis and again ended up in hospital, seriously dehydrated, and Francesca had been in the middle of her O-levels. Of the two claims, Rachel had felt then that Francesca's was the greater (especially since any kind of satisfactory explanation for her departure was clearly impossible) and had stayed with her, while nevertheless deeply concerned for Mary, wanting to be with her, to soothe and comfort her. There had been little doubt that the recovery then had been slower because of her distress at being in hospital; this time, Rachel felt she could not fail her.

'Well, darling, I am in a bit of a rush –'

'Oh Mummy, please.' Francesca's voice was strained, weighted with tears. 'Surely you can spare me an hour. I can't be much longer than that anyway, Nanny's away and Sandie's looking after the children. What's Joan got to be down about?'

'Oh – she's just not been very well. Yes – yes, all right. But I don't want to let her down. Tell you what. I have to get to Paddington, silly for you to come down here. Why don't we meet somewhere up there, what about the Pâtisserie Valerie in the High Street?'

'Yes, all right. I'll be there in fifteen minutes, so you get there when you can.'

It took Rachel almost half an hour to get to Marylebone High Street; Francesca was sitting at the table, pretending to read *The Times*. She was wearing a T-shirt and jeans and dark glasses; she had no make-up on and she was very pale.

'Hallo darling. You look rotten.'

'I feel rotten,' said Francesca. She took off the glasses; her eyes looked sore. She had clearly been crying.

'What is it? Tell me. Espresso,' she said to the waitress who was hovering. 'What do you want, darling?'

'The same,' said Francesca, and then added, 'It's Bard. Of course.'

'What about him?'

'He's – oh, I don't know. I just feel utterly – bewildered by him. Despairing.'

'He hasn't – he isn't –'

'Mummy, don't be coy. It doesn't suit you. And no, he's not having an affair. At least I don't think so.'

'What does that mean?'

'It means I don't think so. Or maybe I do. Oh, God, it's just a mess. A horrible, horrendous mess.' Her eyes filled with tears; she brushed them impatiently away, blew her nose. Rachel took her hand, stroked it tenderly.

'You're not exactly making any sense, darling. Come on. Tell your old mother.'

Francesca sniffed loudly, looked at her and then said, 'I'll try. The thing is we haven't been getting on at all well lately. Lots of rows. About Kitty, I suppose … I mean, not about Kitty. But that's what seems to have started it. We're both worried. All that business about Kirsten in the newspapers didn't help either. Bard was very upset –'

'I should think you were quite upset too,' said Rachel briskly. 'That girl needs a good spanking.'

'Well, whatever she needs, she's not going to get it. The point is we've been quarrelling. Bard and I. A lot. Nasty quarrels. Rows, really. One leading to another, endlessly.'

'As they do.'

'Yes.' She took a sip of coffee, looked down at her wedding ring. 'Married life, I guess.'

'Indeed. So –'

'Anyway, he's been away for a few days. I was so determined it would be better when he got back last night. And then – oh, Mummy, I don't know –'

'Darling, you really are going to have to do better than this. I can't help you otherwise.'

'No. No, I'm sorry. Well, the thing was –'

Slowly, falteringly, the story of the previous evening came out. A rather odd story, Rachel felt. Very odd. She dismissed totally any notion of a relationship between Bard and Teresa Booth; they quite clearly loathed one another. On the other hand, the arrangement of a simple financial transaction didn't seem quite explanation enough for the situation Francesca had walked into.

'And then he wasn't just annoyed, I could understand that, not even just startled. He was furious. Furious and I think scared.'

'Scared? What of?'

'Mummy, I don't know, If I did, I wouldn't be sitting here,' said Francesca irritably.

'Where is he now?'

'I don't know. I've tried Stylings, tried the office –'

'And it's Saturday –'

'Yes, exactly.'

'What about the Booths?'

'Oh no!' said Francesca. 'I'm not ringing them.'

'No I suppose not. But Duggie might know –'

'Mummy, I can't.'

'I could,' said Rachel.

'I don't want you to. What would you say? "Is my son-in-law there? Could you send him home at once? Or has he run off with your wife?" No, it's really silly. And I couldn't bear it.'

'I'm sorry, darling. It was only an idea. Well, if there's one thing I'm quite sure of, it's that Bard hasn't run off anywhere with Teresa Booth. Uness he's going to push her over a cliff –'

'Oh don't.'

'Well, what *are* you going to do?'

'I don't know,' said Francesca fretfully. 'That's why I wanted to see you. To ask you what you thought.'

Rachel looked at her watch; she couldn't help it. Francesca noticed.

'You'd better go,' she said irritably. 'I don't want to keep you from your friend.'

'Darling, I am sorry. It's just that I promised her, she's expecting me on that train and –'

'Yes of course. I understand.' Her tone made it clear she didn't. 'Don't worry about me, I'll just go home and wait for the phone to ring.'

'Francesca –'

'You know what makes me most upset, about our life in general? It's the way Bard seems more and more determined to turn me into some kind of a bimbo. It's always been that way, but it's got worse lately. I don't understand him, I really don't. It's real don't bother your pretty little head about anything stuff. That's not what he married, Mummy, not what he fell in love with –'

'I know,' said Rachel soothingly, 'but men are all the same, you know. That is what they want. Correction, what they think they want. Just someone there, to run their lives and be waiting in a lace négligé when they get home.'

'Did you have to do that?' Francesca's voice was interested.

'Things would have been a lot worse if I had. But it's what your father wanted me to do. To be. And you have to add to the equation Bard's compulsion to keep things to himself. It's not just a closed book you're married to, Francesca, it's one with a lock and key on it, like one of those diaries ...'

'Yes. I know.' She sighed, was silent. Then she said suddenly, 'Do you know what a letter of wishes is?'

'Yes. Well, more or less. It's an instruction that's not quite an instruction to a lawyer or a fund manager. Your father was rather keen on them.'

'Mummy, you sound about as lucid as Bard,' said Francesca, amused. 'I don't understand.'

'Well, it is a bit complex. What the letter says quite literally is, "It is my wish that you do and so and so" – usually with funds – without actually spelling out that it's an order. But of course the recipient of the letter almost certainly will do whatever it is because he's being paid to. It's like all these things, a hook that can be wriggled off.'

'And you'd write one of these to who?'

'Oh – someone who was running a trust for you, a fund, usually offshore.'

'But it wouldn't indicate, would it,' said Francesca slowly, 'that something dodgy was going on?'

'Well, not dodgy, no of course not. A bit creative perhaps. Honestly darling, I'm not an expert. Anyway, why do you ask?'

'Oh – nothing. I – just came across one. When I was in Bard's office the other night, a fax came through. I just wondered what it meant, that's all.'

'Well, not a lot,' said Rachel.

'You seem to understand a lot more about business than I do,' said Francesca irritably. 'Maybe I am a bird-brain. Maybe that's what the problem is.'

'Darling, of course you're not. That company is hugely complex, you couldn't possibly be expected to understand the running of half of it. Unless Bard gave you an intensive course of instruction.'

'Which he certainly isn't going to. Especially now he's disappeared.'

'I'm absolutely sure,' said Rachel soothingly, 'that he'll be back soon. I can't believe he's just run off and left you, or that he's had some accident, if that's what you're worried about. Bard loves you and he cares about you, very much, I do know that ...'

'How do you know?'

'Because he told me so. Only the other day.'

'When? When did you see him?'

'Oh – I can't remember now.'

'Mummy, you can always remember everything. You're being very mysterious suddenly. First Teresa Booth, now you, what is this?

'Oh –'

'Mummy, I know when you're lying. You'll have to tell me. Come on, when did you see Bard?'

'I – I went to see him a couple of weeks ago.'

'What, to the office? Why?'

'Oh – I was going to tell you. Of course. But you know I have this charity I'm involved with, in the West Country, the convent, where my friend's mentally handicapped daughter is –'

'Yes?'

'They're in trouble. They need help. And I – well, I asked Bard if he could do that. Help. Come onto the board or something.'

'Mummy, that is outrageous.' Francesca was flushed, two spots of colour high on her cheeks. 'You can't do things like that, not without telling me –'

'I thought it was better that way. I thought he'd probably say no, anyway, so what was the point –' She was floundering now. 'Obviously, if he'd said yes, I would have –'

'And did he?'

'Did he what?'

'Say no?'

'He – said he'd think about it.'

'I think it's too bad of you. Honestly. He gets furious if he's bothered in the office, by anything outside the business, I wouldn't dream of it even, and then he takes it out on me. I know a lot about charity, Mummy, it's my rather pathetic life's work, I could have helped you with it, I just don't understand –'

'I'm sorry. Very sorry. I didn't mean to upset you. Just to reassure you really. That he does love you. Very much.'

'I'm afraid you haven't reassured me at all. You've upset me more.'

Rachel was silent. She put out her hand; Francesca shook it off. 'Don't.'

'Well,' she said, trying to sound bright, 'there doesn't seem a lot more to be said now. Or a lot more that I can do. Would you like me to –'

'No, it's all right. You'd better get off to your train.' Her voice was very cold.

'Yes,' said Rachel, looking at her watch again, relieved at the excuse, the respite, 'yes, I think I had. It's at eleven fifteen and I'm cutting it fine already.'

'I'll give you a lift,' said Francesca. 'My car's out there. I'll pay the bill; here's the keys, go and get in.'

Her voice was cold and unhappy; she followed Rachel out, started the car, drove it very hard down the street, turned right.

'Darling, left to Paddington.'

'Mummy, I don't know why you think it's Paddington. It's Euston for Leicester. Isn't it?'

'Well –'

Rachel was silent. This was absurd; it was also irremediable. She thought wildly of saying Joan Duncan had moved, or that she was meeting her somewhere along the line, but it would sound clearly nonsensical. She would have to get out at Euston, and get a cab back to Paddington. She would probably miss the train, but she could get the next. There was no alternative.

'Bye, darling,' she said, kissing Francesca briefly on her cheek as she got out of the car. Francesca did not even look at her. 'Try not to worry. I'm sure Bard will be back, very soon, with a huge armful of flowers. I'll ring you later and –'

'You haven't listened to a word I've said,' said Francesca. 'Goodbye. I hope you enjoy your stay.'

She pulled off with a screech of tyres. Rachel watched her safely out of the concourse and then hailed a taxi. 'Paddington,' she said, 'I'll double the fare if you can get there in seven minutes.'

'Blimey,' said the cabbie. He was young and cheerful; he clearly saw it as a challenge. He cut out into the Marylebone Road and put his foot down, weaving in and out of the outside lane, crashed one red light, pulled up swearing at the next. Rachel sat back, slightly alarmed, buckling up her seatbelt; she was too distracted to notice the driver of the Mercedes pulled up alongside looking in. It was a very large Mercedes, the number plate was BC 2345, and the driver was Francesca.

'Oliver, dear, this is Teresa Booth.'

Oh God, thought Oliver wearily, this is all I need. Bloody woman. 'Yes, Mrs Booth, good morning.'

'I just got your mother's letter. I was a little hurt.'

'I'm very sorry, Mrs Booth. It honestly was nothing to do with me.'

'No, dear, I don't suppose it was. But I'd gone to a little trouble to get the house organised for her, and – well, that doesn't matter too much. I'm much more disappointed she doesn't want to see me. Have you any idea why not?'

'No, Mrs Booth, I haven't. Really. But I am sorry. Now if you would –'

'Bard Channing didn't have anything to do with it, I suppose? Her changing her mind?'

'Oh – no. No I don't think so. Of course she likes to go along with his plans, but –'

'Of course. Thank you, Oliver. Well, I hope the trip did her good.'

'Yes, it certainly did. She's feeling much better.'

Which is more than I am, you interfering old bat. 'And now, Mrs Booth, if you'll excuse me, I'm awfully busy.'

'Yes. Of course, Oliver. Thank you, dear. I'll see you soon.'

It sounded more like a threat than a polite platitude.

'God,' said Toby, 'for a girl who's always in trouble, you spend an awful lot of time doing good works.'

'Oh piss off,' said Kirsten. 'I'm not always in trouble and I don't call going to lunch with my grandmother doing good works.'

'I wouldn't have lunch with mine.'

'Yes, well, you're a selfish little shit, aren't you?' said Kirsten, smiling up at him, twisting her fingers through his dark hair. They were in bed; they had just had some extremely good sex, and Toby wanted her to go out to lunch in the country with some of his friends. Kirsten said no, she was going to have lunch with Jess, and anyway, having lunch in the country on a summer Saturday meant sitting in a traffic jam. A boiling hot traffic jam.

'Not necessarily. Not if we leave now.'

'Well, I don't want to leave now. I want to have a very long bath, have lots of orange juice and croissants and read the papers.'

'I'm amazed you can bear to read the papers, after what they've done to you,' said Toby.

'Oh stop talking through your arse,' said Kirsten cheerfully. 'I have to read them, it's part of my job. I want to see if the *Mail* magazine has mentioned a new suncream that I told the girl about.'

'Such an important job, too,' said Toby.

'It is to me,' said Kirsten earnestly. 'I'm not fucking another one up. Anyway, it wouldn't be fair on Gray.'

'Who's Gray? Oh, the chap that got it for you. I think you fancy him.'

'Don't be pathetic. He's not for me at all. He's quite old for a start, and –'

'What's he look like?'

'Well, he's quite good looking, in a rather old-fashioned way.

Brown floppy hair, big grey eyes, rather appropriately, tall, nice clothes. Very nice clothes.'

'You do fancy him.'

'I don't, I swear,' said Kirsten. 'But he is nice, and I don't want to let him down. OK?'

'Or your granny?'

'No, nor my granny. She's been so good to me, rang me up the day after that story came out, said she knew I must have been tricked into it and that she'd speak to my dad.'

'And did she?'

'I don't know. I expect so. She does everything she says she will, Granny Jess does. She's great. And anyway, she's a bit uspet today, about my stepbrother, Liam. He's had a car crash.'

'Serious?'

'Yes, quite. He's in hospital, I mean he's OK but quite badly hurt, apparently, and I know she's worrying about him.'

'Is that the one your father doesn't get on with?'

'None of us gets on with him. He's a bit of a nightmare. Cut himself off from us all. But – well, he is her grandson.'

'Could I come too? To see your granny? No, no, forget I said that, I can see you're about to say yes.'

'You could if you liked,' said Kirsten seriously, 'and she'd be really nice to you, and want to know all about you. She wouldn't approve of your background, she's very left-wing. But you'd like her a lot and –'

'No honestly,' said Toby, 'sweet of you, but I'll give it a miss. Look, I'm going to go and have a shower.'

'OK,' said Kirsten. He kissed her, rather slowly and sweetly, and then clambered out of bed and disappeared into the bathroom; she lay there thinking about him for a bit, about his body and the pleasure it gave her, that it had just given her, and suddenly felt a strong desire to follow him. Kirsten often felt most like sex when she had just experienced it, when the memory was still almost physical; sexual desire to her was self-generating, and the more violent, the more prolonged the pleasure, the more swiftly she wanted it again. A week or so without it, and she could shrug the idea off easily; it was something her boyfriends often found confusing. Not to mention difficult to cope with. But then Kirsten was altogether confusing and difficult to cope with, as she frequently acknowledged herself. She lay there for a little while, tensing and relaxing her body, wondering if the desire would pass, but it didn't; she wanted Toby again and she

194

wanted him badly. And she knew him well enough to know she could probably have him.

She walked into the bathroom; she could just see him, through the steamed-up shower door, his back turned to her, his head thrown back. He was quite tanned, except for the stark whiteness of his buttocks; his back was very muscular, his legs long and strong.

Kirsten opened the shower door, and he didn't even hear her, so loudly was the shower thudding, at full power, full heat; she put her arms round his waist, pushed her fingers down over his flat stomach, reaching into his pubic hair, kneading, tangling at him, thrusting herself gently against his buttocks. They were almost the same height; it made standing-up sex much more comfortable and fun. For a moment nothing happened; then he said, and she could hear the smile in his voice, 'Darling! Have you come to help me wash my back?'

'Sort of,' she said. She started moulding her body against his, bending, flexing, pushing at him, the snarls of desire uncoiling within her, feeling now his penis rising under her fingers; she started kissing, biting his back, pushed one hand between his legs, cupping his balls. They were very soft and heavy, in the heat; she heard him moan quietly. He turned to greet her, smiled at her through the water, lifted her slightly, held her against him; she sank slowly, joyously, down on him, easing herself onto his penis. The thudding water confused her senses; she felt at once languid and frantic, relaxed and desperate for him. He pressed her back against the wall, bracing himself, started pushing, thrusting into her almost at once; she felt herself gathering quickly, sweetly, could feel the apexes of pleasure forming within her, started riding them, each one higher, the fall deeper, climbing, climbing towards the height, the peak, the pinnacle, and there it was, there now, she reached for it, grasped it, had it now, now, in her hungry, grasping, giving, yielding depths, pushed hard, harder onto him, yelled out again and again with pleasure, with the strong, triumphant, glorious pleasure, always the same, always different, and then slithered, laughing, exhausted, shaking, onto the floor of the shower.

Her body was still savouring the pleasure when she drew up outside Granny Jess's little house, two hours later.

'You look very thin,' said Jess severely, handing Kirsten a hugely piled up plate of rabbit stew and mashed potato. Suppose you're not eating. It's this living on your own, I really don't approve of it. The place for a girl is in her father's house, until she gets married. Then it's in her husband's.'

'Granny Jess, don't be silly,' said Kirsten. 'How could I possibly live in my father's house?'

'Yes, well, I can see that. And I blame him almost entirely for what's happened, I'm afraid. He's a spoilt, selfish, amoral man. I'm the first to admit it, much as I love him. Not that I spoilt him. Life's done that. And he's made an appalling mess of at least one marriage. And his relationship with his eldest son. You been to see Liam?'

'No,' said Kirsten, 'you know he doesn't like me. But I have sent him a card. And he's all right, I spoke to Naomi.'

'So did I. And it seems he might not have been. I'm afraid he's a very misguided, mixed-up young man. Anyway, that's another discussion, and nothing really to do with you. All I'm saying is that ideally your father's house is where you ought to be. Not racketing round London, up all hours. I know what you girls get up to. I was young once.'

'I know you were, Granny,' said Kirsten, smiling at her, thinking what a very good thing it was she didn't know what she actually got up to. 'But surely you were living in your father's house? So you couldn't have got up to very much.'

'Well, we didn't have sex, if that's what you mean,' said Jess. 'We waited for that, and a very good thing it was too. Made it all the better when it came.'

'Granny! I'm surprised at you,' said Kirsten, and she was. She had always imagined her grandmother lying and thinking of England, enduring her grandfather's embraces, and that none too often.

'What about? Me enjoying sex? Of course I did. Kirsten, you young people are all the same, think you've invented the whole thing. But you didn't, and I can tell you, there's a great deal of extra pleasure to be had, discovering it together, just the two of you, a purely private delight.'

Her gaunt old face was suddenly softer, her dark eyes distant. Kirsten put down her fork and stared at her, as astonished that she should discuss such a thing as that she had so plainly enjoyed it; Jess saw her staring at her and smiled, flushed a little.

'Well, that's enough of that. Now I daresay you'd like something to drink with that: lemonade? Or ginger beer?'

'Oh – just water,' said Kirsten. She had hoped, briefly, wildly, for some wine, but she should have known better. Jess's disapproval of what she called strong drink was only matched by that she felt for the English class system.

'Good,' she said, 'good girl. Adam's Ale, wonderful stuff. You can't beat it.' She brought a large jug to the table, filled her own pint tankard and a more modest glassful for Kirsten.

'I've talked to your father, as I said I would,' she said, after eating in silence for a while, 'and I think in time he'll come round, forgive you.'

'I don't want him to forgive me,' said Kirsten sharply. 'I don't deserve to be forgiven, and anyway, he's totally impossible, we're much better kept well away from each other.'

'I would doubt both those statements,' said Jess. 'I think you're very fond of your father actually, and I certainly think you deserve to be forgiven. The reason your father was so angry, you know, was that there was more than a small grain of truth in it all, it hit home … It was a terrible time for you, and he had no business to leave you there with your poor mother. When you weren't off at one of those dreadful schools,' she added, 'mixing with those terrible people.' She spoke as if Kirsten had been at an inner-city comprehensive, rather than first Benenden and then St Paul's. 'Just the same, you have been extremely silly, and I'm sure you can see that now.'

'Yes, yes, I can,' said Kirsten humbly.

'Does he know that?'

'Well, I told him so, of course I did, but −'

'He wouldn't listen?'

'No. He said such awful, terrible things −'

'Kirsten, he will come round,' said Jess, 'he always does. He'll want you back in the family with him.'

'What family?' said Kirsten, and to her great irritation found her eyes filling with tears. 'I don't want to be part of that one, that precious little one of his, with Francesca −'

'Francesca is an extremely nice girl,' said Jess severely, 'and the sooner you can admit that the better. Your father's marriage to your mother was long over when he met her, she should bear no responsibility for any of it. Should she?' she added rather fiercely, as Kirsten sat silent.

'No. No I suppose not. But she's got so much and Mum's got so little and −'

'Your mother has a great deal, actually,' said Jess. 'Your father has been very generous to her. That house, all her bills paid −'

'Yes, except she never has any money,' said Kirsten, feeling her colour rising, angry suddenly.

'Kirsten, if she had any money, she would only spend it on drink. You know she would. And in any case, none of that is Francesca's fault. And she has had her own crosses to bear.'

'Like what?' said Kirsten sulkily.

'Like your father's bad temper, for one thing. And now the baby being ill. So you should think before you speak badly of her next time. Now the best thing you can do, in my opinion, is get back to your studies. I never thought it was a good idea to go and work for your father. I don't approve of nepotism in any form. You got a boyfriend at the moment?'

'Yes. Yes I have,' said Kirsten. 'I nearly brought him today, only I don't think you'd terribly like him.'

'What's wrong with him?'

'Oh, his background. Eton, Granny, I'm afraid.'

'Well, he can't help that, I suppose,' said Jess. 'I'd blame his father, not him. Is he clever?'

'Yes, quite.'

'You going to marry him?'

'Good Lord no. Of course not. I'm not in love with him. I don't believe in love anyway, I've told you that before.'

'You will one day,' said Jess. 'Now look, I want you to phone your father, say you're sorry –'

'Granny, he'd put the phone down on me.'

'He might not. Go on, Kirsten, do it for me. And for him. He was very hurt you know, as well as angry ...'

Kirsten looked at her; she had been very generous about it, over-generous really. And she shouldn't have talked to Judy Wyatt, no matter what her father had done.

'Yes all right. But it's only for you.'

'Doesn't matter who it's for. It'll start building a bridge. That young Oliver's a nice boy,' she added suddenly. 'He phoned me the other day, coming to see me soon.'

'Oliver who?'

'Oliver Clarke. Heather and Nigel's boy. You know.'

'Oh, I can't stand him,' said Kirsten, 'he's such a creep. Although I must say he is rather good looking these days. I don't usually like fair-haired men but he's not all wishy-washy like they normally are. I suppose it's the dark eyes. And at least he's tall. Granny, can I have just a tiny bit more stew? It's so delicious.'

'You must come here more often,' said Jess, smiling at her, 'get a bit of flesh on you. And he's not a creep, he's a charming, well-mannered young man. I'd be very proud if he was my grandson.'

'Well, he's not,' said Kirsten. 'Thank goodness.'

Chapter Ten

Francesca awoke to the sound of gunfire, mingled with the telephone ringing; surfacing confusedly from sleep, she realised it was after midnight, and there was a most unpleasant death taking place in front of her, a man writhing on the ground, clutching at his stomach, from which was issuing a great deal of blood. She winced and switched the television off, and then groped for the telephone.

'Hallo?'

'Francesca.' It was Bard: Bard sounding, as he always did when he was guilty, knew he should apologise, disgruntled and short.

'Bard, where the hell are you? Where have you been? I've been so worried, so –'

'I'm in a hotel.'

'Where?'

'Oh – near Manchester.'

'What on earth are you doing there?'

'I wanted to look at the new development. I thought I might as well do that today.'

'I see.' She struggled to keep calm, not to start reprimanding him, to make things worse.

'Francesca, I'm – well, I'm sorry if you were worried.'

That was as near as he would get to a proper apology; from Bard it was a lot.

'Well – at least now I know you're all right.'

'I'm fine. You all right?'

'Yes. Yes, thank you.'

'And the children?'

'Yes. Yes they're fine.' No point even mentioning Liam.

'Good. I'll be down in the morning. About midday.'

'Fine. How will you come?'

'Oh – I'll get a plane.'

'Shall I meet you?'

'No, no. I'll get Horton.'

'Bard, not on a Sunday! He is allowed a life of his own. I'll come. Ring me when you know a time.'

'Yes, all right. Well – I'll see you tomorrow. We can talk then.'

From Bard that was another form of apology: an acknowledgement that there was something to be talked about. She forced some warmth into her voice.

'Yes. That'll be nice. Um – are things OK up there?'

'They're fine. Yes. Why shouldn't they –' There was a loud crackling and she could hear him swearing: then the phone went dead.

He rang again a few minutes later. 'Bloody thing. That was my mobile. Keeps losing power ... I told Marcia to get it fixed and she said there was nothing wrong with it, it's too bad –'

'So what are you speaking on now?' said Francesca, feeling a most unusual pang of sympathy for Marcia and what she would have to endure on Monday morning.

'The hotel phone. So yes, I'll see you tomorrow.'

'Yes.' A long silence.

Then: 'Well, good night, Francesca.'

'Good night, Bard.'

And he was gone; after a conversation, she thought, that hardly acknowledged what she had been through, what he had put her through.

Gray was eating his breakfast – brioche, figs with warm honey, and a large steaming bowl of milky coffee – and trying to convince himself that life on his own was not all bad, when the phone rang. Briony, he thought, reaching for it, knocking over what was left of his orange juice: Briony ringing, saying she missed him.

It was Briony: only not to say she missed him.

She wanted to know if he had made up his mind, and said that she would like to come over later that morning and see him, to discuss things. Gray said he'd love to see her, and then put the phone down, feeling more frightened than he ever had in his life. And still not knowing what he should say to her, or what he was going to do.

Bard phoned mid-morning; she thought he must already be at Heathrow, but he wasn't, had called to say he wouldn't be back until early evening after all. 'I'm sorry, Francesca, really sorry, but I had to meet John Waters first thing, and it dragged on a bit and now there isn't a flight I can get on until after three.'

'I really don't know why you're bothering to come at all,' she said, and put the phone down. And burst into tears.

'What's the matter?' said Jack, who had come in to her sitting room, holding what looked like a very dead bird. It was a very dead bird.

'Oh – nothing. Sorry, darling. I was disappointed because Daddy won't be back till this evening. Why have you got that bird?'

'It was in my tunnel. I think it must have tried to get down it and got stuffocated. Sorry,' he said to the corpse, stroking it tenderly.

'Darling, I don't think that's what happened. I'm sure it's not your fault the bird died. Birds don't really go in tunnels.'

'Well, it might have thought it was a short cut for it to take.'

'It might, but I really don't think so, I think it's much more likely it' – she sought for a comforting answer – 'it was very old and it died in its sleep. In your tunnel. So you did it a good turn, not a bad one.'

'Oh. Oh, well, that's good, then. I'm going to go and make a grave. Want to come and help? Oh, no, it's OK. George is there, he can help. See you, Mum.'

'See you, Jack.'

She watched him go out of the door and her heart turned over with the familiar, painful, joyful love; she thought about the small boy who had once been Liam, and his sad tortured childhood, and about the sadness of his estrangement from his father, and the harshness of a man who could be estranged from his own son. And then she thought that since Bard was not going to be home until evening, she might go and see Liam; it would be at least something she could do. She phoned St Mary's, asked to be put through to Liam's ward. A nurse told her that Mr Channing was comfortable but still not at all well.

'He said to thank you for the flowers if you called. They're beautiful.'

'Good. Has he had any visitors today?'

'No, not today.'

'Is his wife coming?'

'No, she's phoned through. It seems she can't come till tomorrow.' The nurse clearly found this hard to understand.

'I might pop along myself for five minutes. If that would be all right. I am – family.'

'Well, I'll have to ask,' said the nurse doubtfully. 'Just wait a minute, can you?' She came back after a lot more than a minute, sounding breathless.

'Sorry, Mrs Channing. Sister says it'd be all right for you to come, as long it is only a few minutes. He does seem a bit better.'

'Right. I'll be there in about half an hour.'

Liam looked ghastly. His face was greenish-white; one side of it was very swollen and both his eyes were black. He had a drip in his arm, and a tube coming out of his side, she presumed from the punctured lung. A large cage arched over his legs. He was very drowsy.

Francesca took the hand on the dropless side and squeezed it gently. 'Liam. It's me, Francesca. How are you?'

'Foul,' he said. His voice was slurred. 'Thank you so much for the flowers. It was really nice of you.'

'My pleasure. Bard sends his best wishes.'

'Liar,' he said, and his face moved into what she presumed was a smile.

'Well – you know.'

'I do know. Was it in the papers?'

'Yes, I'm afraid so. A couple.'

'Let me tell you what the headline said.'

'Liam, I don't –'

'No, let me. It said something like "Tycoon's unemployed son accused of drunk driving." Am I right?'

'Sort of right,' she said. 'Um – is Naomi all right? As she's not coming in, I wondered –'

'She's fine,' he said. 'She's just making a point, I think. About my behaviour. She wants a divorce.'

'Oh,' said Francesca. She felt very shocked; she didn't know what to say. She looked at Liam; his eyes were closed again. Then she saw a tear trickling from under one of the lids.

'Oh God,' she said. 'Liam, I'm so sorry.'

'Yeah,' he said. 'Yeah. Me too. I think that's why I'm here.'

Sister came up to the bed. 'That's long enough, Mrs Channing,' she said. 'I did say only a few minutes –' She looked stern.

'Yes,' said Francesca. 'Yes of course.'

She squeezed Liam's hand, and then suddenly bent and kissed his poor swollen face. 'I'll come again,' she said.

He smiled and then closed his eyes. There was a pause, then: 'Please do,' he said. 'Please, please do.'

Briony had moved out. Gray had sat and watched her all that afternoon as she packed, piling things into the huge boarding-school trunk she kept in the hall cupboard – I'm only taking my clothes, Gray, and my books and tapes and things, and my cushions, the rest is yours really.'

He had protested, had told her she must take at least some of the pictures they had bought together, the tin signs in the kitchen, the birdcage that they had got in Camden Market and which housed the asparagus plant that trailed through its fine white bars, the *New Yorker* covers she had had framed and hung all the way up the stairs; but she had said no, she didn't want them, they were part of their shared life, they didn't feel like hers any more.

'Well they're not mine either, in that case,' he said. 'That's silly, Briony, of course you must take them.'

But she wouldn't, had piled everything ostentatiously untidily into the trunk (it had taken him four years, and five holidays, to teach him to pack tidily) and had then sat on it, looking at him.

'This is very sad,' she said.

But it was Gray who cried, in fact, not her: who when she had gone, driven away in her beloved Cherokee Jeep, to stay with her sister while she found a new flat of her own, had sat down on the big bed where they had been so lovingly happy, and stared at the wall, remembering Briony, remembering the way she looked, her long straight brown hair, her small, pale face with its large blue eyes, her slender, graceful body – one of the things he had most shrunk from when he thought about her having a baby had been seeing that body changed out of all recognition, the small breasts heavy, the flat stomach hugely swollen, no longer familiarly his, no longer a source of their joint pleasure but invaded by an all-consuming stranger. He thought of how she always came to greet him when he was late home, smiling with pleasure simply to see him, never stayed watching TV or chatting on the phone like other people's wives and girlfriends, how she was always genuinely interested in what he had done that day, whom he had talked to, what he had worked on – 'And then what happened?' she would say, as he told her stories over supper, putting down her knife and fork to listen; he remembered how she was always just very slightly slow to get his jokes, anyone's jokes, pausing puzzled while everyone else started laughing, and then would throw her head back and go into peals of such genuine mirth that everyone laughed at her as well as whatever had amused them in the first place; he thought of how good natured she was, never snappy, never complaining at the awful hours he kept, never all those things other women seemed to be, never moody, never pre-menstrual, never sulky, never bossy. What had he done, how could he have let it happen, condemned himself to loneliness, bleakness, an empty house, an unshared bed? But he knew, deep down, beneath the misery and the onset of loneliness and the fear of never finding anyone he loved as much, as tenderly, as happily as he had loved Briony, he knew he had still done the right thing. He would have lost her, if she had had a baby, as surely as he had lost her when she drove away from the house, away from him; she would not have been the same person, a stranger would have walked back into the house when she came home with her baby – their baby – and he did not want, could not imagine, living with that stranger. Those two strangers.

What was the matter with him, he wondered, what strange bit of disharmony had settled in his genes that he had no wish for progeny, quite the reverse indeed, no desire to see himself reproduced, to see his foothold assured in immortality. He had had a perfectly ordinary happy childhood, with no traumas that he could think of, and had been a much-loved child. His parents had had an averagely good marriage, he had had no especially difficult love affairs. It was all quite beyond him really. Maybe if he went to an analyst or something, or did that rebirthing rubbish – but no. What was the point? He'd have to change and he didn't want to change. Whatever the reason, however loony he was, he liked the grown-up life. He didn't like children and he didn't want to give his house, his lovely ordered, pristine house with its skilful mixture of styles, and his life over to them, their noise and their mess and their general disagreeableness.

Nevertheless, the decision had been hard and telling Briony harder. He had thought about little else, after leaving Teresa Booth; her words had had a huge influence on him. He had really liked Teresa Booth. Underneath the sexy nonsense, and the undoubtedly ruthless streak, there was someone who was at least in part kind. Kind and thoughtful in its true sense. He wondered what on earth she would say if she knew he had acted on her words, thrown out his girlfriend on her say-so. Probably be horrified. After drinking one bottle of wine, he rather wanted to tell her; after getting through the best part of a second, he knew he had to. If Duggie answered, he could say it was about the feature he was writing about timeshares.

But they weren't there; there was no answer. Probably away. He left a message on the answerphone, just to say he'd called, and could she give him a ring some time, and then phoned the number in Birmingham and left the same message there. She would pick it up when she got back and he could tell her then. There was no hurry. Absolutely no hurry at all. Briony was gone, gone for the rest of his life: not for the first time since he had told her his decision, had met those hurt, gentle blue eyes, heard her voice saying, 'Well, Gray, I'm sorry, but I wasn't playing games, I don't think I can go on,' had reached for her and felt her turning away from him, Gray buried his head in his hands and wept.

'Don't you believe me?' said Bard.

'No,' said Francesca.

'Silly bitch,' he said, and kissed her. 'Let me try again. I love you.'

His hand was on her stomach, smoothing it, his fingers massaging the tender, responsive areas he knew so well; unwillingly, almost grudgingly, she rose just very, very slightly beneath them. He felt the movement, increased his pressure, probing downwards; she felt herself softening, easing dangerously; turned her head imperceptibly towards him, looked into his eyes. They were fixed absolutely intently on her face, great, dark, fierce eyes; he did not smile at her, did not even move a muscle of his face, just continued to study her, to gaze into her, as if he could learn more of her, important, crucial things.

'I love you,' he said again. 'Christ, I love you. I love you so much. Never forget it, Francesca, never ever.'

And then quite suddenly he was on her, in her, urgent, seemingly afraid he would lose her, lose the moment, driving, pushing, working at her and in her, kissing her, greedy, hard, holding her head in both his hands; she could feel him, feel his penis reaching in her, for her, and she could hold back from him no longer, could feel herself almost as if for the first time budding, unfolding, blooming, flourishing in great frondlike branches of pleasure, feel the lightness, the spangling of sensations spreading outwards and inwards at one and the same time, feel her arms, her legs, her entire body invaded with the violence of it, her mind bleached of everything but this great reach of pleasure that was at once so focused and yet so wide and wild and pervasive.

She felt him come too, the deep, long throbbing of him, heard his groan, felt his hands lift himself up from her, looked at him, saw his head thrown back, raised upwards, and then almost at once, saw him look down at her, and smile, and say again, 'I love you. I love you.'

They had talked: not very much by absolute standards, a lot by Bard's. She told him she had been to see Liam; he hadn't said very much, except that he could not imagine why she should have done such a thing, and had, nonetheless, asked albeit rather grudgingly how he was.

'I'll write him a note,' he said. 'He won't want to see me.'

'He might.'

'Francesca, he won't.'

She gave up on that one.

He said then he had been thinking; that he could, after all, understand why she had been so upset; that what he had told her about Terri Booth had been true; that he could see finding her in the office had been a shock; and she had said (trying not to smile at the difficulty he had making even so minimal an explanation, so faint an apology) she was sorry if she had over-reacted, had seemed to him to be unreasonable in her distress.

'The thing is, Bard, if you would only tell me more, I would be left to imagine less.'

'But there is nothing to tell,' he said, staring broodingly out of the window, 'nothing that you need to know.'

'It's not what I need to know, it's what I want to know.'

'But I don't see why you want to,' he said, and there was genuine puzzlement in his eyes.

'Oh dear,' she said, laughing in spite of herself, 'we seem to have a very basic problem here. I want to, because I am interested. Can't you understand that?'

And 'Yes,' he said finally, 'yes, I suppose I do. But I spend so much of my time on that company, it is so very nice for me to come home and be free of it. I cannot, Francesca, I really cannot, start going through my day all over again when I get home. It's more than flesh and blood – well, my flesh and blood anyway – can stand.'

And she had to leave it at that: knowing it was unsatisfactory, but recognising at the same time that for now at least she must be satisfied with what he had presented her with. Which was an apology – of sorts; and which was an explanation – of a kind.

'But Bard, I do warn you,' she said, and heard her own voice, very solemn, totally sincere, 'if I ever found there was something serious, something that mattered that you were keeping from me, then I would not be able to bear it.'

She awoke in the morning, to find him already dressed. 'I'm afraid I have to go,' he said, and then, clearly with a huge effort, 'I've got a meeting about Coronet Wharf this morning. With some potential tenants. It could run right over lunch. Which might make me late tonight. But I'll ring you.'

'Thank you,' she said, 'thank you for telling me. And thank you again for the suit. It's beautiful.'

The suit had been a present he had brought her back from Stockholm and only given her that morning: it was honey-coloured suede, very simple, exactly what she would have chosen herself. It was one of his more unexpected qualities, that he was able to buy clohtes for her, in exactly the right size, always in perfect taste.

'You'll look beautiful in it. I'll see you later.'

And he was gone, leaving her feeling at once slightly abandoned, and happier than she had for some time. He was difficult, impossible even, arrogant, manipulative – but at that moment she knew, clearly and sharply, with both her physical and her emotional self, exactly why she had fallen in love with him, and why she had agreed to marry him.

And it came to her, as she lay there, that she would like to show him that she did love him, that she wanted to please him, to do something for him, and that quite soon now it would be his birthday. She would plan something special for that. Not a party, there had been the big one for his fiftieth and besides with Kitty being ill, the thought of organising anything major seemed horrendously inappropriate. But a weekend away – even twenty-four hours – on their own, that would be lovely. And Bard would appreciate it enormously. More than anything. She knew that. He often said (either wistfully or irritably according to his mood) that he had forgotten what it was like to be on his own with her. She would have to tell Marcia, enlist her help. She would phone her during the morning, while Bard was in his meeting.

Half amused, half embarrassed at herself, thinking this was exactly the sort of thing that she would once have most disapproved of – being the sort of woman for whom social organisation was a major occupation – she got up, had breakfast with the children, and drove Jack to school, and when she got back suggested Nanny took Kitty for a walk. 'It's a lovely day, it will do her good. She looks so much better, doesn't she?'

'Well, she does,' said Nanny, determinedly gloomy, 'but I don't like these drugs going into her. It isn't natural. Not for a child.'

'Nanny, of course it isn't natural. But she'd – well, she'd be a lot more ill if we left her to what was natural. Anyway, a walk I think. You could go down to the park, maybe pick up Jack on the way back. The thing is, I have a lot to do this morning, and I can't collect him.'

She wasn't often as firm; Nanny liked to plan her own routine, and it didn't include walking in the morning, she preferred the afternoons, when she could meet her peers in Regent's Park – indeed she never tired of telling Francesca that when Kirsten and Barnaby and Victoria had been little they had lived in Kensington and had been able to go to the Round Pond every day, so much better for them. Francesca had never challenged her on why the air near the Round Pond should be better for children than that by the Regent's Park lake, but she had promised herself that one day she would. She knew the real answer:

that the best nannies, by nanny-standards, were by the Round Pond. But it would be fun hearing Nanny proffering something more acceptable.

Nanny went off to get Kitty ready, disapproval hanging about her like a large, Norland-uniform-brown cloud; Francesca smiled at her broad, retreating back. Getting the better of Nanny even in the most minimal way made her feel good.

She was just about to ring Marcia when her phone rang.

'Francesca? This is Miranda Scott.'

Francesca liked Miranda; she was a kindred spirit, and shared Francesca's views on the basic futility, however pleasant, of their lives. She had been an interior designer, and still worked as a favour for friends; her husband was an extremely expensive gynaecologist, frequently described by Miranda as having been inside every woman in SW3. She was also a brilliant mimic; Miranda being Diana was more like Diana than Diana herself.

'Hallo, Miranda.'

'Look, I wondered if you could help. This dinner on Friday, with the auction, you know? We need a bit of press coverage, and I thought maybe you might know someone. Being in the meeja and all that. I tried Dempster, but he said it was a frightfully busy night and he hadn't got anyone to send. Got any ideas?'

'Well – I'll have a think. I could ask my husband's PR, she's always full of ideas. I'll get back to you.'

'Good. Thanks. And you haven't got any marvellous little extras for the tombola, have you? We need something small, couple of tickets for a theatre, that sort of thing.'

'I've got a ghastly Hermès scarf my mother gave me for Christmas,' said Francesca. 'You can have that, gladly. Only one careful lady owner; never taken out of its box.'

'You're an angel. Thank you. Well, I'll hope to hear from you. Do you want to come for a drink here first on Friday? With your wickedly attractive husband?'

'More wicked than attractive as far as I'm concerned at the moment,' said Francesca briskly. 'I'll have to ask him, Miranda, the way things are going at the moment he could be coming to the dinner via Bahrain. Or not coming at all.'

'Oh don't say that. I couldn't bear it.'

Sam was very helpful about coverage for the dinner; she said she'd have a think. 'Presumably you want someone very respectable. Not a tabloid.'

'Absolutely not. And don't tell Bard, whatever you do. He thinks all journalists should be target practice for firing squads at the moment.'

Sam laughed. 'I have a sneaking tendency to agree with him. And I promise I won't. I'll get back to you.'

'Thanks, Sam. Can you have me put through to Marcia now, please?'

Marcia sounded more condescending even than usual. 'Good morning, Mrs Channing. I'm afraid I can't possibly put you through to Mr Channing at the moment, he's –'

'No, Marcia, I don't want to speak to my husband, I want to speak to you. It's his birthday in July, the twelfth, as of course you know, and I want to whisk him off to Ireland. To the Dromoland Castle, I thought, for just forty-eight hours –'

'How nice,' said Marcia. Her tone implied the darkest foreboding about the plan, as if Francesca had proposed a brief stay in Alcatraz.

'So I just wanted to know if he was free that day, and if not if you could manage to clear it for him.'

There was a long silence. Marcia was obviously anxious to impress upon her that what she had asked was far too difficult to accomplish by a quick glance at Bard's diary.

'No,' she said finally, 'most unusually, Mrs Channing, there is nothing in the diary that day – oh, except for a query on a lunch with Mr Booth. I could speak to Mr Booth about that if you like. He's coming in later.'

'No, it's all right, Marcia. I'll do that. I want to speak to him myself. Thank you.'

'Francesca! How nice. How are you, darling? Sorry about young Liam, we sent some flowers and a little something.'

'That was very kind of you, Duggie,' said Francesca. 'He's going to be all right, apparently. I went to see him briefly yesterday and –'

'That was very nice of you,' he said, 'very nice.'

'Oh – I don't know. Anyway, Duggie, I'm glad I caught you, I thought you might be in the meeting this morning.'

'Oh – no.' He sounded wary and something else – hurt? Had he been kept out of it deliberately? She knew Bard was inclined to be contemptuous of his negotiating skills. 'His only value is in pulling in contacts,' he'd once said, 'and in that he's worth his weight a hundred times over in gold.'

It was true, she knew. She'd watched Duggie at work, at parties, dinners, even on holiday. He could spot a potential client, a source of finance, at a hundred yards. Especially on a golf course. And then draw them into his warm, welcoming web. Dear Duggie; she missed him, they didn't see nearly so much of him these days, with the arrival of Teresa. They had had such fun together when Suzanne had been alive, she had mothered her, had mothered them all. It was all very different now, she thought sadly; Terri was about as motherly as Boadicea.

'Heard the baby hadn't been too well. How is she? Dear little thing. It was lovely seeing her at Easter, you must bring her down here.' He sounded wistful; Francesca felt guilty.

'She seems better. And I keep telling myself the doctors must know what they're talking about. Yes, Duggie, you must come and stay at Stylings one weekend. With Terri of course. Er – how is she?'

'Oh, she's fine. Very occupied with her business this week. Some big trade fair. Up in Birmingham. That's where her head office is, you know.'

'No I didn't.'

'She's a very high-powered girl. Big turnover, that company.' He said this proudly. 'I don't see as much of her as I'd like. Spends a lot of time in Birmingham. Working on her company, you know?'

'Oh – yes, of course.' And then she said – purely to make conversation, of course, not to check up on Bard, of course not – 'I understand Channings have put some money into her company. She must be pleased.'

There was a long silence: very long. For some reason she felt unnerved by it. Then he said, carefully, 'I – hadn't quite realised that.'

'You hadn't? Oh, I see – well –' She was confused, embarrassed. 'Well, Bard just mentioned it. Maybe I misunderstood. Yes, that must have been it. It's very easy to misunderstand Bard, isn't it? He probably just said he was thinking about it. In fact, now I come to think about it, that was what he said. Sorry, Duggie.'

'That's all right, darling.'

And now she was not just embarrassed, but something else: lost again in the swirling mist of half-knowledge, of unease. Damn. Why had she said anything? Why couldn't she have left things alone? And why had Bard told her something that was untrue?

She switched to the real purpose of her call, trying to distract herself, to distract Duggie. 'Now look, Duggie, I need your help. I'm planning to whisk Bard off on his birthday this year. For a little forty-eight-hour idyll, probably to Ireland.' She felt rather less keen on the idea suddenly, but she felt compelled to go on with it, for now at least. 'And he has a query in his diary on lunch with you. Can I quietly cancel it? And could you keep quiet? Say you've got to do something else?'

'Yes of course. No problem. Forgotten it was his birthday. Only a possibility, that one, anyway. Take that as read, Francesca my dear. And mum's the world.'

'Thank you, Duggie. And you're all right, are you?'

'Who, me? Good Lord, I'm absolutely tickety-boo.'

Dear Duggie; walking time-warp that he was. She felt terrible about upsetting him, worrying him. And yet, she still wanted to go on; she had to go on ...

'Good. Um – Duggie –'

'Yes?'

Suddenly it seemed silly not to try and find out why Teresa might have been at Channing House that night; surely Duggie would know. 'I – I just wondered, Duggie. Does – does Terri go into Channing House much?'

'Channing House?' The carefully bluff voice sounded guarded suddenly. 'No, of course not. Not unless I'm there. Why do you ask, darling?'

'Oh – well, she was there the other night. I popped in with something for Bard and she was there. I was surprised, that's all.'

'Which night? When was she there?' Different again, the voice: not even guarded, but edgy, irritable.

'Oh – it was last Friday, actually. Just after Bard got back from Stockholm. Honestly Duggie, it doesn't matter, I just thought –'

'Didn't she say? I mean, how could I know? Didn't you ask her yourself?' The irritability had extended towards her now; he didn't like this, didn't like the situation.

'Well – well, no, not really. The thing is, Bard was in a frightful bait, just for a change, and I was rushing and –' God, she had got herself into a tangle now; silly to have started it. It was obvious she was suspicious, that she was trying to pry. Inspiration hit her. 'Probably she was discussing her company with him, don't you think?'

'Yes. Yes, of course.' He sounded grateful himself for the suggestion. 'Yes, that'd be it. I think, now I come to think of it, she did mention something. Yes, that would be the explanation. Definitely.'

'Yes.' All she wanted now was to get off the phone. 'Anyway, Duggie, you take care, and don't forget about the twelfth, will you?'

'Of course not.' He sounded abstracted still. 'The twelfth. That'd be fine. Absolutely fine.'

'Thank you. Bye, Duggie. Lovely to talk to you.'

'What's that? Oh, yes, very nice. Yes. Goodbye, my dear.' He hauled himself back into the present with an almost audible effort. 'Yes, I won't forget. And bring that little darling to see us. And the young chap. Terri would love it. She's wonderful with children, as you know ... Wonderful girl altogether. Given me a new lease of life.'

'Good,' said Francesca, 'that's marvellous. Bye, Duggie.'

She put down the phone and sat looking at it, telling herself everything was fine. Of course it was. Terri obviously hadn't wanted Duggie to know she had asked Bard to put money into her company. That was all. Well, if she'd made things awkward for her, that was fine by her, thought Francesca. Although she was sorry if she'd upset Duggie. Dear Duggie. She got up, made herself a cup of coffee, and made a call to the Dromoland Castle. And then looked at her watch and thought she might just have time to go and visit Liam again before lunch.

Longman and Drew, the firm of chartered accountants sent in by Methuens to examine the affairs of the Channing Corporation, had made an interim and most reassuring report to Desmond North at Methuens. They had done an extensive survey of the accounts and held exhaustive discussion with both Mr Channing and Mr Barbour, and found everything absolutely in order; a full report would follow within a few days. Desmond North breathed a sigh of relief, realised he had been more anxious than he had admitted even to himself, and booked a two-day break in Florence with his mistress on the strength of it.

Gray sat in his office, feeling raw with misery. Tricia had made him some tea which he had drunk almost without noticing the taste; it was only as he set the cup down on his desk that he realised it was so dark in colour that it had stained the cup. Perversely he promptly felt sick. He had felt sick quite a lot that day: morning sickness, he thought to himself, and tried to find it funny. He didn't. He tried to concentrate on work; it didn't seem very important. In any case, it was Monday, there was no pressure, nothing to set the adrenalin flowing. The only thing on his desk was a note from the editor saying could he think about doing an update on his piece about the EMU, which was hardly going to distract him very much from his misery. That was unfortunate; usually it was the greatest solace, his work: a second wife, his mistress Briony had often said, exciting and revitalising, intriguing and interesting, soothing pain, lifting depression, quite often replacing, or certainly running alongside, physical desire. He really loved it. He was always telling people he would do it for nothing (something of a lie, but they knew what he meant and so did he). He could never quite imagine how anyone could want to do anything else, felt against all logic that every other job had to come second to it, that everyone would wish to do it if they could; and he saw it as the greatest piece of good fortune to possess the kind of talent that made it possible. Briony had always said – God, how long, how painfully, horribly long was he going to go on thinking that? – that it was because he was such a show-off, such an egotist, that it was simply seeing his name in print every week on the top of his column, and of course she was right, but there was more to it than that. It was the sheer satisfaction of taking a starting point, an idea, a personality, a situation, and building a story on it, of talking to people, listening to people, probing, thinking, sorting: nothing necessarily exciting, but nonetheless genuinely creative, colouring in, fleshing out, bringing into focus.

He felt sick again suddenly, violently so, and got up and went to the gents'; sat there for a long time, his head in his hands, wondering (yet again) why, how, he could have done what he had, wondering what Briony was doing, wondering if she was all right, if she felt as bad as he did, hoping, praying almost he had not made a mistake, taken hold of happiness and hurled it away, thrown the baby (God, why did he keep coming up with these images?) out with the bathwater.

And then he began to think again of Teresa Booth: and that led him back to thoughts of Duggie and Channings and Sam Illingworth and the story he was so convinced was there; and a tiny, sweet seam of excitement, of interest, entered his consciousness. He got out Saturday's *Financial Times*, examined the Channings share price; it had been drifting downwards just slightly. Friday had seen more than a drift: seven points. He pulled himself together and went back to his desk and dialled Sam's number.

'Sam Illingworth.'

'Sam, hi. It's Gray Townsend. I wondered if you were free for lunch today. We could discuss trends in property, or your unsinkable share price, or the servant problem, anything you'd like really.'

' 'Fraid not, Gray. I'd love to, but – bit hectic here. Heavy meetings going on all day.'

'OK,' he said, disproportionately disappointed. 'Another day maybe. It is unsinkable, isn't it?'

'What? Oh, the share price. Yes of course.'

'Although not quite so good on Friday.'

'Not quite. Better today though.'

'Oh really? Anything to do with the heavy meetings?'

'No of course not. Gray, don't pump me, you know it's pointless. But it's funny you should ring. I wanted to ask you a favour. Nothing very exciting and I don't suppose you'll be interested, but I'll have done my duty –'

'I know. Bard Channing wants me to go and stay for a few days.'

'No-o. But you're warm in one respect. Mrs Channing phoned me this morning, asked me if I knew some nice friendly journalist who might be able to cover a charity do. This Friday.'

'Oh Sam, for God's sake. I'm not a bloody diarist.' His misery was making him irritable.

'I know, Gray. Sorry. I did say it wasn't very exciting. But – well, forget it. Sorry.'

She sounded so embarrassed he felt quite sorry for her. 'What sort of a charity do?'

'An auction. Tim Kennedy's doing it. Should be fun. If you know anyone who'd like to go, he – or she – would get a free dinner. At the Grosvenor House.'

'Can't be all bad.' He thought of the Friday evening: alone, as all his Fridays would be from now on. The whole fundraising thing did intrigue him; the big business aspect of it. And then – 'Would Mrs Channing herself be there?' he said.

'Oh yes, of course. I think you'd find she'd be very friendly and helpful, as well. She's really very nice. Would you like to call me back, if you can think of anyone?'

Gray reached a decision. 'I've just thought of someone,' he said. 'Me.'

Suddenly he felt better, distracted at the thought of meeting Francesca Channing.

Alan Ferrers was a rising star on the trading floor at Jones Oldbury. He was one of that new and select breed of electronic barrow boys; he'd grown up on a council estate in Dalston, the son of a bus driver, left school on his sixteenth birthday against a background of dire warnings of unemployment and bankruptcy from his father and his headmaster, got a job within weeks, running errands on the Stock Exchange and was now making, in an average year, four times the headmaster's salary and eight times his father's. He was of a cheerful disposition, good looking, randy, foul mouthed and could, he often said with modest pride, smell a deal like a dog could smell a bitch on heat.

He was just pulling up the ring of his third Diet Pepsi of the day, ripping open his second packet of cigarettes and trying to decide whether he should ask Carole Harding, who sat opposite him and had the most sensationally large tits he'd seen for a long time outside the confines of the *Sun* newspaper, if she'd fancy a drink after work, when his screen flickered and a few rows of numbers moved and shifted in their familiar corn-in-the-wind rippling sequence. 'Interesting, my darling,' he said (for he was very fond of his machine and always addressed it thus), and reached out for his telephone to speak to Graydon Townsend, of whom he was very fond and who had for the past two years, or even a little longer, paid him for the odd piece of useful information in bottles of champagne. Vintage. Obviously.

Gray went out at lunchtime to a pub on the corner of High Holborn, drank rather nastily warm ice beer, and thought miserably that in the old days, when Fleet Street had been a place rather than a concept, there would have been a great mass of warm drunken bonhomie to fall into and thus forget himself. Now newspapers were scattered across London like so many isolated hotels, there was precious little of that, and a dangerous falling-off in useful gossip as well. Life generally, he thought, munching a soggy pickled onion, didn't seem to have a lot going for it.

There were three messages for him when he got back to the office. One was from Teresa Booth, saying she'd got his message but was now going away for a couple of days on business, 'but thanks again for a nice time at the Ritz, if that doesn't sound too compromising, and I hope you didn't take too much notice of my advice. It was probably bad.'

'Thanks, Mrs Booth,' said Gray aloud.

The second message was from Kirsten Channing; she was having a party on Saturday, would he and his girlfriend like to come? 'Yeah,' said Gray to the machine, 'and feel like Methuselah. Don't think so, thank you.' He'd drop her a nice regretful little note; it would save having to explain, to make excuses.

The third was from Alan Ferrers at Jones Oldbury, to say the share price of one the firms they had been discussing the previous week had just jumped up fifteen points. Gray forgot about Kirsten and Briony, forgot about everything, dialled his number.

'Channings, would this be?'

'It would indeed.'

'And what would have done that, Alan?'

'Only one thing. Someone's bought a ton of 'em.'

'What's a ton?'

'Oh – say about a million quid's worth. At least.'

'Blimey,' said Gray. 'Any idea who?'

'Nope. But I've been asking around for you. If I get any news, I'll let you know. You owe me a few drinks anyway.'

'You'll get them.'

He rang off and sat staring at the phone; he suddenly felt quite different, excited, phsyically energised. Something was up; his instinct had been right.

'Mr Clarke!' It was Marcia's voice. 'Mr Channing would like to see you in his office please.'

Oliver's heart lurched. Now what had he done? 'Now?'

'Of course. If it had been another time I would have specified it.' Old bag. God, he hated her. One day, one day, he'd tell Bard Channing what she was really like, behind his back. He pulled on his jacket – a new one he'd bought that lunchtime, from Paul Smith, too expensive really, but he didn't have anyone else to spend his money on, Greece had failed him in that respect – and hurried along to Bard's office.

'Go straight in please.'

Bard was on the phone; he waved at Oliver to sit down. He didn't seem angry. He didn't even seem cross. There was a glossy brochure on the coffee table, with details of an organisation called the World Farming Federation. Oliver started flicking through it.

'That sort of thing interest you?' Bard had put the phone down.

'What? Oh – yes, it does, actually. If I'd been able to do a gap year I'd have gone and worked for someone like that.'

'You should do it still. You're very young. Take a leaf out of Barnaby's book.'

'Yes,' said Oliver, thinking of Barnaby, drifting about whatever bit of the world took his fancy, cushioned by his father's money, untroubled by any urgent necessity to finish his course, earn his living.

'I'm serious. If you want to do that, I'd help you. It's important, do that sort of thing while you can.'

Oliver stared at him. 'Thank you, Mr Channing. Thank you very much.'

'It's one of my favourite charities, that one,' said Bard, 'people doing something positive, not just sitting about on their arses, waving collecting boxes.'

'But surely, aren't they waving one at you?' said Oliver looking at the brochure.

'What? Oh, yes, in a way. I have a charitable trust and they're a major beneficiary. But they do something useful with the money. That's what I mean.'

'Yes, I see.' Yes, and save yourself a lot of tax at the same time. Don't be so cynical, Oliver; he's just made you a fantastic offer.

'Anyway, I just wanted to have a chat,' said Bard, 'see how the holiday went.'

'It was great,' said Oliver, who had indeed enjoyed it, in spite of the shortfall on its romantic content: the scuba diving, the windsurfing, the heat. 'And Mum is really much better for it. Thank you very much, Mr Channing, we all really appreciated it.'

'Good. Excellent. And I understand your mother isn't after all going to see Mrs Booth?'

'No. No, I believe that's right,' said Oliver awkwardly. He had hoped it wasn't going to be mentioned.

'She told me in her letter that you'd explained I wasn't keen on the idea. And that therefore she wasn't going to do it. Very sweet of her, and I appreciate that, Oliver. I think between us we saved her quite a lot of distress. Not that Mrs Booth would have meant any harm, but –'

'No,' said Oliver. 'No, I really don't think she would. I think she's really nice, as a matter of fact.'

He spoke firmly; Bard was looking at him, amusement in his eyes. 'You've got guts, Oliver,' he said. 'I like that.'

What did you say to that? Oliver was silent.

'Anyway, that was all. Oh, and I've told Mr Barbour to put your money up. Just a couple of grand a year. You weren't on a proper salary before; more of a probationary thing. You've worked very hard, done well. You're an asset to the team. I hope you'll stay.'

Oliver was so astonished he dropped the brochure. It fell onto the floor and he sat staring at it, thinking he would never again see the WFF logo without feeling a mixture of pleasure and unease. Pleasure that Bard Channing should value him, and say so and show his appreciation in so extremely generous a way, and unease at the feeling he was being rewarded for rather more than being a good runaround boy for Pete Barbour.

'Mr Townsend? Hallo, young fellow. This is Douglas Booth.'

Duggie sounded odd; slightly strained and shaky, while clearly trying to sound jocular. Gray had been doodling rather lethargically, waiting for Alan's call; he sat up sharply.

'Hallo, Mr Booth. How are you?'

'Fine, fine. Could do with a bit more sun, of course, but so could we all. Look – you've been tallking to my wife, haven't you? I heard your message on her answerphone.'

'I certainly have, Mr Booth.' Christ, this was difficult. He shouldn't have done that. How to play it, what to say? Thank God for the original lie; he went for it feverishly. 'I'm doing a piece about timeshares. Hers was an obvious one to include.'

'Yes indeed. Clever girl. Very clever.'

'She certainly is,' said Gray, thinking even in his distraction that 'girl' was hardly a label he would attach to Teresa.

'But – well – look.' Booth sounded embarrassed, awkward. 'Look, she's got some funny ideas. About – well, about Channings. I don't know what she said to you, but I wouldn't like you to – well, to get us all wrong.'

'Mr Booth,' said Gray carefully, 'I do assure you I would never think Channings was anything but absolutely pukka, blue chip, gilt edged, all the right things. You know?' Christ, this was difficult; like working your way through a quicksand. One false step and you were down, done for.

'Yes, well, that's what I hoped you'd say. Thing is, in your section of the profession, you have to get things absolutely right. Well, don't you? Black and white. No half truths, no rubbish. Not like the tabloids.'

'No, absolutely not.'

There was a very long silence. Then, 'Look,' Booth said very quickly, as if he didn't want to be able to change his mind, 'look, I don't suppose I'm making a lot of sense. I wonder if we could meet. I'd like to – well, talk a few things through.'

'Yes, of course we can. When would you –'

'Well, I'm tied up all day here. Lots of meetings and so on. And I've got to go away for a few days. But maybe next week – say a week tomorrow? How would that be?'

'Fine, Mr Booth, absolutely fine. Let me buy you lunch.'

'Oh no, no need for that. And do call me Duggie. Everyone else does. No, this is on me. Shall we say the Reform at one? Rather than a restaurant. Quieter, and all that. And I hardly need say, this would be –'

'Confidential? Of course. Don't even think about it any more.'

'And you've nothing planned on – well, on Channings, for the next week's paper, then?'

'No Duggie, I promise you. My word. As a journalist. You know how valuable that is. Seriously, I promise. Nothing planned at all. Although –'

How to play this exactly: didn't want to frighten the old chap off.

But while he was rattled, while his defences were down, it was a good time for a question.

'Yes?'

'Well, I did notice your share price was down a bit. Earlier.'

'Really?' And there was the old Duggie again, smooth as a putting green. It was the instant change that told Gray he was lying; he was back on course, playing his usual role, the one in which he was word perfect. 'Oh, I never take much notice of all that. It goes down and then it goes up again. Bit of a rollercoaster that whole thing, as you well know. I daresay by tomorrow morning you could see something different.'

Yes, and I bet you know why, thought Gray. God, this was a sexy old business. God, he loved it.

He smiled into the phone. 'I expect you're right. It's all OK there, is it? With the Docklands thing and so on. Must be a hell of a burden, that.'

'Oh, not really. We've come through a lot worse. And you know Bard. He's very good at pushing water uphill, you know. Very good.'

Yes, thought Gray, while appearing to walk on it; and then, getting lost in his own metaphors, said, 'I'll see you next Tuesday, Duggie.'

'Yes. Tuesday, that's right. Now look, let me say again' – less smooth again now, not with the old script – 'I don't want you getting the wrong idea. There's nothing wrong, you understand. It's just – well, you know, it's the old two and fourpence scenario.'

'What's that one? I don't think I –' said Gray. He was beginning to think he was going mad himself.

'Oh, surely you know it? Famous case of Chinese whispers. Someone in some battle or other, out in India I think it was, this was in the old days before radio communications of course, sent a signal down the line saying "send reinforcements, ready to advance", and by the time it reached HQ it had become "send two and fourpence, we're going to a dance". You see what I mean, don't you?'

'I certainly do,' said Gray carefully. 'No, we certainly wouldn't want any of that kind of confusion, Duggie. I'll see you next Tuesday, then.'

Now what the hell was all that about? And what kind of desperation would drive Douglas Booth to ring him up? What on earth had Teresa been saying to him? And how had he found out she had been talking to him anyway? Unless she had told him herself – and if so, why should she try and rattle him, get him worked up?

He flicked back his answering machine, listened to her message again. Listened to her voice, amused, relaxed, thanking him for a nice time at the Ritz, and wondered what the hell Duggie had thought she might have been going to say to him.

Alan Ferrers called him at five.

'You'll like this.'

'What? About the shares?'

'Oh, I'm not telling you now. I want you waiting for me at Corney's in half an hour with a nicely cooled bottle of Bolly.'

'I'll be there,' said Gray.

Alan came in looking very cheerful. 'How are you, my son?'

'I'm fine, Alan,' said Gray grinning at him, thinking that actually with a touch of poetic licence and the merest tweak of biological possibilities, he could actually be Alan's father, rather than the other way round. 'And yourself?'

'Good, good. Hiked the old bonus up a bit. Partly thanks to your friends at Channings.'

'Oh really?'

'Yeah. Bought and sold a few of their shares, made a tiny bit. Price has gone up again. Right back to three quid.'

'Well, in that case you should be buying this,' said Gray.

'Should maybe, but shan't. Taking a very nice girl out to dinner. Very nice indeed. Excellent prospects there, I'd say. Can't be long.'

'So who was it?' said Gray.

'Who was what?'

'Alan, don't fuck about. Who bought the shares? You'd better tell me, otherwise I'm going to stuff this bill right up your arse.'

'OK, OK. Two offshore trusts, apparently. One in the Cayman Islands, one in Jersey. And you can work out what that just might mean, I'm sure. Given the little hiccup earlier.'

'I wouldn't even think such a thing,' said Gray.

Chapter Eleven

The pain was particularly bad that morning. It had been a filthy night. He had hoped it would be easing by now: it was, after all, five days since the crash. But it wasn't. It seemed to be getting worse. It waited for him, lurking darkly, building up steadily towards the end of each four-hour period, as the dope wore off. The leg was the worst: a hot, searing agony. He could almost see the fractured, jagged bone pushing against his flesh. He had begged the little night nurse for an extra jab, the wonderful exquisite jab that took him floating away from it, and she had asked the sister, but Sister had simply told him he was already having more than was good for him, that he should try and relax and take deep breaths when it got really bad – 'Sounds like childbirth,' he had said, grinning at her – but that made the pain in his chest and his ribs worse. The nights were terrible: the long hours of dark, lonely wakefulness, counting the minutes until his next fix. It wasn't bloody fair; he felt sure if he had been in some smooth private hospital he could have had all the stuff he needed. And then there were all the attendant miseries, humiliations: the bedpans, the blanket baths, hearing the other patients groaning, snoring, being sick. Christ, it was awful. Awful.

Naomi had been to see him twice now; she didn't say much, didn't stay long, just brought a lot of books, some fruit, told him he was lucky to be alive and other such uplifting clichés and left again. She hadn't brought the children, which would have cheered him up; he knew she was still angry with him for leaving them alone while he went to get Hattie's Calpol.

'If Jasper hadn't gone next door to the Duncans they'd have been alone for hours. Anything could have happened. Why didn't you at least ask someone to listen out for them?'

'I didn't think of it,' he said. Clearly Martina Duncan hadn't mentioned the vomiting. That was extremely nice of her.

He looked at his watch: eight o'clock. The day seemed to have gone on for hours and hours already; it felt like mid-afternoon. He looked at the lad in the next bed; he had been brought in during the night concussed, both arms and a leg broken, in need of surgery after falling off a drainpipe. Burgling no doubt. He was unconscious still from the anaesthetic: lucky sod, thought Liam. You just wait, mate.

The nurse came over to him, looking officious.

'Good morning, Mr Channing. How are you today?'

'Bloody awful,' said Liam.

'Dear oh dear,' she said. 'Pain any better?'

'No. Worse. What are you doing?' he said as she started to pull the curtains round his bed.

'I'm going to check your dressings. For infections. We don't want you getting gangrene, do we?' She was smiling at him, clearly thought it was funny; he could have hit her.

'I wouldn't care,' he said.

'I think you would. Now then, let's have a look. And then it's time for your wash. Your bottle need emptying?'

'No,' he said wretchedly.

'You're not drinking enough,' she said severely, 'you must get more fluids down, it's very important. Now then, off with that jacket. Come along. Oh and by the way Mrs Channing, Mrs Francesca Channing that is, phoned. She's coming in this morning to see you. A very nice stepmother you've got. That's the third time, isn't it?'

Liam lay back on his pillows and the pain didn't matter any more, nor the prospect of having his dressings changed, nor even the desperate daily misery of having his private parts washed, none too gently, by an outspoken Australian junior nurse.

He felt suddenly filled with pure pleasure, and for two reasons; the first was the simple and indeed delightful prospect of seeing Francesca, spending time with her, studying her, talking to her. The second was a rather more complex one, of savouring something that had been conceived in the long hours of pain and misery and resentment at the person who had actually brought him to this, was ultimately responsible for his accident: his father. It was intriguing and brilliant and delightful, that concept: when it had first come to him, after she came to see him the day after his accident, as she had kissed him, and as he lay there, looking up at her, taking her in, the warmth, the closeness, the smell of her, when he had realised what he might be able to do, he had felt it physically, a slug of shock and delight, and he had lain for hours, distracted from his suffering, working it over in his brain, examining it for potential of which there was plenty and flaws of which there seemed few. It was a relationship between him and Francesca, the beautiful, desirable and not entirely happy Francesca –

and what it would mean to him in terms of revenge against his father. Delicious, glorious, and hitherto unimaginable revenge.

It really had had been a stroke of genius, Gray thought modestly, coming to this charity auction of Francesca's. It was a glorious opportunity to do a little background research. His slow progress on his story was beginning to drive him mad. Perhaps if he met Channing this evening socially, he might even agree to talk to him after all. Although probably with this latest débâcle, his son all over the papers after his undoubtedly self-inflicted car crash, he would probably be more wary than ever.

He had been put on a table with, inevitably, the PR for the charity, a reporter from one of the glossy free-sheets and a terrible woman called Daphne something who, she told him, was social editor on some magazine or other. He was greatly enjoying watching Tim Kennedy quite literally squeezing money out of people. Tim was clever, very clever. He had already charmed, cajoled, flattered, eased £20,000 out of the occupants of the ballroom of the Grosvenor House and was set to at least double that before he had finished. He was one of that small, elite breed, the charity auctioneer; capable of persuading people (as he had that evening) to pay up to £5,000 for a rather worn teddy bear (provided it had just a bit of a well-publicised past with an aristocratic owner), £6,000 for a very mediocre picture (provided it was signed by the celebrity who had painted it), £10,000 for a weekend for two at the Sandy Bay Hotel in Jamaica (providing the weekenders were photographed enjoying it within the pages of the *Tatler*). And now he was working them up, with an almost sexual fervour, for the *pièce de résistance* of the evening: a part share in a racehorse, by the name of Sweet 'n' Sour Charity.

He started gently. 'Come along now, ladies and gentlemen, can we have a start of – what – ten thousand pounds for this magnificent animal. A two-year-old, several wins on the flat this season, an entire horse – so potential for breeding. Ten thousand to start bidding for this superb creature. Correction, part of this superb creature. That part, indeed, for all I know. (Much laughter.) Yes, I'm told that that part is included in the price. That and a twenty-five per cent share in the rest of him. And yes, I'm told a share in the fruits. A twenty-five per cent share in the fruits. That is extraordinarily generous. So come along, ladies and gentleman, do I hear ten thousand? No? Nine? What was that, sir? Five? Oh, per-leese. That is a serious insult. To the horse, to me, to the charity. Come along now, please. Seven? Six then? Ladies and gentlemen, I'm going to lose my job: yes, Mr

Channing? Six? Excellent. Who is going to offer me more than six? Six thousand pounds for this gorgeous animal. Thank you, sir, six thousand five hundred, seven, thank you, madam ...'

Gray saw Francesca smile quickly, gratefully at Bard; he smiled back. He would probably bid twice more, then back out just in time. His sense of timing was very good; it was, after all, how he had made all his money.

The bidding rose slowly but steadily; at fifteen thousand, Gray looked amazed round the room. Here they were in the middle of what was still considered a fierce recession, and people were bidding fifteen thousand pounds for part of a horse ...

He had actually enjoyed the whole evening; there was nothing he liked more than observing such occasions and feeling no obligation to say a single word. He watched the women with particular fascination: sharply and clearly divided between the more earnest ladies, the chairs of various regional committees, county ladies in full-skirted dresses and pearls, and the London crowd, clearly friends of Francesca's and of the Chairperson of Heartbeat. They were subdivided again; into the sliver-thin, icy chic English and Americans, dressed mostly in silk suits or slithery shifts and rather ostentatious fake jewellery, and the foreigners, Japanese and Arabs who, he presumed, had brought most of the money. They, or their husbands, were certainly the most in evidence at the auction.

But it was Francesca Channing on whom he was concentrating, and with considerable fascination: she really was extraordinarily attractive, he thought, beautiful even, and immensely stylish. She was wearing a long narrow Grecian-style dress in white silk, one slim shoulder bare, with an elaborate pearl choker round her slender neck; her dark hair was drawn sleekly back into a knot on the nape of her neck, and her make-up, pale and dramatic, emphasised her large dark eyes, her fine straight nose. She was very thin – almost too thin, he thought – but strangely graceful; he watched as she moved between the tables, bending over one person here, taking a hand of another there, kissing, smiling, carefully attentive as each person required. She must be beyond price as a high-profile wife, he thought: Bard Channing would be mad not to value her. He hoped he did; and fell to thinking too that were she to feel lonely, unhappy, neglected – as these women so often were – she would not lack for consolation, admiration, most fervent attention, indeed was probably in receipt of much of it already.

She had greeted him charmingly, taken his hand, thanked him for coming, introduced him to several people, including Tim Kennedy, and of course to Bard. Who had been friendly enough, remembered him even, but by no stretch of the imagination forthcoming.

The toastmaster had announced that dinner was about to start and Francesca had excused herself and said she would see him later. And now here she was, smiling down at him, apologising for not having been near him all evening. She really was, he thought, extremely nice. Not just beautiful, not just rich, but nice. A most rare combination.

'Don't apologise,' he said, 'I've had a very good time. Met a lot of nice people.'

'It was a huge success, wasn't it?' said Francesca. 'Forty thousand, twenty for a bit of that horse. I can't believe it. Tim is a genius.'

'People will do anything to get in the papers,' sad Gray, grinning at her. 'I should know. But yes, Tim is. I've seen him in action before, actually. Marvellous. How long have you been working for Heartbeat?'

'Oh – a couple of years.'

'And you're the – chairman?' He knew she wasn't, but it was important to go through the charade, to appear to be working on his feature.

'Oh, goodness no, just a humble committee member. Miranda is the chairman.'

'Oh, yes. The sparkly blonde. Very charming. Do you enjoy doing this sort of thing?'

'Well – yes. Yes, of course I do.'

'You don't sound very sure.'

'Sorry. Bit tired.'

'I don't expect you've had an easy week,' he said, 'with your stepson in hospital.'

'Oh – you read about that. Bit tough, yes.'

He could imagine how and why tough: Bard's estrangement from Liam had been famous even before Kirsten had drawn further attention to it.

'But yes, I do enjoy the charity work. And it's nice to be involved in something as productive in cash terms as this auction. You feel you've really done something useful.'

The words 'for once' hung heavy in the air. Gray looked at her. 'You know, you don't strike me quite as a Lady who Lunches.'

'Don't I?' She looked at him warily, as if debating whether she should talk to him or not, then visibly relaxed, smiled. 'Maybe because I'm not. At heart. I was career girl once, you know. Before I married my husband.'

'And you miss it?'

'Yes I do,' she said suddenly. 'I miss it quite a lot. I was in advertising. Quite good at it, too.'

'I'm sure. You should go back to it.'

'Tell my husband that. No don't. Only joking.' She smiled, rather too brightly, looked round his table for a glass. Gray took his cue, found her one, filled it with wine.

'Thank you. So do you think you'll be able to do something for us? About this, I mean?'

'I'll try, very hard,' said Gray. 'I think possibly, yes.'

Actually he thought he could; they had a Financial Diary page on the *News*, and the money raised at the auction had been considerable. Especially for the horse. It was worth a small item.

'It would be marvellous,' she said, 'if you could. But I do realise it might not be easy.'

'I'm surprised you're talking to the press,' he said, 'after that little débâcle with your stepdaughter.'

Her face tautened. 'That was –' She hesitated. 'Unfortunate.'

'Very. But not entirely Kirsten's fault, I think.'

'No?' She sounded cynically doubtful.

'No. Really.'

'Do you know Kirsten?'

'Very slightly. But I do know the journalist in question. I would lay most of the blame at her door.'

'Well,' she said, 'I'd like to think you were right. But –'

'I know I'm right, Mrs Channing. Honestly.'

She looked up at him and smiled. 'You mustn't be influenced by Kirsten's appearance.'

'Oh, I'm not. Although she is very beautiful.'

'She is indeed. Too beautiful for her own good.'

'Now there is an interesting concept. Do you think people can really be too beautiful?'

'Yes, I do. I think it's a dangerous commodity.'

'Then you should take a look in the mirror, Mrs Channing. And see the danger there.'

'Well, thank you,' she said lightly.

'So tell me,' he said, 'does your husband not approve of working women?'

'Well, certainly not working wives. And most certainly not his wife.'

'How very old fashioned.'

'Yes. I mean – this is off the record, isn't it?' she said, suddenly anxious.

226

'Of course it is.'

'Because – well, I don't want to sound rude, but I have to be careful.'

'Naturally. And you don't sound rude. But I have to say that although I admire your husband greatly, I don't quite approve of his chauvinist attitude. I think you should fight that, Mrs Channing.'

'Oh – I've given up.' Her voice was heavy suddenly; heavy and sad. 'It's not something I even think about any more.'

'I don't believe that,' he said.

This was perfect: really very good. They were on deliciously intimate ground and she had had just too much to drink; he could work on this. He was about to refill her glass when she said, 'Oh God,' and a quartet of women bore down upon her.

'Francesca darling, we're off. Can't thank you enough, you're an angel. Wasn't Tim marvellous? Such a sweetie. Bye to Bard, lovely to see him. Bye, darling.'

They nodded coolly at Gray and moved off; Francesca met his eyes and grinned. 'Ladies who lunch,' she said briefly. 'You see what I mean.'

'Francesca.' It was Bard. 'I think we should go. It's late and I have work to do when I get back.'

'Yes, of course. Well, Mr Townsend, thank you again. And –'

And then it happened. An ice-blonde woman, her face skull-like in its boniness, came rushing over to Francesca.

'Francesca. I'm so glad I caught you. And you too, Bard. I wanted to speak to you about something.'

'Diana, perhaps not now –'

'Francesca, of course now. When better? Now listen –'

'I am listening, Diana. Could I just introduce –'

'I was sitting next to a charming colleague of yours at dinner, Bard. One of your directors. Well, ex-directors.'

'Oh really?'

'Yes, Brigadier Forsyth.'

'Ah yes. Yes, he resigned four years ago.'

'He was telling me that. About his gout.'

'How fascinating,' said Bard.

She ignored this. 'And I was telling him about my plans for later in the year, which include a charity golf tournament. Such a good idea, don't you think? And of course he was most interested in that, used to play a lot, and he mentioned your having bought a golf course for development, well, something like that, a few years ago. And I thought well, that's it.'

227

She looked at Bard expectantly; his face was blank, completely blank, oddly still. On the side of his forehead, Gray noticed, a vein throbbed.

'What is "it", Diana?' he said. His tone was extremely mild.

'Well, obviously, that we could have it there. The tournament, I mean. The venue is so important, and of course most places would charge a lot of money and I imagine you would let us have it for nothing or certainly at cost, and –'

'Diana,' said Bard, 'I do assure you there are two misconceptions here. One, I have no golf complex. As such. Two, if I did, I would have no control over whether or not it could be used for an entire weekend free.'

'Oh. Oh I see. Not even for charity?'

'Not even for charity. I really think you people make too many assumptions.'

'Oh. Oh I see.' She was clearly totally nonplussed. Gray could see it didn't happen very often. 'Well, we shall have to find some other source of help. Another venue.'

'I'm afraid so. Goodnight, Diana. Mr Townsend.'

Gray smiled, shook his hand and Francesca's and watched them leave; then he looked back for Diana. She was, as he had known she would be, talking earnestly to a rather stiff-backed red-faced gentleman and gesticulating across the room to where Bard had been. He waited until she had left him, and then moved across to him himself.

'Brigadier Forsyth?'

'Yes.'

'Brigadier Forsyth, my name is Graydon Townsend. Please forgive me for approaching you, but I'm a financial journalist, on the *News on Sunday*, and I believe you once worked with Bard Channing?'

'Indeed I did,' said the Brigadier. 'Had to come to a halt though, not well, you see. Only non-executive of course, but still I enjoyed it. Fascinating business that.'

'Indeed,' said Gray. 'Now, I'm preparing a piece on the property scene, and I wondered if I might phone you one day next week? Just for background information, you understand.'

'Well, you can,' said the Brigadier doubtfully,' but I don't know how much I'll be able to help you. I had to resign that one, oh – four years ago now.'

'Well, that's exactly the period I'm interested in,' said Gray, 'the end of the big boom. I'd love your overview on that.'

Brigadier Forsyth was clearly delighted at the prospect of giving his overview on anything. His life was probably a desert of tedium, thought Gray. 'Well, of course you're very welcome to it. Very. I suppose I did get a pretty clear view of it. Look, here's my card, ring on Tuesday, that's the best day.'

'Thank you very much,' said Gray. 'It's been a nice evening, hasn't it?'

'Very nice. Well, I'll look forward to your call. Goodnight, Mr Townsend.'

Gray took a cab home, and had a very large whisky to help him sleep; he found the large empty bed disturbing. But the whisky didn't help, and he lay awake for hours; thinking about Briony, wondering how he was ever going to recover from the parting; but thinking also about the evening, and about Bard Channing and the expression on his face when he had been denying the existence of his golf complex; and perhaps most interesting of all, the expression on Francesca's lovely face too – sharp, wary, as she looked at him, and then carefully, almost instantly blank.

There was no doubt about it, Gray thought, as he fell finally asleep as the birds on Clapham Common announced the arrival of dawn; Bard had been lying. About something which didn't seem remotely important, but which clearly actually was. Worth investigating. Without a doubt.

'Bastard,' said Kirsten, 'bloody poncy bastard. What a load of total shit –'

'Kirsten?'

She jumped, turned round; she'd been standing at the sink, viciously rinsing out glasses. It was better, anything was better, than watching Toby making a total fool of himself with that creature. It had been all right till then, her party; really quite a good one. A bit grown up of course, but that was what came of having a boyfriend who was twenty-six. With a lot of friends who were also twenty-six. Or even older. On the other hand, he'd seen to the wine, which was not half bad, and insisted she had proper food, not just hacked-up French bread, and so she'd got the Thai place down the road to bring a whole lot in, she certainly wasn't going to do a lot of cooking and that was really nice. Everyone was drunk, but not disgustingly so, and a few people were smoking dope, but Toby who was famously anti-drugs in her circle had made her tell everyone not to bring anything else, and she didn't think they had. If they had, well, it wasn't her fault. He was a bit of a pain, old Tobes, but he was nice. And a good laugh, most of the time. And very good looking; she'd watched him chatting up two of her girlfriends who obviously thought he was gorgeous, making complete idiots of themselves actually, and felt a pang of proprietory pleasure.

Everyone had seemed very happy, in spite of being grown up, about a third of them dancing, the others sitting and chatting. It struck her suddenly that the music (Happy House mostly) was a bit loud for chatting, and she'd just been thinking maybe she should turn it down a bit, and then remembered the old joke about if the music was too loud, you were too old, and had grinned to herself, decided to turn it up.

And then Victoria had arrived, Victoria looking very sweet, in a black silk shift over a white T-shirt, clutching a couple of bottles of wine and some flowers, followed by her new boyfriend, John, an earnest redhead studying anthropology, and another couple. Neither of whom Kirsten had liked the look of at all. The man was pallid, almost pasty, wearing a black leather jacket and leather trousers – God, he must be frying in those, thought Kirsten – with fair hair pulled back in a ponytail and rather blank, very light blue eyes, and the girl was black, Jamaican, very tall, taller than she was even – that always annoyed her for a start – with close-cropped white-bleached hair, and as near naked as it was possible to be in clothes. She was wearing red silk shorts that just covered her buttocks and a boned black top which hung perilously off the edge of her nipples and ended about three inches above her navel, and very high platform red sandals. She looked, in Kirsten's opinion, perfectly ridiculous and as she came in, every man in the room stopped what he was doing or saying and stared at her.

'Hi Kirsten,' said Victoria rather breathlessly, depositing the flowers in her arms, and the bottles on the table. 'I took you at your word and brought a couple of friends. This is Martin, who's at college with John, and this is Tiffany' – indicating the black girl, who nodded at Kirsten rather briefly, and then looked pointedly round the room clearly casing it for talent.

Tiffany, thought Kirsten, nodding at them both, forcing a smile, how corny, how predictable. 'Do get yourselves drinks,' she said, taking the flowers. 'I'll try and find something to put those in, Tory. You OK?'

'Yes thanks.' She followed Kirsten out to the kitchen. 'Sorry about those two,' she said. 'We met them in the pub this afternoon. John seems to think Martin is wonderful. He's in the music business.'

'Yes, well, all the men in that room certainly think Tiffany is wonderful,' said Kirsten coolly.

'She's all right,' said Victoria staunchly, 'honestly. She works at some rape crisis centre.'

'Yeah? I should think she'd cause a few rape crises herself. Hasn't she heard of clothes?'

'Oh Kirsten don't be cross. I'm sorry.' Tory's face became anxious, 'I'm really sorry. Anyway, you're not wearing that much yourself.' This was true; Kirsten had spent much of the afternoon selecting and rejecting clothes and finally settled on a red shift, not a lot longer than Tiffany's shorts and very little higher cut than her bodice. Nevertheless there was a huge difference and she knew it and Tory knew it; her dress had class and style, and was designed to charm and flatter, not provoke. But she managed to smile and say 'sorry' and take Victoria back into the room, where Tiffany had already been dancing with Martin, a glass of red wine in one red-taloned hand, a cigarette in the other.

'Tory!' It was Toby. 'Nice to see you. And your friends.' His dark eyes roamed over Tiffany briefly, then came back to Tory. 'You're looking lovely. Easily outshining your big sis tonight, I'd say.'

'Oh Toby, don't be silly!' said Victoria, blushing; Toby always flirted with her and flattered her, he had told Kirsten she needed it. Normally she liked to hear it, thought it sweet, but tonight she felt a sudden stab of irritation.

'Toby, we're running out of beer. Want to go and get some?'

'Not specially. But I will. Mr Nice Guy, that's me.'

Tiffany walked past him, looked at him rather pointedly, and then grinned. 'Is that right?' Her voice was deep, almost hoarse, with a South London accent; sex on the vocals, thought Kirsten irritably.

'Yes it is,' said Toby lightly. 'Coming with me then, Kirsten?'

'No, I'd better stay.'

'Where are you going?' said Tiffany.

'Oh – nearest off-licence.'

'Get me some cigars, would you?' she said. 'Just ten. Here's some dough.'

'Oh that's all right,' He waved it away. 'Yeah, sure. See you.'

'Your boyfriend?' said Tiffany to Kirsten.

'Yes, my boyfriend,' said Kirsten.

'Uh-huh,' said Tiffany, and moved away.

And when Toby came back, he gave Tiffany the cigars, and Kirsten watched her offer him one and he refused, and then she said something and he laughed and said something back, and she went to fetch herself another drink and when she came back he was dancing with her: really dancing, her arms round his neck loosely (she was as

231

tall as him), her large black eyes fixed on his mouth, her body moving sweetly liquid in perfect rhythm with his. She leant forward and whispered something in his ear and he put back his head and roared with laughter; Kirsten, angry suddenly, turned away. He must have seen her, seen the gesture, for he left the floor at the end of the track and came over to her.

'You OK?'

'Yes, of course.'

'You look a bit – off.'

'I'm fine,' said Kirsten irritably. God, what was the matter with her, why did she have to be so fucking jealous and insecure? She wasn't even in love with Toby, for Christ's sake.

'Good.'

'What did she say to you then? That made you laugh?'

'Oh, she said I danced like a black man.'

'Oh, I see.'

'Big compliment, you know.'

'Yes,' said Kirsten, 'I do know.'

'You sure you're all right?'

'Yes I'm perfectly sure.'

And then he said, 'Oh for Christ's sake, Kirsten,' and went back to the room where the dancing was, and in a very short time was dancing with Tiffany again. And that was when Kirsten went into the kitchen. And heard someone saying her name. And realised it was Gray Townsend and that she had never been so pleased to see anyone in her life.

'Gray! Hi. Nice surprise. I didn't think you were coming. How are you?'

'Fine. I wasn't coming, like I said. Then I thought I was being a bit of a wimp. So I did. But I'm on my own ...'

'That's OK,' said Kirsten. She looked at him, thinking it was actually perfectly OK. He was getting on a bit, must be mid-thirties at least, but he was very good looking with his streaky brown, floppy hair and his grey eyes, and he looked well, as if he cared for himself, tanned and fit looking; and he was wearing a really nice linen shirt and some extremely battered 501s. She didn't usually like old guys in jeans, but he did have a nice body, and they were exactly the right size, not tight, not straining over a middle-aged arse; it was quite sweet really, he'd obviously thought he ought to dress young and *very* casual, and he'd slightly overdone it, but still ...

'Let me get you a drink,' she said.

'Thanks. This is for you.' He gave her a bottle of champagne. 'Not

232

for now, probably. Maybe tomorrow. Nothing like champagne for hangovers.'

'Gray. How lovely. Veuve Clicquot. My goodness. Come on in and meet some people.'

'I really almost didn't come,' he said, taking the glass of wine she gave him. 'Just settling down to a lonely takeaway, I was, in front of the movie channel. Then I thought I was being a bit chicken, and took myself by surprise.'

'Did you and your girlfriend – well – is it permanent?'

'I'm not sure,' said Gray with a sigh. 'I think so.'

'Sorry. You obviously don't want to talk about it.'

'Not now, certainly.'

'Well, anyway, I'm sorry.'

'Thank you.'

'And I hope we can improve on the movie channel. What was on?'

'*When Harry Met Sally.*'

'Oh yes. I think we can. Well, except for that bit –'

'Good. Now where is your nice boyfriend?'

'There,' said Kirsten briefly, indicating Toby. He was now dancing slightly more energetically with Tiffany, and had one of her cigars in his mouth. He was fiercely anti-smoking; he never let Kirsten have a single cigarette. She wanted to go and ram the cigar deeply down his throat.

'Mmm. Who's his friend? She must be feeling very warm.'

'She's a friend of Tory's,' said Kirsten, laughing in spite of herself. 'My sister.'

'And which is your sister?'

'There. In the black and white.'

'Oh yes. Very sweet. Oh dear, I feel very old suddenly. Maybe I should have stayed with Meg Ryan.'

'No you shouldn't,' said Kirsten, putting his glass down, pulling him gently onto the dance floor. 'You're going to have a really nice time, I promise.'

Francesca was re-reading a story in the *Sunday Times* financial section headed 'Bard Channing in crisis talks with bankers' over a very strong cup of coffee. She was re-reading it because she had read it once and then asked Bard about it, as it seemed to imply there was some kind of problem with the Channing Corporation, and he had started shouting and saying there was absolutely no problem, it was just that when he had gone to Stockholm for a perfectly standard meeting with the bank to discuss the ongoing situation, a journalist had heard about it and the entire British press had now got the wrong end of the stick and smelt trouble where there was none, adding that they all ought to be put up against a wall and shot. 'There is no problem,' he had said, 'absolutely none. I've just had some crowd of accountants in who could bear witness to the fact, no-one wants to report on that though, do they? There is no crisis to have talks about, Francesca, and I would be grateful if you wouldn't join the press in inventing one.'

Francesca said she was glad there was no crisis, and (thanking whatever powers thanks were due to, that the article was not in the *News on Sunday* and nothing to do with Gray Townsend) thought she should read the article carefully anyway. It did seem (on second reading) to be about very little, although there was a quote from Pete Barbour about restructuring the loan which seemed slightly more serious and not what Bard had said; she wished now she hadn't said anything to Bard, since it had clearly put him in a bad temper and what she really wanted to know were his plans for the afternoon. He had said at breakfast he had to go into the office: if he did she had thought she might go and see Liam. He was having such an awful time and had told her her visits were the only thing in the world keeping him sane; it was nice to be doing something useful. She had also intended to tell Bard she had been to visit Liam a couple more times, just so that it was all public and above board. Not that she was doing anything wrong, obviously, but she would just prefer Bard to know. But this was clearly not the time, and it didn't look as if she was going to find out what Bard was doing either. She sighed and looked out of the window: Jack was working on his tunnel, his small bottom stuck in the air like Pooh in the rabbit hole.

She went out into the garden to join him. 'How's it going?' she said. 'Can I help?'

Funny thing, love, thought Rachel, watching Mary as she buttoned up her cardigan with infinite slowness. It took you by surprise, showed you things about yourself you'd never have suspected, turned your life over, saw you doing all kinds of things you'd never have thought of.

She who was so impatient, so worldly, so urban a creature, had spent over a week now with Mary, this sweet, loving, grown-up child, three days in hospital and the rest at the convent, caring for her, comforting her, watching videos with her (mostly comedies, but a few Hollywood musicals, most notably *The Wizard of Oz*, four times over now), reading to her (Mary liked poetry best), talking to the others; had become caught up in the routine, the careful order of life at the

Help House, had helped with the laundry even (and she hated ironing above all things), changed wet beds, sorted out socks, had helped in the garden too, picked strawberries, cut lettuces, hoed weeds, and worked in the kitchen, although the food was scarcely her style, good, wholesome but very very plain, because the residents liked it that way. She had left home in such a hurry she hadn't packed properly, left behind the most basic things; the nuns had lent her some under-clothes, strange baggy pants, a voluminous nightdress and a pair of brown leather sandals, and after the first day or so she had simply stopped minding. The only thing that really bothered her was that she had left her absurdly expensive and complex skincare stuff behind, her moisturisers and skin foods and revitalisers and oils; she could feel the wrinkles furrowing more deeply into her face each day. She had mentioned it, laughing at her own foolishness, to Reverend Mother who had left a jar of Pond's Cold Cream in her room and a little note saying 'I find this excellent,' and she had expressed great gratitude and pretended to use it, but did not, preferring to wait until she got home. If it had not been for the wrinkles and a growing worry about Francesca she would have stayed for another week, but she had decided that it was time she left.

'Besides,' she said to Reverend Mother, who had come to her room to try and persuade her to stay, 'there is a lot to talk to Bard Channing about. The planning permission still seems a problem, we have to sort out an architect pretty quickly, and we aren't yet formally established as a charity. I shall still be very much part of you.'

'You should come and live here,' said Reverend Mother, looking at her and smiling. 'It suits you. You look a different woman from the one who got off the train. You've even put on a little weight.'

'I feel different,' said Rachel, trying to accept this last comment as the compliment it was meant to be, 'but I really don't think that would work, Mother. And besides, I'm much more use to you up in London.'

'I suppose so. And Mary is certainly perfectly all right now. She won't mind you going at all.'

'No,' said Rachel. It was at once a source of pleasure and pain to her that Mary accepted her comings and goings with a calm, happy detachment; she was briefly sad when the car disappeared down the lane and then at once distracted by something as simple as laying the table for tea or collecting eggs with Richard.

'And your daughter: does she know you're here?'

'No,' said Rachel quickly. 'No, she doesn't. She thinks I'm staying with a friend.'

'Supposing she rings the friend?'

'She won't. She doesn't have a number.'

'Rachel!' Reverend Mother looked at her, shaking her head gently. 'This can't go on, you have to tell her. What are you so afraid of, will she really mind so much?'

'Yes, I'm afraid she will,' said Rachel slowly. 'She'll find it very hard. She's such a truthful person.'

'Then you should tell her. Before she finds out for herself.'

'She won't. How could she?'

'Very easily, I would have thought. And especially now. She, is after all, married to Mr Channing. I can see it will be a shock, Rachel, but it will be a worse one if she is not told carefully. I think you have to do it.'

'Yes all right,' said Rachel with a sigh, 'I promise I will. Once we've got the planning permision and it's all up and running. But until then – well, I don't want a lot of emotion and drama. Anyway, I'll phone her, I was thinking I must, and tell her I'm coming back, make sure she's all right. Her life isn't easy.'

'No I'm sure,' said Reverend Mother. 'Come and use my phone, Rachel, if you like.'

'Thank you, Mother.'

Reverend Mother had a copy of the *Sunday Times* on her desk. Rachel started leafing through it idly while she settled at the phone, and found herself staring at an article on the front of the financial section headed 'Bard Channing in talks with bankers'.

'Oh my God,' she said aloud, 'dear God,' and then said 'Sorry' aloud, just in case the Almighty might happen to be listening, fearing such words uttered in the study's pure and pious air might be deemed blasphemous. If the press had got hold of this story, it was serious. Not just because she knew that the *Sunday Times* at least wouldn't publish it unless there was some real substance behind it, but also because the property business was, and especially at the moment, a game of poker. It was fine while everyone thought you had a handful of aces; you could stay in the game and if you were clever enough – and lucky enough, there was a lot of that – you could go on to win. But if just one other player suspected you had a duff hand, and wanted to make you declare it, you were done for. Bard seemed to be running out of aces.

But what the press had got hold of was actually a rather upbeat version of the story. Thanks no doubt in part to Sam Illingworth. God, that girl was worth her weight in five-pound notes. Channing had gone to Stockholm, but only to restructure the loan and to firm

236

up on a tenancy offer for Coronet Wharf, and he was also looking at a new development in Leeds; meanwhile the share price which had been dipping slightly had not only steadied but rallied.

' "Everything is fine," Peter Barbour, Channings' Finance Director, was quoted to have said that morning, "we simply wanted to restructure the deal. We have several new projects in the pipeline and several parties extremely interested in leasing Coronet Wharf, and expect to announce a deal very shortly." '

'Amen,' said Rachel fervently, grateful at least in a small part on her own account, as well as Bard's and Francesca's; she dialled the St John's Wood number.

The phone rang for a long time; finally Francesca's voice answered.

'Francesca? Darling, it's Mummy. I've just seen the story in the *Times*. I'm so glad it seems to be all right.'

'I really don't know,' Francesca sounded very cold and distant. 'I would be the last to be told if it was or not.'

'Well, hasn't Bard talked to you about it?'

'No of course not.'

'Is this story in all the papers?'

'I'm afraid I couldn't say.'

Why was she being so unfriendly? It couldn't be just because Rachel had failed her the other day when she had wanted to talk. She felt a sudden pang of panic. Something had happened.

'I see. Well, I'm coming back to London now. Joan has been greatly cheered by my visit, I can't think why, and –'

'Mummy, can we stop this silly game? I know you haven't been with Joan Duncan, I rang her. And I saw you in your taxi that morning going in the opposite direction after I'd dropped you at Euston. If you've got a new boyfriend or something I can't think why you couldn't tell me about it. He must be very unsuitable. Anyway, I've got to go now, I'm busy. Goodbye.'

'Oh dear,' said Rachel, looking at the receiver as Francesca rang off. 'Oh dear, Rachel, now what have you done?'

Gray woke up at midday, feeling very unwell indeed, with a headache that seemed to come from the depths of his body, and a strong sensation of nausea, wondering where he was. He opened his eyes cautiously; found himself gazing into a tangled mane of red-gold curls, found his arm resting across a narrow back, his hand curled tenderly round a full, firm breast. And remembered. Remembered all of it.

He moved gently, pulling away from her; she shifted slightly, smiled in her sleep. He looked at her for a while, exploring his feelings, then turned onto his back. The pain in his head moved, re-settled; the nausea churned, then mercifully settled too. It was bad, but at least he knew he wasn't going to throw up. Everything hurt; even his toes. Even his cock. Yes, certainly his cock, he thought, concentrating on it briefly. Well, not exactly sore, but weary, old. He felt like a very old man altogether. Which was no doubt how Kirsten saw him.

The worst thing of all was knowing he'd made a complete fool of himself. First he had been the object of some curiosity by being at the party at all, a good ten years older than anyone else; then he'd got extremely drunk and allowed himself to smoke that bloody grass – or rather a spliff, as they called it these days – and danced uninhibitedly and rather badly with Kirsten, and then he'd started pouring out his troubles to her, telling her how much he loved Briony and how he missed her, and then she'd had a fight with her boyfriend, and ordered him to get out with the black girl (who had started laughing at her and telling her to chill out, which hadn't made matters any better), and then he had joined in and taken Toby forcibly by the shoulders and pushed him out of the door. He hadn't behaved in so adolescent a manner since – well, since he'd been an adolescent.

And then, when everyone else had rather swiftly departed, Victoria in tears, he had sat down and tried to comfort Kirsten and, without having much of an idea how, had found himself in bed with her. And it had been fantastic. Bloody fantastic. She had taken possession of him, used him and his body through a long, long night, and he had loved every fucking minute of it. Looking back, every minute did seem to have been spent fucking. Obviously it could not really have been, but a hell of a lot of them were. The energy, the imagination, the lack of inhibition Kirsten put into her activities in bed were astonishing. Her body seemed inexhaustible, fathomless; he seemed to grow literally into it, into its greed, its powerful, grasping depths. Not once but twice he had thought himself entirely spent; twice she began to work on him, with her mouth, her hands, her legs, her breasts, urging him, teasing him, drawing him on. She talked to him, talked wonderfully, savagely sexy, savoured him, enjoyed him with a raw, seductive lack of inhibition; he felt himself bewitched, enthralled. Every so often, and despite himself, Gray thought of Briony, of her sweet, tender lovemaking, of the soft, yielding opening to him, the fluid movings of her body, the gentle lapping of her orgasm surrounding his, and even as he mourned her he marvelled that he could have found it enough.

'You make love like a man,' he had said to Kirsten, lying exhausted finally beside her, winding the long lion's mane of her hair round his fingers, smiling into the sea-green depths of her eyes, and 'Yes,' she said, just slightly complacent, 'Yes, I believe I do.'

'You're lovely,' he said, kissing her neck, her breasts (thinking even in his pleasure that she meant she had been told so before, setting the thought determinedly aside). 'Quite extraordinary.'

'Not really,' she said drowsily now, 'just tall.'

'What do you mean?'

'I mean just that, because I'm so tall, and kind of noticeable, people think I'm more different than I am. Imagine I'm six inches shorter and see if you can think of anything else really different about me.'

'You're more beautiful than most girls.'

'That's not different though. And anyway, there are lots more beautiful than me. Anyway, I'm not. I can look really dire.'

'I'll take that on trust,' he said, 'but I find it hard to believe.'

'That was great,' she said, looking at him consideringly. 'Really great. I enjoyed it.'

'Good,' he said. He was afraid she didn't really mean it.

She had kissed him briefly, and turned away and fallen asleep; it was almost five. He had slept too, curled round her, echoing her long body, almost as long as his, thinking how different it was from encircling Briony's small frame.

And as he lay, enduring his physical misery, he kept returning to Briony, to thoughts of Briony, and to the sort of man who could turn from a beloved partner of four years and within a week of her leaving his life could find himself not just enjoying another woman physically, but disturbed, emotionally troubled by her; and thinking how shallow, faithless, worthless such a man must be. And unable to endure those particular thoughts, he got up, the better to leave them behind him, found a towel, showered, dressed – God, how he hated not having clean clothes – and made Kirsten a cup of tea, laid it by her bed, kissed her tumbled hair slightly awkwardly and went back into the kitchen. It was a horror movie: heaped up, overflowing ashtrays, dirty glasses with dregs of wine and fag ends in them, plates piled hastily on every surface including the floor and the windowsill, dirty knives and forks parked in the kind of places that make sense to people at parties, in empty saucepans and beer mugs, jugs, plant pots, on magazines, even a few in the slots of the toaster. The living room was similarly accessorised (knives and forks in vases, plates parked unsteadily on the books in the bookshelf), with cushions stripped off sofas and piled on the floor, presumably to provide more sitting space, various clothes that people had left behind, including inexplicably a pair of brand new men's shoes, and for some reason which had no doubt seemed good at the time, one of the curtains was caught up in a huge knot. There were a couple of burns on the arm of a sofa, and a very nasty looking bit of spillage on the beige carpet, but it could have been much worse.

He had started tidying up, because he felt he had no option, could not leave it, but she suddenly appeared in the doorway, stark naked, mug of tea in hand, and told him to stop.

'Don't spoil some very good memories. I would truly, hand on heart, rather do it slowly, on my own, when I'm feeling better. Tory said she'd come and help, not that I feel too fond of her, bringing that slag round, but please, Gray, don't you do it.'

'Well,' he said, fairly easily persuaded, for his queasiness had been increasing with his task, 'well, if you're sure.'

'I'm sure. Come and talk to me. I'm going back to bed.'

'OK. As long as it's only talk. I don't think I could manage any more.'

'You disappoint me,' she had said, smiling, pushing back her hair. He followed her into the bedroom, aroused again to his own surprise by the sight of her high, taut buttocks, her long, long thighs, and the fall of her breasts as she got into bed, pulled the quilt up and lay back on the pile of pillows.

'You're lovely,' he said again.

'Thank you. And thanks for the tea. Gray —'

'Yes?'

'Gray, it was lovely. Really lovely. I mean it. But I think — well, I think that should be that, don't you? I mean we don't want to start thinking it's serious, or that we're in love or anything, do we?'

'No,' he said, carefully careless, 'no of course not. And anyway, you don't believe in it, do you? In love?'

'How do you know that?' she said, staring at him.

'You told me so. The first time we met.'

'I did?'

'Yes.'

'Oh. Well, I don't, no, it's true. Oh God —' And she began to cry.

'Hey now,' he said, moving nearer to her, pushing her hair back from her face, 'don't, don't, what's this about?'

'I'm such a cow. Such a bitch. I just go crashing through life, doing terrible things to people, taking what I want, I'm so selfish, so bloody immature —'

This last was so patently true that he had to smile. 'Well, I don't quite agree with all of that,' he said.

240

'Don't you?'

'No. Not at all. Not one bit. I think you're wonderful. Warts and all.'

'I haven't got any warts, have I?' she said, half-anxious.

'Of course you haven't. Old saying.'

'So you don't think I'm awful?'

'No,' he said tenderly, passing her a handkerchief, 'I don't think you're awful at all. I hope you don't think I am either.'

'Of course I don't. Why should I?'

'Well – one minute I'm crying on your shoulder about my girlfriend and how I miss her, and the next I'm in bed with you. Not very gentlemanly behaviour.'

'You seem quite gentlemanly to me,' she said, unexpectedly. 'I like it. I really do like it. And you. But now you must go. Please, Gray. Thank you for everything, but please go.'

And that, it seemed, was that: dismissal. No messing: just dismissal. He had served her (probably, in spite of what she had said, not very well) and distracted both of them from their individual miseries, and now he was to go.

'Fine,' was all he said, and kissed her briefly on the mouth. It stirred memories of the first time he had kissed her, in the Harbour Club the day after the story broke in the *Graphic*, strong sensual memories; he would have given a great deal to be back there, at that point in time again.

Chapter Twelve

'Got some change, lady?'

'No,' said Kirsten briskly, looking at the huddled figure in the sleeping bag with distaste, 'and please get off my doorstep at once, or I shall call the police and —'

'Kirsten, you have a heart of stone.'

'Barnaby! Barnaby, you slime bag. God, you almost gave me a heart attack. What on earth are you doing here, and why didn't you tell anyone you were back? Come on inside, oh God, it's good to see you —'

She took his hand, pulled him out of the sleeping bag and into the flat, hugging him, kissing him. She adored her brother. Even though he was so undoubtedly the favourite. Of both her parents. Even though he was never there when you needed him. Even though he got away with murder, over and over again ...

'Right, now,' she said, pushing him down into a chair in the kitchen, 'beer?'

He nodded, grinning at her. 'Several. Please.'

'It's so good to see you. But you look awfully thin —'

'I am awfully thin. That's India for you. Talk about Delhi Belly —'

'I didn't even know you were going to India.'

'Nor did I till a month ago. It seemed like a good idea. Now not so good —'

'Do you feel OK?'

'Just about. Bloody tired. Long flight.'

'Why didn't you let me meet you?'

'I couldn't get hold of you. Or Tory. Or even Horton.'

'Francesca?'

'Out. When I phoned anyway. And Sandie said she didn't know how long she'd be.'

'I bet Sandie was glad you were back.'

'Yeah, she just about had an orgasm,' said Barnaby modestly. 'Said she'd drive down and meet me herself, but Francesca had left the kids with her. In the end I got the Tube.'

'Oh poor Barnaby. What a welcome. But why are you so suddenly home? I thought you were staying at least another month.'

'I just felt so lousy I had to get back. I don't just have gut-rot, Kirsten, I don't have any guts left. They've gone right down the pan - literally.'

'Yes all right,' said Kirsten hastily, 'spare me the details. Do you think you should see the doctor?'

'Nah. I'll be OK. I'd like a meal though. Got anything in the house?'

'No I haven't. I'll go down to the Europa. What'd you like?'

'Something totally bland. Like chicken soup and – yeah, really gooey white bread. The sort that bungs you right up, you know?'

'Yes Barnaby, I know. I'd forgotten how disgusting you were.'

She sat watching him eat it, studying his gaunt sunburnt face, his tangled long blond hair, his bony wrists and thin arms.

'Barnaby, you look as if you've got – well, are you all right?'

He laughed. 'Yeah, I swear. Haven't got anything really nasty. You should have seen the other fellows.'

'What other fellows?'

'Oh, the ones I came back with. That was good, Kirsten. Really good. Thanks a lot. How's things?'

'Oh – all right. Nothing you want to hear about,' said Kirsten. 'Not yet anyway.'

'How's Tory?'

'She's fine. Terribly busy, of course –'

'Of course.'

'And in love with some ghastly person. Spends most of her time at his place.'

'What about you? You in love?'

'No of course not. Not love. You know I don't believe in it.'

'Anyone around even, then?'

'I – well I –'

'Come on, Kirsten, tell me. What's going on in your life?'

'I really don't want to talk about it.'

Not quite true; she did. She wanted to very much, but not with Barnaby. However much she loved him. He was hardly going to understand that once again she had fouled up everything, put a perfectly good fun relationship in jeopardy by going to bed with someone else in a fit of pique, someone else she really liked and moreover to whom she owed a lot, someone she had no business using in such a way, someone who really didn't deserve to be hurt ...

Barnaby shrugged. 'OK. Later maybe.'

'Maybe.'

The phone rang; please, please don't let that be Gray, she thought, please don't make me have to handle that now.

It wasn't Gray, it was Toby.

'I just called to let you know I'd been thinking about you,' he said.

'Nice for you,' said Kirsten carefully.

'Not very. I really didn't like what you did on Saturday, Kirsten. I thought it sucked.'

'Oh really? Well, I'm very glad you shared that with me, Toby. I didn't like what you were doing too much either.'

'Oh for fuck's sake. I was only dancing with the bloody girl.'

'Funny sort of dancing, Tobes. Your hands in her knickers, your tongue down her throat ...'

'Oh shut up,' he said, 'you sound like some pathetic jealous schoolgirl. Anyway, I really think we've reached the end of the road, don't you? Well, speaking for myself I have. I feel pretty sorry for that poor geezer. No doubt he's been totally taken in by you, thinks you're no end of a nice girl. Well, he'll find out, no doubt. Poor old guy. How old is he, Kirsten? Thirty-five, forty? Your father complex is really beginning to show. Does he know about your father complex yet? I suppose if he's got any brains at all he'll be able to work it out. Cheers, Kirsten. I won't say see you around because I'd rather not.'

Kirsten slammed the phone down and went very quickly over to the fridge, got out a bottle of wine and started stabbing rather blindly at it with the corkscrew.

'Hey, let me do that,' said Barnaby. 'What's wrong?'

'Nothing. Nothing at all.'

'Who was that? Sounded like Toby to me.'

'It was,' said Kirsten.

'You still seeing him then? I'm amazed.'

'Not any more,' said Kirsten, trying to smile.

He came over, handed her a glass of wine, gave her a hug. 'It's really nice to see you,' he said, and grinned at her. Kirsten hugged him back and thought if she did love anyone on earth it was probably Barnaby. She poured him another beer, sat down and looked at him.

'What are you going to do next?' she said.

'Oh – I don't know. Going to uni again in October. Till then bum around. I'll have to get some money pretty quick. I'm broke. Owe one of the lads a few hundred. You got any?'

'You have to be kidding. And if you're thinking of asking Dad, don't be too hopeful. He's off family life, he's not speaking to me, he's in a permanently foul mood, Tory says, and he seems to be away most of the time. Oh and the baby's ill, got something wrong with her heart.'

'Really? That's bad. How's Francesca coping?'

'I really wouldn't know,' said Kirsten coldly. 'We're not exactly bosom friends. Especially since –'

'Especially since what?'

'Oh – I blabbed to some ghastly woman journalist one night when I was drunk. And she published it all in letters a foot high in some Sunday rag. Not good.'

'Not good. Kirsten, you are an airhead sometimes.'

'Thanks. Oh, and Liam's in hospital. Had a car crash, drunk driving.'

'Blimey. What a family. How's Granny Jess?'

'She's good. She's been great to me. Stuck up for me to Dad and everything.'

'Dear old Gran. Now I might go and see her tomorrow. She'll tide me over financially, won't she?'

'I hope that's not the only reason you're going to see her,' said Kirsten severely.

'Listen to you!' said Barnaby. 'You always did have a pi streak. How's Mum?'

'She's been bad,' said Kirsten briefly. 'In – in the clinic again. But all right at the moment. She'll be so pleased you're back.'

'Yeah, I'll go and see her too. In a day or two. God, I feel better suddenly. Tell you what, Kirsten, I'll have a couple of hours' kip and then let's say we go out. I'd really like that. To a club or something?'

'Oh I don't know,' said Kirsten. 'I don't feel like going out. And I've got a big day tomorrow at my new job, I can't afford a hang-over –'

'Kirs-ten!' said Barnaby. 'What's with this stuff? Turning into Daddy's good little girl, are you? He won't mind if you're late, surely.'

'I'm not working for Dad any more,' said Kirsten. 'I got fired.'

'You what! Did he catch you with your fingers in the till or something?'

'No of course not. It was the stuff in the paper. He's not speaking to me at all.'

'Well,' said Barnaby, throwing himself back on the sofa, 'I never thought to hear you refusing to go out because you had to get up in the morning. What happened to you, Kirsten? Did you reach middle age or something while I was away? I hope it's not catching.'

'Oh shut up,' said Kirsten. She sat and looked at him; behind the teasing there was a serious note. It was true; she had changed, had begun to be less carefree. She thought of the Kirsten of even a year ago, still at university, who would stay up all night, drinking, smoking (anything), dancing. She looked at a picture of herself stuck on the fridge; she was at a ball at Bristol, head thrown back, laughing, her hair flying round her like a halo, the bodice of her ball dress hanging perilously on the edge of her nipples; what had happened to her in just a year? What was she doing, getting even half involved with some guy twice her age, what was she missing out on, throwing away? It was scary. She looked at Barnaby and said, 'OK. You're on. Where d'you want to go? The Gardening Club? You go and get some kip and I'll wake you at one, OK?'

'That's my girl,' said Barnaby.

The trip to the Gardening Club was not actually a good idea. Kirsten hadn't enjoyed it at all, had felt irritatingly distanced from it, the noise, the heat, the darkness in the three underground rooms, even of the Happy House music; maybe, she kept telling herself, she was just out of sorts, tired. Barnaby was all right at first, found a couple of friends, danced a bit, smoked a bit, and then suddenly appeared in front of her looking terrible. 'I've got to get home,' he said, 'can you get a cab?'

Kirsten got him outside somehow, sat him down the pavement, where he sat doubled up, clutching his stomach, groaning, and hailed a cab. The driver looked at Barnaby, then at her and shook his head. 'Oh no,' he said, 'not in my nice clean cab. Sorry, love.'

This happened twice more; she was just beginning to despair when a police car pulled up by her.

'You all right?'

'Oh – yes,' said Kirsten hastily, 'yes, I'm fine.'

'Your friend doesn't look fine. What's the matter with him?'

'He's got a terrible stomach upset,' said Kirsten, 'he's just got back from India. He's my brother,' she added; she felt they should understand that, without knowing why.

'Yes?' The younger of the two looked at her and grinned. A cynical grin, but nonetheless a grin.

'Yes, honestly. I shouldn't have let him come out tonight, I know. Now I can't get a cab to take us home.'

'Been drinking, has he?'

'No,' said Kirsten firmly, 'he hasn't. And nor have I. Or doing anything else, if that's what you're thinking.'

Barnaby looked up, his face haggard in the darkness, contorted with pain. 'I'm sorry,' he said through clenched teeth, 'I've just got to get to a bog –' and then collapsed again onto his arms.

'Dear oh dear,' said the young policeman, who seemed genuinely nice. 'Looks like he should be in hospital. Tell you what, you get in the car, both of you, we'll run you up to Casualty at the Middlesex. Be there in five minutes.'

'Oh but –' said Kirsten.

'Otherwise, miss, I think it's a call to the parents, don't you? If you've got any.'

'Of course we have,' said Kirsten with dignity.

'Yes, I thought you probably had. Which, then?'

'We'll go to the Middlesex. Thank you.'

'Right. Come on, then. And put him near an open window, there's a good girl.'

Three hours later, as Barnaby lay still groaning spasmodically in a cubicle, Kirsten rather nervously phoned the house in Hamilton Terrace. Sandie answered the phone.

'Sandie! Thank God it's you. This is Kirsten. I'm sorry to phone so early, but we need a bit of help. We're at the Middlesex Hospital, and Barnaby's ill. No it's not serious, but they say it's dysentery and he ought to be properly looked after, you know, and I really think he should go home there. Could you possibly ask Francesca if that would be all right? And then I'll try and get a cab. Only they mostly don't seem to fancy him too much as a passenger. Thanks.'

She waited; after a few minutes Francesca came on the line. 'Kirsten? I'll come down and get Barnaby. I'll only be about half an hour.'

'Thanks,' said Kirsten, adding reluctantly, 'that's very kind of you.'

The Mercedes pulled up outside the Middlesex in under fifteen minutes; Kirsten was waiting outside. She waved at Francesca, went to fetch Barnaby. He needed help in walking; it wasn't difficult to support him, he was appallingly thin.

'He looks ghastly,' said Francesca, getting out to help her. 'What's wrong?'

'Dysentery, apparently. From India.'

'Why did you take him to Casualty?'

'The police insisted –'

'The police? How did they get involved, for God's sake?'

Kirsten told her.

'Kirsten really! Fancy going clubbing when he was so ill. I cannot believe such stupidity.'

'It was his idea,' said Kirsten, aware she sounded like a sulky child.

'I really don't think that's a very good explanation. I dread to think what your father will say. Here, Barnaby, get into the back. Then you can lie down, more or less. How do you feel?'

'Terrible,' he said, lying back, closing his eyes. 'I've got these terrible cramps and I can't stop shitting, you know?'

'Yes, thank you, I think so,' said Francesca.

'Sorry,' said Barnaby humbly. 'I'm very sorry, Francesca, for everything. You must be really glad I came home.'

'Well, not entirely happy,' she said, smiling, albeit slightly coolly, at him. Kirsten looked at him; she had forgotten how diplomatic he could be, how good the results. Of course he always had brown-nosed Francesca, he'd always been her favourite. And everyone else's.

'Let's get you home and into bed,' she said, 'and I'll get the doctor. Are you hot?'

'No, freezing. Shivery.'

'Yes, well, that's probably the temperature coming on.'

'Francesca,' said Kirsten carefully. 'Did – does Dad know about this?'

'Yes, I'm afraid he was there when you called. He had an early meeting, but he said he wanted to hear about it later. He couldn't understand why you were in Casualty. I should tell him you panicked, called the ambulance, if I were you. He probably won't believe it, but it's worth a try.'

'Yeah,' said Kirsten, looking at her, making an effort to smile, to be gracious, 'yeah, that's a good idea. Thanks.'

'Anyway, he said he'd phone me later, find out what had happened. Do you want to get a cab, go back to your flat, or will you come back to the house with me and Barnaby?'

'I'll go to the flat. I've got to get to work. You OK now, Barney?'

'Yeah, more or less. Thanks for looking after me, Kirsten.'

Kirsten had already started to walk away, but she turned, reluctantly, knowing what she must do.

'Thank you,' she said. 'Thank you for coming. And for – for everything. I expect Dad will phone, though. Tell me himself how stupid I am.'

'Yes, he probably will.'

But he didn't. At least not that morning. Or even that afternoon. And when he did, in the early evening, her stupidity was not even mentioned.

Brigadier Forsyth enjoyed his conversation with Graydon Townsend.

He had been waiting for it all morning, had told his wife not to disturb him, that he was being interviewed by the press. She had been very impressed. And Townsend did seem so extremely interested in everything he had to tell him. Well, of course, he had got many years of experience under his belt, had formed some very strong views on the property business. He had actually personally advised Bard Channing not to buy Coronet Wharf, but he hadn't listened. Luckily for him it had turned out all right.

Mr Townsend asked him if he had worked with Douglas Booth at all, and he had said yes, of course, and Mr Townsend had then asked if he had also played golf with him, adding that he was surprised Booth had never persuaded Bard Channing to get into the leisure business and particularly into golf. 'Such a vastly burgeoning industry.' It was funny he should say that, the Brigadier said, because there had been talk of a golf course and complex, some land and property had been found, indeed the company had paid a great deal of money for it, but he assumed it must have been sold again.

'Up in Scotland, it was,' he said, 'some place with a ridiculous name, sounded as if he'd made it up, what was it now, Loch Multyre or something like that. Just a minute, I'll remember it. Anyway he seemed very excited about it at the time, said he knew he could get planning permission, and that Arnold Palmer was going to design the course. Interesting project.'

'I don't know much about land values up there,' said Gray. 'I mean, what would a great deal of money be?'

'Oh – well over a million. Actually I think it was nearer two. But you can bet your life Channing wouldn't have paid over the odds for it. Very shrewd. And I expect he sold it at a very good profit. Anyway, Booth would be the man to talk to about that sort of thing if you were interested. Auchnamultie,' he addded suddenly, 'that's the name of the place.'

'Oh, right,' said Gray. 'Yes, it's a good idea, talking to Douglas Booth. I'm having lunch with him soon, I'll ask him about it then. It's those little details that make a piece so much more interesting. Thank you so much, Brigadier Forsyth.'

'My pleasure, young fellow. My pleasure entirely. Nice to have something to do. It gets very tedious, you know, just killing time. Now you follow up that lead I gave you on the Docklands railway. I think you might find there's a story there.'

'I will indeed,' said Graydon Townsend.

Sandie was putting some clean towels into Francesca's bathroom, checking on the supply of cotton wool and tissues and loo paper and replenishing the two small bottles of perfume (one Coco, one Mitsouko) with which Francesca unwittingly kept her supplied, when the phone rang in the bedroom. That would be Colin, she thought, glancing at the clock on the fireplace; he had said he'd phone at ten. He was always very punctual. Colin was her boyfriend; Colin Douglas he was called, very smooth, very good looking, she liked him a lot. He was divorced and he worked as a sales rep for a big pharmaceutical company. She always rang him back; no point him making expensive phone calls when the Channings could pay for them. He rang from public call boxes, all over London, so the number was always different, just in case the Channings checked their phone bill. She tucked the two bottles in her pocket and settled down on the chair by the bed for a nice lengthy chat.

Only it wasn't Colin. It was Liam Channing. Sandie liked Liam; she thought he had had a raw deal from life. He was very sexy looking too, a bit like his father she supposed, the same colouring, the almost black eyes, the heavy eyebrows, the thick dark hair, but he was a good six inches taller and a great deal better looking. She hadn't seen much of him recently, but when she had first arrived, he had come to the house occasionally, and she had met him at various family parties. He had always been extremely nice to her.

'Hallo Liam,' she said now. 'How are you? I was so sorry to hear about your accident.'

'Oh – on the mend, Sandie, thank you. I'm actually out of bed now, hauling myself about on crutches. Very sexy. And Sandie, thank you so much for your card. It was very sweet of you.'

'Oh goodness, it was nothing. You don't have to thank me.'

'Of course I do. It was one of the reasons I phoned, I thought I might catch you. Is Fr–' He seemed to catch himself short. 'Is Mrs Channing there?'

'No Liam, I'm afraid she's not.' This was a turn-up for the book. Liam and Mrs Channing had always been at daggers drawn. 'She's gone to fetch Kirsten from somewhere.'

'Kirsten? Since when did Kirsten need fetching from anywhere?'

'I don't know. Anyway, I don't know when she'll be back. I think she might have one of her charity things after that.'

Sandie took a very dim view of Francesca's charity work. 'It's therapy,' she said to Colin, 'gives her something to do, makes her feel useful.'

'Oh, I see. Well – never mind. I just wanted to speak to her.' He sounded sad suddenly. 'She's been so sweet, coming to visit me almost every day in hospital.'

'Oh really?' Curiouser and curiouser. She wondered if Mr Channing knew about that. He certainly hadn't been to visit Liam.

'Anyway, could you tell her I rang? And give her my l– my best wishes. I'll ring again.'

'Yes, of course I will. Well, bye Liam. Take care. Glad you're all right.'

'Bye Sandie.'

Now what was that about, thought Sandie. She could have sworn Liam had been about to say to give Francesca his love. Surely there wasn't something going on between them? No, that was ridiculous. But Liam was very charming; they'd obviously become friends, the two of them. Maybe Mr Channing was finally getting her down and she was just looking for a little light relief, bit of a flirtation. She could hardly blame her.

Not that Sandie didn't like Bard; she did, although she was very frightened of his tempers. But no-one, she thought, could call him attractive. And she really couldn't imagine how Francesca could have married him. He must be at least twenty years older than she was. And the thought of going to bed with him turned Sandie up: how could someone who looked like Francesca do that? Well, it had to be the money she was fucking. It was perfectly obvious that was all she wanted. It had to be. Well, good luck to her; who wouldn't do that if they got the chance? Just the same, Sandie found it hard to feel anything for Francesca but a certain distaste, and she didn't find her exactly easy to work for; she was demanding and very critical. Of course Sandie had been spoilt in a way, she was the first to admit it, not having a woman boss for several years; had had a chance to queen it really, and the kids had all been fond of her, and when they'd all been at home they'd had a good laugh together in the evenings; it had been a shock getting used to having to do things Francesca's way. Every so often she thought she'd leave, but it really was a very cushy job. There was Mrs Roberts to do the cleaning, and there was Nanny Crossman, and there was Horton, and most weekends she had the house to herself; she got a car and a good salary, and rarely even had to babysit on account of the old dragon not wanting any time off; and there were lots of hidden perks like the perfume and the odd T-shirt she could hive off into her own collection – not one of the classy Joseph ones of course, but ones from Gap and Marks and Spencer – and there was no need for her ever to buy tights or even knickers, Francesca had a huge supply of both and it was really easy to take a few pairs every now and again – and obviously she fed Colin every weekend from the housekeeping money, they ate like lords. So it was worth putting up with a bit of high-handedness from Madam. Just the same she didn't like her, and she just had this feeling – and Sandie was very strong on feeling – that one day she was going to get her come-uppance, be revealed for what she was: a gold-digger. Nanny Crossman didn't like her either, she knew; she thought she lacked class, was always comparing her to Pattie Channing and some of her other mothers, as she called them. She also thought she was incompetent, and they both agreed she was what Nanny called over-strung and Sandie called neurotic. You certainly never knew when she was going to snap, get all hyper over some minor matter. And they both felt, for slightly different reasons, there was no excuse for that: Nanny worshipped Mr Channing, explained away his most violent rages as exhaustion and worry and said if he could cope, then Francesca certainly ought to be able to: Sandie simply felt if you got all that luxury and no responsibility you ought to shut up and put up when the going got a bit rough.

Sandie put the phone down and looked at it thoughtfully. Very interesting. Very interesting indeed. She went back into the bathroom and helped herself to a liberal spray of Coco. She couldn't wait for Colin to ring.

'Come on, you poor old thing,' said Francesca, 'you look absolutely terrible. I'm going to put you to bed and then call the doctor.'

Barnaby opened his mouth to tell her not to, he'd had enough of doctors for one night, and then another agonising cramp clutched at him, and he had to run from the room. He was lying on the sofa in the small upstairs sitting room, clutching what seemed like a raw empty space where his guts had been, when she came in. She looked down at him worriedly.

'Feel really bad?'

He nodded, tried to smile.

'I've rung Dr Hemmings, he'll be here quite soon. Now look, a bath might be an idea. Could you manage one, do you think?'

'If you wash my back,' said Barnaby.

'Barnaby, don't be silly.'

'I'm not being silly. I'd love you to wash my back. And I might faint or something in the bath and drown, then think how you'd feel.'

'Irritated,' said Francesca briskly. 'Come on, I'll run it for you, and I'll stay within calling distance just in case.'

'Oh all right. You're a hard woman, Francesca.'

'And you're a hard case, Barnaby. Now come on, take my hand, I'll pull you up. Can you make the top floor, do you think?'

'No, I think I should use your bathroom, I'd be safer there. And then maybe I should sleep in your bed, for a few days, just till I'm better. That's what little boys are allowed to do, isn't it?'

'Oh Barnaby,' said Francesca, laughing. 'Barnaby, in spite of everything I'm glad you're home.'

The doctor examined him, prodded and probed at his stomach with his cold hand, which was agonising, took a sample of his blood, asked him to provide samples of various other unpleasant kinds, and then said as far as he could see he only had mild dysentery and a few days' rest and starvation diet should see him on the mend.

'And I do mean starvation,' he said to Francesca. 'Clear soups, nothing remotely solid, maybe some dry toast with something like Marmite on it, no dairy products, just plenty of water. And several sachets of this stuff every day, in the water, it'll help rehydrate him.'

'Beer?' said Barnaby hopefully, from his pillow. 'Beer is very rehydrating, rum, gin –'

'Barnaby, don't be naughty,' said Francesca. She looked at him severely; he grinned back at her. He'd forgotten how pretty she was. He liked her hair longer, and what she was wearing, a T-shirt and shorts, made her look really young. She had a great figure. Fantastic legs. How his father had managed to pull her he'd never know. And he didn't think it was the money either; well, not just the money. She had too much of a mind of her own to have done that; and anyway she'd had a job, been really successful. She wasn't just up herself, like most of the women that came to the house. He hoped his father appreciated his good fortune. Probably didn't.

'Thank you so much for coming, Dr Hemmings. I'll see he does everything you say.'

'Yes, well, it's very important. Especially no dairy products. And no alcohol, young man. And no smoking!' He was obviously trying to look fierce; he failed totally. Barnaby grinned at him.

'Scout's honour, Dr Hemmings. Just cigars.'

When Dr Hemmings had gone, Francesca came in and put a large jug of water by his bed.

'You're to drink all that by lunchtime. Then if you're very good, I'll make you some chicken noodle soup.'

'Fantastic,' said Barnaby. 'Oh Francesca, don't go. Stay and talk to me.'

'I just want to ring Duggie Booth, then I will for a bit. How are you feeling?'

'Terrible. I probably won't even live till you get back.'

'I think you will,' she said, and went out of the room laughing. She was back in a few minutes.

'He was out. Pity. I wanted to arrange to go and see him at the weekend, with the children. I've been meaning to do it for so long.'

'How is he?'

'Oh he's fine. Just the same. Old darling.'

'And Attila?'

'Who? Oh, you mean Teresa. Barnaby, you are naughty. She's all right. Yes, she's fine.'

'How's Dad?'

'Oh – busy. You know.'

'Yeah. I know. How's his temper?'

'Oh – you know,' she said again, laughing. 'I'm learning to live with it.'

'Me too. Still learning, I mean. And Francesca, what about the baby? Kirsten said she'd been ill.'

'She has. She's not really very well at all. She's got a problem with her heart. May have to have surgery, when she's a bit bigger.' She sighed. 'It's very frightening.'

'I'm sorry,' said Barnaby. 'I haven't even seen her since she was about a week old. Is she pretty?'

'Very,' said Francesca.

'Does she look like you?'

'A bit, yes.'

'Well, she must be extremely pretty then.' He smiled at her, put his hand out, took hers. He felt rather sleepy suddenly. 'Thank you for everything you've done this morning, Francesca. You've been great.'

'That's all right. We must try and keep it from your father that you went out clubbing, though. And got picked up by the police – dear oh dear –'

'Oh, I expect he'll be so overjoyed to see me he won't even care,' said Barnaby.

'I really wouldn't bank on that one. Now you have a little sleep, Barnaby, and –'

'Will you sit here and tell me a story? A story about a dead horny bloke and his beautiful stepmother who couldn't resist him.'

'No Barnaby, I won't.'

It was all so bloody awkward, Gray thought: he didn't even now know what to do next, how to handle it. Flowers? Surely not. Too corny, and she would really despise them and him. Little note? But what the fuck would it say? 'Thanks for the memory' or 'that was fun' or 'let's still be friends'? He felt he really should do something. Nothing at all seemed very brutal.

He sighed heavily and tried to concentrate on his morning zap through the papers. It didn't work and he couldn't.

No matter how you looked at it, what had passed between him and Kirsten had been extraordinarily intimate. Not to be set aside with a quick wave and no glance backward. Or was that how they were, her generation? Did they regard sex as exactly that, a delicious meal, a feast, that once enjoyed could be remembered fondly, but with complete detachment? Briony certainly wasn't like that, but Briony was several years older that Kirsten. And light years apart from her in attitude. He tried to imagine Kirsten yearning for a baby and couldn't. She'd view the whole thing with total horror and revulsion. Oh God, now he was just avoiding the issue. What should he, ought he to do? He just didn't know, didn't know enough to handle it at all. In which case, then, he thought, the best thing was to take his lead from her. If she wanted to talk to him again, see him again, she would tell him so. If she didn't, she wouldn't. There was nothing coy, nothing inhibited about Kirsten. Just as she had in bed, she could take the lead and he would follow.

He felt better for a while after that. But still uneasy, still decidedly unsure of how to act. Still feeling wretchedly shocked at himself for his swift betrayal of Briony. And still unable to cast Kirsten off, to set the memory of her and the night with her aside; he felt disturbed, in some way rearranged by her. And he wanted, he knew he wanted, to see her again.

He wrenched his mind determinedly away from Kirsten Channing, and fixed it on Duggie Booth. Duggie and their lunch. Which was hopefully going to answer a few questions.

A few infinitely intriguing questions. Not least why Duggie felt it necessary to talk to him at all, and explain the behaviour of his wife. It showed a fairly desperate concern, did that, especially when the explanation was to a fairly high-profile member of the press. Duggie obviously knew something, or had some very major anxiety. Or both. And it wouldn't be about anything trifling: he might not be the brain of the century, but he was a wily old bird, who'd held his own in a fairly cut-throat business for going on four decades. Gray, contemplating the two hours or so ahead of him, felt a thud of excitement, a surge of adrenalin, Kirsten Channing suddenly of little importance, the pain at the loss of Briony sweetly eased. It was the Reform, the

Reform at one, wasn't it, he thought, rifling through his diary; or had Duggie said twelve-thirty? He hadn't written it down; he'd better ring and find out.

He called Duggie's number at home but there was no reply, not even on the answering machine which was unusual; he tried Channings, where his secretary said he hadn't arrived yet, but she was expecting him any minute. 'He has a big meeting pencilled in for eleven-thirty,' she said, 'and so I should think your lunch would be one or even one-fifteen. It's in the diary for one. I'll confirm that, Mr Townsend, the minute Mr Booth arrives, and ring you back.'

'Thank you,' said Gray.

But eleven and then eleven-thirty came and then it was noon, and still Douglas Booth's secretary did not ring.

It was another heavy morning at Channing House. Bard had come roaring into Pete's office twice, had shouted at Oliver three times, once to tell him the wires from his computer were trailing on the floor in front of his desk and sooner or later someone would break their bloody neck on them, once to get out a copy of the contract with the Cardiff developers, and finally (roughly thirty seconds later, as Oliver was still calling it up on the computer) to ask him if he was taking his lunch break before doing what he had been asked. He disappeared finally for a meeting in the boardroom at eleven-forty-five; even Pete Barbour, normally the embodiment of discretion and formality, met Oliver's eyes and shook his head gently, and then went rather quickly into his office and closed the door, as if to protect himself from further disloyalty.

Oliver returned to what he had been doing, which was an updating of various staff contracts, and wondered if he dared take another walk round Paul Smith's at lunchtime, when Barbour appeared in the doorway.

'Come in a minute, Oliver, would you? Those spreadsheets you just gave me, I'd like to check something on them with you –'

Oliver went in; he was always amused by Barbour's office, its determined resemblance to a library, with its heavy fake antique desk, the leather chairs, the bound volumes on the shelves – not classics, but Simon's Tax Manuals. An analyst, Oliver thought, would have said Pete clearly fantasised about being an academic rather than an accountant.

He went over to the desk, took the papers Barbour held out to him.

'It's this lot here,' he said, 'if you could just – Bard, you OK?'

The door onto the corridor had opened and Bard Channing had come in. His face was ashen, and his almost-black eyes were dull, dead, expressionless. He walked over to Barbour's desk, leaned heavily on it, head bowed, looking down at his own hands. Nice hands, Oliver noticed irrelevantly, not for the first time, long fingered and slender, not at all in keeping with Bard's stocky frame.

'Bard, what is it, what's the matter?'

'It's Duggie,' said Bard finally, very quietly.

'Duggie? What about him? Where was he this morning, he hasn't had an accident, has he?'

'You could say that. Yes, you could. He's – he's had a heart attack, Pete. Duggie's dead.'

Chapter Thirteen

Coffins always looked so small, Francesca thought. You could never believe the person you had known could possibly fit into them. What had happened to Duggie, that his six-foot-long, quite solid shape had been somehow shrunk into this politely neat, hexagonal box? She tried not to think of him in there, it was unbearable: silent, white, confined, himself yet not himself, lying eyes closed, hands composed, dressed in some awful white garment, no doubt, instead of his scratchy tweeds or his old-fashioned City suits, lying there beneath the great mass of white and yellow flowers, roses and lilies, shaped in an absurdly oversized cross, that was Teresa's offering. She thought of him as he had been, as he still was to her, so kind and affectionate and good humoured, and felt saddened, ashamed, that the very last conversation they had had, she had promised to take the children to see him and had never done so. Had considered herself too busy, too distressed, her concerns too important, to give up a day, an afternoon, to give him the kind of easy, affectionate pleasure he had so longed for. Had made the excuse Teresa, Teresa whom she did not like, whom none of them liked, had told herself that Duggie had Teresa, had chosen Teresa, that he was therefore perfectly happy (when the evidence of her own eyes, common sense, told her quite otherwise), and that it was of no importance therefore if they neglected him, ignoring his patent sadness at his estrangement from them all. And that when finally she had found the time, had phoned to arrange it, it had been too late by only perhaps minutes.

She looked over at Teresa; she was sitting on the other side of the memorial chapel, very pale, her blue eyes expressionless, fixed on the coffin, dressed in a black silk suit, a large feathered black hat on her silver-blonde hair; her son Richard was next to her, his face rather grimly set. He was suntanned, handsome in a rather vapid way. The estranged daughter had not come.

Francesca looked then at Bard, whose own face was stern, raw with grief at this loss of his oldest friend, his colleague, with whom he had shared not only much personal pain and joy, but professional concerns too, success and failure, risks taken, ground won, lost and then won again. He had known Duggie before his children had been born, before Marion had died, before Channings had been even dreamed of; it was not only Duggie he was saying goodbye to, but a great multi-emotioned mass of his life. He was singing now loudly, tunelessly, 'Jesu Lover of My Soul', determined not to give in, to weaken. Why, Francesca thought irreverently, why, if she was going to have so heavily religious a ceremony, did Teresa have to opt for this plastic chapel; why not a good, honest, and infinitely more beautiful church? He had to make a speech in a minute; she had been anxious earlier that he would not get through it, would break down, but of course he would cope superbly. Bard could get through anything; nothing broke him.

He had been more distant from her still since Duggie's death; she had expected him to turn to her in his grief, had hoped they would become closer again, that she could comfort him, but it was as if he had decided she could not share the grief, and the effort of trying to make her understand was simply not worthwhile. She had found him the first night in his study, his head buried in his arms, but when she had gone in, put her hand gently on his shoulder, he had shaken her off, quickly, roughly even, said, 'Don't, don't, Francesca, I want to be alone,' and every day since then had moved further away. She had wanted to talk to him about so many things, about Duggie, about their shared past: but it was all quite impossible. She might almost be a widow herself, she thought, staring at the coffin, for all the companionship, the closeness she experienced these days.

Jess, who was sitting next to her, suddenly patted her hand and smiled at her gently, as if sensing her loneliness and distress. She had been deeply saddened herself by Duggie's death – 'another son he was to me, in a way, Francesca' – had aged in the time since, looked somehow less upright, less sprightly, as if some of her strength had gone with Duggie, as if some of her life too had gone along with the memories.

Teresa she had hardly spoken to, after the first awful, awkward conversation, when she had been calmly, almost briskly, in control; she had phoned, of course, to invite them to the service, to ask Bard to speak and then again to ask him what he thought he might say, and who else she should ask, but there had seemed nothing she could say to her that would not seem either trite or hypocritical. She sent her some flowers, and a letter saying she would be there if Teresa needed company or someone to talk to (knowing that she was the last person who would be chosen for either purpose), and that had been all.

Thank God, thank God, Pattie hadn't come; she had been invited, but had refused, obviously unable to face them all. She would have admired her for coming, but it would have added to the tensions of the occasion horribly. There were dozens of people there she didn't know, business colleagues, golfing companions of Duggie's obviously. And rather surprisingly Graydon Townsend was there: she couldn't imagine who had invited him. He really was very good looking, she hadn't really taken it in the other night, and wearing an extraordinarily nice suit. He had the sort of looks she liked best, a slightly hawkish, intelligent face: very attractive. Exactly her type – until she'd met Bard. Patrick had been that type. Gray kept looking at Kirsten, she noticed. Well, most men kept looking at Kirsten. She was hard not to look at.

She supposed Liam would have come under normal circumstances. He had sent some flowers; she had seen them. She had told him about Duggie herself; he had been patently upset.

'He was so good to me,' he said, after a long silence. 'Like another dad. Well, like a dad. When the real one failed me.' He looked at her and smiled rather feebly. 'For years and years he was always there. I used to go there in the holidays, he used to come and see me at school. God, it's a shame. If only I'd –'

His voice had cracked; he stopped talking. Francesca had been touched by his very real grief.

The hymn ended; Bard stood up, paused, took a great breath that was more a sigh, and walked forward to stand by the coffin.

Well, at least, Rachel thought, she had been invited to sit with the family: she was next to Victoria, in between Kirsten and Barnaby. Francesca had forgiven her thus far. But she was still distant, avoiding her; when Rachel had got back from the convent, she had gone straight to see Francesca, planning to make a little speech, to try to explain. But Francesca had been tearful, distracted over Duggie's death, and worried too about Barnaby, who was ill; had said, 'Look, Mummy, not now. Whatever it is you want to say, I'd rather it waited. I really can't cope with anything else at the moment.'

And she had respected that, with some relief, seeing that whenever she did tell Francesca it had to be the right time, she had to be feeling strong and resilient, if there was to be any hope of her accepting the situation. But she had not been allowed near Francesca in the following week, her offers of caring for Jack, for helping with arrangements – 'What arrangements, Mummy?' had been the cool, slightly amused response. 'I'm not arranging a funeral, I haven't got anything to do' – rejected.

And so today was the first time she had seen her, since the first, difficult meeting; and she was worried, frightened at the gulf between them. She had phoned Bard, said how sorry she was, and he had been oddly warm, grateful for her call. 'Duggie was very fond of you, Rachel,' he said. 'He said you were one hell of a woman.'

'Good gracious,' said Rachel, accepting this as the compliment it was clearly meant to be, 'well, I was very fond of him. I just wish –'

'Yes, yes, I know,' he said, 'we all wish. We all wish it very much. But it's too late. Bless you for calling, Rachel. You'll be there on Friday, at the funeral, won't you? I'd hate it if you weren't.'

She had been touched by that, very touched; had written a note to Teresa, wishing she liked her more, and was pleased when she received a formal printed card of thanks, inviting her to the funeral.

Rachel had another worry too, apart from her estrangement from her daughter; a bigger, more tangible worry. Bard had still not finalised arrangements for the money, had not signed the forms of association for the charity; time was winging by, there was so much to do, and how could she chase, chivvy him under these circumstances? She supposed she must simply wait, patiently, the thing she found always most difficult.

Bard was beginning to speak now; she glanced briefly round the chapel, at the many faces she did not know, as well as the familiar ones. The Clarke family were only two rows behind. Oliver had positioned his mother's wheelchair very carefully, so that she could see. He had real charm, that boy, an easy, surprisingly confident charm; Heather Clarke had done a good job under the most appallingly difficult circumstances. He was good looking too, and bright: the sort of son Bard should have had, rather than that layabout Barnaby. Goodness, he was delicious, though, Barnaby: if she were twenty, maybe only ten years younger, she'd be seriously tempted by him. Those marvellous deep blue eyes, the bronzed skin, the corn-coloured hair, blonder than his sister. Far too long, of course, although tied back neatly for the funeral today, and he was wearing a suit which looked rather too big for him; he was terribly thin, no doubt the legacy of India. He was clearly an absolute nightmare, irresponsible, lazy, as much trouble in his own way as Kirsten – but infinitely more agreeable. Which probably made Kirsten worse, she thought. She didn't like Kirsten, but she was clearly the family scapegoat.

Barnaby saw her looking at him and smiled at her, a wide, glorious smile, then swiftly sobered his face again into an expression more suited to the occasion, and fixed his eyes on his father.

She followed his example, turned her attention back to Bard; his rough, strongly pitched voice, its South London tang still about it, reached clearly and easily to every corner of the building. He spoke affectionately, but not mawkishly, of Duggie; told funny stories, described incidents, smiled as he described his passion for golf as his life-force, took them all back through the years, the long years of their association; paid tribute to his loyalty, his courage, his constancy as a friend, his talent for fun, his passion for good food, his capacity for whisky, 'and above all, the sheer goodness of the man. There was nothing shabby about Duggie, nothing cheap, nothing frail. He was a rock; we shall have to manage without him somehow, but it will not be easy.'

He stood there in silence for more than a minute, his brilliant eyes fixed on the coffin, and then he rejoined Francesca, sat down without looking at her, at any of them, head bowed. Oh God, thought Rachel, fishing in her bag for a handkerchief, hearing from every part of the chapel the humdrum sounds of sadness, of muted grief, throats cleared, noses blown: Victoria was crying, openly, tears streaming down her face; Kirsten's eyes were closed, her mouth tightly compressed; Francesca was biting her lip, her eyes welling over; even the terrible Marcia Grainger's eyes were brilliant with tears. And then rather slowly Teresa Booth got up and took Bard's place, and surveyed them all for a long time, her blue eyes almost amused, before starting to speak herself.

It was something of a shock, that speech. To all of them. And extremely clever. Without saying anything very much at all, really, she had managed to make them all, all the family at any rate, feel terrible. It was out of order, totally out of order: but they did deserve it, and she knew it, and so did they.

And she had said absolutely nothing untrue.

Only that she knew she was still not seen as quite a part of Duggie's life, yet, not by most of them, his old friends, his colleagues at Channings, the Channing family – 'And how could I expect to be?' (This with a quick smile.) 'We'd only been married two years, he had been with Suzanne almost thirty, she was still his wife to most of you. I can understand that. But that was not the case, I know, thank God, to him. I was his wife, and I believe I made him happy. I tried to. I tried very hard. Not in the same way as Suzanne had, of course, but in my own way. It wasn't easy. I had hoped to ease his loneliness and in a way of course I did. We had fun, we did things together he hadn't done before, things he certainly enjoyed. But I am very aware that my arrival in his life was not all for the good. There were those of you who had known him for so long, who found the changes hard to accept. The base of his life inevitably changed. I did not try to come between him and his golf – good God,' she said, smiling almost cheerfully, 'no man and certainly no woman could have done that. What did happen, and only a fool could have not seen it, was that he had to give up quite a lot for me. Old friends, old ways, old haunts. Well, it happens, with every new marriage. It's just harder when the new one follows a very old one. And it troubled me at times; I thought perhaps I had taken from him more than I had given, and I thought that others might have felt that too. But I stand here now to put the record straight as I see it: to tell you I loved Duggie, and he loved me, and that he did die a happy man. His last words to me were that he loved me. I am proud of that. Very proud. You should be glad for him and glad for me. Thank you.'

She went back to her front-row seat; her son put his arm round her, but she looked at him almost happily, nowhere near tears. There was a long, almost stunned silence; then the priest stood up and announced the last hymn, and people got quickly, gratefully, to their feet.

God only knew why she'd done it, Rachel thought, what kind of crude satisfaction it had given her, to deliver, with consummate skill, a hard slap in the face for all the old guard, the Channings, the erstwhile colleagues – without saying a word against them. Callously destroyed the goodwill and warmth and happy recollection that had been so tangibly present at the end of Bard's speech: and also cut through the hypocrisy, brought some honesty into the situation, she thought with a sense of near-shock, told them they had not been good friends to Duggie at the end, had stayed away from his home, had not spent time with him, brought their children to see him, had added to any unhappiness he might have been feeling. And told them also that she knew they didn't like her, and she didn't give a shit.

And as the coffin slid slowly away, through the ghastly blue curtains, as Duggie left them finally, Rachel felt, through shock and remorse, and genuine grief, something else. A sense of admiration for Teresa Booth.

So quick, so simple, it was, it had been, the moment: the one that Kirsten always thought afterwards had changed her life, when she had stopped saying quite so categorically she didn't believe in love, had admitted there might be something in it after all, when a drift of an entirely new emotion, gentle, sweet, warm, came across her, into her. And at such a filthy, hideous moment, on such a foul occasion, outside that gross chapel place, why not a church, why, why not? when the awful Booth woman had done her worst, when everyone was feeling wretched and awkward and far worse than they had before, when there was the reception to get through, Francesca being tearful and gracious, and that ghastly mother of hers in that ridiculous hat, flitting about outside the chapel, chatting to everyone and shaking and patting the Booth woman's hand, as if she hadn't just delivered what amounted to a bollocking to the entire congregation or whatever it was called, and kissing her father, and even going over to Barnaby, Barnaby, for God's sake, and kissing him, and taking his arm and walking him away down the path. God, she was a nightmare; a shallow, embarrassing two-faced nightmare, imagine being her daughter – just for a moment Kirsten felt a stab of sympathy for Francesca. And she was vulgar, there was no other word for it, for all her frightful drawly voice, her double-barrelled name. As vulgar as Teresa Booth, in her own way. Not an ounce of genuine feeling in her, she felt quite sure of that.

She tried to distract herself from Rachel; looked at Granny Jess, who was standing in the porch, blowing her long nose rather hard on a very large men's handkerchief; she was clearly waiting for Bard to fetch her, but he was talking to Heather Clarke, bending over her wheelchair. Why did he have to make such a fuss of her and those two children of hers: she'd noticed Melinda gazing at Barnaby across the chapel, silly cow.

She would go over and talk to Granny Jess, take care of her until a car could be found. Gray was somewhere: gone to get his, perhaps. She'd been surprised he was coming, but he'd said, when he rang her to tell her, that Teresa had specifically invited him, had phoned him. 'I was going to have lunch with Duggie that day, and she knew, said he'd been fussing about it just after he collasped and before he lost consciousness, said she must be sure to ring me, it was one of the last things he said. Dear old chap,' he added.

'Yes,' said Kirsten, and then, 'Why were you going to have lunch with him?'

'Oh, to discuss business, developments in the property scene, that sort of thing,' he'd said, just slightly too vaguely, she'd thought.

'Anyway, Mrs B. has asked me to come, so I thought it was the least I could do.'

'Well, it'll be nice to have you there,' said Kirsten, and she'd thought it would be, but actually it felt odd; obviously they couldn't sit together, and people would think it funny if they were together at the reception or whatever it was called. They'd all got to go back to the Booth house: or 'residence', as that silly housekeeper of theirs answered the phone. And she still felt awkward with him, still regretted what she had done, the way she had seduced him, almost entirely to hurt Toby, although she did like him, did find him attractive. He hadn't been exactly interesting in bed, but it had been all right. Well, better than all right, good even. But it had been bad of her, especially knowing he was unhappy, in turmoil himself. He had told her briefly about his girlfriend, about why they had broken up; it was a sorry little tale. She was surprised at Gray, actually; she would have thought he was quite the new man, doting-father type. Well, you never could tell. Anyway, she shouldn't have gone to bed with him. God, she was a tart. A self-centred, stupid tart. Still behaving as if she were fifteen; she had to grow up. Only she didn't want to grow up either; there didn't seem a lot of benefit in it. Shit, what was the matter with her? Suddenly, sharply, she thought of her mother, who had never really grown up either, whose alcoholism was a desperate lurch back into irresponsibility, a place where she was safe, taken care of, where reality was kept at bay. Was she going to go the same way: only was sex, not alcohol, going to be her refuge?

Panic gripped her, standing there alone, panic and at the same time a perverse longing for her mother, and grief too for Duggie, who had been so much a part of her childhood; tears filled her eyes again, hot, fierce tears, and as she turned to wipe them away, she realised she didn't have a hanky, she'd given it to Tory at the service. And it was while she was rummaging in her pockets miserably, trying to find one, her nose starting to run, that it happened, that the moment came, while she was actually wiping her nose surreptitiously on her sleeve, praying no-one would notice, and a voice, a very nice voice, with just a touch of amusement in it, said, 'Here, do you want to borrow mine?' and she turned and there was Oliver Clarke, holding out his, his eyes genuinely sympathetic.

Her first instinct was to say no thanks, and to hurry off; she really had never liked him, had always thought he was a mealy-mouthed creep, and she was sick of hearing from Granny Jess and her father how wonderful he and his sister were. But that seemed too rude, and it was extraordinarily thoughtful of him to have noticed her dilemma, even if he was a creep, so she smiled, rather reluctantly, took the handkerchief, and then noticed that her hand was shaking violently.

'Are you all right?' he said, and there was real concern in his voice. 'You look very pale.'

'Yes, yes, I'm fine. Just – well, you know. Bit shaky.'

'Horrible, isn't it?' he said. 'So unfair. Such a nice old guy. He was always so kind to me. To us.'

'Yeah,' she said, sniffing, blowing her nose again, 'me too. A second dad to me, really. No, you're right, it isn't fair.'

'Life isn't though, is it?' he said. 'Or death, for that matter.'

'No,' she said, 'no, not at all, I'm afraid,' and then she found herself looking at him, looking at him properly, giving him her attention, rather than a quick graze of a glance, for the very first time. He was watching his mother, and the expression on his face was very sweet, concerned, anxious that she was being taken care of; it was obviously totally habitual to him, that sweetness, that concern, it touched her in spite of herself. And then he turned back and smiled at her.

'Sorry,' he said, 'I was just checking on Mum.'

It was his mouth she noticed first and most forcefully; it was wide, almost too wide, and his teeth were very even and well spaced. Kirsten did like nice teeth: one of the things she had first noticed about Toby were his teeth, but Toby's were too perfect, a tribute to the orthodontist's art; Oliver's looked as if they had grown obligingly that way. His jaw was wide too, wide and generous looking, and his nose was extremely straight which she liked, she couldn't stand turned up noses on men (and turned-under ones still less), and then she reached his eyes. She'd always thought of Oliver as fair, and his hair was indeed fair – not blond, but very light golden-brown – but his eyes were dark, not the intense almost-black of her father's, but a soft, dark brown, with black lashes that might have looked girlish but somehow didn't. The other thing he had, which she really liked, was freckles: not too many, but a heavy smattering on his nose and forehead, quite large splodgy ones. They suited him. It was a strange thing to think about freckles, she thought confusedly, blowing her nose hard again to disguise the fact she was examining him so closely, but that was what Oliver's did, they somehow completed his face, made it look less formal, more lived-in. Oh for Christ's sake, Kirsten, she thought, what is the matter with you, drivelling on, this is Oliver, Oliver the dweeb; but she couldn't help it, she just went on taking him, drinking him, in, and noticing that he was tall too, taller than her, by about two inches, and nicely dressed in a dark grey suit and blue shirt. And when he said, 'You OK now?' she heard his voice as if for the first time too: light, easy, completely accentless, a bit like

266

Gray's, she thought irrelevantly, only somehow with more warmth in it.

'Oh – yes,' she said. God, she must stop this, poor guy must think she was a complete moron. 'Yes, thank you.'

And now he was studying her, politely, briefly, but nonetheless studying; to break the silence, she said, slightly awkwardly, 'It was very kind of you to come to my rescue.'

'Well,' he said, grinning again, 'I just noticed you, standing there, and I didn't have anything else to do at the time.'

'Oh.'

'And it is quite bad, not having a hanky and your nose running. It happened to me in an interview last week. I just didn't know what do do.'

'What did you do?'

'Sniffed. Didn't get the job,' he added.

'Why are you going for jobs?' she said.

'Oh – to pass the time between dawn and dusk,' he said lightly, but she could see he was irritated.

'Sorry, I didn't mean that. You seem quite settled at Channings.'

'Not really. I'm only working for Peter Barbour for a bit,' he said, 'just to tide me over. Till I can find something else. That's official,' he added, clearly anxious she shouldn't think he was two-timing her father.

'Yeah?'

'Yes. I really don't want to work for your father long-term. However kind he is.'

It was clearly important he got both those points over; it interested her.

'Well, he's not easy to work for,' she said. 'I should know.'

'Yes.' There was a silence, then he said, 'Bit of a strong speech, that, wasn't it? Mrs Booth's, I mean.'

'Yeah. But – well, if she meant to make us feel bad, she certainly succeeded with me. I felt terrible. I felt guilty already anyway, I never went to see him and he was always asking me, and she's made me feel much worse.'

'Well,' he said almost cheerfully, 'that's what funerals are about, isn't it, guilt? I must get back to Mum.'

She was so struck by what he had said she wanted to pursue it, was going to follow him over to Heather's wheelchair, to say hallo to her, when Gray suddenly appeared at her side.

'Hallo, Kirsten.'

'Oh, hi Gray. Gray, this is Oliver Clarke, a – a friend of the family. Oliver, Gray Townsend.'

'How do you do?' said Oliver, and then, 'Excuse me, I'll maybe see you at the house. Keep the hanky,' he said as she held it out to him, 'I've got some more.'

'Nice young man,' said Gray.

'Yes,' she said absently, looking after him, noticing the way he moved, walked, rather quickly but heavily, noticing that he had very long legs, noticing –

'You OK?'

'Oh, yes. Yes, thank you. I was going to go and get my gran, could we take her –'

And then Oliver turned, and across the expanse of the car park looked at her, above the heads of most of the people there, and smiled: not as he had before, politely, carefully, but with warmth and generosity, and an extraordinary feeling came over Kirsten, a sense that she had just made a discovery, learned something deeply important, only she had no idea what it was or might be, and she smiled back, and then Gray said, 'Come on, let's get it over with,' and without even thinking what she was doing, how it might be interpreted, she took his hand and kissed him briefly, because he too was so kind, and allowed him to lead her to his car.

'Graydon dear.' It was Teresa, smiling at him, across the large hallway of her lush, plush Tudoresque house. 'Graydon, could you help me with some of these canapés? Passing them round. I've slightly undercalculated on the staff, I can see I'm going to have problems. And they've all come back, the vultures. Bottoms smacked or not, they want some of Duggie's best champagne.'

'Er – yes,' said Graydon. He smiled at her suddenly; he had actually rather admired her speech. He had thought it very clever and probably well deserved. He knew what these clans could be like, and he was sure Teresa had not fared well at the hands of the Channings. Not that she couldn't take care of herself, and anyone who could administer the reprimand that she had, and in such a situation, needed no sympathy. And she was hardly the fragile type. But then he looked at her rather more carefully; noticed the shadows under the brilliant blue eyes, the slightly grim set of her smile, the plump, heavily ringed hand shaking as she lit a cigarette, and felt ashamed of himself. She had loved Duggie in her own way, no doubt, and she was hurting much more than she was letting on.

'Of course I will.'

'Come into the kitchen, everything's set out there.'

He followed her in; it was a vast, over-equipped place, the woodwork done in the current mode for distressed colour, in bleached-out pink, the floor elaborately tiled in some kind of mosaic. Heavily ruched blinds hung at the windows, totally out of sympathy with the large green Aga, clearly seldom used; by the Aga was a basket with two snarling poodles in it. Well, she would have poodles; it was inevitable.

'Horrible little things,' she said briefly. 'They're not mine, they're my cousin's, I like real dogs, I've just been looking at some Old English Sheepdog puppies.'

'Oh,' said Gray.

'Duggie was against the idea. Said it would wreck the lawn. Over his dead body, he said.' And then her eyes filled alarmingly with tears and she leant briefly against the wall.

'Sorry, Graydon. Sorry.'

'That's OK,' he said, kicking the door shut quickly, putting his arm round her, noticing the same over-heady perfume, the same intense warmth that had struck him at the Ritz. 'You have a cry. You've been very brave.'

'It's been easy so far,' she said. 'Lots to do, plenty of drama. The tough time starts tonight. When everyone's gone.'

'Well,' he said, and was amazed and almost annoyed to hear himself saying it, 'if you ever want a shoulder to cry one, mine's here. You have my number.'

'Thank you, Graydon. That's very sweet. I have a feeling I'm going to need a few friends. And it's such a very nice shoulder,' she added, patting his chest gently, 'in such a very nice suit. Now, take these two, will you, and I'll go and find that damn Philippino of mine and wind her up a bit.'

It was quite nice, being able to move around the room, with a licence to talk to everyone. He had a quick word with Sam Illingworth, who had just arrived, and with Peter Barbour who looked terrible, white and exhausted, and who introduced him to Marcia Grainger, 'without whom we would all be lost, wouldn't we, Marcia? Marcia, I don't think you've met Graydon Townsend, from the *News on Sunday*.'

So this was Marcia Grainger, thought Gray, studying her with interest: Bard Channing's bodyguard, as she was known on the street, tall, stiff backed, shelf bosomed, dressed in a severe brown suit, her salt and pepper hair apparently glued to her head, and dark red lipstick on a full, very firm mouth.

She looked at him with a degree of polite distaste. 'I have very little to do with the press,' she said. 'I find it better that way.'

Gray, assuming (correctly) that this was meant to be a rebuke for his calling, told her she was quite right, asked her to excuse him, and moved away.

He was just trying to locate Francesca Channing, who had spoken to him briefly outside the church, clearly surprised to see him there, when he found himself near Kirsten. She was standing with her brother – don't like the look of him, Gray thought, over-charming and over-indulged – and a tall gaunt woman in black. Kirsten introduced her to him as Jess Channing – 'My grandmother, practically brought me up.'

'Well, I don't seem to have done a very good job,' said Jess Channing. Her voice was quite low, Gray noticed, and her London accent strong, but it was a very attractive voice. 'Now Barnaby, you could make yourself useful, I'd have thought, passed some of those plates round. Poor Mr Townsend's got his hands very full there.'

'Oh Gran –'

'Barnaby, do what I tell you. How do you know the Booths, then, Mr Townsend?'

'Oh – I've known Duggie from way back. I'm a financial journalist.'

'Gray, what on earth were you doing, just now, locked in the kitchen with Terri Booth?' said Kirsten.

'She was – upset.'

'Oh really?' Her voice was sarcastic, heavy; for a moment he disliked her.

'Kirsten, don't be so harsh,' said Jess Channing, 'it doesn't suit you. I'm sure Mrs Booth is very upset. And I have to say I thought that speech of hers was well deserved. We have all ostracised her. It was wrong of us. And Douglas was very happy with her, he told me so. Now you must excuse me, I have to speak to my son. Isambard,' she called across the room, 'Isambard, I'd like a word, please.' She moved away from them.

Gray had never heard Bard's full name before; it sounded very incongruous. He looked down at Kirsten and grinned. 'Some lady.'

'Yeah, I told you she was great.'

'You all right?'

'Mm. Think so. Bit – well, you know, shaken.'

'Of course. You on speaking terms with your dad yet?'

'Not really. I tried to talk to him about Duggie, but –' Her eyes filled suddenly with tears; she fumbled for her handkerchief. He could see she was genuinely and slightly surprisingly upset.

'You really liked him, didn't you?'

'Yes I did. And I can't bear to think he's gone and I never – never –' Her voice wobbled.

'Oh Kirsten. You are in a bad way. How would you like to have dinner with me tonight? No more than that, just dinner, cheer you up.' And me, he thought wondering at the same time if it actually would.

She looked at him and smiled suddenly, her oddly sweet smile. 'Oh – no, I don't think I should, Gray. Thanks for asking me. But I won't be good company, and –'

'I'm not looking for good company. I just thought it might help.'

She hesitated, clearly tempted. Then she said, 'Well – yes. That'd be really nice. But –'

'It's all right,' he said, hoping he meant it, 'I got the message last time. I understand. Just friends. Don't worry, Kirsten, I'll deliver you home to your door and I won't even kiss you.'

She laughed. 'I'd hate that. Yeah, OK. Where d'you want to go? Or – tell you what, why don't I cook for you?'

'Can you cook?' he said carefully.

'No. But I could get some steak, and –'

'I'll cook for you,' he said. 'Because I can, and there's nothing I like doing more. What do you like? Italian, French ... ?'

'English,' she said, surprising him.

'OK. Steak kidney and oyster pie. How'd that be?'

'Great. Only I don't want you getting any ideas about the oysters,' she said, laughing.

'I swear I won't,' he said, and went off to the kitchen to recharge his tray.

On his way back, he bumped into Terri; she had clearly had more than one glass of champagne and was looking a lot more cheerful.

'You're an angel,' she said, kissing his cheek briefly, 'thank you. And before I forget, Gray, give me a call tomorrow, would you. I think we most definitely have some unfinished business to discuss.'

'We do?' he said, slightly nervous.

'We do. Little matter of a story about one Bard Channing ...'

'Good God,' said Gray. He had not exactly forgotten the puzzlement of Duggie's invitation to lunch, Terri's veiled hints about a story, but he had consciously put it out of his mind, had tried not to think about any of it. He came back to it now with a sense of almost physical pleasure, as to a long-delayed drink.

'You're on,' he said. 'I'll call you in the morning.'

'Oliver, please! Please try!'

'What?' said Oliver irritably. He was watching Kirsten Channing chatting and laughing to that smooth bastard of a journalist, and wondering why it irritated him. Probably because she was so bloody sure of herself, well, she would be, looking like that, with all her father's money behind her, that over-privileged upbringing, everything coming her way. Silly girl she was, slinging the family mud all over the newspapers; it merely confirmed what he'd always thought about her, that she was a shallow, spoilt bitch who didn't know when she was well off. It was just that –

'Oliver please, you're not listening to me.'

'Sorry. What's the matter, Mel?'

'I want you to take me over to Barnaby. Think of some excuse –'

'Melinda, you're ridiculous. You don't want to waste time even talking to that bloke. He's bad news.'

'How do you know?'

'I just do.'

'You were talking to his sister. Looking pretty keen about it, as well.'

'Of course I wasn't,' said Oliver wearily. 'I was just being polite.'

'Oh yes?'

'Yes. You know perfectly well how I feel about Kirsten. I can't stand her.'

'It didn't look like that to me. Not just now.'

'This is a stupid conversation,' said Oliver. 'Can we drop it?'

'When you've got me talking to Barnaby, we can.'

'Oh for God's sake. Look, he's got two trays of canapés, why don't you go and offer to help him with one of them.'

'I couldn't,' said Melinda, flushing violently. 'I really couldn't.'

'Well, go and ask him to take a couple over to Mum. She's talking to his gran, shouldn't be too difficult.'

'Oliver, that's brilliant. Yes, OK. I will. Wish me luck!'

Poor silly little thing, thought Oliver; it was hard to believe that she was twenty-one, she seemed about sixteen most of the time. He hoped to God Barnaby wouldn't do or say anything at all that gave her the slightest encouragement. Because if he did, he'd –

'Oliver! How very nice to see you. How are you, dear?'

'Oh – hallo, Mrs Booth. Yes, I'm very well, thank you.' He'd been dreading this moment, had known it had to come.

'It's very sweet of you to come. And to bring your mother.'

'No, really, we wouldn't – that is – well, I'm so sorry, Mrs Booth. About Mr Booth. He was so – so nice.'

'Yes,' she said, 'yes, that's exactly what he was – nice. I shall miss him dreadfully. But – well, life has to go on. Oh dear –' She smiled at him. 'Not a very appropriate remark, that. Sorry.' She was drunk, he realised; she put out her hand and patted his cheek. He had to concentrate very hard on not brushing the hand away. 'Now are you all right, Oliver, being looked after?'

'Yes. Yes, thank you. We're all fine.'

'Good. I hope that Barnaby doesn't start moving in on your pretty little sister. Nasty piece of work, he is, if you ask me.' God, she was sharp.

'Well – she thinks he's terribly good looking. Got a bit of a crush on him.'

'Silly girl. I suppose he is. Good looking, that is. Not as stunning as his sister, though.'

'Oh – I don't know.'

'She is one gorgeous girl,' said Terri Booth, studying Kirsten, who was now talking to her grandmother and Heather Clarke. 'I don't actually like those sort of looks, I prefer the younger one, but she is a stunner.'

'Yes, she's very pretty,' said Oliver politely.

'I don't actually mind her too much,' said Terri, surprising him. 'I think she's honest. Everyone said it was so dreadful, talking to the papers like she did, but I wouldn't blame her. She's had a tough time, with that mother of hers. Not too surprising she took to drink, of course, being married to Bard Channing –'

'Mrs Booth, I have to –'

'Oh, I'm sorry, Oliver.' She smiled at him, patted his arm, removed a hair from his lapel. 'I shouldn't be talking to you like this. I'm a bit – overwrought. Is your mother all right, being looked after? Perhaps after all she and I can become friends now.'

'Yes, perhaps,' said Oliver.

She looked at him thoughtfully for a moment. 'You work for Mr Barbour, don't you? It must be very interesting. All the internal machinations, eh? Fascinating. You never know what you might unearth there, Oliver.'

'I'm sorry, I don't know –'

'Oh take no notice of me,' she said. 'I'm rambling. Bit too much excitement for an old lady. But let's just say you should keep your eyes wide open, Oliver. Now then, I must go and say hallo to dear

Francesca, I suppose. Before she makes her rather feeble excuses and leaves.'

She was gross, thought Oliver; he felt very sorry for her, but God, she was embarrassing. And always talking in those riddles of hers. He decided that next time – if there was a next time – he was going to come right out and ask her exactly what it was she was always going on about.

'Oliver! Hallo again.' It was Kirsten. 'I'm just leaving. Gray – Gray Townsend, you know – is taking Granny Jess home, and I'm going with him to show him the way.'

'Oh. Oh, I see.' Why the hell did she think he'd be interested in that? Silly bitch.

'I just wanted to – well, to thank you again for the hanky. And for being so kind. I really appreciated it.'

'That's all right.'

'I'll – well, I'll send it back to you. What's your address?'

'You don't have to.'

'No, I want to. Really.' She smiled at him; she looked genuinely friendly. And she smelt gorgeous, some sexy, raw scent she'd just put on: he hadn't noticed it before. For the benefit of that berk, he supposed. Christ, she was beautiful. He'd never known any really beautiful girls, not known them well. Certainly not in the biblical sense – and then, briefly, piercingly, a vision came to Oliver of knowing Kirsten in the biblical sense, of looking at that body unclothed, of touching those breasts, those full, high breasts, of parting those endless thighs, of – get a grip, Clarke, for God's sake. He felt himself blushing. He was worse than Melinda. Only unlike her, he had not the slightest desire, not really, to know Kirsten Channing biblically or unbiblically. It was just that she seemed – well, at least a bit nicer than he'd thought. Softer. More vulnerable.

He gave her his address, said goodbye briefly, and went to help Melinda and Barnaby – Barnaby, for Christ's sake, this whole thing was turning into a nightmare – ease Heather into the car.

'Thank you so much,' said Melinda. 'It is really very kind of you, Barnaby.'

'My pleasure,' he said, smiling at her, his teeth very white in his brown face. 'Nice to see you again. See you around.'

'Yes,' said Melinda, 'yes, see you around, Barnaby.' She waved to him rather overenthusiastically as the car pulled away. 'Do you think he meant that, Mum, do you think he really did?'

'I don't know, dear,' said Heather Clarke. She leant back in her seat. She looked very tired. 'Poor Mrs Booth. She was very upset really, you know. When she said goodbye to me, she looked terribly strained. I feel so sorry for her. It's the shock, you know, when it's sudden.'

'Yes. Yes, of course. Mum, do you like Barnaby?'

'Well, he seems very nice, dear. He was certainly most kind to me. Poor Kirsten is a much nicer girl than I'd thought, too. I was talking to her grandmother about her, earlier. She says she's actually very sweet, just very mixed up, got a bit lost along the way. And Kirsten was charming to me. Told me how good looking she thought you were, Oliver, that she hadn't really noticed it before, and said you'd been really kind to her, and she'd enjoyed talking to you.'

'Don't make me spew,' said Oliver.

'That's a horrible expression, Oliver.'

'Sorry.'

An absurd, but nonetheless sweet warmth had settled somewhere around his consciousness, a totally ridiculous desire to go on talking about Kirsten.

'What was she doing talking to you anyway? What did she have to say? Apart from how incredibly cool and fascinating I was?'

'Oh, not very much. She came over to talk to her grandmother, really. And she promised to come and see me. I don't suppose she will, but it's nice she should even think of it.'

'If Kirsten Channing goes to see you, Mum,' said Melinda, waking briefly from her reverie about Barnaby, clearly casting her mind for something drastic enough, 'I'll enter a convent.'

'Talking of convents,' said Oliver, 'Mr Channing is becoming trustee of some convent in Devon. I saw the papers about it the other day. Getting involved in building some new home for the disabled attached to it. Doesn't that strike you as pretty surprising?'

'Not at all. He really is one of the kindest men in the world,' said Heather.

'Mum,' said Melinda, 'I sometimes think you're in love with Bard Channing. Or were, anyway.'

'Don't be ridiculous,' said Heather.

Francesca was walking past Terri's pink kitchen, on her way to the loo, when she heard one of the poodles yelping. She liked dogs; she went in, bent down to stroke it. 'Hallo,' she said, smiling. The poodle bit her: not hard, but enough to make her flinch, draw back.

'That was horrid,' she said to it severely. She had never liked poodles anyway; silly little over-dressed things.

'Francesca, dear, are you all right?' It was Terri, standing in the doorway, cigarette in one hand, glass of champagne in the other. She didn't look exactly grief-stricken, more like a pet poodle herself, Francesca thought, and felt perversely irritated.

'Yes. Thank you. One of your dogs bit me.'

'Not mine, dear. But I'm sorry. We'd better get it washed. I'm sure the dog's not rabid, but you never know.'

'Well, I certainly hope not,' said Francesca lightly. She moved over to the sink; Terri stood beside her, turned on the tap.

'Give it a jolly good scrub, I'll get you some Savlon or something. Here —' she rummaged in a drawer, produced a tube.

'Thank you,' said Francesca.

'It doesn't seem to have drawn blood, anyway.' The ginny voice was slightly ironic, amused even.

'No, No, of course not. It was just a bit of a shock. Thank you. Er – Terri —' She really felt she must say it, however she might feel, however hostile to Teresa for her outburst in the chapel. 'I just wanted to say, again, I'm so sorry about Duggie. You must be —'

'Must be what?'

'Well,' Francesca felt slightly nonplussed, 'feeling so sad. Lonely. Lost. I —'

'Well, I daresay I will be, Francesca,' said Terri, and the voice was harder now. 'Right this minute, I just feel numb. Which is probably just as well.'

'Yes,' said Francesa, 'yes, of course. Well, if there's anything I can do —'

There was a silence. Then: 'No, I don't think there will be,' said Terri. She drew heavily on her cigarette. 'I find that quite impossible to imagine. Actually. That you could do anything for me.'

'Oh, I see,' said Francesca. She had no idea how to cope with this; this strange, almost open hostility.

'In fact the best thing you can do for me, Francesca, is exactly what you've done so far. All along. Ever since I married Duggie. Keep away. Leave me alone. Ignore me. I haven't liked that, any more than I've liked what your husband has done to Duggie. But it'll suit me just fine now.'

'Teresa, what are you talking about, what has Bard done —'

'Very little,' said Teresa, draining her champagne glass. 'That's the whole point. Or of course if you looked at it another way, rather a lot. Seeing to his own rather well-lined nest. Not giving a bugger about anyone else's. I've got your husband's measure, Francesca, and I don't like it. In spite of those very touching words at the service today.

Everyone sitting there, gazing up at him, the great Bard Channing, hanging on his every utterance. That's the way he likes it, isn't it?'

'Teresa —'

'I think you'd better go,' said Teresa. 'Otherwise I'm really going to say too much. And then, I can tell you, neither of us would like it. I think the best thing you can hope for from me, Francesca, is that you never see or hear from me again. But I wouldn't depend on that if I were you. It's gloves-off time now, you see, now that I don't have to worry about Duggie any more ...'

'I'm sorry, Teresa,' said Francesca, surprised at the cool, the self-control in her voice, when what she was really feeling was the ever more familiar sense of unease, 'but I really have no idea what you're talking about.'

'No,' said Teresa, looking at her very intently, and there was something like sympathy now in her eyes, sympathy and at the same time scorn. 'I really don't think you do.'

Chapter Fourteen

It was a terrible sound; she couldn't think what it was at first. Heavy, muffled, halfway between a groan and a wail. It sounded like an animal in pain. Then she realised: it was Bard. Bard weeping.

Francesca looked at the clock: only one. He had said he was going to sleep in his dressing room, had told her to go to bed early, that she looked exhausted, and feeling at once relieved and faintly ashamed of herself (for what had she to be exhausted about, she had done nothing that day except say foolish vapid things, smile foolish false smiles), she agreed. That had been ten-thirty. He had been in his study since coming in from the office at seven. He had said he didn't want food. He had been curt, withdrawn from her in his grief; helpless to comfort him, at the same time hurt at the continuing rejection, she hadn't known what to say. He had carried a bottle of whisky and a jug of coffee upstairs and shut the door.

Barnaby had gone out with Kirsten, it was Sandie's evening off, Nanny had put the children to bed early, and had retired into her own small sitting room next to the nursery. Francesca felt very alone. Alone with her thoughts. With the memory, too, of the episode with Teresa which, however much she tried to shrug it off, tell herself it had meant nothing, that Teresa had been in an irrational, wretched state of mind, had upset her very much. She hadn't seem irrational or wretched: simply angry. And almost – no, not almost, actually – enjoying it. Well, Francesca told herself for what seemed like the hundredth time since then, grief took strange forms, did strange things. That was all it had been. Of course. There was no point thinking about it any further. What she had said, or what she had meant. No point at all.

The noise came again, from Bard's study. This was a far more immediate, real concern. Francesca got out of bed and pulled on a robe; it was a very hot night and she had slept naked. She quailed slightly at what she had to do, but knew, just the same, she couldn't leave him alone. She walked quietly down the corridor, stood outside the half-open door. The noise went on; he didn't hear her.

She pushed it open carefully; he was sitting at his desk, his head buried in his arms, his great shoulders heaving. She went forward, moving very steadily, and when she reached him put out her hand, onto the shoulders, said 'Bard' quite quietly. She half expected a rebuff even then, was prepared to retreat; but he looked up at her, his face raw with grief, wet with tears, and suddenly put his arms round her waist, burying his head in her breast.

'Oh God,' he said. 'Oh God, Francesca, how am I going to bear this? I loved him so much, he was my only real friend, our entire lives were spent together, the business, everything was ours. I can't do it alone, I can't, I feel so alone, so utterly alone.'

She couldn't think of anything to say; she felt helpless, useless in the face of such pain. She held his head to her, stroking his hair, murmuring wordless nonsense to him as she did to little Jack when he had hurt himself, just listening, letting him talk.

'It was such a good friendship,' he said, 'we were so good for each other. He taught me to be patient, to think before I spoke' – you could have fooled me, Francesca thought – 'to wait for people to make their own judgments, and I put some fire in his belly, gave him ambition, drive. He often said if it hadn't been for me he'd have been a golf pro meandering round some course, spending his evenings at the nineteenth hole. Oh God, Francesca, and if he had, maybe he'd be alive now, maybe I drove him to it, drove him to his death, always forcing him on, demanding things of him, impatient when he was tired or wanted to move into the slow lane for a bit. Christ, what have I done, what have I done?'

'Bard, you haven't done anything. No that's not true, you've done a lot, a lot for him. Duggie loved the company, loved being part of it' – she pushed the memory of Teresa's words away – 'Do you think he'd have been happy being a golf pro?'

'Yes, I do. I really do.'

'For a little while, maybe. Then he'd have been bored, he'd have atrophied. Duggie liked the good life, Bard, as well as anyone. What you did was help him fulfil his potential, give him –'

'No,' he said, brushing the tears impatiently away, sitting back in his chair, looking up at her, 'no, that's not right. He wouldn't have been bored, and he wouldn't have minded not being rich. He was a modest fellow, in every way, he had the sweetest, happiest nature. He'd have been perfectly happy in a little Tudor semi somewhere, I know he would.'

'Well maybe. But –'

'And now I'm on my own. Completely. As I should have been from the beginning, maybe. Maybe this is my punishment –'

'For what?' she said.

'I'm sorry?'

'Your punishment for what?'

'Oh – for everything. Everything wrong I've ever done.'

'Bard, you haven't done anything wrong.'

'Oh really?' he said, looking up at her. 'And how would you know that?'

Francesca didn't know why, but she found the question frightening; then she told herself he was talking nonsense, that he was drunk . . .

'Because I know you. That's how. And I love you.'

'Oh Christ,' he said, 'Christ, I hope you do.'

'I do.'

He sat back and looked up at her for a moment, his eyes absolutely unreadable, and then he pushed aside her robe and cradled her breasts in his hands with infinite care, as if they were fragile, in danger of breaking.

'Lovely,' he said, 'so lovely, you are.'

He bent forward and kissed them, one at a time, his tongue lingering on the nipples, and then moved his mouth down, down to her stomach, her pubic hair. She felt his tongue working at her clitoris, felt the sharp, leaping streaks of desire; she closed her eyes, concentrating utterly on the moment, the sensation of it, the deep, rich, unfurling pleasure: and then he stood up briefly, dragging impatiently at his clothes, kissing her hard, fiercely, and then she was on him, astride him, his penis forcing into her, savagely, sweetly strong, and she rode him, rode the pleasure of him, felt each push, each thrust, felt herself growing, moulding round him, felt the great circles spreading, reaching on and on, out and out, felt herself travelling with them, with him, felt the great dark force of release begin, and she threw back her head and cried out aloud, heard herself, a strange wild cry, the cry of sex, the cry of love.

She stayed there for a long while, holding him, holding him to her; in the months that followed she thought of it often, that night, an isolated piece of happiness preserved, suspended in time, to be looked at, treasured, wondered at.

In the morning he came in, kissed her briefly, said he had to go; he had never followed her to bed, as he had said he would.

'Will you be back tonight?'

'Yes, but very late. Don't wait dinner for me.'

'No, all right.' Her voice sounded even to her forlorn, disappointed. The distance between them was there again, increasing fast.

'Look,' he said, 'I'm not going to be around much for a while. Why don't you go to Greece for a few weeks? The house is there, the staff are there. Take your mother maybe.'

'No,' she said, 'it will be terribly hot and anyway, I don't want to be so far from Kitty's doctor. And I'm not getting on too well with my mother.'

'Oh really? Why on earth not?'

'Oh – she's acting very oddly. I suppose she's got some new boyfriend, won't talk about it, doesn't have any time for me, lied about where she was going one day, said she was going to stay with an old friend and she wasn't there at all ...'

'Yes?' He was bending over, putting on his shoes. 'Well, she's a law unto herself, your mother. Always has been.'

'Yes. Incidentally, Bard, I'm sorry about her pestering you for money for that convent place of hers. I've told her to back off.'

There was a silence. Then he said, very casually, 'Oh, it didn't matter. It was only a cheque. Don't worry about it. I'll see you later.'

'Yes. And Bard –'

'Yes?'

She had been going to say something loving, make some reference to the previous night, but his expression was impatient, distant.

'Nothing. Doesn't matter. Goodbye.'

When he had gone she lay staring at the door after he had closed it, feeling absolutely desolate, no longer loved, warmed, comforted as she had done just a little earlier. And something worse even than desolate: she felt used.

On the other side of London Gray Townsend was also lying alone in bed, also staring at a closed door, also feeling used, although less desperately, less unhappily so. Gray's primary emotion that morning was bafflement, and the person who was baffling him was Kirsten.

She had arrived for dinner the evening before, after the funeral, looking rather subdued, wearing a long, floaty skirt and a white linen shirt: almost girly, Gray thought, apart from the inevitable heavy boots. She was carrying a bottle of wine, and a bunch of flowers.

'I thought this'd be nice. Toby left a few bottles and he never drank rubbish, and the flowers are to cheer your house up. Female-less houses are always so – oh. Oh Gray. You don't need a lousy bunch of flowers. What a lovely house.'

She had come into the hall; Gray was particularly proud of the hall, hated the way most people used them as little better than passages; had made a room of it, papered it with brown parcel paper (the striped sort, his own idea), set a low table just underneath the stairs, covered with small silver frames holding sepia pictures of his aunts and uncles and parents and grandparents as children: 'Great for burglars,' Briony had often said, 'seeing them through the letterbox,' but the burglars hadn't seem to fancy them, nor the heavy brass pot containing the parlour palm that sat beside them, nor the rather nice Victorian watercolours of churches and country houses that hung on the walls, nor the extremely fine barometer gracing the far wall, nor the oak chest that stood at the bottom of the stairs.

He followed her, smiling modestly as she moved from room to room, exclaiming with pleasure.

'It's lovely,' she said again, wandering out into the conservatory, her tour completed. 'How clever you are.'

'I grew up,' he said, 'in a very ordinary little 1930s house. It was nice, but even then I knew how I would like it to be. Having my own house has been a great self-indulgence. Anyway, I'm glad you like it. Now then, glass of champagne?'

'Please,' she said, 'I feel I need it.'

And they sat down in the conservatory, and she smiled at him and said, 'This is so kind of you, cheering me up like this.'

'Not entirely kind,' he said, 'I plan to have a lovely evening.'

He had cooked the promised steak and kidney pie 'with only a few oysters' served with potatoes so tiny they were like marbles and almost raw broccoli, and got one of his summer puddings out of the freezer; they had drunk the champagne and then moved onto Toby's Burgundy which had indeed been extremely good, and had chatted easily about many things, but mostly their childhoods; his had been happy and entirely normal, he said, very dull really, only child, much loved, lived in a country town in Surrey, gone to Charterhouse and then to Warwick, got a 2:1 and then, with extraordinary ease, found his way into Fleet Street via a graduate training scheme. 'I was on the *Guardian*, and I loved it, was a sort of jobbing general reporter, moved onto the arts page and then discovered Mammon, or rather Mammon's pages, and felt I'd come home. Worked on the *Observer*, the *Sunday Times*, been on the *News* four years now. No real traumas, lots of fun, very uninteresting. How about you?'

He had been afraid hers would be tedious, a catalogue of neglect and misfortune, but she was funny about it, sent herself up, describing the horrors of Nanny, of Benenden, even of her mother's alcoholism with a sweetly considered maturity. She adored her brother, she said, while half resenting his charm. 'Even my father thinks he's wonderful' – and loved Victoria 'like an old mother hen. But the person I love best, I suppose, who we all do, is Granny Jess. She was so good to us, so loving and forgiving, so stern and strict, and she had such ambitions for us, encouraged us, urged us on. I don't think there is anything, anything at all that she doesn't know about any of us,' she added, 'and that includes my father. And nothing shocks her, and she never judges us. But even she was no match for the rest.'

'The rest?'

'Oh, you know, the bad things,' she said vaguely. 'I've failed her dreadfully I'm afraid, she so wanted me to be good.'

Then, without warning, she started to cry, heavy bitter tears, her face dropped in her hands; Gray sat staring at her, and then tentatively put an arm round her

'Kirsten,' he said gently, 'Kirsten, you must not be so hard on yourself.'

'But I must,' she said, 'I'm dreadful, awful, so spoilt, and greedy, I use people all the time, look what I did to you. Oh Gray, I'm so ashamed.' And she had buried her head in his chest and cried for a long time.

'You don't have to be sorry,' he had said, smiling down at her, stroking back the wild hair, when she had finally stopped. 'I'm over twenty-one, you know, I can take care of myself. I could have gone home that night, but I didn't, I chose to stay. And it was very nice. Well, I thought so, anyway.'

'Really?' she said, looking up at him in a kind of wonder, hiccuping slightly. 'Did you really not despise me afterwards?'

'Not at all,' he said. 'It was the last thing I thought to do. I think you're lovely, and I was flattered and pleased, and you were very honest with me in the morning, you didn't fudge it –'

'I'll go to hell,' she said miserably, chewing on one of her strands of hair, 'I know I will, I was thinking about it this morning in that foul chapel; when I die, I'll go to hell –'

'Kirsten, really! You don't believe all that –'

'Of course I do. I'm a good – well, a bad – Catholic girl. I've committed most of the mortal sins already. There's no hope for me.'

'You really are ridiculous,' he said and then, because she looked so sad, so forlorn, he bent to kiss her gently; and then, somehow, she had kissed him back, and then, well, then he had started stroking her breasts (which were rather clearly visible through the fine linen) and she had started to respond, and a little less than half an hour later, he was leading her upstairs. 'This is not to make me feel better, is it?' Kirsten had said.

'No, it's to make me feel better,' he said, laughing, 'but only if you really want to.'

'I really want to.'

It had been so different this time, so different from that wild, hard night; this time he had led and she had followed, her body soft, pliable, infinitely willing, wonderfully, gloriously responsive, her orgasms greeting his in what seemed an endless rising, falling, movement and stillness, capture, and release; and when finally they were done, she lay, smiling sweetly, her eyes closed, her hair splayed wild across the pillow, and said simply 'Oh Gray, that was good' and fell fast asleep.

And then in the morning she left, quickly, almost hastily, still slightly distanced from him: said she had to get home, she had so much to do, and promised to phone him later in the day.

Well, perhaps she would.

'Francesca? This is Liam.'

'Oh,' she said. 'Oh Liam, hallo.'

'You sound rotten.'

'I feel it,' she said. She was too miserable to pretend.

'What's the matter? Tell me.'

Oh – no. I can't. I'm just being – silly.'

'I doubt that,' he said and his voice was very gentle, very concerned. A most poignant contrast to Bard's brusque, impatient tones, an hour earlier.

'Yes I am. I'm just – upset about yesterday. About the funeral.'

'How was it? That was why I phoned.'

'Oh – you know. Very dreadful really. So sad. And Teresa Booth delivered what Barnaby would have called a bollocking to us all. For cutting Duggie off, after she married him.'

'What, in the church?'

'Yes. It was awful.'

'Golly,' said Liam. 'I wish I'd been there.'

'No, Liam, it was awful. We all felt bad, I think. Because it was true.'

'Did my father speak?'

'Yes he did. Incredibly well.'

She tried not to think about Teresa's words on that particular subject. She felt better about that at least this morning, more able to dismiss it. But it was still there, at the back of her mind, troubling her.

'He's very good on those occasions,' he said. 'I can still remember when my mother died, how he spoke at her funeral. I was crying, all the time, and somehow I stopped then. He made me feel I could be brave.'

'Oh Liam. I can't begin to think how awful that must have been for you.'

'Not good,' he said, 'but I got through it. Somehow.'

'You must have been very good for each other. Comforting each other.'

'Not really,' he said, and his voice was cool suddenly, surprised. 'I hardly saw him. He sent me off to school.'

'Yes,' she said, 'I was thinking about that. You were only seven.'

'Yes. Yes I was.'

'It must have been terrible. So – so bewildering.'

'Yes. That's exactly the word. I didn't know who or where I was, what I was supposed to be doing.'

'I feel a bit bewildered,' she said, 'this morning. I don't know why.'

'Well, come and see me,' he said. 'Tell me about it. It might help. And it would be lovely for me.'

'Well –'

'Please! It would take my mind off this afternoon, too.'

'What's happening this afternoon?'

'Visit from the big man, who's had a look at my latest X-rays. Going to assess my case, tell me how it might turn out. Whether I'm going to have a limp for the rest of my life. Whether I've got to have further surgery.'

'Oh, Liam!' She hadn't realised that was a possibility. 'How horrendous. Well – yes, all right. Of course I'll come. At about –' she looked at her diary, glanced at her watch – 'eleven.'

'I'll be counting the moments.'

'Mr Channing!' said the Australian nurse. 'You're always on that phone. Come on, I've got to check that dressing. Good news about your leg, isn't it?'

'I'm sorry?' said Liam.

'Well, that it's healing so well, that you'll be out of here in another week or so. I heard Mr Bertram telling you when he was on his ward round.'

'Oh – yes,' said Liam. 'Yes, I suppose so.' He had been so engrossed in his fiction about further surgery he had almost come to believe it.

Kirsten didn't phone. But a letter came, three days later: 'Dear Gray,' it said, 'It was lovely, and you're very special. But this time, I do mean it. It's wrong of me to use you like this. We can meet in a little while, when we have both recovered ourselves: meanwhile thank you again and again for being such a true, good friend. Kirsten.'

A friend, he thought, a good friend; not a good lover even, simply a friend. And realised that there was neither future nor reality in their realtionship: he was, to her, a nice man, not of her generation, nor her way of thinking or doing things, and if he were wise, he would set all of it behind him. And felt not so much hurt, not used even, but dreadfully and deeply sad.

She really couldn't go and see Liam again, Francesca thought: she'd been every day for a week, except the weekend when she and the childen had gone to Stylings and Bard had promised to come if he possibly could and didn't; it was ridiculous, goodness knows what the nurses must think. He was probably beginning to dread her visits: at this rate they'd run out of things to say. Only every day he said please, please Francesca, come again tomorrow, you're my only visitor, and it's an awfully long day, and every day she said she would if she could, only she wasn't making any promises, and then every day she found she really wanted to go again, and of course she could, she had plenty of time, all the time in the world, Bard was working ridiculous hours, and when he did come home, he went to his study and then told her to go to bed without him, that he would be working late, would sleep in his dressing room.

And since she was really rather lonely, and not actually terribly busy, there didn't actually seem any reason not to go. She was at least doing something useful, which was more than could be said of much of the rest of her existence.

And there certainly didn't actually seem to be any danger of their running out of things to say; they chatted easily, endlessly, and every visit she found she had stayed longer. They had much in common, they discovered through those conversations: they found they were charmed and amused by the same things, the same gossipy stories in the papers (both suckers for anything about the Princess of Wales), John Major's Diary in *Private Eye*, the *News Quiz* on the radio, the same films (Best this year so far? Oh, *Somersby*. Really? Me too) the same music (Not Mozart and Clapton and Ella Fitzgerald, not all three, I don't believe it); that they were both reduced to tears by any cheap sentimentality ('I once cried over a wedding on *EastEnders*, can you believe that?' said Francesca, ashamedly, and 'I can believe it, because I did too,' said Liam, laughing at her shame); the same book – '*Brideshead*, I read it every year, and anything, anything at all by John

Updike' – 'Which one, don't tell me, *Couples* is my all time favourite.'
'Mine too, mine too, most people don't even know that one.') They
liked the same food and there was much talk of it, of Indian carry-
outs, and steak tartare and jacket potatoes and apple charlotte – 'Not
crumble, I mean charlotte' – 'Yes, yes, I know, I do too, – and
raspberries rather than strawberries, pears rather than apples,' and Liam
teased her about her passion for figs – 'I told a journalist about that the
other day, I'm sure it was silly of me, D. H. Lawrence and all that.'
'Yes I'm sure it was too' – all this over the mince and carrots that
passed for stew and the dried-up fish and watery mash that was called
fish pie and the tinned fruit cocktail that they swore was fruit salad
which Liam dutifully swallowed for want of anything better. Except
of course for the grapes and the peaches and the nectarines that
Francesca brought him, and the oatcakes and the Dolcelatte, and the
Mars ice cream she had taken in on the Friday: 'Next week if you
come, we'll have one of these,' he had said, indicating a metal blue
and gold attaché case, filled with half bottles of Veuve Clicquot;
'Present from dear old Duggie and Teresa, I feel so terrible, I never
thanked him.'

'We all feel terrible about Duggie,' she said, very sadly, and it was
true, she did, more terrible every day; and then, making a great effort
because after all he needed support, cheering up so much: 'Liam, we
can't drink champagne here, I'll be expelled, expelled from your
bedside, and then you'll be sorry,' and 'Yes,' he said, suddenly serious.
'Yes, I would, so very sorry. But the nurses are all extremely fond of
me now,' he said, grinning at her, 'and dreading me going, so they
won't actually mind a bit.'

'Don't be so sure,' she said, punching him gently, 'and be careful, I
don't like conceited men.'

She loved those conversations: they were so unlike any she had had
for a long time. Bard never chatted these days, certainly never
gossiped, and most certainly never listened to her on such matters as
films she liked, food she adored, books that made her laugh aloud.
Well, not any more, she told herself, struggling as always to be loyal:
what husband of five years did, such comparisons were dangerous,
deeply so. She felt quite sure Naomi Channing would hardly
recognise her husband from these conversations either. Nevertheless
they were wonderfully soothing, marvellously restorative; they
soothed her hurts, restored her morale, eased her loneliness. And as he
recovered, became more of a person, less of an invalid, she found
herself increasingly fascinated by Liam, by his likeness to Bard as well

as his unlikeness; it was impossible not to compare them, not to set one against the other.

Physically they were strangely similar, and at the same time utterly different: Liam's face was in some ways Bard's only somehow made lighter; the same brilliant dark eyes, the just slightly too long nose, the hard jawline. But Liam's eyes were wider spaced, the forehead higher, the mouth tauter. Only the hair was exactly the same; thick, dark, unruly hair, that defied every cut, every piece of hairdressing skill. Bard's was streaked with grey, and Liam's was longer, but it was the same hair.

Their voices were the same in essence too, deep, strong voices, slightly throaty, but Liam's was musical, an actor's voice, shaped into perfection for the Bar, Bard's faster, rougher, more emotional.

But there the similarities ended; Liam was still where Bard was restless, patient where Bard was impatient, as swiftly interested as Bard was easily bored. Liam was courteous, easily charming; Bard was brusque, frank, dismissive of anyone or thing that did not interest him. But the biggest difference of all, she thought, was that Liam was so straightforward, so easy to read, Bard so complex and inscrutable.

'Nice weekend?' he said as she went in that morning to the hospital, found him in the day room, with a suspicious-looking bundle on his lap, under a blanket.

'Mmm. Quite nice. What on earth have you got there, Liam, it looks like a bedpan.'

'Ssh,' he said, 'did you bring the glasses?'

'What glasses? Oh, the champagne glasses. Do you know, I did.'

'Excellent. Let's go over to the corner and tuck ourselves in. No-one will come anyway, they're all watching the royals arriving at Ascot.'

She followed him to the corner, smiling indulgently at him. He seemed to her at that moment exactly like Jack.

He removed the blanket, produced two half bottles of the Veuve Clicquot. 'Even cold. I chatted up the little Indian nurse and she let me put it in the fridge. Here –' he eased the cork out of the first one – 'here's to us. Thank you for a very happy time.'

She held out the glasses, laughing. 'Liam honestly! Hardly happy.'

'Oh, but it has been. I can't remember when I've enjoyed a time so much. Only because of you. You've been wonderful, Francesca. I feel so ashamed of how I used to treat you, so sad to think of all that wasted time when we could have been friends.'

She smiled at him, sipped at the champagne. 'Don't be silly,' she said, while regretting it herself.

'So you forgive me?'

'Of course I forgive you.'

'I'm so glad,' he said. 'Thank you for that, too. As well as all the rest.'

'Liam, I haven't done anything.'

'Of course you have. Giving up all your precious time –'

'Not very precious,' she said, 'I'm afraid.'

'Oh really? Not with two little children and a very demanding husband and some equally demanding stepchildren and –'

'Don't go on, Liam, it makes me feel depressed.'

'Why?'

'Because my time isn't precious. Because quite often I'm bored to tears. Because – oh, it doesn't matter. I shouldn't be talking to you like this.'

'Of course you should. You've put up with a lot of shit from me. Let me put up with a bit from you.'

'No, Liam, it's not fair. Not to you and not to – well, not to anyone.'

He shrugged. 'OK. This is nice, isn't it?'

'It's lovely. Let's drink to dear, dear Duggie.'

'To Duggie.' They touched glasses, smiled; she met his eyes then looked away. The expression in them, intent, probing, made her uncomfortable.

'Tell me about your weekend,' he said.

'Oh – it was all right. We went to Stylings.'

'All of you?'

'Mmm. Barnaby came too.'

'How is the little sod?'

'He's a little sod. But he's also a life enhancer. I can't help liking him. Anyway, he's fine. Well on the mend now.'

'How does he get on with my father?'

'Very well,' she said. 'Bard adores him. Definitely his favourite. Well, apart from Jack. I – oh Liam, I'm sorry. I didn't think, how stupid, I just –'

'It's all right,' he said, and his voice was harsh suddenly, harsh and heavy. 'I'm quite used to it. Have been for a long time.'

'Liam, I – I know he'd like to make amends, if you'd –'

'Francesca, he wouldn't. He hates me. It's all right. Not your fault. Let's talk about something else.'

But he was very quiet for the rest of the time she was there, and when she left, still anxious, his face was sombre, he hardly smiled, even when, to try and comfort him, she kissed him goodbye. All the way back to the house, she reproached herself, wondered how she could have been so insensitive. When he was so sensitive.

'What are you looking so cheerful about?' said Sister. 'Nice visit from Mrs Channing?'

'Very nice,' he said, 'very nice indeed. Sister, would you like to share a glass of champagne with me? I think I have something to celebrate.'

'I killed him,' said Terri Booth. Her voice was very heavy and flat, and she looked exhausted, white and drawn beneath her heavy make-up. She had also clearly lost weight in the ten days since the funeral; she was a very different woman from the defiant one who had stood up and castigated the congregation for being less than good friends to her and Duggie.

'You did?' said Gray, his voice carefully, deliberately light. 'And exactly how did you do it, Terri? Not arsenic, I hope, because –'

'Don't joke, Gray, I did. Of course not arsenic, of course not anything like that. I mean I was responsible for him dying. I caused the heart attack. I nagged and nagged and worried and worried him, and I made it happen. Don't look at me like that, Gray, it's true.'

'I can't help how I'm looking,' he said gently, 'and I know it can't be true. You just don't seem like a nag-hag to me; Duggie looked like the cat that had got the cream the last few times I saw him, I reckon you made him very happy. As you always said. I think you're displaying classic widow's remorse, you feel guilty just because he's – dead, and you're alive. I know that sounds crude, and I'm sorry, and it's not meant to, but it's true. My mother adored my father, she worshipped the ground he walked on, and he never had to so much as pick up the paper for himself, or fetch his own slippers from the fireside, but she said exactly the same when he died. She sat with tears pouring down her poor face, just like you are, and told me it was all her fault. So honestly, Terri –' he took her hand, stroked it gently – 'I really think in a little while you'll know what nonsense you're talking, and you'll feel better. It's all part of the grieving process. As the counsellors say.'

She smiled wearily at him, blew her nose. 'You're such a nice man, Graydon. But I'm afraid you're wrong. I know all that, and I know I made him happy in some ways. But I did worry him to death. Literally. I was – well, I was doing something that was troubling him a lot.'

'Yes? Tell me. Seeing one of the Chippendales?'

290

'Graydon, please don't joke. It isn't funny.' She didn't look as if it were funny.

'All right. Tell me. I promise I won't joke.'

'I was – well –' She hesitated, took a very large slug of the whisky she was drinking. They were sitting in the saloon bar of an extremely vulgar pub, all ruched blinds and elevator music, which she said was her local; Gray, lured some twenty miles and over an hour from his desk by the increasingly urgent sense of a story, had agreed to meet her there.

He leant forward, smiled at her. 'Go on. Confess. If it'll make you feel better.'

'I was trying to find out about – about what happened. To –' she hesitated – 'well, in the early days of the company.'

'Ye-es? Doesn't sound so very terrible. You'll have to do a bit better – or worse – than that.'

'Well – Graydon, I'm convinced that – well, something suspicious was going on.'

'When?' And what sort of suspicious?'

'In the 'seventies. When – when Nigel Clarke died.'

'Uh-huh.'

'You know about that, I suppose. I mean what was supposed to have happened?'

'Yes, I think so,' said Gray. He felt extremely sick suddenly; he knew what it was. Excitement. Raw, physical excitement. He spoke carefully and calmly. 'Nigel Clarke was killed, wasn't he? In his car? I can't see how Bard Channing could be held responsible for that.'

'No, I know. And it was a foggy, icy night, and he wasn't even speeding. And he had been drinking. But – well, I don't know, Gray. Duggie would never talk about it, always glossed it over just a bit too much. That whole time.'

'So what do you know?' said Gray carefully. 'About it all, I mean.'

'Well, Duggie just told me Nigel Clarke and Bard had a meeting, late that night in the office. The company was doing really well, they were flying high, it was the peak of the first big property boom, new contracts and buildings going up all over the place; a real success story. They'd had a few whiskies, Bard said, and then Nigel left, and went on his own to a pub. Which was in itself a bit odd; he had a pregnant wife and a baby, and he was by all accounts a real homelover.'

'Yes, but – well, I can easily imagine wanting to go to a pub, if I had a wife and two small children at home,' said Gray lightly. 'Doesn't sound too serious to me, Terri.'

'No, I know. But – well, that's not quite the point. Duggie hated

291

talking about it. Hated talking about those days at all, as a matter of fact. Just made it all sound too easy. Which it wasn't. It really wasn't. Nobody ever made the fortune those guys did without one hell of a struggle. So I tried talking to Bard.'

'Yes, but why? I don't see why you were so suspicious.'

'It was the Clarkes,' said Terri. 'Bard Channing is so terribly good to them. Out of order good.'

'Well, I expect he felt guilty. A bit like you do.'

'Yeah, well, maybe. But do you know, for instance, he picks up the tab for the nursing home Heather Clarke is in. And she doesn't know, she has no idea. None of them does, they all think it's paid for by some insurance policy.'

'How on earth did you find that out?' said Gray slowly.

'Oh – I'm a very good detective,' said Terri, smiling complacently at him. She was looking better; telling the story was obviously cheering her up. 'I snooped about at the office a bit.'

'You did?' said Gray, remembering with amusement Kirsten's story of seeing her at Channing House late one night. 'You're quite a girl, aren't you? Did Duggie know about this – snooping?'

'Some of it, I'm afraid,' she said, and her face was sad again; then she visibly pulled herself together. 'Anyway, it was all done very skilfully, no doubt to cover their tracks, there's some special fund at the office which paid into an offshore charitable trust. And my God, they've got a few of those. All over the place.'

'Really?' said Gray. 'Can you remember where?'

'Oh – the usual places, Netherland Antilles, Cayman Islands, Bahamas –'

'Any in Jersey?' said Gray, thinking sharply of the large purchase of shares in the Channing corporation, that had restored the share price so efficiently that day.

'Not that I can remember. Why?'

'Oh – just wondered. Anyway, there's nothing illegal about offshore trusts, you know. They're just nice easy ways of fighting off the taxman.'

'Yes, I know that. But they're also nice easy ways of throwing up a smokescreen, moving money around. Lot of that going on at Channing, believe me. Anyway, the money from this particular smokescreen seemed to find its way to various places, but one called Staff Benevolent Care which is actually Mrs Clarke's nursing home. You'd never have found it if you hadn't been looking.'

'Well, I expect the Clarkes are very proud,' said Gray, 'Mrs Clarke wouldn't have taken the money if she'd known.'

'No, I daresay she wouldn't. But there were endless other things – he used to give Oliver extra money on top of his university grant, paid for Melinda's secretarial course, sends them on holiday ...'

'I still think that sounds like just kindness, born of guilt,' said Gray. 'I really don't think you can read much into it.'

'OK. Maybe not. But my God, Channing was sensitive about it.'

'He was?' Gray's stomach churned harder. He stared at Terri. The room seemed very bright suddenly, and the elevator music (the Carpenters now, for Christ's sake) had somehow got very loud. 'What sort of sensitive?'

'Well, he tried to stop me seeing Heather Clarke. He did stop me seeing her. Via Oliver. Told him it might upset her or something.'

'Well, I expect he didn't want her worried,' said Gray.

'Didn't want himself worried, more likely. I talked to her briefly at the funeral. Poor soul. Poor deluded soul. She thinks the sun shines right out of Bard Channing's over-sized arse.'

'I still don't think this adds up to much,' said Gray, only slightly untruthfully.

'OK. Forget that for now. There was something else,' said Terri Booth, 'something much more interesting.'

'And what was that?'

'I found out Duggie only had half the shares Bard did. Between them they hold – held – thirty per cent. I always thought it was fifty–fifty. Not a bit of it. Bard has twenty per cent, Duggie ten. Barbour five. And I didn't like that.'

'I can see that,' said Gray, 'but maybe –'

'I know what you're thinking. That Bard is the star and Duggie the warm-up act. Well, in a way that's right. But my God, he's given his life for that company. Risked his own money several times. Worked his arse off, twenty-five hours a day. And he gets a lousy ten per cent.'

'Yes, it seems a bit hard.'

'Duggie didn't want me to to do anything about it; said he was perfectly happy, that Bard was the brains in the outfit, that we weren't exactly hard up. But like I said I didn't like it. It made me very angry. So I talked to Bard about it, told him it stank.'

'And what did he say?'

'He told me to mind my own fucking business,' she said briefly, 'that it was nothing to do with me, that he and Duggie had always worked together perfectly fine. That was when I started really disliking him. It was mean, you know? And kind of – patronising. It was as good as saying Duggie wasn't worth more than ten per cent, that he looked down on him.'

'So – ?'

'So, by way of a little exercise, I said I wanted some shares. To even things up a bit. He said there was no way I was getting any, that he didn't just hand over shares for nothing, and so I told him I was very interested in the early days, in Nigel Clarke's just slightly mysterious death, in all the things he did for the Clarkes, and a few other things, and I was thinking of doing some investigations. Of getting a private detective on the job. And I said I had contacts in the press who might well be interested. He said I was bluffing, and I told him I'd got your home number and that I intended to ring you.'

'Which you did,' said Gray, remembering with horrible sadness that beautiful evening, when the mysterious phone call had come through and Briony had first broached the big B.

'Yes, I did. And when he realised I meant it, he panicked. And suddenly, do you know, he wanted to invest in my company.'

'Christ,' said Gray. He suddenly remembered the riddle of the Scottish golf course.

'Incidentally, Terri, did Duggie ever mention a golf complex? Up in Scotland.'

'Hundreds,' said Teresa, and laughed.

'No, I mean owned by Channings.'

'Ah,' she said, 'that one. Another little puzzle. I never got to the bottom of it. But there was something fishy about it. They bought some place up there, for a lot of money, and it never came to anything as far as I could make out. Never was developed. Duggie hedged about it, I even asked him to take me up there to see it, but he wouldn't. Said there was nothing there yet. Bit odd. Channing was very evasive when I asked him about it. Got that dead-eyed look of his, you know? You should take a look into that one as well, Graydon.'

'Ah. Then I will. Interesting. Because I heard about it from some ex-director of theirs. All happened about three years ago, would that be right? Place called Auchnamultie?'

'That's the one. Anyway, back to Channing. Just days before Duggie's death, he suddenly made over a great slug of shares to him. Five per cent of his holding. Had us both in, to make sure I knew about it, dished out some crap about how he felt bad Duggie hadn't had more before. Of course Duggie practically wept with gratitude. Now how does that sound to you, Graydon?'

'Bit funny,' said Gray. 'Just a bit funny.'

'I've instructed my solicitor to sell them when they come through,' she added, smiling.

'What on earth for?'

'Oh, anything to reduce Bard Channing's power over that company. And telling him about it really cheered me up. He was beside himself.'

'Teresa,' said Gray, 'you're a clever girl.'

He was quite glad he had a longish ride back to London (he had seen the day as a nice litle outing for the Harley Davidson); he had a lot to think about. What Teresa Booth had said made a certain kind of sense, suited his hunches, fitted his instincts. And the facts: it was just about the time of Teresa's first phone call that Channing had suddenly, and so inexplicably, turned interview-shy. It was good when that happened; it boosted his professional confidence. And if it had been her revelations, or possible revelations, to him that had worried Duggie enough to drive him to inviting him to lunch, then he had almost certainly had something to hide. Or to tell. He had been carefully vague about the lunch to Teresa: had said they were going to meet to discuss the future and Channings' problems, it seemed safer, wiser, and she seemed to have believed him. It also seemed rather sadly clear that if Duggie had been as worried as that, then there was some truth in Teresa's claim that she had killed him. God, what he would give now to know what Duggie had been going to tell him! To his shame, frustration had been as powerful an emotion as sadness when he had heard of Duggie's death.

But poor, dear old Duggie; he didn't deserve such distress at a time when life should have been made calm, easy for him. Gray thought of him, of his agitated voice on the phone, and sorrowed for him, and hoped Terri had been worth it for him in other ways.

But it was exciting. Exciting and intriguing. There was nothing he loved more than this, stumbling on a story, working, worrying away at it, hacking through the undergrowth of past events, of lies, of misrepresentations, and arriving, slowly and often with great difficulty, at the truth. Or the partial truth: that was the best you could hope for much of the time. And this was a tough one: twenty years of undergrowth to clear. What on earth could have happened, twenty years ago, that Bard Channing was still anxious about, or could be made anxious about, anxious enough to do something as out of character as make over part of his shareholding? Well, he could do it, find out. He would just hack away until he got there. And he would start that night, with the press cuttings: go through them all again, force some answers out of them.

It was a lovely evening; even the M40 looked nice, with great shafts of sun shooting down on miserable, hot carloads of holiday travellers, cars jammed with people and luggage on their way to and from docks and airports, with children and mothers on their way home from picnics and outings; with bored, resentful fathers, driving home from work, sweating in their shirtsleeves. He rode, gloriously free, between the static rows, on and on into London, past the factories, along the flyovers, over the bridges and finally, as he was zooming along the Embankment – for he had no intention of going home; he craved, junkie-like, his files and cuttings and all that they could tell him about Channings in those early days – as he rode up through the City and down towards the docks, a tiny phrase of Kirsten's came back to him, crystal clear, infinitely important – 'I don't think there is anything Granny Jess doesn't know about any of us.'

Chapter Fifteen

Liam was sitting in a brown plastic chair that smelt faintly of urine in the hospital day room, trying to find something remotely interesting to read in a copy of the *People* which someone had left there, when Teresa Booth suddenly appeared, carrying an enormous basket of fruit. His first reaction was horror, followed by a stab of guilt that he had never written to thank her and Duggie for the champagne. Although he had managed a rather stilted note when he had heard about Duggie from Francesca.

He looked up at her (noticing that she had lost a lot of weight since the last time he had seen her, that she looked very tired), and switched on his warmest smile, stretched out his hand.

'Teresa! How lovely to see you. I wish I could get up, but –'

'Don't even think about it,' said Teresa. She bent down, kissed him briefly. Her perfume was very rich and strong; he hated it. 'How are you, Liam?'

'Oh – much better. Almost mended. How about you? I was so very sorry –'

'Yes, well, thank you. I'm fine, thanks. Considering. But I was feeling pretty sorry for myself, sitting at home, and I thought what can I do take my mind off things, and then I thought of you. Yes, you don't look so bad. Here, what shall I do with this?'

'Oh – put it down over there for now. How absolutely marvellous, Teresa, a real cornucopia. You are kind. Shall we steal something from it now? Those peaches look wonderful.'

'Good idea,' she said, passing him one. 'I'll have a strawberry or two if I may.'

'Of course.'

'Treating you all right, are they?'

'Absolutely fine,' said Liam, adding (anxious not to miss an opportunity to badmouth his father), 'pretty basic of course, it's not Dad's beloved London Clinic, but –'

'Yes, but you can't beat the NHS when things are really serious,' said Teresa Booth, 'and things don't get much more serious than what happened to you. How did it happen, Liam?'

She looked like a pampered cat, Liam thought, even though she wasn't at her best; one of those hugely fluffy things that lay on satin cushions and wore elaborate collars. She was wearing a white skirt and a gold-coloured shirt, and very high-heeled white shoes, and there was a lot of make-up on her pale face; her silvery blonde hair was freshly set in a great bouffant cloud. She certainly wasn't letting herself go in her grief.

'Oh – long story. But yes, I was going too fast, and yes, I had been drinking. So I got my just deserts. Just lucky no-one else was hurt. Oh dear, this is no place to entertain you, I'm afraid –'

'It's fine,' said Teresa, 'and I haven't come to be entertained, I've come to entertain you.'

She went over to the table, where the fruit was, and fetched a chair; she placed it quite close to his, and sat down. A couple of other people in the room looked at them with interest.

'Bard been in to see you, has he?'

'No,' said Liam. 'No he hasn't.' He left it at that. He was buggered if he was going to make excuses, proffer explanations.

'Ah. Well, I expect he's been busy.'

'Yes.'

'Just the same – blood ought to be thicker than water. Which reminds me, did you get our champagne?'

'Oh, I did, and I've been feeling absolutely terrible about it. About not thanking you.'

'Oh for heaven's sake. And that was a nice note you sent me when Douglas died. I appreciated it. Have you drunk all the champagne yet?'

'Not quite: one left. Perhaps we should have it now … It is the most gorgeous stuff.'

'No, you keep it for a rainy day. When are you going home?'

'Oh – pretty soon now, I think. In a day or so.'

'I hear your wife's got a new job. Does she like it?'

'Well, it's not a proper job. It's while someone else is on maternity leave. So it won't last, and she's still looking, but it's something. At one point she was talking about taking one in Scotland, dragging us all up there. But she changed her mind, thank God. It's been pretty hard for her, trying to get in here and see me of course –'

'Yes of course. So you've been pretty lonely, have you?' Her blue eyes were sharp, even while they were sympathetic.

'A bit. But I'm used to that.'

298

'And I'm getting used to it. Not a lot of fun, is it? We'll have to keep each other company, Liam, from time to time ...'

Christ almighty, he hoped she wasn't making a pass at him. 'Er – yes.'

'Don't look so frightened, I'm not going to eat you. I quite like you, Liam,' she suddenly said, surprising him. 'You're one of the more interesting of that clan of yours. Duggie liked you too. Thought it was a damn shame your father and you didn't hit it off better. I'd have put it rather differently.'

'Oh really?' said Liam.

'Yes. I'd have said it was your father treating you not so well. Bloody badly, in fact.'

'Oh I don't know –'

'Come off it,' she said, her blue eyes sharply amused, 'you don't have to pretend with me, Liam. Neither of us does. Neither of us likes him very much and with good reason, I'd say. Different reasons, but equally good.'

'So what are yours, then?' said Liam.

'Oh – let's just say I find him arrogant. High handed.'

'Yes, I heard you delivered a few well-chosen words at the funeral,' said Liam with a grin.

'Oh really? News travels fast, doesn't it? Yes, I enjoyed that, I have to say. I don't care how he treats me, but I did care about Duggie. Mind you, he continued to think the sun shone out of your father's every orifice.'

Perversely, Liam felt a pang of hostility towards her. She seemed to him quite arrogant herself. 'Well,' he said, 'it's a view a great many people share. I suppose it's easy for him to start believing it.'

'Yes. Anyway, I thought it was disgraceful, the way he treated you. When your mother died, I mean. Sending you away like that. He was a grown man, for God's sake, and you were a little boy.'

'Yes. Well, people are very complex.'

'They are indeed.' She looked at him, paused and then said, 'Do you know anything much about those days, Liam? When they were starting up the company? Has your father ever talked to you about it?'

'No. Not much. He liked to tell me how tough it was, of course. Like all fathers do. The struggles he had, all that sort of thing.'

'What sort of struggles?'

'Oh – mortgaging the house to raise capital, working twenty-five hours a day –'

'Walking thirty-five miles to work with his Hovis sandwiches.' She grinned. 'Do you remember Nigel Clarke, then?'

'Of course. I was thirteen when he died.'

'What was he like?'

'Oh – nice enough. He always seemed a bit – feeble to me. Like his son.'

'I wouldn't call Oliver feeble. He's a very nice young man. Impressive, I'd call him.'

'I hardly know him,' said Liam. 'I know Kirsten and Barnaby get a bit of a mouthful about him from my father. Hearing how wonderful he is, how hard working, all that sort of thing. Very irritating for them.'

'Won't do them any harm,' said Teresa briskly. 'So you think he was a bit of a yes-man, Nigel Clarke?'

'Oh, definitely. My dad said jump and he jumped.'

'Just the same they did pretty well, didn't they, the three of them?'

'Yeah, I suppose they did.'

'Did your father feel responsible in some way for Nigel Clarke's death, do you think?' The question came out suddenly, surprising him.

'I – don't know. I don't think so. Why should he?'

'Oh – I don't know. I've just got that impression. He does a lot for the little Clarke family.' She looked at him for a moment as if she were weighing something up, then said, 'Did you know he pays her nursing home bills?'

'No,' said Liam. 'No I didn't.'

'She doesn't know, she thinks it's covered by some insurance policy. But he does. Lot of money, that. Hundreds a week.'

'Well, he can afford it,' said Liam briefly. He smiled at her, but he felt violently, hotly angry. His father had refused him help, of the most basic kind, and was shelling out thousands a year on a family with no blood ties, no proper claim on him. Bastard. How could he do that? How dared he? It was outrageous. God, how he hated him. He wondered if Francesca knew about that; he was pretty sure she didn't.

'Did – did Duggie tell you that?' he said.

'Oh – no. I discovered it, going through some of his papers. It was all very complicated, done through some sort of a trust. It's something they both seemed to want to keep a little bit quiet. Anyway, it's very – good of your father. I suppose. Unless –' She looked at him, her blue eyes shrewd.

'Unless what, Teresa?'

'Oh – nothing. Well, I was going to say unless he does really feel he owes her something.'

'Like what?'

'Oh – I don't know. That's why I was asking you if you knew anything about that business. If perhaps –'

'Hallo Mr Channing!' It was his tormentor, Karen, the Australian. 'Would your visitor like a cup of tea? Trolley's coming round now.'

'Thank you yes, that'd be very kind.'

She disappeared; came back with two evil-looking cups of tea, slopping onto a tray. 'There. That'll put some hairs on your chest. There's sugar in that bowl.'

'Thank you,' said Liam.

She stayed, hovering, obviously hoping for a chat.

'So how's he doing, then?' said Teresa to her finally, into the silence.

'Oh – very well. He'll be going home soon, I'm afraid. We'll miss him. I will anyway. Nice to have someone decent to talk to. Only patient in our ward for a very long time who's had champagne, I can tell you. He's obviously got some very nice friends.'

'Like me,' said Teresa, 'I sent it. It ought to be on the NHS in my view.'

'That'll be the day,' said Karen. 'But anyway, he's enjoyed it. Although I didn't say that, of course. I shared one of them, didn't I, Mr Channing? Buying my silence, he was.'

'Yes,' said Liam. He smiled at her with an effort. 'Yes, you did.'

'And who shared the rest? Matron?' said Teresa, winking at Karen.

'That'd be telling,' said Karen, grinning back. 'Oh, she just phoned, by the way, Mrs Channing did, said she can't get in today, has to go and meet her husband at the airport later. Sent her love.'

'Francesca's been visiting you, has she? Well, that is nice,' said Teresa.

'Oh, she's been in loads. Nearly every day. We've all got fond of Mrs Channing,' said Karen, 'She's a very lovely person.'

Liam met Teresa's eyes. Which were thoughtful, brilliant with amusement.

'Well,' she said finally, 'how very, very sweet.'

She left soon after that; she said she had things to do, and it was nearly supper time on the ward. She bent and kissed him again, pressed his hand. 'I'd like to talk some more,' she said, 'some time,' and was gone, leaving her heavy perfume hanging in the air. He was half relieved, half sorry to see her go. The conversation about his father had been hugely intriguing, even while it had been upsetting. She obviously had some bee in her bonnet about him, seemed to think he had something to hide, something about the Clarkes. Which was an interesting concept. God, it would be good to get something on his father. Add that to running off with his wife and he really would see him start to sweat. Well, not actually running off, probably. That would be too much like hard work. But getting into bed with. That was an expression used as much in a business context these days as in a personal, a sexual one. Very appropriate. Under the circumstances. Anyway, thanks to Nurse Karen Fisher, Teresa was on to that. Or rather the possibility of it. She was a very smart cookie; she had twigged instantly. Well, that didn't matter: it could suit his cause very well. In the fullness of time, that was. The situation did need rather careful orchestration ... Francesca was scarcely aware herself yet that she felt anything for him except sympathy and a rather happy friendship. But she would. She certainly would. And then, then Teresa could be handed a gun, and a great deal of ammunition which he personally would provide her with. It was all beginning to look rather promising.

Liam suddenly felt tired; he decided to go back to the ward for a rest before supper. It really had been a rather exhausting day.

If anyone had asked Oliver what he thought the odds were against this happening, he would have said a million, probably a billion to one. But here she was, Kirsten Channing was, sitting smiling at him in his car, and he had just kissed her, and that had been an amazingly interesting, not to say moving, experience; and they had had a really good evening, dinner at some place she'd suggested, Harvey's Café in the Fulham Road, he'd been scared it would be some over-priced Sloaney place, but it had been nice, unusual and nice. And then they had walked back to his car, and on the way she had slipped her arm through his and when they had reached it, she had slithered swiftly in beside him, turned his head to her and kissed him very gently.

'I really enjoyed that,' she said. 'Thank you.'

'My pleasure,' he said, and sat staring at her, almost in surprise; at her face, at her strange, beautiful eyes; surprised that he should be here with her at all, surprised that she should have kissed him, surprised above all that she was so nice, not really the brat he had always imagined: awkward possibly, difficult probably, spoilt certainly, but as well as that funny, interesting, interested, and – well, nice. And having thought it, found the courage to kiss her too: a little less gently, rather more determinedly indeed; and she had responded, also less gently, and all he wanted to do now was learn more of her. In every way.

'I really like that jacket,' she said, sitting back in the car, looking at him with great attentiveness. 'It suits you. Where did you get it?'

'Paul Smith,' he said.

'Oh really?' She looked faintly surprised. He knew why; she wouldn't have expected him to shop anywhere so expensive. It half amused, half irritated him.

'I buy quite a few things there,' he said. 'I know what you're thinking.'

'Of course you don't.'

'Yes I do. You're surprised the poor relation – well, poor friend of the family – can afford such a posh shop.'

'Well – OK,' she said, grinning at him, pushing back her hair. 'Just a bit.'

'I like clothes. I always have. I do spend too much on them. But also I'm not really such a poor relation any more. I've got a house and a car and a – well, a sort of job –'

'You don't like that, do you?'

'Oh the job's all right,' he said. 'I don't like that I'm working for your dad. I told you. And it is very kind of him,' he added hastily.

'He doesn't do kind things,' said Kirsten, 'only things that suit him.'

'That's a very harsh judgment.'

'He's a very harsh man.'

Oliver left it at that. 'What shall we do now? We could go to a club.'

'No,' she said, and shuddered, 'I'm a bit off clubs. As I told you.'

'Yes,' he said, 'sorry,' and laughed.

She had been coming out of her father's office the previous week, as he had been going to lunch, walking down the corridor; he heard one almighty, albeit slightly muffled slam, and then a nearer, louder one, and she had emerged from Marcia's office, her head very high. She was, he realised, looking at her more carefully, crying. She looked at him, and then away, brushing at her face, her nose with her hand.

'Want a hanky?' he said, smiling at her gently, and she had smiled, awkwardly through her tears, and shaken her head, fishing in her large, satchel-like bag for one of her own; then lifted her head, shaken back the great waterfall of hair, and said, sniffing loudly, 'Oh well, maybe yes, please. If you've got one.'

'Here you are,' he said, handing it to her, waiting patiently, tactfully not looking at her while she blew her nose, and dabbed at her eyes.

'Has my mascara run?' she said.

'Yes,' he said truthfully, looking at the huge black smudges, 'a bit.'

'I'll go and see to it in the bog,' she said. 'Can you wait?'

'Yes of course. I'm not going anywhere. Well, only to get a sandwich.'

When she came out, she'd looked more cheerful, although still pale, clearly shaken, and 'You wouldn't fancy a drink, would you?' she said.

'Yes,' he'd said, slightly startled, but nonetheless pleased, 'yes, all right. Just a quick one. There's a nice wine bar just off Albemarle Street. Would that do you? Or did you have something grander in mind?'

'What, like the Ritz you mean? No of course not. I'm a working girl. No allowance even. Thanks to darling Daddy.'

He found that slightly hard to believe, but he smiled in what he hoped was a convincing manner, and walked along beside her to the wine bar in silence.

'Want to tell me about it?' he said, having struggled back to her in a particularly crushed corner, with two glasses of warm and mediocre Chardonnay. 'You don't have to, but —'

'Oh, it's nothing really. We were just having one of our cosy little chats, me and my dad. About my misdemeanours. One in particular.'

'Which was?'

'Oh — something so minimal you wouldn't believe anyone could make a fuss about it.'

'Oh, I see.'

'No you don't. All I did was go clubbing with Barnaby when he was ill and the police picked us up because he was collapsing, and took us to Casualty. You'd think I'd been found with a hundred grams of coke on me. That's what he thinks, I know.'

'Oh, I see,' he said again.

'I hope,' she said suddenly, 'you don't think that. That I do a lot of drugs.'

'No of course I don't.'

'Because I don't.'

He was silent; he felt uncomfortable.

'Oliver, look at me.' He looked at her. She was wearing a beige slub silk jacket, a very short black linen skirt, and her legs were bare. Bare and golden brown. Her hair was hanging round her shoulders, and she wore no make-up, apart from what was left of her mascara. He thought again how he had never known anyone even nearly as beautiful, and the very fact made him feel insecure, less confident.

'You do, don't you? Oh, God. Oliver, I want you to believe me very much. It's important. Not because I give a — a toss if you think I do drugs a lot, which actually I don't, I used to, but not any more. I want you to believe me because it happens to be true.'

For some reason, and quite suddenly, he did believe her. 'I know,' he said. 'I can see that.'

'Anyway,' she said, clearly feeling better at having cleared this up. 'He's pathological about it. Questioned me, cross-questioned Barnaby – separately, of course, that's one of his brain-washing techniques – oh, it was awful … He's such a nightmare.'

He couldn't imagine what to say that might be helpful or comforting: punitive parenting was not something remotely within his experience. 'I suppose,' he said finally, 'he's still pretty upset about Mr Booth. Everyone is. So maybe that's made him – well, extra unreasonable.'

'No,' said Kirsten briefly, 'he's always the same. Honestly. I mean, obviously he is upset about Duggie, but it wouldn't make the slightest difference. He's always like this. And the thing is, in my more rational moments, I really can't blame him. Not too much. I am a running sore in his side. Everything I do turns out wrong. And I've done some pretty stupid things lately. What hurts so much though, is that he goes on and on making excuses for Barnaby, whatever he does, and Tory, well, there's nothing to make excuses for there, she's such a goody-goody, and he never gives me even the smallest benefit of the doubt. It's not fair.'

'Well, maybe really you're his favourite,' said Oliver. 'Isn't that what the shrinks would say?'

'They might say it but they'd be wrong,' said Kirsten. 'If he has a favourite, it's Barney. Out of us three. But really now, I suppose those two brats. God, it's all so unfair. Sorry. Won't talk about it any more. Can I get you one now? Oh and look, there's a table. Go and grab it.'

The table was pushed right against the window and there was very little room; Oliver found himself pressed very close to her, his thigh against hers. He could smell her; a strong raunchy fragrance. He liked it.

She smiled, raised her glass to him. 'I bet you think I'm a frightful brat myself,' she said.

'No I don't. I used to think so, to be honest, but I don't any more.'

'Well, you're allowed to. I am really. God, I'm sick of myself. Let's talk about you.'

'Not a lot to tell. Certainly not a lot you don't know.'

'Oh, I'm sure there is. I'm sorry I always hated you before. I was always quite rude to you, wasn't I?'

'Quite,' he said, and smiled again.

'It was having you rammed down our throats, about how hard you worked, how well you did, how polite you were. Granny Jess especially dotes on you.'

'Not my fault,' said Oliver.

'No, not your fault. Tell me about yourself, Oliver, what do you like doing?'

'I like,' he said, reluctant to lose her, the closeness, the smell of her, but realising what the time was, 'I like sitting in wine bars, talking about myself. But I have to get back to work.'

'Shit,' she said staring at the clock on the wall, jumping up, 'so do I.'

'Do you really?'

'I really do. You don't believe it, do you, about the allowance? It's true. But we could talk about you another time. We could have supper one night. Would you like that?'

'I would,' said Oliver, feeling the same sense of disorientation as he had experienced briefly at the funeral, 'yes.'

'And then I could give you your handkerchiefs back. Thank you for the second one.' And she had bent down, kissed him briefly on the cheek and gone.

'So what would you like to do now?' he said, looking at her across the car. He supposed, strictly speaking, he could just have taken her home, but he was reluctant for the evening to end.

'Well – I'd like to see your house. I like seeing people's habitats. Where is it?'

'Ealing.'

'Oh. Bit of a long way.'

'Yes, and Melinda will be there.'

'Ah. Well, you could come and see my flat. Have a coffee. A brandy. And I've got some really good coke we could line up … Don't look like that, Oliver, I'm only teasing you. And it's not a proposition either. I'd just like to talk a bit more.' She sat studying his face thoughtfully, as if she might read something in it, and then smiled suddenly, clearly pleased by what she saw. 'It's been so nice.'

'OK,' he said, smiled back, and started the car.

He liked her flat. It was a typical Sloaney flat, he supposed, big mansion block, lots of Mummy's furniture, a few old-fashioned-looking pictures, dozens of photographs, underwear all over the bathroom, but it was homey and comfortable.

'Dad bought it for us. He's just bought one for Tory, as well. He doesn't want us sharing any more, he thinks I'll be a bad influence on her. Probably right.' But behind the quick smile, he could see resentment, hurt.

'That was quite – kind of him, wasn't it?' said Oliver.

She shrugged. 'Not really. Guilt money. He just wanted me off his conscience.'

'Well,' he said, 'at least he hasn't turned you out.'

'Not yet. Give him time. Coffee? Tea? Hot chocolate?'

'I'd love some hot chocolate.'

She came back with two steaming mugs and a plate of HobNobs – 'My favourite, real nursery supper this, isn't it?' – and put some music on: Simply Red, which surprised him. He said so.

'Oh I get so sick of that house music. Would you kiss me some more, Oliver? I really liked it.'

He started to kiss her, self-consciously at first, then relaxed. She was interesting to kiss; exploratory, responsive, oddly careful, as if she didn't want to appear too assertive. She smelt gorgeous, she was warm, her hair was everywhere; she pulled him closer, began to push her body, almost imperceptibly, at his. And he at hers, feeling his erection begin, feeling its heat and its hunger, kissing her harder, harder, his tongue probing, working at hers.

And then suddenly she pushed him away, sat up straight, smiled at him, rather embarrassed, and reached for her cocoa mug.

'Sorry,' he said, miserable, sure he had offended her. 'I didn't mean to –'

'Oh Oliver, don't. I meant to, and I wanted you to mean to. But I've promised myself, no more sudden sex. It's my mid-year resolution.'

'Oh,' he said, trying to calm himself, shifting on the sofa, crossing his legs gingerly. He wasn't sure he was happy with that; it seemed to imply an endless promiscuity.

'I keep doing it,' she said, 'and it's wrong. Next time, the very next time I have sex, it'll be because I really really know I like the person.'

'Or love them?'

'Well – I don't think I believe in love. I used to say I knew I didn't, but I'm not quite so sure now. Do you?'

'Oh yes. Yes, I think so.'

'Have you been in love?' she said, looking at him interestedly.

'Well – yes. Yes I have.'

'And do you have a lot of sex?'

'Not a lot. Well,' he added hastily, not wishing to be written off as cold, or, worse, a wimp, 'only when I really like the person.'

'I wish I did believe in love', she said. 'But –'

307

And then the phone rang. Oliver looked at his watch. Only just after eleven. He'd thought it was later.

'Hallo,' she said, smiling at him over the receiver, and then slightly more warily, 'oh, hi Gray.' Gray. The journalist guy at the funeral. Smooth sod. Hadn't liked him. 'Yes, fine thanks. How are you? Yes I enjoyed it too. It was nice.' An awkward silence. What was nice? thought Oliver, startled by a stab of rather fierce hostility to Gray Townsend. Jealousy? Already? How ridiculous. After a first date!

'How's work?' Kirsten was saying. 'Oh really? Oh I see. What? My gran? What on earth do you want to talk to her for? Well, I could ask her. I doubt if she would. She mistrusts the press.' She laughed. 'Can't think why. Yes, course I will. Yes, I'll tell her. That'd be good. Bye, Gray. I'll get back to you.'

She put the phone down, curled her legs under her, looked at Oliver. 'Bit weird. That was a guy I know, he's a journalist – oh, you met him at the funeral, didn't you, he knew Duggie. Anyway, he wants to meet Granny Jess. Says it's a feature he's writing on socialism.'

'Socialism?' said Oliver.

'Yes, well, I suppose it's not quite as odd as it sounds, what with her job at the Walworth Road and everything. And she's a great character, as we both know. But – oh well, I can ask her. He said he'd buy us both lunch. What do you think?'

'I think I'd be a bit suspicious if I were you,' said Oliver.

'You're the best,' said Jack. He was sitting looking consideringly at his mother over the breakfast table, in between spreading lemon curd extremely thickly on a piece of Shredded Wheat. This was his latest culinary passion, consumed not only at breakfast but at tea, and at lunchtime as well, if Nanny was away and he nagged Francesca enough.

She smiled at him, kissed his sticky yellow face rather gingerly. 'Thank you, darling. You're pretty good yourself.'

'I think you're the best too, Francesca.' Barnaby was eating his own rather idiosyncratic breakfast: a banana, a Diet Pepsi and a cup of hot chocolate, to be followed shortly by a cigarette smoked on the front steps. This was his way of telling the world how harsh was the regime under which he lived; he could have perfectly well sat in the garden, but that would have been too discreet.

'Thank you, Barnaby.'

'Don't I get a kiss too?'

'No, you don't.'

'God, you're a hard woman. No wonder I have such constant crises of confidence. Francesca, as it's raining, do you think I could have a cigarette in here? Just this once?'

'No Barnaby, you couldn't.'

'But I'll get wet. And I might have a relapse, I'm only just recovered from dysentery after all.'

'I don't think so, Barnaby, honestly. And you could stay dry and go without your fag. Horrible things.'

'You'll be dead soon, if you go on smoking them,' said Jack.

'I'll be dead soon anyway, of pneumonia,' said Barnaby. 'Francesca, could I possibly borrow the little car this morning?'

'OK by me. You'll have to ask Sandie, she might want it.'

'Thanks a lot. Dad away?'

'Yes, he went off yesterday to New York for a few days,' said Francesca briefly. He had: at ten minutes' notice and without any kind of an explanation beyond 'I'm having a very difficult time.'

'Sandie's in the nursery if you want her,' said Jack helpfully. 'And she might give you a sweetie if you're good.'

'Sandie gives you sweets, does she?' said Francesca. 'I'm not too sure about that.'

'I'm sure,' said Jack cheerfully. 'Kinder eggs mostly. If I'm good and don't bother her when she's on the phone.'

'On the phone!'

'Yes, she loves the phone.'

'Does she now?' said Francesca. 'There's the postman, Jack, want to get the letters?'

'Cool!' said Jack.

He came in with a small pile; Francesca flicked through them. Nothing very interesting: bills, junk mail, an invitation to join a chain charity luncheon – what the hell was a chain luncheon, she wondered – another to buy tickets for a ball, and at the bottom of the pile a rather fanciful envelope with deckle edges. The postmark was Guildford: Heather Clarke. Poor woman. She'd liked her at the funeral. She must go and see her soon.

Dear Mrs Channing, (the note read)
Just a quick note to say I was so sorry I wasn't able to speak to you for longer at Mr Booth's funeral. My son seemed intent on rushing me away! But it was very nice to see you.

I thought Mr Channing spoke so well. He really brought dear Douglas Booth alive for us all again. How you will all miss him – and how the company will too.

Please send my best wishes to Mr Channing also, and tell him how much we all appreciate Oliver being given a job there. And thank you for your help in that matter too. I know he is enjoying it very much, and certainly doesn't take it for granted ... And I know he will work hard; he was simply unfortunate losing his other job.

Incidentally I was so interested to hear that Mr Channing has become a trustee of the convent and the home for the disabled in Devon. What a very worthwhile project, and what an extremely kind, good man he is.

Thank you again for your own kindness,

Yours sincerely,

Heather Clarke

Francesca put the letter down and sat staring at it. She felt icy cold and very shocked. Bard a trustee of a home for the disabled! Which meant giving up quite a lot of time and underwriting its debts; she spent enough time on her various charity committees to know that. A trustee of this place of her mother's, the one where this handicapped child was – it must be that one, it was too much of a coincidence to be anything else. What the hell was going on? Why had neither of them told her, what kind of conspiracy had they hatched between them, and why should it matter in the least if she did find out? And what was Bard doing, getting so heavily involved in something so outside his sphere of interest? And a convent, for God's sake, Bard was famously hostile to convents, to anything to do with the Catholic Church, largely because of Pattie and her devout adherence to it.

It just didn't make any kind of sense, any of it; and it was outrageous, the two people closest to her, in some kind of conspiracy behind her back. She felt angry and, worse than angry, extremely hurt. And for the first time since Duggie's death he was away: in New York, so she couldn't ask him about it. And anyway, she wasn't sure if she wanted to,

'Mum! MUM! You deaf or something?'

'What?'

'You are deaf. You'd better get an ear trumpet. I said can I get down?'

'Oh – yes. Yes of course.'

'Is it time to go to school?'

'Um – I don't know.'

'Well, look at the clock, then. Oh dear. She's gone deaf, Barnaby. And I've got to go to school.'

'I'll take you. Shall I, Francesca?'

'What?'

310

'You're right, Jack. She has. I said shall I take Jack to school? In the car?'

'Oh – yes. Yes please, Barnaby, that's very kind.'

'Only Sandie needs her car, so can I borrow yours?'

'Mmm? Oh – yes. Yes of course.'

Barnaby grabbed Jack's hand, and ushered him swiftly towards the door. 'The – the Merc?'

'Yes, if you want to.'

'And – keep it till lunchtime?'

'Yes. Yes of course.'

'Blimey,' said Barnaby. 'Come on, Jack, quick as you can.'

'Blimey,' said Jack. 'Blimey blimey blimey.'

Francesca sat down at the table when they had gone, spooning yoghurt into Kitty and trying to stop herself minding so much about Bard and her mother. She supposed in some ridiculous way she was jealous. That they hadn't told her. Maybe it wasn't right; maybe Heather Clarke had got the wrong end of the stick. She wasn't the brightest woman in the world and her devotion to Bard was such that if she'd been told he'd run away and joined the Moonies she would say what a wonderful thing to have done. Who would know, how could she check on it? And who would have told her in the first place?

And then she realised: Oliver. It was exactly the sort of thing he would be dealing with, in his new position, in the financial office at Channings. She could ask him.

She looked at her watch: only half past eight, too early to ring him. He probably wouldn't get in until nine at the earliest. Shit.

Sandie came in, started clearing the table round her. 'Sorry about the car, Mrs Channing. It was very nice of you to lend Barnaby yours.'

'What? I lent Barnaby the Mercedes?'

'Well, he just drove off in it. With Jack.'

'Oh Lord. I wasn't thinking, how extremely rash of me. I – oh well. I hope Mr Channing doesn't find out, that's all. We'll have to get Barnaby a car of his own, we can't go on like this, playing box and cox with them all the time. Why couldn't he have had yours, Sandie? Well, I'll have to take it, I'm afraid. I need a car this morning.'

'I'm afraid I need it,' said Sandie, 'to do the shopping and collect all that dry cleaning for you.'

'Well, you'll have to manage in taxis, I'm afraid. I have to go and see –' She stopped.

'Liam?' said Sandie.

There was something in her voice that Francesca didn't like: it was insinuating, over-familiar. For some reason it bothered her.

'Mr Channing, yes,' she said coldly. 'In hospital. And Sandie, I don't want you giving Jack sweets, they're very bad for him.'

Sandie looked at her. Her voice was polite, but her expression was coolly blank. 'If you say so,' she said, and walked out of the room, pulling the door shut just too loudly behind her.

Francesca went upstairs and handed Kitty over to Nanny, feeling upset. And then sat down in her bedroom, the door firmly shut, and rang Channings' number. A pause: then a slightly nervous-sounding Oliver.

'Oliver, hallo. Don't sound so anxious. It's just a silly little thing, but Mr Channing is away, as you know. Oliver, there's some confused message here about a trusteeship. You know, of the convent in Devon. You know about that, do you? Yes? Oh – oh, good. That is right is it, Mr Channing is to be a trustee? Oh, and there's a new building as well? Oh yes, of course. Yes, yes, I thought so, but I thought I'd better double check, a friend of mine wanted to help with some of the paperwork, as it's a charity, you know, so I thought before I put her onto Mr Channing, well, you know what he's like if things aren't a hundred per cent right, and it's early days – yes, thank you, Oliver. Yes, of course, I'll tell her to talk to my mother, what a good idea. Thank you again. Well, sorry to have disturbed you, and I'll see you soon, yes, bye Oliver.'

She slammed the phone down, feeling near to tears; she hadn't handled that at all well, had heard her own voice getting louder and more foolish every moment. But at least she knew. And putting up a new building as well. He was obviously very deeply involved. Bloody hell. How dared they? How dared they?

She picked up the phone again, dialled her mother's number. Rachel's throaty voice answered it immediately.

'Mummy, it's me.'

'Francesca sweetheart! How are you? And how is that darling baby? I was so sorry to –'

'The darling baby's fine, thank you. Mummy, would you kindly tell me what the hell is going on? Just why are you and Bard in league behind my back, on this damn convent or home or whatever, and would you mind telling me how it can possibly be so terribly important to you that you've managed to persuade him to do it at all?'

Chapter Sixteen

'Mr Townsend? This is Jess Channing. Kirsten tells me you want to talk to me. What's it about?'

'Oh – hallo, Mrs Channing. It's very good of you to ring me. Yes, I did. I'm a journalist –'

'Yes she told me that. She seems to think quite highly of you. I wouldn't see you if she hadn't, I don't trust the press. But your paper seems quite decent, not one of those rags. Now what is the article about exactly?'

'It's about socialism, Mrs Channing. About its changing face. And people like you, who have made it your life's work.'

'Oh yes? Hasn't done it much good, has it?'

'I'm sorry?'

'The party. Hasn't done it much good, making it our life's work. Dreadful mess it's in and it's getting worse. Smith and now Blair, nothing more nor less than Tories. I don't understand people, I really don't.'

'No,' said Gray carefully. 'No indeed.'

'Are you a socialist?'

'I'm afraid not, no.'

'Never be afraid of declaring your politics,' she said sternly. 'If you're a Tory then just come out and say so, don't apologise. Anyway, I don't think there's much point you talking to me. I can't tell you much. Talk to Barbara, she's your girl.'

'Barbara?'

'Yes, Barbara Castle. There's nothing she doesn't know about it all. Want me to ask her for you?'

'Oh – yes. Yes please.'

He was so engrossed in his fictional piece, so delighted at the prospect of talking to Barbara Castle, that he forgot, briefly, his real reason for wanting to talk to Jess Channing. Just as she was ringing off he realised what he was doing.

'Mrs Channing, don't go. Please. I really do want to talk to you as well. I feel you're a bit of living history. It's so marvellous, talking people of your generation.'

'Living history!' she said, and emitted what he imagined might be a laugh. 'I'm very old, if that's what you mean. You'll have to use plain language if you're going to talk to me. Well, you can come if you like. I don't want to be taken anywhere, I don't like the sort of place I imagine you're thinking of and I don't approve of expense accounts which is what I expect you've got. You come here and I'll give you some lunch'.

'Oh, but –'

'Look, it's either that or nothing. It's all the same to me. I'll give you good meal. Not that men seem to eat properly any more.'

'Well – thank you. I'll try to be worthy of it. Thank you very much. Will Kirsten be there?'

'I don't know. She said she was very busy with her job. I think you helped her get it, didn't you?'

'Yes I did,' said Gray.

'Very good of you. She's a nice girl, under all the nonsense, Isambard and her mother between them have given her a rotten start.'

'Er – well –' Gray heard his own voice floundering.

'Come tomorrow, that suit you, one o'clock? Don't be late.'

'No, Mrs Channing. Thank you.'

Just before he left for Kennington, he had a quick graze through the Channing file. He had been through it so many times now he was beginning to know it by heart. And the early cuttings. But there was nothing. No clues, no leads, nothing even remotely suspicious, just a long catalogue of success. Always less interesting than failure. He was no nearer making any kind of progress with his investigations, about what might have happened twenty years ago. Hopefully today would help.

Teresa Booth had just finished turning out Duggie's desk when she discovered an old Ordnance Survey map of what appeared to her to be a remote district of Scotland. Closer examination confirmed that it was a remote district of Scotland, with an area heavily circled in pencil. On the edge of the pencilled circle was a small town called Auchnamultie. Intrigued, she lifted her phone and dialled Graydon Townsend at his office. He was out, but his nice assistant said he would be back after lunch.

'Just tell him there's a place in Scotland called Auchnamultie,' she said, 'and I'm sending him a map. He'll know what it's about.'

'Fine,' said the nice assistant.

Jess Channing was waiting for him in her small house. She was wearing the same stark black as she had at the funeral; it was obviously not purely for purposes of mourning. She was a very tall woman, he realised, as she ushered him in, and he realised too where Kirsten's fine bones came from – and her wild hair. Jess Channing's was white, drawn back into a large bun and kept most severely under control with what looked like over a hundred hairpins, but there were tendrils escaping nonetheless around her neck, which was long and delicate (again like Kirsten's) and her forehead, which was high and hardly lined.

'Drink?' she said. 'No alcohol, but there's plenty of water and some ginger beer. Which I made.'

'I'll have ginger beer. Thank you.'

'We'll start straight away,' she said, leading him into her dining room. He was surprised by how pretty it was.

'Kirsten looks like you,' he said as he sat down, shook out his napkin. 'I expect lots of people tell you that.'

'They don't and I'm delighted to hear it. If she dressed a bit better she'd be a nice-looking young woman. I worry about her though. No inner resources. All emotion, no intellect.'

'Oh I don't know,' said Gray, 'she seems very bright to me.'

'I didn't say she wasn't bright,' said Jess severely, 'I said she had no intellect. There's a difference. Ill-read. Do you read?'

'Well – not very much now. No time. I did though.'

'You should make time for it. What takes all your time up, anyway? Your work I suppose. Dangerous that. It's what my son does. Works and nothing else. You've met Isambard, have you?'

'Oh – yes. Once or twice.'

'Do you think that company of his is in trouble?' she said suddenly. Gray was so startled he dropped his tape recorder. Fiddling about with it, re-setting it, gave him something to do, and he hoped concealed his real feelings. This looked as if it would be better even than he had hoped.

'Well, I really have no idea,' he said.

'Oh come along. Of course you have. You work on the financial pages, don't you?'

'Well – obviously it's having a tough time. All property companies are. And it doesn't seem to be getting any better for any of them. But he's very clever, is Mr Channing. A survivor.'

'I think,' she said calmly, ladling soup into a bowl, 'it would be the best thing in the world for him if it crashed.'

'Oh,' said Gray. 'Oh I see.' He smiled at her uncertainly. 'This is very nice soup.' It was: delicious.

'Leek and potato. Nothing fancy. Yes, it would bring him back to basics. He's lost sight of everything that matters. He could start again, he'd be fine. What did you think of that service, incidentally?'

'Oh – very nice. Yes.'

'I thought it was shocking,' she said, 'really shocking. Dreadful plastic place, piped music. You need a church at your departure whether you believe or not. Some good hymns to send you on your way and a sense of eternity. That place felt like a supermarket that opened yesterday and will close tomorrow. More soup?'

'Yes, please. Did you make the bread?'

'Yes of course. And what did you think of Mrs Booth's little outburst?' The black eyes, so like Bard's, were gleaming with pleasure.

'I – well, I thought –'

'You like her, don't you? I saw you with her at the house. Nothing wrong with that, I like her too as a matter of fact. I think she's honest. Very important, honesty. Kirsten's honest, you know. Just the same, she shouldn't have done it. Teresa Booth I mean. Not then. If poor Douglas was anywhere there, he'd have been very upset. So let's hope he wasn't. Now then, what can I tell you about the old days? I can remember Mosley coming to the East End, you know, him and his Blackshirts. I was only just married, my husband was in the party as well of course, and two of his friends got hurt in the fighting. That wasn't about politics of course, that was gang warfare.'

'So what is about politics?' said Gray. He really wanted to know, his genuine quest set aside.

'People. People and their needs and their ideals. And balancing those things. That's where the party's gone wrong. It's all about needs and not about ideals. Thatcher, she got it right, in her way. I didn't approve of her of course, but she knew about that balance. You know what Nye Bevan said? The Tories are hard on the outside and hard on the inside, whereas we're hard on the outside but soft inside. Quite true.'

'And when did you join the party?'

'Oh, when I was eighteen. Wonderful years. To be working in it, watching it grow, seeing the Trade Unions getting strong, looking out for the workers, for the unemployed ... But perhaps the most exciting time was after the war. When we got in finally. They sang "The Red Flag" when they met in the Commons for the first time ever you know, the new government. The officials were horrified, hurried on with things, as if they were covering up some dreadful social gaffe.' She smiled at Gray. 'Is this the sort of thing you want?'

'Oh – yes. It's wonderful.' He was already writing this piece in his head; it was far too good to waste.

'Right. Fish pie? Just wait a minute and I'll carry on.'

She did carry on; it was wonderful. Gray's tape ran out twice. She had known them all, Bevan, Morrison, Attlee, Stafford Cripps. She saw the birth of the National Health Service – 'Disgraced now, Nye would weep' – the burgeoning of the welfare state – 'Out of hand these days, I'm afraid' – the housing boom –

'Ah,' said Gray, seeing his chance, 'and when did Bard – Mr Channing – become involved in the property scene? Was he involved in housing from the beginning?'

'I suppose so. Not what I'd call housing. He worked for an estate agent. Profit-making, that's all that was.'

'And when did he get into the development side of things?'

'Oh – not until the late 'sixties.'

'When he went in with Dunsford?'

Jess Channing looked at him for a long moment without speaking. Then, 'Mr, Townsend,' she said very firmly, 'if you wanted to talk about Isambard, you should have said so. And I probably wouldn't have seen you.'

'But you were talking about him earlier,' said Gray reasonably.

She stopped, thought again, then nodded. 'Perfectly correct. But I said what I chose to say. I don't want to be questioned about him.'

'Sorry.'

'That's all right.'

'So – you still work for the Labour party?'

'Of course I do. Shall till I drop dead. Now that'd not be a bad place to go, the Walworth Road. The local parties are the lifeblood, you know. The veins that feed the arteries.'

She talked on; Gray listened enthralled. Finally, after a meltingly good apple pie, he sighed and said, 'That was marvellous. Both the food and the talk. But I think I shall have to get back to my office.'

'Have a cup of tea. Or I suppose you like coffee?'

'No,' said Gray, 'I like tea. Very very weak.'

She chuckled. 'No wonder you're a Tory. Come into the other room.'

'This is such a pretty house,' he said.

'I know. They tried to pull it down once, this street, put up some awful high-rise rubbish, but thank heavens they couldn't get planning permission. Duchy of Cornwall all round here of course. Only thing that family's good for, if you ask me, preserving things. That was what was wrong with the first property boom, you know, the way all those awful high-rise blocks and development went on. Right through the 'seventies. And dreadful shopping centres in the middle of towns. Destroyed communities. People lost touch with each other. Isambard made his money that way, of course. I didn't approve then and I don't approve now. He should never have got permission to build half of them, in my view. I never could quite see how and why it happened.'

Gray managed to go on holding his cup and smiling at her and nodding, as if nothing at all had happened, nothing important had been said; and thought that this must have been very much how St Paul had felt on the road to Damascus.

Without knowing why, Francesca felt slightly frightened. Ridiculous, when all she was going to see was some convent and meet a few nuns – and probably a few of the residents of the home as well. But everything to do with this venture of her mother's had been so mysterious – more than mysterious, totally baffling – that she found the prospect of actually confronting it unnerving. Yes, that was a better word. Unnerved. She glanced at her mother who was sitting next to her, extraordinarily quiet: that was probably what was really unnerving her. No chatter, no nonsense. She had wanted to bring Jack, but her mother had said it was a bad idea. 'It's a convent, darling, and the nuns are – well, a bit fuddy-duddy, some of them. And he'd get terribly bored, it's a long way.'

'Oh Mummy, don't be silly. He'd love it, he likes meeting people, and we can stay the night somewhere, go the beach, make a proper trip of it.'

'Francesca,' said Rachel, and the tone of her voice was the same as when Francesca had wanted to go somewhere when she was a teenager and there was no way she was going to be allowed, 'Francesca, it is not a good idea. Leave Jack with Nanny. We shall need plenty of peace and quiet to talk.'

That too had been unnerving.

They were on the A30, following the coast; 'About another ten miles,' said Rachel, 'then we turn off onto the Hartland road. Then it's some very difficult Devonshire lanes, I'm afraid.' And fell back into her strange silence.

The lanes were difficult: so narrow, so high-hedged and banked they were quite dim, in spite of the brilliant sunshine, beneath their overhanging trees. The hills were steep, and there was no room for cars to pass – certainly not when one was a Mercedes and the other a tractor. The tractors gave no quarter; twice Francesca had to back downhill, round sharp blind corners for what seemed like miles. It added to her sense of unease.

But then, suddenly, the landscape opened up, and they were facing a wide, wide valley leading down to the sea: immediately in front of them was a great grey house. 'That is what we call the Help House, or will be,' said Rachel, crossing her fingers. 'Isn't it lovely? We'll come and look at it later. Now take the right fork, darling, and we reach the convent in about five minutes.'

The convent was situated at the end of a no-through lane; a young man, beautifully polite, saluted them and opened a five-bar gate. 'That's Thomas,' said Rachel. 'Hallo, Thomas, how are you?'

'Very very well,' said Thomas carefully, smiling at her. 'Very very well. Thank you.'

'Sweet,' said Rachel briefly. 'Birth defect. Mental age of five, maybe four.'

Francesca was shocked; he had looked absolutely normal. No-one would have guessed there was anything wrong with him.

She eased the car through the gate into a wide, cobbled courtyard; the convent, which was grey stone, like the house they had just passed, was built round it on three sides. It was Victorian: Victorian Gothic, with stone mullioned windows, and a ravishing wisteria growing over the great arched door.

'What a lovely place,' said Francesca, smiling.

'Isn't it? Park over there, darling, look,' said Rachel. 'Ah, here is Reverend Mother now.'

A nun, aged at the most, Francesca thought, about forty, came out of the building, smiling at them. She was, quite simply, beautiful. Lovely skin, almost unlined, dazzling blue eyes, perfect straight little nose, full, smiling mouth. She wore the modern dress, and wisps of fair curly hair escaped from beneath her headdress. Her legs, exposed from mid-calf, were slim, her ankles elegant above her stout shoes – not so different, Francesca thought wryly, from the ones Kirsten and Victoria wore.

'Hallo Rachel. And you must be Mrs Channing. Welcome. It's a great pleasure to have you here.'

'Thank you. But do please call me Francesca.'

'Now Rachel, there is lunch ready, in the dining room, but I wasn't sure how you envisaged the day going.'

Even she, even in her sweet serenity, looked a little strained. What is this, thought Francesca, what on earth is going on?

'I thought what would be best,' said Rachel carefully, 'is for me and Francesca to meet Mary. Has she had her lunch?'

'She has indeed. And is in the library, waiting for you. But aren't you hungry, both of you?'

'Francesca, are you hungry, darling?'

'Not specially, no.' It was true, she wasn't; her inside felt as if it was curled into knots.

'Nor me. Well, Mother, we'll go and find Mary, take her for a walk perhaps, and then come back.'

'Very well.' Reverend Mother leant forward, kissed Rachel suddenly on the cheek. 'I hope you have a nice afternoon.'

The entrance hall of the convent was wood panelled, with a vaulted white ceiling, and a corridor leading off it on either side; they walked down one, past a small chapel and a vast dining hall with long refectory tables, and into a large room, its walls lined with books. In the corner several people were sitting in a circle, a nun in the middle of the group. She was reading aloud: Francesca recognised *The Owl and the Pussy-Cat*. As they approached, a young woman saw them, jumped up, hugged Rachel. Rachel hugged her back. 'Hallo Mary,' she said quietly.

Mary put her finger to her lips. Rachel nodded, smiling; Mary took her hand and led her outside. Francesca followed.

'This is Mary,' said Rachel. 'Mary, this is Francesca.'

'Hallo,' said Mary.

She was small, with brown wispy hair, and wide blue eyes. She had Down's Syndrome. She smiled at Francesca.

'Hallo Mary,' said Francesca.

'We thought we'd all go for a walk,' said Rachel. 'Would you like that, Mary?'

Mary nodded enthusiastically; took her hand. She signalled Francesca to go the other side of her, and took her hand too. She peered up carefully into her face, examining it, then turned to Rachel.

'Pretty,' she said.

Rachel laughed. 'Very pretty.'

'Thank you,' said Francesca, slightly awkwardly. She felt she didn't know quite how to react, what her role was in this strange drama.

'Get the eggs?' said Mary hopefully.

'No, not without Richard,' said Rachel. 'That wouldn't be kind. Richard is Mary's best friend here,' she said to Francesca. 'They collect the eggs together. Always together,' she added firmly, looking at Mary. 'What about the woods?'

Mary nodded. 'The woods,' she said happily, and started walking more purposefully, ahead of them, pulling at their hands. It was like going for a walk with Jack.

They went out of the convent gate, down a track; through a split in the hill, Francesca could see the sea, brilliant, dazzling in the sun. So why did it look to her somehow menacing, troubling?

Mary suddenly dropped Rachel's hand, tapped her head, smiled radiantly. 'Head all right now,' she said.

'Good,' said Rachel. Mary took her hand again and kissed it; then she kissed Francesca's too.

'Poor Mary had a fall,' said Rachel, 'didn't you, Mary?'

Mary nodded vigorously. 'Down the cellar.'

'Yes, down the cellar steps. Concussed herself and ended up in hospital.'

'You came,' said Mary. 'She came,' she added, turning her face to Francesca. 'Came to see me in –' There was a long pause while she was clearly struggling to get the word out right: 'Hospital.'

'Oh,' said Francesca uncertainly. 'When was that, then?'

'Oh, a couple of weeks ago,' said Rachel casually.

So that was where she had been. Not with a boyfriend. Here, with Mary.

They walked for about half an hour. Francesca felt increasingly tense. Mary was very sweet, she could see why Rachel was fond of her, but there didn't seem quite the need for this. There was obviously an end product, an explanation: but why couldn't it have come earlier?

As they walked back up the lane, she pulled ahead; she didn't want to be part of them, she wasn't part of them. They were in some incomprehensible way a unit, and she felt awkward, misplaced in it.

'You go back to Sister now, Mary,' said Rachel. 'I'll see you later.'

'Later for tea?' said Mary hopefully.

'Maybe. We'll see.'

Mary kissed her again and skipped off. Her legs, Francesca noticed, were slightly mottled, in spite of the warmth of the sun. She looked at her mother and smiled warily.

'Now what?'

'I'd – like to talk to you. Then we can go back to see Reverend Mother.'

'Talk to me. Mummy, what is this about? We've had all day to talk.'

'I wanted you to meet Mary first.'

'But why? What is this? And what is Mary to you? I don't understand, any of it'.

Rachel was staring rather fixedly at the door Mary had just disappeared through. She looked pale. There was a silence, then she took a deep breath and, as if bracing herself for a physical blow, turned to Francesca.

'Mary is my daughter,' she said. 'My daughter and – well, and your sister.'

What upset her most was her own outrage. She felt ashamed of it, even as she raged at her mother, fearing that it was for the wrong, the worst reason, that it was because she could not bear the thought that she should have such a sister. She knew, she was sure indeed, that it was not: she had done work for Mencap, it was one of her charities, she had attended functions, raised money for them, gone on Fun Days. She was unfazed by the mentally handicapped, or so she had always thought; had managed to communicate with them, had expressed and meant huge admiration for their carers, their families, and the heavy burden they bore. So why, now, did she feel phsycially nauseated, wretched, and so furiously, frantically shocked by her mother?

'It's not Mary herself,' she said carefully, trying to remain calm, negotiating herself into the heavy, weaving traffic on the A30. 'Of course it's not. It's that she's been there, all these years, and you've never told me. An immense, terrible secret. I don't know how you could do it. Did my – my father know?'

'No. No he didn't,' said Rachel quietly, 'and so therefore of course I couldn't tell you. Until he died. And then it seemed impossible, it was much too late.'

'How could you marry someone and not tell him you had a child? How could you, it's unthinkable, dreadful –'

'Francesca, things were very different then. When I was married. You simply couldn't imagine it, you don't understand. My parents never spoke of it, they forbade me to speak of it. I was eighteen years old when Mary was born: I had no job, no status. I made a mistake, a stupid mistake. Her father was almost as young as I was: both he and his parents refused to help in any way. All I was equipped to do, had been trained to do, was get married. That was what life was about then, for a girl like me. You left school, you did the season and unless you were very plain or very lacking in charm, you found a husband.'

'And these husbands, they didn't like used goods, is that right?'

'I'm sorry?' Rachel had become very white, her face drawn.

Francesca knew she was hurting her and she couldn't stop. It was helping.

'If he'd known you'd had a baby, my father, he'd have backed off. You'd have failed your test, wouldn't have graduated properly. So you kept your mouth shut. Good God.'

'Francesca, I would ask you at least to try and understand. Life was totally different then. An unmarried woman with a child was an outcast, and the child too. And a mentally handicapped child – well. Impossible. Beyond the pale. There was no way I could have supported myself and Mary, and no way my parents were going to do it for me. Adoption was out of the question, too, because of – well, because of how Mary is. The Community seemed to me the only answer. Was the only answer.'

Francesca was silent, trying at least to appear rational. 'Well,' she said finally, 'no, perhaps I don't understand. But a child, a person; denying her existence, just pretending she wasn't alive, didn't exist ...'

'I never pretended that. I did my best for her. Always.'

'You pretended it to the world. To your husband and your daughter. It's horrible, it's obscene.'

'That's not fair,' said Rachel.

'Well, it may not seem so to you,' said Francesca. 'That's how it looks to me. And yet you told Bard. You told my husband. He was the only person, sharing this awful thing with you. How could you do that, Mummy, how could you make him party to it?'

'I didn't want to. I tried not to. But he made me tell him. I think – well, I think he guessed anyway.'

'When?'

'When he went down to the convent.'

'Bard went there? With you? And met Mary?'

'Yes. Yes, he did.'

'When?'

'Oh – a couple of months ago. That was when I – I told him.'

'My God,' said Francesca, 'this is really unbelievable. I don't think I can stand much more.'

'I had to take him,' said Rachel, 'because I needed the money. He wouldn't give it to me without visiting the place. Obviously.'

'No. No of course not. But he still visited it without telling me. Without you telling me. And knew. And never said anything. God, it's – it's outrageous. I feel such a fool. What else do you think he might be keeping from me?'

'Darling –' Rachel put her hand out, gently touched Francesca's arm. She shook it off violently.

'Don't. Just don't. This isn't something you can charm your way out of. It's too big, too serious. And I hope you realise, I do hope you do realise, that this is my marriage you've been playing games with.'

'I have not been playing games with your marriage. And you're driving much too fast.'

Francesca ignored her.

'Asking a husband to be an accomplice in a deception of this kind is playing games with a marriage. In my book. I'm sorry. And I'm shocked and appalled you should do it. And that he should agree.'

'Francesca, you're over-reacting.'

'Oh am I,' she said, and she was near to tears now, could feel them rising, painfully harsh, in her throat. 'Over-reacting. How silly of me. Over such a small, unimportant matter. A sister, aged – what thirty-five, is she? Whom I've never known about. Whom my mother and my husband have known about. Lied to me about. Sorry. Of course I shouldn't react very strongly at all about something like that. God, don't talk to me any more, Mummy, please. I can't handle it.'

All she wanted now, she realised, as finally they reached the haven that was London, as she dropped her mother, with a terse goodbye, at the taxi rank at Hammersmith Broadway and headed the car in the direction of St John's Wood, all she wanted was to see Liam. Liam would understand; he knew about rejection, about estrangement. Liam could ease her pain.

Rachel poured herself a very strong gin and tonic, and sat staring over the hot, dusty wastes of Battersea Park and tried to fight off an intense rising panic. She had been right all along, and they had been wrong, Bard and Reverend Mother; it was as impossible to explain as she had known it would be, and Francesca clearly found it impossible to understand. And how indeed could she, how could she possibly be expected to understand, a child of the easily permissive age, how could she grasp the absolute impossibility of keeping a baby, any baby, without a husband, and especially a baby such as Mary? And as she sat there, shaking now with misery, reliving the nightmare of it all, thirty-five years ago, she felt along with her remorse and grief a fierce, wild resentment that she had not been allowed to keep Mary and to love her, as she had so longed to do ...

Chapter Seventeen

Francesca had sent Nanny and the children to Stylings. In her raw, distressed state, even Jack's cheerful company jarred, made her feel worse. She needed peace, solitude, to be able to think. Bard had phoned, at midnight, after she returned from Devon, to say he wasn't coming back until Saturday: she had managed to sound calm, to express regret, not to mention the convent – it would have been fruitless, frustrating even – and his voice, even across the Atlantic, was exhausted, heavy. But when she put the phone down, she raged at him, silently, pacing the house, unable to sleep.

In the morning, Liam phoned: 'I'm being sent home today,' he said. Francesca burst into tears: she had been so longing to see him, to talk to him, to get some sympathy, some understanding.

'Hey,' he said, 'what's this about, you should be pleased for me.'

'I am,' she said, desperately dragging her voice back under control, 'of course I am, I just needed – well, wanted to see you so much, something's happened –'

'What sort of something? Not Kitty?'

'No,' she said, smiling through her tears, thinking even in her misery how thoughtful, how sweet he was, 'no it's not Kitty. Something quite different.'

'My father?'

'No. Yes. Oh, Liam, I – God, you must think I'm neurotic.'

'Of course I don't. If you're upset it must be something important. Look, I can't talk now, I'll ring you later from home, if I possibly can.'

'Yes, all right.'

God, she was neurotic. Beautiful yes, desirable certainly, but quite neurotic. Neurotic and spoilt. Well, never mind. It actually made everything rather easier. Neurotic women were far more inclined to rash, reckless behaviour than level, placid ones.

He phoned her at midday; she picked up the phone immediately. 'Hallo?'

'Hallo, Francesca. That was very quick.'

'Yes, well, I didn't want Sandie picking up the phone.'

'Oh don't worry about Sandie,' he said easily, 'she likes me. I could always pretend I was ringing her.'

'Oh,' she said. She sounded surprised, almost shocked. Careful, Liam, he thought. Don't rush this, won't do to sound too practised, too self-confident.

'Now then,' he said, 'what is it, what's happened?'

'Oh – it's so hard to talk about, so hard to explain.'

'I'm very good at listening.'

'Is Naomi there?'

'No, she's not. Haven't seen her yet. She sent a cab for me. Very caring.'

'Oh Liam! That's really – well, that isn't very nice.'

'Well,' he said carefully, 'well, she is working. And she is very high powered.'

'Yes. Like Bard.' She laughed, clearly trying to sound cheerful. 'No place in their lives for us ordinary folk, Liam.'

'When's he back?'

'Oh – not till the weekend. And I've sent the children to Stylings with Nanny. I'm beginning to regret it, it's very quiet here. I'll go down tomorrow, I think.'

'Please tell me what the matter is.'

'I will. Soon. How are you?'

'Bit tired. But fine. Come on, tell me.'

'Well – I've just had an awful shock.'

'What sort of a shock?'

'Oh – oh God, this is so difficult on the phone. I wish you were still in hospital, wish we could still talk. Is that very mean of me?'

'Very. Tell you what, why don't I come down there and see you? I'm dying to test out my freedom.'

'Oh don't be absurd. How can you, you can't walk, you can't drive.'

'I could get a cab. It's not far. Providing you pay for it,' he added, laughing. 'Haven't had my pocket money yet.' (Nice one that, stressing his situation, setting out Naomi's arrogant attitude towards him.)

'Oh, Liam, I'm sure you – well, I'm sure she doesn't –'

'Doesn't what? Treat me like a child, make it plain she holds the purse strings? Of course she does. And I expect I deserve it.'

'Of course you don't. It's not your fault if – well anyway, Liam, of course you mustn't come down here. What if – hang on a minute – yes, Sandie, what is it? Oh – yes, all right, fine. No, you go, there's only me here. Bye. Sorry, Liam. Sandie wanted to know if she could have the rest of the day off.'

'And what did you say?'

'I said she could – there's no-one here, even Barnaby's gone away for a few days. I miss him.'

'Well, then, I shall definitely come. You shouldn't have told me all that,' he said, laughing.

'Liam, I –'

'I'm on my way. I need to talk to you anyway. I'm feeling pretty blue myself, deep down. Put the kettle on.'

He arrived twenty minutes later; she ran down the steps, paid off the cab. She was looking very pale, scruffy almost, her dark hair dragged back off her face, dressed in jeans and a T-shirt. She was obviously very upset. This was good.

'Come in,' she said. 'Can you manage the steps, do you think?'

'Oh yes. I got up ours this morning. I'm very nifty with these things now,' he said, waving one of his crutches. 'Lead the way.'

'I still think this is crazy,' she said, walking slowly beside him into the kitchen.

'I don't see why. Who would care? This is my father's house, you're my stepmother – what a strange thought that is – and anyway there's no-one here.'

'I – I suppose so. Do you want some coffee?'

'Yes please. Now come on, tell me what the matter is.'

'Oh – it's – it's just – oh God, Liam, this so hard.'

'Come on,' he said, fighting down the impatience now, settling on the rather battered old sofa that sat in the corner of the kitchen – he remembered that sofa, he had sat on it with his mother even. 'I haven't come all this way for nothing.'

'All right. Well, I've just found out something horrible. Well –' she tried to smile, he saw her lip tremble. 'Sorry,' she said. 'I'm just being such a wimp.'

'You're not a wimp at all,' he said. 'I think you're very brave. Now what is this horrible thing? Come and sit over here and tell me.'

She told him, and he could see it was indeed an extraordinary, a literally shocking story. And that she was deeply upset and shaken – and with good reason. On the other hand, the crucial thing, Liam thought, was not to seem too obviously on her side. To appear to be taking a balanced view, to be examining both sides of the situation – and at the same time to make sure she knew how he did understand, that he knew all too well how much it must have hurt her. And – and this was crucial – to stress that nobody understood better than he that there was no-one more masterly than Bard Channing at most brutally sweeping the emotions of others aside when he was concerned with his own.

'I wouldn't mind,' she said, 'I wouldn't mind nearly so much if Bard hadn't known. That's what hurts most. That he and my mother should have – well, I feel so totally discarded, humiliated, I suppose. Why did they do it, Liam, why? And why didn't he talk to me, tell me about – about her? Why not do that, why not tell me?'

'Well,' he said, carefully truthful, 'I presume he'd promised your mother. That's what she said to you, isn't it?'

'Yes. But – but I'm his wife. How could he keep something so enormous, so important from me?'

'Well, I suppose because he was in this instance concerned with this convent place. The latest intrigue. The deal.'

'Hardly a deal. It's not going to make him any money. Absolutely the reverse.'

'I don't think,' said Liam slowly, 'that's got much to do with it. What turns my father on, if you like, what excites him, keeps him happy, is anything new, any new concept. Isn't that right? A new deal, a new company, a new toy, a –' He stopped himself, quickly. 'Well, anything.'

He saw in her eyes she had read that pause, knew what he meant by the 'well, anything'. Saw the hurt, the fear, saw he had touched a nerve, didn't like doing it, was glad he had. He picked up her hand, to comfort her from the hurt.

He had never touched her before, except to kiss her briefly when she arrived or left the hospital; he saw her look at his hand, holding hers, saw her look at him, startled, flush, pull her hand away. He went on talking, quietly, steadily.

'And this is a new game, that intrigues him, but he has to play by the rules. Your mother's rules. A chance to play benefactors. Another favourite game, of course. It eases a very guilty conscience.'

'Yes,' she said absently, 'yes, I suppose so.'

'I mean,' he said, and he had been waiting a while to find out if she knew, saw his opportunity, 'look at the Clarkes.'

'What have the Clarkes got to do with it?'

'Well, the way he looks after them.'

'Oh, Liam, he doesn't do anything out of the way for them. Helps Oliver, the odd present.'

'Oh,' he said, carefully flustered, 'oh, I –'

'Liam what is this; what are you talking about?'

'I – I thought you must know.'

'Know what?'

'That he pays for practically everything for them. I mean it's wonderfully generous of him. The flat the kids had, expensive holidays, and of course Mrs Clarke's nursing home –'

'Liam, are you sure about this? I mean surely it comes out of some insurance or other, that's what I always thought –'

'Well – well, no, it doesn't. Actually. No, he pays for it himself. Personally. Always has done. They don't know, but – I thought you would.'

'No,' said Francesca slowly, 'no, I didn't. Bard's always said – well, it doesn't matter what he's always said. I'm very surprised –' She hesitated, clearly shocked again by this new piece of information, the revelation of this new secret; then, clearly making an effort to set it aside or at least to explain it, 'but I suppose it's the sort of thing he would do. He's so incredibly generous.'

'Yes, of course he is. His worst enemy couldn't deny that. And it's the same with this thing of your mother's. And also, Francesca, you're angry because he didn't tell you, but it really wasn't his secret. To tell. Was it? Be honest.'

'No. No, I suppose it wasn't.'

'Well then. You have to like him for that at least.'

'I don't like him for anything at the moment,' said Francesca. 'I can't.'

She spoke quite lightly; but her eyes were shadowy. She looked very unhappy. 'Oh Liam. It's all gone wrong so fast, we're growing so far apart, he seems a stranger half the time these days, he shuts me out so much, won't tell me things, I suppose he's always done it, but it's got so much worse lately. And I thought – I thought after Duggie died he would come back to me, at least some of the way, but he hasn't, he seems almost hostile to me a lot of the time, and – oh God.' Her lip trembled; she looked away. 'I'm sorry, it's very wrong of me to talk to you like this, very disloyal, I don't know what's got into me –'

'Nothing's got into you,' he said. 'You're upset.'

'Yes,' she said, and her voice was almost unbearably heavy, filled with pain and tears, 'yes I am, so very upset.'

He suddenly felt guilty, sick at himself, stopped playing with her, playing on her vulnerability. 'Don't cry,' he said. 'Francesca, please don't cry.'

'I can't help it,' she said, breaking down, really crying now, her face dropped into her hands. 'I can't bear any of it, any of it at all. Not Kitty, not Bard, not my mother –'

He put his arm round her shoulders, very gently; he was afraid of startling her, sending her away. She didn't react in any way, neither shrugged him off nor responded, and for a long time neither of them moved. Then she suddenly looked up at him, her face tear-stained and smudgy, and said, through the tears, 'Oh Liam, I'm sorry, I'm being pathetic. Please forgive me.'

'There's nothing to forgive,' he said, wiping her face tenderly. 'Come on, blow your nose.'

She did, laughing weakly; he put the handkerchief away in his pocket. 'I shall keep that for ever.'

'How disgusting.'

'Nothing you did could seem disgusting to me,' he said, laughing back at her. 'Absolutely nothing. I think you're wonderful, nice, kind and very, very brave. So try to stop fretting, try to set all this aside. Tell you what, what about a proper drink? What about a glass of champagne? I'm sure you have plenty, nothing like champagne for raising the spirits.'

'Oh dear,' she said dashing her hand across her eyes, 'what a pain I am. Yes, I'd like some champagne, how clever of you to think of it, it suddenly seems the best idea in the world.'

She opened the fridge and there were three bottles lying on the top shelf; he'd half forgotten about the way of things in his father's house, the day-to-day luxury, the careless extravagance. A wave of resentment rose in him; he found it hard for a moment to smile as she handed him the bottle, asked him to open it. He poured two glasses, handed her one.

'To you,' he said.

'No, to you, and your continuing recovery. Thank you. And thank you for listening.' She looked at him, for a moment, and then said, 'Oh God, I'm a self-centred bitch. Going on and on about myself. You must feel pretty bad. Can I listen to you now?'

'Well,' he said, hurriedly concentrating his thoughts, 'I'm not too bad. A bit low I suppose; I mean I don't see where, how, I can get any sort of a life together. It was hard enough before; I thought I might seem a useless, pathetic failure, but there was still something I could do about it. Now I'm a cripple as well – even my children seem to have written me off, and as for Naomi –' He heard his voice shake; he wasn't surprised, he wasn't acting. The old familiar sense of futility, of self-distaste, of anger as much at himself as the forces of fate that had brought him to it overwhelmed him; he felt physically sick, infinitely weary of himself. There was a stinging of tears in his own eyes now; he brushed them away impatiently. 'Sorry,' he said. 'Sorry, Francesca.'

'Liam, don't. I – oh God, Liam, don't cry.' And then her arms were round him, gentle, tender, and her voice, soft with sympathy, was talking to him, foolish, soothing nonsense, such as she spoke to her children, as he spoke to his, and he sat there, very still, drinking her in, her closeness, the feel, the smell of her, and then he turned in her arms and looked up at her and said, 'I think you're very lovely, Francesca. I really do. I – well, I seem to be falling in love with you.'

He had not meant to say it, had known it was not really time to say it; but having said it knew also that it was true, that whatever might be false in this complex, dangerous game he was playing, he did indeed most genuinely feel if not love, then certainly tenderness, tenderness and desire for her.

She dropped her arms away from him, drew back. 'Of course you're not falling in love with me,' she said, and the expression in her eyes was wary, almost afraid, but at the same time tender, welcoming. 'You can't be.'

'I can. I am. I'm sorry, I didn't mean to say it, to tell you, but –'

'Liam, please!'

'But Francesca, I am. I know I am. The last few weeks all I've thought about, dreamed about, wanted, was you. In some ways it's been the happiest time in my whole life. The only thing I don't know, that I'm not quite sure about, is what I want to do about it. What I can do about it.'

'Liam, you can't do anything about it, the whole thing is ridiculous, you can't –'

'Please stop saying that,' he said, and leant forward and kissed her on the mouth. A gentle, tender kiss, warm, not in any way sexual – for that would be frightening, threatening, he thought, noticing how much even in the very real emotion of the moment he was enjoying this, enjoying orchestrating it, directing it; and hers in return was gentle too, gentle and very sweet, and then, 'You must go now, at once,' she said, staring at him, her eyes very wide, starry with tears.

'Now I've made you cry again,' he said.

'Yes, you have. Liam, this is awful, terrible, you have to go, straight away, and I must never, ever see you again. You shouldn't have come. No, don't,' she said, jumping up as he took her hands, turned them over, kissed the palms, 'don't, don't, don't. Leave me alone. I'm going to call the cab now, this minute.'

But she hesitated just for a moment before pulling them away, and he knew then that he had won; that he could have her, and whenever he chose.

He was just settling into the minicab, waving to Francesca who was standing at the top of the steps, when he saw Sandie coming round the corner of the street. Liam leaned right out of the cab window, and blew Francesca a kiss. She laughed and hesitated and then blew one back. She hadn't seen Sandie. But he knew Sandie had seen both of them.

The Easterhope Council offices, Gray thought, were the worst yet. Some of them had been very smart, notably in places like Westminister (obviously), some even lavish (Esher), mostly not very nice. Easterhope, situated south-east of Romford, could only be described as fairly nasty: all right outside, 'sixties concrete, with an attempt at landscaping, Easterhope's coat of arms planted out rather inexpertly in pansies, miniature roses and a particularly rigid variety of cineraria in a circular concrete surround in the middle of the car park. But inside dinginess ruled: grey walls, grey lino and green paint, with an overall odour that Gray could only describe as the opposite of fresh air and new polish. He stood patiently behind a rather timid little man while an overbearing woman told him that if he wanted to see someone about his council tax he would have to come back with his most recent demand, plus what she called all the prevalent documen-tationing – Gray, who found bad English as excruciating as some people find chalk scraping down the blackboard, had some difficulty in not correcting her on this – and then waited further while she went off to, as she put it, 'consult a colleague on a point of issue.'

Finally she came back, looked at him blankly and said, 'How may I help you?'

'I'm interested in the history of a building,' said Gray politely.

'If it's history you want the library. High Street, second on left –'

'No, not that sort of history. Of a building in Easterhope, put up in the early 'seventies.'

'Well, there were lots,' she said. 'You'll have to be more specialised that that.'

'Specific,' said Gray

'Pardon?'

'Sorry. Nothing. It's the development on South Avenue, just near the Ring Road, the flats, you know, and there's a school and an old people's home –'

'That'd be South Farm Estate.'

'Ah, yes. Yes, that's the one.'

'What do you want to know, the history did you say?'

'Yes, the planning history, and then when it was actually built, all that sort of thing.'

'Is your interest professional?'

'Yes, it is,' said Gray humbly. 'I'm a journalist and I phoned to say I was doing an article on –'

'You on the *News*?'

'Yes,' said Gray, cautiously. He hadn't thought he'd mentioned that.

'We had two blokes here yesterday, wanting to photograph the new statue. You people ought to be co-operative together a bit more.'

'Oh,' said Gray, 'oh, no, not the *Easterhope News*. The *News on Sunday*, national paper.'

'Oh well,' she said, clearly uninterested again, 'you should have gone through the press offfice at the town hall.'

'I did. And they told me to come straight through you. Said you were always exceptionally helpful.'

It worked every time, this one. In fact, he rarely spoke to press offices, who tended to be not only unhelpful, but suspicious of the press.

She smiled. 'Oh, well, in that case. Down there, the planning offices. Tell them Jackie said it was all right.'

The planning offices were even dingier; beyond the mottled plastic counter that was Reception, he could see endless, floor-to-ceiling bulging brown files on racks, rows of grey tin filing cabinets, men in short-sleeved shirts and women in cotton dresses either thumbing listlessly through sheaves of paper or tapping slightly less listlessly onto computers. Gray was just yielding to serious depression when a very pretty girl in a tight T-shirt and a Lycra mini with the longest, blackest, false eyelashes Gray had ever seen came and smiled at him over the mottled plastic.

'How may I help you?'

'I'm told you may have what I'm looking for,' he said choosing the double entendre carefully, giving his most careful, easily charming smile.

'Depends what it is,' she said and looked at him beneath the lashes.

'Well, it's rather boring, I'm afraid. Just a file on the South Farm Estate.'

'That is boring,' she said, 'you're right. What you want that for, then?'

'I'm a journalist,' said Gray. 'I'm writing an article on architectural development in the 'sixties and 'seventies.'

'Oh I see. Your paper doesn't do those page three type things, does it?'

Gray paused before answering, trying to gauge her reason for asking; he didn't want to offend her. 'No, not really,' he said trying to imagine a pair of oversized and bouncing boobs on the austere pages of the *News*. It seemed, bizarrely, a rather good idea.

'I think they're disgusting,' she said.

'Oh, me too.'

'Not that I'm one of those women libbers,' she said firmly. 'But I just think it's awful, men ogling away at them, in the canteen and that. You feel really awful, as if they could see you like that – and also –' warming to her subject; she clearly felt Gray was in a position of some authority in such matters – 'also, why do they choose such awful models most of the time? There are loads of really pretty girls walking about with really nice bodies and they choose ones who look like they're deformed or sort of.'

'Yes, I couldn't agree more.'

'I mean, I wouldn't do it, of course, but I think if they had girls who were more, like, normal, it would be a lot better. Anyway, you want the files on South Farm. Would that be right from the beginning?'

'Yes, please. If it wouldn't be too much trouble.'

'Haven't got anything else to do,' she said, shrugging.

You could never quite believe it, when something suddenly worked, when a hunch came good, when things fitted even better than you'd hoped. It was like the first mouthful when you were really hungry, the first drink at the end of an endless, tough day, tipping over the brow of a hill and taking off down the other side on a bicycle: a mixture of such physical and emotional pleasure it could be savoured and remembered for a long time. And in those grey and dingy offices, sitting at a table, thumbing through dirty files, Gray found himself staring incredulously at the names on the sheets of paper before him and looked up at the sun, shafting down in great dusty lines through the grubby windows, and at one and the same time was unable to believe it, and knew, without more than a nought point one percentage of real evidence, that he had his answer.

★

334

'Could I have the early files on Bard Channing again? 'Sixties and 'seventies,' said Gray.

The girl in charge of what was left of the cuttings library at the *News* grinned at him. 'You'll wear those things out. Hang on.' She handed them to him; battered brown files filled with yellowing papers. 'Here you are. We're closing in half an hour. That OK?'

'Sure. Thanks.'

He sat down at a table and started methodically from the beginning. She was right, they were becoming very familiar. The young Bard, thin then, the very first time he had hit the press, grinning, flanked by an equally cheerful-looking Duggie Booth, and an earnest young man in spectacles called Nigel Clarke.

'Three young Davids defeat Goliath,' said the headline. They had won a contract to put up a small but prestigious development in South London, against some stiff opposition from the big boys. No details, no more names. The year was 1970.

A couple more like that. One of the articles was more detailed, a short history of the partnership – Gray knew that one literally by heart, how the young Channing had been working for an estate agency, called McIntyres, along with Clarke, and how one of his clients, impressed by the two of them, had offered them a corner of the deal and a percentage of the profit. That had got them up and running; Booth, working for another agency, had joined them a few months later.

Then a bigger piece in the *London Evening News* about how they had landed a contract to build a large shopping centre in the Croydon area in '72, and another for a huge office block near Bromley towards the end of that year. Channing's name was mentioned in several general articles about the boom, about the absurdly escalating prices of property, about single buildings bought and sold three, four, five times in as many weeks, about the almost manic enthusiasm with which banks were lending money, afraid of being caught liquid, with large sums not invested, about the massive demand for office buildings, largely created by the policy of the Labour party to discourage commercial development in the late 'sixties, and to direct all the available funding into building homes. And Channing was quoted too: a surprisingly sober voice for one so young and in such a heady climate, counselling against too much greed, too much profiteering.

It was a counsel that saw him through the massive property crash of '73.

And – yes, there it was, also in the *News* and the *Standard*, and a small piece in the *Telegraph*, the announcement of the contract to build South Farm Estate in Easterhope, in Essex. And another in the same area, a year later, a block of flats and a shopping arcade. A small paragraph in the *Evening News* about the tragic death of Surrey businessman Nigel Clarke in a road accident, and quite long fulsome articles about him, his family, with reports of his funeral in the *Guildford News* and the *Surrey Gazette*. A picture of Heather Clarke, leaning heavily on Channing at the funeral, with Duggie Booth looking shattered just behind them.

And so it went on. And on. The years of consolidation: developments: the public flotation in 1980: the formation of the Northern company in 1985. But no mention anywhere of – 'Shit!' said Gray. He said it aloud, and then he said 'Fuck me' and then he sat and read and read and re-read, half aloud, his lips moving, a report in the *South East London Press* on a dinner given in July 1987 to mark the early retirement, due to ill health, of one Clive Hopkins, a planning officer who had been involved, amongst other things, in the prestigious South Farm development at Easterhope, built by the Channing corporation, and who was a prominent member of the Round Table, the Freemasons and several other charitable organisations for whom he had worked tirelessly. The Mayor of Easterhope, who had been the guest of honour, had wished Mr Hopkins well in his retirement and his new life in Torquay, South Devon, where he was sure Mr Hopkins would find peace and happiness, not to mention the good health which had been denied him of late.

Ten minutes later (having found nothing more), Gray handed back the files and went outside the building and gazed up smiling at the sky for a moment before roaring off on his bike, filling the lovely golden air with exhaust fumes.

When he got home, Briony was waiting on the doorstep.

'So how are you, Gray?'

She looked, irritatingly, extraordinarily well. Well and pretty. He had somehow imagined her to have lost weight, to look drawn and pale. But she was tanned, had obviously been away; her hair was streaked with the sun, and there was a dusting of freckles on her small nose. She was wearing a linen jacket over a long navy and white silk dress, and a big straw hat; she looked, sitting sipping a Pimms in one of the wicker conservatory chairs, exactly like some refugee from the 'thirties. She smiled at him very sweetly; he felt disturbed, upset by her, by the realisation that he still loved her, had missed her horribly.

'Oh,' he said, hearing the silence he had created as he studied her, 'oh, I'm fine. Yes. Very busy. Very busy indeed.'

'Really? Me too.'

'Good. That's good. It's usually a quiet time for you, isn't it?'

'Yes, but I've had a couple of commercials. One for kids, a breakfast cereal, it's been just the best fun. And a travel firm, shooting out in Jamaica —'

'Hence the tan?'

'Hence the tan. Yes. So what have you been up to?'

'Oh — you know. This and that.'

'Uh-huh. Not been away?'

'No, no I haven't been away. I've been very busy, and — well, no-one to go away with. Have I?' He smiled in what he hoped was a careless, jokey manner.

'Well, I wouldn't know, Gray, would I? I mean, two months is quite a long time.'

'Not really, Briony, of course it isn't,' he said, setting aside determinedly the memory of two rather long, exhausting nights with Kirsten Channing. 'I wouldn't call it long at all. Would you?'

And, 'No,' she said seriously, her large blue eyes fixed on his, meeting his gaze steadily, 'no, I wouldn't. Not really.'

Another silence, then he said, 'Anyway, yes of course you must have your prints. I told you to take them at the time.'

'I know, but I was — well, anyway, I didn't want to. But the walls in my new flat do look rather bare, and I did specially like them.' She looked at him and smiled. 'I can't tell you how many times I lifted the receiver to call you, put it down again. It was only because I was actually driving past the road, with half an hour to kill, I plucked up my courage. And I thought I might as well kill it sitting outside your house as anywhere.'

'Well, the half hour is well dead now,' he said.

'I know. Can I make a phone call?'

'Of course.'

He heard her saying, 'Bit held up. Sorry. Be about another thirty minutes. Is that all right? Good, yes, great. Bye.' And who was that she was talking to, he wondered with a stab of jealousy so fierce it was a physical invasion, some new boyfriend?

'Sorry,' she said, coming back in. 'Have to go pretty soon. Photographer waiting. Wants to brief me on a job for some cruddy interior I've got to do next week. So shall I just go and get them, Gray, or have you moved them?'

'No, no, they're still there. Of course.'

She ignored the slight reproach, the emotional tug in his voice. 'Good,' she said quite coolly. 'Well, I'll just pop up and —'

'I'll come with you,' he said.

They went up together, to the small room she had used as a workroom; she smiled at him, unhooking the pictures, handing them to him. They were very nice prints of London bridges; eighteenth century. He had never specially liked them, they were not really to his taste, but they had bought them all while she had been living at the house, and she had always insisted (slightly to his irritation at the time) that they were a shared possession. He would have expected to be glad they were going; actually he felt, looking at the bereft hooks, forlorn, rather sad, as if they had been objects of particular value to him.

'Right,' she said, in the awkward silence after they were stashed on the passenger seat in the jeep, 'well, I'd better go.'

'Briony —' he said. 'Briony, I'd like to — well, perhaps we could have dinner or something. Just for — for —'

And, 'No, Gray,' she said, her blue eyes very steady, setting her hat back on her streaky brown hair, 'there really wouldn't be any point, would there? Not really. I mean nothing's changed, has it? Not for me, not for you, I don't imagine.'

Her voice tailed away; for a moment, just a moment, he was tempted to say no, no Briony, let's talk again, let's think some more, reassess. But he knew it would be pointless, that it would simply open the way to more pain, more frustration; he did not, could not feel differently, and nor did or could she. There was no hope for either of them, no hope at all.

'No,' he said, 'no, I'm afraid not. I'm sorry.'

And he bent and kissed her gently and then went inside and made himself a very strong whisky and sat watching the sky grow dark outside the conservatory, and could not find it in his heart to ring Teresa Booth to tell her what he had only two hours earlier found quite extraordinarily interesting and compelling, and which now suddenly seemed boring and totally unimportant. Well, at least he had his trip to Scotland to distract him over the weekend.

Francesca had spent most of Friday and Saturday forcing herself into a positive frame of mind. What had happened, she told herself, over and over again, was her mother's fault primarily, not Bard's. Liam was quite right; it hadn't been his secret. She would have been just as shocked if he had betrayed Rachel's confidence and told her about Mary. She should, she did, respect him for what he had done. It would be very wrong to blame him, to make an issue of it even. She would just refer to it briefly, so that he knew that she knew, and then leave it. They had enough problems at the moment without her wilfully adding to them; he was having an appallingly difficult time with the company, she could see that, he was still grieving over Duggie, he looked exhausted. Far better to leave things be, harsh things unsaid, reproaches unaired. Least said soonest mended, as Nanny would say: like all clichés, it was true. She found herself repeating this to herself over and over in her head like a mantra all through Saturday, as she waited for his return. He was coming straight to Stylings; she had suggested it, and he had agreed with surprising ease. They could have a quiet weekend with the children and then, she thought, on Tuesday they would escape to Ireland for forty-eight hours. Which could – which would, she knew – heal a lot of wounds.

He was due at teatime, but his plane was delayed; it was almost six when Horton delivered him, and she was reading on the terrace, a bottle of wine on ice beside her.

'Welcome home,' she said, kissing him, smiling carefully.

'Thank you. That looks nice.'

'Here.' She poured him a glass. 'How was your trip?'

'Oh – you know. Bit of a curate's egg really. Where are the children?'

'Both in bed.'

'Jack's in bed! At six!'

'Yes, he fell off his pony. Oh, he's fine, but he was a bit bruised and shaken. It's all right, I've had him checked.'

'Fell off! But Megs only moves at about one mile an hour.'

'Yes, I know. But he's decided to join the circus, and he was riding her bareback –'

'Even so –'

'Standing up,' said Francesca. He smiled at that, properly, for the first time; she smiled rather uncertainly back.

'Oh. Oh, yes, I see.'

'So we can have a nice quiet dinner.'

'Lovely. Just what I need.'

He sat down, threw his head back, closed his eyes; he looked at the furthest edge of exhaustion. She stood there, looking down at him, feeling awkward, wanting to help, not knowing how.

He seemed to drift away from her for a few moments; then visibly pulled himself together, smiled up at her. 'It's nice to be here,' he said and he sounded as if he meant it, reaching out for her hand.

'It's nice to have you here.'

Another silence, while he seemed to be studying her; then he smiled again. 'Maybe an early night,' he said.

And, 'Yes,' she said, smiling slightly awkwardly at him, relieved to find that in spite of everything she wanted him, 'that'd be nice.'

She went up to look at Jack; he was fast asleep beneath his Thomas the Tank Engine duvet, his thumb in his mouth, the muslin cloth he still loved and kept hidden under his bed during the day, clasped in his small brown hand. He looked fine. She bent and kissed his intently sleeping face, adjusted his covers and then went into her bedroom to get ready for the evening, and for Bard.

They ate in the conservatory, and Bard put *La Bohème* on the stereo; they didn't talk much, for things were not easy between them. Francesca kept looking back, wistfully, at only a few months earlier, when they had talked endlessly, easily, and hated that they had come to this, the polite question and answers, the 'oh reallys?' the 'did I tell yous?' But the music helped keep awkwardness, embarrassment, away, and she was able to say, lightly, coolly, into one of the silences, 'Oh by the way, my mother took me down to Devon. I've met Mary and heard all about it, I think it's marvellous what you're doing.' It seemed better that way, to imply she had known all along, even though he knew she had not and even though it was the most difficult thing she had ever said; it avoided any kind of recrimination or reproach and she could tell from his slightly embarrassed smile that he appreciated it, knew what she was doing.

'Well,' he said, 'she's very persuasive, your mother. Even if you don't entirely agree with what she's doing.'

And she knew that came close at least to an apology, even to an expression of sympathy, understanding, and they left it at that. It had cost her dear, in emotional currency; but it had been worth it.

Jack appeared halfway through the meal, fretful, his head aching; they let him stay, grateful for his determined presence, sitting on Bard's knee picking at his plate. 'I don't know what Nanny would say,' said Francesca, looking at them both and shaking her head: and, 'I do,' they said in such absolute unison that she laughed aloud. She took Jack up finally, and put him back to bed, and then went straight to their room and got into bed and lay naked, waiting for him, hoping he would come, nervous that he might not.

He did: he came in, looked down at her in silence for a long moment; then took his clothes off rather slowly, his eyes still fixed on hers. And then got in beside her, and pulled her close to him; they were very ready for one another, he hard and impatient, she soft and liquid. His silence was oddly erotic in itself, shutting out all else, all superfluous emotions, just a total concentration on her and his need, close to a desperation, for her. He was in her swiftly; there was no need for arousal, for preliminaries. She felt him moving, working, sinking within her, felt her own desire becoming fierce, taut, wildly sweet. The great throbbing pleasure began, beating, pulling at her; she was scarcely aware of him, of what he was doing, only of her response to him. Everything else was gone, all the emotions; she was filled, possessed entirely by only one thing: a total concentration on her own pleasure, and there was nothing else in the world for her. She curved, grew round him; she seemed to be part of him, and he of her: one body, one movement, and then, as she rose to him, as she felt herself climbing, climbing to him, heard herself cry out over and over again, felt the waves breaking, wider, broader, higher with each succeeding one, as he came too, so deep within her she felt she must break, she said as she had never done before, 'Bard, look at me, look at me now,' and he did, and his eyes were filled with a dreadful, intense misery.

It meant nothing, she told herself, nothing at all; in a moment of extraordinary tension, emotions were not predictable, not normal. Afterwards he seemed himself (although unusually silent; normally he talked to her, it was the one time she felt they were properly close these days); kissed her briefly, held her for a while, then turned away and slept as he always did when they had made love, deeply, determinedly, like little Jack. And she lay beside him, staring into the darkness, thinking about him, thinking about their marriage. and she felt, despite the closeness, the pleasure he had given her, still estranged from him, still lost and confused.

In the morning she felt better, more normal: Jack was cheerful again, covered in bruises, proud of a lump on his head the size of a duck's egg.

'I think I might not join the circus after all,' he said. 'I might be a racing driver instead. Cars are safer than horses, don't you think, Mum?'

'Definitely,' said Francesca.

'Or I thought I might be a stuffer.'

'A what?'

'A stuffer. Stuff dead animals for money. Granny Jess has got some birds, in that glass case thing, you know.'

'Oh. Oh I see.'

'So like when people's cat died, or their dog, I would stuff it and they could keep it always on a chair. Or I could do their granny or their auntie or something. Or even their husband. What do you think?'

'What a good idea,' said Francesca carefully. 'Another entrepreneur in the family,' she added to Bard.

He was reading the papers, grazing through them as he put it, discarding great heaps as he went; he took them all, hated them all equally. He looked up at Francesca suddenly over a copy of the *News on Sunday*.

'That chap Townsend,' he said, 'the one who came to the auction, the one who appeared at Duggie's funeral. There's a big article of his here about the single currency. It's very good.'

'Really?' said Fancesca. 'Should I read it?'

'Not unless it really interests you. But he is clever. Did he write anything about the auction? And was it the usual unpleasant crap?'

'Yes, he wrote a paragraph or two, and no it was quite nice. I don't think he's the sort of person who'd write anything unpleasant about anything or anyone. He's much too nice himself.'

Gray Townsend stood at the top of a high, overgrown drive, descending quite steeply to an extremely large, ugly and unarguably derelict Victorian Gothic house set on the edge of a very murky-looking lake, covered in weed, edged in tall grasses. Or was it what was in these parts called a loch? Probably not, not quite big enough. He began to walk down the drive; it was lined on either side with thick, unkempt conifer woods. The air was heavy with birdsong, with the wild cries of moorbirds, the less attractive cawing of rooks and crows. Several rather depressed-looking groups of fowl paddled about on the lake, ducking and diving into its dense waters.

At the bottom the drive widened, and opened out into an uneven semi-circle in front of the house; presumably it had once been paved, but all that could be seen now were great straggling clumps of grass and thistle. There was a great studded front door, the hinges rusty, padlocked on the outside; many of the windows were broken, and as Gray stood there, several pigeons flew out from the top floor. The windows at ground level were all sound; he peered in through a couple, set at the right of the door, at a great empty room, with a fine stone fireplace and a wooden floor, the boards broken in several places. To the side of the house were outbuildings, doors hanging open creaking in the wind; he went over to inspect them. One contained a heap of rusting tools, half-bald brooms, rakes, an ancient mower, scythes, and another an old mangle, a couple of stone sinks, some filthy saucepans. Nettles grew amongst them all, reaching high to the broken windows.

He went round to the back; what clearly had once been a vast lawn was a waist-high meadow, the grass fighting with thistles, wild roses, overgrown sorrel, and to the right a row of ruined glass houses filled with rotting seed boxes. The view from there was breathtaking: hills, woods, a shimmer of water, and beyond that a range of purplish black mountains.

He turned again, looked up at the back of the house; the roof had great gaping holes in it where slates had fallen in, and there were still more broken windows, the ones that were intact glinting, and somehow menacing, in the brilliant sun.

'Well well well,' said Gray aloud. 'Channing Leisure. Very impressive. Very impressive indeed.'

He drove into the nearest village; it was hardly that even, a collection of grey stone cottages, a chapel, a pub. The entire area looked as if its creator had said 'Few too many hills round here, let's drop in a lake and a couple of villages,' and had done just that. The landscape was glorious, fold upon fold of purple and black hills, going on seemingly for ever, great sheets of bleached-out sky, the air filled with wind and the cries of birds, not the neat tidy song Southerners know, but wild, strong, haunting. It was a wild, glorious place, but it did not seem an ideal location for a luxury golf complex.

He went into the pub, ordered a Scotch, engaged the landlord rather determinedly in conversation. It wasn't easy.

'Lovely place, up here.'

'You could say that.'

'I'm from London.'

Silence, a brief, uninterested nod.

'Making my way down. Any hope of a bed for the night?'

'Not here.'

'So where's the nearest town, or large village where I might find –'

'Forty miles south.'

'Ah. Bit of a drive, then.'

'It is.'

There was a long silence while he stared morosely at the bar.

'I was just looking at the old Manse up there,' said Gray. 'I'm a writer, it would suit me down to the ground. It's not for sale, is it?'

'It is not. It's sold. Although what for God knows.'

'Why do you say that?'

'Bought by some man from the North of England. Four, five years ago. Never been back.'

'Good Lord. Who owned it before?'

'The old lady. Daughter of the laird.'

'Is she still around these parts?'

'Not precisely, no. She's passed on.'

At this he walked away, clearly feeling he had imparted quite enough information; Gray settled down in a corner, drank the Scotch, and wondered how cold it had to be in Auchnamultie before they lit a fire. Sub-zero probably.

After about half an hour an old woman came in; she was wearing a long black skirt, a shawl, and a black scarf draped over her head. Gray looked at her incredulously: she looked so like an extra in a film about the Highlands he found it hard to believe she was real. She said something unintelligible to the landlord, and he gave her a glass of what looked like Guinness. She stood at the bar drinking it, staring at Gray. Then she spoke to the landlord again: '... from London' was all Gray could hear. Being a topic of conversation was as good an introduction as any; he stood up, went over to her, smiled. 'Good afternoon.'

She nodded, addressed herself to finishing her Guinness.

'It's beautiful round here,' he said.

Silence.

'Gentleman was talking about the Manse,' said the landlord, in a burst of communicativeness.

'Oh aye?'

'Wanted to buy it, he did.'

'Too late,' she said. 'The old lady sold it years ago.'

'Yes, so I understand.'

'For a lot of money. Lord knows what she did with it, eh Rob?'

'No. Lord knows.'

'Really? I would have thought it would have gone quite cheaply,' said Gray.

The landlord made a sound that was halfway between a spit and a snort. 'Cheap! That place went for two hundred and fifty thousand pound, didn't it, Ba?'

'That's right,' she said, 'quarter of a million. No-one could believe it.'

'Good Lord,' said Gray, 'that is a lot of money.'

Chapter Eighteen

'Bard darling, there's something wrong, isn't there?'

Not many people would have the courage (or, as it might be perceived, recklessness, or even lunacy) to say that to Bard Channing. His staff, his children, even his wife, would all have known better; would have anticipated the violent rage, the roaring denial, the instruction to get out of the room, to leave him alone, to be asked if they had nothing better to do than interfere in matters which had nothing whatsoever to do with them and about which they could not possibly have anything constructive to say.

But Rachel, who had spent much of her life rushing blithely in where whole hosts of angels would have feared to tread (with, roughly speaking, a fifty per cent success rate) had looked at his ashen face (thinner than she could ever remember it), his shadowed eyes, red rimmed with tiredness, noticed his slightly shaking hand, his heavily weary voice, and said it. And Bard stared, glared, at her, and as she continued to sit there in his office, smiling calmly, he looked slightly shamefaced and said yes, there was a possibility that there was a problem or two in his life, but it was absolutely nothing to do with her, and he certainly had no intention of discussing it now or at at any other time.

'Well, that's a pity,' said Rachel, 'because whatever it is is obviously eating you up and spitting you out again. Discussing it might help.'

'I'm afraid,' said Bard, 'that's out of the question.'

'Why?'

'Rachel, I don't want to have to ask you to leave my office, but I might have to, if you persist with this.'

'All right,' she said equably. 'When and if you do, I'll go. But I'm a very good person to talk to. You'd be surprised. Unshockable, that's me.'

'I hope,' said Bard heavily, 'Francesca hasn't been talking to you.'

'No,' said Rachel, returning the look steadily, 'she hasn't. She isn't speaking to me at all, I'm afraid.'

'Because of Mary?'

'Because of Mary. I'm very surprised she's taken it so badly. I knew it would be a shock, I knew it would hurt her. But I thought she would be more – mature – about it than this.'

'She was pretty – mature about it to me, I have to say,' he said.

'Oh really? What did she say?'

'Oh, that she was grateful that she knew about it. Very brief, very to the point.'

'Well, I'm delighted to hear it. I haven't been in contact with her at all. Anyway, I'm sorry, deeply sorry, if it made things awkward in any way between you.'

'It seems not to have done,' he said briefly. 'Now look, you and I have work to do here, business to discuss. We can't waste time on irrelevancies. I can't quite believe I agreed to see you this morning anyway. I don't think Marcia can either. She's obviously slipping.' He looked at her and half smiled. 'You're very persuasive, Rachel. I think perhaps I should invite you onto my board.'

'I wish you would. And it is so good of you, Bard, to see me. It's just that – well, the bank have delivered an ultimatum. They've had another offer for the priory, and they've given us forty-eight hours. I have to go back to them with a proper proposal, I'm afraid.'

'Yes, all right. I understand. Now look, Rachel, I know what this place means to you. But financially it's a nightmare.'

'You're not –' She hesitated, almost unable to speak the words, 'You're not pulling out, are you?'

'Not exactly out, no. But out of the original plan, quite possibly. You've seen this report, it's terrible. I was reading it on the plane. The place needs to be virtually rebuilt. Apart from anything else, your people would either be living in appalling conditions while the work was done, or they'd have a very long wait in the convent. As I understand it, neither is practicable.'

'Well – Reverend Mother might be able to keep them for a while longer.'

'She'll have to anyway, even if my scheme can be made to work.'

'You have a scheme?'

'I do. I'm very strong on schemes, Rachel. The point is that for the price of putting that place to rights, we could build several modern houses. Or rather units. I know your heart's in the priory, and it's all very romantic and beautiful, but what matters is your people. Isn't it? They're not going to care whether they're under a fifteenth-century roof or not ...'

'They might.'

'Rachel, please. Don't be awkward. I can't afford the time. We can get finance to put up new buildings, I can organise it myself. I can't get it to put that place to rights. It'll be quicker and easier my way. And you'll end up with what is actually a more suitable outfit.'

'But what would you do with the priory?'

'Knock it down.'

Rachel winced. The thought literally hurt her; the beautiful grey, graceful house by the sea, that had sheltered people with love and care for centuries, bulldozed down, replaced by a series of modern buildings: no doubt in what she called supermarket style, red-tiled, yellow-bricked monsters that were gracing – or rather disgracing – so many in- and out-of-town sites all over Britain. Defacing the valley, her valley: it was unthinkable.

'Would you be allowed to do that?' she said, grasping desperately, frantically, at an extremely small straw. 'I mean, aren't there rules, restrictions –'

'My dear Rachel,' he said, grinning, 'nothing we can't get round. Believe me, I should know.'

She supposed he would. 'But Bard, it seems so – brutal. Terrible. That lovely house – I don't see how we can ...'

He shrugged. 'OK. That's fine. But that's my offer. Take it or leave it. The alternative is out of the question. I'm sorry.'

Rachel looked at him. She knew he meant it. He wasn't playing games. It was new houses or nothing. She took a deep breath.

'Yes, all right, I'll take it. Well, what I mean is, I'm sure we would go along with it, if it was really necessary.'

'Good. I'm sure it's the right thing to do. Now then, I've told Marcia about it, so in future any detail can be channelled through her. If I'm crucially needed for meetings, I'll make myself available but on the day-to-day front, as I told you, it's out of the question. Let me know what the next step is. Presumably, we must get some more trustees. And I'd like to propose Peter Barbour is on the board. Very sound, experienced with charity work, and we do need an accountant.'

'Yes, if he's willing, that would be splendid. And Reverend Mother has a local candidate, which I think is important, don't you?'

'Yes, I do. Anyway, keep in touch with Marcia, she'll be expecting your calls.'

'Fine. Bard, I really am grateful. I just don't know what to say.'

'Well,' he said, grinning at her, 'that must be a first.'

He sat back in his chair then, looked at her, his dark eyes very intense. 'Rachel, what – what made you think that there was – might be – a problem?'

'Bard, I was married to a man whose entire life was a series of problems. I got to know the signs.' She stood up, walked round the desk, and bent and kissed him on the forehead.

'You're a very nice man, Bard Channing. Francesca is lucky to have you.'

'Oh Christ,' he said, 'Christ, I don't know that she is.'

In the heart of the City that golden Monday morning, Desmond North at Methuens Bank received a report from one of the members of his department that the Channing Corporation was yet again behind on the interest payments on their loan.

'This is the third time in six months, Mr North. I just thought you ought to know. I realise the report from the accountants was OK, but –'

'Yes, thank you, Tim. I'll have a look at it straight away.'

If Desmond North had not received that very morning the final details and tickets for the cruise to the West Indies that he and his wife were taking in exactly six months' time (to be followed by a longed-for move to the West Country and the thatched cottage with its large garden that he had recently purchased), he might not have acted as he did. In the event he decided nothing could be allowed to come between him and the certain happiness of that: he had spent forty long and very tough years in the devoted service of Methuens, and he wanted his reward.

He called a meeting of the other board members at a mutually convenient time to discuss the Channing account: six that evening was the earliest they could all attend.

Francesca had just come in from the gym when Liam phoned. Half exasperated, half guiltily pleased by his voice, she sat down on the bed, started pulling off her shoes.

'I just wanted to talk to you,' he said.

'Ah.'

'How are you?'

'I'm fine, Liam, thank you. How are you?'

'Oh – all right. Lonely. Are you missing me?'

'No of course I'm not missing you,' she said. But she was: she knew she was. Missing the long, easy, charming conversations, missing the edgy, near-guilt of being with him, missing the light, heady pleasure of sensing a new attraction, a new desire.

'Well, that's a shame. I'm missing you. What are you doing?'

'Sitting on the bed,' said Francesca, 'taking my – my shoes off.'

'Only your shoes? I wish I was there, to help with the rest.'

'Oh, Liam, really!' she said, laughing. 'Yes, only my shoes. Well – at the moment. I've been to the gym.'

'Yes, Sandie said you were there.'

'Sandie! You talked to Sandie! Liam you shouldn't, it's awfully silly.'

'Why?'

'Well, because – because you shouldn't. And she doesn't like me.'

'Look,' he said, laughing, 'you can't have it both ways. You can't say we're just friends, and then that I shouldn't ring you up. Or are you saying I'm more than a friend after all?'

'No! Yes. Oh Liam, I don't know. I just think it's silly. That's all.'

'Could I see you today?'

'No, you can't.'

'Why not?'

'Well, because I'm busy.'

'Doing what? You make time for your other friends, you were having lunch with lots of them last week. Please, Francesca! Can't we meet for a picnic or something? I'm awfully lonely and I'd like it so much.'

Francesca hesitated. She looked at the day ahead: an empty, silly day. Nanny had already taken Kitty out for a walk, Jack was at school, later he was going to a party. Bard was probably going to be very late. She had to work on her advertising sales for the charity brochure, she had to get her hair done, she had thought of having her legs waxed. What a day, what a way, for an intelligent woman to pass. And she was, she had to admit, nervous, edgy now about the trip to Ireland, of the new, sternly distant Bard, of the heavy silences, the lack of ease.

And she thought of meeting Liam, of the fun they would have, how much she would enjoy it, how much he would tease her, how much she would laugh. And the very fact the temptation was so strong, so heady, made her say no.

'I'm sorry, Liam, I really can't. I'd love to, but –'

'Would you? Would you really? Because I'd really really love to. Love to see you, be with you, talk to you, look at you. Just as a friend, of course.'

'Well, I'd like to, she said firmly, her resolve strengthened further by her leaping pleasure at his words, his tone, 'but I can't. I really can't. I'm sorry.'

He sighed. 'All right. You're a hard woman. But I shall try again. I can't live without you now.'

'Liam, of course you can,' she said, laughing. 'You have to.'

'Francesca darling, I can't.'

'Liam, don't call me that,' she said sharply, shocked as much by a small sweet rush of pleasure at the word – Bard never called her darling, never called her by any endearment – as that he had said it all.

'Sorry. Francesca, then, I can't live without you. How about tomorrow?'

'Tomorrow,' she said, 'I'm going to Ireland. With my husband.'

'Ah yes, the birthday treat. Well, I hope he enjoys it, the lucky old sod, I hope he knows how lucky he is. Ring me when you're back.'

'Liam, I'm not going to ring you.'

'Then I shall ring you,' he said, and then, his tone much more serious, 'I have to, Francesca, you just don't seem to understand.'

'Hopkins,' said Gray. 'Babbacombe, South Devon.'

'How are you spelling that?'

'I am not spelling it,' said Gray, 'it is spelt –'

'Pardon?'

'Sorry,' he said wearily. He really should know better than to try and teach grammar to the staff of Directory Enquiries. 'It is spelt H-O-P-K-I-N-S.'

'No, not Hopkins,' said the voice, sounding almost as weary. 'Babbacombe.'

'Oh, I see. B-A-double B-A—'

'Oh, yes. One moment please.'

The robotic voice came on the line. 'The number you require is 01803 777912 ...'

Gray punched the air. He couldn't believe it. They hadn't moved, they were still there, sitting there, sitting ducks. This was much too good to be true. He was so excited he forgot to thank the robotic voice. He always did that. He knew it was absurd, but he couldn't help it. He was an only child, into whom formally good manners had been dinned from his first breath.

'Mrs Hopkins?'

'Yes?' The voice was light, pleasant.

'Mrs Hopkins, I wonder if Mr Hopkins is there?'

'Not just at the moment. Who is it wants him?'

'My name is Graydon Townsend. He doesn't know me. I'm writing a book about 'sixties architecture. I found his name in some old records. I would really like to talk to him.'

'Oh – oh, I see. Well, I can ask him, Mr Townsend. He retired quite a long time ago, I don't know how much use he could be to you.'

'Well – it's worth a try. I'm told he is a mine of information on the subject.'

'Oh, really?' She sounded pleased. 'Well, as I say I can only ask him. He's out now, playing golf.'

'I see. Er – how is he? I understood he'd not been well, that he retired early.'

'Yes, that's right, he did. About eight years ago now. Well, he's not too bad considering. He had a couple of heart attacks, not too serious thank goodness, and since he came down here and got rid of all that stress, he's been a lot better.'

'Good. Excellent. I'll hope to hear from you, then. Thank you, Mrs Hopkins.'

If he ever heard from Clive Hopkins, Gray thought, his name was Bard Channing.

As she drove home, Rachel thought about demolishing the house, what it would really mean. She thought of the house and how much she loved it already, thought of walking through it as she had with Mary, as well as with Bard and Reverend Mother, of the atmosphere it had of grace and serenity, of the chapel, the outbuildings, the lawn sloping down to the cliff edge; and then she thought of Mary and Richard and all the others, who needed security, who needed to be together, safe with people they loved and who loved and cared for them, and when she got home, she phoned Reverend Mother and told her what Bard had proposed and that she had been forced to agree unless Reverend Mother felt there was a very strong reason for not doing so.

Reverend Mother smiled down the phone: Rachel could hear it. 'Rachel,' she said, 'I don't suppose the stable at Bethlehem was particularly beautiful. It served a very good purpose, wouldn't you say?'

Oliver had been trying to sift through the expenses incurred by the PR department all morning; he was just thinking he might suggest that all restaurant bills went onto the Company Amex account, rather than the rather haphazard system employed at present, of cash when people had it, cheques when they didn't, company cards for the chosen few allowed them, when Bard Channing walked through his small office and into Pete Barbour's. He was clearly, even for him, in an exceptional hurry; as he passed Oliver's desk, something dropped from within the great sheaf of papers he was carrying. Oliver bent to pick it up; it was a gold Mont Blanc fountain pen. He looked into the room; the door was not shut (his signal to stay out at all costs), and Bard was rifling now through his papers, clearly looking for something; probably the pen, thought Oliver, and knocking gently first, went into the room.

They did not hear him: Bard was leaning across Pete's desk, tapping into his small personal computer, pointing something out to him; Pete was shaking his head.

'What about some of the offshore accounts?' he said. 'What about the Antilles? Is there something we can do there?'

'Christ Pete, I really don't want to start on those.'

'Why not, for God's sake?'

'Because they're some kind of insurance, that's why – Oliver, what the fuck are you doing there?'

Bard had seen him suddenly; Oliver was startled, almost scared, by the strength of his reaction.

'I'm sorry, Mr Channing, I found –'

'I don't care what the fuck you found, don't start creeping round this place like some fucking toad out from under a stone. Get out of here, at once, and don't come in again unless you're actually invited. Which is extremely unlikely.'

'I'm sorry, Mr Channing, very sorry.'

He left the room quickly, shut the door carefully, sat down at his desk feeling very shaken. The man really was a monster. If that was the sort of thing Kirsten had had to put up with all her childhood, no wonder she was a bit of a nutter.

'Is that Mr Townsend?'

'Yes, it is.'

'Mr Townsend, this is Clive Hopkins. My wife said you'd phoned. About some book, was it?'

Five minutes later, Gray put the phone down and smiled radiantly across at Tricia.

'In future,' he said, 'you're to address me as Bard Channing.'

'Sorry?' said Tricia.

'You look depressed, Francesca. Shall I tell you a good bogey joke?'

'Barnaby, I'm not depressed, I'm fine,' said Francesca wearily, looking at him over the lunch table, 'and if I was depressed, a bogey joke wouldn't exactly cheer me up.'

'I want to hear it,' said Jack, 'tell me it, Barney, go on, then I can tell it in News tomorrow –'

'Barnaby, if you dare to tell Jack any more bogey jokes I shall throw you out of this house,' said Francesca. 'And what are you doing this evening, because your father's very tired and he'll want some peace and quiet.'

'I won't spoil his peace and quiet,' said Barnaby, his face a study in innocence, 'I'll just sit reading quietly in a corner.'

'Barnaby, you never do anything quietly,' said Francesca, 'and you never read anything either, except those horrible girlie magazines.'

'What, with their bosoms and bottoms showing? They're funny!' said Jack.

'Barnaby, you haven't been letting Jack see them, have you?' said Francesca. She could feel a flush rising in her face. 'That is really naughty, I can't –'

'He couldn't help it,' said Jack staunchly. 'I went in his room, to get my worms –'

'What worms?'

'From my tunnel. I hid them there, cos Nanny doesn't like them. Barnaby didn't even know. They're for Dad's birthday.'

'Now what is worse, I ask you?' said Barnaby laughing. 'Worms dumped in your room, or girlie magazines?'

'Honestly,' said Francesca, 'sometimes I think I'm going completely mad in this house.'

'You're the sanest person in it,' said Barnaby, giving her a hug. 'It's all right, I'm going out now. Won't be back till late. Going clubbing with Morag – remember Morag, great legs, big ti— I mean, eyes.'

'You were going to say tits,' said Jack, 'same as the ones in your magazines.'

'Jack, go and find Nanny,' said Francesca wearily. 'She wants to take you to the swings.'

'Has Nanny got big tits, Barnaby?' said Jack. 'Under her blouse, what do you think?'

'Barnaby,' said Francesca, 'please, please go and destroy those magazines immediately.'

'I will,' he said, 'sorry. Really sorry. I didn't know he was going to be in my room. Oh, and Francesca –'

'Yes, Barnaby?'

'If I don't see you before, good luck tomorrow. With Dad's birthday.' She looked at him sharply, but his blue eyes were sweetly thoughtful as he looked at her. He was, in spite of everything, kind and extremely perceptive. And deep down, nice.

'Thank you, Barnaby.'

'Damn!' said Jean Rivers, putting the phone down. 'Damn damn damn. Sorry, Oliver. Excuse my language!'

Oliver grinned at her. 'I've heard worse. What's the matter?'

'Oh, it's these wretched documents. Mr Barbour asked me to get them ring-bound in time for a big presentation in the morning and they're not ready. They say I can have them at half-past eight, but I can't be there then. I have to take the girls to school. Oh dear, Mr Barbour's going to have my guts for garters.' She was much given to such old-fashioned clichés.

'I'll pick them up for you,' said Oliver.

'Oh Oliver, I can't ask you to do that.'

'Why not? Honestly, I don't mind. And I don't have anyone to take to school –'

'Oliver, you're an angel. Anything I can ever do for you –'

'I'll think of something,' said Oliver. 'Where's the firm?'

'Off Broadgate. Here's the address. Are you sure you don't mind?'

'It's no problem. Honestly.'

Jean Rivers smiled up at him. 'That's really nice of you. Thank you.'

Francesca was eating her supper in front of *Panorama* when Barnaby came into her room. Bard was at some City dinner, but had rung to say he wouldn't be late. His mood was still odd, distant; she was struggling not to resent it, to appear the same herself. She was worried, almost fearful, about the next day, hoping against hope it would be all right, that it would work some magic, bring them close again; fearing it would not, that her lovely plan would misfire, be misunderstood, make matters somehow worse. Bard was becoming each day more of a stranger; she felt unable to predict in any way what he would or would not like. She had already packed her bag, had phoned the Dromoland, asked them to be sure there was champagne on ice in their suite when they arrived, extra flowers, a car available. There was nothing more she could do now, except hope absurdly, irritatingly nervous, for the best. And she was very pleased to see Barnaby.

'Hallo Barnaby. Everything OK?'

'Yes. No.'

'I thought you were out on a hot date.'

'I was. It turned out to be rather a cold one.'

'Oh Barnaby, I'm sorry. Here, have a glass of wine.'

'Thanks.' He drank it down as if it were milk, held it out for a refill. 'I wish I could go to Ireland for forty-eight hours with you, Francesca,' he said, looking at her and grinning. 'We'd have a *really* good time.'

'Are you implying your father and I won't have a good time?'

'Not as good as you'd have with me,' said Barnaby. He spoke with enormous confidence. Francesca laughed.

'Well, if anything goes wrong –'

'I'm afraid it won't,' said Barnaby.

'Happy birthday, Bard.'

He had just woken up; she had scarcely slept herself, had been lying beside him ever since dawn broke, worrying, absurdly.

'What? What are you talking about?'

'I said happy birthday.' She leant over, kissed him; he returned the kiss perfunctorily. 'It's today.'

'Good God, is it really? Do you know, I had completely forgotten.' He smiled at her slightly uncertainly. 'Thank you. How –'

'Happy birthday, Dad.' Jack burst through the door, zoomed onto the bed, flung himself into his father's arms. 'Lots of happy returns.'

'Thank you, Jack. This is very nice. Here I am an old man of fifty-four, I shouldn't still be having birthdays.'

'You have to have birthdays,' said Jack, 'everyone does, that's why you *do get* old.'

'Very true,' said Bard. 'And do you have a present for me?'

'Yup. I made it myself. I'll get it.'

He disappeared, came back with a jam jar apparently filled with earth.

'How very nice,' said Bard. 'Er – what is it? Exactly?'

'It's a wormery,' said Jack proudly. 'There's lots of worms in there, Dad, and you can watch them, while you're having your supper or something. They eat the earth, you see, and poo it out again, it's really clever –'

'That is a great present,' said Bard solemnly. 'I shall keep it always.'

'You can't keep that exact one always,' said Jack, ''cos the worms 'll die. But you can put new ones in, I'll help you catch them.'

'Thank you,' said Bard, 'thank you very much.' He turned to Francesca, smiling. 'And do you have some breathtaking present for me, that you made yourself?'

'Well – not made. Well, sort of made, I suppose. Here –' She handed him an envelope. This already felt wrong, wasn't at all the joyful occasion she had imagined two months ago.

'What's this? A pair of roller skates?' This was a family joke. 'No, envelope's too flat. Bus pass? My God, airline tickets. Just what I always – oh Francesca. How lovely. But –'

'Yes?'

'When do we go?'

'In about an hour and a half. From the house. All fixed.'

'Francesca,' said Bard, and there was just a touch of tension, of – what? reproach, even? – in his voice; reproach that she should not have thought of such things, should have assumed he could simply leave, walk away from everything, 'I can't just drop everything, you must realise that, I have meetings, appointments –'

'No you don't,' said Francesca, determinedly blithe. 'All cancelled.'

'But –'

'Ask Marcia. She's been, I have to say, an absolute brick. Rescheduling furiously, lying away. All you have to do is pick up your bag and follow me.'

He looked at her, and she could see for just a moment he was still resistant, still half inclined to feel he had to refuse; and then he smiled, a little reluctantly to be sure, but still did smile, visibly gave in, relaxed.

'Good God! Well, in that case, I suppose I can only say yes –'

'Bard,' she said, unable to hide her hurt, 'Bard, I thought you'd be –'

'I am. Very. Whatever it was you thought. I am seriously chuffed, in fact. As Barnaby would say.'

'Good. Now look, I have to go and see to Kitty and so on. See you for breakfast in – half an hour?'

'Half an hour, yes,' said Bard slightly absently. He was already rifling through some papers that he had been looking at in bed. Francesca sighed and went out of the room.

Halfway through breakfast, the phone rang; it was Victoria.

'Sweet of her,' said Bard. 'Dear little thing.'

Jess – who had been in on the Irish plan – phoned too; cards arrived from friends, from Teresa Booth – 'My God, that is unexpected!' – from Oliver and Melinda and Heather Clarke, from Rachel, and one he looked at, jaw taut, and pushed beneath his paper. Francesca recognised the writing, predictably huge and sprawling. Kirsten.

Barnaby appeared, looking slightly dishevelled, holding out a card to his father. Francesca looked at the slightly tacky envelope and knew exactly what had happened: he had, unusually for him, failed to buy one until this morning, in spite of her innumerable reminders, and had dashed out to the nearest garage to get what he could.

'Hi, Dad. Happy birthday.'

'Thanks, Barney. I must say I'm being very spoilt. Everyone remembering.'

'Dad! As if we'd forget!'

'As if you would,' said Bard, looking at the card; it showed a man holding a set of golf clubs, and said 'Happy Birthday to a good Dad' in gleaming gold letters. 'Very appropriate. Thank you.'

'That's OK. I've – well, I've got your present on order. It'll be here when you get back.'

'Fine,' said Bard, 'thank you. Very thoughtful of you. Back from where?'

'Ireland,' said Barnaby patiently. 'Oh shit, shouldn't I have –'

'Yes of course you should,' said Francesca quickly.

'God, how many more of you were in on this?' said Bard. He smiled at Francesca, determinedly cheerful. 'Well, I'd better go and pack. How long have I got?'

'Half an hour,' said Francesca. 'Horton's coming for us.'

'OK, I'll be ready.'

He went out of the room. Well, at least he was coming. Nothing had intervened. He might not be over the moon, but they were getting away together on their own, and once they were on their way he would probably relax and start to enjoy it.

She looked out of the window: a perfect morning. Blue sky, sun shafting down onto the garden. Kitty's pram was already out, its sunshade up; Francesca could see two small brown feet waving beneath it. Jack was driving his pedal car round and round the kitchen, making Brands Hatch noises; he grinned up at her.

'Hi, Mum. Don't get run over.'

'I won't,' said Francesca, looking down at him, at his face already filthy, at his shock of shining dark hair, his sturdy little legs pedalling furiously, and felt her heart turn over with love.

'Good luck,' said Barnaby, bending to kiss her briefly, 'I'm sure it'll be fine.'

'Thank you. You off somewhere?'

'Yeah, got some sleep to catch up on.'

'Good,' said Francesca absently. 'Bye, Barney.'

She rummaged under the paper when he had gone, pulled out Kirsten's card. 'Happy birthday and I'm really, really sorry. Love Kirsten.' Poor Kirsten. Bard ought to forgive her. She was still very young and she needed his support. She would try and make him. Once he had relaxed, once they were closer again.

And then she heard the phone ringing. Bard's phone. In his study. Heard him running down the stairs to answer it; heard him ring off, quite soon, heard a long, chilling silence. And then he came into the kitchen. His face was pale, very set. He had his jacket on and he was holding his briefcase; he looked at her and there was something like anger in his eyes.

'I'm sorry,' he said, briefly, 'I can't come.'

'What! But Bard –'

'Francesca, I've said I'm sorry. I can't.'

'Why?' she said. 'Why, why not?'

'It's very – complex,' he said. 'I can't go into it now. I'll phone you later if I can.'

'Bard, you can't just – just go like this. I understand if you can't come, but you have to tell me why. I think you owe me that at least.'

There was a silence; he looked at her, as if trying to decide if he could still avoid it, avoid telling her what he so clearly did not want to. Then finally he said, speaking slowly and painfully, every word hurting him: 'There's a problem with – with one of our bankers.'

'What do you mean? What sort of problem?'

'Oh for God's sake,' he said, 'I told you it was complex, I simply don't have the time to go into it, to explain. Look, I'll talk to you about it later, if I can.'

Francesca sat there for a moment, staring at him in total silence, trying to work out precisely how she felt, how she could and should react, and then suddenly lost her temper. It wasn't so much the trip being cancelled, not the waste of all the arranging and planning and the careful consideration. That was disappointing, but it didn't really matter. What did, what mattered very much, was that this was yet another rejection, that not only was he not prepared to spare the time, any time at all, to tell her what had happened, but he was also making it very plain that it was none of her business, that it was part of his other life, the one he would not share with her, that she was not allowed even to try to understand.

'If you can,' she said, her voice heavily ironic. 'Well, that's very good of you, Bard. If you can. Just forget it. Don't bother. I'd hate to think you had to give up any of your valuable time and attention to me.'

'Oh for fuck's sake,' he said, 'don't be so bloody childish.'

She was silent.

'Look,' he said again, 'look, I said I was sorry. I'll get Marcia to cancel the Dromoland, she can book it for some other time. All right?'

'No,' she said, 'not all right. Not some other time. I'm afraid I don't have the stomach for it. You'd better go. Goodbye, Bard.'

He left and she looked after him, and mingling with all her other emotions came the now familiar thud of unease, and more than that, the suddenly certain knowledge that there were things that she was not to know, not allowed not to know, things she would do best to turn away from. She hesitated, and then, making a conscious effort and because the alternative was too painful, too dangerous, she managed it. She turned away.

She was sitting in her room, trying to calm herself, to make some sense of her own thoughts and feelings, when her phone rang. It was Liam.

'Hi,' he said, cautiously, 'bad time? When are you off to Ireland?'

'I'm not,' she said, 'and it's not a bad time.'

'Really? What's happened? Want to tell me about it?'

'Yes,' she said, 'yes, I think I do.'

Oliver had collected the documents, and was standing on the corner of Broadgate and London Wall looking for a taxi when he saw Bard's car pull up outside Trenchards and Bard himself leap out and disappear inside very swiftly. Oliver was mildly intrigued; Trenchards was one of the more successful American investment banks that had arrived in the City with Big Bang. It had recently attracted a lot of publicity, due to the arrival of a new Chief Executive from New York who had stated it as his personal ambition to build his own small corner of Wall Street in the heart of the Square Mile, 'and I don't care what it costs.' What was Bard Channing doing there? Some new deal, no doubt; God, the man never stopped. Most people would have thought he had quite enough problems already.

He found a taxi, got to Channing House with the files just in time, to Jean Rivers' intense relief, and was sitting having a coffee and studying the markets in the *FT*, when his phone rang. It was Kirsten.

'Hi. You OK?'

'Yes, thank you,' said Oliver.

'Want to go to the movies tonight? Everyone says *Four Weddings* is the best film ever.'

'Yeah, why not. As long as I don't have to work late. Things are a bit hectic here.'

'Oh really? But my dad's in Ireland with Francesca, it ought to be really nice and peaceful.'

'He's not in Ireland,' said Oliver, 'I saw him myself, going into Trenchards half an hour ago.'

'Really? That's funny. What's Trenchards anyway?'

'Merchant bank. Very high profile. Into high-risk loans. If you care.'

'Not really. Anyway, we'll do the cinema, yes?'

'Yes. Thanks for calling.'

'My pleasure,' she said.

'No, mine, actually,' said Oliver. He put the phone down and sat staring at it, a faint smile on his face.

Gray decided to call Kirsten. He really felt he should. It seemed just a natural, friendly thing to do, to say hallo, to see if she was all right. He still felt uneasy about cutting off from her completely. It wasn't – well, it wasn't polite. After two false starts, he dialled her number.

'Hi.'

'Oh, hi, Gray.' She sounded slightly awkward.

'I just – thought I'd say hallo. Make sure you were all right.'

'Yes, I'm fine. Thank you.'

'Good.'

There was a silence.

'How's everything, then?'

'Oh – good. Yeah.'

'Enjoying the job?'

'Yes, I really am. Thank you again for it, Gray. It beats working for my dad, I can tell you that.'

'How is your dad?' He might as well try and get something positive out of what was clearly otherwise an abortive phone call. 'It must be a huge adjustment, working without Duggie.'

'Yeah, I suppose so.' Her voice was very uninterested.

'Is he – in London at the moment?'

'Oh, I think so, yes. Actually, he's supposed to be in Ireland, it's his birthday, Francesca was taking him as a surprise, but Oliver – you remember Oliver Clarke from the funeral? – Oliver said he just saw him in the City. So I don't know what he's up to. Going into some bank or other.'

'Oh really?' said Gray. This was interesting. Very interesting. 'You don't remember which one, do you?' he added, carefully casual. 'I was trying to track him down.'

'Um – no. Something beginning with T. Very high profile, Oliver said.'

'Trenchards?' said Gray.

'Yeah, that's it. Look, Gray, sorry, I must go. Speak to you some time.'

'Yes, fine.' He was so excited at the thought of Bard Channing going to Trenchards, he hardly noticed her cool dismissal. 'Bye, Kirsten. Take care.'

Alan Ferrers was eating his pasta salad, and wondering how he might fancy a little yen and games, as he called his bolder dealings with the Nikkei, when Gray Townsend called him to ask him what he would say if he told him he had understood there was a vague possibility that Bard Channing had been having an early-morning meeting with Trenchards.

'I'd say do up your seatbelt, my son,' said Ferrers. 'I'll get back to you.'

Francesca arrived home mid-afternoon; she was shaking violently. She parked her car at least a foot wide of the pavement, ran up the steps, let herself in, praying no-one would be around: her prayers were not answered.

'Hi,' came Barnaby's voice from the kitchen, 'you OK?'

'Yes. Yes, I'm fine, thanks.'

He wandered out, grinned at her, then as he studied her, looked more concerned. 'You don't look it. You look all shook up. What's the matter?'

'Nothing. Honestly.'

'You sure?'

'Yes, of course I'm sure.'

'OK, OK. It was just that I thought –'

'Yes, Barnaby, what did you think?'

'Well, you know, that as Dad didn't go to Ireland with you that you might be –'

'Might be what?' Shit, her voice sounded strange, shaky, even to herself.

'Well, upset, of course. I'm sorry, Francesca, really sorry.'

'Barnaby, I'm fine. Honestly. It was no big deal. As you would say.'

'OK. Fine. That's good.' He shrugged, turned away from her, obviously hurt at the rejection. She ran upstairs, guilt at that added to the rest, telling herself he couldn't possibly have known, have told from her face, what had been happening to her: could not have known she had arranged wilfully and calculatedly to go and meet another man, a man other than her husband (her husband's son indeed, most dreadfully, shockingly worse), had wept, been held, in the arms of another man, been kissed by another man, over and over again, returned those kisses, found them alarmingly, profoundly erotic, had felt the hands of another man on her hair, her face, her breasts, had heard him saying things, dreadful, wonderful things, had fought back words of her own, wicked words of betrayal, had even spoken some of them, had acknowledged desire, longing even, and if not love then tenderness, had sworn both to him and herself that none of it must ever happen again, and known at the same time that it was possible, more than possible, that it would.

Alan Ferrers listened to his new girlfriend giving him a large piece of her rather small mind for as long as he could stand, on the subject of the cancellation of a dinner date at two hours' notice, and then put the phone down firmly, having told her he would be able to buy her dinner in Barbados in a week or two if she'd only let him get on with his work now. The nature of this particular work was fairly pleasant, and would take place in the wine bars of the City and later quite possibly a restaurant or two; but it was nonetheless essential, and essential that it was done that night. So that within a very short period of time, thirty-six hours at the most, he and a handful of other young fortunates could have earned enough money for their companies to ensure bonuses quite big enough to go to Barbados and back with their girlfriends several times over. First class, of course.

Just before midnight, in the boardroom of the Stockholm head office of the Konigstrom Bank after a very long and gruelling day, the directors phoned Bard Channing and told him that it was with great regret they felt they could, despite earlier assurances, only give him another forty-eight hours before calling in their loan. News had reached them, via their spies in London, that Methuens had made the same decision.

The Chief Executive, reporting on this to his wife when he got home, said he had been most impressed by Mr Channing's response, which had been calm and positive, and that Mr Channing had seemed to think, even at that stage, it was most unlikely that he could not still save his company.

He added that he certainly hoped that would be the case, since not only the bank, but he personally, had staked their reputation on the Channing Corporation, and they would be considerably exposed if

Channings did indeed go down. His wife smiled at him soothingly and said she was sure everything would be perfectly all right.

Chapter Nineteen

'So what would you like to do this evening, then?' said Kirsten. 'Cinema again?'

'No, it's much too nice for that. What about a picnic in the park, that'd be much more fun.'

'If you think it would be fun, let's do it,' she said. 'Pick me up here about six, OK?'

'OK.'

She put down the phone and sat smiling at it slightly foolishly. The feelings that were invading her, increasingly strongly and happily, for Oliver were such as she had not known before. There was no impatience in those feelings, no mistrust, no desire to dominate him, to see her will override his: none of the things that had wrecked so many of her relationships with so many men through her short life. The point being, she supposed, that he was so different from all those men. She had grown up with the ultimate example, in her father, of someone arrogant, demanding, opinionated; had come to see that, inevitably, as the model of how a man should be, and sought it for herself, dislike it increasingly as she might. And then whenever she had chosen the reverse, chosen sweetness, gentleness, consideration, she had found the possessors of those qualities seriously wanting. Oliver managed, somehow, to combine the toughness with the sweetness; he was surprisingly firm with her, said what he thought, did what he wanted, told her when he disapproved of her – when she did something he didn't like, behaved in a way he found unacceptable: shouted at a taxi driver, talked loudly through a film that bored her, bawled out an incompetent waiter – 'You sound like your father,' he had said on that occasion, only the third time they had been out together, and she had promptly burst into tears. But no-one had done that before; the one breed of men (like Toby) had thought it amusing, the others had not dared to criticise.

Oliver was simply quite unlike anyone she had ever known before (he explained it to her, when she remarked upon it, as the possible result of having to grow up very fast and very thoroughly), and everything she knew of him, each fresh thing she discovered, charmed her more. He was of course very good looking, and that was nice, she really could not have gone out with someone plain; and his liking, his eye for, stylish clothes pleased and surprised her. And she enjoyed his honesty, his surprising independence of spirit; he was never afraid to argue, to hold an unfashionable view, he was for instance surprisingly traditional in his moral outlook, deplored the breakdown of the family, the ever-burgeoning army of single parents, and she teased him about it, called him an old man. And then there were other entirely delightful qualities: his sense of humour (unpredictable and slightly quirky), his capacity for enjoying the most ordinary things (a mediocre film, a walk, the rollerblade lesson she had given him), a rather charming greed, a considerable physical energy. He was never tired; however long and demanding his day, he was always ready to go out, and then to prolong the evening, never wanted it to end. He got up early, went running across Ealing Common, was always in the office before anyone else, worked out three times a week, played tennis and squash regularly (by his own admission with more enthusiasm than skill), and liked to walk briskly round the streets to, as he put it, slow himself down before finally going to bed, never before one-thirty or two. Kirsten, fairly inexhaustible herself (a legacy from her father), found herself frequently defeated by him. She also, putting all these qualities together into the equation – the energy, the greed, the capacity for pleasure – found the thought of going to bed with him increasingly tantalising. And she felt the time had come: she had qualified, she felt, under her own rules; she knew him very well, she liked him very much (although 'like' as a label did not seem quite adequate now for the warmth, the intense pleasure of what she felt for him), she found him desirable. And she knew he found her so too, despite his wariness of her, his constant surprise that she was, as he told her, as nice as she was ('Bit of a half-cock compliment, that, Oliver'), she could feel it, as he kissed her, held her, feel the wanting, the desire in him.

And so how, now, did one go about it, she wondered: it seemed arrogant, presumptuous in the worst possible way, the old Kirsten, the one he had always thought she was, to say to him, however subtly, 'Right then, Oliver, I've decided, it's time, you can have sex with me now.'

She thought about it a great deal: whether to set up a situation, ask him back to the flat, pretend surprise, sudden ardour, drunkenness even, but that seemed wrong, at odds with the honesty in their relationship that she was enjoying so much. She kept hoping he would make the first move, would suggest they moved on, would try to seduce her, but he didn't; he seemed prepared to be patient, to wait, to consider her feelings. That in itself seemed charming, a novelty; it was only when she forced herself to realise that few, if any, of the men she had known had been given the opportunity for such delicacy, that she realised also what a strong, an irresistible sexual force she was. And besides, she was not at all sure that the person she now knew to be Oliver would like it, would welcome her usual approach: thinking of the last time she had used it, with Gray, poor, nice, undeserving Gray, she felt abashed, and more than that, ashamed.

Well, she could wait a bit longer, she thought; it wouldn't do either of them any harm. And they had all the time in the world, after all.

'Brandy?' said Gray.

He didn't know about Clive Hopkins, but he certainly needed one. He had been listening to him for over two hours now, in the dining room of the Palace Hotel, Torquay, and he thought he had rarely come across a man of such overweening vanity.

He had been told of Hopkins' vision, his foresight, his aesthetic sense; of his willingness to be unpopular, to fight for the buildings he believed in, to set his own inclinations aside for the common good; of the architects he had encouraged, the talent he had fostered, the standards he had set. Had Nash and le Corbusier pooled their resources, worked together for a hundred years, they would not have achieved more – indeed rather less, Gray was given to believe – than Clive Hopkins.

'I chose not actually to qualify myself, Mr Townsend,' he said, leaning across the table. 'I felt I could achieve more for the architectural scene in this country in my own way. And I have to say to you, I think I was right. Yes, a brandy would be very nice. Thank you.'

He had drunk a great deal for a man with a heart problem, Gray thought: two gin and tonics before lunch, the lion's share of a bottle of claret, and now a brandy. Gray, who had been holding back himself, keeping his head clear, had watched him with some awe. Hopkins had remained sober for some time too; but he was just tipping over now, into a slight slurring of speech, a just discernible glazing of the eyes. Gray, practised at observing such things, felt a huge relief; he had thought it was never going to happen.

The first brandy (a double) was half drunk now, the first coffee cup drained. Just a few more minutes of this, then he could move in for the kill. He braced himself.

'Tell me, Mr Hopkins – excuse me, I have to put a new tape in, this has been so marvellous – yes, tell me, what criticisms would you make of the architectural schools?'

'Ah, now you're asking.'

Yes, I am, you little twat, thought Gray, and I'm very much afraid you're going to tell me.

'Lack of realism. That's the first thing. Improper attention to function. Architecture should be function-led. That's what I tell all my trainees. It's no use having the most beautiful building in the world if the toilets are in the wrong place. Architects don't listen, you see, to the people who know. There is no-one more arrogant than the architect, and the schools encourage that. There is not a building in this world that couldn't have been improved, to my mind, made just that bit better by what I would call editing. By an outside eye.'

'What, even the Nash terraces?' said Gray, unable to bear this any longer.

'Certainly the Nash terraces. Nash went bankrupt, of course. Not many people know that. There is a lot of space wasted in those buildings. A lot.'

'Well, that's an interesting view,' said Gray. 'Another brandy?'

'Oh, well – just a small one. Since you're twisting my arm.'

'And what developments are you personally proudest of?'

'Oh – some of the early shopping precincts. A housing develop- ment near Croydon, very nice that one. Most successful. One of the Larkston chain. And a very nice residential complex out Romford way, two low-rise blocks and then a mixture of two- and three-storey houses. Very well landscaped, they were.'

'Was that one you worked on with the Thompson Corporation?' said Gray.

'No, not Thompson they weren't. Forster, that was, I think.'

'Oh yes, of course. And then you did quite a lot of work with Channings, didn't you?'

'Oh, a fair bit, yes.'

Well, he certainly wasn't sensitive about the name.

'Wasn't there something at Easterhope?'

'Yes, that's right. Quite a nice estate there. South Farm.'

'It was from Easterhope you retired, wasn't it?'

'Yes, that is correct. Mother Nature gave me a couple of warnings, and I thought it was time to go.'

'Did you find Bard Channing easy to work with? I had heard from some other sources he was a nightmare.'

'Oh no, not at all. I can get on with most of these boys, you know. In my experience, those who complain about people being difficult are difficult themselves. People say Chris Forster, for instance, is impossible to work with, but I never had any trouble with him, all the buildings we put up. No, I liked Bard Channing, as a matter of fact. We go back a long way. He was always ready to listen, you see, take advice. He came to my retirement dinner, as a matter of fact. And I played golf with Douglas Booth very often. Nice chap.'

'Oh really? So do you remember Nigel Clarke?'

A different expression came over Hopkins' face suddenly; wary, cautious. 'Hardly knew him. Our paths never crossed. He wasn't in the same league as Bard Channing and Douglas Booth. None too bright, in my view. I don't like to speak ill of the dead, of course, but –'

'Of course not.' This had gone on long enough. Gray moved in on his prey. 'Er – tell me, Mr Hopkins, and I know this is a bit of a delicate question, but it's relevant to my premise –'

'Ask away,' said Hopkins cheerfully. 'I'm not backwards in coming forwards.'

'What sort of salary would a planning officer, such as yourself, earn these days?'

'Oh – not a tremendous amount. These days, I suppose about thirty thousand, possibly forty.'

'Good heavens. That sounds pretty poor to me. Especially compared with what the architects get. Cigar?'

'Oh – yes, thank you. Well absolutely. You're quite right. Pretty unfair, some would say. As at least fifty per cent of the responsibility for the developments is down to us. And frankly it riles me. It really does. But there it is – there is no justice, is there?'

'Not a lot. But it didn't bother you?'

'Oh well, I certainly wouldn't say –' He visibly checked himself, hauled himself back into line – 'No, no, not too much. It was the job satisfaction, you see –'

'And the perks?' said Gray.

'I'm sorry?'

'I said the perks. Surely there must have been some.'

'I'm afraid I don't know what you mean,' said Hopkins. He had become very still suddenly; his hand frozen round his brandy glass, the cigar clamped between his teeth.

'Oh come on. We all get them,' said Gray cheerfully. 'For us guys, it's the freebies – holidays, that we then write books or articles about, I went on a sailing trip in the Caribbean only last spring – and there are endless lunches, all that sort of thing. People writing biographies of famous people get put up for months in luxury. Bank managers get crates of wine, bottles of whisky at Christmas. Same for solicitors. Now you're not going to tell me that nothing like that ever came your way. Come on, Mr Hopkins, you seem like a man of the world to me. I've heard of all sorts of scams in your business, expensive cruises, luxury cars, houses abroad, all given to planners by grateful developers. I can't believe you never came across anything like that.'

He was completely unprepared for Hopkins' reaction. He stood up, his face white with rage, threw his napkin down on the table. 'I think this interview should end right here,' he said. 'And I think moreover, Mr Townsend, you should be extremely careful what you say. There are laws of slander in this country you know, and –'

'Mr Hopkins, calm down,' said Gray soothingly. 'I wasn't for a moment suggesting you were *personally* involved in anything like that.'

'Well, I'm extremely glad to hear it. But I don't like your tone just the same. And I do assure you you could not be more wrong. After Poulson, people thought we were all into that and of course we weren't. Aren't. We're professional men, doing a decent job.'

'Yes, of course,' said Gray soothingly. 'Now look, Mr Hopkins –' he switched off his tape recorder – 'this is strictly off the record, just chatting. I'm not from the *Sun* or the *Mirror*, you know.'

'And how do I know that?'

Christ, he was sharp. 'Well, you have to take it on trust, I'm afraid. You could ring them and check. And surely you got the letter. From my publishers.'

'I did, yes.'

Nice one that. Good old Tricia. The letters she'd written in her time. 'Well then. And I'm sorry if I've upset you. It's just the psychology of it, if you like. It intrigues me.'

'Well, you'd better find something else to intrigue you. All right? Good afternoon, Mr Townsend. And I think you should know, I do have a very good solicitor.'

'I'm pleased to hear it,' said Gray. 'Anyway, you get off now, to your golf course.' He paused. 'Your membership of Gleneagles, that you've had for years.' This was a wild card, but it was time to play it. 'That can't be cheap. Does Bard Channing pick up that tab for you? That and the timeshare in Portugal, on the golf complex there?'

He could see by the dazed look on Hopkins' face, the full flat flush, that wild as it was, it was right. He smiled at him very sweetly. 'Sorry if I startled you. Don't let me keep you now. You get off to your nineteenth hole. And thanks a lot for your help. I've enjoyed it very much.'

Long after Clive Hopkins had disappeared, without a word, long after he had paid the immense lunch bill even, Gray sat at the table, gazing over the lovely blue of Torbay and thinking. So Bard Channing had been – no doubt still was – into bribery: that in itself was not so spurprising or even shocking. It was an important element in the story, insight into the man and how he operated. But he still felt a very long way from an explanation of Nigel Clarke's death – and why Channing felt so extremely guilty about it.

It was not until he was halfway back up the M5 that he remembered Hopkins' contemptuous dismissal of Clarke, and realised what it probably meant.

It was a rather chilly evening for July: Marcia Grainger, who had arrived home late after a particularly difficult day, discovered that was not only the thought of the hard-boiled egg salad she had planned to make distinctly unappealing, but she was also extremely hungry. After a brief struggle with temptation, temptation won, and she picked up the phone and ordered a chicken vindaloo from the Indian takeaway just down the road. She changed into a tracksuit, took a can of lager out of her fridge (thinking as always how astonished those whom she dealt with all day would be to see her now), and picked out *Brief Encounter* from her vast selection of videos.

The curry was a little while arriving, and she had opened a second can of lager before she settled down to it. She was feeling a little light headed by then, and told herself therefore that the very slightly odd flavour of the chicken was due to that, rather than anything more sinister.

And at eleven-thirty, the traumas of her day having been most effectively banished, she had a hot bath and went to bed.

Liam was uncertain what to do next. He had, since his marriage, had several affairs, and in each of them had been in bed with the woman in question within a couple of weeks. This was quite different: more difficult, more complex and a great deal slower. There had, of course, been considerable complications and impediments: not many seductions were conducted from a hospital bed in a public ward, and over the considerable physical obstacle of a badly broken leg; few potential mistresses were their putative lovers' stepmothers. But that made the situation all the more interesting, gave it a raw, sexual edge; the combination of the genuine desire he felt for Francesca, and the joy of knowing its fulfilment would hurt and damage his father irreparably, was intense. But he did have to be very patient with her. He knew she wanted him, knew that she was charmed, very seriously tempted, by him, knew that by her swift, physical response to him the day before. She was like a tentative small bird on the edge of the nest, the nest of her marriage, the nest that had become so uncomfortable; almost ready, but still afraid to try her chance on the air, for a short while at least. If he started nudging her too hard, she would tumble back determinedly into it, and refuse even to look out of it again. Especially as the situation was, by any standards, so extraordinarily complex.

This was not, he decided, hobbling across to the sideboard to pour himself a drink, a seduction at all: it was a piece of psychological warfare, and timing was everything.

He stood, glass of whisky in hand, thinking now about his father: he was clearly in serious trouble, any fool could see that, obviously yesterday there had been some immense crisis that he'd had to attend to. Possibly, probably even, he had the skids under him, was about to go right under. He had always sailed extremely close to the wind; it was his instinctive style. Liam could remember, dimly, early discussions with Duggie Booth, Nigel Clarke, with Granny Jess, just casual ones, outlining his philosophy, over the kitchen table, across Jess's parlour, could remember him saying, 'You have to take risks, you have to go out there, nobody ever achieved anything sitting by the hearth.' But it looked as if he had risked too much this time, strayed too far from the hearth. If he lost his wife at the same time, that would be very painful for him.

The racing pulse, Liam thought, contemplating this course of events, was not just a vividly descriptive phrase; it was a physical fact. He could feel his racing now. Very fast indeed.

Marcia Grainger sat in her perfectly ordered office, thanking heaven that Bard was not coming in that morning, and trying to concentrate on her work and ignore the persistent rumblings of her stomach, a growing nausea, and an increasingly vivid memory of the chicken vindaloo of the night before – and its just slightly odd taste.

By half-past ten, she had had to rush into the ladies' several times, and when at a quarter to eleven she heard Bard Channing's direct line ringing, she could scarcely find the strength to get across his office to answer it.

The voice on the other end of the phone did not serve to make her feel any better, being arrogant and ill educated at the same time, the sort she liked least, and the name it gave was only faintly familiar to her.

'So I want him to ring me urgently,' it said, 'most urgently, on this number. It's very important. Now did you get that?'

It was at this point that a fresh spasm gripped Marcia; the combination of that, the caller's tone and the fact that he was addressing her as if she were a half-witted school-leaver meant that he got the treatment so familiar to Oliver Clarke and Rachel Duncan-Brown and indeed a large number of other unwelcome callers, and his message was consigned to oblivion.

If it was really important he would phone again, she told herself, rushing desperately, her handkerchief pressed to her mouth, along the corridor; and Bard Channing would simply not believe him if he told him he had phoned before. He never did. He couldn't afford to.

'I tell you what I long to do,' said Kirsten to Oliver, as they sat over a very protracted meal at the Pizza on the Park, waiting for the jazz to begin. 'Go through the tunnel, go to Paris on the train. Don't you?'

'Not specially,' said Oliver.

'You've got no soul.'

'I have a lot of soul, actually,' he said, more than half serious, 'and I don't know that I like the thought of that tunnel. We're not an island any more.'

'Oh Oliver, honestly, you really are an old fogey. Oh, go on, it'd be such fun, such an adventure. And romantic. Let's go, shall we?'

'All right,' he said, smiling at her, taking her hand across the table and kissing it. 'Let's go. I'll book the tickets on Monday.'

It was her using the word romantic that he really couldn't resist. She was still a constant surprise to him.

At much the same time, Mrs Clive Hopkins stood in the immaculate lounge of her house in Babbacombe, dialling 999, willing it to answer, her own heart beating desperately hard as she watched her husband enduring the now familiar traumas of a major heart attack. He was lying on the floor, his head supported on cushions, his collar loosened (as she had learnt to do for him on previous occasions). Still held loosely in his hand was the previous week's copy of the *News on Sunday*; face uppermost and right across three columns on the front page was an article on the rising economic crisis, the byline of the journalist Graydon Townsend.

★

Kitty wasn't well. She had seemed so much better and for such a long time that Francesca had almost stopped worrying about her. Or at least worrying in an active, gnawing way; it had become a more passive, more background emotion, something she never stopped being aware of, but which didn't actually dominate everything, overshadow her life as it had in the early days. Also, she thought, looking anxiously into Kitty's cot, castigating herself for the fact, she had had rather a lot of other things to dominate her life recently. The baby was lying listlessly, snuffling and even coughing a little, instead of bouncing up and down holding the bars as she had started to do, and her eyes were dull and heavy. Francesca looked at her and her heart contracted with fear; she called Nanny, who said she thought it was only a cold.

'And she's teething as well, I really don't think –'

'Yes, but Mr Lauder said colds were dangerous, you know he did.' She bent down, stroked Kitty's dark curls; she lay looking up at her mother, smiling rather half-heartedly, rubbing her small fists across her snotty face. 'I'm going to take her to see him.'

'Mrs Channing, I really don't think it's necessary.'

'Nanny, I don't care what you think or don't think. I'm going to call him.'

Mr Lauder was just slightly terse on the phone, carefully polite. 'Does she have a temperature, Mrs Channing?'

'No, she doesn't. But she's very listless, and she's a bit wheezy. I'd really like to bring her to see you.'

'I'm very busy, Mrs Channing. It's my operating day, I really would rather you saw your GP. Unless you honestly think it's an emergency, in which case –'

'No, it's not an emergency. But I'd so like you to look at her. As you know her case so well, as you spotted it in the first place. Listen to her chest, check her heart. Please. You did say a cold might be a problem.'

'Look,' he said, 'you might have quite a wait, and I can't see her in any case until this afternoon. Surely –'

'Mr Lauder, I want you to see her,' said Francesca firmly. 'Please. I don't mind waiting.'

'Very well, Mrs Channing. Come at three-thirty. But I can't promise to be there.'

'No. I mean yes. That's fine. Thank you very much, Mr Lauder.'

He rang off without even saying goodbye.

'What did the doctor say?' said Nanny when she went back into the nursery.

'Oh – that yes, of course he would like to see her.'

'He didn't suggest the GP?'

'Nanny, Kitty isn't an ordinary baby,' said Francesca, struggling to keep her voice from rising, 'she has a hole in her heart. We have to take enormous care. The GP missed that in the first place. Of course I want her to see Mr Lauder.'

'Yes,' said Nanny, 'of course you do.' Her tone and her expression made it very plain that Francesca's opinion was entirely foolish.

When they reached Mr Lauder's consulting rooms, his receptionist said she was very sorry, he was still not back. 'The hospital phoned with an emergency admission. I'm sorry, Mrs Channing.'

'That's all right,' said Francesca, looking at the hour ahead with foreboding, Kitty wailing and fidgeting endlessly. 'He did warn me. We'll just sit here and eat a few magazines.'

The receptionist smiled knowing at once what she meant. 'Mine were just the same. I've got a few old ones she can tear up. I'll go and get them. And would she like some orange juice or something?'

By the time Mr Lauder returned, Kitty had cheered up enormously; a drink and a few magazines, shredded carefully across the waiting-room floor seemed to have cured her, apart from her small nose, which was by now extremely red and runny. Francesca looked at her with a degree of irritation. 'You seem to be fine,' she said aloud. 'Looks like Nanny was right, damn her.'

Nanny had indeed been right; a weary-looking Mr Lauder, clearly struggling to be patient, examined Kitty, listened to her chest and pronounced her perfectly well. 'She has a cold. That's all.'

'Oh. I'm sorry. But –'

'It's perfectly all right, Mrs Channing,' he said, smiling at her with a distinct effort. 'Quite understandable, that you should want to have her checked. And it's always wise to make sure. But next time, if it is a cold, then there's really not too much need to worry. Especially now her medication seems to be working so effectively.'

'Yes. Yes I see,' said Francesca humbly.

'Anyway, I should take her back home now if I were you. Give her a nice long bath, the steam will help to clear those tubes, and I think you'll find she'll be right as rain in the morning.'

Maureen Hopkins sat by her husband's bed in the hospital; his breathing was laboured and he was a ghastly colour, but she had been assured he was almost certainly going to be all right. She found it hard to believe.

He opened his eyes and looked at her; she smiled into his face, took his hand. He pulled her down towards him.

'You must –' His voice was hoarse, hard to hear. 'You must ring Mr Channing.'

'Yes, dear.' She patted the hand soothingly. 'Yes, I will. You rest now.'

'Promise.' He seemed agitated. 'It's very important.'

'Yes, dear, I promise.'

'Tell him – tell him I must talk to him. Tell him I'm here, that it's very important.'

'Yes, darling, I will. Next time I go home.'

'The number's in my address book. His home number. On the desk. Don't wait, Maureen, go home now and do it.'

'Yes, dear, I will.'

When she got home, she found the number, and dialled it. After three rings an answering machine came on. Maureen Hopkins didn't like answering machines, they made her nervous. She rang off and marshalled her thoughts, jotted down what she needed to say and then rang again. She did her best but she was afraid it wasn't very impressive. Anyway, she could report to Clive that she had done what he had asked and perhaps now he would now calm down a bit. It really couldn't be very important, probably about some dinner or other. He hated letting people down.

The house was very quiet when Francesca got home; Sandie had gone out, and the dull thud of rock music that indicated Barnaby's presence was still. Nanny had obviously taken Jack out somewhere. He was filled with restless energy these days; more and more like Bard.

Kitty had fallen asleep in the car and she managed to ease her into her cot without waking her. Little fraud, she thought, smiling indulgently down at her; frightening me like that. Making Mr Lauder cross with me. Well, next time she'd know. If it was a cold.

She went slowly back downstairs, and as she passed the study she heard the answering machine bleeping. She went in and pressed the button: three messages. One was clearly for Barnaby: short and to the point. 'Take your invitation, Channing,' it said, 'and stuff it up your own arse.'

'Charming,' said Francesca aloud: she supposed Barnaby couldn't really be held responsible for his friends, but he'd have to ask them not to leave obscenities on the phone in his father's house. Jack might listen to them, or still worse, Nanny.

The second was from Diana Martin-Wright, saying she was very surprised that Francesca had still not reached her advertising sales target for the ball programme – 'I bet you are,' said Francesca aloud – and wondering if she and Bard would like to come to a charity performance at Covent Garden on 9 September. 'Let me know as soon as possible, won't you, I have a huge queue of chums wanting to come.'

Francesca decided two others from the huge queue could accompany the Martin-Wrights, and concentrated on the third message. It was from a woman, a very nervous-sounding woman.

'This is Maureen Hopkins. I'm very sorry to bother you, Mr Channing, but my husband is ill. He's in hospital, getting better now, and he wanted you to know that. Oh, and the hospital is St Mary's, Torquay, if you want to go and see him. Thank you.'

Poor Maureen Hopkins, thought Francesca, she was obviously very worried about her husband. She wondered who she or indeed who Mr Hopkins was: probably someone who had once worked for Bard. Well, she could pass the message on to Bard; presumably he would appreciate the significance of it.

She went down to the kitchen to make herself a sandwich and some coffee, and to wait for Kitty to wake up.

'Damn damn damn,' said Kirsten, 'where is the bloody thing?' The bloody thing in question being her camera, which she really wanted for the weekend and for their trip to Paris (booked by Oliver for a fortnight's time), and which she had turned her flat all over for. And then she remembered: she'd lent it to Tory, who had wanted to take some pictures of Jack on his pony one day in the summer; and Tory had managed to leave it behind, assured her she would ask Francesca to bring it up to London.

She phoned her at the scruffy boutique in the Fulham Road where Tory was earning some holiday money and asked where it was now.

'Oh God,' said Tory, 'I'm sorry, I forgot, it's still at the house.'

'Well, you'll have to go and get it for me, I don't want to run into either of them, specially Dad after our last little encounter. I don't think that'd be a good idea. I told him I'd never speak to him or see him again, and I meant it.'

'Very unlikely you'd see him, I should think,' said Victoria. 'He's hardly ever home at the moment. Barnaby says he comes home to sleep occasionally, and leaves again at dawn. He's having a nightmare time,' she added. 'I wonder if the company's going to crash.'

'Who cares?' said Kirsten.

'Kirsten! That's horrid.'

'Tory, I don't give a shit if it crashes. And even if it does, Dad'll rise from the wreckage, holding a gold watch, you know he will.'

'You might give a shit if it did crash.'

'Why? I don't get anything from him. And I certainly don't care about him, or his precious little family.'

'Oh, Kirsten,' said Tory with a sigh, 'all right, have it your own way. What does Oliver say about it?'

'Oliver? How should I know?' said Kirsten carelessly.

'Because you're seeing him, that's how you should know.'

'I'm not seeing him.'

'Funny,' said Tory, 'I could have sworn that was him in your car the other night, when I drove past your flat, holding hands over the steering wheel. Poor Oliver.'

'Why poor Oliver?'

'Because he's so nice. And so vulnerable. And you'll break his heart.'

'He's not all that vulnerable, actually,' said Kirsten, 'and I have no intention of breaking his heart. Look, don't worry about the camera, I'll ring Sandie and ask her to find it, and post it or something. I'll never lend you anything again, Tory, I really won't.'

Sandie found the camera.

'I've got it here, with your sunglasses. Want me to post it to you?'

'My sunglasses! God, she must have taken them too. Well, you certainly can't post *them*. Look – is Mrs Channing there?'

'No, she's out, getting her hair done and God knows what. They've got a big dinner party this weekend. In the country.'

'And my dad's not there?'

'No, course not. He's never here, I've almost forgotten what he looks like. He works much too hard, poor bloke.'

'Right. Well, I think I'll pop up at lunchtime, Sandie.'

'Fine,' said Sandie.

She took a taxi from the office, ran up the steps. Sandie let her in.

'Here you are. And I found that T-shirt you were asking about last time. I think Tory had that as well.'

'Bitch. Thank you. Thank you very much. How are you, Sandie?'

'I'm fine. D'you want a quick coffee?'

'Um – yes, why not? As long as you're sure my stepmother won't suddenly appear?'

'She won't. Not till much later. Then tomorrow she's off to the country. I've got to go down there too, help with the flowers and so on. And I've got to do some puddings for the dinner party. She asks a lot of me, I must say. One house is enough, I'd say.'

'I would too. Surely they have someone down there?'

'Well, yes, they do, but I don't think she's much of a cook. Usually they get someone in to do it, but she's away. And Mrs Channing is very strong on the flattery. You know, there's a lot of "Oh, Sandie, that is just wonderful, thank you so much," and "Oh, Sandie, I don't know what I'd do without you." It's all very well, but she never seems to think of giving me extra money.'

'You don't terribly like her, do you, Sandie?' said Kirten casually.

'Well, she's all right. But she's a bit thoughtless. And high handed. Been worse lately. Ticking me off for giving Jack sweets, went mad because I'd not got her dry cleaning. Well, she didn't say it was urgent. "I have to have the red dress for the dinner party, Sandie, and that's that," she said. "You'll have to organise it somehow." '

'Silly cow,' said Kirsten. She knew it was silly, to badmouth Francesca to someone who worked for her, and who didn't like her very much, but she found it almost irresistible. 'Why can't she get her own dry cleaning? She can't have that much to do. She's got Nanny as well, for God's sake.'

'Oh, you'd be surprised,' said Sandie. She got up, fetched the coffee pot, refilled Kirsten's cup.

'Oh I know, all that crappy charity stuff of hers and her dinner parties. Big deal.'

'I didn't just mean that.'

There was something in her voice that caught at Kirsten's attention. She looked at Sandie sharply.

'What did you mean, then?'

'Oh – nothing much. She seemed to find plenty of time to go and visit Liam in hospital.'

'Liam! Francesca visited Liam in hospital?'

'Oh, two, three times a week.'

'Good Lord. What did my father have to say about that?'

'I don't think he knew,' said Sandie, carefully casual. 'Well, certainly not how often she went.'

'How extraordinary.'

'Yes.' She paused, looked at Kirsten over her coffee mug, then said, 'He was here the other day.'

'Liam! Here? You're kidding.'

'No, he was here.'

'Was my father?'

'Oh no,' said Sandie, 'your dad wasn't here. He was away.

Everyone was away. They were here on their own. He was just leaving when I came round the corner. Blowing each other kisses, they were. Drinking champagne too, empty bottle on the kitchen table.'

'Good Lord,' said Kirsten. This was the most intriguing, unlikely thing she had ever heard. Liam, who so famously hated Francesca he would never even speak to her, coming to the house, visiting her alone. How bizarre. What on earth was going on? Surely, surely not – But no. That really was unthinkable. And then she suddenly felt, intriguing as this was, it had gone far enough, even for her. She stood up.

'Sandie, I must go. Could you possibly call a cab for me? Put it on the account, no-one'll ever notice.'

'Course I will.'

All the way back to the office, and indeed all afternoon, she kept turning this extraordinary conversation over and over in her head, trying to make sense of it, wondering if what Sandie clearly saw as the explanation could be at all possible, and deciding again and again it simply couldn't be. Simply couldn't. Could it?

Bard phoned Francesca late on Thursday afternoon and told her he was going to New York and wouldn't be back in London until Monday.

'But Bard, there's the dinner on Saturday, at Stylings, it was all your banking people, how am I –'

'Oh for God's sake,' he said, 'I can't come rushing back there for some bloody stupid dinner. You can entertain them yourself, for God's sake, can't you, they'd much rather talk to you.'

'But –'

'Francesca please. I really can't waste time like this. I'll be there until Sunday, then I'm flying over to Munich. Get the numbers from Marcia. Everything all right?'

'Yes. It's fine,' said Francesca, 'absolutely fine. Don't you worry about us, Bard. Goodbye.'

She put the phone down, too angry to be upset. Hours later she remembered the message from Maureen Hopkins. Well, she certainly wasn't going to risk his wrath delivering that. It couldn't possibly be important anyway.

Maureen Hopkins sat holding her husband's cold hand and assured him that she had done exactly as he said.

379

'I told him you'd been ill, where you were, and that you'd like to speak to him,' she said, 'so don't worry.'

'And you actually spoke to him?'

Maureen hesitated. She knew if Clive had any idea his important message had been consigned to an answering machine he would become extremely agitated again. And there was no doubt whatsoever that Mr Channing would have got the message. The answering machine had told her that both Bard and Francesca Channing would be returning later that day.

'Yes,' she said firmly, 'yes, I actually spoke to him. And he was very nice, very sorry.'

'But is he coming to see me, is he going to ring me?'

'He's not coming to see you,' she said truthfully, 'but I'm sure he'll ring you. Please Clive, don't worry about it any more. I gave Mr Channing your message. Just like you told me.'

Gray had decided to go to Jersey. If Ferrers was right – and it seemed fairly likely – and Channing had been buying shares in his own company, to support the price, then the two companies that had made the purchases must somehow be linked to him. David Guthrie, his editor, had given him a flat no to a trip to the Cayman Islands – 'The fare alone is two grand, Gray, what do you think this newspaper is, some kind of a benevolent society!' – but had grudgingly agreed to a trip to Jersey. 'But you'd better bloody well deliver, Townsend. The last little investment I made in one of your hunches crashed rather, I seem to remember.'

'I will,' said Gray and hoped he felt as confident as he sounded. He'd wanted to go immediately, but it was now Thursday afternoon, and if Ferrers was right, and Channings really was about to go down, the activity around it would be intense and he needed to be in London. He would need to talk to Sam, to Alan Ferrers and his cronies, try and talk (fruitlessly he was sure) to Bard himself; he would try them all, Barbour, Francesca – he might just catch her off her guard – Kirsten – she might have some tasty little detail for him: at this stage any quote at all was useful, potentially valuable. Meanwhile he could only wait. He felt excited, that evening, almost fretful; drank too much wine, went to bed early, and dreamed dark, brooding dreams, of huge ugly buildings dwarfing grey city streets; he dreamed that he was driving down roads he did not know, waiting endlessly at airports for flights that never came. And then he dreamed of Briony, standing far away from him, smiling, just out of reach; and then he did reach her, took her hand, pulled her towards him and it was not

Briony at all who stood there, but a tall old woman with white hair, dressed all in black, holding out her arms to ward him away.

He woke shaking, sweating; it was only four, still not light. He decided there was little point in staying in bed, and he dressed and got out his bike and went for a long ride out into Surrey; as he drove back over Albert Bridge (thinking as he looked at the Thames, gleaming in the misty golden air, that London at its best really was every bit as beautiful as Paris) his mobile rang, it was Alan Ferrers.

'Time to do it up now, old boy,' he said.

'Do what up?' said Gray stupidly.

'Your seatbelt. And watch the screens. Could be something quite interesting happening any minute now. Only could, mind you. Be in touch.'

Gray promptly forgot about the beauties of the City of London, about Briony, even about Clive Hopkins, and put his foot down, weaving in and out of the traffic on the Embankment, his mind fixed only on the office and the importance of getting there as fast as he could without actually endangering his life. He knew what the phone call had meant: the bear raid on Channings had begun.

Chapter Twenty

Rachel put the phone down after a long and anxious conversation with Reverend Mother and decided that whatever the complexities of the conversation – and they would be considerable – she had to speak to Bard personally. She knew he'd been away all weekend, that Francesca (as she had informed her mother in a curt voice) hadn't even seen him, that he'd failed to make an appearance at a dinner he'd asked her to organise at Stylings, had been first in New York then in Munich, and had flown in late the night before and had still not appeared home.

Rachel quailed from her task, from speaking to him, bothering him: apart from the fact he was bound to be hostile to her, for exacerbating an already difficult situation with Francesca, he was having what was clearly an appalling time with the business. Even as she dialled Channings' number, she saw a piece in the *Telegraph* headed 'End of the line for Channing?' The papers had been full of the story all weekend; how his shares had fallen in price to some all-time low, how he had been holding crisis talks with his bankers; she had read estimates of how much Coronet Wharf, his great gleaming white elephant in Docklands, had cost him, and the figures, running into dizzy millions, had read doomsday-style, prognostications of the length of time it would take to recoup the losses on the loan, running into hundreds of years. There had been several 'no comment' quotes from Bard himself, and several slightly longer ones from Pete Barbour, admitting yes, there were certain difficulties, but he had every confidence that it should still be perfectly possible to salvage the company. And several well-informed articles by financial pundits, including one by the charming young man she had met at Douglas Booth's funeral, explaining that salvage was not only extremely unlikely, but barring a miracle impossible now: now that the shares had tumbled, the cash-flow was out of control, the rolled-up interest into astronomical figures, the confidence of the bankers and the shareholders at rock bottom. But in spite of all this, there was still her small helpless community in Devon, looking to her for help, the bank down there looking to her for reassurance; and in spite of it all, therefore, she had to do it, had to talk to him. If only to be able to tell Reverend Mother the whole thing was off, she had to do it: had to make sure.

Marcia picked up the phone: 'Mr Channing's office.' She sounded quite normal.

'Oh, Mrs Grainger. I'm so sorry to bother you. But this is very urgent. Could you possibly ask Mr Channing if he could spare me just literally two minutes. I realise it's not the best time but – yes, yes, I'll hold. Thank you.'

That in itself was extraordinary: for Marcia simply to ask her to hold on, without a long litany of warnings ('It's very unlikely he will be able to speak to you now'), reproaches ('I don't think you can quite realise how busy Mr Channing is') and crushing put-downs ('I'm afraid he can only take calls of the highest priority this morning'). Still more extraordinary was that she came back, said, 'I'll put you through, Mrs Duncan-Brown.'

She hadn't been expecting that, hadn't got her speech quite ready; she pushed the paper aside, adjusted her glasses – Rachel found it very difficult to speak succinctly when she couldn't see – and said, cursing the shake of nervousness in her voice, 'Bard, I'm so sorry to bother you, when things are obviously not easy, but –'

'That's all right, Rachel. Is there a problem?'

'Well, it's just that – well, I really have to know what to say to the bank.'

'The bank?' he said, and he sounded puzzled, as if a bank was unfamiliar to him, something quite outside his experience.

'Yes,' she said, puzzled herself by his reaction. 'The bank who are dealing with the convent. You know?'

'Oh,' he said, 'oh, yes, that bank. Look, Rachel, I – Christ, you'd better come over, we have to talk.'

'What – now?' She looked at her watch; it was two o'clock. How could Bard possibly have time to talk to her at two o'clock in the afternoon? 'Yes, all right, Bard. Fine.'

She got in a taxi, feeling the extravagance entirely justified. When she arrived at Channing House, Hugh saluted her, phoned up to Bard; told her to go up to Marcia's office. It all seemed perfectly normal: maybe they were just having a quiet day.

She walked rather slowly and carefully up the polished staircase, knocked warily on Marcia's door. Marcia called her to come in, and rose to greet her graciously. She also looked quite her usual self, calm, imposing, immaculate. 'Mrs Duncan-Brown. Good afternoon. Mr Channing won't keep you a moment.'

That was unusual too; normally she told all visitors, with the possible exception of Eddie George, that she would have to ask them to wait, adding, if they had the temerity to ask, that she had no idea how long. Rachel sat down and smiled at her.

'How are you, Mrs Grainger?'

'Perfectly well, thank you.' She returned to her word processor, making it plain that Rachel would be ill-advised to interrupt her further. Rachel picked up the *Wall Street Journal*, her favourite paper, purely on grounds of its appearance – 'like *The Times* used to be when it was a proper paper,' she would say to anyone prepared to listen – and had scarcely started to read the first article (on the subject of Clinton's Benefit reforms) when Bard's door opened and Sam Illingworth came out. She smiled bravely at Rachel, and said hallo to her, but her voice was odd, and she looked as if she had been crying. Dear God, thought Rachel: this was worse than she had thought.

'Rachel, good afternoon. Come along in.'

Bard stood in the doorway: he looked appalling. White faced, heavy eyed, and somehow bowed, stooped. He was wearing no jacket and his white shirt was open at the neck, his tie hung loosely. Everything about him seemed to hang loosely, she noticed confusedly, even his skin; his face looked jowly, heavy, there were bags under the black eyes, and his arms, usually outstretched in welcome, hung limply at his sides.

'Bard, hallo.' She kissed him briefly. He smelt strongly of whisky – odd, she thought, Bard never drank during the day, it was one of his most stringent rules.

'Hallo, Rachel. Marcia, we'll have some tea.'

'Yes of course, Mr Channing.'

She followed him into his office, he shut the door.

'Bard, is everything all right?'

'No,' he said heavily. 'No it isn't. It's all wrong, I'm afraid. And I'm very much afraid I won't be able to help you any more. With your – project. Certainly not in the short term.'

He looked so dreadful, so wretched and something else – what? ashamed – Rachel felt only the merest pang of panic for her project. 'Don't worry about that,' she said, 'we can sort something out. Tell me what's happened, Bard. I'd like to know.'

'It's all over,' he said, and his voice was quite cheerful suddenly. 'All the reporters and analysts were right, as they always are. Usually are, anyway. The major bank, that is the Swedish one, has called in the loan, as have Methuens, here, and that means the others are all following suit. And that means the end of the Channing Corporation.'

'But surely they can't give up on you just like that? They'll give you time to sort yourself out ...'

'Oh I've had that,' he said wearily. 'Months of time, they've been very fair. Very good to me, as a matter of fact, I can't fault them. And until very recently I thought I could get by. They rescheduled the interest payments, restructured the loan itself, all the constructive things – but of course word of that gets out, and has an effect on the share price. Anyway, it had got insane. We've been bleeding cash, as they say. The interest on that loan, on Coronet Wharf, was breathtaking, I don't think we could ever have recouped it. So – today, this morning, they called it in. The receivers will be here any minute. Channings has gone belly up, Rachel. There's no more I can –'

He stopped; Marcia had come in with the tea tray. Rachel looked up at her, smiled awkwardly.

'Thank you, Marcia,' he said. 'Yes, put it there. And I'll have a clean glass, please, as well. Rachel, d'you want some whisky?'

'No. No thank you.'

Marcia, looking deeply disapproving, fetched a clean glass from the cupboard by the fireplace, gave it to him. 'Anything else, Mr Channing?'

'No. No thank you. And I don't want to be disturbed.'

'No. No, of course not. Unless –' Her voice tailed discreetly away.

'Yes of course. If they arrive let me know.' He smiled grimly at Rachel. 'The receivers.'

'Ah.'

He filled his glass, sat staring at it morosely. Rachel picked up a cup of tea. 'Look Bard, if you'd prefer I went –'

'I can't think of anything I'd prefer less,' he said. 'It's good to talk to you.'

'Where's Francesca?' she said. She couldn't help it, felt somehow that her daughter should have been here, doing what she herself was doing, shoring him up, keeping him company.

'She's still down at Stylings. I was meant to be there this weekend, for some damn dinner – oh, it was one I'd asked her to organise – and didn't show. Because of all this, obviously. But I'm not her favourite person, I'm afraid.'

'She should be here,' said Rachel, ashamed of Francesca suddenly, ashamed she should be so self-obsessed, that she couldn't see that Bard needed her, that however hurt she was over the dinner, Mary, Ireland, what she saw as Bard's neglect, she should be able to set it aside for now.

'Well – perhaps. We've not been communicating too well lately. As you know.' His voice was emotionless, he seemed not to care.

'Bard, I'm sorry. For my part in that. So sorry.'

'That's all right. One of those things. Anyway – that brings me back to it, the convent –'

'Bard, please don't worry about that. It should be the least of your concerns. Can I do anything? Anything at all?'

'Yes,' he said, 'just stay here. Be here. Keep me company for a few minutes. I can't bear to be alone. Alone with it.' He dropped his great head onto his hands; his voice was muffled. 'Christ, I could –'

Rachel stared at him feeling shocked and helpless. 'Oh Bard. Bard, I'm so sorry. So desperately sorry.'

'Thank you,' he said, and his voice was raw with pain. 'I'm only glad Duggie isn't here. It would have broken his heart.' He looked up at her and she saw tears in his eyes; one rolled slowly down his cheek.

'It's the waste, Rachel, all those years of work and effort and investment, and I go and fuck it all up with a piece of arrogance, bad judgment, thinking I could walk on water. How could I have done that, how could I have been so stupid?'

'We're all stupid, sometimes,' she said, thinking of all her own follies, thinking of the most recent, 'we all make mistakes. You just got the opportunity to do it on a larger scale.'

'I know, but it's not just me. It's all the others. Marcia, Pete, Sam, Charlie. I've failed them all. Stupid fucking, arrogant idiot. I – oh Christ –'

Rachel stood up, walked over to him, without even thinking what she was doing, put her hands on his shoulders, tenderly, gently. He sat up, looked at her, startled, clearly ashamed, embarrassed, then suddenly, put his arms round her waist, buried his head against her. She stood there, stroking his hair, talking quietly, soothingly to him, as if to a child; and then she heard the door open, and Marcia's voice and someone else's, as if from very far away, and looking up found herself staring straight into Francesca's eyes.

Chapter Twenty-one

'Sit down there,' said Jess, 'and stop fidgeting. You know I don't like fidgeting. If you make an effort to appear calm, you feel calm.'

Bard glared at her. 'I have no desire to feel calm. This is not a situation for calm.'

'Well, what is it a situation for? Making a ridiculous, hysterical fuss? Upsetting everybody? What good is that going to do?'

'I have not,' said Bard, very slowly, 'been upsetting anybody. Well, not directly.'

'You've been upsetting Francesca.'

'Francesca has been upsetting me. And how do you know, has she been talking to you?'

'She has, but not in the way you mean. And only because I telephoned her, asked her to come and see me if she wanted to. And she said she couldn't, just at the moment. But she's clearly at the end of her tether. Doesn't know what to do to help you. Wants to very much. And something is upsetting her very badly. I don't know what it is.'

'She could try talking to me about it,' said Bard quietly.

'Isambard, I have known you much longer than Francesca has. And I know how difficult it is to get you to talk about anything when you don't want to.'

'I do want to.'

'No you don't. You don't want to talk. You just want people to listen to you. That's quite different. You should try listening to her.'

'Mother —'

'Isambard, please.' Her gaunt old face was less stern, very distressed suddenly. 'I beg of you, don't shut Francesca out. Don't risk losing her as well. She is such a lovely woman. She can help you so much, if you allow her to.'

He was silent, clearly struggling to keep his temper, to appear at least to be listening to what she said. Then finally he said, 'Yes, all right. I'll try, I promise. Mother, do you have any whisky in this house?'

'I do not. I'll make you some strong tea, much better for you. No use looking for the answer to things inside a bottle. That's what Pattie did, poor girl, I should have thought it would have taught you that lesson at least.'

Bard glared at her. There was a sudden shrill bleeping from his pocket: his mobile phone.

'Yes?' he said, pulling it out. 'No. Yes of course I do. Obviously. Christ Almighty, it would all be so much simpler if they let me be in there. Bloody nonsense. Yes, all right, tell them to ring Pete. No I do not. No. None of them. Bloody vampires.'

He switched his phone off sharply, slammed it down on the table.

'Who was that?'

'Mary Forbes, Charlie Prentice's secretary. One of the fortunate few allowed to be in the offices.'

'You were very rude to her,' said Jess. 'It's not her fault, any of it. I think you should ring her back and apologise.'

'Oh Mother, for Christ's sake. I have better things to do than start making bloody silly phone calls to secretaries.'

'Isambard, probably that woman is going to lose her job because of what has happened. The least you can do is be pleasant to her while you can.'

There was a silence. Then he said, 'Yes all right. I'll ring her later. Don't look at me like that, I swear I will.'

'Good. Now I want to know why you're not allowed in. If Charles Prentice is there. What's going on?'

'Oh God, I don't know.'

She looked at him over her tea cup. Her black eyes were softer, more anxious. 'You haven't done anything wrong, have you, Isambard?'

'What? Oh for Christ's sake, of course I haven't done anything bloody wrong.'

'Please stop swearing. And explain to me what is happening at Channing House.'

He sighed, made a clear effort to sound more patient, less harsh. 'The accountants, that is the administrators' accountants, are going through everything. All the assets, all the debts. They have to try to salvage what is left. So that they can do what they can for the creditors.'

'And they don't want you to be involved in this? Why not?'

'Because that is the procedure. They have a skeleton staff in there, picked by them, don't ask me how, one senior person, that's Charlie, one junior, who just happens to be young Oliver, doing some admin for them, photocopying and so on, one of the surveyors –'

'Not Peter Barbour?'

'No,' he said shortly. 'No, not Pete.'

'That seems very strange to me. He must know more about the finances of the company than anyone.'

'Mother, for God's sake, it is not strange.'

'There is no need to shout.'

'I'm not shouting.'

'Isambard, you are shouting. Now then, there's something else I want to know. Does this mean personal ruin for you?'

'It could,' he said carefully, 'I don't know.'

'Why don't you know?'

'I'm sorry?'

'Isambard, it's a very basic piece of information. Either you're liable for the company's debts or you're not. I would imagine you are: certainly you should be.'

'Thanks.'

'If I were a small shareholder in Channings,' said Jess firmly, 'and I lost all my savings, and I could see you still living in your big house driving around in your big car, I would personally wish to come and throw bricks through your window.'

Bard stared at her, a flush rising up his face: then he said quite calmly, 'Yes, well, of course most of it will have to go. But there is so much to be sorted out, there are various funds put away for the children and so on, we may – salvage a little.'

'Well, a little would be fair, I should say,' said Jess. 'So what are you doing with yourself, while they go through all these papers and so on?'

'Not a lot. There isn't a lot to do. I don't know what – oh Jesus.' It was the phone again. 'Yes? No I will not speak to the press. No, no exceptions. Not Murdoch himself. Tell them to go and play with –' he looked at Jess, paused – 'play with their computer systems. Oh and Mary, I didn't mean to be rude. Earlier. Sorry.'

He switched the phone off, looked at his mother. 'That do you?'

'I've heard more gracious apologies, but it will have to, I suppose. I saw a very nice journalist a week or so ago, incidentally. They're not all bad. He came to lunch here.'

Bard looked at her; his face was ghastly, ashen. 'You what? What are you talking about?'

'I had a very nice journalist to lunch,' said Jess patiently. 'Oh, it's all right, he didn't want to talk about you. He was interested in politics, in the early days, what I did for the party.'

'A journalist! You had a journalist here. Who the hell was it, and why was he here —'

'He was from the *News on Sunday*. You must know it, it's a very good paper. Kirsten arranged it.'

'Kirsten! Kirsten arranged for you to see a journalist? What was his name? For Christ's sake, Mother, have you no sense?'

'Don't swear. He was a friend of Kirsten's, in fact he helped her get her new job. I liked him very much. His name was Townsend. He was at Douglas's funeral, as a matter of fact. He seemed to know him quite well. And Teresa.'

'Ah, yes,' said Bard, slowly, 'Mr Townsend. He's doing a very good job, inveigling himself into my family.'

'Oh don't be absurd.'

'I'm not being absurd, that's exactly what he is doing. I don't like him and I don't trust him. And how dare Kirsten arrange for you to see him at all? Will that girl never learn anything? She ought to be bloody thrashed. After everything I — she —'

'Isambard, do stop this. You're being ridiculous. Mr Townsend is a very nice young man, he works for an extremely respectable newspaper, and he's writing an article about the socialist party. Or what used to be the socialist party. I was very careful not to say anything whatsoever about Channings, and he was at pains to stress he wasn't interested in it.'

'I bet he bloody was,' said Bard. 'I cannot believe you did this, the pair of you, after the last fu— wretched fiasco. How dare Kirsten do such a thing to me, how dare she?'

'Kirsten didn't do anything to you,' said Jess. 'Now drink your tea and calm down. I do what I like in my own house, Isambard. I know you're used to telling large numbers of people what to do, and it's a pity they let you get away with it. But I don't. Now then, you'd better pull yourself together, there's a beef stew in the oven and I want it eaten properly. It'll do you good. And I don't want you getting angry with Kirsten, either, for arranging for Mr Townsend to come here.'

'Oh for God's sake,' said Bard. 'I won't get angry with Kirsten, as you put it, for the simple reason I'm extremely angry with her already.'

'Well, you're not to start shouting at her,' said Jess, 'because there's nothing to shout about. Are you listening to me?'

'Yes,' said Bard, struggling patently to be calm. 'Yes, I'm listening to you.'

Without knowing precisely why, Francesca felt frightened. Well, she supposed she knew the main, the prime reason: that Bard was in serious financial trouble, was probably going to be declared bankrupt. But somehow that did not seem enough; not for the fear that stalked her, that woke her at two in the morning, and would not allow her to go back to sleep, that followed her wherever she went, that sat in her car, shared her table, was present in every ring of the phone, every knock at the door. In fact she didn't actually think she minded very much about the bankruptcy; she had seen it before, with her own father, she knew the worst it could do, and it was not really, in her book, so terrible. She realised, of course, that it was one thing to think it might not be terrible when she was still living in her large house, or even houses, with people to take care of her and her children and her every physical need attended to, and another were she to find herself on the street, or rather in a small house (if she was lucky) on a quite different style of street, but she still felt she could easily cope with it. She had never cared about Bard's money; she had enjoyed it, had enjoyed the considerable pleasures it had brought her, the beautiful possessions, the seeing of much of the world, the removal of herself from such small everyday unpleasantnesses as standing at bus-stops in the rain, cleaning her own house, balancing her bank account (sometimes with great difficulty), but she would have given it up with only the briefest regret. Indeed, she thought (as she lay awake, tossing and fretting), without even the briefest, if she could have all that was good of her old life restored to her, along with the bad. She had tasted huge wealth and she knew very well (as in all the best moral tales) it had brought her no real pleasure.

No, it was not the fear of bankruptcy that frightened her: it was her sense of loneliness, of isolation, of being set aside, seen as of no use any longer to Bard, having no importance in his life. The scene in his office, when she had found her mother comforting him, clearly far closer to him than she had been for weeks, had distressed her deeply; had made her feel humiliated and ashamed. She felt even worse at the memory of what had happened next; of shouting at her mother on the stairs, ordering her to leave her alone, of refusing to take her phone calls for twenty-four hours. She had gone to see her then, tearful, deeply distressed, had apologised, told her she knew Rachel had only been doing what she should have done, and Rachel had been (of course) generous, gentle, understanding. But she still knew she had been deeply in the wrong.

And when Bard had come home that night, late, exhausted, avoiding her, to sleep in his dressing room, she had lain awake, staring into the darkness, trying to summon up the courage to go to him, to say she was sorry, to ask how she could help. But he had been fast asleep, snoring drunk, a half bottle of whisky on the bedside table; in the morning he had gone early, without a word to her, only to return, humiliated, wretched, two hours later, having been barred from Channing House. She could hardly bear to look at him as he told her, so hideous had been his shame, his fall from grace as he saw it, the transformation of Bard Channing from legend to mortal, from success to failure, from walker on water to drowning man. And he had seen that she could not look at him, and had misinterpreted it; had turned away from her and walked out of the room, out of the house, and she had heard his car start, heard it driving away; much, much later when he returned she tried to explain, to apologise, but he saw it as an excuse, a feeble attempt to cover her distaste, her disdain even. And since then they had hardly spoken: he had moved about like a great restless ghost, from room to room, always on the phone, always in a hurry, never available to her. After a couple of days Marcia arrived, spent long hours locked in the study with him; she was as always perfectly, distantly polite to Francesca. She too had been banned from Channing House.

The banishment was another reason for Francesca's fear; dark, shadowy, ever more familiar. Bard had explained impatiently, Pete Barbour (who had also been to the house, having been banished also) more gently when she had, carefully careless, asked him about it, had explained that it was quite customary in such cases, that there were various anxieties about security on these occasions, that the directors might manage to salvage more than they should, 'shred documents, shunt money around, all sorts of exciting things', Pete had said with a weary smile; but the unease, ever more insistent now, stayed. What were they going to find, these people, sifting through the minutiae of the company, what were they looking for, what might be there? She kept hearing Terri's words again, in her kitchen, after the funeral, the very clear implication that she knew something about Bard, something dangerous. 'It's gloves-off time, Francesca.' What had that meant, what did she know, was there some connection with it all? And then, as she had trained herself to do so often and so carefully over the past few months, she would crush the fears, calm her panic, tell herself it was all normal, to be expected, that Terri had been overwrought, saying inevitably things that made no sense, that what was going on was, of course, as Pete had explained, a statutory procedure, something that under these circumstances had to be done.

And then too, she was lonely; her own phone was silent, people were clearly embarrassed, most of them not knowing what to say. A few of her closer friends had phoned, expressed an awkward sympathy – Miranda Scott had been marvellous, phoned her several times, taken her out for lunch, teased her about moving to Cardboard City, made her laugh – but most of them had simply stayed away. If she saw any of them at the gym, or at a restaurant, or even phoned someone unexpectedly, they carefully avoided the subject, were falsely, clumsily bright, as if she had been stricken by sudden bereavement or a terminal illness. It was, she could see, something not covered by most etiquette books, most social experience, the correct thing to say to someone whose husband's company had gone bankrupt and was now under investigation. Although after the last few years, it must have happened that most people had been confronted by it, somewhere in their circle. And it was hardly a crime, an offence even, simply a piece of misfortune. And of course mismanagement. She supposed that was what lay at the heart of the embarrassment: the implication that Bard must be a fool, incompetent, or it would not have happened. Whatever the reason, she felt rebuffed, alienated.

She also felt frightened, without knowing why, about Liam. She supposed it was fear of discovery, but that was absurd (she told herself): discovery of what? Several conversations, a few hospital visits, an hour at the house, some brief, almost innocent embraces: nothing wrong, nothing for which she could really be blamed. Except perhaps a little secrecy of her own. And yet – yet when she woke, in her midnight vigils, and thought of Liam, it was fear she found alongside him in her head.

Dear Dad
Sorry to read about your problems in the papers. It must be very distressing for you, and I hope things are not too tough. What a shock! Obviously the press are giving you a hard time; I hope your shareholders don't follow suit!
Yours, Liam.

The pleasure he got from writing that letter was, Liam thought smiling, as he finally sealed the envelope, almost, if not quite, orgasmic. The thought of his father humbled, brought so low, reduced from mighty Colossus to puny mortal, stripped of dignity, of position, no longer riding his vast fortune, his huge power, but dragged helpless along in his creditors' wake, more beggar than benefactor, useless, impotent – and at that thought, that particular label, Liam threw back his head and laughed aloud. It was a long time, a very long time, since he had felt so good, so powerful, so omnipotent himself. All the years of hurt, of rejection, of belittlement, were suddenly, sweetly avenged: the past and his endurance of it infinitely worthwhile, that he might savour this most marvellous present.

And there remained for him still the ultimate prize.

He had not been able to speak to Francesca since they had parted on his father's birthday; she had returned none of his calls, had been away all weekend and not answered the phone herself once. She had – most foolishly, had she known it, but having been assured quite wrongly that Naomi was away – sent him a note, saying they must not meet again, and thanking him for all that he had been to her 'at a difficult time', signed simply 'Francesca'. It wasn't much, but it could still be quite useful.

And since the news of the company's crash, all the lines, all the ranks had been closed, getting near to her was impossible. Finally, late on the Thursday afternoon, he had spoken to Sandie, briefly; she had sounded excited, clearly enjoying the drama. Mr Channing was beside himself, unable to do anything, banished from his office – 'it's what they call sealed, Liam, he literally can't get into it' – holed up in his study at home, emerging occasionally to shout at Francesca, at her, Sandie, at the children.

'And how is Francesca?' he said.

'Upset, but she's not actually with him much, they're hardly speaking. Nanny's being sent with the children to Stylings tomorrow, apparently the atmosphere's bad for them. Bad for them!' she added, her voice rising. 'Not too good for any of us. And Barnaby's gone off to stay with Kirsten, I think I might go mad.'

'Poor you!' said Liam. 'And poor Mr Channing! It must be very hard for him. No point you sending him any good wishes from me, Sandie, but you could give Mrs Channing my – my sympathy. And my love, if you can do it discreetly.'

Another little kitten, he thought, sent out padding innocently amongst the pigeons.

Oliver was hating the whole thing. For lots of reasons. It was terrible to see the place disintegrating: nice people like Sam Illingworth and Jean Rivers disappearing, Peter Barbour banished – that was really odd. If the administrators wanted to keep the company going, wanted to know what all their systems were, what buildings were tied up and so on, then surely Barbour was the one man above all they needed there.

'They just want skeleton staff,' Barbour had said to him carefully, by way of explanation, 'from the various management levels. And Charlie Prentice can tell them what they want to know just as well as I.'

'I don't see how,' said Oliver. 'He's not involved in the day-to-day running of the company, or –'

'Well, they're very experienced,' said Barbour, heavily, 'and I think we must assume they know what they want. I shall be called in from time to time, I'm told. Meanwhile they're retaining you.'

'Me! Why?'

'Oh – they want someone from this office. You're cheaper than I am –' he smiled grimly at Oliver – 'and they want someone to do some dogsbody work. Photocopying, and so on. Sorry, but at least you'll still get paid. Of course if any of those other jobs comes through –'

'Well, they haven't yet,' said Oliver, and then because he felt so sorry for Barbour, he said, 'I'm really sorry, Mr Barbour. Very sorry.'

'Thank you, Oliver. I tell you, I'm sorry too, that we couldn't go on working together. Maybe in another life –'

'Yes, maybe,' said Oliver.

Three days into the administrative procedures, he was sitting trying to sort out some filing when one of the accountants came into the room. He smiled at Oliver. He was quite young, and the only one who had been at all friendly.

'Hi. John Martin.'

'Hi,' said Oliver. 'Oliver Clarke. Is – everything OK?'

'Yes, sure. How about you?'

'Sorry?'

'You'd not been here long, had you? Must have been pretty distressing for you.'

'Oh – well, a bit. It was only ever going to be a short-term thing. I want to go into private practice.'

'Yes, much better. So how come you joined them at all?'

Oliver told him.

'Oh, I see. You're the son of Nigel Clarke. Who helped found this company?'

'Yes, that's right. Only he died. Twenty years ago.'

'Sorry about that. Tough for you.'

'It's OK,' said Oliver. 'It was a long time ago.'

'Yes, I suppose so. So you know old man Channing quite well?'

'Yes, pretty well.'

'And he's kept an eye on you, has he?'

'Yes,' said Oliver, 'and my sister and my mother.'

'Nice of him. I mean obviously he should, but thousands wouldn't. As they say. So you were pretty close to him?'

'I wouldn't say that,' said Oliver. 'It was quite a formal relationship.'

'Uh-huh. Well thanks, Oliver. But there was this business of your mother's nursing home fees? The Staff Benvolent Care?'

'No,' said Oliver, surprised, 'no, that came out of our own – well, my father's own – life insurance.'

'Ah. Is that what Mr Channing led you to believe?'

'He didn't lead me to believe it,' said Oliver shortly, 'it was true.'

'I see. Must have got it wrong, then. Did – well, do you like Mr Channing?'

'Yes, very much.'

'Is he popular in the company?'

'Very,' said Oliver firmly.

'Good. He seems a nice enough guy. Tell me, did he and Mr Barbour work very closely together?'

'Pretty closely, yes.'

'More closely than, say, Mr Prentice and Mr Channing?'

'I really don't know.'

'Did they have free access to each other's files?'

'Well, Mr Channing obviously had access to Mr Barbour's. Whether it was the same the other way round I couldn't say.'

'Who could say?'

'Marcia Grainger, I suppose. She was Mr Channing's secretary. She knew everything there was to know.'

'Yes, I see. You must have found the system here very complicated. All the subsidiary companies, the trusts, the transfers for developments, all that sort of thing.'

'Not terribly. But of course I hadn't been here long.'

'No I suppose not. Well, I've certainly seen much worse. Now then, who would pay all the company phone bills?'

'They came through this office,' said Oliver. 'That was the sort of thing I attended to. Any domestic expenditure –'

'Right. And that included the faxes?'

'Yes, of course.'

'Mr Barbour had a direct line, obviously. Did he use it much?'

'I don't know,' said Oliver truthfully. 'I don't think an enormous amount. It meant Jean – Mrs Rivers – couldn't screen the calls for him.'

'So it rang straight through onto his desk? And was it mostly personal matters, would you say? Calls from home and so on? Or business too, people he worked very closely with?'

'Both as far as I know,' said Oliver. 'Obviously I didn't answer it or use it.'

'And the bill for that would have gone in with the rest?'

'Oh – yes. Certainly yes.'

'Thanks, Oliver. I'd be grateful for that photocopying now, if you could manage it.'

'Yes of course.'

He went off, feeling miserable and somehow, for no logical reason whatsoever, threatened.

'Your dad's been on the phone, Kirsten.' Shelley, the girl in Reception, greeted Kirsten as she came in from a long round-trip delivering products and press releases to the furthest outposts of the media, taking in Wapping and Docklands, and pausing on her journey to gaze up at Coronet Wharf in all its harsh, glittering beauty, see what a temptation it must have been, and marvel that something so solid, so tangibly valuable, should have been the instrument that finally reduced her father to ruin. 'I told him you probably wouldn't be back today. Sorry!'

'Don't worry,' said Kirsten, 'that's just about the best thing you could possibly have told him. Unless it was that I'd left the planet for good. What on earth did he want?'

'Well, he didn't say. But he was ever so nice to me. And I mean, he didn't sound cross or anything. Probably just wanted to take you out to lunch or something.'

'Yeah, and probably pigs are about to fly right past that window. No, I'll have done something wrong, that's for sure. Anyway, thanks, Shelley, and if he rings again, tell him the same, will you?'

'Yes, sure. Oh, and Oliver phoned. Can you ring him?'

'I will,' said Kirsten, and went into her office smiling. She was even less daunted by her father, now she had Oliver.

The board of the London office of the Wall Street investment bank Fortescue-Tillich were all agreed they were most impressed by Naomi Channing. Her references, her career history, her education, her cool articulateness, her well-groomed (and well-bred) appearance, all reinforced the report from the Personnel Director based on her first interview, that she was the ideal candidate for the job of Vice President they were offering. A package had been agreed (£100,000 basic, plus increments, health insurance, car and five weeks' paid leave), and there only remained the purely nominal interview with the Chairman, Saul Petersen, fixed for the following week, to confirm the appointment.

It was of course well known that Mr Petersen was a devout Protestant who held the strongest possible views on the sanctity of family life, that he viewed his company as an extension of his own family, and regarded any irregularity in their marital arrangements with the utmost seriousness. But as Mrs Channing had gone to great lengths to assure the board that she was happily married with a young family, there seemed no real possibility of any difficulty in that direction.

'Are you OK?' said Kirsten.

'What? Oh – yes. Yes, I'm fine.' They were in a cab on their way to Ealing; Oliver had been unable to find his cash card and become anxious about it, and Melinda had then phoned to say it was in the kitchen drawer, with his car keys.

'Would you mind if we went to get it? It won't take long, and we can pick up my car as well, maybe drive out to the country somewhere, instead of eating in town.'

'I'd love that, all of it, and most of all seeing your house. Let's get a cab though, my treat, I hate that crawly District Line.'

He had been quiet ever since they had met, quiet and distracted; it was unlike him. She asked him again what the matter was.

'Oh – something that happened today in the office. It isn't important.'

'It seems to be.'

'Well, it is in a way. It's horrid there, seeing the place being taken apart, nobody around, like a sort of ghost town.'

'Is my father really not allowed in?'

'No.'

'I wonder why on earth not?'

'Oh, it's perfectly normal in this sort of situation. Honestly. Doesn't mean a thing.'

'Pity,' she said absently, 'I thought maybe he'd been cheating the Revenue or something and was about to be locked up.'

'No of course not,' said Oliver. He sounded irritable. 'You really shouldn't talk like that. You'd hate it if something really happened to him.'

'No I wouldn't,' said Kirsten positively. 'I know you find it hard to understand, but I really don't feel any of the proper things for him at all. As far as I'm concerned he can be locked up for a hundred years.'

'Kirsten, I just know that isn't true. If it was, he wouldn't be able to upset you so much. Anyway, he's been incredibly good to me – to us. Possibly more than I realised, actually.'

'What do you mean?'

'Oh – doesn't matter.'

'Please tell me.'

'Well – from something one of the accountants said today, Channings have been paying for my mother's nursing home bills all these years, not her insurance policy at all. Some staff benevolent fund.'

'So they should. Honestly, Oliver, he's got so much money, it's the least he can do.'

'I don't see it quite like that,' he said, 'but let's not argue about it.'

'No, don't let's.' She leant over and gave him a kiss. 'We're going to have such a lovely evening.'

'It's really nice here,' she said, looking round the small, just slightly overdressed sitting room, 'I like it. Did you buy all the furniture and stuff, or was it your mum's?'

'Melinda chose most of it,' said Oliver, 'and I have to say it's more to her taste than mine. But as she was doing all the work, making the curtains and so on, it didn't seem fair of me to be too fussy.'

'Well, I think it's lovely,' said Kirsten, and meant it. Raised as she had been on her father's austere taste, her mother's fondness for the ethnic, and with a strong hostility towards the kind of restrained chic with which Francesca dressed her houses, this pretty, chintzy, frilled and flounced house enchanted her. She had liked Gray's house, of course, but that had been a show-place, a devastating display of stylish confidence; this one was for living in, being happy in, a normal proper house, for normal, proper people. She smiled at Oliver, slipped her hand into his, gave him a kiss. 'I'd like a house like this,' she said.

He kissed her back, and smiled at her, and, 'You're just saying that,' he said, and she knew that once again he was surprised by her, surprised that she was not the person he had always imagined her to be. She surprised herself quite a lot, these days.

'Right,' he said, picking up the keys and the card, 'let's go. I thought sort of Oxford direction, what do you say?'

'I say Oxford direction'd be fine,' she said (wondering, with a stab of pleasure, if this might be her answer, if perhaps they might find themselves with too much to drink, in some nice country hotel, forced to stay the night), 'but I must go to the loo first.'

'Sure. Down there, end of the hall.'

Kirsten went into the cloakroom; it was decorated in the same pretty, cottagy taste as the rest of the house, with flower-sprigged wallpaper, elaborate ruched blinds at the small window, and a Victorian-style basin and loo, in blue and white patterned china. There were baskets of pot pourri, bowls of shells and tiny guest soaps; it had a delicious rosy, musky smell. The only thing that marred its perfection was an open box of Tampax on the shelf: Melinda had obviously left in a hurry that morning. And as she stood washing her hands, Kirsten suddenly found herself concentrating very hard on that packet, and realising with a stab of faint, but very real, unease that it seemed to have been a long time since she had needed to buy any herself; and then she told herself she was being silly, it probably wasn't long at all, and that when she got home she would check in her diary. Not that she was worried. Not at all. Not in the very least.

'Well, Liam.' Jess looked at him rather sternly over her cup of tea. 'You're looking much better than when I last saw you. Using the leg, are you?'

She had summoned him to her house for tea, telling him it was time she had a chat with him; he had gone slightly nervously, for she seldom wanted to chat about nothing, there was usually some other agenda. He had arrived in a taxi (for walking was still painful), with a bunch of flowers for her and a carefully prepared script on the subject of his career and his marriage. And thought, as he travelled through the hot London afternoon, that he might, if he put his mind to it, learn a little more about the background to the early days of the company in which Teresa Booth had shown so much interest. Jess would know all about that, if anyone did.

'Oh – yes. I look less like Hopalong Cassidy every day. And I feel really extremely well.'

'Good. How's Naomi?'

'Oh – she's fine. We think she's got a new job. A proper one, I mean. Fingers crossed.'

'Hmm. What about you? When are you going to get back to work?'

'Oh – pretty soon now, I hope. As soon as I'm properly mobile.

Got a couple of interviews, at least. In-house jobs, which isn't really what I want, but I can't go on living off Naomi for ever.'

'Good for you. Well said. And when's your case coming up?'

'Oh – in about a month. Not looking forward to that, I must say. But I deserve it, whatever I get. I was just lucky no-one else was hurt.'

'Yes, you were. Very lucky. Might have been your children. But we talked about that before. No point raking over old ground.'

'No. Anyway, how are you, Granny Jess?'

'Oh – I'm pretty well. Busy, of course, with this leadership election, you know.'

'Yes. What do you think of Tony Blair?'

'I think he's a very good Tory,' said Jess severely. 'Prescott now, he's more what the party needs. But I fear they won't get him. I liked Kinnock, of course. A genuine socialist, he was. The last one. But that showbiz rally of theirs, dreadful. He deserved to lose, agreeing to that.'

'Is that what you think? I'm not so sure.' Liam was genuinely interested in politics, it was one of the close bonds between them, he the instinctive Tory, she the rational socialist, and they would roam the subject in all its aspects and ramifications for hours, incorporating such absorbing philosophies and arguments as the incompatibility of Conservatism and Christianity, economics and socialism.

Today, Liam having postulated that the Tory party had lost its way and its philosophy under the classless banner of John Major as thoroughly as the Labour party would do the same under Blair, and Jess having mourned the cynicism of the young – 'the true danger in politics' – towards both parties, Liam realised that it was after six and at seven he had to collect his children from their friends in the Terrace. Or had to unless he phoned, asked if they could stay on.

'Phone if you like,' said Jess, 'but won't they be disappointed not to see you?'

'Good Lord no,' said Liam. 'They're with me all the time at the moment. I'm the new man, Granny Jess, not an absentee father, like my own.'

'Yes, and I always thought that was a great pity. Isambard wasn't a bad father at all, he could have been a good one given a little more time with you all.'

'Well, I think that's a slightly over-charitable view,' said Liam lightly, 'but I suppose the circumstances in my own case were rather extreme.'

'Yes they were. Which is not to say I approved of what he did, because I didn't. You needed one parent at least, and he should have recognised that. But he had to survive somehow, and I'm afraid throwing himself into his work was the only way.'

'Yes. Well, I suppose I had you.'

'You had me. And Douglas and Suzanne. And Heather Clarke, she was very good to you as well.'

'Poor Heather,' said Liam, tipping his voice over into the honeyed liquid sympathy that, on the rare occasion it had been put to use in court, had invariably led his witnesses into a sense of false security, 'I really must go and see her again. I feel very bad about her, she must be horribly lonely.'

'Yes, I think she is. But she's as well looked after as she could be.'

Liam made a great performance of shifting his injured leg about, so that Jess couldn't see his face. 'I didn't realise until the other day,' he said, 'that my father paid her nursing home bills.'

'And who told you that?' said Jess. A spot of colour burned suddenly on her high, sallow cheekbones.

'Teresa Booth. She was going through all Duggie's papers and so on, and –'

'It seems a rather strange thing to tell you,' said Jess. 'Confidential, I'd have thought, that sort of thing.'

'Well – she did tell me. For whatever reason. She's a funny woman. Not to my taste, but I understand she made Duggie quite happy.'

'I think she did, yes,' said Jess, 'and I quite like her. I find her honest. As you get older, you value honesty more and more.'

'So you knew that, did you?'

'Well, I knew there was some provision made for her. By the company. And at your father's suggestion, she was not to know.'

'Why on earth not?'

'Because she's very proud, that's why not, and she wouldn't have taken it. It seems Nigel had left her rather badly provided for.'

'I see. Well, I suppose we shouldn't begrudge her anything. Poor woman.'

'No,' said Jess, 'we certainly shouldn't.'

'And after a purely temporary spell as a cripple, I'm even more sympathetic towards her. Just the same –'

'Yes?'

'It still seems a very generous thing to do. Paying all those bills for her. I mean –'

'Liam, your father is a very generous man. And besides –'

'Yes?' He hardly dared to move, to breathe, for fear she might draw back.

'Oh – doesn't matter.'

'Granny Jess, go on. You know I have a lot of trouble relating to my father. Coming to terms with what's happened between us. Anything that helps me to understand him better –'

'I do wish,' she said apparently irrelevantly, 'the two of you could become friends. It's a source of great regret to me, this feud between you. So unnecessary, such a waste of time and emotion.'

'It doesn't seem that way to me,' he said, and he was speaking with genuine passion suddenly. 'He rejected me when I was a small boy, when I needed him, and he's been rejecting me ever since. And he might have helped the Clarkes, but he's done precious little for me.'

She was silent. She knew he was right.

'And I have tried,' he said, 'I really have.'

'I haven't seen much evidence of that,' she said. 'Certainly not lately. And I really don't approve of the way you behave towards Francesca.'

'Well, you're very wrong there,' he said, 'she and I are quite good friends now.'

'Is that so?'

'Yes. She came to visit me in hospital, several times, and I have made it very plain that I'm sorry about – well, about my attitude to her.' God, this was fun. Talk about exquisite irony.

'That rather sounds to me as if she made all the running,' said Jess.

'Not really. In fact we'd started to build bridges before that. I met her at Channing House one day, long before the accident, and we had a long talk. I was wrong about her; I don't mind admitting it.'

'Well, that's very nice of you,' said Jess, 'and I'm pleased to hear it. She's never mentioned it to me, but there's no reason why she should, I suppose –'

'Not really, no. We're both a bit embarrassed about it, I think. Well, I certainly am. Anyway, if it's any comfort to you, I wrote to my father after the crash, told him I was sorry.'

'And has he responsded?'

'No,' said Liam, with a carefully light sigh, 'but I'm sure he's very busy.'

'I'm afraid he is. And very upset. His pride's hurt as much as anything.'

'Yes. Poor old Dad.' And I know all about pride being hurt, he thought, a lot more than he does.

'Anyway, back to the Clarkes. You were going to give me your view of all that.'

'I was?'

'I think so. Trying to whiten Dad's reputation a bit.'

'I would never try, as you put it, to do that,' she said, with great dignity, 'I would only tell the truth. As I know it.'

'And what is that? Is there really some more to it, something that I – that we all should know?' Again, he held his breath: literally.

'Not – not really,' she said after a long pause. 'But I do know he felt – still feels personally guilty for Nigel's death.'

'Guilty?' And now the astonishment was genuine. 'Why should he feel that?'

'He and Nigel were drinking that night. In the office. He felt responsible for letting him go out and drive home. It wasn't illegal then, of course,' she added, sternly. 'Thanks to Barbara, things are different now.'

Barbara? Barbara who? What was she talking about? Maybe she was getting a bit past it after all. Then he realised: Barbara Castle. 'Oh. Oh I see,' he said carefully, very quietly. 'Well, I wouldn't have thought that was so very terrible.'

'Wouldn't you?' she said, and her sharp old face was softer suddenly, almost grateful. 'Wouldn't you really?'

Liam seized on the gratitude. 'Granny Jess, of course not. Nigel was hardly a kid, he could decide whether or not he was in a fit state to drive.'

'Yes, I told your father that. But he couldn't accept it. And it's been eating away at him, all these years.'

'That really is ridiculous. I wish I could tell him I think so myself.'

'Perhaps you should,' she said.

'If ever the opportunity arises, I will. I promise. I wouldn't wish that sort of burden of guilt on anyone.'

'Well,' she said, stern again now, 'I do feel he has to bear some of the responsibility. Obviously. I like it that he does. It always encourages me that he still has a conscience. But perhaps he need not take on quite as much as he does.'

'No. No indeed.'

There was a silence; there had to be more, he thought; his father wouldn't have been eaten up with remorse for twenty years over feeding a colleague a few drinks. Even if the colleague had then gone out and virtually killed himself. He waited, patiently. Silences were very potent, certainly in court: witnesses felt bound in the end, even subconsciously, to say something, anything, to break the silence. Graydon Townsend could have told him the same thing about interviewing subjects.

'They'd had a quarrel, you see,' she said slowly. 'Well, not a quarrel, a disagreement.'

'Not so surprising. Partners often have those.'

'I suppose so. But that was why they were having the drink; they'd sorted it out, and were – well, relaxing, I suppose.'

'Oh. Yes of course.'

Yes of course. That was it. It was the quarrel that had made his father guilty; the quarrel that had been fatal. The quarrel that had caused the crash. Not the drink. From what he remembered of Nigel Clarke, he was the mildest, most self-contained of men, most unlikely to drink himself into the sort of stupor that would cause him to crash his car. He sat there, very still, looking at Jess, watching her carefully, his key witness.

'Do you know what this row was about?' he said gently.

'Oh – no. Not in detail. Something about the way the company was being run.'

'Yes. Yes, I see.'

'So you see,' she said briskly, standing up, 'your father is not so unfeeling. Not conscienceless. Try and make up with him, Liam. You'll regret it if you don't.'

'I will,' he said, 'I promise.'

'And try to feel a bit less sorry for yourself,' she added. 'Self-pity is a very destructive emotion.'

It was very hard to maintain the ruefully regretful smile at that, but he thought he'd just about managed it.

He wondered if he might share this new information with Teresa Booth; she had seemed interested in it all. He stopped the cab at a phone box on the way home to call her, but her housekeeper informed him she was out for the evening. He didn't want her phoning him, and when he got home Naomi was there. What looked like a very long weekend lay ahead of him, deprived as he was of making any progress in his campaign; but Naomi was in surprisingly friendly mood, and he supposed he did have a great deal to think about.

John Martin sat back wearily in the chair that had once been Marcia Grainger's and decided to leave Channing House for the weekend and go home to his wife and baby in Guildford. It had been a tough four days, and he wasn't thinking properly any more. He was as sure as his name was John Martin there was something going on here, that Channing had something – a lot – to hide, but he was buggered if he could find it. So far everything seemed totally in order. Yes, there were a lot of complex goings-on; yes, there were dozens of different bank accounts; yes, there were all sorts of insurance funds and pension schemes and offshore trusts; yes, a great deal of money was sent on apparently circuitous journeys round the globe, ostensibly in order to finance foreign developments; yes, Channing did personally hold an enormously high percentage of the shares; yes, he and the poor old bugger who'd copped it, Douglas Booth, had been dual signatories on a great many of the company accounts; yes, there was a house in Greece that was clearly something of a tax dodge; and yes, that pompous twit Peter Barbour was living in a house that appeared on the face of it to be rather beyond his fairly modest salary; but none of it was actually seriously illegal. None of it. So far he hadn't found anything, anything at all. Of course there were still the shareholders to dredge through, but the register appeared, on the face of it, in order. Anyway, he was bushed. And he couldn't think straight any more. He'd leave it now till Monday. He wanted to go home and have the nice supper that his wife had told him she'd prepared several hours ago, and sit and listen to the new CD they'd bought of the Pavarotti concert in Hyde Park. And tomorrow he would get up early and go to the golf course.

He was just walking through Reception when he saw the pile of photocopies and print-outs young Oliver Clarke had been working on all that day for him. Nice lad; slightly funny business about his mother's nursing home fees, but there was nothing illegal about paying for a crippled old lady's comfort out of your own pocket. He could hardly get Channing on that one. He picked up the envelope, went downstairs, said goodnight to the porter and hailed a taxi. As it wove its rather tortuous route to Waterloo, he pulled out the first sheaf of papers, which was a breakdown of company purchases and assets for the year 1989. All pretty predictable. All in order. Nothing that would interest him: shopping malls, blocks of flats, office blocks, exactly the sort of stuff that left the Martin pulses running pretty slowly. Except – well, except for this. This would be very nice indeed, by the sound of it. Something to be personally checked out, perhaps. A golf complex, up in Scotland in a place called Auchnamultie. He hadn't realised Channing had one of those. Bought by the company, undeveloped, for two million. Must be worth three, four times that now. If it was any good. He loved playing golf in Scotland. The air was so marvellous. He had once, only once, played at Gleneagles, on a corporate day's entertaining, and had told his wife afterwards it was the nearest thing to heaven he'd ever known. She hadn't been terribly impressed.

Anyway, he had a week's holiday coming up. He'd investigate it on Monday, find out where it was and see if he could book into it.

Before it had to be sold, which it undoubtedly would be, to benefit Channings' creditors.

The cab had reached Waterloo. Thank God. John Martin put the file back into the envelope, found his train, got into the first class compartment that was one of the few perks of working overtime for Muir Whitehead, and fell asleep.

Chapter Twenty-two

Kirsten sat in the bath, gazing down at her stomach (so flat, so reassuringly flat), and tried not to panic. Of course she wasn't pregnant; she couldn't be. It was impossible. Quite impossible. She'd been taking her pills. Hadn't she? Regularly. Well, quite regularly. Of course she did forget from time to time. And since she hadn't been having any sex lately, she'd been getting quite sloppy about it. But mostly she took them. Probably she was just late because her system was all mucked up, simply because she was always forgetting to take them, and then taking two or even three. That was it. She didn't feel sick or anything. Last time she'd been terribly sick. And her boobs were still just the same. She seemed to remember they'd got bigger and sore before. No, she was just being silly. It wasn't even worth doing a test. But she might, just to set her mind at rest. She would, just to set her mind at rest. But she'd only missed one. Well, one and a half. Yes, she'd get a test and do it and probably that would bring it on. It was a pity, her being so worried – well, not worried, but distracted – because it had spoiled the evening with Oliver, scuppered her plans for finally seducing him. He'd known there was something up, had even asked her (slightly embarrassed) if she was feeling OK. Probably thought she had her period. *That* was an irony. Well, she was seeing him later that day; she'd have done the test by then, the chemist was just down the road, and then she'd know she was OK and could go along with his suggestion for another jaunt into the country and reset the scene.

She smiled happily to herself, reached for the razor, started shaving her legs.

Reverend Mother had received two letters that morning; it was hard to say which gave her more anxiety. The first was from Rachel, a sad, careful letter explaining that there was no longer the slightest hope of Bard Channing putting any money into their project and explaining why. She said she had written personally to the bank, to apologise and explain to them, thanking them for their patience; and she also said that Bard had suggested a few other people who might help. 'But I feel, honestly, that having to go back to square one, we will lose so much time we have no hope of getting the priory, or the land for that matter, now. The property developer has been waiting in the wings, and is now bound to rush on stage, waving wads of notes. I am so sorry, Mother; and Mr Channing has asked me to apologise and to tell you that he intends to write himself in a few days. I think things look very bad for him, and his problems are extremely complex and severe; please bear with him, therefore, if the letter is a while materialising! My love to Mary; I feel I can't leave London and Francesca just at the moment, but I will be down in a few weeks. Yours ever, Rachel.'

The second letter was from the Department of Health and Social Security, and it said that its Mr Rutherford would be calling upon Mother Felicia within the next few weeks to discuss with her certain aspects to the running of the convent and the community in the light of new EEC regulations as they applied to residential accommodation. If Reverend Mother would care to phone Mr Rutherford on the above number then a mutually acceptable meeting could be arranged.

The meaning of this, despite its excruciating grammar, was very plain; the countdown to the dissolution of the Help House in its present form had begun, and the happiness and security of at least some of the residents was seriously under threat.

Reverend Mother went to the chapel for a while and sought guidance, and then, with a very heavy heart, sat down and wrote a letter back to Rachel, saying that while she understood Rachel's presence in London was clearly very desirable, she would like her to come to the convent as a matter of urgency, so that they could discuss matters further.

'Bard,' said Francesca tentatively, 'is there anything at all that you'd like to do? This weekend?'

He glared at her. 'Short of taking a sawn-off shotgun to those morons who are raking over the ruins of my company, no, there isn't.'

'Well, just supposing you don't do that, do you want to go down to the country? Would that help?'

'Help? How could it help?'

'Well, I don't know. It would give you something to do.'

'Francesca, I've got a great deal to do. Thank you. And I don't think wandering round discussing the roses is going to be particularly therapeutic.'

'Bard, you never discuss the roses. Or anything else to do with the garden, except to complain about poor Mr Parker.'

'I'd like to go sailing,' he said suddenly. 'That really would be worthwhile.'

She knew why he'd said that: to hurt her, because he knew she couldn't or wouldn't go with him.

'Well,' she said calmly, refusing to rise, 'why don't you go? I don't mind. Take Charlie, or Henry. I'm sure they –'

'Charlie and Henry have their own lives to lead. I can't expect them to drop everything at a moment's notice to come sailing with me.' Francesca didn't point out that under different circumstances Bard expected everyone to drop everything to do what he wanted; she simply smiled at him and said, 'Well, what about Barnaby? He likes sailing.'

'Well –' He hesitated. 'I could ask him I suppose. No doubt he'll think he's got better things to do. Where is he?'

'Asleep I suppose. It's only half-past ten. That's what the morning is for, when you're twenty.'

'That's ridiculous. I didn't spend all my time in bed when I was his age. I wasn't allowed to and nor did I want to. He ought to be up, sorting his life out, not lying there, doing nothing. Has he organised next term, where he's going to go, yet?'

'Bard, I don't know. He's not my child. I can't be –'

'Yes, so you're very fond of telling me. Especially when he's not doing what he ought to be doing. Which reminds me, I have to get hold of Kirsten. Bloody girl's done it again.'

'Done what?' said Francesca, a procession of possible events ranging from arrest to pregnancy drifting past her eyes.

'She's talked to the press. I know it's hard to believe, but she has.'

'What? But –'

'Oh, it's not quite as bad this time. But almost. Fixed for that bloody Townsend man – your friend – to see my mother.'

'He's not my friend,' said Francesca, keeping her temper now with a huge effort. 'But I don't see why –'

'Nor do I. Whatever her reason, she must be half-witted. I tried to get hold of her yesterday and she wasn't in the office. Skiving off somewhere, no doubt. Anyway, I'm going to go and kick Barnaby out of bed, and see if I can get him to come sailing with me.'

Half an hour later, grumbling loudly, but actually quite pleased at the prospect, Barnaby was being bundled into the car by his father, en route to Chichester harbour and Bard's latest water-based toy, a state of the art thirty-five-footer ULDC – 'short for Ultra Light

Displacement Craft', he had told Francesca, one of the many times he had tried to tempt her onto the water, 'incredibly fast, so light it skims through the water, almost planes in fact.' Francesca had said she was sure it was wonderful, but she'd rather go on just hearing about it.

Bard had promised Barnaby, who had been longing to experience the delights of the ULDC – christened *Lady Jack*, much to Jack's resentment, since he had not been allowed on it once – that given a following wind – of which there seemed considerable promise – they would sail across to France and spend the night there. Francesca breathed a sigh of relief, put in a brief prayer for the wind back to England to be light, if not non-existent, for several days, and decided to go and see her mother.

Oliver put the phone down, feeling rather depressed. He had been looking forward to his day with Kirsten; they had been planning on a long drive out to the country, dinner somewhere nice and – well, who knew what might have happened after that. He was beginning to feel rather physically obsessed with Kirsten, not to mention frustrated. It just wasn't easy, being so close to her, feeling so – so involved with her, wanting her, really wanting her now very badly, wanting to explore her, to enjoy her, to feel her enjoying him.

But he liked, on the other hand, her attitude towards sex; well, the one she presented him with, anyway; he felt quite sure she was not always so circumspect, but that, in a way, made him feel he mattered to her. It was a rather weird, back-to-front judgment to make, he supposed: that because she wouldn't go to bed with him until she knew him (and presumably liked what she knew), then she saw him as important. But he felt it was the right one.

He was still slightly fazed by what had happened between them; still amazed that this girl, the beautiful, difficult, disagreeable girl he had grown up watching, observing, disliking, should have become the beautiful, interesting, and agreeable one he now knew rather intimately. And he did know her intimately: OK, they hadn't been to bed, but they had spent a lot of time together. He knew how she worked, what made her happy, what made her sad, what pleased, what angry; he could tell a bad mood from a good, within minutes of saying hallo to her; he knew her views on things, what she felt about matters large and small. He knew that she was a mass of contradictions, physically reckless, emotionally cautious, self-opinionated, unsure of herself; that she had huge phsysical energy, and was acutely intellectually lazy; that she was generous, good humoured – until she lost her temper, and then she was unreasonable with rage; that she was swift to judge, slow to change a view, dismissive of those she disliked, intensely loyal to her friends. And he knew she liked him, and he knew she wanted him, and he felt they had known each other long enough now to take things further. To get into bed together. To have sex. And even while he was nervous of the event itself – for he felt instinctively her sexual energies would be enormous, that her experience probably far outstripped his own – he thought it would still be all right. More than all right, good. Her rather touching attempts to defer to him, to let him take the lead, to please him, to be seen to be a great deal more compliant than he knew she actually was, all conspired to make him think so.

And he had really thought that they were there: that she had decided the time had come, was waiting, slightly impatiently even, for him to make the move, to go beyond the kissing, the caressing, the rather tumultuous closeness they had reached; and had planned the last time, when they had gone out to Oxford, to do so. Only she had been strange that evening, distracted, slightly edgy: probably PMT or something. Melinda made much of such issues; he had grown up respecting them. Had understood, been patient – and thought today would see it happen.

And now she had phoned, clearly not herself, saying she felt lousy, could she cry off, she had a foul headache – Kirsten never had headaches, she had her father's impatience of sickness, as she had so many of his other such arrogant qualities – she just wanted to be on her own, she said, she'd be bad company. And he felt miserable and disappointed, and something else: worried. Worried that maybe she was telling him that after all there was nothing for them, the two of them, that it was best stopped now, quickly before it was too late. Only she had said she'd ring him in a day or two, and added she was sad and sorry too.

Well, there was nothing he could do about it. Maybe it had been PMT the other night, he thought, so now it would be her period; yes, that must be it. They really didn't know each other well enough for her to feel she could discuss such matters, he thought, while setting aside the uneasy idea that actually she would have confronted it head on, said that was precisely what the matter was.

Oliver got out his mountain bike and set off down the street, heading in the direction of Richmond, telling himself very firmly that it would be perfectly all right in the end. He only had to wait a few more days. He really was quite sure of it.

Kirsten sat by the phone for a long time after Oliver had rung off, hearing over and over again in her head the echo of disappointment in his voice behind the bright, light, 'Well, speak to you in a day or two, then.' And then she went back into the bathroom and looked down at the long white plastic stick with two identical pink circles on it, two pink circles that meant she was indeed pregnant, and thought that there was only one person who could possibly be the father, and that was Graydon Townsend.

'I've got to go to Devon,' said Rachel, 'to see Reverend Mother. Why don't you come with me?'

'Oh, no, I couldn't possibly do that.'

'Why on earth not? Of course you can, it would do you good. Make you realise there are other problems in life besides Bard Channing.'

'Mummy, don't start on that tack, please.'

'Well, I'm sorry, darling. But he is a large, spoilt child, and I have a rather less spoilt one to worry about. And several more. And I feel I've let them down and I don't know what to do about it.'

Francesca hesitated. It was quite true; it would do her good. Bard wouldn't be back; the children were at Stylings, and perfectly happy; she had nothing to do. She couldn't even – she shut her mind hastily away from what she couldn't even do, and said rather feebly, 'What about the children?'

'Bring them. They'd enjoy it.'

'I don't think so,' said Francesca, envisaging the arrival of Jack at the convent with some foreboding. 'Anyway, I want to talk to you.'

'What about?' said Rachel casually.

'Oh – just things.'

'Fine.'

'I must check they're all right. But we're not going to be far away, are we?'

'Much less far than if you'd gone sailing with your husband,' said Rachel. 'Think of it that way.'

'Yes, that's quite true. And they've got Nanny and Mrs Dawkins and Horton down there. All right, Mummy, I'll come. We'll take my car, it'll be much more comfortable.'

It was a glorious day, too glorious to be on the M5. The sun beat down relentlessly on the procession of cars, caravans, trailered powerboats and motorbikes that were beating their way to the coast; after a while they gave up, turned off just before Taunton, had a leisurely lunch at a pub, and resumed at three when the worst was gone.

It was five-thirty by the time they turned into the lane that led to the convent; the residents were having their supper. But Reverend Mother was waiting for them in her study, with tea, freshly baked bread, warm scones with clotted cream, chocolate cake: as one woman Francesca and Rachel waved temptation way, took small cucumber sandwiches.

'It's absurd,' said Reverend Mother. 'You look like half-starved birds, both of you. Well, I shall eat cake for us all.'

Francesca looked at her, thought inconsequentially how in another life, another age, she would have been called voluptuous, with her thick, creamy skin, her bosomy figure, her lovely full-lipped face, the fair curls drifting from beneath her headdress onto her high, unlined brow.

'I am sorry, Mrs Channing, about your husband's business. We have prayed for him.'

'Thank you,' said Francesca, thinking rather nervously, even at this distance, of Bard's likely reaction to this piece of information.

'Has he taken the event badly?'

'Not too well, I'm afraid. It is quite – serious. And –' She smiled at Reverend Mother. 'He is a very – emotional man.'

'But a very strong one, I would suppose.'

'Yes.' She had forgotten Bard had been to the convent; it made her feel odd, more of a stranger herself.

'Well now, Rachel, we have a problem,' said Reverend Mother, Bard Channing and the downfall of his multi-million-pound empire having been dismissed as a minor matter: and he wouldn't like that either, thought Francesca, amused in spite of herself.

'Yes,' said Rachel, 'yes, indeed we do.'

'You see, I know that we shall not be permitted to continue to house all our residents. Our facilities are simply not adequate. If we lived in Italy, or France, no-one would so much as lift the smallest finger to keep these new regulations, if it was known that all was running well, and everyone was happy, but I'm afraid in England, we feel rules are to be obeyed.'

'So, what will happen?' said Rachel. She sounded calm, but Francesca could hear an echo of panic in her voice.

'Well – those who have families who we feel can cope will be asked first to remove them. To find alternative accommodation, or to take them in themselves. That is the sensible thing.'

'Yes. Yes, of course.'

'And Mary has a family. Does she not?'

'Yes, Mother. She does.'

'A family who can cope. Cope very well, it seems to me.'

A longer pause: then Rachel said, 'Yes.'

Later they walked on the cliffs by the priory; Francesca stood and looked at it, its lovely outline etched against the brilliant evening sky, so sheltering, so safe and strong looking. A refuge: she wished she could go into it herself, stay there, for a long time. The air was clear, salty, still warm; she could hear the waves below beating on the rocks, the gulls crying overhead. She looked at her mother; she was standing still, staring at the sea, her face troubled, her eyes dark.

'The thing is,' she said to Francesca, 'Mary will be so unhappy in London, with me. She has only known the country, the community, Richard, the bakery, collecting the eggs, helping everyone, helping her friends; that is her life. She will hate it. Hate it.'

'I suppose,' said Francesca gently, 'that's what everyone will say.'

'Yes. Yes of course it is. And if she goes to another community, that will be strange, she will know no-one. At least in London she would have me.'

'Well – yes. And – and me,' she added carefully.

Rachel looked at her thoughtfully, then smiled. 'That is very sweet,' she said, 'very sweet indeed. And I am proud of you, and I know I don't deserve it, the way I've handled all this. I hope one day you'll understand.'

'Well – let's say I think I'm beginning to,' said Francesca.

They were staying at the pub in the village: over a dinner of baked mackerel 'and vegetables grown at the convent,' said the landlady, beaming; new potatoes, peas and tender runner beans, and then a wonderful French apple tart, served with clotted cream, she talked to her mother about her unhappiness with Bard.

'It's not his temper, not even his high-handed attitude to me, it's the way he won't tell me things, even now, now when I want to help, when I know I should be helping. He just loses his temper whenever I ask him about any of it; I can't bear it.'

'Your father was much the same,' said Rachel briskly.

'He was?'

'Yes. Information is power, darling; keep it to yourself, and you have something no-one else has. Then you can deal it out in whatever proportions you choose, to whomever you choose. Be a puppet master, pull strings, watch people jump. Only your father was rather stupid and it did him no good. Bard is extremely clever and I daresay it works for him.'

'Not for me it doesn't,' said Francesca, 'I can't stand it. Not now, now all this has happened. I feel as if I'm on a quicksand. Not knowing which way to go, which way is safe. It's horrible.'

'How bad is it, does he think? Is he going to be personally bankrupt?'

'Mummy, I don't know. He won't talk to me about it.'

'Not at all?'

'Not at all, no. You see what I mean. It's impossible for me to do anything, anything constructive or helpful. He just behaves as if there's nothing to discuss. If I try he starts shouting at me. We don't have a marriage any more, we're just two people meeting occasionally, not knowing what to say. I hate it so much.'

'Francesca,' said Rachel slowly, 'are you trying to say you think Bard is – well, is concealing something major from you?'

'Like what?' she said, her voice suddenly sharp. Sharp with fear, that Rachel had guessed what she was really afraid of. Wanting her to be the one to say it, to spell it out.

'That he's doing – done – something wrong.'

'You mean with the company? Something fraudulent?'

'Well yes, obviously that's what I mean. I didn't think he might be running around with some floosie –'

'No of course not,' said Francesca, and her voice, even to herself, sounded surprisingly steady. 'Of course I don't think that. He wouldn't. He couldn't. He may be difficult, he may be devious, but he's not dishonest. I would know, if he was, obviously. I couldn't be married to him and not know. I'm surprised at you even thinking such a thing, Mummy, really I am.'

'I didn't say I thought it,' said Rachel carefully, 'I asked if it was what you thought.'

'Well, I don't. Absolutely not. It's the last thing I meant. I trust him totally, in that way. If I didn't I'd leave him. Immediately. I'd have to.'

'Yes, of course you would,' said Rachel. 'I'm sorry, darling, I didn't mean to upset you. Really I didn't. I just felt – well, you're under a lot of strain. It helps to air things, talk them out.'

Francesca looked rather helplessly round the dining room. They were the only people in it: fortunately, she thought, given the direction their conversation had taken.

Rachel put out her hand, touched her cheek gently. 'Are you all right, darling?'

'Yes. Yes, I'm all right. Just – tired, I suppose. Sorry. And I've got a bit of a toothache. That doesn't help.'

'Do you want to go on talking about it? We don't have to.'

'Oh, God, I don't know. No, I don't think so. It's all so hopeless, you know? But he's always been the same, as far as I can make out, he's just got worse lately. Liam says –'

'Liam?'

Damn. She hadn't meant to mention him. It was the sense of security induced by the closeness restored between her and her mother, her tiredness, the long day, the bottle of wine …

'Yes. Liam,' she said with a quick smile. 'Surely you realised we were quite good friends now.'

'Darling, I realised no such thing. How did that happen? I mean I know you visited him in hospital, after the accident, I thought it was very nice of you then, but – well, he's always been so horrid to you.'

'Well, he isn't any more.' She could feel herself blushing, getting flustered. 'I met him at Channing House one evening, and we got talking and then yes, I went to visit him in hospital, a few times actually, and – well, anyway, yes, we're friends now.'

'And what does Bard have to say about this? Is he pleased? I imagine he must be.'

'Bard doesn't really know,' said Francesca, and then, realising this sounded more incriminating still: 'I mean, it never seemed worth mentioning. Talking about. And the way he's been behaving recently, you never know what might send him into a bait, he's almost pathologically hostile to Liam –'

'Francesca darling,' said Rachel lightly, 'there's no need to justify your friendship with Liam to me. Probably best for Bard to know about it, though. Whatever his reaction, it would be better to hear about it from you. Than from someone else.'

'Well, I don't know who you think he might hear about it from,' said Francesca irritably, 'and hear about what, anyway? You make it sound as if there's something sinister about it, Mummy. It's only a friendship, for God's sake.'

'Well, that's all right then,' said Rachel.

She smiled at her, the quick brilliant smile that Francesca knew meant she hadn't quite left a subject, and turned with the apparent irrelevance that was one of her trademarks to the question of whether the new curtains for her drawing room should be made with simple French pleats, or with a swagged pelmet.

In the morning they went to Mass at the convent: Rachel stood in the shafting sunlight, and looked at her two daughters – at the one, sweetly, and securely innocent, singing her heart out, unconscious of the dark fate that hung over her, and at the other standing silent, her lovely eyes ranging round the chapel, so worldly yet so insecure – and was all too conscious of the one who truly concerned her. In spite of her denials.

Barnaby and Bard had had a good trip. The sail across had been idyllic; just a sweet, fast-running wind, easily manageable, perfect for the *Lady Jack*. They reached Bard's favourite port, Sainte Vaas, by eight in the evening, had a superb meal of moules, lobster, and peaches poached in white wine, drank the best part of a bottle of wine each, and slept extremely soundly. Barnaby, waking once in the night for a pee, listened, smiling indulgently, to his father snoring, and thought that no-one would have thought he had a care in the world.

But in the morning, the wind was high. 'Be fine,' said Bard briefly, tearing into his second pain au chocolat, 'exciting, much more fun.' They set sail at around ten-thirty; two hours later they had not made a great deal of progress. Bard seemed perfectly happy, roaring out instructions, battling with the elements, but Barnaby looked at the rising and plunging sea with increasing anxiety and wished most fervently that he was safely at home in London, downing pints at the Pheasantry ... or even just downing pints ... or even just at home ... 'Pull yourself together,' roared Bard suddenly. 'Let that sheet out and bloody concentrate. Or do you want us to capsize?'

'Yes, Dad. I mean no, Dad. Sorry, Dad.' God, and there were another eight or nine hours of this at least.

They had sailed for another half hour, still only following the coast as far as Barnaby could make out, when the weather suddenly got worse. They were heading straight for a stretch of darker water, stronger wind, Barnaby knew that, recognised it with foreboding and – 'Shit,' said Bard, 'holy shit, Barnaby, for God's sake lean out, out, right back – that's better. Right, now pull on that sheet hard. Hard. Christ, bloody thing's broaching. Fucking weather, the sea's so bloody heavy behind us, that's what's doing it –'

Barnaby looked up at the great sail, straining above him, heard the wind screaming in it, felt the boat suddenly rear almost vertically beneath him, watched the sail lying now almost parallel to the water, felt he was sitting on a perilously narrow wall; felt terror, felt violently sick.

'Barnaby, concentrate. The bloody thing's going to go right over if we're not careful. Lean out further. That's right. The sail's going to get wet in a minute, then we'll be done for. Oh Christ. Christ Almighty.'

'What is it?' shouted Barnaby. 'What's wrong?'

'Mast's broken above the spreader. Look. There, see?'

He could see: it had snapped, almost at the top.

'So now what do we do?'

'So now it's almost impossible to sail. We'll just have to head back. Make for the nearest safe harbour. Sorry, Barney, but it's the only thing to do.'

Relief flooded Barnaby, violent, hot relief. 'That's OK.'

'Damn shame. But I can't risk the boat in this ... Get ready to go about.'

'Sure, Dad.'

After lunch that Sunday, Naomi sent the children next door to play and told her husband that she thought they ought to have one last stab at making their marriage work. She said she had given it a great deal of thought, and now that they were under less strain she could see things more clearly.

'We owe it to the children, and I still think it should be possible. I know I said some very harsh things to you, before you had your accident, and I'm sorry.' She added that she was still very fond of him.

Liam said he thought it might be worth trying, and that he was still very fond of her as well. He said that he had been very hurt by some of the things she had said, but he could nonetheless understand her saying them.

'And as soon as I'm back on my feet – literally – I really will carry on trying to get a job. Even if it's selling insurance.'

Naomi said she didn't think he would need to sell insurance, he was much too clever for that, and suggested they had a glass of wine to seal the pact. They drank the best part of a bottle and ended up in bed having some extremely good sex.

'Bard? Yes of course I can hear you. Where are you?'

'I'm in bloody France, that's where. Weather's awful, mast's broken. I've got to get it fixed, it may take a day or two. I probably won't be back till tomorrow afternoon at the earliest. Let everyone know, will you? I've called Marcia.'

'Yes, but if you've called her, then surely –'

'Francesca, can't you just do what I ask?'

'Yes, Bard, all right.'

'Children OK?'

'The children are fine. Thank you.'

The phone went dead. Francesca looked at her mother and smiled wearily. 'There is a God after all,' she said.

She decided to go back. She wanted to see the children 'and this tooth is giving me real gyp. I'm afraid I'll have to get it sorted.' Rachel was going to stay on at the convent for a few days: 'I need to think and to talk to Reverend Mother some more. And to be with Mary, see if I can make her understand just a little. It's difficult, I don't want to worry her or frighten her.'

Francesca, who had observed an attention span in Mary of little more than twenty seconds, didn't think this was very likely, but she didn't want to say so; Rachel was distraught enough about the situation as it was, and she didn't want to make her feel worse by arguing. Or displaying a hurtful and probably unhelpful ignorance.

'I think I'll go to Stylings tonight,' she said, 'and stay there for a few days. There's no point my being in London.'

'Well, there is if Bard wants you to be.'

'Mummy, he doesn't.'

Rachel looked at her thoughtfully. 'I wouldn't be too sure,' she said. 'He's very upset, darling, probably terrified, and he loves you very much.'

'Do you really think so?'

'I know so.'

'I wish I did,' said Francesca.

The children were both asleep when she got back to Stylings; Nanny was in her most self-righteous mood.

'We had a very nice weekend, Mrs Channing. Quiet, but not dull. Kitty has been extremely good and seems very well, as I told you, she always responds to a strict routine, and Jack and I have gathered a great many flowers which we are going to press. Once his interest is aroused in something he becomes much quieter and all that upper activity disappears.'

'Hyperactivity, Nanny, not upper. And he isn't hyperactive, he's just an ordinary lively little boy.'

'Just as you say, Mrs Channing.'

She went in to look at them both. Kitty was sound asleep, breathing sweetly and steadily, but Jack was restless; she pulled his duvet up and he opened his eyes, looked at her, smiled sleepily.

'Hallo, Mum. I missed you. Grandma all right?'

'Yes, she's fine. How are you?'

'All right. We had such a boring time, Nanny made me pick about a hundred stupid flowers and then she put them in a big book in the library to press.'

'Well, that sounds a nice idea.'

'It's stupid,' he said. 'Flowers are for growing, and being looked at, not squashed in books.'

She bent to kiss him. 'Well, thank you for being so good.'

'That's all right, Mum. Anyway, Horton gave me a driving lesson.'

'A what?' said Francesca faintly.

'On the grass cutter. I sat on his knee and drove it. We had a crash, it was great.'

'A crash?'

'Yeah, into a tree. Only a little one. But it's all right, the cutter can probably be mended.'

'Oh good. And the tree?'

'I thought we could press it,' said Jack.

Francesca checked her answering machine in London. There were very few messages; there was still silence from all but a very few friends. But there was one from Graydon Townsend. Could she call him? He thought she had his number, but just in case here it was.

Francesca thought for a bit and then dialled it. He answered it immediately.

'Graydon Townsend.' He sounded as if he was eating something.

'Mr Townsend, it's Francesca Channing. Sorry, have I interrupted your supper?'

'Oh – hallo. Thank you for ringing. No, don't worry. Only an omelette,' he said and added, as if it mattered, '*fine herbes*.'

'How nice for you,' she said, amused.

'It is, very nice. How are you?'

'Fine. Thank you. Er – if this is about what I think it's about, I really can't say anything to you at all. I'm not allowed to.'

'Not allowed to! By whom?'

'Well, obviously my husband. And my husband's lawyers.'

'Well, you have to do what lawyers tell you, of course. But I'm only ringing you on behalf of someone else. As I know you personally.'

'Who would that be?'

'Our woman's editor. She would like to do an interview, obviously we were hoping for this week's paper, but next would do. The crash from the woman's angle.'

'Mr Townsend –'

'Please call me Graydon,'

'Mr Townsend, you can't really think I'd agree to that?'

'Well – I've learnt never to think – or rather assume – anything. You never know, in this business.'

'Well, you know about me,' said Francesca firmly, 'and I have to say no. I'm sorry,' she added, 'I know you were very kind to me, about the auction, and that you were extremely kind to Kirsten, and I appreciate it, but –'

'Is Kirsten well?'

'Yes, she's fine.'

'Good. And it was a pleasure being kind to her, I do assure you.'

'And that's something else,' she added, trying to sound severe, finding it very difficult when he was so charming, so civilised, so unlike any journalist she had ever met.

'Yes?'

'My husband has discovered you went to see his mother. And he's fairly cross about it. And –'

'Your husband being fairly cross is quite something, I would imagine.'

'Well – Kirsten shouldn't have done it. Without checking with him.'

'Whyever not? I'm writing an article about politics, and Mrs Channing was kind enough to talk to me about it from her viewpoint. She's a remarkable lady, a walking, talking history book.'

'I know that,' said Francesca, 'but she's still Bard's – my husband's – mother. And things are very – delicate at the moment.'

'Yes of course. I'm sorry. But I saw her before – before things got delicate, you know.'

'I appreciate that. But just the same – I hope it is only about politics, your article.'

'I do assure you that that particular article is only about politics.'

'Good.'

'And thank you for the warning.'

'That's all right.'

'And I really can't persuade you to talk to our woman's editor? Not even try to persuade you personally, over the most delicious lunch at, where shall I say, Ceccone's?'

'Not even there. Sorry! Much as I'd love it.'

'Ah well, I have to say I'm not honestly so surprised. Give my best wishes to Kirsten, won't you? If you see her?'

'I will. Thank you. Goodbye, Mr Townsend.'

He was so nice, she thought. Good looking too. Now why couldn't Kirsten have an affair with someone like that, instead of the riff-raff she normally went around with? Graydon Townsend could do her nothing but good.

John Martin and Peter Ford of Muir Whitehead had an oddly telepathic relationship. They were slightly sheepish about it, being accountants by training and profession, with all that that implied, but they had found that in several cases in the past they had both became first intrigued and then troubled by various aspects of an investigation at roughly the same time.

And that Monday it happened again. It was not John Martin's discovery that the Channing golf complex did not seem actually to exist, despite such a large sum of money having been paid for it, nor even Peter Ford's growing awareness that the dates of some of the statements of the Channing accounts with their various bankers did not entirely line up with some of the others, and that their system for the presentation, clearing and paying of cheques into the accounts seemed more than usually complex; it was none of those things that alerted them to their anxiety; they agreed there were many perfectly reasonable, indeed highly satisfactory, explanations for all of them. It was the thud of unease they both felt, and recognised in one another, at the news that Bard Channing was not in the country that day, that he had sailed his boat across the Channel at the weekend, and clearly could, if he so wished, and thought it desirable, sail it on ever further away from them and their investigations, that made them agree over their ploughman's luncheons that the time had come for them to get him into the offices and have a little chat.

'Just to elucidate things,' said Martin, pushing his last bit of french bread round the plate in search of his final piece of pickle.

'Sure,' said Ford, draining his glass of low-alcohol lager and shaking the last crumbs of his ham and pickle crisps out of the bag and into his palm. 'On the other hand, we don't want to alarm him. Not while he's over there. Or he might decide it's all getting so uncomfortable he – well, he might not want to come back ...'

'True. Which would be very unfortunate. So on second thoughts, we'll keep things ticking over quietly. Maybe we should have a few more words with the individual managers of the banks as well. That chap at Methuens, I felt he was a little edgy. Didn't you?'

'Just a bit,' said Martin. 'Anyway, I have no doubt it can all be explained as yet another example of eccentric accounting. All these entrepreneurial chaps go in for that. What about the Scottish development though? Possible case of leapfrogging, do you think?'

'Well, let's say it does seem possible,' said Ford, 'although of course

423

we shouldn't jump to any conclusions. What's the name of the subsidiary that actually conducted the transaction?'

'Border Leisure. Haven't found it yet. But of course it's early days. Now, should we talk to Barbour, do you think? About the accounts?'

'Could do,' said Ford, 'after the banks. Get him in tomorrow, maybe, or the next day. Has Mr Channing got any other boats, do you know?'

'I'm not sure. Yes, I think he has. We'd better get a full list drawn up of all that sort of thing. Young Oliver Clarke could do that for us. Nice boy, that one.'

'Very nice. Channing obviously does a lot for the family, did you take that in?'

'I did indeed.'

The recognition that they were both speaking with this identically cheerful, if rather heavy, irony, was the next stage in the telepathic process. It was interesting, they both agreed later, that it had followed on the first rather more quickly than was usual.

'No honestly, everything's fine,' said Pete Barbour. He shifted in his seat, in an effort to ease the pain in his abdomen that seemed to have been with him ever since he could remember, intensifyng daily. 'Sorry about your boat. But really there's nothing to worry about. Well, nothing more. Nothing's happening. They still haven't even asked to talk to me. So I really don't think there's any point you rushing back. Get your boat fixed, take your time. I wish I was over there with you. What? Well, I don't think Vivienne would be too pleased about that. But thanks for the offer. Another time, maybe. What? Oh, Marcia's fine. How's young Barnaby? Good. Right oh, Bard. See you Thursday or Friday. Enjoy yourself, I would.'

Kirsten sat at her desk trying to keep her mind on her work. She wasn't having a great deal of success. She felt sick now; misery she supposed, there was no other reason why she should have felt sick today when she'd been fine yesterday. Morning sickness didn't come on that quickly. Sick and totally miserable. She just didn't know what to do. Presumably have an abortion; that was the obvious thing. She'd had two already. Physically it was no big deal. But God, they'd screwed her up: she was only just properly recovering from the last one. She knew why: it was her Catholic upbringing. No amount of logic, of intellectual reasoning, of common sense, could rid her of the dreadful guilt she endured. Abortion was murder: that was the Church's teaching. It also just happened to be true. Inside her now, growing, growing fast, was a person. At eight weeks – which was about what it was – a person with a head, a body, a brain – she should know, she'd studied the subject often enough. It was sitting there inside her, growing steadily, with its funny little curvy body, its big head, its strangely smiling face. It was safe, warm, comfortable, it trusted her; what she was going to do was drag it out, kill it, throw it away. It wasn't just that it was a mortal sin, and she would go to hell for it: it was a barbaric act, a dreadful, savage crime. It was murder.

And she wasn't sure she could face all that again. The guilt, the fear, the revulsion.

On the other hand, how could she not do it? How could she have it, look after it, bring it up? She could scarcely look after herself, let alone a baby. A child. God, she was a stupid fucking cow. How could she had been so stupid? And with Gray of all people. If only, if only it were Oliver's – that would be different. Quite different; Kirsten stopped to think, dangerously, of what might happen if the baby were Oliver's. He would be pleased, proud, happy, all the normal things. He'd want to marry her, live with her, bring it up. She could start again, be a nice person, a good person. Instead of a killer, a murderer. Even if it had been Toby's it might have been all right. She could have married Toby. They could have had a lot of laughs. He had loads of money. They could have worked something out. But Gray! OK, she liked Gray, he was very sweet, but he was – old. Old and really a bit hopeless. She'd even wondered, until that night, if he might be gay, what with the cooking and the nice house and the ridiculous fuss he made over his clothes.

Not that Oliver didn't fuss about his clothes. Thinking of Oliver again made her feel sicker. Very sick. She was going to be sick. Oh Christ. This was awful. This was absolutely awful ...

Francesca had woken up very early on Monday morning with something feeling terribly wrong somewhere inside her head. She couldn't think what it was at first, then realised it was her tooth, throbbing deeply, regularly, in time with her pulse. She touched it gently with her tongue: it stabbed violently. An abscess, it felt like: she'd have to see her dentist.

She phoned him, and he said he could fit her in at noon.

'I'm sorry,' she said to Jack, 'I just have to go to London. I've got really bad toothache.'

'You don't have to go to London,' said Jack, 'I'll do it for you. You just tie a bit of string round it and tie the other end to the doorknob, then slam the door. It's easy. That's how George's brother got his tooth out.'

Francesca was beginning to feel even that would be preferable to continuing to house the tooth in her head.

On her way to London, her mobile rang. It was Liam.

'Hallo, darling. How are you, I've missed you so all this long weekend.'

It was so nice to hear his voice, his lovely, caressing voice, she didn't even reprimand him for calling her darling. Anyway, she liked it. And it was harmless, lots of people used the word all the time, it didn't mean anything, anything at all ...

'I'm not very well,' she said, 'I've got an abscess, I think, on one of my teeth. On my way to the dentist now.'

'Oh, you poor angel. There is no pain in the world worse than that. I'm so sorry. Well, I hope your husband will be very kind to you.'

'I'm afraid he won't be,' said Francesca, 'he's in France. His boat's broken.'

'Oh really? How long will it be broken? Long enough for me to see you, to comfort you, to kiss your poor hurt face better?'

'No Liam, certainly not,' she said, laughing (while thinking how nice that would be), 'he'll be back any hour, I should think.'

'Oh, dear. Well look, phone me the minute you get out of the dentist, because I shall be worried. Otherwise I shall phone him myself, it's Mr Porter isn't it, yes I thought you'd go to him, and make sure he's taking really good care of you.'

'Yes, Liam, all right,' she said, 'I'll phone you. But –'

'Don't say it. Good luck, my darling. Be brave.'

She phoned Hamilton Terrace, to see if there was any further news of Bard. Marcia answered the phone.

'Oh, Mrs Channing, yes; I was about to leave. Mr Channing has just rung and asked me to tell you he won't be back till Thursday evening. His boat requires major repair work.'

'Oh,' said Francesca. 'Is that – I mean is there any other message? Does he want me to ring him or anything?'

'No, Mrs Channing, that was the only message.'

'Thanks,' said Francesca, and slammed the phone down. 'Damn you, Bard Channing,' she said aloud, 'damn you. Just don't bother talking to me at all in future, get Marcia to do it all.'

The dentist was very skilful, very gentle, but even the examination hurt her a lot. He said it was probably an abscess, prescribed some very strong antibiotics, and told her to come back first thing in the morning. 'I may have to take it out, if it's no better. Or open it up and drain it. All right? Now you'll need some strong painkillers as well, I'll give you some.'

She came out into the sunlight slightly hazy with pain, got into the car and sat there for a while, leaning her head against the window. She felt rather sick and very unhappy.

Her mobile suddenly rang; she picked it up. Perhaps it was Bard, phoning after all.

It wasn't Bard; it was Liam.

'Francesca? How did you get on, how is it, your poor tooth?'

'It's terrible,' said Francesca, and burst into tears.

Looking back, afterwards, she could see it was all absolutely inevitable from that moment on. That Liam should say he was going to come down to the house and look after her; that she should say he mustn't, it was quite out of the question; that he should say well he would phone Sandie, tell her to have hot-water bottles, warm milk, all ready; that she should tell him, no, he mustn't ring Sandie, it would be very foolish, very foolish indeed; that he should insist, and having rung Sandie, and spoken to Mrs Roberts, and discovered that Sandie had, of course, been given the Monday off in lieu of the Saturday she had worked in the country, had gone away in fact until Tuesday evening, discovered also from a worried Mrs Roberts that she was about to leave, and not even Barnaby was around to look after Mrs Channing; inevitable that therefore soon after Francesca arrived at the house, and was sitting in the kitchen, feeling a little better already as a result of the strong painkillers, a taxi should pull up outside and there would be a ring at the door, and Liam should be standing on the doorstep, a basket over one arm and a bunch of white roses in the other, smiling at her, tenderly, anxiously; that she should slightly feebly tell him to go away, and then allow him to come in, just for a moment, while she looked to see what was in the basket (a quarter bottle of brandy, some oil of cloves, some camomile tea, a video of *Somersby* and a copy of *Couples* – 'Liam, I don't know how you manage to remember everything I tell you.' 'It's because I care about you so much'); that she should sit down, rather shakily, on the sofa and he should make her a cup of the tea, bring it over to her saying 'Now I'm going to fill you a hot-water bottle, and you are going to lie there and watch *Somersby* while I watch over you'; that she should laugh and say no, he must go, she would watch it by herself, and could he put the roses in water, very kindly; that he should point out that they were white, not red, because although he might love her, their relationship was so pure, so sadly unconsummated that it had seemed the only colour.

427

And then she had started to laugh, and because she was rather confused, to cry again, and then he had sat down to comfort her, had held her, kissed her gently, tenderly on her hands, hair, her forehead, 'because I don't want to hurt your poor face,' and then suddenly, everything changed within her, and the pain of her tooth became part of something much more urgent, much more interesting, and all the hurt of all the rejection from Bard made her angry instead, and wonderfully, powerfully strong, and the gratitude for Liam's sweetness, his gentleness, needed to be expressed, and the only way to express it seemed to be to kiss him back; and she did, tentatively at first, then hungrily, hard, and he pushed her head back suddenly, his hands in her hair and looked at her and said only 'Francesca, I want you so much,' and she was lost.

'Not here,' she said, 'not here, in Bard's house,' and he said, white faced, his voice shaking in his urgency, 'here, yes, it has to be, here, now,' and they had gone upstairs, quickly, very quickly, and she had led him far down the corridor, away from her room, the room she shared with Bard, away from his dressing room, into the guest suite, and slammed the door, locked it and stood there, leaning against it, shaking with fear, fear and desire.

And 'Oh, God,' he said, 'Oh I love you, I love you,' and had pushed her back onto the door and begun to kiss her, as he never had before, harsh, hard, disturbing kisses, his hands moving on her breasts, pushing his body against hers. She returned those kisses, waiting for the guilt, the sense of wrong, and it did not come; she felt only hunger, a longing for him so acute it was like a great heavy pain, spreading outwards from her centre, piercing her; she closed her eyes, and heard herself moan, quite loudly, again and again.

'Oh God,' he said, 'dear God,' and pulled away from her and then they were on the bed, he tearing at her clothes, she at his, kissing, saying words that meant nothing, that meant everything, and then his naked body was against hers and she leapt quite literally within herself and cried aloud with the force of it. And he began then, and it was no sweet seduction, no tender, careful demonstration of love; it was a taking, a plunder of her body, that stunned in its violence and its speed and that she greeted in her turn with a raw, hot delight.

She felt something then, something that was not quite guilt, not quite fear, rather something extraordinary, a sense of abandonment of herself: it was not Francesca who lay on that bed in her husband's house, with her lover, with her husband's son, pushing her, forcing her with this strange harshness into a pleasure almost beyond endurance; not Francesca who welcomed the harshness, greeted, it liquefied, dissolved within herself at it; not Francesca who moulded, grew, tautened round him; not Francesca who felt the great mounting, invading surge, created with a swiftness, a savagery she had never known before; not Francesca whose body clenched and flexed and arched with pleasure; not Francesca who called and cried aloud as she came.

It was only afterwards as she lay looking at him, at peace finally with him, that she became Francesca again, and realised what she had done.

He left quite soon; she made him go. Terrifed that Sandie, Barnaby, would return, Bard even, his boat restored by some kind of swift sorcery, blown back across the sea by some fierce, malevolent wind. 'When will I see you again?' he said, and 'I don't know,' she said. 'How do you feel then?' and 'I don't know that either,' she said, and meant it. She did not know; part of her shocked, disturbed even, by what she had done, part of her joyfully, triumphantly defiant. She felt she had in some way repossessed herself and her life, ceased to be in Bard Channing's thrall; felt guilt mixed with honour, shame with an odd, awkward pride, knew that what she had done was by any standards wrong, shocking even, and felt also that by some strange perversity, it was right.

Her tooth was hurting again; she took some more painkillers and went to her own bed, fell asleep, resurfaced into the memory, lay there for a long time forcing herself to think about it, to confront what had happened. The force, the violence of Liam's lovemaking, had shocked her, even as she had enjoyed it (and been shocked that she could enjoy it); there was something close to cruelty there, oddly at variance with the man she had thought she knew. Bard, for all his toughness, his need to dominate, was most tenderly, patiently skilful in bed; he urged rather than led, took her with him, carried her into pleasure. It was very odd, odd and morally most uncomfortable to compare them; but she could not help it, it had to be done indeed, an inevitable consequence of what had happened to all three of them. And what the final consequence might be she dared not think.

Graydon Townsend and Teresa Booth had spent a long day sifting through Duggie's complex affairs; now that they knew what they were looking for, it seemed suddenly rather obvious. There was an account entitled Channing Golfing and Leisure to which he and Bard were dual signatories (as indeed they were to most of the company accounts), and which made regular payments to a wide variety of

people and organisations, including the Gleneagles Golf Club in
Scotland, the Belfry near Birmingham, the Wentworth in Surrey and
the manager of a timeshare complex on the Quinto di Largo in the
Algarve. Other beneficiaries of this wing of the company were the
owner of a ski chalet in Meribel, a house in Carmel, California, and an
apartment and mooring in Il Cuppusco, on the Costa Smerelda,
Sardinia.

'What a lot of happy planning officers. Amazing they were able to
do any work at all, spending time in all those places,' said Terri.
'Graydon, who else do you think might be involved in all this? At the
company?'

'Well, Pete Barbour without a doubt, I'd say. What Channing has
undoubtedly been doing is moving funds around all his different
accounts, as and when the need arises. You can't do that without a
very friendly financial director.'

She stared at him, clearly astonished. 'Pete! Stuffy old Pete, with his
waistcoats. I can't believe that.'

Gray laughed. 'You shouldn't be deceived by appearances. You of
all people. But I would say that's probably all. Anyway, no-one else
needed to know, they didn't have any power. And the fewer the
better, of course.'

'Yes, I suppose so. You're very up on all this, aren't you?'

'It's my trade, Terri. I've seen a lot of it.'

'So do you think the fact Bard Channing's been locked out of that
place means they're suspicious?'

'Yes of course. Raking over every tiny bank account. If there are
any tiny bank accounts.'

'Getting tinier by the minute, with luck,' said Teresa.

'Well, maybe. Is there any of that gorgeous Brie left? I could kill it
if there is.'

'Sure. Would you like me to make some soup or something?'

'No thank you,' said Gray, 'it's very sweet of you, but the cheese'll
do fine.'

He had sampled Teresa's soup; you could taste the stock cubes. He
thought wistfully and irrelevantly of Briony's watercress soup, her
speciality. Well, that was something he was unlikely to savour again.
He hauled his mind determinedly back to the Channing Corporation
and asked Teresa, not for the first itme, if she was quite sure Duggie
had had no contacts in Jersey. Not for the first time, Teresa said he
might have done, but she couldn't find any: no names in his address
books, no phone numbers, no bank accounts, no memberships of any
golf clubs.

'I reckon that's our dog that didn't bark,' said Gray. 'Anyway, I'm off there next Monday. I'm absolutely convinced I'll find what I'm looking for.'

'Which is what exactly?

'I – don't know exactly.' He was never sure how much to tell her. 'But I've got a lead of sorts, and like one of Macbeth's witches, I have a pricking in my thumbs about it.'

'Oh yeah? And what was that about a dog not barking?'

'You know, famous Sherlock Holmes story: Holmes knew who the criminal was because the dog didn't bark.'

'Oh, that one,' said Teresa, 'yes I remember. My dog's arriving next week,' she added irrelevantly, 'sweet little golden spaniel. It'll give me something to do.' She smiled at Gray. He looked at her carefully.

'You really miss Duggie, don't you?'

'Yes, I really do.'

'You sure you're not going to mind all this coming out?'

She paused, then said, 'No. Can't hurt him now. And seeing Bard Channing brought down will be pretty good therapy. Excuse me, there's the phone.'

She came back wearing her cat-got-the-cream expression.

'That was Liam Channing. He's been doing a bit of spying for me. Said he would. Apparently Channing and Clarke had a row the night Clarke was killed. And they'd been drinking. According to old Mrs Channing, he's always been very guilty about it. Now what do you think that all adds up to?'

'I'm not absolutely sure,' said Gray slowly, 'but I'll tuck it into my back tooth, as my mother used to say, and see what happens. It does happen to tie in with a theory I have. Actually. Funny chap, isn't he?'

'Who?'

'Liam Channing. I mean it's very helpful of him to share his information with us, but hardly filial behaviour.'

'He hates his father,' said Teresa briefly, 'and with good reason, I'd say. And a little bird told me that he and the saintly Mrs Channing have got the hots for one another.'

'What!' said Gray. This was one of the most extraordinary things he had ever heard.

'Yeah. She'd been visiting him in hospital and –'

'Oh Terri really! That doesn't mean a thing. She's his stepmother.'

'I know. But there's visiting and visiting. There was a little nurse there who'd obviously got the same impresson. What's more, Liam didn't make the slightest attempt to disabuse me of it.'

'How very interesting,' said Gray. 'God, I wouldn't like to be Bard Channing. He's got more enemies that I've had nicely seasoned dinners.'

He was hugely intrigued: not so much at the thought of Francesca having an affair with Liam, but at Liam encouraging people to think she was. The whole bloody family seemed more and more like the Borgias. Which reminded him, for no good reason, of Kirsten; he asked Teresa if he could phone her.

She shrugged. 'Go ahead.'

He rang her office; a nice girl on the switchboard said Kirsten had gone home early. 'She's not well. I'm sorry.'

'I'm sorry too. I'll try her at home, then.'

He rang Kirsten's number, but she didn't answer and neither did her answering machine. She was obviously between the office and home. Unlike Kirsten to be ill; she had told him her father had never allowed her to be ill as a child, and certainly not to stay off school, and it had become second nature. He wondered what the problem was. Women's stuff, probably.

Francesca woke up on Tuesday, her tooth much better. Clearly the antibiotics had worked. Her relief was intense; she wanted only to get away from the danger of being alone in London, alone in the house. As time passed, guilt and fear (of what Bard might say, might do, were he to find out) grew, mingled with something else. A longing, that was near desperation, to be in bed with Liam Channing again.

She went back to the dentist, who confirmed that the antibiotic was working, and said he wouldn't need to see her again unless the pain returned; got into her car and drove rather too fast down to Stylings. She told everyone there she didn't want to speak to anyone on the phone, apart from Bard, and devoted herself somewhat feverishly to her children.

By the end of the day, when Liam had not phoned, she felt, in spite of herself, rather bleak.

She slept badly, woke up feeling irritable. She was drinking a second rather strong coffee after endeavouring to exhaust herself with fifty lengths of the swimming pool, when her mobile rang. She had meant to turn it off and clearly hadn't: Freudian, she thought grimly to herself.

'Yes?'

'Good morning. How are you today?'

'Liam! I'm fine. Thank you.'

'Tooth better?'

'Yes. Much better, thank you.'

'Come and see me, Francesca. Please!' His voice was very serious, very intense. 'I can't think of anything else but you, making love with you. Come today, come now.'

The swiftness of the attack surprised her; she had thought he would be more circumspect.

'I can't, Liam. You know I can't. It – it mustn't happen again.'

'And I know you can. And it has to happen again.'

'Liam, no.'

'Francesca, yes.'

She was silent.

'Ah,' he said, and he was more like the old Liam now, the one she knew. 'You're weakening. I knew you would. Darling Francesca, please.'

'Don't call me darling.'

'Why not? You are my darling. And why not? In the name of heaven, why not –'

'You know why not.'

'No, Francesca,' he said, and his voice was very intense again, almost sombre. 'I don't know why not. I know no reason why not.'

'I have a husband.'

'Yes, and you don't love him.'

'I do,' she said staunchly. 'I do.'

'Oh dear,' he said, and sighed, 'we seem to be back where we were before. Only of course we're not. Are we, Francesca? Darling Francesca.'

'No,' she said quietly. 'Not quite, no.'

'Please come and see me. We need to talk. If nothing else.'

'If I thought it was nothing else,' she said, and laughed, 'I might come.'

'Very well, it will be nothing else. I swear. We will talk and talk, we're good at that after all, and see what we are to do about everything. Tell you what, let's have tea at – at Brown's Hotel today. There now. Nothing could be more innocent than that, I can hardly ravage you on the floor of their very expensive drawing room, can I? In front of a lot of old ladies eating scones.'

She hesitated. 'I'm busy today. I'm taking Jack to a gymkhana.'

'My goodness, what a hectic schedule you have. What about tomorrow, then? Providing he's not back, of course.'

'Well –'

'That's settled. My treat, don't argue. I've never bought you so much as a cup of coffee. And then you can explain exactly why we can't meet ever again, try and convince me even, and I'll explain why we can. All right? Good, see you tomorow at four.'

The team from Muir Whitehead held a formal meeting at the end of Tuesday, and agreed that having talked further to Mr North from Methuens and with Jon Bartok of the Konigstrom Bank in Stockholm – and given the small but interesting matter of the purchase of the land and property in Scotland and the apparent disappearance of the £1.75 million which the company had paid for it, not to mention the rather timely sale of a large block of shares by a charitable trust in the Dutch Antilles, there now seemed to be a clear case for calling in their forensic division.

'And meanwhile John and I'll talk to Mr Barbour,' said Peter Ford. 'He could clear up a few things for us.'

'One way or another,' said John Martin.

Pete Barbour spent two hours at Channing House on Wednesday afternoon. He had been, they agreed afterwards, extremely helpful, and had, as they had anticipated, satisfactorily answered most of their queries. He didn't look at all well; he suffered intermittently, he told them, turning away the Dundee cake they offered with tea, from a duodenal ulcer which flared up at times of stress. 'And as times go, this one is pretty stressful.'

'Yes, of course. Well, we're trying not to prolong the agony at least,' said John Martin, 'sorry, bad choice of words. How long have you worked with Mr Channing?'

'Oh – almost twelve years.'

'So you think pretty much as one?'

'I wouldn't say that,' said Pete Barbour with his rather formal smile. 'Nobody could possibly know quite how Bard Channing's mind worked.'

'But you probably better than most?'

'Well – yes. Probably.'

Late on Thursday morning, Marcia Grainger had a call from Mary Forbes, who was still working at Channing House. She said she was sorry to bother Marcia, but one of the new team that had come in were asking for more details of the Channing Charitable Foundation, and she couldn't find them in the computer files.

Marcia told her exactly where the details were, checked that Mary had them, and then asked her who the new team were. Mary said she wasn't quite sure, they were still from Muir Whitehead, but a different lot.

'They're going through everything, though, all the phone bills, faxes, everything. Poor Oliver's having a terrible time with them. But they're all very nice, I'm sure there's nothing to worry about.'

After Marcia put the phone down she decided to go and have tea at Fortnum's and perhaps do a little shopping. She was unused to leisure and finding, greatly to her surprise, that she rather liked it. As she walked down Albemarle Street and neared Brown's Hotel, she saw a taxi pull up and the tall, slightly saturnine figure of Liam Channing got rather painfully and awkwardly out and limped inside. He was obviously recovering well from his accident. She had just turned to walk back down towards the Ritz, when she saw another taxi pull up outside Brown's and Francesca Channing get out of it and hurry inside. One of her endless charity meetings, Marcia presumed. How very odd, she thought, what a strange coincidence that they should be arriving there at the same time; she hoped in the light of their well-known hostility to one another that they wouldn't find themselves at adjacent tables.

At much the same time, David Sloane, who was heading up the new forensic accountancy team, was sitting at Pete Barbour's desk, sifting through some auditors' accounts, when John Martin put his head round the door. He was holding the printout of some phone bills. 'I think we've got something here,' he said, 'look. And the dates do tally. With the sale of those shares.'

Sloane looked.

'Excellent,' he said, 'but how on earth did you get onto that so quickly?'

'Oh —' Martin tapped the side of his nose. 'It's not what you know, is it?'

Bard Channing arrived back at Chicester late on Thursday afternoon after a very satisfactorily exciting sail, tanned and more relaxed than he had looked for weeks. His car was parked at Chichester harbour; he and Barnaby drove to Stylings.

Nanny was bathing Kitty for her nap and Jack was sitting in front of the television in the breakfast room, watching *The Jungle Book*; he was joining enthusiastically in the chorus of 'King of the Swingers' when his father walked in. He flung himself into his arms.

'Dad, we thought you was in France still. Was it fun, Mum said you nearly capsized, I wish I'd been there and you really had, next time will you take me, promise, promise you will ...'

'I might,' said Bard cautiously, returning the hug. 'Where is your mother?'

'She's in London. She went this morning. She had one of her stupid meetings, and then she phoned to say she was staying up there. I want to go back though, Dad, I can drive now, can I show you?'

'Ah, Mr Channing,' said Nanny, coming in, Kitty in her arms, damply sweet, smiling radiantly at her father, 'welcome back. We weren't expecting you until tomorrow. I do hope you had a good trip. You look very much better, if I may say so. A couple of messages: we did try to contact you, but of course as you were on the boat —'

'Yes, yes, Nanny. Are they urgent?'

'Well, one did seem to be a little urgent, yes. From Mr Barbour, could you phone him at home. And also a Mr Sloane from —' she looked at her notepad, 'Muir Whitehead. He said could you ring him as soon as you get back, at Channing House. Providing it's before six. Does that make sense?'

'Yes,' said Bard, 'yes, it makes sense. Thank you, Nanny. I think I may have to go on to London tonight after all.'

'Cool,' said Barnaby.

'Can I come?' said Jack.

It was after ten when Francesca got home. The house was in darkness; she stood at the bottom of the steps, breathing deeply, trying to calm herself, praying it was as it seemed, empty; that he wasn't there.

She opened the door very quietly: no lights on anywhere, not even the landing. She listened for a long, long moment. Total silence. Not even the answering machine was bleeping. Thank God. It was going to be all right. It was all right. She kicked off her shoes, made her way very quietly up the stairs, pulling off her heavy gold earrings. They were tight; her lobes came slowly back to life, throbbing horribly. She winced.

Something suddenly shot out of the darkness, and she jumped violently; then there was a loud purring and something warm rubbed against her legs.

'Oh, Cat. For once I'm pleased to see you,' she said, and picked him up, stroked him briefly, then carried him along towards her bedroom. As she passed Bard's dressing room, she realised the door was ajar: that was odd. She knew it had been shut when she went out. Well, maybe Sandie had put some things away. But Sandie hadn't been here; it had been her afternoon off.

She pushed it open gently, cautiously, but there was no-one inside.

She must have been mistaken. Still stroking the cat, she walked towards her room; again the door was ajar. Now she knew *that* had been shut, because she had left a lot of clothes lying on her bed and hadn't wanted Cat to get on them.

She felt very frightened suddenly, could feel her heart thudding violently.

And then she heard a voice. Bard's voice. From inside her room. Talking on the telephone.

'I'll talk to you more tomorrow. You can come here, if you feel up to it,' he was saying, 'otherwise I'll come down there. What? No, no she's not here. So —'

Francesca pushed open the door. He looked up, saw her, and slammed the phone down.

'Where have you been?' he said. 'What have you been doing?'

She didn't say a word, just looked at him sitting there, on their bed, in the dim light of her reading lamp, he looked terrible, white, exhausted, slumped in a defeat even more patent than the day he had first come home, been sent home, after the crash.

And then, before she could say a word, even think what to say to him, he held out his hand, pulled her towards him. 'Sit down,' he said, 'I need to talk to you.'

Chapter Twenty-three

'So you want me to lie for you. That's what you're asking, isn't it?'

'I suppose so. Yes,' he said. Very quietly.

There was a long silence. They were in the kitchen, sitting at the table, on opposite sides, facing one another. Appropriately she thought, as if in court.

'It's a lot to ask.'

'Of course it is,' he said, 'and I hate asking you. I hate it.'

'So why –'

'There isn't any other way.'

'Bard, of course there is.'

'Well – there isn't anyone else. I couldn't ask anyone at the company. It wouldn't work. I can't ask one of the children. Or my mother. So it has to be you.'

Francesca felt intensely bewildered suddenly; if someone had asked her name, she could not have told them. She looked at Bard, who was telling her black was white that two and two made five, and she almost wanted to laugh, it was so ridiculous.

'Bard, no-one has to lie. You could tell the truth.'

'But you don't understand,' he said. 'If I tell the truth, I'm done for. Our lives will collapse. Yours, the children's, my mother's.'

'But I thought that was going to happen anyway. Everything will have to go, surely, the houses, all that sort of thing.'

'Yes, most of it probably will,' he said, 'but I'm not talking about that.'

'Well, what *are* you talking about?'

'You know what I'm talking about. I'm talking about the fact I'll be – I'll be personally done for.'

'You mean everyone will know you're a crook?'

She knew it was coarse, cruel, but she couldn't help it. What he was doing to her was cruel. She expected him to shout at her then, to start on some long tirade, some piece of self-justification, but he met her eyes very levelly.

'Yes,' he said, 'yes, that's right, they will.'

'And then?'

'Well, then, I suppose – I'll be tried.'

'For fraud?'

'Yes.'

'Would you be sent to prison?'

'Possibly. Probably. Yes. If I was found guilty.'

'Oh.'

'Think about that for a moment, Francesca. Think about what your life would become. I would be in prison. The children would have to live with that. Kitty wouldn't care, yet, of course, but she will, it will haunt her all her life. And little Jack, think how he'd suffer. And Barnaby and Tory and Kirsten, they've had enough to cope with already. And my mother. Think what it would do to her.'

'I think,' she said, 'your mother would far rather you told the truth.'

He was silent.

'So – so would I have to give evidence in court?' she said.

'Well – ultimately, yes. Though you certainly can't be forced to. As my wife, you can't be subpoenaed. And even then you're what's officially known, I believe, as an unreliable witness,' he said, and despite himself he smiled.

'So when do I have to tell this lie? First?'

'Oh – I don't know. Exactly. Some time within the next few weeks. They will be asking, I know that.'

'Because –'

'Because it's inevitable. They've already asked me if I knew about the sale of those particular shares.'

'And you said –'

'Well, obviously that I had no idea. But they're into the printouts of the phone calls and faxes. There were allusions to those. It's all rather veiled at this stage, of course. Almost coded. I must say I'm surprised –' He stopped.

'Surprised about what?'

'Oh – nothing. Doesn't matter. They're very efficient. Surprisingly so. I have to be impressed.' He smiled again, briefly.

'And who do I lie to? In the first place.'

'Well – I suppose in the first place to whoever was doing the investigation. The forensic accountants, possibly the SFO.'

'The who?'

'The Fraud Squad.'

'Oh God,' she said. In that moment, it became reality, in all its horror and ugliness. Until then it had been almost a philosophical

439

discussion, a what-if, a would-you. Now suddenly she could see it; Bard and a crime and the police and prison, and her involved by her unique ability to save him.

'Who else knows about it?' she said. 'In the company? I think I should know that.'

'Pete Barbour,' he said quietly.

'Pete? Bard, he can't be, it isn't possible, he's so –'

'Straight?' he said, and he almost smiled. 'I know. And he is, in his own strange way. But he's up to his neck in it. Same as I am.'

'Anyone else?'

'Nobody else. Nobody at all.'

'Tell me again,' she said, 'exactly what you want me to say, and how it would work.'

She felt him thinking the wrong thing; that she had said she would do it, saw his face change, relax, his eyes lighten.

'All I want you to do,' he said, 'is say I wasn't in London that day. That I was with you. In the country. Or somewhere, anywhere. That surely isn't so very much to ask.'

'So that you couldn't possibly have made that phone call? The phone call to the people, telling them to sell your shares.'

'Yes. Yes. That's right. It's as simple as that.'

'And they'd believe me, would they?'

'Yes. Of course. Well, I suppose they might want –'

'Evidence?'

'Well – you know. Nothing heavy. A diary entry, perhaps.'

'But Bard, everyone would know you weren't at Stylings that day. Nanny, Sandie, Horton –'

'Oh for Christ's sake,' he said, and banged his fist on the table violently; she jumped, stared at him, almost frightened: 'Don't look for difficulties, don't make problems. We can do it, we can find something, somewhere we could have been. If only you'll say you'll do it. Do it for me. It would mean all the difference in the world, Francesca; it would mean I could salvage something, quite a lot, go forward, start again. Otherwise, I'm done for. Out for the count.'

There was a very long silence; she sat there, waiting, listening to it, trying to think, to think straight, to find some sort of sense, some sort of answer. And she couldn't.

'You're not going to do it, are you?' he said, finally, and his voice was cold, heavily hostile. 'You're not going to help? You won't do it for me, just this one thing, you're saying no.'

'Bard, I didn't say that. I didn't say anything. I don't know. I can't think, I can't decide anything. You've got to give me time. You've got to. And you've got to tell me more. More about it, all of it.'

'I don't know what you mean,' he said, and his expression was genuinely baffled. 'I've told you everything.'

'No Bard, you haven't. You've told me about this – this phone call. About selling the shares. But nothing else. I need to know it all. Everything to do with it, everything you've done. From the beginning.'

'Oh no,' he said, 'no, that really would be very unwise.'

'Well then, the answer is most definitely no.'

'Francesca, I don't think you understand.'

'Don't say that,' she said, and she was shouting now. 'Don't, Bard, don't tell me I wouldn't understand. Because I swear to you, if you do, I shall walk out of that door and you'll never see me again. Ever. You've done this to me all through our marriage, told me I wouldn't understand, belittled me, surrounded yourself in this ridiculous mystique. I want to know everything. I want you to tell me everything. About Teresa Booth, she's involved in some way, and Nigel Clarke – there's something there, isn't there? – and –'

She stopped, frightened suddenly that she could allow herself to think, to say all these things, that she no longer had to push them away.

'Francesca,' he said, and his voice sounded quite normal suddenly, 'you really don't understand, you don't understand at all. Can't you see, I haven't told you because it's much much better that I don't. Much better that you don't know everything, or even anything at all.'

There was another very long silence; she sat there absorbing this, absorbing the fact that what he had told her was only the beginning, not the end at all. It was quite literally shocking: she felt bruised, weakened, as if he had physically hit her. Then she stood up, and moved away from him towards the door.

'Where are you going?'

'To my room,' she said. 'I need to think. I need to think very hard, about all of it. I'm sorry, Bard, but I can't possibly give you an answer. Not yet. It's too complicated.'

'Well,' he said finally, 'I can only say I would do it for you. Without hesitation. Goodnight, Francesca.'

He stood up and walked past her into the hall, up the stairs to his study; she heard the door close behind him. After a while she went upstairs herself and got into bed, and greatly to her surprise, after a while, she slept.

★

In the morning, Bard was gone. There was a note for her, outside her door, saying he would be at Pete Barbour's house all day. 'There is no great urgency, you must take your time,' he had written, and signed it simply 'Bard'.

She phoned Stylings and, knowing even as she did so the distress it would cause Jack, told Nanny not to bring the children up that day. She needed to be alone.

She felt very odd. If anyone had asked her to guess how she would feel in such a situation, she would have said she would feel distraught, or wretched, or frightened. In fact she felt none of those things. Her prime emotion at that particular moment, she discovered, was a kind of shock that Peter Barbour could be involved. Peter, with his stiff manners, his formal clothes, his old-style courtesy. The fact that it was possible, that he too could be guilty of such things, made her realise how seriously her own judgment must be at fault. Otherwise, she felt oddly calm, as if she were suspended from real life altogether. She did find herself wondering, quite seriously once or twice, if she might be dreaming; had to stop indeed, haul herself back to reality, go through the whole thing in her mind again, the whole ghastly scenario. It was strangely like watching a film, or a television programme: she watched herself with her husband, in the house that night; heard what he was saying, that he had illegally sold his own shares, to save his own skin; observed herself as she discovered she was married to a crook – she had to keep using that word, rather than the more acceptable fraudster, it helped keep her on course, not getting swept up in some romantic fantasy – learnt what she was required to do, to become an accomplice, to lie for him possibly under oath – and there it stopped. She longed for the film to go on, to watch this person making their decision, acting upon it, living with the consequences. But of course she could not.

She kept remembering all the times she had said that of course wives must know, wives of burglars, of train robbers, murderers' wives, people like Sonia Sutcliffe, that it was impossible that you could live with someone and not see, not guess what was going on; that it was impossible to believe that a wife could be so stupid, so blind, that she could not see the person she lived with could be lying, cheating, stealing, had actually discussed with her friends how extraordinarily unlikely it was that the wives involved in some of the big financial scandals had continued to think that their husbands were conducting their businesses in an entirely honest, straightforward way, that nobody could be that naive, that gullible. Now suddenly she could see exactly the truth of it: how it really was, and how it been for

442

her, which was that she had known, of course she had known, and had been at the same time quite sure that she had not, had crushed the doubts, ignored the fears, denied the terrors, had told herself it could not be, had turned her face to the wall and said no, it was impossible, that a man she had loved, slept with, borne children to, known intimately, could be at best duplicitous, and at worst dishonest. And at the root of it had been a kind of arrogance, a determination that all must be well, otherwise she had to be naive, gullible: laughably, pathetically so. She had known, of course she had known, she had seen, heard, read the evidence for herself, and while she had not understood it, had turned her back most resolutely on what it meant, had forced herself to assume that Bard's secrecy, his erratic behaviour, his often inappropriate reactions, had been symptoms of the complex, high-handed arrogant attitude towards her and indeed everybody else that she accepted as the norm.

And that had been made easier because he had never actually lied to her; she had accepted, gratefully, while pretending she did not, the lack of explanation, of information, could see it had been used deliberately to confuse, to divert her, and had allowed that because it was what she had needed it to do.

And so she was implicated; and so she must now, perhaps, accept the implication and do what he asked. The dilemma she found herself confronted with now had, through her own fault, actually existed for some time: it had merely been polarised by Bard's request. She thought sharply, wretchedly, now of the night not so very long ago, when Bard had asked her how much she loved him, and whether she would do something dishonest, something wrong for him, and how definite she had been that she would not. Now suddenly, it was reality, not a piece of idle, amusing speculation, and she felt a great deal less certain about her answer. Had he known then, she wondered, had he been thinking even then of what might be required of her, what she might do?

Her sense of isolation, strong already since the crash, seemed dreadfully increased: she was quite, quite alone in this dilemma, it was an entirely private matter, concerned only with her own conscience, affected only by her own intellect and emotions – but relevant, most dreadfully relevant, not only to herself, but to a great many others. Others, some dear to her, some less so: she tried not to think of them, knowing their influence on her decision to be dangerous and confusing, and failed. Jack, Kitty, her mother, Jess, Kirsten, Barnaby, Oliver, Melinda, Heather Clarke – all with a requirement for her to do what Bard asked, to keep him as they had always known him. She wondered what each of them would have told her to do: Jess, she knew, would have told her to say no, to tell the truth, as she would have done. But Jess did not know; and the pain she would be caused by learning of it would be immense. She could save her that. Her own mother she was less sure about; pragmatism was Rachel's creed.

The children's opinions she hardly considered, with the exception of Liam. Liam: her lover, her partner in adultery, in an almost incestuous crime. Liam who had become so central to her life within the space of days that she could no longer imagine it without him. And yet she had not thought of him for hours; she remembered him now and what he had become to her with a sense almost of shock. She found it impossible to imagine what he would counsel. He would hardly be surprised; his opinion of his father was already so low. She had left Brown's Hotel that night shattered, profoundly disturbed, both physically and emotionally; had closed the door of the room still hearing his voice, telling her she was mad in her loyalty to Bard, mad to continue to protest her love for him.

'You don't love him, I know you don't. And he doesn't deserve you.'

'Liam,' she had said, 'he's my husband, and the father of my children. And I can't leave him now.'

But if she did not do what Bard had asked, then she would have to leave him anyway.

And her dilemma was as much about her marriage as it was about anything else.

Chapter Twenty-four

Oliver had hardly ever cried. Having been told he was the man of the family from the age of three, he had always known he couldn't. Men didn't cry. Just very occasionally he had: he had cried, he couldn't help it, when the coffin had been carried out of the church at the end of the funeral service, because that had been when he felt his father had actually finally gone from him. He had cried the first Christmas morning he had woken up after his father had died, thinking of the day ahead without him (but had hidden the tears most successfully, he knew, from his mother); he had cried when his mother's wheelchair had arrived, sitting in the porch, so hideous and uncompromising, with its dreadful implied message, that she was now actually and unarguably a cripple; he had cried when she had finally had to go into the nursing home; and he had cried for some reason and to his intense shame when he had got straight As in his GCSEs because although he could phone his mother at the nursing home and tell Melinda (who burst into tears herself), it just all seemed rather bleak and empty when all his friends' fathers were clapping them on the back and shaking them by the hand and giving them drinks and buying them mountain bikes.

And he had cried (with still more shame and misery) after his first sexual experience, because it had been a disaster and although obviously he didn't think he would have told his father about it, he felt he was growing up without any proper male support, even of the most tacit nature, and – well, that had been about all really. Until that Friday morning, when he had got a letter from Kirsten, saying that she really thought it was best if they didn't see each other any more: 'or not for quite a long time, anyway,' he read in her extravagant handwriting. 'I just don't think it's going to work out, but thank you for a great time anyway. Please take someone else to Paris, don't waste the ticket! And I hope you get a really good, proper job soon. Kirsten.'

Oliver stood in the hall, the hall where Kirsten had kissed him and told him how much she liked his house, looking at the letter, reading it over and over again, trying to make sense, to find sense in it, and failing totally. In the space of one day, less than one day, they had moved abruptly from closeness to distance, warmth to coolness, ease to tension, and in the space of a week, their relationship, their warm, loving, lovely relationship, stretching before them with all its promise and delight, had been ended. How, why, where had it happened? What had he done, what had he said? It had to be his fault, he had to have offended her, hurt her, damaged things between them. He thought again of that evening, the evening she had come to the house; of the long taxi ride, laughing with her, telling her some stupid incident in the office, hearing of some equally stupid one in hers, remembered her turning to him, kissing him first tenderly, then with more passion, of her resting her head on his shoulder, slipping her hand into his, of her voice, her husky, gorgeous voice saying, 'You're so nice, Oliver, I like being with you so much.' That was the last time really, the last time they had been happy; he saw her vividly now, standing in the sitting room, the sun behind her, haloing her wild hair; saw her smiling at him, the funny, rather lopsided smile that made her face so much less beautiful, so much more desirable; remembered every tiny detail of her: she had been wearing a short white dress, her legs and arms bare, quite tanned, she was, there were even some freckles appearing on her nose – and as he stood there, concentrating so hard he felt he could summon her up in actual physical fact, he realised that he couldn't actually see very clearly, couldn't see the flowers that Melinda had put on the hall windowsill, couldn't see the letter, couldn't read the awful words any longer, even though they were written so large, and the reason was that his eyes were full of tears.

'Anyway, it was brilliant,' said Barnaby, pushing back his long blond hair, still tangled from the wind. 'Bit scary on the Sunday night, before we turned back, but we had some great meals, and a gorgeous trip back yesterday. You've got to hand it to Dad, he's one hell of a guy in a crisis.'

'Well, he certainly needs to be that at the moment,' said Kirsten irritably. She was slumped in a chair opposite him, picking at a hole in her sweater, a habit of hers when she was out of sorts. She was very pale. 'Did he say anything to you about it all? The company, I mean?'

'No, not really. Just that it was a bit tough, but he thought it would be all right in the end.'

'Well, I'm glad someone believes in him,' said Kirsten. 'Anyway, I hate sailing him with him, he's such a bully.'

'No he isn't. He just knows what he wants, there's no time for saying would you mind awfully, or excuse me please, when the boat's about to go over. Which it nearly did. And he's got a lot of guts, and I – You're awfully pale, Kirsten, you all right?'

'Yes of course I'm all right.'

'You don't look it. You look rotten.'

'Barnaby, I'm all right, OK?'

'Yes, OK. Want to come out tonight? I've had enough of the simple life for a bit, we're going clubbing.'

'No. No, I don't, thanks.'

'Going out with Mother's Boy, are you?'

'No,' said Kirsten, 'no I'm not. And just shut up about him, Barnaby, will you? He's – I'm – oh God.' And she found herself, to her huge irritation, bursting into tears.

'Hey,' he said, 'what is it, Kirsten, what's the matter?'

'Oh – I don't know. Nothing. Nothing really. It's just –'

'He hasn't chucked you, has he? Because I'll break his nasty little neck if he has.'

'No, he hasn't chucked me. I – well, I don't want to talk about it.'

'OK'. He shrugged. 'Have it your own way. But you're not looking good, Kirsten.'

'Thanks. Thanks a lot. Just fuck off, Barnaby, will you, leave me alone.'

'Yeah, OK. If you change your mind, we're meeting over at Tory's. She's coming with us tonight.'

'God. Not with that slime-bag of hers?'

'No, that's finished. She's got some other little gnome now. I really don't go for her blokes.'

'Just as well,' said Kirsten, with a ghost of a smile.

'Yuk! Don't even think about it. Anyway, you can get me there.'

'Who are you going with, anyway?' she said. 'Morag?'

'No,' he said, 'I tried her, but she seems to have decided I'm not worthy of her. Silly girl.'

'She's such a slapper anyway,' said Kirsten, 'I don't know what you ever saw in her. She ought to be stuck up her own arse.'

'I'll tell her that,' said Barnaby, grinning, 'if I see her. Bye, Kirsten.'

'Bye, Barnaby.'

After he had gone, she made herself a mug of tea and sat down, huddled into the corner of the sofa. She half wished she'd told him. It might have helped. He was unshockable, Barnaby was, and he always made her feel better. In spite of being such a nightmare in lots of ways, he had a lot of common sense: more than she did herself. Well, maybe she could tell him another time.

'I think Kirsten's in trouble,' said Barnaby cheerfully to Tory, scooping a tinful of baked beans into a microwaved jacket potato.

'What sort of trouble?'

'The usual sort.'

'What – pregnant? Oh, Barney, surely not! Not again.'

'Think so. She's gone all moody, she looks like a corpse – I just think she is.'

'I just can't believe it,' said Tory, her small pretty face distraught. 'She never learns. This is the third time. And whose is it?'

'God knows.'

'I hope it's not Oliver's.'

'Might be, I suppose. What about that berk Toby, she still seeing him?'

'No. No, they broke up ages ago. Well, at her party. I suppose that's not ages ago, actually. And there hasn't been anyone since. Except Oliver. Oh God, Barnaby, this is terrible. Dad hasn't got over the press thing yet. What can we do, how should we –'

'Easy!' said Barnaby. 'We don't know yet. I'm only guessing. And you'd better not rush over with that worried look on your face, or she'll bite your head off. But I think it's a bit likely. That's all.'

'I'm off to Jersey on Monday,' said Gray to Alan Ferrers over a glass of rather indifferent champagne – God, these City bars ripped you off – 'Got any contacts?'

'Because?'

'Well, because of those shares of Channings' which got bought there that day, by the offshore trust. That you alerted me to. Just before the crash. I've just got to crack that one. Then I'm there.'

Ferrers shook his head. 'Tough one. They're very close over there. Worried about their reputation. You'll never find it.'

'Well, I've got to try. And I'm actually quite good at finding things.'

'Yeah, I know that. Thing is, those trusts are absolutely confidential. No-one knows who's running them, they're not registered, it's real needle-in-a-haystack stuff. And anyway, it might have been a bona fide purchase. You never know.'

'Alan! You don't really think that. Half a million quid's worth at that stage in the game!'

'No, you're right, I don't. So what are you going to do, just wander

448

about asking if anyone runs a trust for Channing and if they bought some of his shares?'

'That sort of thing,' said Gray with a grin. 'No, I think I can do a bit better than that. I just need a tiny leg-up, that's all. I thought you might give it to me.'

'Well, I do have a chum there,' said Ferrers, 'as a matter of fact. I'll give him a bell. I'm sure he'll help if he can. As long as it doesn't implicate him in any way.'

'I'll try not to let it,' said Gray.

Clive Hopkins was recovering fast. He was out of Intensive Care and in a side-ward now, bored, irritable, chastising poor Maureen for bringing him cherries when he had wanted grapes – 'What am I going to do with the stones, dear, just tell me that' – his cotton dressing gown when he had particularly stressed towelling – 'It's after the shower, Maureen, I did explain most carefully why I needed the towelling one' – the new John Grisham when she knew he preferred Jeffrey Archer – 'You know I don't like American authors' – his reading glasses when he had stressed the bifocals – 'I'm being constantly interrupted, Maureen, and I need to be able to see properly without taking my glasses on and off.' And the last straw had been the *Daily Mail*, which as he pointed out to her, he would have finished by mid-afternoon, when he had said the *Telegraph*. 'Surely you can see I need a proper paper at least, if I haven't got a book to read.' Fortunately the nurse who brought in his lunch was waving a *Spectator* about, asking if anyone wanted it; although it was a little extreme in its comments at times, Clive Hopkins liked the *Spectator*, its politcial views coinciding so neatly with his own. He read the Portrait of the Week and Auberon Waugh's column and then turned to the City page, where he read, with mounting distress, an article on what the writer called the minefield of Docklands, citing the collapse of the Channing empire as the latest example.

Realising that this was clearly why Bard Channing had not responded in any way to the messages he had sent him when he had been ill – which had been, he was able now to admit, a little hurtful – he reached in his bedside table for his writing paper and envelopes and wrote Bard a note, saying how sorry he was and how he quite understood that he must have been too busy and preoccupied to respond to his earlier messages. And when Maureen arrived, bearing grapes, a towelling bathrobe, the latest Jeffrey Archer and the *Daily Telegraph*, he sent her out immediately to post it.

'Because I want it to arrive at his home tomorrow. Without fail. Poor Mr Channing, what a terrible thing.'

Maureen arrived at the letter box to see the van disapearing with the last post in it. She saw no reason to tell Clive this; it really wasn't going to make the slightest difference to Bard Channing if he got one of what were presumably hundreds of letters at the end of the weekend, rather than the beginning of it. And since he clearly wasn't nearly as interested in Clive as Clive seemed to think he was, it wouldn't matter at all.

Kirsten had phoned the surgery, as she had been told to do, and was told, as she had known she would be, that her pregnancy test was positive: just the same, on hearing the news she burst into tears and cried for a long time. And then she found herself shivering violently: she had a bath, and then climbed into bed on that hot summer evening, with a hot-water bottle and a big mug of warm milk, and fell fitfully asleep; an hour later, she woke, sweating, to hear the phone ringing. Thank God, thank God she had left the answering machine on; when it had done its work, she went to listen to it.

The message was from Oliver. 'Hallo Kirsten,' he said, 'it's me, Oliver. I just rang to say I got your letter and of course I quite understand. I'll maybe see you around.' She knew why he had rung, of course, for she knew him so well, and knew what the message had meant; he had rung on the off-chance that she would be there and he could persuade her to talk to him, to tell him what the matter was, and it must have been immensely hard for him to do that; since she was not there, clearly out enjoying herself, he was not prepared to look foolish, had dismissed her therefore with a cool, detached explanation. And standing there, listening to his light, easy voice, seeing him with horrible vividness, his heavy fair hair, his dark blue eyes fixed on hers, playing the message over and over again, touching the machine as if it could convey him physically to her, she began to cry, only this time not from shock, but from grief and as if her heart would break.

'I thought I'd go off on the boat again for the weekend,' said Bard to Francesca on Saturday morning. 'Just sail along the coast a bit. Unless you want me to be here.'

The meaning was very plain. She looked at him and said, 'No. No, that's fine. I might go and see your mother. I haven't seen her for ages.'

He looked at her, uneasy suddenly. 'Francesca, I hope –'

'Oh, for Christ's sake, Bard,' she said, her voice low with distaste, 'what do you take me for? Just go off on your boat and leave me alone.'

'Right. Well, I'll be back tomorrow night, then.'

'Fine'.

He left without another word, without even the briefest embrace. She watched him leave, still feeling absolutely nothing. She wondered when it was going to end, the nothingness. Perhaps it never would.

'You're pregnant, aren't you?' said Tory tenderly.

She had arrived at Kirsten's flat that morning to find her glassy-pale and tear-streaked; shortly afterwards she disappeared into the lavatory. Tory could hear her vomiting. When she came out she sat down, smiled at Tory sheepishly. And Tory asked the question.

'Yup. 'Fraid so.'

'Whose is it?'

'Tory, I don't want to talk about that. And I don't want you making any wild guesses either, OK?'

'All right, I won't. Does he know?'

'No,' said Kirsten briefly.

'So what are you going to do?'

'I don't know. I just don't know. I suppose have an abortion – oh, I don't know. Oh God, Tory, how could I have done it again?'

'Kirsten, I – look, how far gone is it?'

'About – about seven, eight weeks. Not that far.'

'Are you quite quite sure? That means only one period, it can't be that definite –'

'Yes, I've had tests done. But anyway, I know, I've been through it enough. I keep being sick, my boobs hurt, I keep crying.'

'It's not – Toby's, is it?'

'No it isn't Toby's. Look Tory, I said I didn't want to talk about that. Just tell me what you think I ought to do. Please.'

'Kirsten, I don't see how you can possibly have it. But I do think you ought to tell him. Whoever he is.'

'I can't,' said Kirsten wretchedly, tearing at her handkerchief. She saw Tory looking at it, stuffed it hastily up her sleeve. 'I just can't. It would be the most awful thing to do.'

'Some people would think it was awful not to,' said Tory.

'I know. But this is so complicated. You couldn't begin to understand. But I just don't know that I can face another abortion. I really don't.'

'Well, look. You have a bit of time. Don't rush into it. Talk to –'

'Yes? Who do I bloody talk to, Tory? Who do other girls talk to in this situation? Their mothers? Fat lot of good mine would be. Their best friend? You and Barnaby are my best friends. Oh shit, Tory, it's not fair, why do I have to be so fucking fertile?'

'She is pregnant,' said Tory to Barnaby on the phone much later that day, having left Kirsten asleep on the sofa. 'She told me herself. She's in a terrible state.'

'Whose is it?'

'I don't know,' said Tory slowly, 'she won't tell me. Says we're not even to try and guess. But I do think it's Oliver's, honestly. She was using a handkerchief of his this evening, it had his intials on it and when she saw me looking she stuffed it up her sleeve. But she made me promise not to tell him. Well – not him. Whoever it was.'

'I'll tell him,' said Barnaby, 'self-righteous little turd –'

'Barney, you're not to. Absolutely not to. It would be a terrible thing to do. Promise, promise me you won't.'

'Yeah all right, all right, calm down. What do you think she's going to do?'

'She doesn't know what to do. You know how screwed up she gets each time she has an abortion. I wish I could think of someone sensible to talk to about it. I mean it's no good talking to Mum –'

''Fraid not. Well, we'd better keep an eye on her. Poor old Kirsten. Bloody shame.'

'I'm just worried,' said Rachel, 'about Mary living in London. I don't know how she's going to take to it. What she'll do.'

'No, she's very much a country girl, I'm afraid. But –'

'She has to leave you, does she? I mean, she's one of the prime candidates?'

'She doesn't have to, no. But as I said, a third of them will have to go, and I'm afraid there are many others who have no families, no homes to go to. I have to keep them.'

'What about alternative homes?'

'Well, there are none in the area. In the immediate area, that is. The nearest alternatives, and the most like ourselves, are the Dunlop Trust communities; there are several of them. Mostly full, with long waiting lists. It could mean going into somewhere much less suitable, for a time, while they waited. For some, Peggy for instance, I fear it might even be a nursing home.'

'A nursing home? But they're full of old people. Peggy's only – what, in her forties?'

'I know that, Rachel. But she is quite helpless, she is doubly incontinent, she wanders unless she is watched all the time ...'

'But surely, then, she should stay here.'

'Of course she should. But not everyone can stay here. I have to make some very difficult decisions. And I thought for Mary at least, it would not be so hard.'

'No,' said Rachel, 'no, of course not. Er – might it be a nursing home for her? If – well, if she didn't have a family?'

'Hopefully not. But you see all the better places – and many of them are not nearly as good as ours – have waiting lists. I mean, there is a place in Taunton I've been talking to. It's not so bad. Go and have a look at it, if you like. You can borrow my car.'

Rachel went. She was appalled. The residents were kindly treated, but the place was in the centre of the town, there was nothing to do but walk endlessly round the shops and the small parks, and no activities apart from housework and weeding the patch of garden. There was a sewing room, but it was largely unoccupied, a few books in the dining room, and the cooks discouraged patient-participation, as they called it. Long hours were spent by most of the residents watching the television, which blared incessantly, horribly loud. She drove back, deeply upset, went and found Mary who was painstakingly sticking labels onto jars of honey.

'Mary darling, what would you think about coming to live with me?'

Mary smiled at her sweetly. 'Have you got bees?' she said. 'Bees made this honey, our bees.'

Francesca was drinking some rather nice white wine and watching television when Barnaby came in. It was a classic Saturday evening documentary on BBC2, about a tribe in West Africa, principally designed, as far as she could see, to make the people watching it feel they were in some way superior to the people watching the game shows on BBC1 and ITV and the soap opera on Channel 4. She looked rather doubtfully at Barnaby; she was very fond of him, and he made her laugh, but he was also very demanding and demands required resources. And she had no resources left, none at all.

'Hi,' he said, 'is everything all right?'

'Yes, of course it's all right,' she said, knowing why he had asked, knowing she and Bard were scarcely speaking to one another, unable to acknowledge the fact even.

'Good. I just wondered. Um – Francesca, can I talk to you? About something?'

'Oh, Barnaby, not now. I'm sorry. I'm terribly tired.'

'Oh,' he said, and for a moment he looked just like Jack, crestfallen and totally dejected. 'Oh well, never mind. Doesn't matter.'

'I'm sorry,' she said again (telling herself how easily he could turn on such performances, that it was quite possibly only a rejected cash card, a request for a loan for the evening), 'maybe another time,' and then promptly felt filled with remorse. What was the point of her struggling to make some kind of responsible, thoughtful decision for her family, and then turning her back on one of her favourite members of it? She patted the sofa beside her, smiling up at him.

'All right – come on,' she said. 'Tell your wicked stepmother.' (And oh, God, if only he knew how wicked.) 'What have you done?'

'I haven't done anything,' he said, sitting down, crossing his long legs in their ripped jeans, 'it's Kirsten.'

'Oh Barnaby. What's happened to her now?'

'Nothing. Well – oh God. This is really hard.'

'Barnaby, come on! It isn't like you to be so lost for words. Here, have a glass of wine, maybe that'll help.'

'I'm not sure I should be telling you at all. But Tory said if only we had someone sensible to talk to –'

'Tory!' said Francesca. 'Is she involved as well?'

'Only – only indirectly,' said Barnaby carefully, taking the glass. 'Go on.'

'Like I said, we wanted someone sensible to talk to. And we – well, I – thought of you.'

'I'm very flattered. Now tell me what it is. Come on, drink your wine.'

'Thanks. The thing is, Francesca – and this is terribly confidential and you're not to say anything to her. Promise?'

'I very seldom get a chance to say anything to Kirsten,' said Francesca, 'but yes, I promise.'

'Yes, well, she's – she's pregnant. Kirsten's pregnant.'

'Oh Barnaby. Not again!'

'That's what everyone says. But yes, again.'

'Oh God. Who's the father?'

'I don't know. For sure. We think we do, me and Tory, but –'

'Well, let's leave that for now. What does she want to do about it?'

'She doesn't know. The thing is, Francesca, I know she's a bit of a nightmare, and I know she's awful to you, but actually deep down she's pretty vulnerable. And very mixed up.'

'I buy the mixed up. I'm not so sure about vulnerable.'

'Well anyway. She gets so upset when she has these abortions –'

'Barnaby, anyone would get upset when they had an abortion,' said Francesca sternly. 'Unless they had a heart of steel.'

'Yes, I know, but really upset. I mean I was really worried about her last time, she was talking about taking an overdose —'

'What?'

'Yeah. Tory and I stayed with her night and day for weeks. It's the Catholic thing you see, she knows it's murder and —'

'Well —' She hesitated. She didn't want to sound critical, reactionary. 'I can see why she should feel like that, and with the Catholic doctrine thrown in —'

'Exactly. She was put on anti-depressants by the doctor, everything. And now it's happening again.'

'Yes, Barnaby, I can see that. And I can see why you're worried. But if she felt so terribly strongly about it, I can't understand how she can have let it happen again. Getting pregnant. I mean it isn't very difficult to avoid these days.'

'I know, I know. But she's — well, she really is terribly unlucky —'

'I'm afraid I don't call that unlucky,' said Francesca drily. 'I call it careless.'

'Yes, I know. And I can see why you're not too terribly sympathetic, but — well, we really are so worried about her. And she hasn't got anyone to go to, I mean Mum's useless, but if you don't feel you can help I'd understand, I mean I know she's behaved really badly, of course —'

'Look,' said Francesca, her mind entirely engaged now on this new crisis, her own briefly forgotten, 'look Barnaby, let's be a bit practical abut this. How pregnant is she?'

'Oh, about six weeks. Seven weeks at the most.'

'Right. So we do have time. And is she quite sure, had tests done and so on?'

'Yeah.'

'And what does she want to do herself?'

'She doesn't know. That's the whole point. She can't make any sort of sensible decision, because she's so fu— screwed up. And there's no-one to talk to. Only us, and her friends, and the priest of course, but he'll just tell her to have it, or she'll go to hell. Which she thinks she will anyway, because of the other two times.'

'Yes, I do see.' For the first time that she could remember, Francesca felt genuinely sorry for Kirsten. 'But the trouble is, Barnaby, I don't see how I can help. She hates me. It's not just that she won't want to talk to me about it. She *wouldn't* talk to me about it.'

'Well, that's exactly why *I'm* talking to you,' said Barnaby. The simple logic of this touched Francesca; she smiled at him.

'OK. That's sensible. Now who do you think the father is? It must be relevant. If it's someone she's really fond of, then she should talk to him. And anyway, he certainly has a right to know.'

'Do you think so?'

'Well, of course I do. It's not just her baby.'

'Yeah. Yeah, I suppose so.'

'It's not that brash Toby creature, is it? I really didn't like him, the one time I met him.'

'No. No it isn't. She did say that. For definite.'

'Is it someone she's been having a steady relationship with? Because if so, then I would have thought, given all these psychological problems of hers, then keeping it, staying with him, is an option.' Poor chap, she thought, whoever it is.

'We're not sure. How steady, I mean.'

'Or is it some one-night-stand thing? Honestly, Barnaby, I can't help her – help you – make a decision without some sort of knowledge. It's crucial. Under the circumstances. So – first bit of advice. From a sensible person –' she smiled at him – 'urge her to discuss it with the father. Whoever it is.'

'Yeah. Yeah, OK. Thanks, Francesca. I knew you'd know what to do.'

'I don't really know what to do. And whatever differences Kirsten and I may have had, I do feel very sorry for her. I don't know if you can convey that to her, tell her if she wants to talk to me she can, and I will really really not be in any way judgmental. But I'm afraid she won't want to.'

'OK. Thanks.' He smiled at her. 'Are you sure you're all right? You look terrible.'

'Thanks, Barnaby. I'm fine.'

'Good. Um – Francesca, you couldn't lend me twenty quid, I s'pose? Just till Monday ...'

She went to lunch with Jess next day; it was a mistake. She had thought, wrongly, that it would prove a distraction from her turmoil; and then she felt fiercely lonely, longing for Liam, dreading his call. As escape from the house seemed an answer, however temporary. In the event, Jess's sharp eyes, and the sense of sternly honest virtue she exuded, were making her feel worse.

'So why are the children down there?' she said, ladling chicken casserole onto Francesca's plate. 'Eat that up, you look as if you need a decent meal.'

'Oh – I thought it would be better for them. It's so difficult at the moment. Everyone's feeling the strain. And Jack's so naughty, and Bard's temper isn't exactly long at the best of times … This is delicious, Granny Jess.'

'Well, I can imagine how he's behaving. But he's a lot more patient with your two than he was with the others, you know.'

'Really?'

'Oh yes. We used to have the most terrible scenes with Barnaby and Kirsten. And Liam, of course. But then he was very, very difficult. And Isambard was under a lot of strain. Just after Marion died. Not that that excuses it, of course, I'm not saying it does. But at least I could understand it. There was a time, you know, when I took over, took Liam home with me for a while.'

'Poor Liam,' said Francesca, carefully casual, her heart, her senses thudding, beating sweetly painful at the simple fact of speaking his name. 'Yes, I know.'

'You do? Yes, well, he had a bad time. It was very hard for him. The whole thing. It explains a lot –'

'Like what?'

'Oh, his behaviour ever since. His attitude to Pattie; his attitude to you to an extent, although there is less excuse for that. And I can't say I greatly approve of the way he lives now, allows Naomi to keep him –'

'He can't help that. Can he?' Careful, Francesca; this is dangerous ground.

'Of course he can help it. If a man can't make a career work for him, he should find another one. He should have some pride.'

'But the Bar is terribly tough. You need time, and luck, and –'

'That sounds like Liam talking to me,' said Jess, looking at her rather sharply.

'Well – we were talking about it, yes. Just one day when I went to visit him in hospital. You know.'

'Yes, he told me you'd been to see him. That was very nice of you, Francesca. After the way he's treated you all this time.'

'Oh – we made it up a while ago. We've become quite good friends, I'm pleased to say. Talked quite a lot.' She felt herself flush, moved her glass from one side of her plate to the other.

'Francesca,' said Jess suddenly. 'Beware of Liam.'

'Sorry?' She was so surprised, she knocked the salt over.

'He's very charming, and I'm very fond of him. In spite of what

457

I've just said. Throw a pinch of that over your shoulder, it's unlucky to spill it. And I'm aware that yes, life has been hard on him, that Bard certainly has failed him. But he was born sorry for himself. And you're very – persuadable, I'd say, and not very happy at the moment, and he's extremely devious. Don't forget that, will you?'

Francesca was silent.

'If his mother hadn't died, if his father hadn't rejected him, he would still have found something to make a fuss about, some excuse for his failures. Naomi's had enough, if you ask me, and I can't blame her. She's kept him for years now, and it's not right.'

'But she earns so much, and –'

'Francesca, you have been listening to him. I thought so. Don't. Or take some of that salt with you next time. What Naomi earns has got nothing to do with it. He ought to have some pride. And some guts.'

'I think it takes quite a lot of guts, to stick to what you believe in,' said Francesca.

'Depends what that is,' said Jess. 'I don't call sitting around letting your wife keep you believing in anything. Except what your own vanity tells you. No, Francesca, Liam sees himself as a special case, and always has done. It's very nice of you to stick up for him, but he doesn't deserve it. I've bought Jack a present, by the way,' she said, clearly deliberately changing the subject, 'one of those transformer things. He told me all I had here was puzzles, and they were girls' things. He's right,' she added. 'This looks much more fun.'

'Granny Jess!' said Francesca, grateful for the change of direction. 'Haven't you heard of sexual conditioning?'

'Unfortunately yes,' said Jess. 'Load of rubbish. Pattie was the same, never let Barnaby have any guns to play with. He used to pull the legs off the girls' dolls, use them for guns instead.'

Francesca laughed, slightly hysterically. She felt tears suddenly stab at her eyes, turned away quickly. Jess looked at her, frowned, then said, her voice rather gruff, 'What is it, Francesca?'

'Oh – nothing,' she said, dashing her hand across her eyes, 'just a bit tired. That's all. It's difficult this, you know, with the company and Bard and everything.' She sounded cross, even to herself.

'Yes, of course it is,' said Jess. 'I realise that. And anything to do with Isambard is more difficult than it need be. But –' She frowned again. 'Is there more to it, Francesca? More than the company going down, I mean?'

'I – don't think so. No. Not really.'

There was a silence, then: 'I think there is,' said Jess, 'and I think you know there is. So does he. I'm not a fool, you know.'

'Of course you're not. But –'

'Oh, you don't have to tell me. And I know how loyal you are. But if you want to talk about it, you can. It would go no further, I promise you that.'

Francesca looked at her and longed more than anything to tell her. To get some of her tough, uncompromising views, to be told what to do. And knew, because Jess loved Bard so much, because he was her son, she could do no such thing.

'No,' she said finally, 'no, it's all right really. Everything's quite all right.'

Oliver went with Melinda to see his mother on Sunday afternoon. He didn't really want to, indeed he could hardly face it, but anything was better than being alone with his thoughts, with thoughts of Kirsten, with the phone silent. He listened to the two of them discussing the clothes in the *Next Catalogue*, wishing they would shut up, and drinking endless cups of the disgusting nursing home tea. He would never have believed anything could hurt so much.

Bard arrived back late on Sunday night; Francesca, lying in bed, heard the car pull up. She switched her light off quickly, so that she could pretend to be asleep. She really couldn't face him now. She felt no further on in her dilemma; she had nothing to tell him, she didn't want to see him.

But then she'd had nothing to tell him for what felt like a long time, and nor had she wanted to see him; and that thought alone was deeply distressing.

She heard him coming up the stairs and tensed, dreading his hand on her door-handle, his figure appearing in her doorway. But the footsteps stopped at his dressing room; she heard the door open and then close again behind him. She relaxed; but she couldn't sleep.

In the morning he was politely distant. 'I've told Nanny you'll ring her this morning, either go down there or get the children back here. I dropped in last night, Jack's missing you.'

'Yes, all right. I'll probably go down there. What are you going to do today?'

'God knows,' he said, pouring himself a cup of coffee, 'but I – oh, thanks Sandie.'

She had appeared with the post; he leafed through the thick heap of letters. 'God. Dozens of them. All commiserating, no doubt, all needing to be answered. Well, you can help with those. I – Christ, what's this?'

He had pulled a letter rather roughly out, thrown the envelope down on the table. It was a heavily deckled job, addressed in a rather uneducated hand. The postmark was Torquay.

'What is it?'

'Ssh,' he said, quite quietly, 'I'm trying to –' He sat, deathly still, reading it, and then, after a moment, looked at her across the table. 'Did you take a call?' he said, and his voice was deceptively light, easy. 'From a Maureen Hopkins? A week or so ago?'

'Oh – oh, God, yes, I did,' she said. 'Well, it was on the answering machine actually. I'm sorry, Bard, I forgot to tell you. It was just before – before the crash. You know, that Thursday? You were away, in New York I think. It didn't seem terribly important. With so much else going on, I just –'

'It didn't seem terribly important?' he said, and his voice now had the deathly quiet tone to it that preceded a violent outburst. 'Is that right? Is that what you decided?'

'Yes. I'm sorry. It was just –'

'You have no right,' he said, and the voice was rising now, 'no right at all, to decide what is important and what is not. Do you understand? It *was* important, as it happens, hugely important. How dare you make decisions about my phone calls, decide what you will and won't tell me ...'

'Bard, I didn't decide. I forgot.'

'Oh, well, that makes it perfectly all right, doesn't it? That you forgot. Christ almighty, Francesca, this is – oh, never mind.'

He turned and left the kitchen; she heard him going along the corridor to his study, heard the door slam behind him.

Five minutes later he came back. He looked very drawn, very strained. 'I've got to go out,' he said, 'I have to go and see someone.'

'Who? This – this Mr Hopkins?'

'Yes. This Mr Hopkins. As you call him. He's very ill. If you hadn't decided he wasn't important, I could have gone sooner. I may not be back until very late. Possibly even tomorrow.'

'Why, where are you going, where is he?'

'He's in hospital. In Torquay. Bit of a long journey. Still, I don't exactly have a lot to do ...'

'Bard, why on earth are you going all that way so suddenly? What's wrong, what's happened?' And then she stopped, staring at him. It was something else, something else he wasn't going to tell her. Something else wrong.

'I can't stop and have some bloody silly conversation with you

460

now,' he said, picking up his keys, 'I've got to go. And if by any chance your friend Mr Townsend should get on the phone, tell him to climb back up his own arse, would you? And that he'll be hearing from my lawyers. All right?'

'Bard,' she said, 'he's not my friend. But yes, all right.'

Graydon Townsend sat in his window seat on the first flight in to Jersey from Heathrow that morning, meditating upon two things: one, that the catering services of British Airways must be in the hands of someone with a profound dislike of and disdain for the entire travelling population, that they would offer for its sustenance at at eighty forty-five in the morning a shrinkwrapped bread roll that was at the same time stale and soggy, filled with ham, tomato and a rather too thickly sliced, over-vinegared gherkin, and coffee that seemed to have already done several hundred hours of flying time; and two, whether his hunch was going to pay off and his insistence that his editor invested upwards of £500 on a trip to back it up was really going to result in a story such as was only granted to a journalist to write once or twice in a lifetime.

Chapter Twenty-five

It was raining when Gray's plane landed; he stood in a rather long taxi queue for rather a long time and thought that if he were a paid-up visitor to Jersey he'd feel pretty much like getting back on the plane and going home again.

He checked into his hotel in the centre of St Helier (called les Deux Jardins, most inappropriately since it seemed to have at best two very small windowboxes, and which was apparently filled entirely with pensioners and Germans), trying not to succumb to a creeping depression, and then walked through the grey, small-town streets, to meet Alan Ferrers' friend Andy Beeston.

Beeston worked in the Jersey office of an accountant's called Crosland and Laing; Gray's sense of disorientation increased as he passed Kensington Place, Charing Cross, Broad Street, found large plush branches of Chase Manhattan, Coopers and Lybrand, Coutts, nestled close to boulangeries, pâtisseries and most bizarrely, an Indian restaurant called La Balti. St Helier, which he had imagined somehow to be cross between Cannes and the City of London, seemed to resemble more closely Reading overrun by seagulls. Office buildings apart, the only obvious luxury were the off-licences, which were glittering and plush, like Duty Frees. Which, he supposed, they precisely were.

Then he arrived at Crosland and Laing and found Jersey's other face. The receptionist was glossy, well dressed, efficient; Beeston was young, charming, Sloane speaking. He had booked a table at a restaurant called the Central Bistro which would have been at ease in Kensington; it was packed, and he seemed to know everybody there. Gray ordered moules, sea bass in white wine and garlic sauce, and at Beeston's suggestion a bottle of Australian Chardonnay, and felt better.

'So what are you looking for exactly?' said Beeston.

Gray looked at him over a mouthful of moules. 'Let's just say I want confirmation of the identity of someone behind a trust.'

'Based here? The trust, I mean?'

'Yes.'

'Any idea at all of the name of the trust?'

'No.'

'Or the firm that conducts its business?'

'No.'

'Is there a company that fronts it?'

'I don't know.'

Beeston grinned.

'Needles in haystacks be easy compared to that,' he said cheerfully. 'Do you know how many registered companies there are in Jersey?'

Gray said he didn't.

'Thirty-five thousand. And of course the trusts aren't registered at all. No way of tracing them whatsoever. You'll need a few years, I'd say. Still it's quite nice here, I'm sure you'll settle down.'

'How long have you lived here?'

'All my life. We mostly have. We jump ship every now and again, usually after qualifying, but then we come back. It's a bit claustrophobic, Jersey, and it's been described as eighty thousand alcoholics clinging to a rock, but it's a pretty good lifestyle. I've got a ten-minute commute, a very nice house, a boat, I pay twenty per cent flat-rate tax, and crime is virtually non-existent. What more could you ask?'

Gray thought quite a lot, but smiled politely and didn't say so.

'Now how can I help?' said Beeston. 'Any friend of Alan's and all that.'

'I don't know quite,' said Gray. 'If you were me, where would you start?'

Beeston looked at him and grinned again. 'No idea. This is a very – shall I say careful? – community. The business one, at least. We're about ten thousand strong, and we look after our own. And our clients. Hallo darling, how are you?'

A very pretty girl had come over to their table; she was tall, dark haired, well dressed in a slightly flashy, 'eighties way, in a red silk suit and just too many gold chains. She smiled at Beeston.

'I'm fine. Just had a very good lunch, bought for me by my boss. He thought I might be going to leave him.'

'And are you?'

'Probably.' She smiled again.

'Shelley, meet Graydon Townsend, journalist from London. Graydon, Shelley Balleine.'

'Hallo,' said Shelley. Her nose wrinkled up rather sweetly when she smiled, Gray noticed, and she had very pretty, small, even teeth. He smiled at her, shook her hand. It had a couple too many rings on it, but it was warm and soft and closed round his immediately. She was sexy as well as pretty.

'Welcome to Jersey. What are you doing here? Not another exposé of our tax laws and loopholes, I hope. We're getting pretty jumpy about all that.'

'No,' said Graydon, 'not exactly.'

'So?'

'Shelley, join us,' said Beeston. 'Glass of wine? Or should you get back, earn that lunch?'

'Oh, no. No rush. I'd love some wine, thanks.' She sat down next to Graydon; she smelt good. 'What are you here for, then?'

'Looking for someone behind a trust,' said Beeston. 'No idea who, what, or what it's called. Really easy. It's all right,' he added to Gray, 'Shelley is very discreet. She has to be, the way she carries on.'

'Shut up,' said Shelley mildly, slapping him gently on the shoulder. 'Sorry.'

'What's he done?' she said to Gray, looking at him curiously. 'This person?'

'Oh – not a lot. He's just interesting.'

'You'll have to do better than that,' she said, 'if you want us to help. We like a bit of excitement in our lives, don't we, Andy?'

'Well,' said Gray, cautiously, 'this person, who shall remain very nameless, has been buying a lot of shares. Through the trust.'

'Why shouldn't he?'

'No reason, except they're in his own company.'

'Uh-huh. Bit more interesting. And you know for a fact it's based here? The trust?'

'Yes.'

'Well, I should think it's almost certainly dealing through a company. Wouldn't you, Andy?'

'Probably. If it's – what shall we say, complex? – in any way. The more tortuous the chain the better.'

'Well, let's put it this way,' said Shelley, sipping her wine, looking at Gray thoughtfully through her large, melting brown eyes, 'if it isn't, you'll never find it anyway. So you'd better put your faith in that one and find the company. If you can't, you might as well go home.'

'And how do I find the company? Or rather its whereabouts.'

'Well, you go to a place called Cyril le Marquand House,' said Shelley, 'and look it up. If the company exists, it'll be there. With its registered address and directors and so on. Then all you've got to do is find out if there's a trust behind it. Which is totally privileged information. Blood out of a stone is easy by comparison.'

'Thanks,' said Gray, smiling at her. 'Well, I've obviously got a really easy time ahead. Where is this Cyril le Whatsit House?'

'Le Marquand. Right on the other side of town, I'm afraid,' said Shelley, 'take you at least five minutes to walk there. I'll come with you, point you in the right direction.'

Tricia was sitting at her desk, sorting out some data Gray had asked her to get on the Docklands, when she got a call from the Sergeant. The Sergeant manned the front reception desk at the *News on Sunday* and its sister paper the *News Daily*. He was not actually a sergeant at all, having seen his last days of active service in Suez in the 1950s as a corporal, and the limp he suffered from was not due to a war injury as he led everyone to believe, but to an altercation with a lawnmower ten years previously. The limp was also not quite as severe as it seemed (as those who had observed him playing snooker in the Pig and Whistle when he had had a few could testify), but it contributed to the widely held impression that he had been injured serving King and Country, and over the years had helped him get several jobs in several reception areas. He had been at the *News* offices now for ten years and was very popular, being respectful to the men and only mildly flirtatious with the women, not so much as to offend any feminist sensibilities, but enough to make them pleased to see him at the beginning (or indeed end) of a bad day. He had a very sure instinct with women, knowing precisely whom to address as Miss So-and-so and who by their Christian names; Tricia was definitely Christian name material.

'Mr Townsend's not up there, is he, Trish?'

'No. No, he's away.'

'For how long?'

'Oh – till about Thursday.'

'Right. Well, I'll tell the gentleman that. Or do you want to speak to him?'

'Well, who is it, Sergeant?'

'Name of Channing, Tricia. Mr Channing.'

'Ah. Well, yes, perhaps I'd better speak to him.'

She waited. A voice came on the phone; it sounded angry.

'Is Mr Townsend there?'

'Er, no.'

'Well, where is he?'

'He's away.'

'Oh really? Are you quite sure about that?'

'Yes, I'm quite sure,' said Tricia briskly. 'I'm his personal assistant and –'

'Can you tell me where it is, this trip?'

'I'm afraid I can't, no. He's on holiday.'

Gray had told her always to say that, just in case someone about whom he was writing decided to try and find him. Especially if it were a delicate matter. Which this almost certainly was.

'Well, will you just tell him to keep his rather unpleasant nose out of my affairs. He'll know what that's about. Oh and you might tell him I have some very good lawyers. He'll know what that's about as well.'

The phone went dead: Tricia looked at it and made a face.

'Charming,' she said.

Maureen Hopkins was sitting with her husband when Bard arrived. She had known he was coming because he had phoned, and she had met him once or twice over the years, but she was still so much in awe of him that she jumped up, dropping several papers and books and a bunch of grapes she had brought Clive; found herself on the verge of curtseying. She told herself she was being silly, and still made a silly little bow with her head, over his outstretched hand.

'Good morning, Mr Channing,' she said.

'Morning, Mrs Hopkins. Nice to see you. Hallo Clive, how are you?'

'Oh – not too bad. Thank you. Making progress.'

'Good. You don't look too bad.'

'No. Of course it has been very unpleasant.'

'Yes. Well, as I told Mrs Hopkins, I had no idea. I'm very sorry.'

There was a silence while Maureen scrabbled around picking up the things she had dropped, trying to think of something sensible to say.

'Maureen; you can go now,' said Clive Hopkins, 'thank you. Mr Channing and I have business to discuss.'

'Yes, dear. Of course. Er – when would you like me back?'

'Try in an hour,' said Clive Hopkins, 'but first check with Sister that Mr Channing has gone. Oh and bring me *The Times*, would you? I've been very disappointed in the *Telegraph* the last couple of days.'

Maureen said she would; she gave them an hour, but when she got back, Sister told her Mr Channing had gone.

'And I think now you should let your husband have a little sleep, Mrs Hopkins. I'm afraid his visitor tired him rather. Upset him even, I would say. Not an ideal situation at the moment.' She clearly felt it was Maureen's fault.

'Oh dear,' said Maureen. 'I'm very sorry.'

'Yes, well, another time, please ask me first. Your husband has been very ill, you know.'

'Yes, I know,' said Maureen humbly.

Marcia Grainger was waiting for Bard, as agreed, in the upstairs bar at the Savoy early that evening. She looked rather pale, but otherwise seemed quite herself.

She handed over various letters that she had typed for him while he had been away, and some documents that he had asked her for.

'Thank you, Marcia, that's very good of you. I do appreciate your doing all this for me.'

'That is entirely my pleasure, Mr Channing.'

'You're extremely fortunate,' he said wearily, 'not to have been subjected to personal experience of those people. They really are appalling.'

'I do recognise that, Mr Channing. I have heard from Mary how very – unattractive some of their behaviour has been. But I imagine they must have more or less finished by now.'

'I hope to God they have, Marcia, I really do.'

'Did you have a good trip to France? You're looking a great deal better, if I may so so.'

'Yes, thank you, it was fun,' said Bard with a sigh, 'only the mast broke, which was a bloody nuisance. Still, it gave me a bit of time over there. Took my mind off things. Bit of a long day today, though.'

'Yes, indeed. Is your friend recovering?'

'Yes, I think so,' said Bard shortly. 'Marcia, you haven't had any calls from some bloody journalist called Townsend, have you? From the *News on Sunday*?'

'No,' said Marcia, her voice heavy with distaste, 'I never speak to journalists.'

'How very wise of you,' said Bard. 'Bloody vermin, the lot of them.'

'I thought Mrs Channing was looking rather tired,' said Marcia. 'It must all be a great strain on her. Such a pity she doesn't enjoy the sailing too.'

'Yes. Yes indeed. And when did you see her?'

'On Thursday afternoon, Mr Channing. She was going into Brown's Hotel. One of her charity meetings, I would imagine.'

'I suppose so, yes. I didn't know Brown's was one of her stamping grounds. Are you sure it was her?'

'Oh quite sure, Mr Channing, yes. I particularly noticed her because just a few minutes earlier your son Liam had arrived at the same hotel. I thought what a strange coincidence it was, given that they were most unlikely to have been actually meeting there.'

'Yes,' said Bard, 'most unlikely. I don't know what the hell Liam's doing at places like Brown's. He can hardly afford a cup of tea and a wad on his earnings. Well, you must excuse me, Marcia, talking of difficult children. I have to go and visit my daughter.'

Cyril le Marquand House was a large, hideous building, all dirty-white concrete blocks and huge staring metal-case windows, which reminded Gray of some of Clive Hopkins' finer creations in Easter-hope. He went in to the Financial Services department, asked if he could do a company search.

'It costs three pounds,' said the perky-looking girl behind the counter. 'What's the company's name?'

'Oh – It's – that is, well, there are several. Actually.'

'Well, it's three pounds each time,' she said briskly. 'Look, go over to that computer there, tap in the name, get the company number, then fill in this form, here, and I'll get you the file. Easy.'

'Thanks,' said Gray, wishing it was, and tried to put himself into Bard Channing's head, and work out what name he might give a company that he just might not want to be entirely open about.

He started, although he knew it was ridiculous, with Channing; it seemed silly not to try. There were no registered companies called Channing: or Isambard: or Booth: or Barbour. There was a Douglas and there was a Grainger, but they both gave their own addresses, not that of their agents. He moved on through the company and Bard Channing's family, always favourites with these guys, there were shades of the Mafia about the whole thing: there was indeed a Francesca Financial Services, and his heart lurched, but again it was a small insurance company, and gave its own address. He tapped in Barnaby, Jack, Kirsten (which gave him an interestingly sharp pang), Rachel, tried Duncan, Brown, and even in a stroke of inspiration, he thought, Lady, in case Bard's boat might be fronting for him. He moved on to addresses; tried Hamilton, Stylings, St James's – no good. He began to run out of petty cash; the perky girl looked at him under her eyelashes …

'You're not getting far, are you? We close in five minutes. You can come back tomorrow.'

It was still raining; he went back to the hotel, had a cup of murky tea, and then went for a long walk on the beach. St Helier sea front lacked charm. It looked to him rather like Slough might have done, had it been based by the sea. There was a vast power station, a hideous fort of a castle at the end of a concrete walkway, and an endless line of boarding houses and private hotels along the esplanade. There was no other life on the beach, apart from endless rows of lugworms, which had left casts, and a rather miserable-looking dog. Gray fought down a rising panic and went back to his hotel; there was a message to ring Shelley Balleine.

'I know what this place can be like if you don't know anyone,' she said cheerfully. 'Want to have a drink? We could talk some more, I could suggest a couple of people you could talk to.'

'That'd be great,' said Gray. If Shelley Balleine had asked him at the moment to sign away all his worldly goods to her, he probably would have done.

Shelley arrived with her car. 'I thought we'd get out of St Helier,' she said. 'I'd hate you to think it was all like this.'

'I'd hate that too.'

She drove him drove along the Slough sea front, westward, towards St Brelade – 'We're going to the poshest hotel on the island.'

The poshest hotel on the island was called L'Horizon. Gray was too depressed by now to believe anywhere on Jersey could be nice, but in fact L'Horizon was a marvellous surprise, lushly decorated, facing an exquisite bay; they sat out on the terrace in an evening that was suddenly and sweetly warm, and drank Bellinis – always Gray's yardstick by which to judge a good bar – and looked at the sea. The rain had stopped and slowly, almost grudgingly, the sky eased, parted, gave up the evening sun; it slanted down onto the beach, and coloured up the sea.

'There, you see,' said Shelley, 'it's not all grockles and plastic macs. How was your afternoon?'

'Terrible,' said Gray. 'I spent almost fifty pounds in bloody useless searches. I've used up every name I can think of, and I can't see what else I can do, short of putting out a broadcast saying unless someone tells me they've worked for – well, for this bloke, I shall drown myself.'

'You'd end up drowned, I'm afraid,' said Shelley. 'No-one'd do that. People are very protective here. It's a very tight little community. But that's no reason you should give up,' she said, smiling at him. 'They're a pig, those company names, I must say.

469

We're always having to find names for them for our clients. Everything you think of is gone.'

'Who do you work for?' said Gray, realising slightly to his shame he hadn't asked her anything about herself at all.

'Oh, one of the smaller law firms. We're one of the few left in Hill Street, that's the one leading up from Royal Square. They were all here once, that was our financial district. Did you see Royal Square, about the size of a postage stamp, our equivalent of Parliament Square? Do you know, if you read palms for money on Jersey, you can be burnt as a witch? There, in Royal Square.'

'I didn't know that, no.'

'Well, you can. Strictly speaking.'

'In that case, I won't ask you to read my palm. You're much too pretty for such a fate.'

'If I did,' she said, grinning, 'I'd tell you you were going to go on a journey. If you had any sense. Back to London. I tell you, we're very good here at protecting our own. Or those who've made themselves our own. Did you know outsiders have to guarantee two hundred thousand per annum in tax for a period of five years – which means an income of a million – to qualify as residents, and even then they don't often get in?'

'I didn't, no,' said Gray. 'Let's have another Bellini.'

'Fine by me. Thanks.'

The second Bellini ordered, Gray said, 'So who did you think I might talk to? Some bent attorney?'

'Certainly not. He'd be the least likely to tell you anything. No, you'll have to box clever. One of the local journalists knows everybody, might feel slightly more like talking to you. Might just have observed your person being here. Funny old chap called Paul le Barre. Talk all evening for the price of a bottle of Bourbon. Only thing, you might not get your money's worth. You think he's actually been here, do you?'

'I don't know,' said Gray. 'I suppose these things can all be conducted by phone and fax.'

'They can, yes. But most people pop over sometimes, to sign things, talk to their lawyers. It's a nice place to spend a few days, after all. Anyway, you could ask Paul. And then there's a guy I –' she hesitated '– well, that I know, who spends a lot of time in a bar in St Helier, very very rich, got a chain of chemist's shops on the mainland, and a few here, and he just might talk to you, if I ask him very nicely, might have got a whiff of your man, if he's at all high profile ... I can't tell him you're a journalist, though.'

'No,' said Gray, 'no, don't. And best not tell your journalist chum either. I think I'm just an old friend of yours from way back, don't you? How about a would-be restaurateur and cookery writer? It's a long-term ambition of mine anyway.'

'OK, fine. Goodness, I'm enjoying all this.'

'So does he live here, this very very rich guy?'

'Oh, yes. He has the most gorgeous house on the north coast, near Bonne Nuit Bay. He's been here for about twelve years. He could afford to meet the residential requirements all right. He's called Jeffrey Tyson.'

'And you know him, do you?'

'I did. Yes.' She smiled again, a brisk smile. It told Gray everything he wanted to know, and that there was no more to be said on the subject.

'Well, it's really nice of you to be so helpful,' said Gray, smiling at her. 'Thank you. I'd like to try either of them.'

'OK, I'll see if I can fix it. Let's go for a walk on the beach, shall we?'

The tide was right out, and they walked the length of the bay. Shelley was wearing trousers and a cotton sweater; she looked much prettier than in her power clothes, Gray thought. She kicked off her shoes and paddled in the rock pools, noisily happy, like a child. It would have been irritating in anyone else — with the possible exception of Briony, he supposed — but she was so cheerful and so genuinely uninterested in the effect she was creating it seemed rather endearing.

'You married?' she said, coming back to him, taking his arm.

'No,' said Gray shortly. Endearing she might be, but he lacked the stomach and even the energy to go through even the most basic early-courtship ritual.

'I was,' she said, 'got divorced last year. I prefer it this way. I'd never get married again.'

'Why not?' said Gray, grudgingly interested.

'I like being totally independent. No-one to worry about, or please, or displease, do you know what I mean? I have a much better time this way. Who needs to belong to someone?'

'I think I do,' said Gray slowly, 'but I fucked the someone up a bit.'

'How?'

He was amazed to find himself telling her.

She seemed faintly familiar, and he suddenly realised why. She was a younger version of Terri Booth: sexy, warm, fun, uncomplicated. She was clearly that rather old-fashioned, politically incorrect creature, a good-time girl. Well, good for her, thought Gray. He got very tired of touchy women.

She listened carefully, sympathetically, then: 'Well,' she said finally, walking back onto the terrace, pulling on her shoes, 'if it's any comfort, I think you did the right thing. I mean you can't give up kids, can you, like you can a job? If you don't like it?'

'No,' said Gray. 'No, that's rather what I felt.'

'Do you fancy dinner?' she said suddenly. 'I'm free.'

Gray hesitated; he knew what that meant; dinner, and then if they both felt like it, bed. He sighed, and with some regret, and because he liked her so much, found her so attractive, said no. She was cheerfully untroubled.

'Fine. I must take you back, then, if you don't mind. Got a friend to go and see. Sort of standing arrangement. It's been nice, Gray. I've enjoyed it. I hope it's cheered you up.'

'Yes it has. Thank you. It was a very kind thought of yours.'

'Purely selfish,' she said, grinning at him. 'It's such a relief, meeting someone different. Every now and again, you just have to get away from everyone. Only you can't.'

'Why do you stay here? If you feel so shut in.'

'Oh, I feel safe,' she said simply. 'There's a lot of mileage in feeling safe, you know. You can do more in the long run, if you know exactly where you are. And who you are. Don't you think?'

'Never looked at it that way,' said Gray.

'Well, good luck,' she said, as she pulled up outside his hotel, 'and I'll see if I can fix those meetings.'

'Yes, thank you.'

'How long are you here for?'

'Well, I've allowed myself three days ...'

'Not enough,' she said. 'Three years, more like it. Bye, Gray. I'll call you tomorrow.'

He looked up at his hotel, his spirits already sinking. 'Thanks,' he said.

Kirsten wasn't very easily frightened. She did the most appallingly reckless things: caught late-night Tubes home, if she didn't have her car, walked through dark city streets, got up in the night to investigate strange sounds while Victoria cowered under her bedclothes. She had, as a child, ridden the most awkward ponies, climbed the highest trees; as she grew up she had learnt to surf on the big waves in Australia, had taken small dinghies out on rough, tough seas, had raced down unfamiliar black runs on her skis. She refused Novocaine at the dentist, dug deep into her own flesh to remove splinters, and once famously ordered a nurse to stitch up a badly cut foot, first taking out the glass, without benefit of local anaesthetic, because she said it would be so much better afterwards than waiting for it to come round. And although she was deeply disturbed and upset by her latest predicament, she was not afraid; she knew she could do what had to be done.

But she was very afraid of her father. It was not only his voice, so rough and raw and powerful, raging at her, nor the things he said, always unbearably hard, often unjust, not even his threats of violence when she had been smaller (never carried out), of deprivation emotional and social when she was older, or even his frequent statements that he was ashamed of her, that he wished her out of his life: it was the force of the emotions he engendered in her, the grief, the pain, the sheer physical terror, the nausea, the deafening thud of her own heart, the hot weakness in her stomach – and above all the sense of isolation, of loss of any sense of identity, and more than all those things, of being removed from love. She never saw his writing on an envelope without panicking, nor heard that he had called without dread; and that Monday evening as she sat in her flat, and her phone rang and it was his voice on the other end of the line – the worst voice, ice cold, heavy with rage and distaste – she closed her eyes and clenched her hands in anticipation of the misery that lay ahead.

'I want you at the house now,' he said. 'Now. Do you understand?'

'I can't come,' she said, amazed at the steadiness in her voice. 'I'm at home, I'm not well and I'm staying here.'

There was silence for a moment, then he said, 'Then I shall come there.'

'Fine,' she said, and knew he could hear the shrug in her voice, that his rage would increase. 'You do that.'

He rang off. She made herself a cup of weak tea, the only thing she could stomach at the moment, then settled down to wait for him.

He had a key; he walked in. It was a crudely arrogant thing to do, and he always did it, on the rare occasions he visited her, making it plain that it was his flat, not hers. He looked down at her with distaste; she returned his look, tried to smile.

'Hi,' she said. He ignored the greeting.

'Do you know why I'm here?'

She shrugged. 'To give me a bollocking, I suppose.'

'Don't swear.'

'You swear.'

He ignored this too. 'What's the matter with you, anyway? You look terrible.'

'Thanks.' He was obviously waiting for an answer: reluctantly she said, 'I don't know. Some bug, I suppose. I was in bed.'

'I see. Well, this won't take long, then you can go back there.'

He walked over to the window, turned round, his back to the light, so she couldn't see his face clearly; it was another trick, employed, she had read, by brainwashers. She sat looking up at him, keeping her own face as blank as she could.

'Kirsten,' he said, speaking quite quietly, 'I have often wondered if you were actually bad, or just plain stupid. I think I have finally decided today. I have to give you the benefit of the doubt. You are stupid. Painfully. Unbelievably. Dangerously. Criminally. Stupid.' The words came out slowly, with a full stop sounding between each one. 'How otherwise can you possibly imagine that after all that happened earlier this year, with you and the press, it would be acceptable for you to arrange for a journalist to come into my mother's home, and interview her? How? How can you indulge in such abysmal behaviour? How can you be so dense, so obtuse, so arrogantly cretinous? Words fail me, Kirsten, they really do.'

'They don't seem to,' she said.

'Don't answer me back.' He stood up, and she thought for a moment he was going to hit her. Then he said, 'Well. Would you like to try and explain?'

'No,' she said.

'Indeed? And why not?'

'Because there would be no point. You'd only distort any explanation I might give you, destroy it.'

'You appal me,' he said, 'you really do.'

'I can see that.'

'But it doesn't greatly trouble you. Is that right?'

She didn't answer.

'No doubt you will tell me that he's a friend, that he meant no harm. He's a financial journalist, Kirsten, and they will stop at nothing, nothing at all, to get a story. And this one, this Mr Townsend, has been doing rather a lot. He is hugely dangerous, and he has been most painstakingly collecting together a great many unpleasant facts about me, in order discredit me further. And you have helped him, by introducing him to my mother, taking him to her home –'

'What?' She was so shocked, so amazed, she forgot to be frightened.

'Dad, I don't know what you're talking about. Graydon wanted to talk to Granny Jess about politics.'

'And you believed that?'

'Yes of course I did. He did talk to her about politics anyway, she told me so.'

'Kirsten, that man is a liar. He'll tell anybody anything, I do assure you. He's inveigled himself into other people's confidence in the same way. And then found out whatever he needs to know. Have you talked to him about me?'

'No. No of course not. Don't be ridiculous.'

'Well, I hope for your sake as much as for mine that is true. I want your absolute promise you will never, ever, have anything to do with this creature, or any other of his kind, again. God in heaven, you are truly pathetic. Mindless, half witted, pathetic.'

It was that which stung her, finally, into saying it. She didn't mind, quite so much, all the rest; she had heard it before, that she appalled him, that she was cretinous, but the total diminishment of that 'pathetic' was too much.

'I am not pathetic,' she said, 'nor am I a great many of the other things you called me. I'll tell you who's pathetic, Dad; you are. Hiding behind that great company of yours, behind your staff, bullying the world. That's pathetic. Only now it's gone, your company, what'll you do? Find another hiding place, or run away, like all bullies.'

'Be careful,' he said, 'please.'

'No,' she said, 'no I won't. You are a bully, a bully and a thug.'

Then he did hit her; he stepped forward and slapped her hard, across the face. 'Apologise for that,' he said.

'No,' she said, facing him, resisting with difficulty the desire to put her hand up, to cover her cheek, 'I won't. You don't deserve any apology.' Amazingly now, she had come through the pain and the fear, felt a strong, a heady freedom and power. And knew suddenly how to hurt him: and wanted to. Wanted to very much. She looked at him, waited for a moment, savouring it, and then said, 'And instead of criticising me, and attacking me all the time, why don't you look a bit nearer home?'

'What do you mean by that?'

'Perhaps you should ask Francesca what she's been doing, visiting Liam in hospital three times a week. Ask Liam why he was at your house the other day, while you were safely in New York or Stockholm or whatever. Ask both of them about the kisses they were blowing each other on your doorstep. The champagne they were drinking from your cellar. Go on. And just get off my back and leave me alone.'

There was a very long silence. She stood there, listening to it, watching him: he was absolutely white, with two brilliant patches of colour burning high on his cheekbones. His black eyes seemed to be probing into her, she could almost feel their force.

'What the hell do you mean?' he said, his voice quite low, and then stepped forward and caught her wrist. 'Just explain yourself, or I swear to God I shall thrash you, right here, where I stand.'

'There's nothing more that I can explain,' said Kirsten, 'and you've done enough thrashing for one day. You'll have to ask them. I've told you all I know.'

He turned away from her, walked out of the room, out of her flat and probably, she thought, her life; she stood there, her eyes closed, shaking violently, half glad, half sorry at what she had done.

Barnaby let himself into Kirsten's flat whistling cheerfully; he had a good evening planned. Morag had phoned him, asked him to a party, and had indicated that she'd like to resume their relationship; on the basis of that, Barnaby felt a few pounds invested carefully before the party would probably yield considerable dividends afterwards. There were only two problems: one, that he had no money at all, and the second, that he would need to square it with Kirsten that he could bring Morag back to her flat for the night. He obviously couldn't take Morag to his father's house, and she lived with three gross blokes whom he really didn't like at all, but Kirsten could be a bit funny over his arrangements. Only a week before he'd been there, having a quiet smoke with a few friends, and playing some music quite low, and she'd come storming in, telling him to shut up and get his friends out of her flat fast. He certainly didn't want that happening when he was in bed with Morag. Or trying to get in bed with Morag.

He'd have to get something of his own sorted soon, accommodation-wise; he couldn't go on living with his father, it was ridiculous. On the other hand it was pretty cushy there, everything done for him, washing, ironing, cooking, and Francesca was always a soft touch when he needed to borrow some money. He really did intend to pay it all back one day; he liked Francesca, she was a real babe. She'd been great over the Kirsten thing, given what seemed to Barnaby some really good advice. He must tell Kirsten what she'd said, maybe even this evening before he went out …

And if he wasn't living at home, of course, he'd need some proper money, for rent and food and so on, and he really didn't fancy the thought of a job; all the things his friends did in the holidays were dire, stacking shelves at supermarkets and humping plants round garden centres, and some of them even cleaning, for God's sake. If you set that against being moderately polite to your father and turning up for meals sometimes and expressing gratitude about three times a week, it was no contest really.

Anyway, he couldn't really borrow any more money from Francesca, not after the twenty quid she'd lent him on Saturday, and the bank had refused his card the last three times he'd tried to get some cash; he'd just have to try Kirsten. She certainly didn't need much money at the moment.

He shut the door behind him, called out to her; there was no answer. Maybe she'd gone out, maybe she was feeling better. That'd be good. He was very fond of Kirsten, genuinely sorry for her in her wretched situation. And if she felt better, it'd be easier for her to make some kind of a decision.

He went into the kitchen, plugged in the kettle, switched on the radio. He was just checking the petty-cash tin, kept in one of the drawers by Kirsten for purchases of such essentials as teabags, milk and alcohol, in the hope that he might find even a small contribution towards his evening, when he heard her voice.

'Hi.'

Barnaby looked up; she was standing in the doorway, looking absolutely appalling, She was ashen-pale, even her mouth; her eyes were great dark sockets in her face, her hair was dragged back from her face. She was leaning heavily on the doorpost, as if she had no strength in her legs. She had, he realised, lost a lot of weight, her face looked thin and gaunt, her arms like sticks, even her jeans loose.

'Hi,' he said, 'you OK?'

'No. Not really. I just – oh Barney, I don't know what to do, I feel so terrible, I –'

She burst into tears, deep painful sobs. 'Hey,' he said, 'come on, it's not that bad,' and went over to her, gave her a hug, led her into the sitting room. She sat down on the sofa, still crying; he looked at her rather helplessly.

'Kirsten, what is it, has something happened, has someone upset you –'

'No,' she said, rocking backwards and forwards, her arms folded over her stomach, 'nothing's happened, well, it has, but it's me, I'm so awful, Barney, I'm so ashamed of myself, I'm such an awful, fucking bitch, God, I wish I was dead, I really really do.'

Barnaby looked at her in silence; he was no good in this sort of

477

situation. And she certainly needed someone, needed them badly. Tory would have done, but Tory was away for a couple of days. Francesca would have done, but she and Kirsten were hardly bosom friends. Who, who on earth could he get to help? Granny Jess? But she might be shocked – well, not shocked, she was unshockable, but upset – about the baby. His father? He'd been pretty good in France, but on the other hand, he did have a lot of problems, and he was still at daggers drawn with Kirsten. Their mother? All she'd do was cry as well and say she blamed herself and then use it as an excuse to get drunk. It struck Barnaby with great force suddenly that he and Kirsten – and Tory for that matter, only rather less so because she somehow needed less help, was more sensible than they were – really were rather alone in the world. It was a scary feeling.

'Look,' he said finally, 'you're not making any sense. Start at the beginning. Tell me what's happened today, at least.'

'I can't,' she said, rocking more violently still, 'I really can't, it's too bad, it's terrible, I feel so ashamed, don't ask me that, Barnaby, please.'

'Kirsten, I can't help you if you don't tell me what the matter is.'

'Nobody can help me,' she said, starting to cry again, 'nobody. Because I'm so bad, I've fucked up my whole life and other people's lives, I just think I ought to be – oh, I don't know, put away or something. Oh, God, now I'm going to be sick again.'

She ran out of the room; Barnaby turned up the radio to drown any unpleasant noises and was just thinking he might try and and get hold of Francesca when the phone rang.

It was Morag.

'Hi. You OK?'

'Yeah, thanks.'

'I mean for tonight?'

'Well, actually I'm not quite sure, now, I might –'

'Oh Barnaby, for Christ's sake.' She sounded extremely cross. 'You're not going to let me down, are you? I've turned down two other things for this evening. Well, suit yourself, I really don't care –'

'Well, I – Morag, don't go.' Barnaby had a sudden vision of her as he had last seen her, stark naked, kneeling above him in bed, her expert mouth doing unbearably exquisite things to him. It had taken quite a bit of work on Saturday, not to mention expense, to get her back. He really didn't want to waste it. Kirsten would be all right. She would be fine. She was only a bit over-emotional because of her condition. And he could be with her all the rest of the week. It was only tonight.

'No, honestly, just a bit of a problem with – with my dad. But I can sort it. Yeah. It's cool. Where do you want to meet?'

'Meet? That sounds very grown up, Barnaby. I thought we'd meet, as you put it, at the party.'

'No, I thought we could go for a drink first.'

'Oh – OK. Where?'

'Um – Covent Garden? Party's in Pimlico, isn't it?'

'Great. See you outside the Brahms and Liszt. In an hour.'

He put the phone down, waited for Kirsten's return. She came in, looking glassy pale, sat down rather uncertainly on the sofa.

'Sorry. Feel a bit better now.'

'Do you really not want to talk about it? Any of it? You see, I really think you ought to talk to –'

'Barney, I've told you, I don't want to talk about it. Not really. No point, I'm afraid. Nothing anyone can do.'

'I suppose not,' said Barnaby, grateful for the reprieve at least. 'Like a cup of tea?'

'Yes, please. That'd be great. You going out tonight?' Her voice was still shaky, but she managed a smile of sorts.

'Yeah,' he said slightly hestitantly. 'If you don't mind.'

'Of course I don't. Need some money? I can lend you a tenner.'

'Thanks,' he said, relief flooding him. She couldn't be feeling too bad if she was prepared to finance him. 'You're OK, Kirsten, you know that?'

'I'm not, I'm afraid,' she said, lying back, resting her head on the back of the sofa, 'I'm not OK at all.'

Just before he left to go and meet Morag he heard her crying again from her room. Feeling slightly ashamed of himself, he left, closing the door quietly behind him.

Melinda phoned Oliver at the office just as he was embarking on another load of photocopying and asked him if he'd like to meet her for a drink.

'It might cheer you up a bit. A few of us from work are going, just to Covent Garden. Sarah's coming, you know you liked Sarah, and Nick, and –'

'No, I won't, thanks,' said Oliver. Sarah and Nick were both workmates of Melinda's and he found them both profoundly irritating, Sarah with her capacity for giggling at everything he said, and her rather vapid prettiness, and Nick who could and did bore for England on the subject of rambling and ramblers' rights of way. 'It's very nice of you, Melinda, but I'm going to be tied up here for ages.'

'Oh. That's a shame. Because I thought then we could travel home together, I'm feeling really tired and not very well –'

'If you're feeling not very well,' said Oliver briskly, 'you shouldn't be going out drinking in Covent Garden.'

'I thought it might cheer me up,' said Melinda plaintively. 'It's only one of my headaches and it's not a lot to ask, Mum said herself she worries about me being alone on the Tube late at night –'

'Yes all right, all right,' said Oliver, 'I tell you what, I'll come and pick you up at – what shall we say, nine? You shouldn't stay out later than that anyway, if you've got a bad headache. Where are you going?'

'Oh – Tuttons, I think. If we're not there, we'll be in Rumours. Yes, all right, come at nine. That'll be nice. Then you can still have a drink with us.'

'No Melinda,' said Oliver, 'I honestly don't want to have a drink with you. I'm sorry. I'll just pick you up and we'll go home. What I'm doing at the moment isn't much fun, you know.'

'I know, that's why I thought of this, it would cheer you up.'

'Well, it wouldn't work, I'm afraid. Thank you for the kind thought anyway. Now, I'll see you at nine, OK?'

'Yes, OK,' said Melinda.

Gray hadn't had the heart to go in search of a decent meal, had settled for the hotel offering. It was dark brown lamb; he ate it because he was so hungry, drank a great deal of indifferent red wine, and found himself pacing his small, hot, claustrophobic room just after ten quite unable to sleep, sweating, with bad indigestion and, for the second time that day, a sense of feverish panic. The panic was so severe he had a urge, rare for him now, but more common in his youth, simply to run away, hide, disappear, wait for whatever problem, whatever chaos he had found himself in, to recede.

'Graydon Townsend,' he said to himself aloud, 'you're cracking up. This won't solve a thing.'

He knew he'd feel better if he went out for a walk, but he couldn't face it, so he made himself some tea (wonderfully weak at least) with the kettle and teabag that are now the mark of the indifferent hotel, the one that cannot afford room service, and settled on the bed, leaning against the cheap, lumpy pillows, trying to think positively. This was a tough one. He hadn't, stupidly, realised how hard it would be, had imagined Jersey would be more forthcoming. In the Cayman Islands, for instance, all the lawyers running offshore companies of various kinds were situated, neatly convenient, in a long line all down one street; it was almost folksy, you had only to get into the offices to start snooping. He cursed Guthrie for not letting him go there. Here, he could clearly snoop for a year and not begin to get anywhere. He knew, he knew Ferrers was right, that Channing had been dealing in his own shares, propping them up, that two pukka, half-million-pound share purchases by anyone else at that point in the game just wouldn't have happened, it was too much of a fairy story, too good, for Channing, to be true. They had been bought here, for Channing, through that trust; he knew it, all he had to do was prove it. But how, for God's sake? How did you find even the registered address of a company whose name you did not know, which could be anything, any word in the dictionary, Alpha to Omega, beginning to end; it was impossible. He sat there, drinking tea, doodling, trying the old trick of forcing thoughts out; wrote down the words Bard Channing over and over again, pushing his pen into the paper. It didn't do any good. The pain in his chest was worse, he felt claustrophobic, almost frightened by it; to distract himself he picked up the *Times* crossword, started trying to do it. He was hopeless at crosswords, always had been; Briony used to tease him about it, say he was always so fussy about words, about their proper meaning, using them right, he should be able to play all sorts of complicated games with them. But two clues was about all he could ever manage and certainly all he could manage that night; there were endless anagrams after that and anagrams always seemed to him to be the most pointless of exercises: words that bore no relation to other words, either in sense or structure. What kind of schmuck would know what 'Easy for example, involving MD in mishap' meant? He lay back crossly on his pillows staring at the paper and then at the words Bard Channing; and suddenly, suddenly he sat up, grabbed the pen and started playing with letters.

'Francesca? It's Liam. You OK?'

She had been longing to hear his voice: she was longing for him in every way. She had never felt like this before, this physical craving; she wondered if it was how an alcoholic, an addict felt. All she wanted was to be in bed with him again, experiencing him, experiencing the strangeness, the raw, relentless force of him. And yet, even as she wanted it, she was afraid of it, this strange addiction; it had a darkness, a threatening quality to it that she couldn't understand, did not recognise.

'Francesca? Darling, are you all right?'

'What? Oh yes. Yes, I think so.'

'You sound very odd. What's the the matter?'

'Oh – nothing really.'

'I can tell there is.'

'No honestly. Well, life's rather – confusing at the moment. Obviously.'

'Yes, of course. Is he back?'

'Well, he is, but –'

'But what? Is he there, in the house?'

'Not yet. It's not that. It's just all so complicated.'

' "Complicated?" In what sort of way?'

'Liam, I'm sorry, but I can't talk now.'

'Why?'

'I just can't,' she said wearily. 'That's all. It's quite late, and I'm desperately tired.'

'I miss you so much,' he said. 'I just want to be with you, all the time, now that I – well, now. It was good, wasn't it, Francesca? So good?'

'Yes,' she said quietly, her body churning again at the memory. 'Yes, it was. Liam –' She had been going to ask to see him next day, had stopped somehow, determined to keep herself, the whole thing in check, until at least she knew what she was going to do about Bard.

'What? What were you going to say?'

'Oh – nothing. How's Naomi? Is she back?'

'Back?'

'Yes, back. I thought she'd been away.'

'Oh – oh, yes. Yes, she's back. I only hesitated because I hardly notice the difference. She never talks to me, she's never here for meals even, I mean she's still out now and it's – well, what is the time? God, half-past eight, well, you see what I mean. I might as well be living completely alone.'

'Oh Liam. I'm so sorry. Well, it's much the same for me at the moment. If that's any comfort to you.'

'Not much. I suppose there's no point trying to persuade you to meet me tomorrow.'

'No,' she said, forcing the words out, knowing if she agreed she was lost, that each meeting was more dangerous than the last. 'No point at all. Now look, I'd better go. I'll – well, I'll call you in a day or two.'

'All right. But please, I want you to know, if you really need me, I'm here for you, any time. Any time at all. Just pick up the phone and –'

'Yes, Liam, all right. Bye now.'

'Goodbye, Francesca darling. I love you.'

She put the phone down, sat feeling very shaken. It was very dangerous talking to Liam on the phone. He had this ability to reach out to her, to make her feel he was there, with her, comforting her, touching her even: it was the voice, of course, the beautiful, emotive, persuasive voice. And just for a moment, a terrible, overwhelming moment, she had wanted to tell him. Well, not exactly tell him, but talk about her dilemma: in the vaguest possible way, obviously. She needed to talk to someone quite badly now; she was beginning to feel she was going mad, the whole thing going round and round physically inside her head, battering ceaselessly against her brain, unable to get out, tormenting her with its presence until she made her decision. It was horrible, awful.

Her phone rang again suddenly. 'Francesca? It's Bard.'

She was surprised to hear his voice: she had assumed he was still in Devon. 'Bard!' she said now. 'Hallo. How are —'

'I'm on my way home,' he said. 'I'll be about half an hour. Please be there when I get back, I want to talk to you.'

He sounded odd: strange, harsh, almost threatening. A shoot of unease uncurled within Francesca, a dart of panic; she put down the phone, stood staring at it taking deep breaths, her heart-of-the-night fears surfacing sharply, vividly, into daytime and reality. Then she told herself she was being ridiculous, that there was nothing to be fearful of, that he probably wanted to talk to her again about what he had asked, and went to her dressing table and brushed her hair. It looked terrible, she thought absently; it needed cutting. But that seemed, like everything else, totally inappropriate at the moment.

It wasn't going very well; Barnaby was beginning to feel depressed. Morag was in a ridiculous mood, terribly hyper; she had been drinking even before they met, and she was talking endlessly about absolutely nothing. He thought she had probably had something else as well as alcohol; her dark eyes had a brilliant, slightly glazed look, and she kept lighting cigarettes and stubbing them out after a few puffs. As Barnaby had bought them, he found this extremely irritating. She was wearing a denim shirt, which was hardly buttoned up at all, and a long black linen skirt with a slit up each side of it, and if she wasn't busy thrusting both her legs out of one slit, she was rearranging them and the skirt and pushing them out of the other. She kept spotting people she knew on the other side of the wine bar and rushing over to them, or shouting and waving at them, and in between she sat, half listening to him, fiddling with her nails and blowing smoke into his face.

They were in a small bar called Backstage, just off Bow Street, near the Opera House; it was very busy for a Monday night, very hot. Barnaby who had already spent the whole of the tenner Kirsten had lent him and six pounds he had found in change in a jacket pocket of hers, was about to suggest to Morag that they moved on to the party when she leapt up with a cry of pleasure and flung herself at a tall man with very little chin and pale blue eyes, with cries of 'Jimbo'. He looked at her rather uncertainly, and hugged her briefly back.

'Jimbo, how lovely. Come and join us, who are you with?'

Jimbo said he wasn't with anyone, just having a quickie on the way home.

'Then you must have it with us. Barnaby, this is James Dunsley-Thompson. Known to all as Jimbo. Jimbo, Barnaby Channing. Not known to many of us, actually.' She laughed loudly at her own joke. 'Barnaby, why don't we have a bottle of champagne, I feel like celebrating. I haven't seen Jimbo for ages, have I, not since that foul ball in Glos. Hey –' she called a waiter, 'can we have a bottle of champagne.'

'Well I –'

'Oh now look, Morag, not on my account, in fact my account wouldn't stand it –' Jimbo laughed loudly at this, a high, braying laugh.

'Oh don't be silly,' said Morag, 'it's on us, isn't it, Barnaby?'

'Er – well –'

'Oh Barnaby, don't be such a pillock. Even if your father has gone bust, he must still have a few millions stashed away.'

'I say, your father's not Bard Channing, is he?' said Jimbo.

'Yes,' said Barnaby shortly.

'Damn shame.'

The champagne arrived; it wasn't even cold. Barnaby watched miserably while Morag poured it.

'We're going to a party, why don't you come? At Sue Birkhead's, you know her, don't you –'

'Oh, no, not tonight, Josephine. As they say. Got to catch up on my kip. Heavy weekend.'

'Jimbo, you're such a party animal. Go on, do come, it'll be fun.'

'Oh – oh, all right.' He grinned at her, pushed back his mouse-coloured hair. Great, thought Barnaby; fucking great.

'Barnaby! Hi! How lovely to see you!'

Jesus Christ. It was Melinda. Melinda Clarke, accompanied by two of the nerdiest-looking nerds Barnaby had ever seen.

'Are you sitting here? Can we join you? Thanks.'

There was a silence while Morag and Jimbo studied the new arrivals and Jimbo smiled politely. Nobody said anything.

'Hi,' said Morag finally. 'Friends of yours, Barnaby?'

'Well, a bit more than that,' said Melinda, 'actually. Barnaby is my – what would you say you were, Barnaby?'

Barnaby was silent, shrugged helplessly.

'We sort of grew up together,' said Melinda. 'My father was his father's partner, and –'

'Was?' said Morag icily. 'What happened?'

'He died,' said Melinda.

'Oh,' said Morag, 'how sad.' She could have said 'how funny', for all the sympathy or emotion she put into it. Melinda looked abashed just for a moment, then smiled at her determinedly and turned to Barnaby again.

'Can we get you a drink, Barnaby?'

'No, I'm fine thanks. We're just going. Aren't we, Morag?'

Morag looked at him coldly. 'Yes, I suppose so.'

'Oh, well, that's a shame,' said Melinda. 'Oliver's coming along in a minute. Well, I hope he is. I hope he can find us. I said Rumours but it's packed, I left a message for him, with the barman, you know, he was very nice but –'

'And who is Oliver?' said Morag. 'Another friend?'

'No, my brother. He –'

'Don't tell me, another blood brother for Barnaby. How sweet.'

'Yes, he works for Mr Channing. My brother does.'

'Not much longer, I shouldn't imagine,' said Morag. 'Look, Barnaby, are we going to this party or not?'

'Oliver! Hi!' Melinda was standing up, waving frantically at Oliver, who was standing uncertainly in the doorway.

'Christ,' said Morag under her breath. 'Barnaby, we'll wait for you outside, OK? Can you settle the bill? Bye,' she said to Melinda, 'really nice to have met you. Come on, Jimbo, let's get some air.'

Barnaby was left, sweating, with a bill for £62. He wanted to run after them, haul Morag back in, make her pay, but his pride wouldn't let him. He knew his card would be refused; he'd just have to hope they'd take a cheque. He walked up to the bar, got his chequebook out with more confidence than he felt, wrote the cheque, adding a fiver for a tip, in the hope it would soften up the staff.

'Thank you, sir. Could I have your card, sir?'

'Oh God,' said Barnaby, making a great play of going through his pockets, 'I don't seem to have got it. How awfully stupid of me. I – but you can you still take that cheque, can't you ... ?'

'Sorry, sir, no I can't. We could take Visa or Access ...'

'No. Sorry. Left those behind as well.' In his father's office, long ago, when he had cut them both ostentatiously in half after discovering Barnaby had run up five grand on each of them.

'Well, I'm sorry, sir, I can't take this without a card. Could one of your friends –' He gestured towards the table. They were all watching. Barnaby, feeling sick, worked his way out of the bar, found Morag and Jimbo. They were already sitting in a taxi.

'Oh at last, Barnaby, I thought you'd never come.'

'I'm awfully sorry, but they won't take my cheque. I've left my card behind. Can you help?'

'Oh Barnaby, honestly. You're so hopeless,' said Morag, looking at him with acute distaste.

'Here,' said Jimbo, pulling a fifty-pound note out of his wallet, 'will this help?'

'Oh – yes. Cheers. Won't be a minute.'

'Look,' said Morag, 'we've been waiting ages. This guy's getting very impatient. If we're gone when you get out, just follow us on to the party, OK?'

'Morag, he'll wait,' said Jimbo. He was clearly embarrassed.

'Not much longer I won't,' said the cabbie. 'Bow Street station's just there, and I've been causing jams here for the last five minutes, thanks to you lot.'

'Well, can't you drive round the block or something?' said Barnaby.

'Big block, this one. Cost you at least another quid.'

'Oh for heaven's sake, then just go on,' said Barnaby, finally losing his temper. 'I'll catch up with you guys there.'

He'd have to get a bus; even with the fifty quid, he'd have hardly any change. Great.

'Fine,' called Morag as the cab pulled away, 'see you there.'

Barnaby walked slowly back into the bar. He felt very angry. Angry with Morag, angry with Jimbo, but most of all with Melinda, who was sitting at the table talking animatedly to her friends. Oliver was beside her; he always looked so fucking smug, thought Barnaby. Tight-arsed little nerd. God, he disliked him. He nodded to him coldly.

'Barnaby, come and join us,' said Melinda. 'I hope we didn't drive your friends away.'

Barnaby finished Morag's glass of champagne, poured himself what was left in the bottle. It had all suddenly gone to his head; he felt very light headed and odd.

'You did, actually,' he said, and didn't smile.

'Oh,' said Melinda. She looked very hurt: like a kicked puppy, Barnaby thought.

'Barnaby,' said Oliver, quite pleasantly, 'please apologise to Melinda for that.'

'Sorry,' said Barnaby, and belched loudly. He knew he was behaving appallingly, being a brat, but he couldn't help it.

'Oh it's all right,' said Melinda. 'I'm afraid we did barge in a bit.'

'Yes, you did,' said Barnaby, and belched again.

'Barnaby, I think you'd better go home,' said Oliver, still pleasantly. 'Shall I get you a cab?'

He stood up, looking, Barnaby thought, like some model for Burtons or something, all neat and well groomed, and utterly, totally naff. Bloody Oliver, with his good degree and his accountancy qualifications and his bloody perfect manners, Oliver the poor relation, who'd wheedled his way into a job at his father's office, telling him, Barnaby, what he ought and ought not to do. And this was the person who'd got his sister pregnant.

Barnaby had a sudden vision of Kirsten as he'd last seen her; ashen, gaunt, leaning on the doorpost; remembered hearing her crying as he shut the door, and felt a wave of violent, white-hot anger.

'Don't you tell me what to do, you little turd,' he said, pushing him down in the chair again.

'I'm sorry?' said Oliver. He still spoke pleasantly, but his eyes had suddenly gone much darker: like his father's, Barnaby thought irrelevantly, when he was about to lose his temper.

'I said don't tell me what to do. And maybe you ought to look to your own behaviour before you start making bloody judgments on other people.'

'Perhaps you'd like to tell me what on earth you're talking about,' said Oliver.

Barnaby did.

Chapter Twenty-six

Francesca heard the front door slam, heard Bard on the stairs, waited, her heart pounding, telling herself over and over again to be calm, not to allow him to frighten her; but as soon as he walked in, shut the door heavily behind him, she knew she was very frightened indeed. His face was white, and in his forehead the pulse throbbed, and the set of his jaw was so harsh, the expression in his eyes so brilliantly angry, she found it hard to face him, to meet his eyes, not to look away.

'Hallo,' she said, trying to sound normal. 'Good day?'

'Fucking filthy day,' he said, 'thanks to you.'

'Me! What have I got to do with your day? I haven't seen you or been near you.'

'Well, who have you been near, Francesca? Perhaps you'd like to tell me that. Or wouldn't you want me to know?'

'Bard,' she said, consciously taking deep breaths, struggling to sound as level, as normal as possible, 'I really don't know what you're talking about.'

'Is that so? I'm afraid I find that rather hard to believe. Perhaps I'd better give you a few clues. Have you seen my son Liam today?'

'No,' she said, her voice so low she could hardly hear it herself. 'No, I haven't.'

'You haven't had him here, drunk some champagne with him, given him a few kisses perhaps? Gone to bed with him, even?'

'No,' she said, 'no, of course not.'

'Well, would you say that was even a possibility?'

She was silent. Trying desperately to think what to say, how to deal with him, the best way to get through the situation.

'Francesca, look at me. Have you or have you not been having an affair with Liam?'

Still she was silent.

'I don't think I need ask any more, then, do I?' he said. 'Do I, Francesca?'

'No,' she said, her voice even lower.

He was silent then; looking at her, an expression on his face of such shock, such absolute dislike, she had to look away.

'How could you have done such a thing?' he said finally. 'Slept with my own son? It's incestuous. It's disgusting, Francesca. You disgust me.'

'I'm – sorry. Very sorry that you should feel like that.'

'Oh indeed? Sorry? And how would you expect me to feel? Would you think I might understand? Pat you on the head, tell you it was quite all right, if it was what you both wanted? For Christ's sake. Use your fucking brain.'

'I'm sorry,' she said again.

There was a long silence. Then he said, 'And how in the name of God did it happen? I really would like to know. When he has so repeatedly refused to see you, to speak to you over the years, how did you manage to end up in his bed?'

'Well – I went to see him in hospital,' she said, more quietly still. 'You know that.'

'Ah yes, of course. And how many times was that? Once? Twice?'

'A – a few times.'

'When you knew, when I had told you, that I didn't want you to.'

'That was absurd,' she said, 'forbidding me to go and see your own son, when he had nearly died.'

'My own son, who was quite happy, it seems, to have an affair with my wife.'

'Bard, you don't understand –'

'Oh, but I think I do. I think I do very well. And from there on you saw him again, did you? Again and again, it seems. Here?'

She thought quickly. If he thought, if he even suspected she had been to bed with Liam in the house, he would surely kill her.

'Yes,' she said, 'yes, he came here once. A long time – weeks ago. Nothing happened, nothing at all, we just – talked ...'

'You talked! How very charming. For fuck's sake, what did you have to talk about?'

'I was – well, I was upset. He – oh God, this is absurd.'

'I agree. Quite absurd. You were upset, so my son, the son I had always been led to believe hated you as much as he hated me, came to visit you. And then you drank champagne with him, and kissed him. Oh, I have all the details, you see.'

How, how did he know, who had told him? There had been no-one at the house, no-one had seen them.

'And have you seen him since then?'

Another silence.

'Francesca, I know you have. I know it. You were at Brown's Hotel with him, were you not? Only last week? While I was away?'

His voice was suddenly a roar; a wild, almost primitive roar. She was so startled, so shocked, she put her hands over her ears.

'Stop it. Stop this, Bard, stop it at once.'

'Why should I stop it?' he said, coming much closer to her, his voice, his face, menacing. 'Why the fuck should I stop it, when you've done this disgusting thing? Sweet Jesus help me.'

Francesca looked at him, at the black dangerous eyes, the heavy face so ugly in its rage, and something overwhelmed her entirely, a sweet hot courage, and she didn't feel frightened any more, didn't want to save herself. She wanted him to know the truth, how she really felt, how it had happened ...

'Yes, Bard, I have. Done this disgusting thing, as you call it,' she said, and her voice was very steady now, she could hear it, was relieved, drew fresh courage from it. 'And I feel in many ways quite horribly ashamed, of course I do. And desperately sorry to have caused you such pain.'

'How very sweet of you,' he said. He drew away from her, dropped into a chair, sat staring up at her, shaking his head in some kind of incredulity. 'I would not have believed it of you,' he said. 'I really would not.'

'Well, let me help you to believe it, tell you how it happened.'

'I don't think I want to hear. I've heard quite enough.'

'Bard, you will hear. You will. If you had heard me, listened to me before, it wouldn't have happened.'

'Oh, for fuck's sake,' he said, 'so now it's my fault, is it? I might have guessed that, I suppose. You've been listening to that self-indulgent, devious pervert of a son of mine, I suspect. You really shouldn't, Francesca, he's extremely dangerous.'

'Of course he's not dangerous.' (Who else had said that? Oh, yes, Granny Jess, at lunch, yesterday, a lifetime ago.) 'Liam is unhappy, hurt, damaged, you seem completely to miss that point. And in one way, yes, it is your fault. Because of what you have done to me. He has been kind, gentle, understanding, at a time when you have ignored me, humiliated me, treated me like a moronic child, blocked me out of your life, refused to share anything of your life with me, refused to discuss your problems, your troubles, when your secretary was permitted to be far closer to you than I am, when you and my own mother shared a secret that concerned me intimately. You cannot call that a marriage, Bard. And you are not what I thought you were.'

'Oh I see.' He looked at her with immense distaste. 'And what was that, what did you think I was? Some kind of indulgent sugar daddy, someone who'd give you everything you wanted and not demand things in return, turn you into a rich wife, buy you nice clothes, enable you to play all those bloody silly games of yours, the charities, the lunches —'

'That is a filthy thing to say,' she said, quite quietly. 'I have no interest in your money, I never did, it is of no importance to me. Actually what your money does, has done, is damaging to me, it's taken away my career —'

'Oh Jesus,' he said, 'spare me that, Francesca, please, that feminist claptrap. You and your fucking career. What did you want of me, then, or perhaps I should say what did you come to want of me, I seemed sufficient for you in the beginning —'

'I suppose,' she said, very slowly, 'I wanted to be what you needed. And I wasn't. It's as simple as that.'

'And Liam? Is he what you — need?' The word was turned into an obscenity.

'Yes. Yes, he is. Exactly what I need. Which is how and why it has all happened. And for a long time Liam has been no more than a loving friend to me, and the credit for that is entirely due to me and to him and not in the least to you. And you can believe that or not as you wish, it is of little interest to me.'

'Well,' he said, 'I'm afraid I do find it very hard to believe. So then what happened, in this touching story?'

'Well,' she said, gathering all her courage about her, 'well, then what happened was that I did — we did —'

'Let me help you here,' he said, 'since you seem to be having trouble finding the words. You fucked him. How will that do? You went to bed with him and fucked him, didn't you, Francesca, that's what you did?'

'Yes,' she said quietly, 'yes, I did. And it was terribly wrong. I know that. But in my defence, I can only tell you that you had hurt me once too often. It was beyond endurance, Bard, I'm afraid. In the end it was as simple as that.'

'Simple!' he said. 'Simple! An incestuous love affair, and you call it simple. Dear God. Well, at least now I know.'

'Know what?'

'Why you won't help me, do what I've asked of you. It would suit you rather well, wouldn't it, to have me in jail, locked up for a few years? While you carried on your little romance —'

'Bard, that is ridiculous. A vile thing to say. How can you even imply such a thing?'

'Quite easily,' he said, 'quite easily actually. It makes perfect sense to me. You've been having an affair. An affair with my own son. Think you're in love with him, no doubt. And here, dropped into your lap, is a nice, neat way for you to be able to pursue it. Now that is what I would call vile, Francesca. Absolutely vile. You horrify me. You really do.'

She sat there absorbing this, absorbing this view of her, this dreadful, ugly view, and thought that whatever she had done, she did not deserve it.

'Well,' she said, 'well, I won't horrify you any longer, Bard. I won't continue in this farce of a marriage. I'm leaving you, now. But I want you to know, not even that has any bearing on my decision. Any bearing at all. If I decided it was right to – to help you, then I still would. Not for myself, or for you, but for the children, your mother, my own even. Perhaps that might serve to convince you I'm telling the truth, about that at least.'

'I'm afraid I don't believe you, Francesca. I can't.'

'Well, and I'm afraid,' she said, 'that is your problem.'

And she walked past him out of the room, went up to their bedroom and packed a few things into a bag, and was in her car, driving away from the house, before she even realised quite what she had done. And remembered then Liam's words of only a few hours earlier: 'I'm here for you, any time, any time at all, if you really need me.'

She really needed him now.

Barnaby decided he had better walk home. Home to St John's Wood, rather than Kirsten's flat. He needed to sober up, to think a bit. What he'd done hadn't been very clever. Not very clever at all.

He'd looked pretty terrible, Oliver had, when he told him. A lot less like a shop window's dummy. Just for a moment it had been worth it, to see that smug, concerned expression wiped off his face; but then it hadn't been so good. He hadn't said anything for a bit, just sat down and stared at him, and his face had gone from its usual colour, changed first to white, then grey.

'Is that what she told you?' he'd said. 'Is that really what she told you?'

'Well – yes,' said Barnaby, just slightly uncertainly. 'Well –'

And while he was trying to think, to form some coherent words, to get his brain in sync with his mouth, which seemed extremely difficult, Oliver had stood up, and walked out of the bar.

'Oh God,' said Melinda, standing up too, 'I'd better go after him. Sarah, Nick, I'm sorry. Please excuse me.'

She glared at Barnaby, her pretty little face set with distaste – and he thought in that moment it was the first time ever he'd seen her looking really sexy – and ran out into the street. He saw her look up and down and then, obviously seeing Oliver, start to run in the direction of the Strand. Barnaby had sat down, and looked rather helplessly at Sarah and Nick.

'Sorry,' he said. 'I hope I haven't spoilt your evening.'

He thought as he walked home it really was the most cretinous remark he had ever made.

He started walking: up to Long Acre, into St Martin's Lane, up Tottenham Court Road. He'd always hated Tottenham Court Road, with its endless line of greasy kebab bars, video shops and knee-deep litter; it looked like his vision of hell.

He cut across Marylebone Road, up into the sudden sweeping elegance of Regent's Park, walked on. His head was clearing a bit now. Maybe it wasn't so bad. Maybe it was even good. At least Oliver knew now. It might not have been the best way to tell him, but he had needed to know, Francesca had been quite right. And now he could decide what he wanted to do. He might even want to – Christ, suppose he wanted to marry Kirsten! At that thought Barnaby stood stock still. That would be really gross. To have Oliver in the family! Oliver with his perfect manners and his goody-goody ways. And not just him, but Melinda. Oh God. He wasn't sure if he could face that.

He looked at his watch: it was still only ten-thirty. He felt as if whole days had passed since he'd left Kirsten. He wondered if he ought to tell her. He supposed he should. But she probably wouldn't be terribly pleased. Maybe he could ask Francesca about that. Yes, she'd know what to do. Thank God for Francesca. He was where the park met the top of Baker Street now: not much further. He'd be home in another twenty minutes. His legs were feeling pretty weak, but his head was clearer. Yes, Francesca would know what to do. No doubt when he'd calmed down a bit, Oliver would go and talk to Kirsten and they could sort something out. He'd probably done them a favour really.

He walked, his legs almost buckling with weariness, past Lord's, down Garden Road and into Hamilton Terrace. But when he finally reached the house, Francesca's car was not outside, and when he knocked cautiously on the drawing-room door, seeing through the crack that his father was lying back on the sofa, listening – in a way most unlike him – to some very heavy, classical music, he looked at him in an almost dazed way and said that Francesca had gone out.

Well, it was all much too late to sort anything out now, and he really didn't have the strength. Barnaby said goodnight to Bard and went up to his room.

Kirsten had gone to bed with two aspirins as a defence against her horribly throbbing head; the noise of the doorbell, ringing insistently, finally broke through her sleep.

She sat up, confused, shaking her hair back. Bloody Barnaby, must have forgotten his key. She pulled on her robe and walked rather unsteadily over to the intercom.

'Barnaby,' she said, 'you're hopeless.'

'It's not Barnaby,' said a voice. 'It's Oliver. I have to talk to you.'

The room seemed to shift round Kirsten; she leant against the door, feeling faint. 'Oliver? Why, what do you want?' she said.

'I told you. I have to talk to you.'

'But –'

'Kirsten, open the door. It's important.'

'OK. Just – just a minute.'

She pulled her robe round her more firmly, wishing she hadn't lost the cord, and pushed the buzzer. The door opened slowly, and Oliver was standing there.

He looked terrible. Really terrible. His face was grey, his eyes dull and heavy. He just stood there, staring at her, his eyes moving over her face and then her body. Heavy, hostile eyes.

'What the hell are you playing at?' he said finally.

'What?'

'I said what are you playing at?'

'Oliver, I don't know what you mean.'

'Of course you do. You're pregnant, aren't you?'

She waited, trying to think, trying to work out who might have told him. Then: 'Yes,' she said very quietly, 'yes I am.'

'And who's the father?'

'I can't tell you that.'

'But you're telling everyone else, aren't you?'

'What? Oliver, I'm sorry, but I really don't know what you're talking about.'

'You're telling everyone else it's me. That I'm the father of your baby.'

'Oliver, I don't know who you've been talking to, but I swear, I swear, I've told no-one who the father is. Not one person.'

'Maybe you don't know,' he said, and his voice was bitter.

'Oliver! Don't!'

'Why not? It seems to me that's quite likely. All that stuff about not sleeping around any more, saving yourself until you knew you really liked someone. Not letting me near you –'

'That's not true!'

'It's true.'

'Oliver, I wanted to, I wanted to so much. But – oh, this is ridiculous. I think you'd better go.'

'I'm not going,' he said, moving towards her, 'until you've told me who the father of your baby is.'

'Then you'll be here a very long time,' she said.

He stopped, looked at her; she met his eyes very levelly.

'And why, in God's name, let people think it's mine? I suppose it's quite likely really, isn't it, the poor relation you've been slumming with, your father's protégé, quite convenient too –' His eyes were glittering now, fixed on hers, his face ugly with rage, with bitterness.

She swallowed, steadied herself. 'Oliver, stop this. Please. How did you get this idea?'

'Does it matter?'

'It does to me.'

'Your brother told me,' he said finally, 'very charmingly, very loudly, across a crowded wine bar.'

'What?' It took a while for the words to make any sense. She sat down abruptly on the chair in the hall.

'Oliver, I just can't believe this.'

'Well,' he said, 'if it's not true, why do you think I'm here?'

'Look,' she said, 'I'm sorry. I don't feel too good. Can we go into the kitchen?'

'Yes, all right.'

He followed her in; she sat at the table, her head on her arms.

'Would you like a glass of water?'

'Yes. Yes please.'

She drank it, then sat back in her chair, looking at him. 'Oliver,' she said, 'I swear to you, I did not tell Barnaby you were the father of my child.'

'Oh,' he said, and sat down opposite her. He looked slightly nonplussed now. She could see he was almost ready to believe her.

'I'll get my Bible if you like,' she said with a ghost of a smile, 'would that help? You know how I feel about all that.'

'No,' he said, and almost smiled himself, 'no, it's all right. I – well, I do believe you. But you must have told someone.'

'I haven't. I swear. They must have – well, they must have put two and two together. And added it up all wrong.'

'Who are they?'

'Barnaby and Tory. Nobody else knows. Nobody at all. And I've told them, both of them, again and again, there's no question of my telling the father. No question at all.'

'Oh,' he said again. 'But why not? I just don't see.'

'Because it would be absolutely –' she hesitated – 'inappropriate.'

And then, most unexpectedly, for she had thought she was feeling quite in control, calm even, tears welled up, filled her eyes; she brushed them away impatiently. 'Sorry.'

'It's all right,' he said, and then, as she made a rather feeble effort to smile, groped for a tissue in her pocket, 'here. Have a hanky. Add it to your collection.'

'Thank you. I'll send it –'

'Don't. Keep it. Doesn't matter.'

There was another long silence, then she said, 'And I'm so sorry, so dreadfully sorry you should have had to go through that. It's appalling. When I see Barney I'll screw him to the wall.'

'Well,' he said, smiling suddenly, briefly, 'I expect I'll get over it.'

'Was anyone else there?'

'My sister. Two of her friends. And like I say, just about the whole of Covent Garden.'

'Oh, God. Oliver, I'm so sorry.'

'Do you think he's told a few thousand other people?'

'What? Oh God, I don't know. I'll speak to him in the morning. I don't know where he is now. At some party, I think.'

'With the most charming people.'

'What? Oh, of course, the terrible Morag ...'

There was another silence, then he said, his voice quite different now, almost gentle, concerned, 'So how do you feel?'

'Terrible. Thank you.'

'I don't know a lot about pregnancy,' he said. 'I suppose you're being sick in the mornings?'

'No,' said Kirsten. 'All day long.'

'Oh.'

'Oliver, I –'

'Yes?'

'I just don't know what to say. To make you feel better. About me, I mean.'

'Oh – don't worry about me,' he said.

'But I do. I have. I can only tell you that this happened before – before we started going out. I didn't know. I didn't know for ages. I really want you to believe that.'

'All right,' he said, with a sigh, 'I do believe you.'

'And –'

'But why didn't you tell me? Explain. It was so awful, the way you just – froze me out.'

'I'm sorry. I suppose it was – well, I felt you'd think worse of me if I explained. And I wanted so badly for you to think well of me.'

'Well, that just shows,' he said, and he almost smiled now, 'how little you know me.'

'Yes. Yes, I suppose it does. Well, we didn't have much time together really. Did we? I so wish we'd had more. It was so –' Her voice shook for a moment, 'so lovely.'

'So – what do you think – well, what are you –' He stopped.

'What am I going to do? I don't know, Oliver, I really don't. I can't decide. It's very difficult.'

'Oh,' he said, and was silent.

She could see him taking in the implications: that this was not something to be dealt with quickly, easily, that she might want to keep the baby, that it superseded any other relationship now; could see that it hurt. There was nothing she could do about that.

'Well,' he said, 'I suppose I'd better be going.'

'Yes.'

She didn't want him to leave; however difficult the circumstances were, it was so lovely to be with him again, talking to him, looking at him. But clearly he had to.

'I'll speak to Barnaby in the morning, then,' she said, 'first thing. I'm so sorry again. It must have seemed so very –'

'That's OK. Don't worry about it.'

He stood up, pushed his chair back; Kirsten stood up too. She had forgotten her robe had no tie; it was very light cotton, and as she moved towards the door, it swung open. And Oliver, formally mannered, considerate, reticent as he was, stood there, staring at her, at her naked body, unable to move. He had never seen her body before, she realised; it seemed very strange that it should be under these circumstances that it had happened, these sad, sorry, cruel circumstances. She wanted to pull the robe back round her, but she couldn't; she stood there, quite still, silent, watching him, and it was a totally emotive moment, erotic even: and after a long time, he sighed a great heavy sigh and looked at her, and then moved slowly towards her and kissed her, very gently, on the mouth.

'The trouble is,' he said simply, drawing back, 'and there's nothing either of us can do about it, nothing at all, but the trouble is, I love you. Goodbye Kirsten.'

Francesca had gone to her mother's flat. She could hardly arrive at Liam's house at eleven o'clock at night, and she had to go somewhere. She phoned from the car: Rachel's husky voice informed her on the answering machine that she was not there at the moment, but to leave a message.

Still in Devon presumably, thought Francesca, and, thanking God her mother had insisted she always had a key to the flat, drove to Battersea.

She smiled suddenly, feeling better as she closed the door behind her; the place was so redolent of her mother, it made her feel as if she had walked into her arms. Stylish, slightly excessive, charmingly cluttered, filled with dried and fresh flowers, the kitchen smelling of herbs and good coffee, the bathroom of Rachel's absurdly expensive perfumes and body lotions that she could not really afford, piles of glossy magazines in all the rooms, the walls covered in pictures, albeit many of them cheap watercolours, every conceivable surface covered with framed photographs of her family: it was Rachel, that flat, in all her warmth and extravagant vitality.

Francesca went into the kitchen, made herself a large mug of the good coffee and sat down in the drawing room. She felt very odd, as if she were some visitor, some stranger who had never been there before. She leafed through some magazines, plumped up some cushions, studied the photographs on the low table beside her. They were a poignant collection; it made her feel normal again, made her feel worse. One of her and Bard on their wedding day, on the steps at Caxton Hall, she in white silk, draped skilfully over her burgeoning bump that was Jack; one in the nursing home, not of her, but of Bard holding the baby; Rachel at Stylings holding an armful of Easter eggs; Rachel with Kitty at the christening – God, thought Francesca, that was when it all began, it seemed a lifetime ago; and, a new addition, a picture of Mary, aged about ten, wearing a pink cardigan and a pink ribbon in her hair, beaming radiantly with a basket of eggs, outside the convent. Francesca sat and looked at her for a long time, that sister of hers, thinking about her, thinking of the burden of keeping her a secret, of the courage and strength of spirit that had enabled Rachel to do so, and wondered at it. She lacked that spirit of her mother's, she knew, lacked the determined sense of joy, the ability to be positive, forward looking. She supposed, she feared, she was more like her father, the father she could scarcely remember, the man her mother had seen so clearly, in spite of her loyalty; the man who had promised her the moon and delivered only a falling star.

For a long time Francesca sat there, staring at those pictures, thinking of her mother, and wondering what she would tell her to do; and finally she fell asleep, in the chair, to wake at dawn cold, aching, and with a sense of desolation greater than she could ever remember.

And at nine, thinking it must surely be safe by then, she rang Liam and asked him to come and see her.

At almost exactly the same time, Gray Townsend arrived at Cyril le Marquand House in Jersey. The perky girl looked at him and grinned.

'Not you again! This isn't a casino, you know.'

'It is to me,' said Gray.

It was the third word he tried: Drab, hardly even an anagram, but Bard, spelt backwards. A perfectly anonymous, dispiriting, uncharismatic little word. Drab. Perfect. Exactly what you'd hide some complex, tax-evading wing of a great glittering company behind. And instead of the tantalising 'O' dancing about under the cursor when he tapped it in, yes, there it was: Drab Financial Services Ltd. He wrote down the number, filled in the form, pulled out yet more of the toytown one-pound notes and advanced on the perky girl.

'Can I have a look at this one?' he said.

Drab Financial Services had been formed ten years earlier, and had, as its registered address, Robinson and Wetherill, on Hill Street, St Helier – handy for Shelley, he thought, and wrote down the names of the two directors: Peter Marsh and Henry Williams. He had found the haystack, he had even found which section of it the needle was in; all he had to do now was actually pull it out. Get someone, anyone, in those offices to admit they knew Bard Channing, and then he would be ninety nine per cent certain. Q.E.D.

He could see the headlines now.

Perversely, Kirsten felt much better the next day. She had no idea why; she could only assume that at least some of the burden had been lifted from her. Oliver knew what had happened; she had seen him, talked to him, and he had told her he loved her. That alone gave her courage: she had no illusions that he was suddenly going to ask her to marry him, tell her he would bring up the baby and they would all live happily ever after; she simply felt that if someone as nice, as intrinsically good, as Oliver could love her, then she could not be all bad. Some small sense of self-worth had been restored to her, and with it, a lessening, however slight, of her physical misery, enabling her to think more clearly.

And the first thing she thought was that she must go to Francesca and confess.

'I don't know, Liam,' Francesca kept saying. 'I don't know who told him. In the first place. But somebody did. And then I did, I had to, there was no point my denying it, no point at all.'

'So he knows we're having an affair?'

'Yes.'

'Ah,' he said, and he looked at her and she saw the most extraordinary expression in his eyes, just for a moment; extraordinary and inappropriate: a look of triumph, of complacency – and then it was gone.

'Well,' he said finally, and the voice was odd too, slightly shaky, not its lovely musical self, 'well, I wonder where that leaves us.'

'I don't know,' she said. 'I really don't.'

She was hoping for something then, she knew not what; she sat quiet, still, just looking at him, studying him.

'How did he take it?' he said. It seemed an odd question.

'Oh – you know. He was terribly angry, desperately hurt, all the things you'd expect. I felt terrible.'

'Oh no,' he said abruptly, 'no need for that. He should feel those things.'

It was ugly, that; she didn't like it. 'Liam, don't. Please don't.'

'Don't what?'

'You sound so – so vengeful.'

'I am vengeful,' he said simply, his face, his voice, both oddly expressionless; and then, clearly seeing her distress, became almost visibly the old Liam, the tender, caring one she knew.

'Oh darling, I'm sorry. It must have been so terrible for you. I wish I could have been with you, helped you sooner. Come here, let me hold you.'

She moved over to him, and started to cry, tears of shock and strain as well as grief, and, 'Darling,' he said, as he took her in his arms, started kissing her hair, her eyelids, gently, sweetly, 'darling, it's not so bad. You've got me, it's all right, you're safe now –'

And: 'No, no,' she said, 'you can't understand, you couldn't, it was dreadful, so dreadful to see him so angry, and so hurt, to know I'd done that to him, and I'm not safe, not safe at all, it's truly, truly terrible, Liam, you don't know what he's asked me to –'

'No,' he said, kissing her again, 'no I don't, asked you to what?'

'Oh – nothing. I can't tell you. I mustn't. It wouldn't be right, it wouldn't be fair.'

'What?' he said, clearly puzzled by her anguish. 'What has he asked you –'

Francesca pulled away from him, went over to the window. She looked out at Battersea Park, through the plane trees, looked at them all, ordinary, lucky, happy people, joggers, cyclists, rollerbladers, men with briefcases, women with pushchairs, girls arm in arm, giggling, people with no dreadful choice to make, no awful dilemma presented to them, just a procession of days, one after the other, some good, some not so good, jobs to do, mortgages to pay, schools to go to, and her envy of them was so intense she could hardly bear it. She looked to her left, up to the elaborate ironwork of Albert Bridge, and beneath it the river, shining in the morning sun, boats moving up it, all so ordinary, all so safe.

'Oh God!' she said. 'God, I want to run away. Just run away somewhere where no-one can find me.'

'Then I'll come with you,' he said. 'But why, Francesca, why do you want to run away, I don't understand –'

'You couldn't,' she cried, 'you couldn't, nobody could, oh God, oh Christ, I can't stand it, any of it, I can't stand it any longer!'

She supposed what happened next was that she had hysterics: it had never happened to her before, the total, cathartic loss of control, the drumming in her ears, the inability to see, the pounding in her head, the great flow of tears that she could not stop, the sound she could hear that was her own screaming, the beating of her own feet on the floor as she stamped, the pain of her own fists thudding against the wall. But that was what she knew, that was what she was aware of, had to endure, and then something else; strong, restraining arms round her, making her be still, a voice, quiet yet very firm, bidding her be silent; hands then, holding her wrists, to stop her beating at the wall, firm hands, pushing her into the chair, holding her there, and gradually through the tumult, a peace came, a stillness, and she could see again, and what she saw was Liam's face, concerned, gentle, infinitely kind.

'You have to tell me,' he said. 'You must tell me what the matter is. Someone has to help you. And I want it to be me.'

And he made her a cup of sweet tea, and found some brandy and poured her a glass, fetched a blanket to put round her to keep her warm, for she was shaking now, shivering violently, and sat and held her hand and stroked her hair while she told him.

Kirsten decided to go to the house and confront Francesca personally. She felt she owed her that. She phoned from the office, to see if she was there or at Stylings: Barnaby answered the phone.

'Barnaby,' she said quietly, forgetting Francesca for the moment, 'you are a total and utter piece of shit. How dare you interfere in my life like that, how could you do that, tell Oliver that, when you didn't even know? And anyway, for your information, what you told him was completely wrong, so you're a double piece of shit.'

'Oh,' said Barnaby. 'Oh I see. Well, I'm very sorry. Very very sorry. I – well, I was drunk.'

'Oh, and that makes it perfectly all right, I suppose,' said Kirsten. 'You were drunk, so nothing else matters. Nobody hears what you say, believes it, gets upset by it, if you're drunk. I really cannot believe it of you, Barnaby, I trusted you, I told you not to tell anyone, and –'

'I know. But Francesca said you ought to tell whoever –'

'Francesca? Barnaby, is there anyone you *haven't* told? For God's sake –'

'It was only because I was so worried about you,' said Barnaby. 'We, me and Tory, we just didn't know what to do.'

'Dad doesn't know, does he?'

'I don't think so. Well, unless Francesca told him.'

'Oh God. He'll just about – oh well, never mind. It's done now.'

'How do you know?' said Barnaby. He sounded extremely subdued.

'Because Oliver came round to see me.'

'Oh Christ. Did you – explain?'

'Well, I apologised for you. Profusely. And tried to explain. But –'

'I'm sorry,' he said again. 'I was only – well, I suppose I was trying to help.'

'Oh Barnaby!' In spite of herself she laughed. 'Next time, don't help. Walk straight past me on the other side of the road.'

'Yes. Yes, all right. But Kirsten, if it isn't his, whose is it?'

'God, do you think I'd tell you? You might broadcast it on Capital Radio next.'

'Toby's?'

'Barnaby, stop it. No it's not. Now can we change the subject, please? Is Francesca there?'

'No,' said Barnaby, 'no she's not. She's moved out.'

'She's what? Moved out!' Kirsten felt violently sick again. 'Barney, when, where, how do you know?'

'Last night. Apparently. I got in, found Dad in the weirdest state. He said she wasn't there, and then this morning, Sandie told me.'

'How did she know?'

'Well, she saw her, apparently. Getting into the car quite late, with a suitcase. She said she and Dad had had a terrible row, and –'

'Oh God,' wailed Kirsten, 'this is all my fault. Oh Barney, I have to find her, have to talk to her.'

'How can it be your fault?'

'Oh – never mind. It is. Does Sandie have any idea where she is?'

'No. But she's not at Stylings, because I've tried.'

'Probably at her mother's,' said Kirsten. 'You don't have the number, do you?'

'No. Sorry. But she'll be in the book.'

'I should think she'd be in *Yellow Pages* in display type,' said Kirsten. 'OK, I'll try her there.'

'OK. You sound better, Kirsten.'

'I feel it,' she said, and her voice was surprised.

Liam finally left Francesca just before lunch; she said she wanted to be alone. She had spoken to her mother, arranged to go down there, to stay at the convent.

'I feel safe there, I can think.'

He was quite glad to be away from her; the strain was intense. He felt nervy, edgy, himself. He wondered what his father would do. Bard had phoned Rachel's flat; they had listened to his voice, heavy, almost emotionless, on the answering machine, asking if Francesca was there, if Rachel was there, and looked at each other like guilty children, feeling in some way he was able to see them.

Somehow, for some reason, he had not thought about that; his vision had taken him only to seducing Francesca, only to his father learning of it, and no further. He supposed because there was nothing Bard could do to hurt him, except possibly physically beat him up. That was always a possibility.

He let himself into the house: the answering machine was bleeping. He poured himself a drink before listening to it.

'I want to talk to you,' came Bard's voice. 'And if you don't get back to me, I shall come and find you. Which won't be nice for Naomi. Or the kids. I'm at the house, ring me there.'

Liam made himself another another drink, and settled down in the big sofa in the drawing room with the phone. Halfway through dialling the number he stopped, went over to the stereo and, after a moment or two's hesitation, put Fauré's *Requiem* on. It seemed appropriate, and it was one of his favourite pieces of music. This was the moment he'd been working towards for a very long time. He wanted to enjoy it.

Francesca had decided to drive to Stylings and set off for Devon early next day. She wanted the children with her, she didn't want to leave them. She was afraid of what Bard might do, that he might take them away somewhere.

She had spoken to her mother, told her briefly that she had left Bard, that she would explain when she saw her.

'I'm too tired to drive down tonight. Especially with the children.'

'Shall I come to you?'

'No. I can't be at Bard's house. I just can't. Well, not after tonight. And I certainly can't ask you there.'

'All right, darling. We'll see you tomorrow. Take care.'

You could say one thing for her mother, Francesca thought: well, lots of things actually. But one particularly: she didn't fuss.

'Hallo, Dad. This is Liam.'

'Ah. Where are you?'

'At my house.'

'Your wife's house.'

'Let's call it ours.'

'Ah. So you believe in sharing, do you? Do you share affairs?'

He didn't answer.

'I don't have a great deal to say to you, Liam. And I hope this will be the last conversation we ever have. I just wanted to tell you that you're a little shit. A pathetic, immature, amoral little shit.'

There was a silence; Liam turned the Fauré higher.

'And as from today you do not exist for me. That's all.'

Another silence. Then Liam said, 'Well, I can only say I think that might be an improvement on the present situation. Although scarcely noticeable. Goodbye then, Dad. She's a terrific lay, by the way. Isn't she?'

The phone went dead. He smiled into it, drained his glass. Those had been without doubt the best few minutes of his life.

And then he picked up the phone and dialled another number.

The trick, Gray had discovered, when you wanted to find something out, was to hit an office at the busiest time. When the important people were all busy, and you got a minion. A minion you could fluster and who would tell you something a more clued-up and important member of a team would never reveal. The busiest time in a company was around eleven-thirty in the morning, when the top people were all in morning meetings, and the lesser ones frantically getting material ready for the afternoon ones. And the next trick was to give people very firmly a piece of incorrect information; they felt bound to give you the correct one.

At eleven-thirty-five a.m., Gray arrived at Robinson and Wetherill. He looked at the long list of registered companies just inside the door, noting a lot of very strange names that made Drab sound quite reasonable – Oral Ltd, for instance, Lookout Ltd, Carpetbagger Ltd – and smiled charmingly but rather distractedly at the receptionist.

'Could I see someone on the Drab account?' he said. 'As soon as possible, it's –'

'Well, I'll see what I can do. Who shall I say it is?'

'My name is Paul Smith,' said Gray, his mind closing gratefully around the label inside his jacket, 'and it's very urgent, well, quite urgent, and –'

'Just one moment, please.' She pressed several keys importantly on her computer, then waited, studied her screen, tapped some more, spoke into her phone; he heard her say, 'Well, I know, but he says it's very urgent. Isn't Peter there? Oh, right. Well, I'll tell him that, yes, but –'

She looked up at Gray. 'I'm sorry,' she said, 'but I'm afraid there's nobody available; everyone on that account is in a meeting now. Mr Jarvis says, though, if you could come back later, or leave a message –'

'No I can't, I'm afraid. Look, couldn't I speak to Mr Jarvis myself, I won't take a second of his time –'

'Well I –'

'Please!' said Gray, smiling at her his most charming smile. 'I'm a dead man if I don't –'

Mr Jarvis appeared in reception; he was very young, with a white face, and badly bitten nails. Excellent, thought Gray.

'Look,' he said, 'I really don't think I can help, I don't have any details about the company at all, and I'm not empowered to –'

'Oh I don't want any details,' said Gray. 'It's just that I wondered if you happened to have seen Mr Channing this week? I'm supposed to be having lunch with him today, and I phoned the restaurant, Central Bistro, you know, to check, and they say he's not booked there, so ...'

There was a long silence, while Mr Jarvis stared at him blankly; go

505

on, you little twerp, thought Gray, go on, say no, he's not in town, or you haven't seen him for weeks, or yes, he was here yesterday or no, he never comes in, but say something, say you register the name at least ...

Finally Mr Jarvis spoke. 'I'm sorry,' he said, 'but I really can give you no information about any of our clients.'

'I don't want information,' said Gray, 'I just want to know if he's in Jersey this week, as I was assured he was. I've flown in specially from Brussels for this, and –'

'Mr Smith, I can't help you. I'm sorry ...'

'Oh come on,' said Gray. 'Look, he'll have me for lunch if I've got this wrong, I've obviously got the wrong place, it's ghastly, and I've tried L'Horizon, where he usually stays, and he's not there either, staying somewhere else, I suppose –'

'Mr Smith,' said Mr Jarvis, 'I'm sorry, but I have absolutely no knowledge of any Mr Channing. And even if I did,' he added hastily, 'I certainly wouldn't be able to pass it on. Now if you will excuse me –'

He left quickly, through the swing doors; Gray sighed and looked at the receptionist.

'This is a nightmare,' he said, in his most melting, anguished voice. 'I just don't know what I'm going to do. You haven't seen Channing, have you? He hasn't been on the phone or anything?'

She stared at him, her face coldly blank. 'I don't know the name at all,' she said, 'but even if I did, we're not allowed to give information about any of our clients ... Would you excuse me now, I'm very busy ... Robinson and Wetherill, can I help?'

At least, thought Gray, she didn't say 'How may I help you?'

He went for a walk, had several drinks in several bars, and then at three went back to his hotel, picked up the phone and dialled Robsinon and Wetherill.

'Oh hi,' he said, in his best American (West Coast) accent, 'this is Jay Brownjohn of Chase calling from San Francisco, can I speak with someone on the Drab account please? Thank you – oh, hi, I wonder if you can help me, just a little hiccup on this one, did you get a letter from Mr Channing giving you a new instruction on this account? I'm sorry? Channing, yes, C-H-A-N-N – oh, really? None whatsoever. Well, that's very odd, I was assured he – well, thank you. Thank you, very much. Yes, I will. Sure. Thanks. Bye.'

He put the phone down. Shit. It was either genuine, and no-one there had had any dealings with Bard Channing, or they were so primed up they'd have to be hung, drawn and quartered before they'd admit to it. The second seemed marginally more likely. This was getting seriously tough.

And if he wasn't careful he'd alert someone to the fact that he was there, looking for Channing, and word just might get back to him.

He dialled Shelley's number, asked her if she'd managed to contact either Paul le Barre or Jeffrey Tyson. She said Tyson would be at Lido's that evening, 'It's a bar in Halkette Street,' and happy to have a drink with him if he dropped by.

'I told him you were over here on a trip and that you were hoping to open a restaurant in London, I hope that's all right.'

'Well done,' said Gray.

'But Paul le Barre's out of town. Drying out, I should think.'

'Doesn't matter. Thanks for trying.'

Tricia was enjoying her week. Gray might be fun, he was very charming, he was nice to flirt with: but he was very demanding. And just lately, he'd been on the low side, irritable even, which was very unusual. And not pleased if she wasn't there when he needed her. Which meant, basically, never being able to leave the office.

So with him in Jersey, she'd been able to catch up on her social life, lunch with her friends, arrange some dinner parties. That Tuesday, she went out for a long lunch. And when she got back, there was a note on her desk, saying a Mr Channing had rung, wanting to speak to Gray Townsend 'urgently' said the note. 'He'll ring again, or ring him on his home number, Islington four-seven-six-nine.'

Another unpleasant phone call, thought Tricia with a sigh. She supposed she'd better call Gray and tell him.

Gray wasn't in his hotel, and his mobile was switched off. She left a message with the hotel and went back to her social life. Gray was coming back on Thursday, she could tell him then.

The new young receptionist at the Deux Jardins Hotel wrote the message down for Mr Townsend and put it in his pigeonhole. Mr Richard Townend, who had just arrived in Jersey for a week's golf, and was also staying at the Deux Jardins, got the message to ring his assistant and duly did so. His assistant said he thought it must have been a mistake. Mr Townend was only too happy to get back to the nineteenth hole, and thought no more about it.

Francesca was just leaving her mother's flat when Kirsten rang for a second time. She listened to her voice on the answering machine, saying she really really needed to talk to her, and was tempted to ignore it, but thinking of Barnaby's anxiety about her, picked up the phone.

'Hallo, Kirsten.'

'Francesca, I've got to see you. Got to talk to you.'

'This is very sudden. What's the matter?'

'I – don't want to talk on the phone. Can't I come over there?'

'I'm sorry, Kirsten, but I'm on my way to Stylings. I'm already late. I really don't want to wait any longer. Is it urgent?'

'Well – yes. Yes, it is. I've just got to see you.'

'All right,' said Francesca with a sigh, 'I'll wait for you. Where are you?'

'I'm at work. I'll get a cab. I'll be about twenty minutes.'

She was shocked at the sight of Kirsten. She had clearly lost at least half a stone; her skin was terrible, her eyes heavy and dark ringed, the glorious hair lank and dull.

'Hallo, Francesca,' she said awkwardly.

'Hallo, Kirsten.'

'I'm sorry to hold you up. But I just had to come and see you face to face. To apologise.'

'Apologise?' She couldn't keep the coldness out of her voice. 'What for this time, Kirsten? What have you done?'

'Worse than anything I've done before,' said Kirsten, and her voice was very quiet. 'If that's possible. And you're going to hate me more than you ever hated me before ...'

'Kirsten, I don't hate you,' said Francesca. 'That was your speciality.'

Kirsten stared at her. 'You must do.'

'I'm sorry to disappoint you, Kirsten, but I don't. I hate the way you behave a lot of the time, but I always thought the raw material was all right. I thought we could have got on quite well. Actually.'

'Oh,' said Kirsten. She sat down suddenly. 'Sorry. I don't feel too good.'

'Do you want a drink of water?'

'Yes please. You know, don't you? About me being pregnant?'

'Yes I do. And I'm sorry. Very sorry. I did tell Barnaby you could come and talk to me about it if you wanted to, but I didn't think that was very likely.'

'Well – you certainly won't want to talk to me after I've told you this.'

'Perhaps we'd better talk before you tell me, then,' said Francesca, trying not to smile.

'Oh – no. I couldn't do that. I have to get it over with.'

'Well, come on then. Shoot. As your father would say.'

'Well, you see –' Kirsten visibly straightened, pulled her courage about her; it was an oddly touching sight. 'It was me told Dad. About you and Liam. And I'm more sorry than I can say. It was unforgivable, horrible, an awful thing to do.'

'Yes, it was,' said Francesca, staring at her, wondering why she wasn't more angry. 'Why did you do it? Do you know?'

'Because I wanted to hurt him.'

'Hurt *him*! What about me?'

'Well, I knew it would hurt you too,' said Kirsten, with a rather engaging honesty, 'but it was him I was bothered about. Or rather not bothered about. Oh God. Couldn't you hit me or something?'

'I don't normally like hitting pregnant women,' said Francesca, with a faint smile, 'and it wouldn't do much good. Why did you want to hurt your father so much?'

'He's so – so horrible to me,' said Kirsten. 'He despises me so much, always sees the bad in me, always puts everything in the worst possible light. Whatever I do, it's wrong. Always has been. And I want to – well, I used to, when I was young – want to please him so much. I want him to be proud of me. And he never will be, never is. He's ashamed of me. He hates me.'

'Oh I don't think so,' said Francesca, 'I think actually he loves you very much. He's just – difficult. I know that's a bit like saying Genghis Khan was assertive, but –'

'Yes. Granny Jess says that. That he loves me, I mean. But I'm afraid you're both wrong. Anyway, he was bawling me out as usual. Misinterpreting something I'd done. Telling me I was pathetic. And I – well, there's no excuse, I just lashed out. And it was awful of me, really awful, and I'm so, so sorry. Which doesn't help at all, I know, but –'

'Yes it does,' said Francesca, surprising herself. 'It helps a lot. Actually. I couldn't think who could have told him, and I kept imagining all sorts of hidden enemies I might have. But Kirsten, who told you? I don't understand, you've never been anywhere near the house or anything –'

'Sandie told me,' said Kirsten. 'She doesn't like you, I'm afraid. I'd think about sacking her, if I were you. I know she's awfully efficient and everything, but –'

'I might possibly do that, Kirsten, yes. Just possibly,' said Francesca briskly. 'But what did she tell you, exactly?'

'Oh, you know, she said he'd been there one day. And that you and Liam had been blowing kisses and stuff. And that you'd been to visit him loads of times in hospital –'

'But she didn't know that,' said Francesca slowly. 'I never told her I was going. Well, except the very first time. I don't understand ...'

'Oh they're very clever, servants,' said Kirsten, with all the authority of one who had grown up with them, 'they see everything, you know. And she's got a bit of a soft spot for Liam, always did have ...'

'Yes, I see. Er – how do you feel about him? As a matter of interest?'

'Oh, well, I'm quite fond of him, I suppose, and I'm very sorry for him, but he's a bit of a wanker. He really is.'

'Oh. I see,' said Francesca, slightly faintly.

'Anyway, it's nothing to do with me what you do. Of course. And I don't really care. I mean, anyone who lives with Dad is entitled to behave how they like, I think.'

'Really?'

'Yes. Definitely. But I just wanted to – make trouble, I'm afraid. I'm very good at that,' she added.

'Yes. Well, that's true.'

'And I don't know why. Not really. Bad lot, I am.'

'I don't think you're a bad lot, Kirsten,' said Francesca. 'I think you're a bit – muddled. Misguided. And you've had some rather – unsatisfactory parenting. I don't think a bad lot would have done what you've just done. I appreciate it. So thank you. Look, I've really got to go. I must get down to Stylings, to the children. We still haven't talked about you.'

'Oh,' said Kirsten. She looked utterly desolate suddenly. 'There's nothing to talk about, really. I've got myself into a fucking – sorry, awful, mess and I've got to get myself out of it.'

'Termination?'

'Well, obviously it's the sensible thing to do. But I'm Catholic, you see. Ties you up in knots, that does. I don't know if I can face it again. Anyway, don't worry about me.'

'Kirsten,' said Francesca gently, 'I do worry about you. Quite a lot, actually.'

'Well, that's nice of you. I'm sure I don't deserve it.'

'You don't want to come down to Stylings with me?' said Francesca. 'We could talk some more on the way.'

'No. No, really, I've got to get back to work. They've been very good to me, I can't let them down. Um – Francesca – you're not going to leave Dad, are you?'

'I don't know,' said Francesca, thinking it was hardly a decision she could make, touched that Kirsten should think she had any choice in the matter. 'I really don't know. I don't know what will happen to us at all.'

'Because he'd go completely mad if you did. Instead of just almost. If you can stand it, I really think you should stay.'

Francesca sat in the early evening traffic on the A24, thinking about the perverseness of a girl who had done everything she could to wreck her marriage, the courage to come and admit face to face that she had done so, and the naiveté to encourage her now to stay in it. And of a girl, careless of the background of great wealth against which she had grown up, who had been given everything she wanted all her life, in material terms, but who refused to take an afternoon off from her very menial job when she was clearly feeling extremely unwell, because she didn't want to let them down. She supposed she was very like her father.

She reached Stylings at tea-time; Jack was doing what he called diving, which meant running very hard towards the swimming pool and bombing in, bottom first, displacing the maximum amount of water as he did so. He saw her mid-jump, waved ecstatically at her with both arms, and disappeared, resurfaced coughing and choking, grinning radiantly.

'Hi, Mum. Your dress is all wet.'

'Good heavens,' said Francesca, looking down at her linen dress, soaked with chlorinated water – which would probably stain – marvelling that so small a body could create so large a wave, 'I wonder how that happened.'

'Don't know.' He gave her a hug. 'It's even wetter now. I missed you.'

'I missed you too. Have you had fun?'

'Well – a bit. There's this boy in the village, he's shown me how to make a shooter.'

'A shooter?' said Francesca. 'What sort of shooter?'

'Well, you have a sort of stick thing, and some elastic, and then you can shoot stones with it. It's really good.'

'Oh I see,' said Francesca faintly. 'How's Kitty, where's Nanny?'

'Oh, stupid as ever,' said Jack, 'she –'

'I'm here, Mrs Channing.' Nanny had appeared, pushing Kitty in the buggy. Kitty waved her small arms and beamed at her mother. 'I watch Jack from behind the hedge, so I don't get too wet. I am quite near enough at hand to see he's safe, I wouldn't wish you to think he was in any danger.'

'No, Nanny, I wouldn't think that. Anyway, they both look really well. Kitty's all right, is she?' she added, reminded of the ever-present spectre of Kitty's health as the baby sneezed lightly.

'Perfectly all right, Mrs Channing,' said Nanny, clearly resenting the implication that something might have gone wrong with Kitty while she was in her care.

'Good. Now look, I'm staying here tonight and then tomorrow I'm taking them down to Devon.'

'To Devon!' said Nanny. 'With the children!' Her tone implied that Sodom and Gomorrah might have been more suitable locations. 'Why Devon, Mrs Channing, is there a reason?'

'Well, my mother is there,' said Francesca lightly, 'and I want to see her.'

'I see. But surely you can't be thinking of taking them on your own?'

'All on my own, Nanny. I won't be needing you for a few days. You can have a little holiday.'

'Yeah!' said Jack, punching the air.

That night Liam phoned.

'Are you OK?'

'Yes. Yes, I'm fine. Thank you. Thank you for everything. I think I'd have really gone off my trolley this morning without you.'

'You did come off it. For a moment or two.'

'Yes. I know. So thank you.'

'Well, you know. I'm always here. Waiting.'

'Yes.' She smiled. 'I'm sorry there's been so much waiting.'

'It's all right. It was worth it in the end. Wasn't it?'

His voice was very intense suddenly, stirring emotions, memories in her; physically disturbing memories.

'Yes,' she said quietly, 'yes it was. Liam –'

'Yes?'

'Liam, you never talked to Sandie about – about us, did you?'

'Sandie? Of course not. Don't be absurd.'

'Oh – well, apparently she said something to Kirsten. It was she who told Bard, incidentally.'

'Kirsten! Little cow. How dare she, I've a very good mind to –'

'Liam don't. She's desperately sorry. And she had the guts to come and see me about it. She's just a silly, mixed-up girl. Anyway, she has her own problems at the moment. And besides, he had to find out sooner or later.'

'Maybe.'

'You haven't heard from Bard, have you?'

'No. Not a thing. I suppose he's just given up on us both.'

'Oh –' She found that hurtful; she had expected, perversely almost wanted, Bard to create total havoc about it. 'Well –'

'Look,' said Liam, 'I know I said it all this morning. But you really cannot – must not – do what he asked. It's an appalling thing for him to do, he couldn't possibly really care about you and place you in that position. I can't believe it, quite honestly, even of him. It's horrific. Dreadful.'

'Liam, you won't –'

'Won't what?'

'Well – I shouldn't have told you. It was so wrong of me. It was just that I – well, I was so upset. But I am worried about it. About telling you. I shouldn't have said anything.'

'Darling! What do you think I'm going to do? Tell the newspapers?'

'Oh don't,' said Francesca with a shudder.

Lido's was a fairly flash bar, it was a sunny evening, and most people were sitting outside. There was man sitting alone in corner, drinking what looked like whisky, who Gray thought was probably Tyson: he was middle aged, grey haired, and wearing the regulation tan and blazer of the Jersey rich. He went over to him.

'Jeffrey Tyson? Graydon Townsend.'

'Yeah, sure. Come and sit down. Shelley said you might be along. What will you have?'

'No, no, let me,' said Gray.

'OK. Bourbon. Thanks. You enjoying Jersey?'

'Very much,' said Gray untruthfully, 'but it's a bit of a flying visit. I'm in the restaurant trade, and I thought I'd take a busman's holiday, check this place out.'

'And? Any recommendations?'

'Oh – several, yes. I had a very good lunch at the Central, and –'

'Good.' Tyson was clearly bored by the discussion already. 'How long are you here for?'

'Oh – till Thursday morning. Then I have to get back. Have you lived here long?'

'About twenty years. It gets a hold on you in the end. St Helier's a bit of a non-event, but the north coast is beautiful, you should take a look at it, if you haven't already.'

'How much time do you spend here?'

'Oh – about two thirds of the year. The rest of it I'm travelling round the world. Seeing to my businesses.'

'Which are – ?'

'Chemists. Got a chain of them. All over the UK and Europe. Tough market these days, you have to be into everything from jewellery to aromatherapy and all that nonsense. But I get by.' He grinned at Graydon. 'So what do you really want?'

Gray was startled. 'Sorry?'

'Come on, Mr Townsend. I do read the newspapers, you know. And your name's pretty big in the financial pages of your paper. Is this a sneak interview or what?'

'Sorry,' said Graydon. 'Pretty silly really. I should have realised.'

'Yes, you should have. But I won't hold it against you. Anyway, I'd do anything for Shelley. She's a lovely girl. Except tell you the island's secrets. Which are many.'

The drinks arrived. He raised his glass. 'Cheers. Thanks.'

'Cheers,' said Graydon. He felt completely poleaxed, incapable of saying anything. Tyson looked at him thoughtfully.

'Look,' he said, 'we don't have to continue with this at all. Or we can talk about the weather, or the financial situation in general, I don't give a shit. It's quite nice for me to have someone new to chat to here. It gets a bit incestuous after a bit. Or you can just go back to your hotel. But you might as well ask me whatever it is you want to know, and get it out of the way. It won't do any harm.'

'OK,' said Graydon slowly, 'I'll ask you. Do you know a man called Bard Channing?'

'Yes, I've met him,' said Tyson. 'We had a tangle over a property, as a matter of fact. Oh, about ten years ago. He won. Clever chap. I've been following his decline and fall in the papers. Bloody shame. It's that government of yours that's to blame, of course. Criminal incompetence.'

'Yes, well, I have some sympathy with that view myself,' said Gray, 'but I don't think they're going to reach out much of a hand to him, or indeed any of the other businessmen they're crucifying with such vigour at the moment.'

' 'Fraid not. Anyway, I've never seen him here, if that's what you want to know. Or heard any talk of him.'

'No?' said Gray. He could feel his stomach churning into panic again. Christ, he'd got himself into a mess.

'No. And that's the truth. Mind you, I'd deny it if I knew, or even thought, he did have any business, any dealings here, but as it happens, I can tell you hand on heart that he doesn't. I have never heard a whiff of the man. You're wasting your time. Got it wrong. Sorry. Do you play poker?'

'No,' said Gray.

'Pity. Got a game tonight. That's how we pass the odd evening here. We're not allowed a casino, you know, they're afraid we'll lose all our money, so poker's the nearest to gambling we can get. Oh well. Look, have another of those, will you, and tell me if you think this damn recession's ever going to end ...'

Fate, thought Gray miserably, as he made his way back to the doubtful refuge of the Deux Jardins, did not seem to be on his side, and his own faith in his hunch was beginning to fade. He had no doubt that Tyson had been telling the truth. Probably the best thing he could do was cut back to London tomorrow, with his tail between his legs. He'd try and change his flight first thing in the morning.

As he waited for his key, he looked idly at the rack of leaflets on the desk; he picked out one that said 'Go Flying' and promised trial flights in a four-seater aircraft round the island. Gray often said he'd had more trial flights than most people had had flights; he had taken them at small airfields all over the country. It was a perfect way of looking over an area, the instructors were always relaxed, uncomplicated and fun, and – most relevantly, he felt, contemplating his sinking spirits – he usually found the experience exhilarating. If he couldn't change his flight, he'd do one next day.

Rachel was waiting for Francesca and the children with Mary at the big gates when they arrived next morning. Mary smiled at them, went round to peer in the car.

'Baby,' she said, pointing at Kitty in her seat.

'Yes,' said Francesca, lifting Kitty out. 'She's called Kitty.'

'Like a cat. I can take her,' said Mary, holding out her arms. 'Show her to Mother.'

'Well, I don't know ...' said Francesca. She hated appearing in any way awkward with Mary, but she was afraid she might drop Kitty.

'Put her in her buggy,' said Rachel quickly, 'and then, Mary, you can push the baby.'

'If you run with her,' said Jack, who had been studying Mary, 'she shakes up and down and laughs.'

Mary shook her head. 'Never run with the baby,' she said

reprovingly, 'be very careful with the baby.' She started very slowly pushing the buggy across the courtyard.

Rachel looked at Francesca and smiled. 'Nothing to worry about there,' she said.

Reverend Mother had prepared a room for Francesca and the children. 'You'll all have to be in together,' she said, 'I'm sorry.'

'That's fine,' said Francesca. 'And I hope my mother told you, I have a cot with me. A travelling cot.'

'Yes, she did. What a pretty baby.'

'She's stupid,' said Jack. 'She can't even talk.'

Reverend Mother looked at him. 'I expect you'd like to help Richard with the eggs, wouldn't you?'

'What, cooking them?'

'No, finding them. All over the barns and so on.'

'Cool!'

'Mary,' said Reverend Mother, 'take Jack to find Richard. Then you can come back, I expect. Can't she, Mrs Channing?'

Francesca looked at Mary, who was stroking Kitty's face gently, with her rather clumsy little hands.

'Yes, of course she can.' She smiled at her mother. 'I feel better already,' she said.

She told her mother about Liam. They sat and talked after supper, when the convent was quiet, when the children were asleep, about what had happened. Rachel listened in silence; Francesca had been afraid she would be judgmental, reproach her. But all she said was, 'How do you really feel about him, darling?'

'Who, Liam?'

'Well, I meant Bard. But we can talk about Liam if you like. Are you in love with him?'

'Yes,' she said after a long pause. 'Yes, I think so. I really do.'

'And Bard?'

'I don't know, is the answer. I don't know how I feel about him any more. Hostile, at the moment. He's treated me so – so contemptuously.'

'Fairly contemptuous, the way you've treated him, I would have thought,' said Rachel briskly.

'I know that,' she said quietly, 'of course I do. But if Bard had been – different, I would never have done it.'

'Francesca, every adulterous wife since the beginning of time has said that.'

She paused, looked at her mother slightly awkwardly. 'Has she?'

'Of course. It's essential to have a justification. It's always different, of course: that you needed the excitement, or the reassurance, or the understanding, or the respect. Otherwise you're just wicked, faithless.'

'Yes Mummy, all right,' said Francesca irritably. 'I get the message.'

'Anyway, you say you're in love with Liam. What does that mean?'

'Oh – I don't know. I just feel happy with him. Safe. You know? He's so much more my sort of person, really.'

'I wouldn't have thought you were quite in a position to make that judgment,' said Rachel drily.

'Well – no. But he's so funny, and gentle and – and civilised. It's hard to explain. And we agree about so much. Enjoy the same things. I just love being with him. It's easy. Happy. That's all. After Bard, being with Liam is like – like a lovely spring day after months of ice and fog and driving rain.'

'And I presume you've been to bed with him?'

'Yes,' said Francesca, meeting her mother's eyes steadily, 'yes, I have, I'm afraid.'

'Well, he is extremely attractive,' said Rachel after a long pause. 'Very good looking in that marvellous tortured way; I fancied him myself the first time I met him.'

'Mummy, you fancy everyone,' said Francesca, laughing for the first time that day.

'Not quite everyone. Mind you, given a straight choice between Liam and that Barnaby – but that's by the way. But Francesca, nobody knows more about the charms of the extra-marital affair than I do.'

'Mummy –'

'No, hear me out. It is heady, wonderful stuff. After all those years of ice and fog and driving rain, of course it's a lovely spring day, as you put it. You're back to courtship, and romance, to gazing across the table at one another and hand-holding and waiting for the phone to ring, and being told you're wonderful again, having your jokes laughed at, your conversation found fascinating. And sex is marvellous too, not boring, and predictable, you're right back to being young, virginal almost ...'

'Yes,' said Francesca doubtfully, remembering Liam's painfully ferocious, demanding lovemaking, thinking her response to it scarcely warranted the description of virginal, 'but –'

'And then it's all forbidden, all so exciting. That adds a huge frisson to the whole thing. And in this case, throw in the fact that Liam is Bard's son, his estranged, ill-treated son, hurt, damaged, and my God, Francesca, of course you're in love with him.'

Francesca was silent. Then she said, and she could hear her own voice defensive, irritable: 'There's more to it than that. I know there is.'

'And is there a future in it? I mean, have you talked about that?'

'No,' said Francesca, 'no of course not, we hadn't even thought that far. But –'

'So what of his marriage, then?' said Rachel.

'What? Oh Liam's, you mean. Well, it's dead. They just live together. For the sake of the children. She doesn't talk to him, she's contemptuous of him, he's in a hideous position, financially depend-ent on her, he has no self-esteem. I've actually seen him in tears at things she's said, things that have happened –'

'Could he not get a job?' said Rachel.

Francesca looked at her. Then she said rather coldly, 'This seems to be becoming an attack on Liam. I don't like you turning him into some kind of – of bit on the side. It's not fair. It's not like that. I love him and he loves me. I think, if you don't mind, I'll go to bed. Goodnight.'

'Liam,' said Naomi, relaxing against him finally, after a tumultuous, climbing, falling, crying, cataclysmic orgasm, 'that was just – just, I don't know, inspired.'

'Funny you should say that,' he said simply. 'It's exactly how I felt.'

Chapter Twenty-seven

Oliver couldn't concentrate. He had sat at his desk all day, hearing over and over again, like some strange dream, Barnaby's voice saying, 'She's pregnant, you little twat, with your baby,' and then seeing Kirsten's face, so thin and drawn and shocked, and hearing her voice saying how lovely the time they'd had together had been, and seeing her body, that long, slender body, so unbelievably holding a child, and then kissing her, for the last, the last ever, time and then leaving her, somehow, and going away from her, aching, hurting more even than before.

He had found a taxi and gone home, told Melinda, sweet, loyal, stupid Melinda who was waiting anxiously up for him, to go to bed, and sat and drunk himself into a stupor; in the morning, had woken late, feeling terrible but still gone to the office. Barnaby had phoned, embarrassed, chastened, full of apologies, of wishes to make amends, to do anything, anything at all, practically take out a page in *The Times* or space in Piccadilly Circus to try and make Oliver feel better, it was funny almost; in the end Oliver had found himself trying to soothe Barnaby, to calm him down.

It was when Barnaby had offered to tell his father what he had done, to prostrate himself on the ground in front of him, as far as Oliver could make out, wearing no doubt best quality sackcloth and ashes, that his sense of humour began to surface.

'It's OK, Barnaby,' he said, 'honestly. I'll get over it. Kirsten's explained. I've seen her. I'd probably have done the same thing.'

'I doubt it,' said Barnaby gloomily. 'You've been properly brought up.'

By the end of the day Oliver was feeling sick and very tired; he wondered if that was how it felt to be pregnant, how Kirsten felt. He was totally weary of the situation at Channing House, it was depressing and tedious, and none of the firms he had applied to recently for articles had come back to him.

He felt so rough that when Mary stood up with a sigh and said she must go and face the horrors of the Albemarle Street post office, he offered to do it for her.

'I'd like to. Honestly. I need some air. Bit of a hangover. And then I can slope off home.'

'Yes. You certainly could. Well, if you really don't mind, Oliver. And actually, then we could both slope off home.'

He was at the station when he realised he had forgotten his jacket. He would have left it, because it was a hot evening, and he had already struggled down the crowded steps into the litter-strewn, evil-smelling hell that was Piccadilly Circus on a hot evening, if his season ticket hadn't been in it. Slightly reluctantly, half tempted to buy a ticket – but then he wouldn't have his season ticket in the morning, and the queues were so awful – he went back.

'Everyone's gone,' said Hugh. 'Shouldn't let you up really. Go on, young man, don't be long.'

'Thanks, Hugh.' He was surprised; the new team usually worked late.

He ran up the stairs, went along to his office, picked up his jacket and walked back along the corridor more slowly, checking the jacket pockets. The door to the office that had been Marcia's, the one that Sloane was now using, wasn't properly shut; he must still be here then; they were locked up like Fort Knox at night. Obviously Sloane had gone out for a break and was coming back. He could hear the phone ringing. And then he heard the answering machine pick it up and something kept Oliver there, kept him standing, listening, trying to hear. And because he couldn't quite hear, he pushed the door open, gently, and put his head in. And heard just the end of the message: '... about the financial routes into Switzerland you were asking for. I'll have those details for you tomorrow. Goodnight.'

It wasn't the words that were intriguing: they could have meant anything. Well, almost anything. It was the tone. The tone which was brisk, efficient – but friendly. Familiar. And the voice. Oliver knew that voice. He knew it very well.

Feeling heady, his heart thudding, he went into the room, picked up the phone, dialled 1471. The number that came up meant nothing to him, but he wrote it down on a piece of paper, stuffed it in his pocket and ran down the stairs.

'Mum! Quick, quick, Kitty's fallen out of the window –'

'What? Jack, where, why –' Rachel and Francesca had been sitting in the convent kitchen; they shot out into the hall, to see Jack sliding happily down the banisters.

'Yeah, got you!' His little face was radiant with pleasure. 'Course she hasn't. She's playing with her stupid posting box thing. And that nice big little girl. Mary.'

'Jack, that was very naughty, frightening me like that,' said Francesca, and burst into tears. Rachel looked at her. She put her hand out, took Francesca's, just as she had when she had been a little girl. 'Let's go for a walk.'

'I can't,' said Francesca, sniffing. 'Jack'll probably start practising his catapult in the chapel next. I can't cope with it, any of it –'

'Don't tell me you're missing Nanny already!' said Rachel briskly. 'I think we'll go and find Richard. Jack, you come with me. You really are very naughty.'

'It was only a joke,' said Jack indignantly.

'Now,' said Rachel, having checked that Mary was playing with Kitty with infinite care in the laundry, and that Sister Mary Agnes was keeping an eye on them both while ironing exquisite linen and lace altar cloths, 'tell me what the matter is. There's more than all this with Bard and Liam, isn't there? There's something else?'

'Yes,' said Francesca, 'but I can't tell you what it is.'

'Why not? You obviously need to talk about it. It's eating you up. I'm not going to tell anyone. And maybe I can help.'

'No one can help,' said Francesca with a sigh.

'Francesca, whatever it is, I won't mind. Whatever you've done, I'll be on your side. That's what mothers are for. Come on, tell me.'

David Sloane, who was now leading the investigation into the Channing Corporation's affairs, phoned Bard that morning and asked him if he could go and see him again, just to run over some ground they had already covered. There were two areas he was particularly interested in, the charitable trust in the Netherlands Antilles, and a particular purchase of two very large tranches of shares just about a month earlier.

Bard said shortly he was really quite unable to give him any information about the activites of his shareholders, and David Sloane said he would still like to see him if he could spare the time. Bard said that unfortunately he had a great deal of time.

David Sloane conducted the interview as usual from Bard's own office, and started by commenting helpfully that he had come to the conclusion that Bard really should have had the staircase carpeted over: 'or perhaps removed and a lift put in, bit more appropriate for commercial use.' These observations clearly not being particularly welcome, the interview did not begin on a very happy note.

When it was over, David Sloane called his secretary in, asked her if the preliminary documentation on the Channing case had been completed, including the official questionnaire which Channing himself had been required to complete in all its painstaking detail, and then lifted the phone to his opposite number at the Serious Fraud Office.

Sandie, who was still greatly enjoying the whole situation, happened to be passing Bard's study shortly after he got back, with a pile of clean towels. She wasn't one to eavesdrop, but she did pause and check the pile just outside his door, and she heard his voice raised in what sounded like genuine anguish.

'I cannot understand it, Pete,' he was saying. 'They seem to be bloody psychics. How have they got onto it all so fucking fast? Look, I'll come down and see you, I think, ASAP. We're obviously missing something ...'

Another little morsel to tell Colin about, Sandie thought, hurrying on to the airing cupboard as she heard the receiver go down. He'd already said she might be called as a witness in any inquiry. She liked that idea.

Gray sat in the co-pilot's seat and watched the green fields of Jersey shrinking beneath him. He hadn't been able to change his flight.

'We'll take a buzz right round the island,' shouted the instructor, whose name was Rob. 'That was a very good take-off by the way. You're a natural.'

Gray smiled modestly; he wasn't about to admit to what must now be twenty trial flights. He wondered, as he always did at this point, why he didn't study for his licence; it was such a heady feeling, just getting up here in the tiny little car-like planes, by what seemed largely faith and willpower; totally liberating, with nothing around you but the sky, a bit like the moment when the first drink of the day hit your bloodstream. And he always felt so safe: aren't you terrified up there in one of those little things, people would say to him, aren't you scared it would crash; and no, he would say, no I'm not, and try to explain that the plane was so small, the sky so welcoming, the entire experience so absorbing, it seemed quite impossible that anything could go wrong, it just felt like driving, rather slowly and carefully on a vast and completely empty highway. A blue highway. His only problem was that he was afraid to take his eyes off the road, as it were; afraid to look down and study the landscape, for fear he was going to bump into something. He knew it was absurd, but the earth-bound driver's anxiety and brainwashing was hard to overcome.

They banked round to the right; he had a moment of giddy fear, aware suddenly of the angle, the sensation of being able at least to fall, then steadied, and forced himself to look down. And it was quite lovely; a brilliant blue and gold day, the cliffs – so small, so sheer, from up here, edged with the brilliant yellow of the gorse, the white of the huge dog daisies, the paler gold of the sand, the toytown castles set on the tiny heads, the absurd neatness of the golf courses, stitched into the wilder landsape, and the smaller islands, Guernsey, Sark and Alderney, looking as if they were floating free in the dancing sea. Bard Channing and the *News*, and the refusal of the two to come together on Jersey at least, seemed a very long way away and almost unimportant.

He did an almost perfect landing and sat in the cockpit for a few minutes, chatting to Rob, sorry to have come back to earth.

'You really should sign up,' said Rob. 'You're very good.'

'Well – I'm only here for a few days,' said Gray.

'Where do you live?'

'London.'

'Well, there are dozens of schools all round the M25. Why not have some lessons there? Look, I've got a list inside, why don't I give it to you.'

Gray hesitated, then he said, 'Yeah, OK. I've left my jacket there anyway. I'll have to come back in.'

He followed Rob in, up the stairs into the office, and while he was waiting for the list to be found looked idly at the notice board. It was covered with details of flying events, and photographs of happily grinning people.

'This your Hall of Fame?' he said.

'Yeah. Mostly people who've got their pilot's licences,' said Rob.

'Lot of females.'

'Yeah, well, they tend to enjoy it more than the men. Not trying to prove anything, I suppose, don't want to be long-haul pilots on their first lesson.'

'Oh dear,' said Gray, 'well, I suppose we –' And then his voice tailed off. He felt as if he was completely isolated from everything and everyone in the room, that Rob and the woman behind the booking desk were very far away. There was an odd rushing noise in his ears, and he could feel his heart thudding, very fast. For on the board, right at the bottom, smiling just slightly less ecstatically than some of the others, but smiling nonetheless, in considerable self-satisfaction, was a face he was almost sure – no, he knew – he recognised. It was not a face that he had imagined smiling thus, indeed, and nor was he accustomed to seeing it with hair round it, falling rather untidily moreover onto its owner's shoulders, with only goggles holding it back from the smiling face, and nor could he ever have imagined those rather stiff shoulders encased in a leather flying jacket, sheepskin trimmed, and certainly not with the friendly addition of an instructor's arm draped round them; but there was no doubt at all whose photograph it was there, in that room, on that board; who had come to Jersey, who had clearly come to Jersey many times, for how else could the pilot's licence have been earned there: and who was a great deal more likely to have come for a purpose than simply having a holiday, or even earning a pilot's licence, to have come here on business. Channing Corporation business.

It was Marcia Grainger.

One of the few good things Pattie Channing had done for her daughters was send them to a first-class gynaecologist at the first signs of their needing one. Meg Wilding, who practised from rooms in Welbeck Street, was forty-five years old, a brilliant surgeon and obstetrician, and the mother herself of eighteen-year-old twin boys and a daughter of twenty. She was thus familiar on the most intimate daily basis with raging hormones and their consequences, and friendly, approachable and non-judgmental. She had known Kirsten since she was fourteen. She looked at her this morning across her desk with some foreboding.

'Oh dear,' she said, 'poor you.'

'Does it show?'

'Well – only to me. Because I know you so well. How do you feel?'

'Terrible. Just terrible. Can't stand it much longer.'

'Do you want to tell me about it? How did it happen?'

'In the usual way,' said Kirsten with a sigh.

'No, I mean why did you get pregnant?'

'Yes, so did I. I wasn't taking my pills properly.'

'Yes, well, they don't work unless you do,' said Meg, 'unfortunately. I think maybe we should consider an implant for you. And – ongoing relationship?'

'No. I'm afraid not. But – oh, God I'm such a mess. Can I – can I tell you about it? Could you bear it?'

'I'd like you to.'

When she had finished, Meg said she was sure Kirsten was going to make the right decision and that she could, if she liked, make the necessary arrangements. 'It'll take about a week. But don't rush it, Kirsten. I know you're feeling lousy, but it's important to get it right.'

'Yeah, I know,' said Kirsten with another sigh. 'Mrs Wilding, if it was your daughter, what would you say to her?'

'I'd tell her she must make up her own mind. But that her own life was at this stage a very important factor. Insofar as it affected her ability to care for a baby. Emotionally as well as practically. Motherhood is the most difficult job in the world, Kirsten. And it's not one you can leave if you don't like it.'

'I know. I know that. But –'

'And I know about the teaching of your Church and what it does to you. And I would be a great deal less fond of you if you didn't get so screwed up about it all. A termination is never nice. It's not nice for the mother and it's not nice for the doctor, I have to say. I hate it.'

Kirsten looked at her. 'Do you?'

'Of course I do. I'm surprised you're surprised.'

'What about the – the baby? What's it like for – it.'

Meg Wilding looked at her steadily. 'None of us can know. Of course. I think – we all like to think – that it isn't like anything for the baby. That it can't feel anything at all. But it would be wrong of me to tell you that categorically, because I don't know. I've never lied to you, Kirsten, and I'm not going to start now. I happen to think the Pro-Life people are an irresponsible lot, with their lurid emotive descriptions of the whole thing, just as irresponsible as anyone who goes into termination lightly. But I could be quite wrong. What I do know is that when I do my NHS clinics and I see young mums, young single mums who are having their second or third baby at nineteen, with no husbands to support them, no money, no back-up, my heart goes out to them – in spite of what the Tory press describe as their cushy living conditions. I don't think a council flat and sixty pounds a week or whatever is adequate recompense for what they have to cope with.'

'No,' said Kirsten quietly. The talk of single mothers was reminding her of Oliver rather painfully.

'Babies are demanding, tetchy, often disagreeable little creatures. It's just as well they can't talk, I often think, or we'd spend all our time quarrelling with them instead of trying somehow to shut them up. Of course they're lovely too, of course they're touching and sweet and intensely rewarding – at times. Nothing in the world like the first smile. Or the snuggling little head against your neck.'

'But –'

'Of course some single mothers are brilliant. You could well be. To be fair, I think you might. But not many are. And believe me, Kirsten, without back-up, it's hard to be adequate, let alone brilliant. Think of the baby, Kirsten, not of yourself. That's the background against which to make this decision.'

'Yes. Yes, thank you. I'll – I'll get back to you.'

'Fine. Now then, let's be practical, shall we? When was your last period, and –'

Oliver had no idea what to do. He felt instinctively he should speak to Bard, but he didn't know what to say. The thing was so slight, so tenuous, and the implications were somehow unpleasant. If detailed information was being given to the investigating accountants on what seemed to be an unofficial basis, and in what could only be described as a rather clandestine way – and, moreover, by someone with a rather intimate knowledge of the company and its workings – then it seemed to indicate that the investigations had reached what could at best be described as a delicate stage. Oliver was not stupid, nor was he an innocent; as the days had passed it had become increasingly clear that the accountants were looking at rather more than a list of the company's assets and its profit-and-loss account. Nevertheless it was hardly for him to say to Bard Channing – of whom he was in any case extremely nervous – look, you ought to know that someone you trust is betraying you. If Channing was honest, if he had nothing to hide, there was nothing to betray. But Channing was more to him than a boss; he owed him a great deal, and what did it matter if he did bawl him out? He couldn't kill him. Well, not quite ...

And if it turned out that he was wrong, that everything was in order, that there was a perfectly reasonable explanation, then that was fine. He'd have some egg on his face, but he had greater miseries than that to endure at the moment.

Bard had been in that morning, to see Sloane. It hadn't sounded a very happy encounter. Oliver didn't like Sloane; he treated him with mild, but very obvious, contempt.

He decided to go out to lunch and have a couple of glasses of wine to give him courage and then phone the house. He had never used the number, had never dared to, but he knew what it was.

Gray could hardly believe he could have been so stupid, not to have thought of her before, to have assumed she was what she seemed. It was obvious, so obvious; these old biddies always knew everything. Loyal beyond belief, they would all go to the rack for their bosses.

And of course she would have known: she would have seen, heard, everything. A perfect accomplice: discreet, slightly forbidding, the embodiment of respectability; if Bard Channing had advertised for someone to help him in his dealings, no-one more suitable could have turned up. She was like the wooden horse of Troy; he could send her in anywhere and no-one would dream of investigating her, of seeing in her more than she seemed. And she was also, clearly, claiming her rewards: a few phone calls (at the busiest times) had revealed a couple of bank accounts and a share portfolio. Clever old trout: she had gone up in Gray's estimation considerably. And it was going to make a marvellous twist to his story. But he still had to finally nail her at Robinson and Weatherill.

He was on his way to meet Shelley in the restaurant she had specified when he had called and offered to buy her lunch. It was called La Capannina and was to Jersey, Gray gathered, what the Caprice was to London, being filled with well-dressed expensive people eating well-dressed and expensive food.

Shelley was waiting for him when he got there, drinking champagne: 'I knew you'd want me to have some,' she said, smiling sweetly up at him. She was wearing stinging pink silk today, rather than red, and her dark hair was looped back with two big slides; she looked delicious and Gray wondered, not for the first time, how he could possibly have turned down her original invitation to dinner.

'Hi,' he said, sitting down opposite her. 'This is very good of you.'

'What, drinking champagne?'

'Well – coming to meet me. At such short notice. I'll have one of those,' he said to the waiter, pointing at the glass of champagne, 'and let's order, because once I start talking I don't think I'll be able to stop.'

'Sounds interesting,' said Shelley, 'and have the lamb, it's magic.'

Gray, who had an aversion to the word magic used in that context, suppressed it and ordered the lamb, because he didn't want to risk displeasing her in any way, preceded by carpaccio.

'Right,' she said, 'tell me what's happened.'

Gray told her, trying to keep his voice low; hearing it rising in volume and pitch, distracted from the story only briefly by the arrival of the carpaccio, which was so perfectly served with such exquisite olive oil and just the right amount of lemon and pepper and parmesan that he felt it deserved a tribute, however brief, of silent appreciation.

'Well,' said Shelley politely, when he had finished, 'that is very exciting.'

He was slightly disappointed, seeing that she was not actually going to lie awake that night thinking about it; but then reminded himself that anyone who did not actually know Bard Channing and his extraordinary company and history, and Marcia Grainger and her legendary formality and ability to daunt all comers, could have been expected to do so.

'And now I need your help,' he said.

'I'll try,' she said, through a rather large mouthful of lamb. 'I told you this was magic. Isn't it?'

'It is,' said Gray. 'Absolutely gr— magic. Yes.'

'So what do you want me to do?'

'Well, first of all, do you know anyone at Robinson and Wetherill?'

'Well,' she said warily, 'a few people. Derek Robinson for a start. But Gray I've told you –'

'Know any of the secretaries?'

'No. None of them. Well, except for Nancy, Derek's PA. Oh, and Maureen, in Personnel. So I'm not much use to you at all, I'm afraid.'

'Oh but you are,' said Gray. 'That's exactly, *exactly* what I was hoping to hear.'

Jackie Morton, who worked for one of the junior attorneys at Robinson and Wetherill, was just struggling her way through the first draft of a complicated new contract on the purchase of a very large and expensive house near Bouley Bay when her phone rang. She cursed the phone more fervently every time it rang, which was frequently, because she had been told by the junior attorney that he had to have the contract by four to take to a client meeting, and it was already a quarter past three. Moreover it had been made rather clear to her that her boss was not finding her work very satisfactory, and he had more or less hinted that if she didn't deliver this afternoon, she might find herself in a slightly less secure position.

'Yes?' she said. 'Yes, Jackie Morton speaking.'

'Oh, hallo,' said a rather hesitant, anxious Irish voice, 'I wonder if you can possibly help me. I'm in the most awful jam and I just don't know what to do.'

'Well, I'll try,' said Jackie, 'but I am very busy. So –'

'Oh, it won't take you a minute. I just want to confirm an address. Er – excuse me, but are you a secretary?'

'I am indeed,' said Jackie, wondering how much longer that might be the case. Certainly for Robinson and Wetherill.

'Well, that is wonderfully lucky,' said the voice, 'because you'll know how I'm feeling, what a predicament I'm in. My name is Mary, by the way, Mary O'Hagan. I work for Greenhills. I expect you know it.'

'Well, not too well, and I'm in a fine old predicament myself,' said Jackie, suddenly feeling a warm rush of sisterly support. 'I have a long contract to type, first draft and an impatient boss waiting to take it into a meeting at four.'

'Oh God, you poor soul. Well, I can't tell you how I sympathise. But how about this one, then? A letter to type, terribly urgent apparently, well, you know how it is, they're all terribly urgent, aren't they? Sorry, what was your name again?'

'Jackie.'

'Oh yes, of course. These men, Jackie, I feel so sorry for their poor wives, don't you, God I'm never going to get married. How long is your contract?'

'Seventeen pages. And I've only done twelve.'

'Oh no! But that is almost impossible. It's not fair, is it, they just don't understand. Well, I promise not to keep you. Now this is just a bit of a wild card, but I thought it would be worth a try. Your boss does take care of the Drab business, doesn't he?'

'Ye-es,' said Jackie doubtfully. 'Yes, I think so.'

'Well now, you see, Jackie, Mrs Grainger – Mrs Marcia Grainger, you know – is coming over to Jersey tomorrow. And I have to have this letter delivered to her hotel and waiting when she gets here. You'd think it was the crown jewels, I tell you. Well now, himself has gone off and never told me the name of the hotel, I thought it would be L'Horizon, but they're not expecting her, and so I suppose it's the Longueville Manor, or there again, it could be Water's Edge or even the Grand, but if I get it wrong I may as well throw myself into the Devil's Hole itself, now do you have any idea where she'll be staying?'

'I have no idea at all, I'm afraid,' said Jackie. 'My boss might, but –'

'Well, can you just confirm that she is coming over tomorrow, that would be something, if I have another day I can get my knickers a bit out of their twist. You do know who I mean, don't you, Jackie, Mrs Grainger –'

'Well, not really,' said Jackie, 'and I really do have to get this draft typed –'

'Of course you do. And I can't expect you to waste time on my predicament. But if you could just – oh, now I have an idea, could you give me the address in London, then I could phone her secretary there and ask her myself, and stop bothering you. Would you just do that for me, Jackie?'

'Well, I'll have to look in the file. It might take a minute. I don't even recall – just a minute, now –'

A long silence; Jackie picked up her pencil and a pad, and went and flicked through the files for Drab Financial Services Ltd. She had an uneasy feeling, indeed she knew perfectly well she shouldn't really be doing this, that all this sort of information was totally confidential, but she was so sick of being shouted at, asked to work through her lunch-break, given her work back to be done again, she didn't care. If they didn't like it, if they wanted to fire her, they could. She might even welcome it.

She returned to the phone.

'Hallo? Yes, here we are now, the address is 4 Frognal Rise Court, Swiss Cottage, London, NW3. Telephone 0171-787-9187.'

'Oh, Jackie, I cannot thank you enough. I'll return the favour one day. You've saved my life. And that is, just to confirm, that is Mrs Marcia Grainger, of Drab Financial Ltd. And the Folkestone Trust.'

'Yes it is,' said Jackie. 'Well, not the Folkestone Trust, no. The – just a minute – yes, the Sandstone Trust. And now if you'll excuse me ...'

'I knew there was a stone in it. Of course I will, and good luck with the contract, Jackie. I'll be thinking of you.'

'Thank you,' said Jackie.

She had put the phone down before she realised that she had never actually heard of Greenhills. Well, she had better things to worry about than that; it was now three twenty-five and there was something she absolutely could not read on page thirteen, and no-one to ask about it either ...

In Graydon Townsend's room at the Deux Jardins Hotel, Shelley Balleine put the phone down and grinned triumphantly at him.

'Wasn't I wonderful?' she said, still in her Irish accent. 'Aren't I just the most brilliant actress?'

'You are indeed,' said Graydon.

'So does that mean you've got him?'

'It means I'm ninety-nine per cent certain I've got him. It was the crucial piece in the puzzle, made sense of all the rest.'

'What do you do about the one per cent?'

'Pray. And use a very careful form of words.'

'I really can't make much sense of it,' she said.

'Just as well,' said Gray.

Shelley went back to her unfortunate boss for an hour or so, and Graydon got out his laptop and began pulling his story together. He felt he could have done anything at that moment: walked on water, flown through the air, spoken Chinese. Drifts of conversation, prompts for his happiness, kept coming back to him: 'Oh, yes, Marcia, she's very good, been coming here for years … rents a little bedsit over near St Peter … Now that is Mrs Marcia Grainger, isn't it, of Drab Financial … Aren't I just the most brilliant actress … Yes, Mr Grainger, we'll send you a bank statement straight away …' His thoughts, the facts, the structure of the piece, jumbled helplessly and hopelessly in his head for so long, suddenly formed into powerful, strong sentences, paragraphs, sections; quotes fell into his memory, questions found answers, it was as if someone else was dictating the piece, so easily, so logically did it all appear on the screen. It was, quite simply, he thought immodestly, terrific. Bribery, corruption, insider dealing; it had it all. He felt very confident about its veracity; his information had been pretty impeccable, his homework exceedingly thorough. But the lawyers would certainly be going through it with a toothcomb. 'The truth isn't what counts,' an editor had said to him once, 'it's deniability. Knowing something is true isn't enough. You've got to be able to prove it.'

Well, he could prove it. Just about. He had the pictures of the Manse, of Marcia Grainger – in her other persona, at the flying school – the recording of his conversation with Clive Hopkins.

The only thing left to do now – and it was a big thing – was go and see Bard Channing, confront him. It was something that had to be done, giving people the right to reply. If they'd see you. Usually they just threatened you with an injunction. And if they did it was inevitably a painful process, particularly if you liked the person. And he did like Channing. He couldn't help it; he was imaginative, brilliant, he had guts, vision, he kept going, didn't whine, wouldn't give up. OK, so now he knew he was a crook, but not, in Gray's book, a very serious one. Set against a drunk driver knocking someone down and killing them, or a rapist, or a bully of a parent knocking a child about or abusing it, a man who'd stashed away a few million ill-gotten quid in a numbered bank account didn't seem to him too terribly bad.

He rang the editor, told him he'd got the story.

'We should use it this Sunday, if we possibly can. But we can discuss that when I get back. We don't want it go off the boil. It'll be really big, Dave, lead story, or certainly second lead, and a spread inside at least …'

'Well, I'll need to know by Friday, Gray. Can't keep all that white space floating about indefinitely.'

'Dave! For God's sake. As my first boss used to say, this is a newspaper, not an annual.'

'Yeah, and I'm the editor, and it's run my way ... Cheers, Gray. Speak to you tomorrow.'

It was only when he realised he had used up all his teabags that he looked at his watch and saw that it was almost an hour after he had promised to phone Shelley.

Rachel had decided she should just arrive on Bard's doorstep. It was the only way. Ambush him. She knew he was based in London, at the house. If he wasn't there, she'd just wait. And give that bit of a housekeeper a mouthful of her own medicine, if she possibly could.

She left Francesca and the children in Reverend Mother's care, telling Francesca she had to go to London to see her dentist, that it was a long-standing appointment to have a crown refitted, that the crown was so loose it had come out twice in the past week, and that since it was a front crown, it being missing gave her a very close resemblance to a witch, and that she couldn't stand it any longer. She said she'd be back next day at around lunchtime.

She knew Francesca would believe that; Rachel's vanity was legendary. She teased her mother about it as she drove her to Okehampton to catch the train, adding that tooth trouble must be catching. Her own was fine now, only the occasional stab reminding her of it. As the pain was linked inextricably now in her mind with Liam and sexual pleasure, she quite liked the stabs ...

Rachel reached Paddington at four and got a taxi straight to Hamilton Terrace. Bard's Aston Martin was not outside the house: damn. Well, maybe he wouldn't be long.

She went up the steps, pressed the bell. Sandie came to the door.

'Oh, Mrs Duncan-Brown. Good afternoon. I'm afraid Mrs Channing's not here and –'

'I know where Mrs Channing is,' said Rachel briskly, 'thank you. It's Mr Channing I want to see.'

'He's not here either, I'm afraid. And I don't know when he'll be back –'

'Has he asked you to prepare dinner? I presume that is one of the things you do, that must have given you a clue.'

'Well, he said he'd be back for dinner, yes,' said Sandie. She looked less friendly. 'But that could be any time. Mr Channing doesn't keep to a strict timetable.'

'Well, I'll wait,' said Rachel. 'That's quite all right. Is Barnaby here?'

'No, he's gone away for a couple of days. Is Mr Channing expecting you?'

'No. I suppose he'd be here if he was. He's not an impolite man, is he, would you say?'

'Er – no.'

'Fine. Well, perhaps you could get me some tea, Sandie. I like Earl Grey. And do you have any cucumber?'

'Cucumber? Yes, I think so.'

'Excellent. I do so like cucumber sandwiches. Could I have a round or two? Oh, and with the crusts cut off, please.'

She sat down in the drawing room. It was untidy, somehow unkempt looking; Sandie was obviously taking advantage of Francesca's absence. And knowing Bard would be too distressed even to notice, certainly to care.

When Sandie brought in the tray, she smiled up at her graciously. 'How kind. Oh, dear, I didn't want milk, though, I wanted lemon. Would you mind? And also, Sandie, I did notice those flowers were dying. And those over there. I'm sure you wouldn't want Mr Channing to come in to that sort of thing. You could do them now, don't mind me. Order some fresh ones, I would. Oh, and did you realise those curtains aren't properly tied back? Shall I help you fix them? The hall carpet could do with a little vacuuming too, I should get it done before Mr Channing gets back.'

It was an hour before Bard came back; there were several phone calls to the house, one plainly for Sandie, since she spoke for long time. No doubt she used the phone a lot herself, was running up a huge bill. Francesca really should get rid of her. She was lazy as well as trouble.

She heard him come in, throw down something in the hall – his briefcase presumably – go into the kitchen, heard Sandie say something. Then he appeared; he looked at her with a kind of wary bravado. It was an expression she had seen on Jack's face.

'Hallo.'

'Hallo, Bard.'

'If you've come to see Francesca, she isn't here.'

'No, I know that. I've just left her.'

'Oh.' A silence, then he said, 'I thought she might come running to you. No doubt with some sob story. Well –'

'No, Bard. No sob story. Let's not get onto that tack. You look exhausted, you poor man, I'll get Sandie to make you something. What about an omelette now, nothing like getting the blood sugar up to help you cope. Sandie, make Mr Channing an omelette would you, cheese, I would think, or would you rather have tomatoes, Bard? and do you want a drink? No. Well, then a bottle of Perrier, I'd like some too. And could I have some more Earl Grey, dear, and another round of these sandwiches. Quite delicious.

'You should get rid of her,' she said, sitting down, gesturing at the seat beside her for him to sit down. 'She's dreadful. You know it was her who imparted the news about Francesca and that son of yours, don't you? Charming. And this place is a pigsty.'

'Rachel, I really haven't come here to be lectured on my staff. Your own daughter has caused me a lot more grief.'

'Possibly about as much as you've caused her, I'd say,' said Rachel, 'but no, that's not why I'm here. Nor have I come to discuss your marriage. I've come with a proposition for you.'

She stood up, walked over to the window, looked out for a bit, then turned round and smiled at him: her most dazzling smile. 'I'll provide your alibi, Bard. It'll be a pleasure.'

'It's nice here,' said Jack to Francesca. 'I'd like to stay always.' He had just come in from doing the egg collection with Richard. 'Can we go to the beach now? I could do some surfing. Barnaby told me about surfing, I know how to do it.'

'Well, we could go to the beach,' said Francesca, 'but I don't think any surfing. Not today, anyway. You need a grown-up with you to show you how.'

'We could take Richard. Or Mary. I like Mary. She's cool.'

'I don't think either Richard or Mary is very good at surfing,' said Francesca, 'but let's go down to the beach anyway. Kitty would like that.'

'Does she have to come?'

'Yes she does.'

'Oh all right. And can we take Mary anyway? I could show her how to dive.'

'Jack, you can't dive in the sea. There's nothing to dive off.'

'There's the cliffs.'

'Er – yes,' said Francesca.

They drove through the village down the lane to the beach. Mary sat in the back, holding Kitty's hand. She smiled at Francesca every time she turned round. She really was very sweet, thought Francesca, noticing absently that she had a rather runny nose. She passed her a tissue; Mary wiped her nose very carefully and tucked the tissue up her sleeve.

As they reached the edge of the village, they passed a large, rather beautiful grey stone house, built high above the lane; it had very pretty wrought-iron gates set in a high brick wall, with roses tumbling endlessly over them. It looked neglected; there was an old man sitting on the steps that led up from the gate, mopping his brow in the hot afternoon sun. Poor old chap, she thought; probably the gardener. Not a time to be working.

There was a path over the dunes to the beach, edged with gorse, brilliant yellow against the blue sky; she had to pull the buggy. Jack and Mary pushed it, which actually drove it deeper into the sand, but their intentions were so good she didn't have the heart to stop them. The beach was no more than a large cove, but the tide was out, the big Atlantic tide, and the wet sand stretched out, shimmering silver in the sun. It was very hot, but the cliffs threw out great shadows, making a shelter, and there were tall caves, Enid Blyton caves, Francesca thought smiling, which they could explore. She looked at the sea, rolling endlessly in, the seagulls circling above it, at the rows of cliffs ranged as far as she could see; felt the warmth of the sand under her feet, licked her lips and tasted the salt. Mary and Jack were making a castle: or rather Mary was making one under Jack's direction. 'Too high,' he was shouting, 'too high. Make it wider. No, wider. Dig fast.' He was very much his father's son.

She carried Kitty down to the water's edge, and dipped her small feet into it; she squealed, giggled, kicked violently. The water was cold, and very clear. A small shoal of tiddlers swerved through the water, moving this way and that in their orderly forty-five-degree progression. Francesca felt soothed, comforted, almost happy. She had always loved the sea; it made her feeel strong. Well, she needed to feel strong. Maybe she should come and live down here, as Jack had said.

She went back to him, him and Mary. They had tired of the castle and were now working on a tunnel. 'We could make it all the way up to the convent,' said Jack, 'and crawl up it.'

Mary nodded enthusiastically.

Francesca set Kitty down on the sand; she promptly started eating it.

'Oh, no you don't,' she said, 'come on, sit on my knee, I'll give you a drink.'

She watched Kitty drinking out of her beaker, her small face frowning in concentration, thinking how well she looked now, brown and almost chubby. It was much too soon to say, of course, but maybe Mr Lauder had been right in his cautiously expressed hope; maybe the hole in her heart would heal itself; maybe she would, literally, grow out of it.

Mary picked up the baby, carried her a little way down the beach, talking to her; Francesca watched her, leant back on the rocks. It was so wonderful to be without Nanny, having her children to herself. Well, she probably would, now, all the time. Bankrupt people didn't usually have nannies.

The trouble was the minute she wasn't properly occupied her dilemma crowded back in upon her, all the aching, exhausting pressure of it. She kept hearing Liam's voice, telling her that of course she mustn't do it, that if Bard really loved her, he would never have asked her to do such a thing. He was right: it was perfectly true. She knew what her mother thought: that she should do what Bard had asked. She would have done it, without a doubt. She hadn't said so, of course, but she had fixed Francesca with her brilliant blue eyes and said poor man, poor poor man, and although then she had hugged Francesca, told her she was desperately sorry for her, that she could not imagine a more terrible situation for any wife to find herself in, it was perfectly clear what she really thought.

But then, her mother was braver than she was. And a lot less intrinsically honest.

Shelley was rather cool when Gray finally phoned her.

'So now I'm no more use to you, you can keep me waiting for an hour.' She spoke lightly, but she was clearly upset.

'Shelley, I'm so sorry. I – well, I got bogged down in it all. Had to phone my editor, do all sorts of things.'

'That's OK,' she said, 'as long as I was able to be of service.'

'Oh God, I'm sorry,' said Gray again, 'I really am a sod, aren't I? I just don't know what I'd have done without you today. Well, right through this. You've been terrific.'

'I aim to please,' she said, sounding more herself.

'Good. Now then, can I buy you the dinner I spurned the other night? We could go back to that nice hotel. I really would like that.'

There was a silence, then she said, quietly, 'No. Sorry, Gray. I've just fixed up dinner with someone else.' There was another pause, then she added, 'Now. But I'm glad it's all worked out so well for you.'

'Oh – yes. Well thanks. If you ever come to London –'

'Don't worry. I'll be on your doorstep. I have your fine card.' She was Irish again now, laughing at him. 'Bye, Gray. Good luck with it all.'

'Thanks,' he said, and put the phone down, suddenly and in spite of everything depressed, seeing a fiercely vivid picture of Shelley, in her white trousers and cotton sweater, standing in a rock pool, her pretty heart-shaped face smiling at him. The whole thing seemed, on a small scale, symptomatic of all his relationships, and his ability to wreck them: by thoughtlessness, selfishness, sheer bloody stupidity. He might be a good journalist, he might have a nice way with words, he might have a fine eye for design and a clever way with a pasta sauce, but when it came to emotional matters he was a blockhead, as Kirsten would have said. A lonely, perfectly dressed, beautifully styled future stretched before him, and he could see no way out of it.

He sighed, tried to return to the flying, triumphant mood of an hour earlier and failed rather dismally. Not even the prospect of the story of a lifetime beneath his byline could quite accomplish that.

'Mr Channing, this is Oliver Clarke. I'm very sorry to bother you, but there's something I really would like to talk to you about. I'm out of the office, I'll have to phone back, maybe this evening. Thank you.'

There was a second message, almost identical. Bard looked at the answering machine with distaste.

'God, what is it now. Wants to know about his job, I suppose. Well, he'll phone again, no doubt.'

He and Rachel were in his study, the door shut; he had not wanted to talk to her in the drawing room.

'She shouldn't have told you,' he said. 'She had no right to tell you.'

'And you had no right to ask her.'

'Well, I know that. But I'm pretty desperate.'

'I can see. I'm quite serious about my offer. And I'm a very good liar, and Francesca is not.'

He was silent for a minute, then he said, 'No. I couldn't let you. There is far less reason for you to.'

'And all the more, therefore, for people to believe me.'

'I don't see why you should, in any case,' he said.

'Well, let's say, for all the reasons she should. To help you. To save the family. The children. Also –' She hesitated.

'Yes?'

'I can't help hoping that if – if you came out of this with something salvaged, you might still be able to help me.'

'Ah,' he said, and he almost smiled, 'so now we have it. A motive. A quid pro quo. Well, that makes me feel a little better.'

'So when did you make this – this phone call? Where were you really?'

'In my office. On the Thursday before the crash. But late. Everyone had gone. It was stupid, sheer panic. I should have gone out, done it from somewhere else.'

'Or not done it all.'

'Well – yes. Obviously. Rachel, I do want you to understand why I did it. It was panic. Panic and a desire to salvage something. Not so much for me, but for Francesca, the children. Sheer, criminal stupidity.' He grinned at her. 'Certainly criminal. You don't seem too troubled by that, Rachel, if I may say so. Having a crook as a son-in-law.'

'Well, I'm a pragmatic soul,' said Rachel briskly, 'and anyway, crook is a very strong word. Too strong. I know so very well how these things happen. What that particular breed of panic can do to you, how those chains of events take you over. I did wonder – no, I'd better not ask any more. The less I know the better.'

'Christ,' he said, 'you really do know this stuff, don't you?'

'Bard, I've been through it all, of course I do.'

He said nothing, just looked at her very seriously.

'How much will you lose?' she said.

'Oh – a lot. Not everything, of course. This house is in Francesca's name. So that's safe.'

'But she's –'

'Well,' he said, lightly, 'she can sell it.' He sighed. 'I won't ask you what she's feeling now. I don't know what I'm feeling myself, God help me ... I thought at first I would never forgive her, never want to see her, be near her again. Now I'm not quite so sure.'

'It was particularly – hideous for you,' said Rachel. 'A terrible thing for her to have done. And for Liam to have done.'

'I would like,' he said simply, 'to kill him. If he walked in here now, I would do that. I know it.'

Rachel looked at him, tried to imagine how he must feel and failed totally. 'Well,' she said finally, 'whatever else, he is certainly extremely clever. He has preyed on Francesca at a time when he knew she was extremely vulnerable.'

'I don't think,' said Bard drily, 'that is quite excuse enough. Actually.'

'Of course it's not. I can't and won't try to excuse what she did. I find it very – shocking.'

'You do, Rachel?' he said, and there was an odd note in his voice, one almost of relief. 'You really do?'

'Yes, of course I do,' she said. 'Very shocking. I may be her mother, but I am not a fool about her. And not without a moral sense. But it is

538

out of character. She is a fiercely honest person. I'm sure she didn't enter into this without a lot of anguish.'

'I would certainly hope not,' he said, his dark eyes heavy.

'But Bard, I do think the background, her unhappiness, her anxiety, Liam's behaviour, does help at least explain it. Not excuse it, of course. And that might make forgiveness a little more possible.'

'A little. Perhaps.'

'Or at least acceptance,' said Rachel. 'There's a huge difference. And in my experience, the one leads to the other. Given time.'

'Quite a lot of time, in this particular instance, I fear,' said Bard with a sigh, 'but yes, you're probably right. You're a wise woman, Rachel.'

'Well,' she said, 'I have had quite a lot to accept, in my time. And to forgive. I've learnt pragmatism. As you know.'

'I do.' For the first time he smiled at her. It was a rather exhausted, grim smile, but it was a smile. 'In any case, I have my own theory about the whole thing. I think it was a deliberate plan of Liam's, a sabotage, a kind of revenge for all the wrongs he thinks I have done him. I think he set out to seduce her. When, as you say, he knew she was vulnerable.'

'Bard, nobody is that devious. Surely.'

'Liam is. Believe me. Of course he would never admit it. But that is what I think. There is nothing, nothing at all, he would not do to hurt me. And I suspect Francesca may never hear from him again. Which will prove my case.'

'Good God.' She was silent.

'The worst thing, you know,' he said, suddenly, 'is not that she slept with him. It's that she could have been fond of him, been close to him, talked to him; I find that almost intolerable. The thought of what he might have told her about me, the thought of them together, discussing me ... And – God. Oh my God.' He was suddenly silent, looked at her, his face horrified. 'You don't think,' he said, and his voice was very quiet, almost inaudible, 'you don't think she'll have told him? What I asked.'

'No,' said Rachel, 'no, I don't. I'm sure she hasn't. Quite quite sure.'

'She told you.'

'I'm her mother. That's different. She trusts me totally.'

'I'd like to be sure,' he said, 'because if he knows that, I'm – well, I'm really done for.'

'Surely he can't hate you that much?'

'He hates me that much. Oh, partly my own fault, no doubt. I was a lousy father to him. But there were – mitigating circumstances. And I did try. For a long time I tried. Oh Christ. Christ Almighty.' He was slumped now in his chair. 'This gets worse and worse.'

The phone shrilled suddenly.

'Yes? Hallo, yes, this is Bard Channing. Oh. Yes, I see.' He stood up suddenly, his face very taut, expressionless. 'Fine. Yes. Well, let me look at my diary. Friday morning would be all right. Eleven. Yes. With –' He scribbled a name down on a pad. 'Yes. Yes, I've got that. Goodbye.'

He looked at Rachel. 'That was the Serious Fraud Office. They want me to go in. Just for a chat, you understand. That's all. Just for a chat.' He put out his hand suddenly, gripped hers. 'Don't go away, Rachel. I don't think I want to be alone just now.'

Well, thought Oliver, pulling the ring off a can of lager, with a hand that he noticed was shaking, he'd agreed to see him, at least. That was something. Although the thought of confronting him, telling him face to face, was pretty terrifying. He'd hoped to do it on the phone. He couldn't imagine quite how he was going to do it. What he was going to say. Maybe he could get Channing asking him questions. That would make it easier. The more he thought about it now, the more unlikely the whole thing seemed, the crazier his idea. But he couldn't go back now. And he'd checked the phone number, from a phone box, and it had been what he'd thought. Who he'd thought.

Every time his mind strayed towards the the next afternoon – at three o'clock, at the house, Channing had said – Oliver felt like throwing up. He'd never sleep that night. Not a wink.

Well, at least it was taking his mind off Kirsten.

Kirsten's conversation with Meg Wilding had made her feel worse rather than better. She was so bloody honest, she thought; why couldn't she have given me the answers I wanted to hear, made it easier for me? She felt now more than ever as if she were on the rack, pulled, stretched this way and that, tormented by primitive visions of perpetual hellfire and more rational ones of perpetual guilt, of dead and dying embryos. And thought that however sensible, however rational, she couldn't do it; she couldn't get rid of this baby. It was impossible; she would have it, manage somehow, make amends for the rest of her life for what had been at best an appallingly reckless, irresponsible piece of behaviour. She could manage somehow; she knew she could. At least she'd be able to live with herself.

She felt better after making her decision; went for a short walk, and then, when she got back to the flat, realised she was out of milk and drove to the Seven Eleven. It was very crowded, mostly with people going home from work, men, girls, young couples. She got some milk and a large packet of crisps – she had a craving for crisps at the moment, they were about the only food she fancied – and was standing in the queue to pay for them, when a girl came in, with a baby in a pushchair and a toddler hanging on to her hand. The toddler was crying and its nose was running, and he was grizzling and swinging on her hand; she kept shaking at his arm, telling him to be quiet. She looked about eighteen years old.

She picked up a packet of nappies and some sweets and joined the queue behind Kirsten. Kirsten smiled at her but she looked back at her blankly. The toddler was on the floor now, fiddling with his shoes, trying to undo them.

'Don't,' said the girl, as if it mattered. He looked up at her, his small face a study in defiance, and started fiddling with his mother's shoes instead. Suddenly she bent down, slapped his hand off her foot; he started to bellow, and she bent down again, pulled him up by his arm. His flailing legs caught Kirsten's and hurt her quite sharply; she winced, tried to say it didn't matter.

'Course it matters,' said the girl, although she didn't apologise, shaking the child now. 'Don't do that, you little bugger, and don't cry, just stand still, shut up.'

He went on crying and she raised her arm and hit him, hard, on his bottom. Kirsten winced.

'Oh don't,' she said, 'don't smack him. He doesn't mean any harm.'

The girl ignored her and, since he was still yelling and kicking, smacked the child again.

'Don't!' said Kirsten more sharply. 'It's not fair.'

The girl looked at her, through mean, exhausted eyes. 'You shut up,' she said, 'keep your opinions to yourself. He's my child, not yours.'

Kirsten turned her back on her, paid the bill and went out to the car. As she reached it, the girl and the children came out; Kirsten looked at her and the girl raised two fingers. Kirsten sighed and started the car; and then suddenly looked at the little boy's face. It was pale, heavy, dull with misery, with boredom, with what she supposed if he had been older would have been called despair. And suddenly she saw his life, that little boy's; days spent interminably with his despairing mother – who was probably not really bad tempered, not intrinsically rude, had merely reached rock bottom in her struggle to cope, to provide, to be cheerful even. And she felt sorry to the bottom of her heart not only for the mother, for that girl, who had lost her youth, her future, her present even, but also, still more so for the child.

And heard Meg Wilding's voice saying, 'Think of the baby, Kirsten, not of yourself,' and realised that she had indeed only been thinking of herself, her own guilt, her own tortured conscience; looked at the kind of life she might in truth be able to offer that baby, and at the spoilt, immature, self-centred person who would be its mother, and knew what she had to do.

She went home and left a message on Meg Wilding's answering machine before she could change her mind.

'What's that pretty house in the village?' said Francesca to Reverend Mother at supper. 'The one set high up, behind the wall. Is it a vicarage or something?'

'No, it's much nicer than the vicarage,' said Reverend Mother. 'It belongs to a charming man, Colonel Philbeach, his wife died a few years ago ... It's actually called High House. Such a lovely family, they were: all grown up now, and flown the nest. I fear he's very lonely. He was going to sell the house last year, but at the last minute pulled out because he didn't like the people.'

'Oh, I can understand that,' said Francesca. 'Houses are like – well, like children. You can't just put them in the care of any old people, people who won't understand them.'

She looked across at Mary, who was smiling at Richard, and thought how lucky she was, to be here, to be safe, to be happy, loved, understood; and then remembered she wasn't quite so lucky or so safe any more. She found it very hard to imagine Mary living in the flat in Battersea; she would pine for the country terribly. Maybe – just maybe –'

'Do you think Colonel Philbeach might put the house back on the market?'

'I don't know. I would think he'll have to. He's very hard up.'

A little later she went to phone her mother. There was no reply from the flat; Rachel had obviously gone out on the town. Francesca left a message on the answering machine to say she'd ring in the morning, and went for a walk round the convent grounds.

She was slightly surprised Liam hadn't phoned. In fact she was – well, quite surprised. Of course it was difficult for him sometimes, but he had her mobile number, he could ring any time. He always had before, and it was safer, easier when she was here, away from Bard. He must know how she'd be feeling, must know how much she'd appreciate even the briefest call. Well, maybe Naomi was home, taking a few days off before starting her new job. Yes, that was probably it. And the children were around all the time, of course, it was the school holidays. She still felt uneasy about telling him about Bard. She shouldn't have done it. Of course he wouldn't tell anyone, obviously he wouldn't, she trusted him totally; but if she had been more in her right mind she would have kept her mouth shut. It wasn't fair on him, apart from anything else. It wasn't fair on anyone, she thought bitterly. Certainly not on her.

She went back to her room and tried to read, but she couldn't concentrate. She kept now hearing her mother's voice asking her if there was any future in her relationship with Liam, and suddenly she wanted to know. Not that he was going to move out and suggest they set up home together or anything; but whether he was going to tell Naomi, so that they could be together more. She supposed he would; after all, Naomi wasn't going to care. And then they could explore their relationship properly, get to know one another, just enjoy one another. It was essential really.

Yes, if he didn't ring in the morning, she might try him. She could always put the phone down if Naomi picked it up. She missed him.

'I thought,' said Naomi, over supper that night, 'we might go away for a few days. Once I start this job, week after next that is, we'll be stuck for the rest of the summer. I mean if we went on Friday, say, we could have ten days. We could go to my dad's flat in Spain, he says it's free next week. I know it's a bit grotty, but at least it'd be a break. What do you think?'

Liam thought fast. It would quite suit him to go away. He had no real desire to pursue the relationship with Francesca any longer; it had served it purpose and he could see her becoming very tedious. If he just wasn't at home, and didn't contact her, she'd presumably get the message pretty quickly. And if she didn't get the message, she still wouldn't be able to bother him. He had this tasty little morsel for the *News* of course, but he could deliver that first thing in the morning and then it would be quite a good idea to get the hell out of things for a bit. Townsend would be back tomorrow, the girl had said so.

'Lovely idea,' he said, 'yes. And I might even stay on for another week or so with the kids, if the flat's still free. They haven't had much fun lately.'

'Fine. Well, I'll ring Dad and clinch it then. And you can sort out the flights tomorrow.'

'OK,' said Liam.

★

Bard had gone to see his solicitor; it was nine o'clock. Rachel felt uneasy, sitting there in the great house. Awkward. Compromised. Well, of course that was ridiculous, but she did want to go home. She needed to go home. Francesca might phone, wonder where she was. Perhaps she should ring her. Tell her she was in a restaurant or something. Yes, that was a good idea.

She tried the convent, but there was no reply; they seldom picked up the phone in the evening. And she had left Francesca's mobile number in her other bag, at the convent. Very sensible.

Well, never mind. As soon as Bard got back — and he'd said he wouldn't be much after eight-thirty, his solicitor was going out to dinner — she'd go. She couldn't possibly stay the night.

She heard the car outside: good, he was back. She had a tray of drinks waiting for him, some smoked salmon and a salad. Sandie had gone out, said it was her evening off. She'd see he was all right, they could share the food, and then she'd go.

She heard the front door shut and then total silence: just nothing. It was unnerving. She went out to the hall. And knew she couldn't go home.

Bard was grey, leaning with his back against the door: appropriate, she thought. His great head was thrown back, he was staring up at the ceiling. Rachel went forward, took one of his hands.

'Bard? Are you all right?'

He looked at her, staring at her as if he didn't even know who she was for a long time; then he said, 'No. Not really.'

'Come on,' she said gently, leading him into the drawing room, 'come on, tell me about it.'

He sat down heavily on the sofa, buried his head in his hands. 'It looks like I've had it,' he said.

Rachel phoned the convent first thing in the morning and left a message for Francesca, to say she had to go back to her dentist and wouldn't be down until the evening.

'Tell her I'll ring later about which train I'll be on. But probably the five o'clock.'

'Poor Mummy,' said Francesca, when she received this information. 'She's obviously having a lot of trouble. I think I might wander up to the village, Reverend Mother, take the children. Kitty didn't sleep very well, I don't know why. Probably over-excited. She might drop off in the buggy.'

'Mary's not too well this morning,' said Reverend Mother. 'She has a very nasty cold. She has a weak chest, you know, we have to be careful with her.'

'Oh dear,' said Francesca. 'I hope that's not my fault, letting her get all her things wet on the beach yesterday.'

'No, no, she was starting the cold before that.'

'Yes, I did notice. I'll see if we can find her a little something in the village, cheer her up.'

She felt tired herself that morning; tired and depressed and with a throbbing headache. Liam hadn't phoned, and she had hardly slept. The pressure of time passing added to the rest; she felt terribly alone. Every time she thought she was coming near to making a decision something tugged her the other way: she would think no, she couldn't do it, and then she would look at Jack, his clear, untroubled little face, and think how he would feel with a father imprisoned for fraud, think that she could save him from it, decide perhaps she should: and then think of doing it, of lying, formally, publicly, for a man she no longer loved, and knew she couldn't.

She was beginning to think she was going mad.

She set out with the children; the village was half a mile from the convent, down a high-banked Devon lane, lush with fern, which opened up suddenly near the church and the village green. They spent some time in the village shop, bought a packet of pretty hankies for Mary, which the lady in charge produced, rather dusty, from the bottom of a shelf piled high with teatowels, dusters, and children's T-shirts. There was a long delay while Jack tried to persuade Francesca that Mary would much prefer some bubble gum and a water pistol; she dissuaded him with some difficulty, finally agreeing to the bubble gum for himself. He walked down the village street blowing huge balls of it, and popping them loudly while Kitty watched him admiringly. She seemed better; probably just over-excited and therefore overtired, Francesca thought. That was certainly what Nanny would say.

As they reached High House, the old man she had thought to be the gardener appeared at the gate with an equally elderly black Labrador. He wasn't quite as old as she had thought: he looked as if he were in his late sixties, and rather good looking, with brilliant blue eyes and thick, silvery hair. He raised his battered panama to her; she smiled at him, said good morning.

'Good morning to you.'

'I was admiring your house yesterday as we drove past. It's lovely.'

'How very kind of you. Yes, I love it too.'

'Reverend Mother, from the convent, you know, we're staying there, said it was on the market last year.'

'It was indeed, but the people who wanted it were rather dreadful. Yuppies, I believe they're called. In the end I couldn't let it go to them. Hanging on a bit longer. But really I should move into something smaller, I'm afraid.'

'Very sad for you.'

'Well, yes and no. Not sure that I can face another winter in this place. Very expensive. And very cold. But the thought of all that business with estate agents, dreadful people coming round – oh dear.' He smiled at her. 'Are you from round here, or –'

'London, we live in London,' said Jack. 'It's horrible. I like it here much better.'

'Of course you do. Any child would. Been on the beach, have you?'

'Yes. I'm going surfing today. Can you surf?' asked Jack.

'I used to be able to. Believe it or not. Oh, not all this Malibu nonsense, but we used to have such fun, on our old wooden boards, me and my lot.' He smiled at Jack, patted him on the head. Jack grinned up at him.

'Charming,' he said to Francesca, raising his hat. 'Well, I must be on my way ...'

'Er – Colonel Philbeach – I'm sorry, Reverend Mother told me who you were – my mother and I – well, that is, I wondered if – if you were serious about selling the house – whether we could come and have a look at it. Later.'

'Oh. I don't know.' He hesitated. 'Oh, why not. Yes, of course you could come. Yes. I've got some chappie coming round to sort out the summerhouse, but – look, can I get you at the convent?'

'I've got a –' Francesca stopped herself just in time; she didn't think the Colonel would approve of a mobile phone. The yuppies had probably had one. 'Yes. Yes you could. My name is Francesca Channing.'

'Excellent. I'll phone you. I have the number, of course.' He beamed down at Kitty. 'Pretty little thing. Good morning to you.'

'Good morning. And thank you.'

Meg Wilding phoned Kirsten at work, and said she had had an operation cancelled for Saturday morning; if she liked she could book her in then.

'I know it's a bit of a rush, but there's no point hanging about.'

'No,' said Kirsten. She had already been sick three times that morning; suddenly even three days seemed a very long time.

Colonel Philbeach phoned the convent and said that he would be delighted to see Mrs Channing and her mother that evening at six-thirty. 'Come for a glass of sherry. Oh, and bring the young chap. I'll show him our surfboards.'

Francesca had already accepted when she realised she still didn't know when Rachel would be back. Damn. She might try and catch her. She phoned the flat: no answer.

Well, she could try the dentist, she thought. She might catch her there, or be able to leave a message; she knew the number, it was the dentist she used to go to herself. Her life recently seemed to be revolving around dentists, she thought amusedly.

She dialled the number. It was engaged. Damn.

And then she looked down at the phone, and thought she would try Liam. Quickily. Before she had time to think.

A child answered the phone. 'Islington four-seven-six-nine.' A little boy: that would be Jasper. He sounded sweet, perfectly spoken, very efficient.

'Oh – oh hallo. Is – is Mr Channing there?'

'No. No he's gone out. Can I take a message?'

'Oh – no. No, it's all right. I'll call again. When will he be back?'

'I'm afraid I don't know. Sorry.'

'Oh. All right then. Thank you.'

She put the phone down, feeling bleak, Absurdly bleak. Then she shook herself. It was obviously terribly difficult for Lim to phone her at the moment. With the children there all the time. Probably he'd gone out to phone her. Probably he'd phone any minute. She'd ring the dentist quickly and then keep her line free.

'Mr Poultney's surgery.'

'Oh – good morning. This is Mrs Channing, Mrs Duncan-Brown's daughter. I wonder is my mother there? Or if not, could you tell me when her appointment is, give her a message from me?'

There was a silence, then the receptionist said, 'I'm sorry, Mrs Channing, there must be some mistake. Mrs Duncan-Brown isn't booked in with us this morning.'

'Oh. Oh I see.' Francesca's sense of disorientation increased. 'But she did come in yesterday, didn't she?'

'No, Mrs Channing. She has an appointment for two weeks' time, maybe you've been confused –'

'Yes. Obviously. Thank you.'

Francesca slammed the phone down. If her mother wasn't at the dentist, where the hell was she? And why should she have lied to her? A dark, unwelcome thought came into her mind; so unwelcome she could scarcely bear it. She got up, walked round the room, kept looking at her phone. Finally, very slowly and almost reluctantly, she picked it up again, punched out the number of Hamilton Terrace.

Mrs Roberts answered it.

'Oh – Mrs Roberts. Good morning. This is Mrs Channing.'

'Good morning, Mrs Channing. How are you?'

'I'm fine, Mrs Roberts, thank you. I just wondered – er – my mother hasn't been there, has she?'

'She was here, Mrs Channing, yes. She was here when I arrived, as a matter of fact. But she's gone now. Can I give her a message if she comes back?'

'Oh – no. No thank you, Mrs Roberts,' said Francesca. 'No, it's quite all right.'

She put the phone down and sat staring at it, angrier than she could ever remember. At being lied to, belittled, manipulated, betrayed. And disregarded. Completely disregarded. Again. And then suddenly, through the white heat of her rage, it came: the answer. Brilliantly, savagely simple: the answer to her dilemma.

Chapter Twenty-eight

'Gray, you look wonderful. You're quite brown. I don't believe you've been doing any work at all.'

'Have you?' said Gray lightly.

'Yes of course I have,' said Tricia indignantly. 'Look at these poor stubby things, worn to the bone.' She waved her hands at him. 'Well? Was it good?'

'It was very good. As stories go, this is going to run and run. Now I have to make a couple of appointments. Starting with Mr Channing.'

'Oh, I thought you'd have spoken to him already. He's been very pro-active. Didn't you get the message?'

'What message?' said Gray. 'And no, no I didn't.'

'Oh. I'm very sorry. I did leave one at the hotel.'

'Well, I didn't get it. What was it, anyway?'

'Bard Channing came here, the first day you were away I think it was. He said to tell you to keep your nose out of his affairs, and that he had some very good lawyers.'

'Charming.'

'Yes. Yes, he was. But then he rang again, said it was very urgent he spoke to you, and could you ring him. So I phoned you straight away.'

'And never thought to make sure I'd got the message? Bloody incompetent,' said Gray.

'Gray, how was I supposed to –'

'By using your bloody brain,' said Gray. 'Anyway, let's not waste time on that now. Get him for me, will you? I presume you've got the number.'

'Well – no. Because after I'd given it to the hotel, I threw it away. But it was an Islington number, I do remember that –'

'You don't remember any such thing,' said Gray. 'Bard Channing doesn't live in Islington. Well, never mind. I've got it here – shit.'

'What's the matter?'

'I've left my bloody Filofax at home. Must be losing my grip. Well, I can get it from Kirsten. Get her for me, will you?'

Kirsten sounded very subdued, startled to hear his voice. 'Oh – hallo, Gray.'

'You OK?'

'Oh – yes. Yes, thank you.'

'You don't sound it. And they said you weren't well the other day. What's the matter?'

'Oh – some bug or other. I'll live.' There was a silence, then she said, 'How's things with you?'

'Oh – fine. Thanks. Look, can you give me your dad's number at home?'

'Well I –'

'Come on, Kirsten, I've rung it lots of times, spoken to your stepmother. But I've left it at home. He's rung me, for Christ's sake, he wants to speak to me.'

'Oh. Oh, I see. Yes, all right. It's four-five-six, double-three, double-three.'

'Thanks. Hope you get better soon. We must have a drink. For old times' sake.'

'Yes. Sure.'

She really did sound rotten, Gray thought. He might ask Francesca about her if she was at the house.

Francesca didn't answer the phone; Rachel did. She remembered Gray immediately from the funeral; she had liked him, he was rather charming, and extremely well dressed, she remembered, and they had had a most enjoyable chat about their favourite London restaurants.

'How can I help?' she said.

'It's your son-in law I'm after. He phoned me, it seems.'

'Oh, he did? Well, I'm afraid he's not here. Tell me what it was about, perhaps I can help –'

'I don't think you can, unfortunately,' said Gray. 'Perhaps you could just tell him I called. I'm at my office.'

'Which is?'

'The *News on Sunday*. He'll have the number.'

'Oh yes, of course, I'd forgotten for a moment you were a journalist, how stupid of me. Well, I have to say I'm a little surprised he called you, Mr Townsend, he's rather hostile to the press at the moment. Understandably.'

'Yes, quite,' said Gray, 'but I definitely did have a message that he'd called. Urgently, was the word.'

'Well, then obviously he did,' said Rachel. 'Look, I'll tell him you rang and I'm sure he'll be in touch. Er – when was this message?'

'On Tuesday. But I've been away.'

'Right. Well, he won't be much longer, and I'll tell him the minute he comes in. Now tell me, have you been to Ceccone's lately, because I thought it had become even better?'

'No,' said Gray, 'but I tried to take your daughter there, to buy her lunch. She turned me down.'

'How very silly of her,' said Rachel, 'on two counts.'

'Well, thank you. Is she there? Francesca, I mean?'

'No, she's away for a few days. And I'm only passing through. Well, goodbye, Mr Townsend.'

She had just put the phone down when Bard came in. He had been back to see his solicitor; he looked slightly better.

'Philip seemed a bit more – optimistic this morning. He's been talking to a barrister, seems to think we've a chance.'

'What did he say?'

'Well, of course everyone actually says very little in these situations. It's all done in a kind of code, as no doubt you know. You can't sit down and say "This is what I did, now how are we going to cover it up", it's much more "This is what they seem to think I've done, but obviously I don't know anything about it". But the barrister was very bullish, apparently, said intent in these cases is almost impossible to prove. Which is the relevant thing. So I'm feeling a bit more chipper. Who was that on the phone?'

'That very charming young man Mr Townsend. You remember him?'

'I do, yes,' said Bard, 'and charming is not quite the adjective I'd apply to him. What did he want?'

'He wanted you.'

'He can take a running jump,' said Bard. 'I'm not speaking to him.'

'Why did you ring him then?' said Rachel.

'I didn't ring him, for Christ's sake.'

'He said you did. Said you wanted to speak to him urgently. He was quite clear about it.'

Bard looked at her. The vein throbbed suddenly on his forehead. 'Did he say when I was supposed to have made this call?'

'Yes. On Tuesday.'

'Christ,' he said. 'Jesus Christ.'

'Christ,' said Gray. 'Jesus Christ.' He had put the phone down, was sitting staring at it. 'Tricia, what did you say about Channing's number? What the exchange was?'

'It was Islington something. I know it was, because it's the same exchange as mine.'

Gray picked up the phone again, dialled Teresa Booth.

'Graydon, hallo! How was Jersey?'

'Hot. Tell you another time. Give me Liam Channing's number, would you?'

'Yes, of course. But –'

'I'll explain later. Sorry.'

'Francesca, darling, this is Mummy?'

'Oh,' said Francesca. 'How very good of you to ring.'

'What?'

'Mummy, don't give me that. I know you're up there with Bard, comforting him, consoling him, letting him cry on your shoulder. Again. And I think it's foul beyond belief. You're making things worse, Mummy, not helping, it's awful, horrible. Just – oh, just go away. Go away and leave me alone. Both of you.'

The line went dead. Rachel looked at Bard.

'Oh, dear,' she said. 'She's very upset.'

'What about?'

'Oh – I'll tell you in a minute. I'm trying to think what to do.'

A hot panic gripped her; she tried to fight it down. Obviously Francesca had rung her flat, rung the dentist, and leapt rather predictably to her conclusion. As circumstantial evidence went it was fairly damning. It was clearly pointless trying to ring Francesca again; she thought for a moment, and then phoned Reverend Mother.

'Mother, I'm very very sorry to bother you, but I need your help desperately. It is quite extraordinarily urgent.'

'Well, I'll do my best. What is it?'

'I want you to go and find Francesca – she will be very upset – and tell her she is quite quite wrong about – about what I'm doing. That is the first thing. And the second is that she must ring me, immediately, at Hamilton Terrace. It's about Liam Channing.'

'Very well. I'll see what I can do.'

Rachel looked at Bard across the interminable silence.

'I don't suppose,' she eventually said, 'you'd consider coming down there to see her? To try and talk to her? This is getting worse by the minute.'

'I don't know,' he said heavily, 'I really don't know.'

After about ten minutes Francesca phoned. She sounded icy cold, distant.

'Yes? What is it about Liam? Has he phoned?'

'No. No he hasn't. Francesca, listen to me. Did you tell Liam anything, anything at all, about – about your conversation with Bard?'

There was a very long silence. It told Rachel all she needed to know. Finally Francesca said, 'Why? Why do you want to know?'

'Because – well, because we think – we think he might have been talking to your friend Mr Townsend. At the *News*.'

'Well, that is ridiculous!' Francesca's voice was low, shaky with anger. 'That is the most ridiculous thing I've ever heard. Of course Liam wouldn't do that. I know he wouldn't. You're making it up, you've dreamed up some plot between you to discredit him, just to hurt me.'

'Francesca darling, I cannot tell you how much I wish that was true. Unfortunately it isn't. Now look, how much did you tell Liam, and –'

But Francesca had put the phone down.

'Mum! Mum, can we go now, go to the beach?'

'What? Oh, no, no Jack, not yet. Sorry. Kitty's still asleep.'

She was snuffling rather. Her nose was a bit runny. She must wipe it, Francesca thought absently. She rummaged in her bag for a handkerchief, could only find the ones they'd bought that morning for Mary. Well, Mary wouldn't mind. She pulled one out, wiped Kitty's small nose. Kitty twitched slightly in her sleep, then settled down again.

'Jack darling, go and find Richard. Please. I'll be with you very soon.'

'OK.'

Very, very slowly, she punched out Liam's number. A little girl answered the phone. Hattie.

'Is your daddy there?' said Francesca.

'No, sorry, he's gone out.'

'Do you know how long he'll be?'

'No, sorry. I don't. Quite a long time, he said. He's gone to see someone and then he's going to pick up our tickets.' She sounded excited.

'Your tickets?' said Francesca. She struggled to sound normal, cheerfully friendly. 'What are the tickets for?'

'We're going on holiday. All of us. To Spain. Tomorrow, really early. Do you want to talk to Mrs Hackett? Our daily? She's here.'

'Oh – no. No, it's all right,' said Francesca, 'thank you. Goodbye.'

She felt absolutely numb, as if she were watching herself, watching some mildly interesting film. So it was quite easy then to find Gray Townsend's number, ring him at the *News*, ask to speak to him. And when his assistant told him he was out, that he'd gone to meet someone, but she'd get him to phone the minute he got back, asked for her number, she still didn't feel anything at all. Anything.

Gray had arranged to meet Liam at the American Bar at the Connaught. It was quiet there, especially at twelve: the only other people likely to be there were tourists. He ordered one of the dry Martinis the Connaught were so rightly famous for, and sipped it very slowly. Silly, really. He should have had mineral water. He needed a clear head. But he had needed the drink; he was beginning to feel uneasy. There was something about all this that was disturbing him, that he didn't quite like.

Liam walked in at about five-past twelve. Gray had never met him, but he had seen photographs of him. All rather old photographs, like the one illustrating the piece about Kirsten. He was much better looking than he'd expected, and rather well dressed. There was something that was Bard about him; the eyes were identical, the almost black eyes, and the dark hair, but it was also the set of the head, and the shape of the jaw. An aggressive jaw.

He stood up, held out his hand. Liam nodded, took it, eased himself into the chair opposite him.

'Martini?'

'Oh. Oh, yes they're supposed to be rather good here, aren't they? Not one of my stamping grounds of course. Can't afford it.'

Gray ordered the Martini, and some mineral water for himself; Liam started munching his way through the olives. He seemed perfectly relaxed.

'Well now,' said Gray finally, 'what did you want to talk to me about?'

'Well, first of all, I want your assurance that this is totally confidential. That you will not reveal your source. As they say.'

'You have that assurance. Naturally.'

'Good. Well now, I understand you've been investigating a story about my father.'

'Yes, I have.'

'I trust your investigations have been fruitful.'

'To a degree. Thank you.'

'Are you intending to publish a story soon?'

'Possibly.'

'You are probably aware that my father's business is not entirely – straightforward?'

'Few businesses are, Mr Channing.' God, he didn't like this man.

'Were you aware of a charitable trust? Offshore? Out in the Dtuch Antilles?'

'I had heard something about it, yes,' said Gray.

'The chief beneficiary is the World Farming Federation. A very worthy cause.'

'Indeed, yes.'

'I have it on very good authority that most of the shares held by that trust in the Channing Corporation have now been sold.'

'Ah,' said Gray.

Channing picked up the Martini, sipped at it. 'This is excellent,' he said. 'It exceeds its reputation.'

'I'm glad you're enjoying it.'

'Yes, the shares have been sold. On an instruction received five days before the company collapsed. An instruction sent out from my father's office.'

'Yes. Yes I see.' This was new; this was really heady stuff.

'You didn't know this?'

'Not all of it, no.'

Channing picked up his glass again. 'Moreover, a person very close to my father – I don't think we need go too closely into who, but I'm sure you can imagine – this person has been asked to lie about his whereabouts that day. At the time this instruction was given.'

'Yes. Yes, I see.'

'So I think that should add a few extra lines to your story, don't you?'

'Possibly,' said Gray, 'just possibly.'

'Good. Well, I hope so, anyway, I wouldn't want it wasted. And I should so enjoy reading it. Are there any other little details you're having trouble with, Mr Townsend? That I might be able to help with?'

'No. No, I don't think so,' said Gray. He wondered what the matter with him was; instead of feeling excited, instead of wanting to rush off and file his story, he felt rather sick.

'Good. Fine. Well, I'm going away tomorrow, for a few weeks, so you won't be able to contact me anyway. So this is our first and last meeting.'

'Yes,' said Gray. 'Yes, indeed. Er – how did you come by this information exactly, Mr Channing? I do have to know, you see. You might have just made it up.'

'Oh – oh no, I do assure you it's absolutely genuine. I got it from –

what shall we say – the horse's mouth. Or rather the filly's. Or to be really precise, the mare's.'

'Yes, I see,' said Gray.

After Liam had gone, he sat there for a long time; the Martini seemed not to have had the slightest effect on him, so he ordered another and listened to a middle-aged American couple dressed in identical Madras cotton shirts and navy trousers arguing about whether they should go to Oxford or Stratford-on-Avon the next day.

They asked Gray what he thought. 'Oxford,' he said, 'much more civilised.' The couple promptly settled on Stratford; Gray left them and took a taxi back to the office.

'Hi,' said Tricia, 'interesting?'

'Very,' said Gray shortly.

'Good. Now then, Dave wants to see you urgently. And can you ring Francesca Channing? She phoned.'

'I bet she did,' said Gray.

He phoned the number; it was a mobile, and the reception was terrible. There was a great clattering of what sounded like knives and forks and china in the background.

'Francesca? This is Graydon Townsend.'

'Oh. Oh, yes. Can you hold on a minute, I'll have to move.'

A brief silence, then she said, 'Sorry. Better now.'

'You sound as if you're in a school dining hall.'

'I was. Well, a convent dining hall.'

'What on earth are you doing at a convent?'

'Oh – long story. Mr Townsend, I have to ask you something, and I have to know the answer. Please.'

'Yes?' he said, knowing what was coming.

'Has – has Liam Channing been in touch with you? With a story? About my husband?'

'I really can't tell you that,' he said carefully.

'That answers it really. Doesn't it?'

'It – could.'

'Yes, I see,' she said. 'I think perhaps I'd better come and see you.'

'No, Mrs Channing, don't. The least said about all this the better. Certainly by you.'

'Oh,' she said. 'Oh – yes. I see. But –'

'Don't even think about it,' he said. 'Coming to see me, I mean.'

There was a long silence. Very long.

'Are you all right?'

'Oh – oh, yes. Yes, thank you, I'm fine.'

Another silence.

'Well −' she said, finally, 'thank you for calling me. I'm very grateful.' She sounded almost eerily calm. Distracted, but calm.

'Are you sure you're all right?' he said.

'Yes. Yes, I'm fine. Honestly. Thank you.'

'Good. Er −' and he wouldn't have asked her then, but he was genuinely concerned, worried about it, 'I'm sorry to − well, to ask at such a moment, but is Kirsten all right? Is something the matter with her?'

'Kirsten?' She sounded puzzled, as if she didn't know who he was talking about.

'Yes. She's been ill − for quite a while now, as far as I can make out. It's nothing serious, is it?'

'What? Oh − no.' Another long silence, then she said, still in her strange distracted voice, 'No, no nothing serious. She's pregnant, that's all. Look, I must go, Mr Townsend. I'm sorry. Goodbye.'

Bard and Rachel drove very fast down to Devon. Rachel comforted herself by thinking, as Bard sat in the outside lane of first the M4 and then the M5 with his foot pressed to the floor of the Aston Martin, that it was better than the last time they had travelled together to Devon, in the helicopter. Just.

He had suddenly said he would come; had stalked into the room, his face set, and told her they would leave at once, without further explanation. Rachel had not asked for any. He had spent most of the journey on the phone, which made the speed, which at times topped 120 mph, still more terrifying. Hearing him shouting at Marcia, who had failed to deliver some form or other to the accountants; at Gray Townsend, whom he had told to get off his fucking back, and then at Oliver, whom he was unable to see now until the next day − which hardly seemed to be Oliver's fault − while overtaking various cars on the inside because they wouldn't get out of his way, was hardly relaxing. She kept longing for a police car to appear, to stop them even, but the entire British force seemed to have their attention focused away from the south-west of England that day.

He was in a strange mood: brooding, intense, absolutely focused on the journey, on what he was going to do at the end of it, but his despair gone; once or twice he even smiled at her. She was puzzled by this, until he said something, just in passing, as they battled through the torments of the M4 extension. 'At least now she knows,' he said. 'She knows what he really is.'

★

It was just after four when they arrived at the lane. 'Now for God's sake, Bard, it's very, very narrow and steep. And tractors have right of way.'

He ground his teeth and braked violently; halfway up the first hill, a vast hay-wagon appeared from a field, began to come down towards them. Bard hooted loudly.

'Bard, don't,' said Rachel, 'please! He'll mow us down.'

'He can go back into the field. I've got to back half a mile.'

'Yes, you have. I presume this car can go backwards.'

'Well, of course it can go backwards, but I don't see why it should –'

'It should,' said Rachel, 'because you're not a farmer, you don't live here, and he's bigger than you are. Now reverse. Please.'

She sat beside him, observing Bard Channing giving in to someone else, and wondered how often it had happened in the past fifty-four years.

As they drove into the courtyard, Jack saw them; he was cradling some eggs in his hands.

'Dad! Dad!' He ran towards the car holding out his arms, the eggs dropping around him like large, messy insects. 'What are you doing here? Dad, I can surf.'

'Surf?' said Bard, getting out, picking him up, hugging him, looking a the broken eggs. 'Whoever taught you to do that, one of the nuns?'

'No, they're not allowed to take their things off. Barnaby told me how, and a nice old man called the Curdle showed me on the beach today. Mum says –'

'Where is your mother?'

'She's in her room. She's tired.'

'Can you show me her room?'

'Bard,' said Rachel, 'Bard, let me go up first. Please. I think it would be best.'

'Oh – all right.'

'Dad, come and help with the eggs. Oh and I've made a shooter, you could try that if you like, I've been trying to hit that –' he pointed at the crucifix set above the wall by the five-bar gate – 'but I haven't yet.'

Bard Channing was not often seen to look nervous, but he did then.

'You can say what you like,' said Francesca, 'I just can't forgive you.'

She looked terrible; her eyes were swollen, she was somehow smaller, shrivelled in her pain.

'Why not?'

'Oh don't be so fucking dense!' She shouted the words: Francesca, who never swore. 'How do you think it feels for me, to know you've been up there in London with Bard, that you sneaked off to be with him, lied to me about it, how do think it feels to know you're much much closer to him than I am, that he talks to you, confides in you as he never did in me? And you in him, for that matter.'

'That's what hurts, isn't it?' said Rachel slowly.

'Yes of course it is. It's horrible. You told him about Mary before you ever told me, you were there in his office the day of the crash –'

'Pure coincidence. I told you.'

'Yes, so you say.'

'Francesca, that's what hurt Bard most, you know, about you and Liam. That you had become so close. Not the sex at all.'

'Oh so you've discussed that as well, have you? Well, I'm glad you've both been having such cosy chats about it all. No doubt I seem perfectly ridiculous to you both. Childish, pathetic. I might tell you, Mummy, you bear some responsibility yourself for what has happened. You really do.'

'Francesca,' said Rachel, 'Francesca, you've got this all wrong.'

'Listen,' said Francesca, 'this whole thing has happened because Bard shut me out. Wouldn't talk to me, share things with me. Can't you understand, every time he gets close to you, it's just another wedge between him and me. It's just as bad as if – well, as if you were having an affair with him.'

'Oh Francesca, really!' said Rachel. She realised in that instant that she had subconsciously feared Francesca might actually have thought that, thanked God that she hadn't. 'Now you're being really absurd.'

'No I'm not. You see, you just don't understand. And anyway, why did you lie to me?'

'Because if I'd told you I was going to see him you'd have panicked. Tried to stop me. Or insisted on coming too. I had to lie.'

'You could have told me once you were there.'

'Darling, once I was there, events took over. Believe me. And I couldn't leave him. Last night. He was – very low.'

'Why? What's happened?'

'He'll tell you, I expect. He's here.'

'I don't want to see him. And why, why on earth did you go and see him? I still don't understand.'

Rachel looked at her, so hurt, so damaged, betrayed, as she saw it, by everyone she was close to and loved, and knew she couldn't possibly tell her the real reason; that she had gone to offer to lie for Bard, to provide him with his alibi – and knew also that could no longer be an option. It would be the ultimate example of what was so deeply distressing Francesca; she would be moving in on her already sick marriage, taking her place, displaying the ultimate loyalty. It might save Bard, but it would destroy Francesca.

'Oh, well,' she said lightly, 'I'm afraid I was just playing marriage counsellors, darling. Interfering, poking my great hooter in. Probably my besetting sin. As you very well know. And I shouldn't have done it, and I'm terribly sorry.'

'No, you shouldn't,' said Francesca. She looked at her mother and then gave her an odd, distorted smile. 'But I suppose I have to believe you meant well.'

'I wish you could. Believe it, I mean.' She looked down at Kitty, who was sitting on the floor between them, sorting out the waste-paper basket, breathing rather heavily.

'Is she all right?'

'Yes, she's fine. Bit of a runny nose, that's all,' said Francesca absently.

'Are you all right?'

'Oh – God, I don't know. No, I don't think I am. I don't even know what I feel. All the worst things. Hurt. Ashamed. Frightened. Humiliated. And just – more unhappy than I can ever remember. Could have thought possible.'

Rachel looked at her, and would have given all she had to have been able to shoulder some at least of her pain.

'Even Granny Jess warned me about Liam, you know,' said Francesca.

'Really? How did she know?'

'Oh – second sight, I suppose.' She tried to smile. 'I don't know. Anyway, she did. "Beware of Liam," she said, "he's dangerous." I was just angry with her, thought that like everyone else she'd got him wrong. When it was me who'd got him wrong. Hopelessly wrong.'

'Well,' said Rachel, 'it's very easy. When you're – obsessed with someone.'

'No,' said Francesca, 'it was just pathetic. I was taken in by him, listened to all his self-indulgent garbage, like some half-witted virgin. Oh, God, how could I have been so stupid?'

'Being stupid isn't a crime,' said Rachel, 'although it can be dangerous. Will you see Bard? He wants to talk to you.'

Francesca sighed. 'There's no point. There's nothing to say. Our marriage, our relationship, is over. Certainly nothing's changed that. I've still been unfaithful to him, with the person he hates more than anyone in the world, and he's still totally rejected me.'

'Francesca, you cannot possibly be sure of that. Not yet.'

'I think I can,' she said, 'and he's only going to say all the same things, again and again. Most of which I deserve,' she added, 'but there is no point.'

'I think he has some different things to say,' said Rachel, 'and before you look at me like that, no, we have not discussed them. Francesca, he loves you still. He wants to – '

'Well, I don't love him,' said Francesca.

'How can you be sure of that?'

'Mummy, don't start on all your marriage-guidance garbage, please. Of course I'm sure. And – oh, all right. Yes, I'll see him. I've got something to tell him actually,' she added, and the expression on her face was interesting, Rachel thought; very careful, almost shrewd. She wondered what it was, if Francesca had made her decision.

'Good. I'll take the children for a walk. Is it all right for Kitty to go out?'

'Yes of course. She's fine. Mary's got a nasty cold though. She's had to stay in bed today. I'm sure she'd love to see you. Don't take Kitty in to her though, will you?'

'No, I won't.'

Whenever Francesca hadn't seen Bard even for a few days, she was struck by the sheer physical force of him. He stood there across the room from her, looking at her, his eyes dark, broodingly blank, and felt him tangibly, as if he was holding her, touching her.

'Hallo, Bard. I'm surprised to see you here.'

'I'm quite surprised myself,' he said. 'I'm still not sure why I've come. I think,' he sighed, paused, looked at her with the same blank look – 'I think I just wanted to see you.'

'I can't think why.'

'No,' he said. 'No, I can't really, either.'

'You must hate me,' she said, 'really hate me. And hate the sight of me.'

'Oddly enough, no, I don't. I hate the thought of what you've done. That's not quite the same thing. Although it has a bearing on it, of course.' He almost smiled, sank down heavily on the bed.

'Yes,' she said quietly, 'I suppose it does.'

'And you, how do you feel about me now, do you suppose?'

'I don't know, Bard. I really don't.'

'I'm sorry,' he said suddenly, abruptly, the words ripped out of him as if by force.

She stared at him; of all the things he might have said, that was the most unexpected, the most unthinkable.

'What for?' she said finally. 'What are you sorry for?'

'For saying what I did. About – about what I asked you. And about your reaction to it.'

'Well,' she said, 'well, it was understandable, that, I suppose. I've been thinking about it.'

'You have?'

'Yes. And you were wrong. Quite wrong. But I was afraid you might be right.'

'Ah,' he said. 'Yes, I see.'

'I did behave very badly,' she said, after a while, 'I know that. It was horrifying. As you said.'

'It was very – painful, yes. But Liam must bear much of the blame.'

The name touched her grief; it was like a physical hurt. She couldn't say anything for a while, then: 'Have you spoken to him yet?' she said. She had to know; it was important.

'Briefly, yes.'

'And did he – deny it?'

'No, of course, not. On the contrary.'

'I'm sorry?' she said. 'What do you mean, what did he say?'

'Well,' he said, slightly impatient, 'obviously he wanted me to know all about it. How very satisfactory it had been, that you had – had – Christ Almighty, Francesca, do I have to go through this? Why do you think he began it all? To hurt me as much as he possibly could. He wasn't going to go quietly, he wanted to extract the maximum mileage from the situation.'

'Oh,' she said. 'Oh yes, I see.' She wouldn't have thought it could have hurt more, but it did.

'Are you still – communicating with him?' he said, and his eyes were darker still.

'No. No I'm not. Not any longer.' She was too unhappy, had come too low for pride. 'It's – well, it seems to be over. Whatever it was.'

'I see.'

'Bard –'

'Yes?'

'Why do you hate him so much? Why have you always hated him so much?'

'Oh,' he said, wearily, 'many reasons. But I suppose mostly because he is mine, part of me, flesh of my flesh and still so – rotten. It's hard to bear, that. That is what I found hardest about you, about what had happened, thinking of you with – oh Christ.'

He looked down at his hands; remorse, grief for him flooded her, she felt physically sick with it. She stepped towards him, then drew back, sensing the revulsion he felt for Liam must extend to her.

'Come here,' he said, reaching out a hand, still not looking at her. 'Come here, please.'

She went forward very slowly, as if she were making some dangerous, difficult journey; took the hand. He did not move otherwise, did not look up, just sat there, his head bowed, holding it.

'I still love you,' he said, 'I think. I wish I didn't but I do. And that is what makes it so – difficult.'

She was silent, shocked that he should feel such an unlikely, an impossible thing; just stood there, looking down at him, at his bent head, his hand holding hers.

'Bard,' she said finally, feeling she must say, do, something into this awful, dreadful silence, 'I'm so sorry, so desperately sorry. Not just for what happened, but that I told him. What you'd – what you'd asked. It was so stupid, so totally stupid. I was beside myself, hysterical, desperate, and he – well, there's no excuse. It was a terrible thing to do.'

'Oh,' he said, his voice almost indifferent, heavy, 'it doesn't matter.'

'Bard,' she said, puzzled, 'of course it matters. He's told – told Gray Townsend.'

'I know that. But it doesn't matter. Francesca, I'm in this thing so deep, I'm in such trouble, it probably can't make much difference now.'

He looked up at her then, and said slowly, very quietly, 'Perhaps – perhaps you should come and sit down. And I'll tell you about it.'

And she sat down beside him, still holding his hand, and listened. To a long, involved story: one that she could hardly follow at times, of tortuous dealings, of shares bought and sold illegally by long complex chains, of money moved across currencies and continents, moved into bank accounts where it had no business to be, of desperate attempts to shore things up at the last minute, to save the company, money secured against non-existent properties.

'It's all I cared about,' he said. 'That company and you. And the children, of course. It's hard to explain; it was me, an extension of myself, I created it out of nothing, took something out of the ether, an idea, a plan, a determination, and turned it into bricks and mortar, buildings and streets, houses and factories, shops and schools, all there because of me. I became part of people's lives, the people who worked for me, directly and indirectly, hundreds, thousands of them, they had security, a future. It makes for arrogance, that sort of thing. I became very arrogant, I'm afraid.'

Francesca looked at him, sitting there, his head bowed, brought down, no longer arrogant, and could find nothing to say. And then he looked up, at her face, and said, 'Do you think you can begin to understand?'

She nodded. 'I think so, yes.' She sighed a sigh almost as heavy as his. 'And – Nigel Clarke? And Teresa Booth –'

'Oh Christ. Of all the – bad things I've done, that was the worst. The only truly bad one. And it's haunted me all my life. I –' He stopped, shook his head. 'I don't think you want to hear this, Francesca.'

'I want to hear it.'

He started talking again, so quietly now she could scarcely hear him. 'We – well, Duggie and I, were – bribing planning officers. Back in the 'seventies. You had to, almost. You felt, rightly or wrongly, if you didn't somebody else would, and they'd get the contract. We weren't prepared to risk it. Anyway, I thought Nigel knew, that he understood. He didn't. He was incredibly straight – you've met Heather, you can imagine what he must have been like. Anyway, he came to me, that night, the night he died, told me he'd found out, that he didn't like it, that he was going to pull the plug. Tell someone. He was pretty self-righteous about it, read me a sermon about dishonesty. I – well, I told him, if he did, he'd go down as well, that no one would believe he hadn't been involved, in fact I'd make sure they knew he had been. We were drinking; he got very drunk. I knew he was drunk, Francesca, and how distressed he was, and I knew he shouldn't drive, and I was so angry with him, so fucking angry, I didn't care, I let him go off, into that awful foggy night, I should have stopped him, and – well, you know what happened. He was killed. And it was my fault. I killed him, Francesca, I killed Nigel Clarke. And not a day has passed since that I haven't thought about it, felt guilty about it –'

Francesca looked at him There were tears in his eyes; one rolled down his cheek. She moved her hand, wiped it away with her finger.

'Bard,' she said, 'you didn't kill him. Of course you didn't. He wasn't a child. He was old enough to know whether or not he should have been driving. It's not true.'

'No,' he said, shaking his head, 'it is true. I should never have said what I did, threatened him like that. It was terribly wrong. And at least I should have stopped him from driving, made him get a cab, you don't understand. And poor Heather, a widow so young, and those children, growing up without a father, all because I was so fucking irresponsible and dishonest –'

'And I suppose,' she said suddenly, 'Teresa had got hold of this. Something of this. Had Duggie told her?'

'No, he hadn't told her. But she was suspicious about lots of things, she's very sharp, Teresa is, and she didn't like me anyway, she felt I was hostile to her –'

'I can't imagine why she should feel that,' said Francesca. She smiled; she couldn't help it. Bard ignored it.

'And she didn't like Duggie having a smaller share of the company than I did –'

'That's understandable.'

'Why?' he said, and for a moment he was the old Bard suddenly, self-justifying, overbearing. 'I made all the running, took all the early risks, he just followed along, bit of a taker, really –'

'Bard!' said Francesca. 'Stop it.'

'What?'

'For a clever man, you're often extraordinarily stupid. Stupid and arrogant. Do you really think Teresa could see it like that? Whatever else, she really loved Duggie. And you did – patronise him. Just a bit.'

'I did?' He looked so astonished, so discomfited, so exactly like Jack, she smiled again.

'Yes. You did.'

'Christ, how awful. I never realised. Poor old Duggie, how appalling of me ...'

'I don't think he minded so very much,' said Francesca. 'He thought you were wonderful. But she minded. As I would have done.'

'Yes, well. And she threatened to get a private detective on the case, and he'd have found out what your friend Mr Townsend did, and a great deal more besides –'

'Bard, he's not my friend. If he's anyone's, he's Kirsten's friend.'

'Ah, yes,' he said, his face heavy with anger again, 'Kirsten. We have a great deal to thank her for.'

'Bard, there's something I have to tell you about Kirsten. She –'

'Have you spoken to Townsend today?' he said, ignoring her.

'Yes. Yes I rang him when I – when I realised what had happened.'

'Probably unwise.'

'I'm – sorry.'

He shrugged. 'And what is he going to do?'

'I don't know,' she said, very quietly.

'Well,' he said, standing up, 'we shall just have to wait and see, I suppose. He's coming to see me in the morning. My lawyer's advised against it, but I think I want to hear what he's got to say. After I've been to the SFO. Christ Almighty, what a mess.'

He looked down at her. 'What were you going to say about Kirsten?' he said suddenly.

'She's pregnant.'

'Oh Christ,' he said, 'not again. God help me. Whose is it?'

'I think it's Kirsten God needs to help,' said Francesca, 'and I don't know. Nobody knows.'

'I'd better speak to her. What's she going to do?'

'She doesn't know that either. She's in a very bad way. Bard, please, please be gentle with her.'

'Why, for Christ's sake?' he said. 'Why should I be?'

'You're beginning to sound better,' she said, with another faint smile. 'Because she came to me, that's why, because she was very brave and told me what she'd done, that she'd told you about me and – well, about me. And apologised. And also because she's desperately unhappy, she needs help and support. And if you said something nice to her, for once –'

'I've been very nice to her.'

'No you haven't. And she loves you very much really. Please, Bard.'

'I wish she did,' he said shortly.

'Bard, she does.'

'Do you really think so?'

'I know so.'

There was a long silence; finally he sighed and said, 'I would like to believe it. But – well anyway. All right, I'll give her a call. I'll be nice to her.'

'Thank you.'

He looked at her again. 'Francesca,' he said, 'Francesca, what are we going to do? How are we going to survive all this?'

'I don't know,' she said quietly. 'Bard, I think –'

There was a sudden knock on the door: 'Mrs Channing!'

Francesca opened it; it was Sister Mary Agnes. 'Sorry to disturb you, Mrs Channing, but there's been a slight accident. Jack's driven Mr Channing's car into the wall – oh he's quite all right, but –'

'We'll resume this later, Francesca,' said Bard. 'Sister, where exactly is this wall?'

★

'Look, Gray,' said David Guthrie, 'I need to have this story. First thing tomorrow latest. Otherwise it'll have to be held over. I can't go on holding those pages.'

'I know, Dave, and I'm sorry. But I have to see Channing, I have to give him a chance to reply, and he's finally agreed to see me in the morning. Twelve o'clock. Then I'll come in here and file it. OK?'

'Yeah, OK. But two's your deadline. Otherwise you lose the slot. And someone else may get the story. If your friend's right and the SFO are onto him, it's a matter of days.'

'Yes, yes, I realise that. Look – I'd like to go now. If that's OK. Got something important to do.'

'Yeah, fine.' He was already pulling some page proofs towards him; Gray walked out of the office and shut the door quietly behind him.

Kirsten had gone home early again. She'd felt so awful that afternoon, she just couldn't stay at her desk any longer. She told her boss she had to go to the dentist and that she'd come in early to make up the time. She could tell she was beginning to use up a lot of goodwill, but it was only another day or so now.

She reckoned she could be back at her desk by Wednesday at the latest. A diplomatic bout of flu till then should see her through. She was trying not to think about Saturday. Trying not to think about any of it. But it was very difficult.

She got home at half-past four, had a bath, lay down on her bed with the remote control of the television, started zapping through the channels. *Blue Peter* was just finishing; she watched it smiling, transported instantly back to her childhood, wondering if she could manage what they were making today, a water garden in a big glass jar. Probably not; she'd never been able to do any of them, had shed almost as many tears over collapsed papier-mâché fortresses and runny jelly rabbits as she had over her mother's drinking habits. Well, in the early days, anyway.

Neighbours began; Helen Daniels was being sweetly firm with one of the teenagers, the dog had got lost again, there was a new arrival in Ramsey Street ... she began to get sleepy, closed her eyes. If only she lived in a suburb of Melbourne, if only –

The phone rang suddenly; she jerked awake, leant over and picked it up. Noticed that it was almost six.

'Kirsten. It's your father.'

'Oh,' she said. Even to herself her voice sounded totally bleak, unwelcoming.

'How are you?'

'All right.'

'Francesca tells me you're not.'

'What? I don't know what you're talking about.'

'Yes you do. I'm talking about you. Being pregnant.'

'Dad,' said Kirsten, her voice rising in warning, 'Dad, I really can't take –'

'It's all right,' he said, and his voice was level, reasonable, 'I'm not going to say anything. Not going to ask any questions. I don't want to know – well, I don't want to pressure you in any way. I just wanted you to know that if you need any help, you have only to ask.'

'Oh,' said Kirsten. She wondered if she was still asleep, if this was part of *Neighbours*. Or was it *Home and Away* now. 'Well – no. No, I don't. Thank you.'

'No money? For – anything?'

For an abortion. To pay the doctor. To pay for the baby to be – dealt with. Got rid of. Killed ... Don't, Kirsten, don't go down that road, concentrate on now, on this conversation.

'Kirsten, are you all right?'

'Yes,' she said, with a huge effort, 'yes, I'm all right. And – well, I'll see. If that's OK.'

'It's OK.'

'Thanks.'

'That's all right. And Kirsten –'

'Yes?'

'Kirsten, I'm – sorry about the other night. I – well, I over-reacted. Said more than I should have done. And I'm very sorry I hit you. It was – very wrong of me.'

God, this was unbelievable. What had happened? Had he had some kind of vision or something?

'Well,' she said finally, 'well – so did I, I guess. Say too much. And I'm sorry too.'

'Right. Well, that would seem to make us quits.'

'Where are you?' she said suddenly.

'Oh – I'm down in Devon. At this convent place. You know about that?'

'No.' Her father at a convent? Maybe he *had* had a vision. 'What on earth are you doing at a convent?'

'Long story,' he said, 'get Francesca to tell you. I'll be back in London tomorrow. Providing my car will go. Jack's just taken to the road.'

'*Jack* has?'

'Yes,' said Bard. He sounded more himself suddenly. 'Bloody child

568

decided if he could drive the lawnmower, he could drive the car. Totally wrecked the offside wing.'

'Is he all right?'

'What? Oh, he's fine. Of course. Bye, Kirsten. Ring me if you need me.'

'Yes. Yes, all right. Bye, Dad. Thanks.'

She lay back on her pillows feeling very shaken. She had no idea what might have happened to him, but something clearly had. Maybe it was just the going bust. Maybe it had done him good.

Her front-door buzzer rang; she sighed, went over to the door picked up the phone.

'Kirsten?' It was Gray Townsend. 'Can I come in?'

Chapter Twenty-nine

'It's lovely,' said Rachel, 'really the most charming house. Thank you so much, Colonel Philbeach, for letting us see it.'

She felt rather confused: life seemed to have taken on a through-the-looking-glass aspect. Here was Bard, with the clear possibility of arrest hanging over him, Francesca apparently hellbent on the termination of her marriage, Jack escaping most narrowly death, or at least serious injury, and what looked like the best part of a hundred-thousand-pound car crushed to pulp, and they were being shown round a house, and asked to admire its cornices and its fireplaces and the breathtaking views of the Atlantic it commanded from the drawing-room window.

'Well,' said Colonel Philbeach, 'I really do have to sell, I'm afraid. And it's very sad. But I would like it to go to a young family. Such as yours, Mrs Channing.'

'Yes, well, it would certainly suit our purpose very well,' said Francesca,' thank you. Naturally, we have a lot to think about. How much was the asking price, last time it was on the market?'

'Well –' Colonel Philbeach hesitated. 'Two hundred and fifty thousand. Or a near offer,' he added hastily. 'At least that's what's the agent said.' He clearly felt this was an outrageous sum of money. Rachel thought of what quarter of a million would buy in Fulham, or Battersea – nice little three-bed bijou job – and felt slightly sick.

'Right,' said Francesca. 'Right, I see.' She smiled brightly at her mother. 'All right?'

'What? Oh, yes, yes, fine. We should be getting back now, I think.'

'Oh, won't you have a sherry?'

'I think not,' said Francesca, 'but thank you anyway. My little boy –'

'Oh the accident, yes. It could have been dreadful, from what I can gather … He's all right, is he?'

'Oh, he's fine. Bit of a bruised leg, where the door hove in on him, but that's all. Lots of guardian angels, Jack has.' She smiled at Colonel Philbeach. 'The car hasn't been so lucky.'

'Well, it's only a car, I suppose.'

'Indeed it is. Come on then, Mummy. We really must go.'

Rachel managed to smile at her, as if it was her idea, not Francesca's they should have come in the first place, and followed her down the steep steps to the lane.

'Lovely, isn't it?' said Francesca, looking back at High House, its grey stone carved into the evening sky. 'Don't you love it?'

'Well, I do darling, yes. But I don't really think it's an ideal proposition for you. You're very much a London girl really –'

'Well, I do,' said Francesca. 'It's exactly what I want, what I need. I love it, I really do. And so does Jack.'

'Well, the Colonel is certainly charming,' said Rachel inconsequentially. 'I liked him very much.'

Francesca looked at her and smiled at her for the first time that day. 'Mummy,' she said, 'of course you did. He's a man.'

Kirsten gave Gray a mug of tea. 'Sorry, no biscuits. Bit of toast, maybe?'

'No, thank you. That tea looks perfect, Kirsten, I'm most impressed. There is – was – only one other person who could make my tea how I like it.'

'Your girlfriend? Briony?'

'Yes.'

He was touched, moved even, that she should have remembered the name. He studied her while she fetched some sugar, set it down on the table. She looked very pale, very thin. Unsure of herself, jumpy. She seemed a very different creature from the Kirsten of two months earlier. Two months. It sounded so harmless. Just a neat little space of time. A dangerous little space of time.

She smiled at him slightly defensively, realising he was studying her. 'How are you?' she said.

'I'm all right. It's you I'm worried about.'

'Worried? Oh, you don't have to worry about me. I'm all right.'

'Kirsten, I know you're not.'

'What?' She looked uncomfortable, almost cross. 'What are you talking about?'

'Kirsten,' he said, and he had not expected to say it so quickly, so easily, had thought he might hedge round it, try to find things out, how she felt, what her situation was, 'Kirsten, is it mine? Your baby, is it mine?'

And 'Yes,' she said, hardly hestitating, 'yes, it's yours,' and it was the most extraordinary moment, intimate, touching, and for the rest of his life Gray thought he would remember it thus, it would be there, set, preserved in time, incomparable, quite literally astonishing.

Gray looked at her as she sat there, her head bowed, staring down at her hands, wondering what he felt, wondering how she felt; and then he reached out and pushed back the heavy hair, stroked her cheek.

'Why?' he said. 'Why didn't you tell me?'

'I couldn't,' she said, staring at him now, her greeny-blue eyes thoughtful, almost amused. 'What on earth would have been the point?'

'Well,' he said, 'it might have helped you. For a start.'

'How?' she said. 'How could it possibly have helped me?'

'Well,' he said uncertainly, slightly shocked at what she saw as his entirely extraneous role in the whole thing, 'I don't know. Quite. But I could have taken care of you, you've obviously been feeling terrible, you could have talked to me about it, we could have –'

'Yes? We could have what?'

'Well,' he said, 'we could have decided what to do. Together.'

'But Gray, it wasn't something we could decide together.'

'Why not?' he said. 'I don't understand.'

'Because – well, because of all the people in the world you weren't going to be interested. And I had no right to ask you to be interested.'

'But Kirsten,' he said, 'Kirsten, it's my baby.'

He heard his voice saying those words, strange, unthinkable words that he had never ever thought to say, and looked at her, and thought of what had happened between them, this most intimate, extraordinary, yet ordinary thing that he had never dreamed would happen to him; that he had made love to her, and because of that there was within her now a new being, a potential person, partly of her, partly of him: he had done that, had created it, had created a life.

'It's my baby,' he said again, into the silence, while he tried to explore the beginnings of what he felt, 'and of course I'm interested.'

'But Gray, you don't want babies, ever, you told me, you told me that was why you'd finished with Briony, how could I expect you to – to –'

'To what?' he said. 'Expect me to what?'

'To care?' she said quietly.

'Kirsten, you obviously have a very low opinion of me. Of course I care. I care about you, I care very much. And I care about this, about what's happened to you, even more.'

'Oh,' she said abruptly.

'And what,' he said, more gently still, 'what do you think you are going to do?'

'Have a termination,' she said, and burst into tears.

Gray stood up and held out his arms, and she looked up and then, reluctantly almost, moved into them, stood against him crying while he held her, stroked her hair, and said nothing, nothing at all, while she cried herself out.

'You see,' she said, when she had finished, sniffing, wiping her eyes and her nose on the thing nearest to hand, which happened to be the teatowel, 'it was so wrong what I did, sleeping with you.'

'Why?' he said, stroking her hair, kissing her gently. 'Why wrong of you and not of me?'

'Well, you were so low, so muddled, and I was just – just piqued. And I did want to,' she said, smiling her funny lopsided smile. 'I don't want you to think I didn't, I thought you were lovely, really horny, I still do.'

'Well thank you,' he said, 'for those few kind words. And did it not enter your tortured, muddled little head that I was wrong too? That I am a great deal older than you and should be a little bit wiser, that I could see you were upset. And that I wanted to, too.'

'Well – no,' she said. 'Actually, no I didn't.'

'Well actually, you should have done. Here, have a hanky. Sit down, and I'll make you another cup of tea. Or would you like a brandy or something?'

'Oh – no,' she said, making a face, 'I'd be sick.'

'Well, I'd certainly rather you weren't that. We'll stick with the tea.'

'And then,' she said, 'I thought, well, I couldn't tell you about it, about the baby, because that would be even more wrong. Putting the responsibility on you.'

'Of course it's my responsibility. You're nuts, you know,' he said cheerfully, 'quite, quite nuts.'

'I know I am. I'm sure I'll end up in a bin.'

'Of course you won't. And if you do, I promise I'll come and visit you. I'll probably be in there with you, actually. Now listen to me, Kirsten –'

'Gray,' she said, 'I have made up my mind. I can't have it. It wouldn't be fair.'

'On you?'

'Yes, on me. But I actually meant on the baby. That's why I decided.'

'I see,' he said, 'but supposing we –'

'Gray,' she said, and her face was alarmed, 'you're not going to ask me to marry you, are you? Because I wouldn't. I couldn't.'

He felt stung, in spite of himself. 'Am I really so repulsive? Such a bad prospect?'

'No of course not. I told you, you're lovely. And horny and really, really nice. But you're – well, you're –'

'Old?' he said helpfully.

'Well – Yes. A bit.'

'I see.'

'Oh God. Now I've offended you. But you are.'

'It's all right,' he said, 'and yes, I am. And there are other – obstacles too, I daresay.'

Like the fact, he thought, I have the power to make sure your father goes to jail; to make his humiliation absolutely public; to wreck the lives of your whole family.

'Yes. It really really wouldn't work, Gray. And I'm sure you wouldn't really want it.'

'No,' he said, 'it probably wouldn't work. Fond of you as I am. But if you wanted to – keep the baby, I would help you financially, help to support it. It and you.'

She sat back and looked at him. 'God, Gray. You're so nice.'

'Hardly,' he said, and sighed.

There was a long silence. Then she said, 'Who told you?'

'Francesca. But only by mistake, you are not to blame her for it.'

'No. I won't. Poor Francesca. She's having a hideous time. And I haven't helped.'

'Poor Francesca. Yes. Here, drink your tea.'

'Thanks.'

'Does – does your father know about it?' he asked. Thinking that, actually, if Bard Channing did know about Kirsten's baby, and moreover if he knew who had fathered it, there would be no hiding place for him anywhere, anywhere at all.

'Yes. Yes, he does actually. I mean he knows I'm pregnant. Not whose it is, obviously. He just phoned me, I thought he was going to bawl me out, but he was really nice.' She sat there, drinking her tea, saying nothing for quite a long time, and then: 'Gray,' she said, looking at him, her face very set, 'Gray, like I just said, you're really, really nice and I so appreciate you coming. But it hasn't changed my mind. I know what I have to do.'

'Well,' he said, 'it's your decision.'

He didn't quite feel that; in fact he hardly felt it at all. But he wanted to make it easy for her. He owed her that at least.

★

He took a taxi home; but then he found he couldn't bear to be on his own with his thoughts, and he got the bike out and rode on and on, out of the dusty wastes of London, through polite, surburban Surrey countryside, into the folds and hills of Sussex and so on back into the seaside suburbia and right on down to the sea. He sat on the beach, the stony beach of Littlehampton, where he had come so often as a small boy, a carefree, untroubled small boy with no idea of the complexities of the life that lay ahead of him and looked out at the just-darkening sea. And thought of Kirsten Channing and her awkward, stubborn courage, and her beauty and how he had almost loved her; and thought of the baby he had made for her and with her, and the fate that was to befall that baby, and was shocked and amazed that he felt as he did.

'Take my car,' said Francesca, 'it's the obvious thing to do. You've got to get back to London, and I can easily hire one in the morning. And Reverend Mother has one, in an emergency.'

They were in the library at the convent; the drama, the shock, had cleared the emotional air, made things easier between them.

Everyone was at supper. Kitty and Jack were both asleep.

'All right. Thank you. Jack seems OK.'

'Jack is fine. Don't worry about him.'

He looked at her. 'I was hoping we could have more time before I left. To talk.'

'Bard, I really don't think there's anything to talk about.'

He stared at her. 'Of course there is. I need to know what you've decided. If you will – give evidence for me. Just in case all is not quite lost. I know I shouldn't have asked you, but –'

'Oh,' she said, 'that.'

'Yes. That. Have you –'

'I have decided, Bard, yes. And you were right, you shouldn't have asked me. But you did, and I think that's the point.'

'I don't know what you mean,' he said.

'Bard, you put me in this appalling dilemma. And now I'm going to make it yours. Because it is really.'

'You've lost me,' he said, staring at her. 'Really lost me.'

'Well, let me help you find yourself,' she said, quite briskly. 'It came to me this morning, when I discovered my mother was with you, when I should have been, when I realised how far apart we really were. Too far apart for me to cope with. I realised that it couldn't be my decision at all. It's got to be yours. You'll have to tell me what to do. I'm prepared to do it, if you really want me to. I'll stand up in court and lie to the best of my ability. Which I have to say isn't very impressive. If you really feel you can ask that of me, I'll do it. But I can't decide for myself and so you'll have to do it for me. All right?'

He sat staring at her, his face blank: finally he said, 'That's very clever. Very clever indeed. And very unfair.'

'I don't think so,' she said. 'It seems very fair to me.'

'I can't possibly tell you what to do. You know I can't.'

'Of course you can, Bard. You spend your life telling people what to do. Manipulating them, moving them about on your chessboard. Just carry on as usual. Anyway, I'll be waiting. Let me know.'

'And you really mean that?'

'I really mean it.'

There was a long silence. Then he said, 'Well, I suppose I should thank you. I shall have to think about it.'

'Yes, I think you should.'

He looked at her, and she could see in his eyes something she had seldom seen before: respect. Respect and uncertainty.

He got up then, went over to the window, looked out at the courtyard for a long time before turning back to her.

'And what are we going to do about us?' he said.

He was staring at her with a quite extraordinary concentration, as if he could force out of her whatever he wanted to hear. She was surprised by it, surprised and shocked; she could think of nothing to say. Finally, she said very quietly, 'Bard, I don't think there is an us any more. It's been battered to death, us has.'

'What? What do you mean?'

'I mean exactly that. There is no more marriage. My fault as much as yours, but it's gone.'

'Oh I see,' he said slowly, 'yes, of course. How stupid of me. Well, that was a very clever piece of rationalisation of yours, Francesca. Very clever.'

'What was?'

'All that crap. Telling me that you only did what you did because – what was it? Oh, yes, because I shut you out. That it was my fault. So I do what you ask, tell you everything, and suddenly it doesn't make any difference. What you're really saying is that you want to leave me and go to Liam but it makes it easier for you this way, to blame me, to say it's my fault, that I don't understand you, for Christ's sake –'

'Bard, that's not right, you're doing it again, not listening to me, you don't understand –'

'Oh, but I'm afraid I do understand. Only too well. It seems very simple to me, an open and shut case, as the lawyers say.'

'Everything seems simple to you,' she said, 'that's the whole problem, you find your nice, easy explanations and make everything fit them. That's what you're doing now.'

He didn't say anything for a moment, just looked at her, taking in what she had said, clearly having difficulty with it. And then something altered between them, and there was something else there, something raw, something dangerous.

'Come here,' he said suddenly.

'What?'

'I said come here.'

Still she didn't move, just stayed, sitting at the table, staring at him. Wondering what to do, how to defuse this strange new mood, feeling something odd, strange within herself.

'For Christ's sake,' he said, and he crossed over to her instead, pulled her up against him. He held both her wrists in his hands; his face was very close to hers. 'For fuck's sake, Francesca, get rid of him. Stop it, let him go.'

'Bard, I keep telling you, it's not – not –'

'Damn you,' he said, 'damn you to hell. Both of you.'

Francesca pulled one of her hands free and hit him: hard, on the side of his face. He winced, but he didn't move, his expression didn't change.

'Don't talk to me like that,' she said. 'Just don't.'

'And why not? Why shouldn't I talk to you like that?'

'Because you have no right to.'

'I have every right,' he said, and pushed her down in the chair, holding here there, 'every possible right. Don't talk to me about rights, Francesca, please. Wrongs are more your style, I think.' He put his hand up, then took hold of her by her jaw, turned her face sideways, staring at her, his eyes boring into her, as if he could read what was inside her head.

'Bard, for God's sake. Stop it.'

'I just can't stand it,' he said, 'any of it. I look at you there, and all I want to do is fuck you, God help me, I want to fuck you more than anything in the world, get him out of your head and your body. And short of raping you I can't do that. And I would rape you, Francesca, I wouldn't hesitate. Here, in this sanctuary of yours, down there, on that floor. And no-one would hear you, if you called out, if you screamed, no-one would come. But I won't, and do you know why not?'

'No,' she said, shaking now partly with fear, partly with – what? Desire? No, surely not desire.

He bent then and kissed her; hard, violently, on the mouth, his tongue probing her mouth, echoing what he might do – what she wanted him to do, she realised suddenly, shockingly, what she wanted him desperately in that moment to do to her body.

'I won't rape you,' he said, pulling away from her, 'because I love you. In spite of everything, everything you've done, everything I've done, I do still love you. I want to be with you again, I want to forgive you, I want you to forgive me. Perhaps that will convince you, Francesca. Think about it, anyway. I'm going now. One day you'll know how much you've thrown away. What a fool you are.'

He started to walk to the door; then he suddenly turned and looked at her.

'This is very sad,' he said, 'very sad indeed.'

And then he was gone, closing the door very quietly behind him; she sat there, motionless, heard him walk across the courtyard and open the gate, heard the Mercedes start, heard it going across the cobbles, through the gate and then a scream of tyres as he put his foot down in the lane. Francesca went out then, walked across the courtyard to shut the gate after him, and she thought that for the rest of her life she would be able to hear that noise, that ugly, screaming noise, the noise of the ending of her marriage.

Gray had hardly slept; he had got back to Clapham after midnight, had sat in the conservatory then for a long time, drinking glass after glass of Bourbon, and finally fallen asleep, fully dressed on his bed. He had not thought he had dreamed, but he woke at six to find himself weeping, the pillow wet with his tears. His head ached, almost beyond endurance; he eased himself up slightly, felt nausea hit him, just made the bathroom, threw up.

And as he sat there on the tiled floor, holding his head, he could see very clearly what he had to do.

Francesca woke up to hear Kitty coughing. Just a little cough, but nonetheless unmistakable. She must have got Mary's cold, she thought, looking at her watch: seven o'clock. How extraordinary. She had not thought she would sleep at all, and she had slept soundly and dreamlessly. Perhaps, she thought, it meant she had been right, that parting from Bard was not an ending but a beginning; then she felt the reality, the sense of failure, of loss, hit her, heard his voice telling her he still loved her, felt again the extraordinary, shocking desire, and with it a hard, physical wrench of misery. And knew it was too late.

And then Kitty sneezed and coughed slightly again. Francesca climbed out of her narrow, high bed and looked fearfully into the cot, but Kitty smiled up at her quite cheerfully, turned onto her stomach and struggled up first onto all fours, then into a sitting position, and then held out her arms to her mother and made the noise that meant 'Get me out of here'.

'Come on then,' said Francesca, reaching in for her; she was very wet, but quite warm – but not too warm, not hot. Nothing too serious; it was just a cold. Only a cold. Not really a cough even. Well, she wasn't going to worry about it too much. Not like last time. Mr Lauder himself had said she mustn't take colds too seriously. Only a cold. Those had been his exact words. Kitty sneezed again. 'Bless you,' said Francesca and, having checked Jack was still sound asleep, took Kitty along the corridor to the bathroom to change and dress her. It was time they went home, she thought, they should go today; and then realised she didn't know where home was any more and burst into tears.

Philip Drew, Bard's solicitor, arrived at the house at Hamilton Terrace at ten the following morning, in order to accompany him to the SFO.

'You look terrible,' he said. 'You all right?'

'Yes thanks,' said Bard shortly.

'Right. Well, I thought we'd run over a few things first. Now I've got George Spackman to agree to represent us. Thought we'd better bag him as soon as possible. He's the best there is and we don't want the other side getting him.'

'You seem very sure we're going to need him.'

'Well, we'll have a clearer idea after this morning. But at least he's ours if we want him.'

'Good.'

'Now then, as I told you, you have to answer the questions these boys put to you. It's like being under oath. And if you lie and they can prove you lied, it can be used in evidence against you later, at your trial.'

'Right.'

'Say as little as possible, naturally; tell them what you told me, and you should be OK. They're not over bright, some of them, but they know how to rattle you. Don't get lulled into a sense of false security.'

'I'll try not to,' said Bard. He almost smiled.

★

'Good morning, Mr Channing. I'm Peter Stainforth. Do sit down.'

Stainforth was unremarkable in every way: brown hair, medium height, accentless voice, pleasant expression. The only thing that distinguished him was a pair of very pale, ice-blue eyes.

'Thank you,' said Bard. 'My solicitor, Philip Drew.'

'Good morning, Mr Drew. Tea? Coffee? Linda, would you? Thanks. Now let me say straight away, this is not an interrogation. It's just that we can't quite reconcile all your bank accounts, and there are a couple of matters on which we require clarification. Shareholdings and so on.'

'Fine,' said Bard.

'Now the first thing, Mr Channing, nothing very major, but this business of the purchase that was made by your company, of a piece of land up in Scotland. For the purpose of building a golf course and leisure complex, all that sort of thing. Very nice idea. Interesting sideline for a company such as yours.'

'Yes,' said Bard shortly.

'However, things don't seem to have progressed very much. Well, these things do take time of course. But it's the money we're interested in. Now your company paid – what, for this acquisition, Mr Channing?'

'Two million pounds. That is the price we paid for it. I was acting on the advice of my directors.'

'Yes, of course. Lot of money for a bit of land and a rough old house.'

'It reflects the potential,' said Bard.

'Yes, I see. But you see, it seems the previous owner, Mrs – oh, yes, Mrs Blair – only received a quarter of a million pounds for the property. Can you explain that?'

'Not without looking into it,' said Bard shortly. 'The negotiation was handled by a subsidiary company.'

'Ah, yes, the subsidiary. Channing Leisure, is that the one?'

'Yes. It was.'

'Why did Channings not buy this land direct? From Mrs Blair?'

'Because that is not the way my company works. Subsidiaries frequently act for the main company.'

'And why would that be?'

'I told you. Channings is a complex company and that is the way it is structured.'

'I see. And so you have no idea why there was a difference between what you paid and Mrs Blair received?'

'Absolutely none. I was acting in good faith, and I left it to the company in question to acquire the land.'

'Yes, I see. But you see, there is something else which puzzles me. The money doesn't appear to be in the Channing Leisure account. It doesn't appear to be anywhere. Do you have any idea where it might be?'

'I'm afraid not. Channings is – was – a vast company, I really can't keep every small detail at my fingertips.'

'I don't think I'd call one and three quarter million pounds a small detail, Mr Channing, but I'm sure we will find it sooner or later. Anyway, we will leave that for now. Now there is something else, which I'm sure you can clear up for us. On the –' he glanced at a piece of paper, a list of dates on his desk; 'on the 30th of May this year, there were two purchase of a large block of shares in your company. Roughly a million pounds' worth.'

'Yes?'

'You have no idea who made that purchase?'

'Of course not. I don't go running round checking on my shareholders and their activities. I have better things to do.'

'Yes of course. Well, it shouldn't be too difficult. They are presumably registered.'

'Presumably. Since the law requires it.'

'Indeed. Anyway, it was very fortunate for the company that those purchases were made. Since they served to steady the share price.'

'If you say so.'

'I do. Now rather interestingly, you took out a loan on the 28th of May. With Engels Bank. Of eight hundred thousand pounds. Almost a million.'

'I did take out a loan with Engels recently. Yes. I have no idea of the precise date. Or the amount.'

'Well, now you do. And it was to fund an option on a site in – let me see, near Munich.'

'Yes.'

'Is that going ahead all right?'

'There have been some problems with it.'

'So it's not going ahead?'

'Mr Stainforth, you don't appear to have a very clear understanding of the property business. It's not like a trip to Sainsbury's. Every purchase is complex. Every development has its difficulties.'

'I wouldn't have thought a man like you would know about Sainsbury's,' said Stainforth.

'What? Oh for God's sake. If you can't follow a simple analogy –'

'Er – perhaps we could leave that for now,' said Drew, 'you must understand, Mr Stainforth, we have just been presented with all this, we must have time to look at it more carefully. My client's business is, as he has said, extremely complex.'

'Yes, of course. I quite see that. But there is one other thing, then I'll let you go. There's a charitable trust you have, out in the Dutch Antilles. Is that right?'

'Yes, there is.'

'The chief beneficiary being the World Farming Federation.'

'Yes. I have a great interest in these matters.'

'I too. There lies the salvation of our planet. Wouldn't you say?'

'I would, yes,' said Bard.

'Now this trust holds – or rather held – a large number of shares in the Channing Corporation. Is that correct?'

'Indeed.'

'But you see, Mr Channing, those shares, as you no doubt know, have been sold. And what we are – interested – in is the date of that sale. Now, I wonder if –'

'Christ Almighty,' said Bard, as they walked up Elm Street, looking back over his shoulder at the SFO's rather sinister-looking, mirrored front, 'how have they got all this stuff so quickly? How have they done it? I just don't understand it. I thought you said they weren't terribly bright.'

'Obviously I was wrong,' said Drew. 'Look – let's go back to my office. We need to talk urgently. They seem to have rather more of a case against you than I originally imagined. Obviously a load of baloney, but we do need to do some thinking.'

'I can't,' said Bard, 'not now. I've got this journalist coming to see me at twelve. Well, I had this journalist coming to see me at twelve, Christ look at the time. 'He'll probably have gone long since.'

'Well, I told you not to see him anyway,' said Drew, 'it's madness. Call me later, Bard, will you. I don't want to alarm you, but I think you might have got a bit of a problem.'

He flagged down a taxi; Bard got into his car. It had a parking ticket on it: it seemed very sinister. He wrenched it off the windscreen, pulled it out of its plastic cover and ripped it into pieces.

Gray sat in his car outside Bard's house, reading his story. It was very good. It was fucking brilliant. It read like a thriller, he could hardly believe he'd done it. It had everything: sex, money, crime, bribery, beautiful women, wronged wives, exotic locations, double dealings –

and a twist in the tale that John Grisham would have been proud of. Shit.

It was always an extraordinary moment, this, when everything had worked, woven into the final whole, all the research, the hunches, the patient trawling through endless documents: all translated into a few thousand words of densely packed prose. You could never quite believe it, that it had worked; more odd still was the point when the story was set in type, had gone to bed, when you knew the machines were running it, that there was nothing more you could do to it, nothing to stop it. You felt powerless then, out of control, nervous, edgy, it was a bit like stage fright. After that, reading it in the paper, seeing it there on the page, was an anti-climax, it seemed to have little to do with you.

He saw, in his mirror, the Mercedes coming up the street: saw Channing get out of it, slam the door, run up the steps. Gray put the sheets of paper in an envelope, got out, called to him; Channing looked down, scowled at him, said nothing.

Gray followed him up the steps, stood right by him, studying him, seeing the wretchedness, the exhaustion, the fear in his face, thinking how closely, how extraordinarily closely and in what extraordinary ways their lives had become intertwined. It was one of the things that never failed to amaze him about his profession; that for a few days, weeks, you became part of someone's life, their present, their past, their work, their family, and then it was over, the knot was loosened, the bond undone. It could be a relief, it could be an anti-climax: occasionally, very occasionally, it seemed sad. At this moment, it seemed sad.

Without saying anything at all, he handed over the envelope to Channing.

Friday was shopping day for the convent; consequently Reverend Mother needed her car, and one of the sisters had taken the only other vehicle, a big pick-up truck, to a market garden twenty miles away to pick up some boxes of fruit. Which in turn meant Francesca was unable to pick up the hire car which would take them back to London. By mid-morning Kitty's cough had worsened: nothing dramatic still, of course, just a sneezy, tickly cough, but just the same to be heard more and more frequently. Francesca was edgy, clearly as much worried about her as she was about her own situation, impatient to get away.

'Perhaps you should take her to the doctor,' said Rachel, looking at

Kitty as she sat on Francesca's knee. Her small nose was red now, her dark eyes liquid, but she still appeared perfectly cheerful.

'I can't take her to the doctor because I haven't got a car,' said Francesca irritably, 'and I'm sure there's no need, it's only a cold. And besides I want her to see our doctor, or Mr Lauder, not some idiot down here.'

'I'm sure he wouldn't be an idiot, darling, and anyway, you just said it was only a cold, so −'

'Yes, well, it is. And Mr Lauder said specifically last time that I wasn't to fuss over a cold, that they weren't serious, so there's no point doing anything. But I do want to get home. As soon as Reverend Mother gets back I want to go and collect this thing. What time is that normally, because −'

'Darling, I don't know. I'm not that regular a visitor.'

'No. Surely she can't be that much longer, I just don't see how on earth a bit of shopping can take over two hours.'

It's a while since you did any real shopping, Rachel thought, realising in that moment how spoilt, how removed from reality Francesca had become. 'Well,' she said carefully, 'it's a way away, the town.'

'Yes, I suppose so. What do you think I should do about that house then? I can't leave it indefinitely.'

'Francesca, I don't think you have to decide that now. We only saw it a little over twelve hours ago, it's not even on the market. I wouldn't call that an indefinite delay.'

'Well, you know what I mean. Oh, God. Do you think Kitty's hot, Mummy? Does she seem feverish to you?'

Rachel felt Kitty's forehead, her small hands, and shook her head. 'No, I really don't. I think she's fine. It is just a cold, I'm sure.'

'I'm not,' said Francesca fretfully. 'Maybe I should see the doctor here, just have her checked. I'll phone, I think, do you know the number?'

'I don't, but any of the Sisters would. I'll go and find out.'

But the local doctor, whose name was Richard Paget, was about to go out on his rounds, and his receptionist informed Francesca she had no appointments until six that evening. 'And then it's emergencies only.'

'Well, this might be one,' said Francesca, her voice rising just a little, 'if I don't see him before then. Or rather if my baby doesn't, she has a heart condition, you see, and she's got a bad cold and −'

'Just a moment,' said the receptionist, and there was a whispered conversation; she came back on the line.

'Could you bring baby down right away, and Doctor will have a look at her.'

. 'No I can't,' said Francesca, 'because I haven't got a car, I'm stuck here at the convent, at Bresholme, you know, could he come here, do you think?'

'Well, possibly later this afternoon. But I can't say when it would be. Really if you could get her down here for six, that might be better, more satisfactory for you –'

'It doesn't sound satisfactory at all,' said Francesca irritably. Kitty coughed again. 'Oh, look, don't bother, I'll just get her back to London, to my own doctor.'

'Very well, my dear. If you prefer that.'

Francesca slammed the phone down, looked at her mother. 'Stupid bloody woman,' she said. 'Oh for God's sake, where is Reverend Mother?'

Gray finally reached the office after two. Tricia looked at him in a mixture of rage and relief.

'Gray. Where the fuck have you been? And I quote our esteemed editor.'

'Sorry. I had to – finish something.'

'What, the story? Well, thank God for that. He's going mad, Gray, absolutely barmy. And I'm not surprised, quite honestly. He's been holding three pages for you for twenty-four hours, and – Gray, are you all right? You look terrible.'

'Yes, I'm all right,' said Gray with a sigh. 'Just. I'm sorry you've had to field all the shit, Tricia. Very sorry.'

'Oh, it's all part of the job, I guess,' said Tricia cheerfully. 'Anyway, go straight down there for God's sake. Want me to do anything for you?'

'No, no, it's all done.'

'Great. Did you see Channing?'

'Yes, I did.'

'And what did he say?'

'Not a lot.'

'I see. Is that the story? Doesn't look very long.'

'It's long enough,' said Gray. 'Could you get me some tea, Tricia, please?'

'Sure. Oh and Gray, by the way, Liam Channing phoned. From Spain. He's going to ring back. He wanted to know whether you'd been able to use that information he gave you.'

Gray thought for a minute. Then he said, 'Ah, yes. Could you tell him it was of enormous help to me and that I'll certainly be making very full use of it.'

'Oh, OK,' said Tricia, 'yeah, I'll tell him.'

'Thanks,' said Gray. He walked rather heavily out of the office and along the corridor in the direction of David Guthrie's office.

Barnaby was not normally much given to doing what he thought he should; most of his actions were directed entirely by what he knew he wanted. He'd gone to stay with Tom in Wiltshire for a few days because he'd wanted to get away from it all, the emotional chaos, but now he found himself thinking, greatly to his surprise, that he ought to go back to London. Back to Hamilton Terrace. The recent events had shaken him: he had been upset by Morag, had genuinely shocked himself by his behaviour in the wine bar with Oliver, he had been very distressed by Kirsten's anguish, and he was horrified by the prospect of Francesca leaving his father. He liked Francesca enormously; she wasn't just pretty and good natured and fun, she had a bit of a brain on her as well. And she'd made the house much nicer to live in. OK, Kirsten hated her, but it had actually been foul before she'd arrived, with first Nanny fussing over them, and then just Sandie looking after them, or rather not looking after them; there'd been no warmth, no affection, no heart to the place. And he could remember life with their mother and that had been absolutely horrible. The five years since Francesca had married his father had actually been the best of his life, Barnaby thought. OK, his father had still been filthy tempered a great deal and the feuding between Kirsten and Francesca, until Kirsten had moved out, or been moved out, hadn't been too good, but on the whole things had been pretty fair. And now Francesca was going. Or threatening to go. He couldn't actually blame her, but still.

Anyway, that morning he'd decided he ought to go home for a bit. His father must be at rock bottom, poor old sod; Kirsten might need his moral support; and if Francesca did come back, even breifly, he could pull out all the stops, really try and make her change her mind. She was very fond of him, he knew she was, in fact he had a pretty good hunch she quite fancied him, and he could be very persuasive if he put his mind ot it.

He phoned Kirsten from Tom's house to tell her he was coming; she was touchingly pleased.

'Barney, I'm so glad. I really really want you to come with me tomorrow. Will you?'

'What's happening tomorrow?'

'I'm having the − the thing done. You know.'

'Oh.' Barnaby was appalled, his good resolutions caving on him fast. 'Oh. Couldn't − I mean, wouldn't you rather Tory went with you?'

'No. Tory's so bloody earnest. She'd keep asking me if I was sure I was doing the right thing, and if I'd seen a priest and everything. I want you, Barney, I really do.'

Her voice wobbled; Barnaby felt instantly guilty. 'Oh. OK, but I won't have to − well, do anything, will I?'

'Of course not, you half-brain. Only hold my hand.'

'What, not while they're −'

'Barnaby, of course not. Beforehand, that's all. And afterwards, maybe.'

'Oh. OK. You feeling all right, then? About it?'

'Yes, I'm fine thanks. Come to the flat about nine, can you? We can go in my car. And you can take it and then collect me next day.'

'Yes, fine. Right. Well, I'll see you tomorrow then. I'll be at the house if you need me. Or shall I come round this evening? We could have a Chinky, get a video out.'

'Yes,' said Kirsten, 'I'd really like that, Barney. Thanks.'

Reverend Mother finally reached the convent after one. 'I'm so sorry, Francesca, to have kept you. I had to go and see Father Brownlow at the church on my way back. If you like I'll take you straight into Bideford now, so you can go on to London, don't have to come back here.'

'No, it's all right,' said Francesca, trying not to sound short, 'Kitty's asleep now, there's no point waking her. We'll have lunch and then go, perhaps. If that's all right with you.'

'Of course. Come along and we'll go straight in.'

Francesca couldn't eat any lunch; her stomach felt like tangled string. Jack had spent the morning in the bakery and had made her a very grey-looking roll; she did her best to swallow that at least, but it was impossible.

'I'm sorry, darling, it's delicious, but I've got a bit of a tummyache. I think I might go and see if Kitty's all right. She's been asleep for ages.'

'I've made her some bread as well,' said Jack. 'A fly got in the dough, look, you can see it there, but it'll be cooked, it'll probably taste nice.'

'Thank you, Jack. That's very kind. I'll see you in a minute.'

She went up to her room. She felt worse every minute, sore,

aching, exhausted, as if she was developing some very virulent form of flu. Perhaps she was developing flu, she thought, perhaps something more serious. Perhaps she was going to be really ill, and have to be rushed to hospital. That seemed oddly welcome; it would remove her from being brave, from trying, from living with herself and her decision, with working out whatever she was going to do next; she could just lie in bed and life would go on around her and everyone else would see to things and nothing at all would be asked of her. She felt so dizzy as she walked up the stairs that she had to sit down, put her head in her arms. Sister Maria, the sweet-faced old nun who did much of the cleaning in the convent, saw her, asked her if she was all right, if she could get her anything, if she could get her mother for her.

'No, the last thing I want is a fuss,' said Francesca sharply. 'We'll have half the convent up here in a minute ... I just felt a bit dizzy, that's all.'

Sister Maria patted her head very gently, and moved quietly away. God, I'm a bitch, she thought, and opened her mouth to call an apology, but then found she didn t have the strength or the emotional resources even for that. She wished she could stop thinking about Liam, and wondered how it could be that she was more upset about him and the way he had behaved towards her, his cruelty, his duplicity, than about the ending of her marriage. She supposed it was because her pride, as well as her heart, had been hurt; she had been totally deceived, made a fool of by him, like some gullible teenager, had listened to him talking endlessly in that bloody beautiful voice of his, playing on her sympathies, preying on her loneliness, and never recognised any of it. Bard was right: she was a fool. God, how could she have been so stupid. So totally, horribly, pathetically stupid. She wondered if she would ever have to see him again; she hoped not. Well, she supposed she hoped not. Actually, Francesca, go on, admit it, if he walked through that door now, with his bloody sensitive face looking at you all tenderly, and gave you some half credible story, some explanation about what had happened, you'd swallow it, eagerly, gratefully, and still want to go off into the sunset with him. It was grotesque, humiliating to realise, but it was true. Mercifully it was extremely unlikely. For the hundredth, the thousandth time, she thought fearfully of what he might have told Graydon, what Graydon might be going to do with the information. Probably it would be all over the papers on Sunday: headlines, progressively more nightmarish, drifted into her head: 'Adulterous wife betrays ruined husband.' 'Wife cheats on husband with stepson.' 'Incestuous pillowtalk sends husband to jail.'

Well, she'd probably read all of that and worse. She thought of how angry and shocked she had been with Kirsten at her indiscretion with the newspapers, and felt ashamed as well as everything else. She suddenly wondered if, wise or not, she should talk to Graydon Townsend. Find out what he was going to do, find out exactly what Liam had told him. Maybe, maybe she could still persuade him; anyway, she thought, she ought to try. It was too important not to. She owed that to Bard, at least.

She looked in on Kitty; she was still asleep. She didn't look too bad; she was lying on her back, her face rather sternly composed, her dark eyebrows, surprisingly heavy for a baby, creased in a near-frown. She looked a bit like Bard. A lot like Bard.

And then she coughed a different cough from the spluttering, wheezy ones earlier, a deeper, more rasping sound. Francesca put her hand down into the cot, felt Kitty's face, her legs. She was warm. Very warm indeed.

Francesca promptly forgot about Gray Townsend.

Chapter Thirty

'What do you mean, there's no fucking story?' said David Guthrie. 'What's happened to it, of course there's a story.'

'No,' said Gray, 'there isn't.'

'But Gray, there was a story yesterday. There was a story this morning even, I understood from Tricia.'

'She thought there was,' said Gray.

'And did you think there was yesterday? Christ Almighty, Gray, have you had some kind of a breakdown or something? I don't understand this. All these weeks, months it feels like, you've been leading me on, telling me it was coming, it was the biggest thing in years, that it was going to blow my balls off, and now you tell me there's nothing there. Are you suffering from some kind of mental impotence, can't you get your head up any more?'

'Something like that,' said Gray quietly.

'Oh I see. You've had an attack of conscience. Well tough. I pay you a great deal of money, Gray Townsend, I've borne a lot of expenses, this Jersey trip alone, fucking fortune. And now suddenly you're wimping out. Did Bard Channing threaten you or something?'

'No, he didn't.'

'Now look, Gray,' said Guthrie, his voice suddenly more reasonable, 'you don't have to write it, it doesn't have to go under your by-line. If you want to disappear for a bit, that's OK. But I want that story.'

'You can't have it,' said Gray.

'I've paid for it.'

'I'm sorry. There isn't a story.'

'Did you get it all wrong? Is that what it is, can't you find the guts to tell me?'

'Dave, there just isn't a story. OK?'

'No, not OK. Nobody does this to me. You're fucking fi—'

'And I'm resigning.'

'What! Oh don't be so bloody pathetic. Of course you're not resigning. We can –'

'Dave, I'm resigning. Sorry. Here's my letter of resignation. And there's no story, no notes, nothing on my machine. So please don't go looking for it.'

'Get out!' said Guthrie, his face white now with alarming scarlet blotches on it. 'Get the fuck out of here. Don't show your face in here ever again. Ever. And I would be very surprised if any other newspaper wanted to see it either, by the time I've finished talking about this.'

'No, I'm afraid you're probably right,' said Gray.

He left Guthrie's office, walked back to his own. An evil-looking plastic cup of tea sat on his desk. He picked it up, drained it. Tricia watched him in astonishment.

He smiled at her, and said, 'Right, well, I'm off.'

'Off? Where to?'

'Home,' said Gray. 'I'm sorry to spring it on you, Tricia, but I've just resigned. I'll come back in next week for my stuff, if Dave hasn't personally set fire to it, and buy you a lunch to die for. Meanwhile, have a good weekend.'

He suddenly bent down to her as she sat, literally open mouthed, staring up at him, and gave her a kiss. 'You've been great,' he said, 'thank you for everything. I'll miss you.'

When he got home, he went straight up to his study, and phoned Briony.

'Hi,' he said, 'it's me.'

'Oh,' she said. 'Oh, hallo Gray.' She sounded wary, almost cold.

'Are you busy tonight?'

'No-o. No I don't think so. Why?'

'I wondered if you'd have dinner with me,' he said. 'I want to talk to you.'

Oliver stood on the doorstep in Hamilton Terrace, thinking he had never been nearer in his life to running away. He kept taking deep breaths, thinking it might help; all it did was make him feel light-headed.

Sandie opened the door.

'I've – I've come to see Mr Channing. I'm Oliver Clarke,' he added, in case she didn't recognise him.

'Oh yes. He's expecting you. Come in.'

Oliver went in. He had been to the house several times, but it never failed to impress him. His own small house would almost have fitted into the hall alone, he thought, gazing up at the immensely high ceiling, the fine staircase at the back of it, the tall window, reaching almost from floor to ceiling. He followed Sandie through the folding doors into the drawing room, running the depth of the house, still almost inclined to run, to claim a suddenly remembered urgent appointment.

Bard Channing was standing by the fireplace. 'Ah, Oliver. Come in. Sit down. How are you?'

He looked very tired, Oliver thought, tired and somehow smaller. He made a great effort to smile at him.

'I'm fine, thank you, Mr Channing.'

He sat down rather suddenly on one of the sofas; it was very soft, he felt engulfed in it, trapped.

'Good. Well, what is it, what did you want to see me about? I'm afraid I can't help you with your job, if that's what you're hoping.'

'No,' said Oliver, 'no it isn't.'

'Well, what is it, then? Ah Sandie, thanks. Put it down there. Tea, Oliver?'

'No thank you,' said Oliver. He thought if he tried to swallow anything he really would be sick.

There was a silence. Bard began to look irritable, visibly struggled not to sound impatient.

'Well, come on, then. Am I really so frightening?'

'Yes,' said Oliver truthfully.

'Well then,' said Bard, making a clear effort to lighten the occasion, 'the sooner you tell me why you're here, the sooner you can leave again.'

This was the sort of logic that appealed to Oliver; he took a deep breath, looked briefly, wildly at the door, and said, 'It's about – about the accountants. About the investigation.'

'Oh yes?' Bard Channing didn't move, nor did his face change, and yet he became visibly, instantly, more alert, tense. 'What about them?'

'Well – you see – I went back there the other night. I'd left my jacket behind. And the phone was ringing in the office that Mr Sloane's been using.'

'Yes?'

'It was your old office. Well, your secretary's.'

'Yes, Oliver, I know that.'

'And he wasn't there, there was no-one there. And I heard the answering machine pick it up. And I could hear – someone's voice.'

'Not unusual,' said Bard lightly. But he didn't look light; he looked heavily, fiercely intense.

'No, of course not. Anyway, I thought I recognised the voice, so I stopped to listen. It – well, it was leaving a message about some financial routes. Into Switzerland. I didn't know what it meant. I expect you do.'

Bard said nothing, but his jaw had tightened, and the vein throbbed in his neck.

'Well, this person obviously knew Mr Sloane. Had talked to him before. Said they'd phone again next day. With the information about these financial routes.'

'Yes. Is that all?'

'Well, it's all they said, Mr Channing. The point was, who this person was. Supplying this information. I mean – well, it seemed rather odd, that's all. And I thought – well, you ought to know.'

'Oliver, I would be very grateful if you could let me know who this disembodied voice belonged to,' said Bard. 'I think I've got the picture now and the gist of what you're trying to say.'

'Yes,' said Oliver, 'yes of course. Well –' He stood up; he thought if the bawling started that would be better than if he was sunk into the great soft sofa. 'Well, the thing is, Mr Channing, and you may very well know this, of course, and if you do I'm sorry, but it was – well, it was Marcia Grainger.'

'Now look,' said the doctor soothingly to Francesca, 'yes, your baby has a cough. It's only slight. Little more than a cold really.'

He smiled at her; an old-style GP, white haired, kindly, all-powerful, dishing out old-style anodyne.

'But she's got a temperature,' said Francesca, trying to keep her voice level, 'and a heart condition, and I've been told –'

'Yes, yes, she has got a temperature. A very, very slight one. Just a hundred. And I know she has a heart condition. I've spoken to your own doctor about her, and –'

'Dr Paget, why didn't you speak to Mr Lauder? Her consultant? That's who I told you to get in touch with –'

'I'm afraid Mr Lauder was away, Mrs Channing. On holiday. But your GP was very reassuring, and –'

'He's an idiot,' said Francesca shortly. 'He missed the hole in her heart in the first place.'

'Mrs Channing, this isn't getting us anywhere.' Dr Paget was clearly put out by this slur on the medical brotherhood. 'The point is, your little girl's condition is simply not very serious. I'm going to prescribe some antibiotics for her and I'm quite sure that in twenty-four hours she'll be right as rain.'

'Well, I'm going back to London tonight, I can get a second opinon then,' said Francesca.

Dr Paget looked at her, a careful patience on his face. 'Now I really don't think that is a good idea. It's a long drive, it will tire her, she's far better staying here, at the convent, resting, and then you can go back when she's recovered.'

'But I want –'

'Mrs Channing, you can do whatever you like, of course. She's your baby. I can only say if she was mine, she would stay here peacefully, getting over her cold, rather than be subjected to jolting around in a car for five hours, inhaling motorway fumes.' He reached out suddenly, patted her hand. 'I know how worried you are. Any mother would be. But she will be all right, I promise you.'

Francesca suddenly felt rather ashamed of herself. 'Yes. I'm sorry if I seem impatient. It's just that –'

'Of course. Now look, give her this sachet in her milk now, and here's another couple, just in case you miss the chemist tonight. Every six hours, wake her at midnight – it may seem cruel, but it's important. And any worries at all, just call me, I'll gladly come any time, middle of the night or not.'

'Thank you,' said Francesca humbly.

She looked down at Kitty, sitting on her knee; she did seem better. She put her small hand up, touched her mother's face as if to comfort her.

'There, you see,' said Dr Paget, 'she's trying to tell you not to worry. She'll be fine, Mrs Channing, just you see.'

Briony was waiting in the restaurant – the Depot in Barnes, one of their old haunts – when Gray arrived. He stood for a moment in the doorway, just looking at her. She was reading the evening paper, looking very pretty in a black T-shirt and a long natural linen skirt, her brown hair falling over her face. She pushed it back behind her ears, looked up and saw him, and smiled. He had managed to get a table window; the river was gleaming in the evening sun, studded with boats, on the other side people walked with their dogs, children cycled and skated. It looked like a painting, as if it had been painted indeed with the precise purpose of making a backdrop for her.

'Hi,' he said, going over, bending to kiss her.

'Hallo, Gray.'

'You look lovely.'

'Thank you. Why are you so brown? Holiday?'

'Few days in Jersey. Researching a story.'

'Good story?'

'Well – something of one in its own right. I'll tell you about it. Let's order. Then we can concentrate.'

They ordered and then sat in a slightly strained silence, punctuated by the bright polite 'What you have been doing?' and 'Seen any good films?' of the once intimate. The starters arrived – goat cheese and rocket salad, the best in London Gray always said, and Gray smiled awkwardly at her, took a deep breath.

'This is – very good of you. To see me at such short notice.'

'That's all right. I wasn't busy.'

'I just needed to talk to you. Terribly badly.'

'Yes. Gray –' She hesitated, looked awkward. His heart thudded uncomfortably; she was going to say she had someone else. He took a very large mouthful of the Chardonnay he had ordered, felt it hit his bloodstream, found himself brave enough to say, 'Yes?'

'Oh – nothing. Doesn't matter, it can wait. How's the *News*?'

'I suppose it's all right,' said Gray. 'I've resigned.'

'You've resigned?' She looked totally stunned. 'Gray, why, how, what happened?'

He looked at her, put down his fork. He couldn't eat this, even if it was the best in London. He reached out, took both of her hands in his.

'Briony, just listen, will you? Till I've finished. You can ask me questions when I've finished. This is very complicated and very – difficult. Just listen.'

Briony listened. She was very good at that. She always had been. He'd forgotten quite how good. And when he had finished, she sat in silence, looking at him for a long time, her clear blue eyes very thoughtful. And then she said, 'I'm sorry, Gray, I need to think about this. Quietly, on my own. I'll – I'll phone you in the morning. If that's all right. Sorry about the dinner.'

Gray sat staring after her as she walked across the restaurant and out into the courtyard, her long skirt floating round her, and wondered why he couldn't see her more clearly. He realised after a while it was because his eyes were full of tears.

'Marcia? This is Bard Channing. I'd like to come and see you, if I may.'

'What, this evening, Mr Channing? Well, I don't know if that would be entirely convenient, I had planned to have an early night, I'm rather tired.'

'It won't take long, Marcia, I assure you. I just wanted to check a couple of details with you.'

'Oh. Very well then. Of course. If it's reallly essential. How soon can you be here?'

'Oh – in half an hour or so.'

'Very well, Mr Channing. But I do hope it won't take too long.'

She would never have said that in the old days; the balance of power had already shifted.

She opened the door to him, smiled her rather awkward smile. She was wearing a pair of dark grey trousers and a beige cotton shirt.

'Mr Channing. Do come in.'

'Thank you.'

He walked past her into her sitting room, as regimentally neat and orderly as her office had been. It was impersonal, but in a rather surprisingly good taste, all shades of beige, like many of her clothes. The only strident note was a painting of the harbour at St Brelade on Jersey: a rather vulgar painting, the colours brilliant.

'Ah,' he said, 'did you buy that there?'

'I did. A local artist, I feel they should be encouraged.'

'Quite so.'

'Would you like a drink, Mr Channing?'

'Oh – yes, please. Whisky if you've got it. I may as well add drunken driving to my list of crimes.'

'Mr Channing, I don't think you should talk like that. It's defeatist,' said Marcia severely. 'All may yet be well.'

'That's what you think, is it?' said Bard.

'Of course, yes.'

'Well, in that case, you're going to be very disappointed.'

'I'm sorry?'

'I said you're going to be very disappointed. If that happens in spite of all your endeavours.'

'Mr Channing, I'm afraid I don't know what you're talking about.'

'Marcia, come off it,' said Bard. 'You've been feeding – shall we say sensitive? – information to the accountants. I know you have. I've been told.'

Marcia looked at him. Her face was very flushed. 'Who?' she said. 'Who's been telling you these lies?'

'Not lies, Marcia. Are they? That is what you've been doing. It all seems extremely clear suddenly. How they've got to it all so fast. Nobody could have worked all that out, not for months. So let's not waste time playing silly games, please.'

She took a large mouthful of her whisky. 'You can't prove it,' she said.

'Oh, I don't know. I have a very reliable witness, who'll testify to it in court.'

. 'Who was it?' she said, her voice heavy. 'One of them?'

'I don't think I should tell you. What was it, Marcia, a bit of plea-bargaining? "If I tell you all this, will you see I get off more lightly?" Something like that?'

'There's nothing for me to be charged with,' she said.

'Oh really? What about Jersey?'

'Mr Channing,' she said, her voice ice-cold, 'I was only – what is the phrase – carrying out orders. I don't think there are very heavy penalties for that.'

'Oh really? What about the little bit of creaming off you did there, Marcia? Your own personal bank account, opened with company money, your nice little bedsit you've been renting over there in St Ouen, your application for the boarding house, only three years away now. I'd call that theft, myself. What happened to honour among thieves, I wonder?'

'Nobody knows about that,' she said, 'nobody. You could never prove it.'

'Well, I could, actually, Marcia. The person who told me found out all by himself. He's talked to someone over there. It's all written into a story, as a matter of fact. A story that's going to appear in the Sunday papers. Featuring all of us, mainly me of course, but certainly you, Marcia. Quite a lot about all that. It might be a bit hard for you to get another job now, I think. And I think your application for the house might not go through quite so easily either, do you?'

She was silent; she was white now, her grey eyes gimlet-hard in her face.

'Why did you do it, Marcia? That's what I want to know. You could have got off, you were only obeying orders, as you so rightly say, you could have pretended innocence. You were well rewarded, well paid, you were able to sell your shares in good time ...'

Marcia drained her glass. 'I wanted to hurt you,' said, quite matter-of-factly. 'I wanted to damage you.'

'But Marcia, why? What did I do? I know I swore at you, treated you badly, but that was just my way. I know it was bad, I don't make any excuses, but you knew I was fond of you, you'd been loyal for so long ...'

'Well,' she said, 'everyone has a breaking point, Mr Channing. Even me. I didn't mind the swearing, as a matter of fact. Or your terrible temper. I knew it didn't mean anything. I thought it was rather absurd of people to mind, as far as I was concerned it was simply another facet of your personality. The personality I had always admired.'

'But, Marcia —'

'Mr Channing, I would like to finish.'

'Sorry.'

'We had a very close bond, you and I, for all those years; I was proud of it. I liked the fact that I was privy to all your secrets, that I knew much of what was going on, I didn't care about it in the least, what you did, so stupid of people not to realise, not to be aware of the way of our world. I thought it was very amusing, rather pathetic, that your own wife could not see it at all.'

'I wish she'd seen it that way,' said Bard. 'But anyway, what was this — breaking point?'

'It was the way you behaved,' she said flatly, 'with that woman.'

'Woman?' said Bard. 'What woman, for Christ's sake?'

'Mrs Duncan-Brown.'

'Mrs Duncan-Brown?' said Bard. 'Marcia, I swear to God, I don't know what you're talking about.'

'Of course you do,' she said. 'On the day of the crash. When I wanted so much to be able to comfort you, when I had — well, clearly it meant nothing to you. I meant nothing to you.'

Her voice shook slightly; she got up, poured herself another whisky, sat down again. 'And then to see you there, with her. In the office, our office. Not your wife, that would have been different, of course a man in your situation has to have a wife, I always accepted that. But her. You holding her, your head on her — her breasts.'

Bard stared at her. She was looking at him with total distaste; he felt rather sick.

'Frankly,' she said, 'I found that disgusting. Humiliating and disgusting. It made me realise the sort of man you really are. I'd like you to go now, Mr Channing, please. But I shall look forward to your court case. I shall look forward to it very much indeed.'

Chapter Thirty-one

Kirsten sat in the car beside Barnaby, her teeth chattering. She felt very cold, and her head ached. She was also terribly thirsty, but was forbidden to have anything to drink.

'You OK?' he said, looking at her.

'Yeah, I'm fine.'

'Soon be there.'

'Yes.'

Soon be there. Soon she'd have it done. Soon it would be over. Soon it would be dead.

'Oh Christ,' she said, and then, struck by the inappropriateness of her words, giggled; a nervous, hysterical giggle.

They arrived at the hospital, a lush, expensive place in North London. Barnaby stopped the car. 'I'll go and park, be with you in a minute.'

'You will come back, won't you?' said Kirsten.

'Of course I will, you silly cow,' said Barnaby with his widest grin. 'Five minutes max.'

Kirsten watched the car disappear with a lump in her throat, thinking how much he must be hating this, how very much she loved him.

The woman in Reception was brisk, cool. Kirsten felt sure she knew what she was there for, disapproved of it. She filled in the admission form, followed a nurse down the corridor, up in the lift.

'My brother's coming back in a minute,' she said, 'you will make sure he comes up to my room, won't you?'

'I surely will,' said the nurse, grinning. She was Australian, plump, freckled. 'How you feeling?'

'Oh – you know. Bit sick.'

'We'll give you something for that,' said the nurse. 'Soon be over. Now you pop up into that lovely robe there, and I'll take your blood pressure and all that and then –'

Kirsten sighed, and started to undress.

★

Barnaby came back, ultra cheerful.

'Hi, all right?'

'Yes. Yes, I think so. Barney –'

'Yes?'

'Do you believe in hell?'

He considered for a moment, then shook his head. 'Nah. Load of bollocks if you ask me. All of it.'

'Barney! What would Mum say?'

'Well, it hasn't done her much good, has it? Her religion?'

'Well no, but –'

'Look,' he said, 'it's all a matter of geography, if you ask me. I realised that in India. If you're born there, you believe in cows and reincarnation; if you get to be born here, you believe in hell. How's that?'

'Not sure,' said Kirsten, 'but it's given me something to think about.'

Peter Stainforth, who had spent a rather restless night, phoned David Sloane first thing on Saturday morning.

'Michael, morning. Sorry to intrude on your weekend. I'm a bit thoughtful about Channing.'

'In what way thoughtful?'

'Oh – you know. The usual way. I just feel he might feel a bit restless, you know what I mean? I thought perhaps we should take the usual steps fairly quickly. He might want to go walkabouts suddenly. Or even sail-abouts,' he added.

'Hardly that, surely,' said Sloane, 'you don't get the sort of places he'd be making for in a boat. But I think you might be right. Yes, OK. I'll have a bit of a think and get back to you.'

Kitty had slept heavily; Francesca woke her at midnight, as instructed, and gave her her medicine, and had to wake her again at six. She seemed no worse, but she was no better either, flushed and wheezy. Rachel had come in at six-thirty, looking anxious. Jack had been moved into her room.

'How is she? I heard her coughing.'

'Not very well,' said Francesca. 'Oh, dear God, I wish we were at home.'

'You don't want to go now? In spite of what that nice old doctor said?'

'I still haven't got a bloody car.'

'Well, I know Reverend Mother would take us into Bideford. Or even lend us her car.'

'Well I – oh, I don't know, Mummy. Kitty's still feverish. The doctor could be right. The journey would exhaust her. I think we should wait until she's a bit better. She's holding her own, at least she's not any worse.'

Kitty opened her eyes and smiled up at them and then coughed, several times, hard; that made her cry, and she coughed more. Francesca sat holding her, stroking her silky hair, trying to crush the panic she felt, trying to tell herself it was just a matter of time. That it was only a cold. Only a cold.

Philip Drew was eating his breakfast when Bard Channing telephoned. His wife, who was getting very tired of Bard Channing's voice and its inevitable effect on what should have been their private life, said rather shortly that she'd get her husband, but they were just going to go out.

'This won't take long,' said Bard.

Drew came to the phone. 'Morning, Bard.'

'Good morning. Look, Philip, I had a bit of a shock yesterday. It seems the SFO aren't quite so bright as we thought. Someone's been giving them information, that's how they've been doing so well. Someone with an inside view, as you might say.'

'Oh really? Important information?'

'Well, they clearly think so.'

'Who is this person?'

'My secretary.'

'What, Marcia?'

'Yes.'

'Christ.'

There was a long silence while Drew took this in, clearly examining its implications. Finally he said, 'How absolutely extraordinary. I thought she adored you.'

'She did,' said Bard grimly. 'That's what seems to be the trouble. Menopausal fantasies at work, I'm afraid. Look Philip, I won't keep you long. I've been thinking, though. What might their next step be? The SFO, I mean.'

'Well, without knowing what she's been telling them, of course, but to be brutally frank, and if they thought there was more of a case, then I think, given your interests abroad and so on, they might well wish to see your passport removed. And put out a port stop. While they continued with their investigations.'

'I thought you might say that,' said Bard. 'Thanks.'

'Bard, you're not going to do anything silly, are you?'

'Of course not,' said Bard.

Kirsten had had her pre-med; she was becoming drowsy. She lay, her hair tucked up into her paper hat, her face tranquil. She was hardly recognisable, Barnaby thought. She still clung to his hand; he was beginning to be afraid he'd have to go into the theatre with her. Kathy, the nurse, had already assured Kirsten he could go down in the lift with her, stay with her until she was under the anaesthetic.

'Barnaby,' she said suddenly, her voice slightly slurred, 'Barnaby, can you give me one of the hankies in my bag? The big bag over there.'

'Sure.'

He rummaged in the bag, found three neatly folded men's handkerchiefs, gave her one.

'Thanks. This is very important to me,' she said carefully, clasping it tightly in her hand, 'very important. Make sure I don't lose it. Don't let them take it away down there, will you?'

'No,' said Barnaby. 'No, I won't.'

There was a long silence. Then she said, her voice hazier still, 'Oliver's, you know. Oliver's hankies.'

'Oliver's?' said Barnaby. Clearly the stuff was making her confused.

'Yes. He – gave them to me. At – the – funeral.'

'Oliver Clarke?' said Barnaby. He was beginning to feel confused himself. Nothing could have been made clearer to him than that this baby was nothing to do with Oliver, and here she was clasping his handkerchief as if it were a lifeline.

'Yes. I love Oliver, Barney. I – think.'

Two tears trickled from beneath her lashes; she wiped them away with the handkerchief.

'You love Oliver?' said Barnaby.

'Think so. And you. Love you.'

'Er – does he know you love him?'

'Mmm? No. Don't know.'

She was silent, drifted off into sleep; obviously hallucinating, thought Barnaby, unconscious already.

Kathy came in with two porters and a trolley. 'Right then, Kirsten, you just pop on to this trolley and down we go.'

'Shall I disappear now, then?' said Barnaby hopefully.

Kirsten's hand shot out, gripped his. 'Don't go, Barney.' Not unconscious. Not hallucinating.

They walked down the corridor, him beside the trolley. She gazed up at the ceiling, still gripping his hand. Barnaby didn't know about Kirsten, but he certainly felt sick. They went down in the lift, along another corridor, and into a brilliantly lit room, the walls lined with boxes of instruments, three people in masks and gowns. Shit, he'd got into the operating theatre, this was a nightmare, his own worst nightmare. He tried to ease his hand away from hers, but she still clung on.

'Hallo Kirsten.' Meg was there, smiling down at her, and then at Barnaby. 'And what a good brother you are. Right now, Kirsten, this is Dr Morgan, the anaesthetist, he came up earlier, he's going to be looking after you.'

Kirsten nodded, smiling rather vaguely. Dr Morgan took her hand, tapped it, looking for the vein. 'Right,' he said, 'now just a little prick.'

Kirsten giggled suddenly. 'That's what did it,' she said, 'just a prick.'

'Shut up, Kirsten!' said Barnaby, embarrassed.

Meg Wilding laughed. 'She's a bit drunk,' she said, 'it's the pre-med.'

'Can you hear me, Kirsten?' said Dr Morgan.

She nodded.

'I'll take that, shall I?' said Kathy. It was the handkerchief, she was easing it out of Kristen's hand.

'No!' said Kirsten sharply. 'No, I want it.'

Meg shook her head at Kathy. 'Leave it,' she said.

'Now Kirsten, I want you to count up to ten,' said Dr Morgan. He was putting something into the needle now.

'Love Oliver,' said Kirsten, smiling seraphically now, her lids closing, 'loves me. One – two –' She was gone.

'I'll take the handkerchief,' said Barnaby, removing it easily now from her limp hand. 'Important to her. Um – I might faint or something, I'm afraid. If I have to watch,' he added, hearing the desperation in his own voice.

Meg smiled at him, her hand on the trolley, walking it gently away from him, towards the double doors at the end of the small room. Of course, that was the operating theatre, not this. God, he was an idiot.

'Of course you don't,' she said, 'but I think you're very brave to have come this far. Not many brothers would have done this. You go off and have a well-earned stiff drink.'

'How long will she be?'

'She'll be back in her room in about forty minutes at the most. But she'll be very sleepy for a while after that. No rush ...'

'OK,' said Barnaby, 'thanks. Where's the nearest phone?'

★

Elaine Briggs had worked for Action Travel in Chiswick for four years. It wasn't exactly exciting, but she liked it; you met lots of interesting people, well quite interesting anyway, although her friend Carol who worked at the Kensington branch met *really* interesting ones, models and so on, and once one of the Breakfast TV people had come in, and Chiswick wasn't really in that league, but still it was a nice job, people on the whole were polite to you and in a good mood when they were booking tickets, which Carol said was more than she could say for some of the models.

Anyway, the man who'd come in that morning had been interesting all right. Obviously lots of money, to judge from his watch and the car he'd parked outside, although he had quite a London accent. Paid with his Barclaycard, nothing flash, no platinum Amex or anything. And it had been quite a complicated request. Complicated, but not difficult. Everyone in France these days spoke English, thank goodness, it wasn't like when she'd been at school and they'd gone on that trip to Brittany, and it had been quite hard making themselves understood half the time.

Anyway, it had been fun doing it, she'd felt a bit like someone in a telly programme. Made a change from package tours to Corfu.

'The thing is, Gray,' said Briony, her large blue eyes very earnest, 'I just wish you hadn't told me all that. I don't know why you did.'

'Well, I felt I had to,' said Gray. He could feel a lurch of unease in his stomach. 'It was all very important. Important in making my decision.'

'Yes, but it's also very hard for me to cope with. I mean, I'd hardly left you. And it wasn't as if it was some scrubber you'd just picked up somewhere. I know you had a soft spot for Kirsten Channing, ages ago. I know what she looks like too,' she added.

'Bri, I know all this. And of course I shouldn't have done it. But I was so — unhappy. Lonely. That's how it happened.'

'Yes, well, I was unhappy and lonely too,' said Briony, 'but I didn't go falling into bed with the first good-looking bloke who came along.'

'Briony, I'm sorry. Terribly sorry. I didn't mean to hurt you even more than I had already. I —'

'Yes, well you have,' said Briony. 'I don't know why you couldn't see it would. Why you couldn't just have told me you'd changed your mind. Without all this detail.'

'Oh, for God's sake!' said Gray. He felt angry suddenly, that she didn't understand, was too caught up in her own distress to recognise his. 'Briony, this is an earth-shattering thing that's happened to me. I felt so strongly before that I could never, ever want – what you wanted. So strongly that however much I loved you, it was unthinkable. If something was to change that, it was going to be serious. Important. Do you honestly think if I'd just come along to you and said hey, Briony, it's all right now, I've changed my mind and I do want a baby after all, you'd have believed me?'

'Yes,' she said, 'yes I do.'

'Well, actually, I don't think you would. It would all have been very hunkydory at first, and then you'd have started wondering. If I really meant it, if I was going to change my mind again.'

'Yes, but –'

'Briony, we've always been so honest with each other. That's why I let you go, for Christ's sake. It would have been much easier to have said yes, OK, we'll do it in a year or two, I give in, and then gone on putting it off, or even agreeing and then telling you I'd changed my mind again. Don't you see?'

She sat staring at him. 'Yes, I do see that. But you obviously really cared about Kirsten, about what happened to her, about the baby, it hurt you a lot. I don't know if I can handle that, Gray, I really don't.'

'Well, is that so terrible? Why can't you be pleased by that? Don't you see, Briony, it can't be so bad, can it, that I find the thought of her being pregnant with my baby so moving? And the thought of that baby being – well, done away with – so sad.'

'I just know,' she said, 'that I find the thought of you going to bed with Kirsten Channing a few days after we – after I left you – very horrible. And then her being the one who got pregnant with your child, not me – it's hideous, Gray, you must understand that.'

He didn't say anything, just sat staring at his hands.

'What would you have done if she'd wanted you to marry her? With this great new discovery of yours, of your paternal instinct. Would you have married her, Gray? Being so fond of her and everything, caring about her so much?'

'I don't know,' he said very quietly. 'I've thought about that, obviously, but it's impossible really to get my head round. She was so – so against the idea.'

'Well, that's very nice for me,' said Briony briskly, 'and very convenient for you. I get her cast-offs. Shit, Gray, I don't like this. I don't like it at all.'

'Briony, *please*. Try and look at it my way.'

'I am looking at it your way. And your way looks pretty damn convenient. Screw some girl you've fancied for ages, get her pregnant, discover you want a baby after all and then go back to your original girlfriend. Well, I'm sorry, Gray, but I don't feel very much part of this decision. And this story you've trashed. Is that because of Kirsten?'

'Yes,' he said quietly, 'partly it is. But it's for all of them, really. I like Bard Chaning, even if he is a crook. I like his wife even more, she's very sweet. Liam Channing's a bastard, I'd hate to contribute to his nasty little scheme. It would have made things so much worse for them all, that story. Dragging things up from the past, hurting people who don't deserve it –'

'Oh Gray, for heaven's sake. I haven't heard you talk like this before. Not when you exposed the Brunning scandal, not when you had Tony Packard all over your front page.'

'I didn't know their families,' he said.

'But they had families, you must have realised that. And Brunning and Packard didn't think of them too much. Any more than Bard Channing thought of his.'

'Well, clearly I'm not the toughie I thought I was. That's why I resigned. I don't want to be in the business of wrecking people's lives any longer.'

'Well, that's very high minded of you,' she said, 'and I suppose I ought to admire it, but I just find it all part of the same thing. A bit hard to take, suddenly. Sorry, Gray. You'll have to find some other high-minded person to mother your babies. Maybe you could even persuade Kirsten to change her mind.'

'Shit,' said Gray, picking up the nearest heavy object (his juicer) from the table and hurling it at the door she had just closed behind her. 'Holy bloody shit.'

Oliver was sitting in the small garden, drinking a can of Budweiser and trying to read the paper; he still felt slightly shell-shocked from his interview with Bard Channing the day before. It had been one of the strangest experiences of his life. The strangest thing had been Channing's calm, the way he had thanked him for letting him know, and then, more courteously than Oliver could ever remember, shown him out of the house. Oliver had looked back once and he had still been standing at the top of the steps, staring after him. Yet he had obviously had no idea; had been very shocked. Poor bloke. Life wasn't exactly good for him at the moment.

Oliver tried again to concentrate on his paper, and also on not listening to Melinda and her friend discussing their wardrobes for their forthcoming holiday in Italy. They had already covered swimsuits and whether the high-cut legs were more flattering than the standard, and the problem of their necessitating a bikini wax and whether a second wax during the course of the holiday would be necessary in which case was the do-it-yourself kit adequate, or would they need to go to a beauty salon somewhere in Italy, and had now moved on to other items.

'I've got a really nice dress for the evenings,' Melinda was saying, 'halter neck, quite short, I got it in the Top Shop sale. And then I've got a couple of pairs of shorts. Oh, and a culotte dress.'

'I've got one of those,' said the friend, whose name was Tara, 'it's really sweet, it's cream with little flowers on.'

'Oh, what, from Next? Oh, no, mine's the same —' there was much giggling at this point — 'we'll look like Tweedledum and Tweedledee.'

'Heavenly twins more like it. Trouble with them is, it's such a performance when you want to go to the loo, you have to take them right off and — Oliver, is that the phone?'

'Yeah,' said Oliver, deeply grateful for the interruption. It was bound to be for Melinda and then he could stay indoors without appearing to be rude; he didn't like to risk hurting people's feelings even if they were unlikely to notice.

The call wasn't for Melinda.

'Oliver? Hi, Oliver, this is Barnaby. Barnaby Channing.'

'Oh yes?' said Oliver. He would have been pleased to hear from a lot of people that day; Barnaby was not one of them. It clearly showed in his voice.

'There's no need to sound like that,' said Barnaby slightly plaintively, 'I've just come from the hospital.'

'What were you doing in hospital?'

'I wasn't in hospital. Kirsten was.'

'Kirsten's in hospital?' Oliver sat down abruptly on the hall chair. 'Why, which hospital, what's wrong?'

'Nothing. Well, you know she's having the — the thing done today. At the Princess Diana.'

'Oh,' said Oliver. He tried to work out how he felt about that and couldn't. 'Oh, I see. Well, is she — is she all right?'

'Yeah, I think so. The doctor woman seemed quite cheerful. Anyway, look, I thought I ought to ring you, and I can't make head or tail of it honestly, but I thought you ought to know —'

'Know what?'

'Well, she said something. Just as she was going under. You know. People get a bit funny then, apparently. Sort of drunk.'

'Barnaby, what are you talking about?'

'Well, she had one of your handkerchiefs. Actually she had three of them. With her, in her case. I thought it was a bit odd, specially when –'

'Barnaby *please*!' said Oliver. He was beginning to feel desperate. 'What are you on about?'

'All right, all right,' said Barnaby. 'I'm only trying to do you a good turn. You and her. And don't blame me if I've got it wrong. But anyway, she said, just as she was going under, like I said, she said she loved you.'

'Oh,' said Oliver. There was a long, bright silence. He was looking at the sun falling on a piece of carpet in the hall by his foot. It was a quite an ugly piece of carpet, or so he had always thought, it had been left by the people before, and it was brown with a yellow circular pattern on it. It suddenly looked extremely beautiful to Oliver, a perfect blend of colour and design; he thought how fortunate they were, to have it there in their hall.

'Did you hear that?' said Barnaby. He sounded slightly put out.

'What? Oh yes, yes, I think so. What was it again?'

'I said, Kirsten said she loved you.'

'Yes,' said Oliver, 'yes, I did hear you. Thank you.'

There was another long silence; this time Oliver's eyes were on a vase that had been given them by an aunt, bright green it was, studded with pink china rosebuds, he'd always hated it … Melinda had stuck some yellow wallflowers into it; they were the wrong colour and the wrong length. Perfect, thought Oliver, quite quite perfect.

'Oh Christ,' said Barnaby, 'I've said the wrong thing again. I'm sorry, Oliver, I just thought –'

'That's OK,' said Oliver, 'don't worry about it. Princess Diana, did you say?'

'Yeah. Sorry, Oliver. Didn't mean to –'

'It's OK,' said Oliver again, 'bye Barnaby.'

He went out into the garden. Melinda and Tara were comparing brands of deodorant. It seemed extraordinarily interesting. He smiled at them.

'You OK, Oliver?' said Melinda.

'I'm fine,' said Oliver, 'I've got to go out. You ought to wear that colour more often, Melinda, it suits you.'

'Olly,' said Melinda, staring at him, 'you've always said I looked terrible in yellow.'

'Well, I was wrong,' said Oliver, 'you look absolutely beautiful.'

★

Dr Paget spent a long time listening to Kitty's chest. Francesca thought, each time he lifted the stethoscope, that he was going to put it away, but then he just moved it to another place and listened again, the intent, blank expression on his face. Kitty didn't seem very interested; she didn't seem very interested in anything. A few days ago, yesterday even, she would have been squirming about, trying to get hold of the stethoscope, gazing round her; today she sat listless, wheezing a bit, coughing occasionally, rubbing irritably at her runny eyes. Every so often she looked at her mother and half smiled, then seemed to change her mind and grizzled instead. She was very miserable.

'She's clearly not herself,' said Dr Paget finally, folding the stethoscope, 'and she's very wheezy. You have been giving her the antibiotic regularly, haven't you?'

'Yes of course I have,' said Francesca, fear and irritation working at her in equal proportions. 'Isn't it working then, isn't she better?'

'She's no better yet,' he said, 'and I had hoped she would have been by now. A bit anyway. But on the other hand, she isn't any worse. Which may sound a bit negative, but isn't really. At her age, they go down very quickly. And up again, of course. She's staying the same, holding her own. I think I'll pop back this evening. Now some Calpol for the temperature might not be bad idea, and that'll help if she's feeling a bit sore and achy as well. Which she probably is. There you are,' he said to Kitty, chucking her gently under her small chin, 'have you quite well again soon. I'll be back at about six, Mrs Channing. Try not to worry.'

Francesca managed to smile at him. Try not to worry! Try not to breathe.

She looked up at her mother, who was hovering, there was no other word for it, in the background, clearly at a complete loss as to what to do.

'Mum!' said Jack, running in, flushed and beaming, 'Curdle Philbeach says he'll take me to the beach, he's here now, can I go?'

'What? Oh, yes of course you can. How kind of him.'

'No, not really, I've told him I'll let him work on the tunnel with me. Do you think he's called Philbeach because he goes to the beach a lot?'

'Yes, I expect so,' said Francesca. 'Mummy, why don't you go with them? You can flirt with Colonel Philbeach and deal with Jack if he's naughty.'

'I think Colonel Philbeach is more than able to deal with Jack,' said

609

Rachel briskly, 'and whatever you may think, Francesca, I don't fancy everything in trousers.'

'But he's wearing shorts,' said Jack, going into fits of mirth at his own wit, 'so you can. Then you can snog him.'

'Jack, be quiet at once!' said Rachel.

'Barnaby snogs all the girls he fancies,' said Jack with dignity, 'he told me so, so there.'

Kirsten was surfacing, slowly and painfully, into confusion. Her stomach hurt, not badly, just ached, dully, miserably, like a period. Maybe she'd got her period at last, maybe she wasn't pregnant after all. She felt sick though, very sick, so maybe she was. The light was too bright; she turned her head fretfully away from it, towards the door. Someone was sitting there, looking at her anxiously. It looked like Barnaby. It was Barnaby. What was he doing in her bedroom?

'Barney?'

'Hi, Kirsten. You OK?'

Reality hit her. 'Awful,' she said and promptly threw up all over the floor. 'Sorry,' she wailed, 'I'm so sorry.'

Kathy came in, smiling good-naturedly. 'You all right, pet?'

'Yes, I think so. I'm really sorry.'

'Don't worry. All part of the fun. For me, anyway. You just lie back and enjoy it, and let me do all the work. You OK, Brother Barney? You don't look so good yourself.'

Barnaby had gone green; he rushed out of the room

'Men!' said Kathy. 'Hopeless! The other one's no better, said he had to get some air. Want a sip of water, pet?'

'What other one?' said Kirsten, but before Kathy had opened her mouth, she had sunk down into sleep again.

When she woke next the room was much less brilliant; she looked groggily at her watch. It said half-past four. God! She'd been asleep for hours. Poor old Barney, waiting all this time. Only now she wanted him, he didn't seem to be there. She raised her head cautiously; she felt much better. She reached for her water, took a sip; her hand was feeble, she couldn't hold it properly, and it toppled over on the sheet.

'Shit,' said Kirsten. She groped for her handkerchief, the one she had known, known was there when she had gone down to theatre, tucked into her sleeve. It was gone.

Oliver's handkerchief, gone. Like Oliver, like the baby. She had lost them all, and she couldn't bear it. Tears sprung to her eyes; she blinked them away furiously. More came, a great flood.

'Oh God,' she said, aloud, and began to wipe her eyes, her nose, on the sheet. She heard the door open, couldn't face the wretchedly cheerful Kathy again, kept her face buried in the sheet, sobbed louder …

'Here,' said a voice. A gentle, careful, anxious voice, a voice she had not thought to hear again, and looking up she saw its owner, looking at her very sweetly, very concerned, but smiling at her. 'Here, do you want to borrow a handkerchief?'

Chapter Thirty-two

Gray was very drunk when Teresa Booth phoned. He had been drinking since Briony had left, at lunchtime, and as far as he could make out, there were now two empty wine bottles and an empty whisky bottle sitting by the rubbish bin in the kitchen. He couldn't quite believe he had drunk the contents of them all: maybe they'd all been half empty. Even so it was quite a lot.

Briony liked whisky: rather surprisingly, it was the only alcohol she actually liked. He'd tried to make her like wine, but she really didn't; well, she said she could take it or leave it, and nice water was better. They'd actually had a couple of rows about her not liking wine: stupid, pointless, rows. Well, he supposed most rows were stupid and pointless, and actually about something quite different. They didn't have many: or hadn't, they were both too easy-going, too level to bother. But when they did they were quite spectacular. Making up was the best, of course: that was really good. Briony always wanted sex when they had quarrelled; she said the adrenalin made her randy. It wasn't the only time she wanted it (although in the last few months, before she had moved out, they had had rather less than Gray might have wished), but when they had been fighting, when her passions had been running high, she tended to be more imaginative, less passive, she often managed – even after two years – to surprise him with her demands and her responses to his.

He thought of her now, wretchedly; not just of having sex with her, but living with her, being happy with her, having fun with her, sharing things, enjoying things with her, and now, thanks to his cocking things up so totally, so appallingly, it was quite over, she would never come back to him now, there was no hope at all, she saw him as the selfish, arrogant, totally insensitive, philandering bloke he really was. He was so appalled by this mental list that he got to his feet, and found a piece of paper and a pen, and actually wrote it down; it seemed important to see it in black and white, fix it in his mind, to have it permanently there, a sort of mental hair shirt, so that in the extremely unlikely event of his ever finding anyone else, he could keep reminding himself of them, the shortcomings, and try very hard to prevent the unfortunate someone else from discovering them.

He had finished the list and replenished his glass when the phone rang. It was Teresa Booth.

'Well,' she said briskly, 'there you are. Thanks a lot for keeping in touch, communicating and all that.'

'Oh Terri, I'm sorry. Been a bit – a bit – faught. I mean fraught.'

'Graydon, you're drunk.'

'Yes,' he said simply, 'I am.'

'You all right?'

'No Teresa, I'm not all right. I'm –' he looked down at the list in his hand, 'I'm selfish, arrogant, insensitive and a pil – philanderer. And unprofessional with it. And unemployed,' he added.

'You're what? Graydon, what do you mean you're unemployed, what happened to the story?'

'Oh,' he said, 'I tore it up.'

'You what!'

'I tore it up. And then I resigned. Terri, don't you be cross with me, I couldn't stand it. Please.'

There was a long silence. Then she said, 'You on your own?'

'Yes, I am. But –'

'I think I'll come and see you,' she said. 'I can be there in forty-five minutes, this time of night, and I certainly can't wait till tomorrow to find out what's going on. So I'm not going to read all about Bard Channing and his misdeeds in the papers, then?'

'Not under my byline, no,' said Graydon.

'Pity. Great pity. I'm on my way,' she said slightly grimly, 'and don't you dare pass out before I get there.'

She arrived, as she had said, in forty-five minutes; he had however passed out, or at least fallen asleep; he could not think who or where he was, who might be ringing at the bell; stumbled to it, forcing himself to move around over the agony of his head, the heaving of his stomach, and lay down again, gazing up at her helplessly like a sick puppy.

'Well,' she said, 'you are in a bad way. Where's the kitchen? I'll make you a cocktail. I have the ingredients with me.'

'Terri,' said Gray, very quietly, 'I do not want a cocktail.'

'You'll want this one,' she said, and disappeared. He lay, with his eyes closed, feeling the room first heave and then spin around him, heard her moving around the kitchen, wondered if he could make the lavatory and knew he couldn't, and then felt her sit down beside him.

'Drink this,' she said severely. 'Duggie's patent.'

It was an evil-looking brew: afterwards she told him it was raw egg, soluble Vitamin C, soluble aspirin, Worcester sauce and a smidgen of vodka. He thought for one ghastly moment he was going to spew, then miraculously his stomach settled, eased. He even managed to smile.

'Now then,' she said, 'you'd better tell me what all this is about.'

Dr Paget looked up at Francesca and smiled: a gentle, careful smile. He had been bending over Kitty, listening to her small chest; she was coughing more now, and her temperature had risen to 101.

'She's no better, is she?' said Francesca. There was a tight band increasing round her own chest, and another round her head; she could never remember being so frightened. She looked back in amazement at the woman of yesterday, even earlier that day, the woman who was so distraught that her lover had betrayed her, so distressed at her husband's failures, who had decreed that her marriage should end, and wondered that such trifling matters could possibly concern her.

'Well – no.' He clearly had difficulty in saying the word. 'No, she's no better, I'm afraid.'

'Well – is she worse?'

Another long silence. Then, 'Perhaps a little. A little worse.'

'Well, what should we do? Who should see her, where should we go?'

'Well –' and this time the hesitation was even longer – 'well, tonight, nowhere. She should stay here, in the warmth, continue with her medication, and hopefully she should turn the corner.'

'And if she doesn't?'

'If she doesn't, we can decide in the morning.' He smiled again, a careful, sympathetic smile. 'There is no need for you to go rushing off anywhere tonight.'

'There's no-one we should get to see her? No-one who could come here, no specialist?'

'Well, no, I see no point in that. No point at all. You see, all her notes, her tracings, everything, are in London. It would mean getting them down, almost impossible tonight, and so anyone we talked to would be working in the dark, and would therefore be compelled to send her off to the hospital, probably at Plymouth, to get more done.'

'Well, I'm perfectly willing to –'

'Mrs Channing, that would not be a good idea. Kitty would be made far more distressed by such a thing, both physically and emotionally, and her condition simply doesn't justify it. So please don't even think about it. Let's give her another twelve hours, and then re-think in the morning. All right?'

'Yes,' said Francesca, giving in because there seemed to be no possible alternative. 'Yes, all right.'

'But if you're worried, as I said last night, call me any time. And I'll be along first thing in the morning to have another look at her.' He patted Kitty's restless little body tenderly. 'You get some sleep, little one. Get yourself well.'

Rachel went to let him out of the convent; came back, looked at Francesca.

'Can I get you anything, darling?'

'No. No thank you,' said Francesca. 'Mummy, what am I going to do, how are we going to get her through this? We ought to be in London, we ought to be with Mr Lauder, at the hospital even –'

'Well darling, you heard what he said. And frankly, if she needed to be in hospital then I'm sure Dr Paget would have her there in a trice.'

'Here!' said Francesca. 'What possible use is a hospital here?'

'Darling, we're not in the Outer Hebrides. There's a large modern hospital at Plymouth, another in Exeter, I've been in them both with Mary, there is no reason to doubt their ability to look after Kitty.'

'But Mr Lauder said –'

'Francesca, Mr Lauder is away. If he were in London, I might see more point trying to get her back there.'

'Well, what about Mr Moreton-Smith? The surgeon, you know, who saw her? We could get her to him, get him down here even ...'

'Maybe tomorrow, yes. But not tonight.'

'Oh God, why did I let this happen?' said Francesca, throwing back her head in agony. 'Why didn't I take her back early yesterday, before it was too late? I'll tell you why, it was because I was so wrapped up in my own troubles, too sorry for myself. I neglected her, she'll get worse, she'll probably die, all because –'

'Francesca, stop it,' said Rachel severely. 'You're being hysterical. You didn't take her back yesterday because you were advised not to. And the day before she was perfectly all right. She had a slight cold. Which, you told me yourself, Mr Lauder had told you to ignore. Or words to that effect. This is all purely a result of happenstance. It is not your fault. Now please calm down. Babies are very susceptible to tension.'

Francesca didn't say anything. She just bent over the cot, stroking Kitty's head, the dry hot forehead, the dark curls falling onto the red little cheek.

'Would you –' Rachel hesitated. 'Well, I just wondered if you'd like to –'

'Like to what?'

'Well, speak to Bard.'

'What about?' said Francesca, genuinely puzzled.

'Well, about Kitty. About her being ill.'

'Mummy, of course I don't want to speak to Bard. What good would that do?'

'It might make you feel a little better. And perhaps he – well, he ought to know. He is her father.'

'Oh for Christ's sake!' said Francesca, and her rage at her mother was so great she spoke louder than she had intended, and Kitty started in her cot. 'Of course it won't make me feel better,' she went on, very low, 'it would make me feel a great deal worse. And don't even suggest she's so ill he ought to know. That really is nonsense. Why don't you go to bed, Mummy, I'll be all right.'

'Yes all right,' said Rachel, almost coldly. 'I was only trying to help.'

'Well, it wasn't helpful. Goodnight.'

'Goodnight Francesca. I'll see you in the morning.'

After she had gone, Francesca sat down in the small wooden chair that had been given to her as a bedside table and looked at Kitty in the cot. She was asleep again now, restless but asleep, her thumb in her mouth. So tiny she was, such a hopelessly tiny little piece of human existence; so tiny to withstand the onslaught of her illness. How could she manage it, Francesca thought, how could she withstand it, how could such a small, damaged, half-helpless heart hold out against what was happening to it?

She put out her hand, into the cot, pushed her finger in Kitty's free fist; wishing, willing her well again, sending out strength, love to her.

She could not even think of going to bed; she was afraid to sleep, afraid of leaving Kitty unwatched over. She just sat there, thinking, looking back over the short life, so filled with anxiety, right from the very beginning.

Well, not from the very beginning, of course. That had been wonderful. Slowly and painfully, for it hurt from her damaged distance, Francesca looked back at those golden days on the Greek island, and wondered at the speed with which her life had darkened.

Jess Channing very seldom visited her son at home. She felt uncomfortable in the excesses of Hamilton Terrace; her socialist soul contemplated the wasted space, the perfectly furnished, overheated, under-used rooms, the wardrobes full of scarcely worn clothes, the cellar stacked with wine that might one day be drunk, the large cars outside the door driven so much of the time by one person, the over-paid, under-employed staff, there to do for Bard and his family things they were more than capable of doing for themselves, and was distressed by it.

She summoned Bard to her, when she wanted to see him, and he visited her when he wanted to see her; and if the meetings were not quite as common as she might have wished, they were not rare either.

But recently, she had not seen him at all: not since the day he had come to lunch, after the crash, three weeks ago now, and she felt uneasy. She had always known when he had something to hide, when he had done something wrong, ever since he had been a very small boy; and she had known by the simple fact he stayed out of her way: up trees, in cupboards, under beds when he had been very young and she had been looking for him to chastise him; in his room, the door firmly shut, when he had been a little older; simply staying away from her house when he was grown up. And in these past three weeks, he had certainly been staying away.

She had phoned a few times, left messages, and he had alway rung her back, told her he would visit her in a few days, that he was very busy, that things were tough; but he had not been. And now she was worried about Liam and what he might be doing to Francesca (who was clearly under his influence), and worried about the business and the people investigating it, and worried about Bard himself and his silence. And so, that Saturday night, she phoned the house.

Bard answered the phone himself; he sounded heavy, flat.

'Isambard, it's your mother.'

'Yes, hallo.'

'You don't sound very happy.'

'Porbably because I'm not.'

He had only admitted to misery twice in his life: once when Marion had died, once when Pattie had finally been admitted to the clinic for the first time.

'I'll come round,' Jess said.

'So what have you done, Isambard?'

She had made him some tea, sat down opposite him in the kitchen, the only room in the house she liked to be in.

'Me? I haven't done anything. Life's been doing some pretty harsh things to me.'

'You make your own life, Isambard. Nobody does it to you.'

'Oh really?' he said, and for the first time for many years he was angry with her. 'Is that so? It was my fault, was it, that Marion died?'

'No,' she said quietly, 'of course not. I'm sorry.'

'I thought I'd found her again,' he said, sitting down, his head between his hands, 'or the happiness of her, at any rate. In Francesca. And she's left me. Told me to go. Now. When I need her so much.'

'Isambard, you've been shutting her out. I told you. That's no way to show a woman you need her.'

'I was protecting her.'

'Women don't need protecting,' said Jess briskly. 'That's what men need. Been having an affair with Liam, has she?'

Bard stared at her. 'How the f— hell did you know?'

'I talked to her.'

'What, she told you about it?'

'Of course not. I'm not stupid. It seemed very plain to me. That she was very taken with him, at least. It went further than that, did it?'

'I'm afraid so, yes.'

'And how can you be so sure?'

'Because they've both made it perfectly clear to me.'

'Both? You've talked to him?'

'I'm afraid so, yes. And he went to great pains to assure me it had been a great – pleasure.'

'That boy is appalling,' said Jess, her face drawn with distaste. 'I can't help being fond of him, but –'

'Oh can't you?'

'No I can't. He's damaged, which is always attractive, don't ask me why, and that excuses a bit of his behaviour, and he's interesting and very good at making me feel I'm interesting. Which is no doubt how he worked on Francesca.'

Bard was silent. Then he said, 'So you think he did that? Actually worked on her? To hurt me?'

'I'm sure of it. Aren't you?'

'Oh yes, of course. But it's reassuring to have it confirmed.'

'He's very dishonest and he has the morals of a tomcat. Which probably insults tomcats. And he's very cruel. He worries me a lot.'

'He worries you!' said Bard. His voice was bitter.

'Yes, he does. What he might do next. Mind you, Naomi's a clever, ruthless girl, she can probably cope with him.'

'What upsets me most,' said Bard with a sigh, 'is not so much that – that she –'

'That she slept with him? Is that what you're saying?'

'Yes,' he said, embarrassed to be having such a discussion with her.

She looked at him, her sharp face tender suddenly. 'You really don't mind that, Isambard? Are you sure? It can't be easy for you.'

'No. No it isn't. Of course not. I could tear him limb from li .b. And her, in my darker moments.'

'Yes, I daresay. Well, she should know you're angry. Something wrong if you weren't.'

'Oh, she knows that,' said Bard, 'of course she does. But what hurts most is that they were so close. Talked to one another. You know?'

'Yes, well, that's largely your fault,' said Jess severely. 'I did try to warn you, you know.'

He looked at her. 'Mother, if you're going to start lecturing me, I'd rather you left. I thought you'd come because you wanted to help.'

'Well, I'm not going. And I do want to help. Of course I do.' She put her hand on his briefly; so undemonstrative was she normally, it was like a caress.

'But you've got to understand. Francesca had this relationship with Liam because she was lonely. Unhappy. Of course it was wrong of her, but she'll know that ...'

'Yes,' he said, with a sigh, 'yes, she does. But it doesn't seem to make any difference. She doesn't want to carry on with the marriage. That's the point.'

'And you do? Are you sure? There's a lot to forgive. It's hard to do that, to forgive. Especially for someone like you. It can lead to dreadful bitterness.'

'I'm quite sure,' he said slowly. 'I've thought about it a lot and I can do it. And besides, there is a lot for both of us to forgive. It's not an – an uneven situation. But she doesn't want to try.'

'Oh I think she does,' said Jess. 'She loves you very much. She may not know it at the moment, but she does. It's very plain to me. She wouldn't be so troubled by you if she wasn't.'

'How do you know she's troubled by me?'

'Because it shows. Any fool can see it. You've got to go and get her back, Isambard, if you do really want her. She won't come to you. It's no use sitting there, waiting, and thinking she ought to.'

'I can't,' he said, 'you don't understand. I've tried.'

'And how have you tried? I've never known you not get what you wanted before.'

'I went to see her. I've said I was sorry for my part in it. Told her I loved her, that I needed her.'

'Oh well, that was very good of you,' said Jess. 'You think she's going to believe that, do you, you think that's sufficient, a few words?

Words come cheap, Isambard, I've always told you that. Easy come, easy go, words are. A few actions, that's what Francesca's looking for.'

'Mother, I told you, she told me to go away, that our marriage was over.'

'Yes, well, she doesn't mean it,' said Jess.

'How do you know?'

'I was always telling your father to go away. I didn't mean that either.'

'But you hated my father.'

'No I didn't. I hated what he did, but I loved him. Very much.' Her gaunt face softened suddenly. 'He was very powerful, very strong. As you are. He persuaded me in the end, however bad he was, that I still wanted him. I couldn't have him in the house, because of you. But I still wanted him.'

'You mean, you loved and wanted a man who knocked you about?'

'Oh yes,' said Jess. She spoke matter-of-factly, as if he had asked her if she wanted another cup of tea.

'Oh,' said Bard finally.

'I'll tell you why. He managed to stop. It was very hard. He had to get help, admit to it. And there wasn't much therapy in those days, and attitudes were very different. But he did it for me. He showed me, you see. And when he was killed, I was very unhappy for a long time.'

'Well,' said Bard finally, 'I wish you'd told me all this before.'

'Well, I'm telling you now. You don't knock Francesca about, I presume. And she still loves you and you can get her back, if you want her. Of course you can.'

'I don't knock her about, no,' said Bard slowly, 'but I –'

'Yes? What have you done to her, Isambard?'

He looked at her, across a long silence; then he said, 'I can't tell you. I really can't.'

'All right,' said Jess, 'don't. But whatever it is, you can make it all right. If you really want to. It's a matter of doing, though. Not just saying, Isambard, doing.' She looked at him, smiled. 'I know you think I'm a silly old woman, but it's true. Do enough and she'll take you back. It's a mattter of finding what's enough. That's all. Where is she, anyway?'

'Oh – she's in Devon with her mother,' said Bard abstractedly.

'With the children?'

'Yes.'

'That'll do her good,' said Jess, 'do them all good. Just what they need.'

'Well,' said Teresa, 'I don't know what to say. I suppose I should be cross. I am cross.' She smiled at Gray. 'I'm bloody furious, actually.'

'You could,' he said, 'take the story yourself. Sell it to some other paper. Or even mine. You've got all the facts.'

She looked at him thoughtfully. 'I could, couldn't I? Then we'd have it all ways. I'd see Channing's goose cooked, and you'd have your conscience clear.'

'Yup,' said Gray.

She looked at him. 'It must have hurt,' she said, 'giving that story up. When you'd worked on it for so long, when it was so good.'

'It was absolute agony,' said Gray simply. 'Every time I think of it, in the paper, on the front page, under my name, I have to have another drink. But I just had to. I'n not even quite sure why myself.'

'I think I am,' said Terri, and her voice was very gentle. 'You're a nice person, Graydon. Very nice. Well, I suppose I could do that. Tell another paper I mean. But I probably won't. As far as I can see, Channing's goose is pretty well cooked anyway. Fancy the old bag being involved like that. Well, I suppose she's in love with him. They always are, you know.'

'Who are?'

'Those old dragons of secretaries. They think they have some special place in the bosses' lives, that they're even closer to them than their wives.'

'Do you really think so?'

'I know so. Very Freudian, or whatever.'

'Yes, I suppose you could be right,' said Gray slowly. 'She looked very different in those photographs, I can tell you. With her hair let down, literally.'

'Oh she's a very sexy woman, Marcia.'

'Sexy!' said Gray. 'Terri, don't be ridiculous, she's not sexy, she's –'

'Old, were you going to say? Of course she's sexy. You've only got to smell her for a start, that perfume she wears, very strong, that's not an old maid's perfume. And that bosom of hers, very voluptuous. Don't make the mistake, Graydon, of thinking we middle-aged women can't be sexy. It's all there still, you know. Sex doesn't end with the first grey hair.'

'No,' he said quickly, 'no, of course.'

He looked at her; she was smiling, but there was hurt behind her bright blue eyes. Suspiciously brilliant blue eyes. He put out his hand, took hers.

'Terri, I'm sorry. I didn't mean to hurt you.'

'Oh, it's all right. I'm a bit low, that's all. Missing Douglas.' She sighed, got up, took a cigarette out of her bag and lit it. For once, Gray didn't mind. 'I think I'm glad that story isn't coming out, you know. In spite of what I said. I want people to remember him as they thought he was. Duggie, I mean. As he really was, actually. Kind, sweet, generous. Just a bit foolish. And a bit greedy, I suppose.'

'Yes, a bit,' said Gray carefully.

'And under Bard Channing's influence.'

'Yes.'

'Oh, dear,' she said suddenly, fumbling for a handkerchief, stubbing out her cigarette, 'sorry, Graydon, bit emotional I'm afraid.'

Graydon looked at her. He felt very strange suddenly. Strange, sad, and very tender towards her. He got up, walked over to her, held out his arms.

'Here,' he said, 'come here, Terri.'

She looked at him, half smiled, and moved into them. She felt, as always, very warm; she smelt heady, rich. Her arms went round him, tightened; only slightly surprised, he felt a response to her. She lifted her face to his, pulled his head down very gently; Gray, still surprised, but wanting to nonetheless, kissed her.

She was very good to kiss; confident, sensuous, her mouth at once soft and very sure. He wanted to kiss her more, he discovered; he wanted to do much more than kiss her. And she wanted to do more to him.

'Good God,' she said, pulling away from him briefly, smiling up at him, an amused, self-assured smile. 'Good God, Graydon, this is very surprising.'

He put his hands down onto her buttocks, felt them, moulded them; they were very full, very luscious. She pressed herself against him, moving skilfully, almost imperceptibly.

'Terri,' he said, 'Terri, I –'

And, 'No,' she said suddenly, pushing him away, 'no, this is most definitely not a good idea.'

'It seems great to me,' he said, half indignant, half amused, 'it seems wonderful.'

'Yes, I know, and to me, I'd like to fuck you into next week, but you're drunk and you're lonely, and I'm lonely, and we'll both regret it like hell tomorrow. And –'

The phone rang shrilly; she reached out, hesitated, then passed it carefully to him. It took just too long.

It was Briony.

'Gray? It is you, isn't it?' She sounded just slightly uncertain. 'Look, I've been thinking, maybe we could talk some more, can I come round? I'm only round the corner, I can be there in five minutes.'

'Well,' he said slightly hazily, pushing his hair back, 'yes, well maybe not now, I –'

There was a silence. Then: 'Gray,' she said, her voice suddenly moving into another gear, wary, quiet, 'Gray, you've got someone there, haven't you? Haven't you?'

'Well – well yes. No. I mean –'

'Fuck you,' she said, her voice thick with anger and tears, 'that's all I can say, fuck you.'

And she slammed the phone down.

'Oh dear,' said Teresa Booth.

'I think,' said Dr Paget gently, 'I think we should perhaps get this baby to hospital.'

'To hospital! Why?'

It was such a stupid question Francesca could hardly believe she had asked it: for a nice morning out, perhaps; for the drive; to fill in a few empty hours. But asking it somehow helped; distanced her, just for a moment, from the awfulness of the situation, the full urgency, helped her pretend that Kitty was not really so ill that it was perfectly obvious she should go to hospital, that Dr Paget had just made a suggestion that they should discuss.

Dr Paget hesitated, looked at her, then said, 'I think she needs increased medication, and greater care than we can give her here. She simply isn't coping, I think she's retaining fluid, her liver is a bit swollen, and I would like to see her getting some extra oxygen.'

Francesca stared at him. 'Well, why the hell didn't you decide this before?' she said. 'I've been saying for days she should go, but no, you kept saying she was fine, that she was getting better –'

'Mrs Channing, I didn't –'

'You did. You said there was no need, you said that last night, it's just plain incompetence, I shall make sure someone hears about this, you clearly –'

Panic flooded, engulfed her; she felt hot, breathless, dizzy, sat down suddenly.

'Francesca!' It was Rachel. 'There is no need for this and it doesn't help. Dr Paget has been so kind, has been doing his very best –'

She looked at her mother, hating her. 'Well, it's not enough, is it? His best just isn't good enough. We all hang around wasting time, and meanwhile a baby gets worse and worse. I – oh, what's the point? If we're going, let's go. Yes, Sister, what is it?'

'I'm sorry, Mrs Channing. It's your husband, on the telephone. He says –'

'Well, I can't speak to him now,' said Francesca. 'I really can't. Please tell him I'm busy. And don't tell him there's anything wrong with the baby either, Sister, I don't want him worried, there's no point.'

'Francesca, shall I speak to Bard?'

'No!' She spun round, glaring at her mother. 'I am absolutely sick of your interfering in my marriage. Now just leave us both alone. I don't want you speaking to him, I don't want to speak to him, I don't want any of us speaking to him. All right? Thank you, Sister, just tell him I'm busy.'

'Yes, Mrs Channing. But he did say –'

'Sister Mary Agnes, I don't mean to sound rude, but I don't want to know what he said. I have a sick baby to worry about, I really can't get involved in complicated conversations about anything else at the moment.'

'Yes, Mrs Channing. Very well. Of course.'

'I think,' said Dr Paget mildly, 'we should call for an ambulance now. The sooner the better.'

'An ambulance?' Something was in Francesca's throat, something painful, something raw. 'Can't we take her in the car?'

'I think an ambulance would be wiser, Mrs Channing.'

'Yes,' said Francesca, calm suddenly, 'yes, very well. Please do call one. I'll change Kitty, get her things ready. Mummy, you'd better stay here with Jack.'

'We'll take care of Jack.' It was Reverend Mother; she was in the doorway, holding Jack's hand. 'You'll need your mother with you, Mrs Channing. He'll be very good, won't you, Jack?'

'Course I will,' said Jack. 'I always am.'

In the hall of his house in St John's Wood, Bard Channing stood gripping the phone until it seemed to gouge into his hand, waiting to speak to Francesca, or at the very least for an answer to his suggestion that he come down to Devon to see her that day, because it was so important he talked to her again, and finally received the information that his wife couldn't come to the phone, certainly not at the moment, that she was too busy, and that Sister Mary Agnes really couldn't say when it might be a better time to phone again.

Briony was sitting in the kitchen of her small flat, pushing a spoon round and round a strong, sweet cup of tea, thinking viciously that only a total wimp like Graydon Townsend would like tea the way he did – 'weak and watery, just like him,' she said aloud – when there was a ring at the door.

She was tempted to ignore it; she was very tired, having slept extremely badly, and her head ached and her eyes felt as if there was gravel behind them, and she had a sneaking feeling it might be Gray and she really didn't want to see him. Indeed, she did ignore it the first time, but then it went again, and very reluctantly she went to answer it.

There was a woman on the doorstep; no-one Briony knew. She was middle-aged and rather flashy looking, just slightly over-made-up, with very bouffant blonde hair. She was wearing white trousers, and a navy and white striped jumper, and looking at her more carefully, Briony could see she had obviously, in her youth, been very pretty.

She looked at Briony now through brilliant blue eyes and said, 'You're Briony, are you?'

'Yes. Yes I am.'

'Well,' she said, 'my name is Teresa Booth. We did speak once, but you won't remember. And I think we ought to have a chat. Can I come in?'

'Well, I – well, I don't know,' said Briony cautiously. You heard very odd things about people forcing their way into other people's flats and houses. The name did sound familiar though ... Teresa Booth, Teresa Booth, why did that ring a bell? 'Um – what should we have a chat about?'

'It's about Graydon,' said Teresa, smiling at Briony very sweetly. 'Graydon Townsend. You know?'

'Yes,' said Briony icily, 'yes, I do know. And I really don't want to talk about him, I'm afraid. So –'

'Well, I can understand that, but I really think you ought to,' said Teresa Booth cheerfully, 'and he is a bit of an idiot, I have to say, but he loves you very much. Very much indeed.'

'I'm sorry,' said Briony, 'but I think I'm missing something here. How do you know what Graydon feels about me?'

'Because, my dear, I've spent most of the night listening to him telling me. And quite a lot of time over the past few weeks as well.'

'Oh, so he's sent you, has he? To try and talk me round. Very nice.'

'No, he has no idea I'm here.'

'Oh really? So how did you get my address? Unless he told you?'

'Oh for heaven's sake,' said Teresa, 'I went through his address book, while he was asleep. Look, it's very important you listen to me. Apart from anything else, I feel a certain amount of guilt about you. I gave Graydon what I can see was a piece of bad advice a few months ago. Now will you please let me come in? And a cup of coffee would go down pretty well.'

Jess woke up still worried about Bard. She had slept badly, most unusually for her, and having tried all her usual remedies for anxiety (a good strong cup of tea, a brisk walk round the block, washing the kitchen floor), she gave in and telephoned him. There was no reply, only the answering machine. She left a message that she had called and would like to hear from him, and rang Stylings.

'Horton, is my son there?'

'No, Mrs Channing, he isn't. I'm sorry. Have you tried the house in London?'

'Yes, I have. And left a message. Could you ask him to ring me if he contacts you?'

'I will indeed, Mrs Channing. Certainly.'

'I expect he's gone down to Devon to see Francesca and the children.'

'Yes, Mrs Channing. Possibly,' said Horton. He tried to sound positive, but everything he had heard and seen over the past few days made that seem rather unlikely.

Jess tried Kirsten's number next. She was a little while answering the phone.

'It's your grandmother here,' she said. 'Have you heard from your father?'

'No,' said Kirsten, 'I haven't. Well, not for a day or two. But it's very nice to hear from you, Granny Jess. Very nice indeed.'

She sounded different, Jess thought; somehow softer and extremely happy.

'Good,' she said. 'Why don't you come and see me later?'

'Well, maybe not today. I'm a bit – tired today. Next weekend, though. I might bring Oliver with me,' she added.

'Oliver? Oliver Clarke, do you mean? Our Oliver?'

'Yes, Granny Jess. Oliver Clarke, that's exactly who I mean. Our Oliver.'

Jess was very sensitive to the inflections in voices. Kirsten's, as she said Oliver's name, each time she said it, was liquid, sweet, echoey with happiness.

'Well,' she said to herself aloud, as she put down the phone, 'how very, very nice.'

But that still hadn't produced Bard. For some reason Jess was increasingly uneasy. She tried the house again; rang Tory; even left a message on Rachel Duncan-Brown's answering machine and then, telling herself repeatedly there was really no reason to be worried, set off for church.

Liam Channing enjoyed a breakfast of croissants and orange juice and very good coffee (one of Naomi's few culinary skills was making coffee), and then said if she didn't mind he was going to wander down to the town and see if he could get a Sunday paper.

'Liam, we're in Spain,' said Naomi irritably, 'don't be ridiculous! You won't be able to get an English paper here.'

'Of course I will. This is the mid-'nineties, Naomi, and we're all Europeans now. I bet you anything they have them.'

He was back in half an hour, looking irritable. 'No papers. It's absurd. Not till tomorrow, they said. Well, unless I drove in to Marbella, I could probably get one there ... I just might do that.'

'Liam, have you gone quite mad? It's an hour and a half's drive to Marbella. Now please go and do something with those children, they're bored already. I really hadn't thought it would be so hot.'

'Can't they play in the pool, for God's sake?'

'They're sick of it already, and it's so tiny. Absurd for a development the size of this one. And the other people here really are rather appalling. We'll just have to go to the beach later on, thank God we did get that car. Liam, you're not listening to me, what on earth is the matter with you?'

'Oh – nothing,' said Liam. 'Sorry.'

Marcia Grainger had also gone out early to get the papers. She bought rather more than usual, a selection of tabloids and broadsheets; when she got back to her flat, she poured herself a large cup of coffee and, visibly straightening her shoulders, settled down at her spotless kitchen table to read them. After an hour's very careful study, she pushed them away, poured herself a whisky and smiled at the rather stiff plant that stood on the windowsill.

'I thought he might be bluffing,' she said to it. 'How very pathetic.'

Mike Langton, who worked in the harbour at Chichester, kept an eye on all the boats and took care of several of them, saw the Channing Mercedes in the car park, and looked across to where the *Lady Jack* was moored. Her mainsail was up and he could see Mr Channing just about to cast off. He waved to him, but Channing hadn't seen him, was manoeuvring the boat out of the harbour with his usual skill. Mike had been wanting to speak to him, see if he was entering the race the following Sunday; he started running round the harbour to try and catch him. But he was too late: by the time he reached the harbour mouth, the *Lady Jack* was already skimming her way towards the open sea. Lovely things they were, those ULDCs; the boat he'd most like to have himself, he reckoned. And so fast, it was like flying on the water. You could get a long way in a day in a boat like that, given a good following wind. A very long way.

It was an endless drive to Plymouth: over an hour and a half, much of it down winding roads, and often behind long lines of Sunday holiday traffic. Kitty dozed most of the time, breathing slightly unevenly and coughing. Francesca had been allowed to travel in the ambualnce with her; by the time they arrived she felt violently sick.

The hospital was reassuringly large, against all odds; she had been expecting something small, a cottage hospital even. The ambulance pulled up in front of Casualty. Somehow expecting to be made to wait, she was startled by a reception committee of a doctor and two nurses, with a small trolley. On the trolley was a large Perspex box; it looked very forbidding.

'What's that?' she said, her voice somehow faint.

'It's an oxygen box,' said one of the nurses. 'We understood she might need some straight away. Now if you just pop her onto the trolley, and we put it over here, there, like that you see, and you follow us ...'

They started to move ahead with the trolley; Francesca followed, numb with fear, shocked at how swiftly Kitty had been removed from her, had ceased to be her own baby, under her own personal care, had become an object, an object for medical care and attention. She felt very alone. Then she felt a hand in hers; it was Rachel, who had followed in Reverend Mother's car.

'Come on, darling,' she said, 'chin up.'

The ridiculous instruction did Francesca good, restored normality for her; she smiled at her mother shakily.

'I'm sorry I've been so foul,' she said.

Kitty was taken up to a side ward; the doctor removed her from her little box, pushed up her dress, listened to her chest and her heart for a long time.

'Yes,' he said cheerfully, 'not too good. Not too bad either, Mrs Channing, don't worry. We'll need to do another echo cardiogram, I'm afraid, and some more X-rays, get the latest picture. She's had that done before, hasn't she?'

'Yes,' said Francesca, 'yes she has. Look, Mr Moreton-Smith at St Andrew's knows her case, and Mr Lauder, but he's away —'

'Mrs Channing, we have to make our own judgments, from how she is at the moment. Frankly, anything they might say would be irrelevant now. Except the medication she's been on, and we've already spoken to your GP in London.'

'Oh,' said Fancesca, She was surprised at their efficiency.

He grinned. 'It's OK. We haven't actually got straw behind our ears.' He was terrifyingly young, but she liked him, trusted him. 'Now we'll get her into an oxygen tent, I think, straight away, she simply isn't getting enough oxygen, look you can see from this measure here, on the box, and we'll give her some extra diuretics, she's retaining fluid, and —' He looked at her suddenly, smiled again. 'Don't look so frightened, Mrs Channing. She'll be all right; they're very tough, you know, babies.'

They all said that, thought Francesca, and it just wasn't true.

Philip Drew had also slept badly. The Channing case was beginning to worry him seriously. Channing's defence hadn't been too good in the first place, and with this latest débâcle, of the secretary giving information, it looked very poor. He was pretty sure Bard would get hauled in again, and that they'd then ask him for his passport. He was simply too good a prospect for the SFO not to go the distance with. They'd had few enough successes lately, and they'd see Channing as a good prospect for one.

He got out his notes, started going through them. There were a couple of things that really weren't clear; he decided to give him a ring. He tried the London number; the answering machine was on. Damn. He'd hoped to be able to see him. He left a message, then phoned Stylings; was told he wasn't there either.

Horton, whom he'd met several times, told him Bard's family were in Devon. 'He might have gone down there.'

'Do you have a number? It's quite important.'

Horton said he didn't. 'I'm sorry, Mr Drew. If he should phone, I'll tell him to contact you immediately.'

'You can't think of anywhere else he might be?'

'Well,' said Horton, 'the last couple of weekends, Mr Channing has been sailing. Maybe —'

A slither of fear made its way into Drew's consciousness; he pushed it resolutely out again.

'Maybe. Do you have a number of the harbour, something like that?'

'Yes, indeed, Mr Drew, I'll just get it for you.'

Drew phoned the harbour, and got put through finally to Mike Langton. He sounded cheerful.

'Yes, that's right, he went out this morning. Saw him go. About nine-thirty, I'd say. I should think he's a very long way away by now. Lovely wind out there.'

'Oh I see,' said Philip Drew. 'Well, thank you very much.'

He put the phone down and sat staring out at his perfectly mown lawn. 'Christ Almighty,' he said.

'There's some new people arrived,' said Hattie, looking out of the window of the apartment. 'Look, they've got children too. Our age, Jasper, come on, let's go and see them.'

'Well, don't be long,' said Naomi, 'we're going to have lunch in a minute, and then we're going to the beach.'

'I don't like that beach,' said Hattie, 'it's boring, and it's so hot.'

'Oh God,' said Naomi.

Liam watched the children running down to the central area of the development, saw them go and speak to the new arrivals, watched the family — mother, father, two boys — smile, clearly pleased at the welcome, saw Hattie indicating where their own apartment was: saw the family disappear inside, saw the children re-emerge, start playing in the pool with Hattie and Jasper; watched them for a while, listened to Naomi banging plates about in the tiny kitchen that led out of the living room; looked out again and saw the father emerging. He had swimming trunks on, and a T-shirt, and was holding a beach bag; under his arm was tucked a copy of the *News on Sunday*. Liam's heart lurched. He stood up.

'I'm just going down to the pool for a minute,' he said, 'get a dip before lunch. I'm terribly hot.'

'Don't you start about the heat,' said Naomi.

He almost ran down the stairs, went out into the pool area. The man was now sitting back in a deck chair, the paper by his side. Liam squinted at it, but he couldn't see anything.

'Morning,' he said casually, 'just arrived, I saw. Good flight?'

'Yes, not too bad,' said the man. He had a North Country accent. 'What's it like here, good weather?'

'Oh – yes,' said Liam, 'very good.' It always astonished him that people cared so much about the weather; that hot sun equalled a good holiday. He hated the sun himself. 'Er – mind if I look at your paper? If you've finished with it? Bit starved of news out here.'

'Jolly good thing if you ask me,' said the man, 'can't wait to get rid of the lot of it. All this nonsense about Blair and Prescott, who bloody cares. Yes, you have it.'

'Thanks.'

He was so nervous his hands were shaking. He sat down on the side of the pool, picked it up. The front page blurred briefly, then settled into legibility. This might make the front page, you never knew. It hadn't. Well, the first inside spread, then. It was big news. Nothing on the inside spread.

Liam turned to the financial section. Of course, that's where it would be. You really couldn't expect something about a failed businessman, however crooked, however dramatic the story, on the front page; not competing with Tony Blair and the Princess of Wales.

There was nothing in the financial section. Nothing at all. He went over it again and again, feeling increasingly angry, turning the pages more and more frantically, crumpling them. He saw the man looking at him curiously, and didn't care. Shit, where was it, what had happened, why hadn't they used it? That bloody stupid secretary of Townsend's had assured him it was going to be used, his stuff; this Sunday, hopefully, she had said. Well, he thought that was what she had said. He retraced the conversation.

'Yes, Mr Townsend asked me to tell you your information was very, very helpful and he had put it into his story.'

Well, it couldn't be much clearer, could it? So what had happened? Liam felt sick: sick with frustration and rage. He'd gone to a lot of trouble to help Townsend, apart from anything else. And he could have given it to half a dozen journalists. He should have done. He really should.

How could he find out, who could he ask?

Of course: Teresa Booth, she'd know. She'd be able to tell him all about it.

He looked up at the window to make sure Naomi wasn't watching him, then walked away from the pool, through the archway that led into the village – village, more like an industrial estate – and the phone.

Teresa Booth answswered the phone at once.

'Oh, hallo Liam,' she said. She didn't seem very surprised to hear from him.

'How are you, Teresa?'

'I'm fine, thank you, Liam. How are you? Where are you?'

'In Spain, I'm on holiday.'

'Nice?'

'No, pretty bloody awful, staying in a grotty flat in an awful holiday village.'

She laughed her throaty laugh. 'You should have asked me, Liam, I've got some very nice timeshares in Spain.'

'Yes, well, perhaps next time. Teresa –'

'Yes?'

'I was – well, I was expecting to read that story today.'

'What story?'

'In the paper. The story of Graydon Townsend's. About my father.'

'Oh,' she said, 'yes, that story. Yes, it didn't appear, did it? Gone off the boil apparently, the whole thing. Editor wouldn't touch it, something like that. Such a shame for you, Liam. After all you did. Never mind, maybe later on. Sorry about your holiday.'

Liam put the phone down and walked slowly back to the apartment. He felt shattered, exhausted and shaky.

'What on earth's the matter with you?' said Naomi.

'Oh, nothing. Got a bit of a headache, that's all.'

'Daddy, do we have to go to the beach this afternoon?' said Hattie. 'Those two new children are really nice, and they're staying here, by the pool. Can we stay here too?'

'Please?' said Jasper.

'Oh – yes. Yes, sure. That's fine.'

'And we can have a little siesta,' said Naomi. She looked at him, and smiled, a confident, determined smile. Liam tried to smile back.

A long hour later, he sat up, looked down at her naked body, then at his own failed, incompetent one.

'I'm sorry,' he said, 'very sorry. Maybe later.'

'Yes,' she said, her face closed, 'maybe.'

She stood up, pulled on her robe, turned to face him. 'I hope it isn't going to be like last time, Liam,' she said.

'I'm sorry?'

'Last time one of your little affairs went wrong.'

'Naomi, what are you talking about?'

'It took months, as I recall. For you to – what shall we say – recover. I don't think I could stand that again, Liam. I might have to

632

rethink the whole arrangement. Even ask you for a divorce. Anyway, I'm going for a swim. Got to do something to dissipate my energies. See you later.'

Gray was dozing on the sofa when he heard the bell. He had slept appallingly badly, had spent most of the night talking to Terri about Briony and then what was left of it moving in and out of a fevered, disorientated sleep. He had an appalling headache and he felt horribly nauseous. Terri had offered to fix him some breakfast, but fearing it might be bacon and eggs and greasy at that, he had refused. She had left mid-morning, leaving a revoltingly strong cup of tea on the table beside him, and told him she'd phone later. That was at least two hours ago.

He heard the bell a second time and decided to ignore it, but it went again, and then again, insistent, boring into his throbbing head. Finally, because it was easier, he stood up, staggered out to the hall, opened the door.

Briony stood there. She was looking very solemn, almost cross; Gray looked at her warily.

'Hallo.'

'Hallo Gray. I heard you weren't feeling too good.'

'Oh really?' He frowned. 'How do you know?'

She ignored the question. 'Honestly Gray, you really are pathetic. Getting so drunk, at your age. It'll land you in trouble, you know.'

'Look Briony, I really would rather not be chastised like this, if you don't mind. Even if I do deserve it. So if you'll excuse me –'

She ignored him. She still looked cross. 'It's about time you grew up, Gray. Got a bit more sensible.'

'Bri, please –'

'But I'm afraid that's a bit unlikely. Actually. What do you think?'

'What? Briony, what are you talking about?'

He looked at her again. She wasn't looking cross any more; she was smiling, the rather reluctant smile he could hardly remember, and had never been able to forget, and her blue eyes were very soft, very amused.

She moved nearer to him, looked up into his face.

'You do look terrible, Gray. Not surprising, really. Two bottles of wine and a bottle of whisky. Come on, let me take you inside and make you a nice cup of really, really strong tea.'

'Oh Christ,' said Gray. 'I feel sick.'

'You deserve to feel sick.'

She walked in behind him, her hands guiding him gently into the sitting room, settled him back on the sofa, and disappeared into the kitchen. Gray lay back and stared up at the ceiling, trying not to think about anything.

He heard her come back in, heard a cup go down on the table, felt her sit down beside him. He turned his head, looked at her; she was looking very serious again, her small face set, her blue eyes fixed on his. He had forgotten how pretty she was. He always did. Oh God. Oh God, he was a fool.

'Oh God, Briony, I'm a fool,' he said. 'Such a fool.'

'Yes, you are,' she said. Then she smiled at him, slowly and sweetly, and nodded in the direction of the tea. 'Drink that.'

It was very, very pale beige; there was a thin slice of lemon floating in it. Gray lifted the cup, and sipped it. It was almost tasteless, slightly scented. He sighed and said, still looking into it, 'Briony, this is perfect, and I love you.'

'I love you too,' she said.

Chapter Thirty-three

It was mid-afternoon. Kitty was asleep, very still and pale now, in her little oxygen tent. She had had some X-rays and some blood tests to establish her oxygen level; she had been given some extra diuretics to try to rid her small body of the fluids it was retaining. The cheerful young doctor had promised to come and see her again and to talk to Francesca the minute he had the results. There was nothing to do but wait.

'Maybe,' said Francesca to Rachel, who had just come back with two plastic cups of something which might have been tea, 'maybe you should get back to the convent. To Jack. Poor Reverend Mother must be at the end of her tether.'

'Apparently not,' said Rachel. 'I just phoned, and the Curdle has taken Jack off to the beach. They're great friends, those two. And this morning he helped Sister Florence with the housework. Apparently he is planning to be a monk when he grows up.'

'Ah,' said Francesca. She smiled in spite of herself. Rachel looked at her, then at the sleeping Kitty.

'She really will be all right,' she said. 'She is having the best possible care, and babies are –'

'Mummy,' said Francesca, 'I don't mean to be rude, but if one more person tells me babies are very tough I shall scream.'

'Sorry, darling.'

The door of the small room they had been given opened and the cheerful young doctor came in, followed by an older, rather less cheerful one.

'Hi,' he said. 'Mrs Channing, this is Mr Bateson. Our consultant paediatrician. I asked him to come in, dragged him away from his gardening actually, because I wanted his view on Kitty's condition.'

Francesca nodded briefly at Mr Bateson. 'Well, that was kind, thank you.'

Mr Bateson looked as if he had been born with a stethoscope round his neck. 'Not really. I am not over-fond of walking up and down with a lawnmower. Now then, your baby. Er – Kitty.'

'Yes?' said Francesca. Please, please just say she's better, she's responding to the treatment, she can go home tomorrow, she'll be fine.

'Now Kitty is nine months old?'

'Yes. Nearly.'

'And the VSD – that is, the hole in her heart – was diagnosed when?'

'In May. By Mr Moreton-Smith. At St Andrew's.'

'Ah, yes. And she's been quite well since then, has she?'

This was bad. When they started going over old ground, appearing to consider it as if it was new, instead of getting to the point, it meant the news was bad.

'Yes, she has, she's been much better. Until she got this chest infection.'

'Yes. Yes, of course. And according to Mr Moreton-Smith, this hole was quite small, is that correct?'

'Yes. He said he was hopeful that it might heal itself.'

'Yes, well, of course, that does very often happen in these cases. But – well, I'm afraid that is not what has happened with Kitty.'

'Oh,' said Francesca.

'The hole is, I would say, of a size not to do that. It is quite possible, of course, that the strain of her recent illness has made it larger.'

'Oh,' she said again. What he meant was that Mr Moreton-Smith had boobed.

'Now, I'm not going to beat about the bush, Mrs Channing. Your baby is quite ill. Not dangerously ill at the moment, but she could become so. Her lungs aren't coping, and neither is her heart. Her oxygen levels are quite low, I'm afraid.'

'So –'

'So I would recommend to you very strongly that she is operated upon. As soon as possible. What we do is quite literally put a patch into the heart. Over the hole. It sounds very alarming, but in ninety-nine cases out of a hundred, the children make a complete recovery.'

'Yes, I see. And would you do it here, the operation?' It was extraordinary how calm her voice sounded; as if she was discussing a dinner party menu, or an appointment with the hairdresser.

'No, I wouldn't. We really don't have the facilities here, and this particular area is very specialised. I would recommend that she is taken back to London, and that Mr Moreton-Smith does the operation at St Andrew's.'

'Yes, I see,' said Francesca again. It sounded very dramatic. 'Would she be all right, travelling so far?'

'Oh, yes, I think so. She is already benefiting from the extra medication, and she would go by ambulance, it would be a pretty quick journey, and she could be given her oxygen and so on on the way. She could go in the morning, I wouldn't recommend it tonight, and in any case if she continues to stabilise, she will be stronger tomorrow. So, that is my recommendation. If you would like me to call St Andrew's and make the necessary arrangements, I will do so.'

'Yes,' said Francesca. There seemed to be very little choice. 'Yes, please, if you think that really would be best. Is it – is it a big operation?'

'Quite big. But not impossibly so.' He smiled at her. 'You really must try not to worry too much, Mrs Channing. I know that's easier said than done, but she couldn't be in better hands, and of course babies are very tough.'

Francesca opened her mouth and screamed.

Later, after she had calmed down and drunk several cups of sweet tea and apologised to Mr Bateson and the young doctor, and they had left, she turned to her mother and said, through the great choke of fear that seemed to have taken up residence in her throat, 'I think, Mummy, maybe we ought to tell Bard.'

It was a perfect evening in France. The *Lady Jack*, flying before the wind, had reached the coast in record time; was now moored in a harbour a little down the coast from Sainte Vaas. Bard had not wanted to go somewhere he was known. Next day he would have to leave her, catch the train to Paris. He didn't like the thought; she was his shelter, his last link with all that he was leaving behind. But it was no use being sentimental about her; she had served her purpose and now she must be discarded. He was very tired; he would find a good restaurant, he thought, have a meal and then hopefully get some sleep. He'd deliberately kept his radio off all day. Apart from the obvious fact of not wishing to be contacted, he found the constant babbling of voices on Channel Sixteen almost unbearable: people calling other people to notify them where they were, where they were going, what time they might get there, some of them at considerable length (as they were not really supposed to do). It sometimes seemed more like a chat-line than a ship-to-ship radio service.

He did look briefly, thoughtfully, at the telephone in the restaurant, wondering if he should for the last time try to make contact with Francesca, but then he rejected the idea. He had burnt his boats now, almost literally; there was no point. She'd made it clear she didn't want to see him, or speak to him; there was a limit to how much pride he could swallow and to what he could do. Whatever his mother might say.

'No, Mrs Channing, I haven't seen Mr Channing all weekend. Several people have phoned, his mother, his solicitor, Barnaby, but he hasn't been in touch. I'm sorry.' Sandie didn't sound very sorry; she sounded as if she was enjoying the situation.

'Oh,' said Francesca. 'Well, all right, Sandie, I expect he's in the country. Thank you. If he does phone or anything –'

'I'll get him to ring you, Mrs Channing. On your mobile, yes?'

'Yes. Thank you.'

'And I do hope Kitty's all right.'

'Thank you.'

Horton gave her the same story. Including the fact that Philip Drew had called.

'As I said to Mr Drew, I thought Mr Channing might have gone sailing. I haven't heard from him since.'

'Oh – thank you, Horton. Fine.'

'They think he might have gone sailing,' she said to Rachel. 'I could phone Mike Langton. At Chichester. See if he's seen him.'

'Yes, what a good idea,' said Rachel. Something in her voice made Francesca look at her sharply.

'What is it? What are you thinking?'

'Oh – nothing. Just that it would be nice to be able to contact him. That's all.'

'Yes, well, we will be able to,' said Francesca irritably. 'It's just a question of finding where he is. There's no problem.'

'No, of course not.'

Mike Langton sounded very cheerful. 'Yes, he went off early this morning, Mrs Channing. I expect he'll be back pretty soon, it's getting late. Unless he's going to stay over in France again.'

'Oh God,' said Francesca. A tight band seemed to be closing on her head.

'Why don't you try the radio?' said Langton. 'Channel Sixteen, you know how to get onto that, don't you?'

'What? Oh, yes, yes thank you.'

'But I expect he'll be back soon, and if I can catch him, I'll get him to ring you immediately.'

'Yes, fine. Thank you, Mike.'

Before trying Channel Sixteen, she decided to ring Philip Drew, to see if he'd already contacted Bard.

He sounded tense, awkward.

'No, sorry, Mrs Channing, I haven't. He seems to have his radio turned off.'

'How odd,' she said, surprised at the calm in her voice. 'His mobile is as well. Damn. Well, look Philip, I'll keep trying. Let me know if you contact him, get him to ring me will you?'

'Yes, sure. Is there anything wrong?' he said, as if the only reasons any of them wanted him were trivial, commonplace; to know when to fix a meeting, arrange supper perhaps.

'Well yes, there is actually,' said Francesca, finding this suddenly irritating, illogically feeling he should have known, should have known something so important, so terrifying. 'My little girl is ill. I wanted Bard to know.'

'I'm sorry,' he said, and he did indeed sound it. 'Is it serious?'

'Um – a bit. Yes. We're coming back up to London tomorrow, she may have to have an operation. That's why –' Her voice shook; she swallowed hard. 'Well anyway, Philip, tonight we're at Plymouth General, but I have my mobile. OK? You've got the number.'

She went back to the small room and to Kitty. Looked down at her as she lay there, pale and listless, in her little oxygen tent. And like all mothers when their children are in danger, whether they believe in God or not, she sat beside her and prayed.

Bard ate well; he was hungry, despite everything. He also had rather a lot of red wine, a bottleful, and then a couple of brandies. He hoped it would help him to sleep. In any event, it put him in a rather sentimental mood; he sat sipping the second brandy, thinking about Francesca, about how much he loved her, in spite of everything, in spite of what she had done; about what a hash he had made of his marriage, about his criminally clumsy request of her, and the brilliant neatness with which she had turned it on its head. She was a clever woman, Francesca. He'd known that, but then he'd rejected the cleverness, tried to turn her into what she wasn't, shut her out, make her a company wife. Stupid. Terribly, horribly stupid. Well, it had misfired, and it served him right.

And now he might never see her again. He had made his decision and now she would be in his past, his old life, lost to him, any last hopes that she might come back to him quite gone. He looked briefly at the appalling loneliness that confronted him, and then set it aside. He would cope with it when he reached it. That was the prime objective now. Reaching it. Getting there.

Sandie was enjoying the drama. She was sorry about Kitty, of course, but Mr Channing disappearing, everyone looking for him, Mrs Channing sounding quite awful, old Mrs Channing obviously worried out of her head; it was all extremely exciting.

She almost wished she wasn't going out with Colin that night, but he'd been getting a bit funny lately, and what with her having to cancel a couple of times, she thought she'd better not do it again. She'd leave the answering machine on, she'd only be gone an hour, two at the most, they were just having a quick drink, and then she could deal with any messages when she got back. She phoned Horton, to say she was going out but would be back, re-set the machine and went to meet Colin.

Philip Drew decided to have one last go at phoning Bard. After all, if he'd got back late Mike Langton would almost certainly have missed him, and he might have been really tired and just ignored all the messages. He tried Stylings again: no, said Horton, still no word. Drew swore and phoned the London number; the answering machine was on.

'Bard,' he said, trying to keep his voice level, 'sorry to bother you on a Sunday, but give me a ring at home, would you? Just a couple of points I wanted to clarify. Thanks.'

He didn't want to sound in any way alarmist; if he did Bard might take serious fright. If he hadn't already.

Bard got up slightly unsteadily from the table, paid his bill in cash and then looked at the phone again. Maybe he would try. Just once more. He heard Jess's voice. It's a matter of doing. Not just saying, doing. If he thought she'd let him, he would; he'd do it still, anything. Yes. It was worth a last try.

He sat down at the table again, punched out the number of the convent on his mobile. It rang for a very long time. Finally a voice he had not heard before answered: a rather old, frail voice.

'Reverend Mother?'

'No. I'm sorry,' it said, after quite a long silence, 'no, she's not here. She's in chapel. Father Benedict is here, saying Mass, and –'

'Oh. Oh, I see. Well, is Mrs Channing there? Mrs Francesca Channing? This is her solicitor speaking.'

Another long silence. Then: 'No, Mrs Channing has left the convent. With –'

Bard interrupted her. 'All right. Thank you. Goodbye.'

Shit. So she'd gone. Well, in that case she was probably at Stylings. Only he didn't want to risk speaking to anyone else. Well, he could put the phone down. He tried the number. Horton answered. He decided to risk it.

'Horton, this is Mr Channing. Is my wife there?'

'No, Mr Channing, I'm afraid she isn't. But where are you, Mr Channing, we —'

Bard felt a rush of panic. They were obviously trying to find him. Probably beginning to get worried. 'Sorry, Horton,' he said, 'can't talk now.' He slammed the phone down again, trying to think what to do. Clearly they were wondering where he was, where he might be. He dialled the London number. It was on the answering machine. He punched in the listening facility; there was only one message on it, from Philip Drew. He sounded carefully, quietly calm, said he wanted to run over a few points. Well, he knew what that meant. He was worried to death, and trying like hell to disguise the fact. And no other messages. Not from anyone. Anyone at all. Certainly not Francesca.

'Fuck,' said Bard aloud, 'fuck the lot of you.' And walked back round the harbour to the *Lady Jack*.

Kitty was a little better in the morning. Her colour had returned, and she even took a bit of her feed.

'Good,' said the young doctor. 'Well done.' He smiled at Francesca. 'She's better. No doubt about it.'

'Do you think ... ?' said Francesca, and he looked at her sitting there, exhausted, ashen, and knew what she meant at once: that perhaps her baby was going to be all right, would get better by herself, wouldn't need the surgery, the journey to London; and he said at once, because he knew it was much better that way, 'No, Mrs Channing, I'm sorry, I don't. She's only better because of the increased medication. She won't be well until she's had this operation. Then she'll be very well indeed, I promise you.' He reached out, patted her hand. 'Honestly. I won't say it, in case you scream again, but it is true, they are, babies, the human race wouldn't have survived otherwise. The ambulance will leave here at about nine, so good luck. Bring her back to see me when she's a teenager, will you, I can see she's going to be absolutely knockout.'

Francesca smiled at him; it was a rather weak smile, but it was a smile.

'Ah, Mr Drew. Mr Stainforth here, from the Fraud Office. I wondered if you could help me.'

'Yes?' said Philip Drew.

'We wanted to have another chat with Mr Channing. Just a few points, you understand. But he doesn't seem to be at home. I wondered if you could help.'

'Yes of course,' said Drew, fighting to sound confident. 'When would you like to see us?'

'Oh – shall we say this afternoon? Two o'clock suit you?'

'Yes, that's fine, I should think. If you don't hear from me, then we'll be there.'

'Good. Excellent. Good morning.' He rang off.

'Oh Christ,' said Drew.

Rachel had driven back to the convent. She was going to collect Jack and then go on up to London. Reverend Mother was waiting for her with coffee.

'You look tired. How is Kitty?'

'She's a little better. But she does have to have this surgery, I'm afraid. She's being taken to London today. By ambulance.'

'Oh, dear. I'm sorry. We said a Mass for her last night. We shall say another today. How is Mrs Channing?'

'All right. Just. Nothing from Mr Channing, I suppose?'

'No. There was one call last night, Sister Ignatius took it, from her solicitor. He left no message, seemed in a hurry.'

'Her solicitor? But why – oh dear. Oh, my God.' Rachel stared at Reverend Mother. 'I think,' she said, 'that was not a solicitor.'

Jack was outraged at having to leave.

'I like it here much better. I'm going to be a monk now, so why can't I stay?'

'Because you can't train to be a monk yet,' said Reverend Mother firmly, 'you have to pass all sorts of exams before you can even join us. But you must come back lots of times, to see Richard and Mary and me.'

'And the Curdle, and our tunnel, what about that?'

'Colonel Philbeach will be here for a long time yet,' said Reverend Mother. 'You can see him again.'

'Anyway, why can't we go back with Kitty and Mum? Is she better?'

'Well,' said Rachel carefully, 'Kitty is a little better. But she has to have a little operation, to make her completely well.'

'In London?'

'Yes, in London.'

'Well,' said Jack with matchless logic, 'I'd be much better staying here. I always make too much noise, everyone says so, and ill people need quiet.'

'Jack darling,' said Rachel, 'Kitty will be in hospital for a while. So you can make as much noise as you like. Now go and say goodbye to Richard and Mary.'

Reverend Mother was driving them to Bideford; as she started the car, turned it in the courtyard, Richard and Mary came out of the house with Jack, each holding one of his hands. Richard had tears rolling down his face.

'Come back soon,' he said, giving Jack a hug. 'Come back to us here.'

'Come back soon,' echoed Mary, 'and your baby. Bring your baby again soon.'

Rachel looked at the two of them, and for a moment she forgot Kitty, forgot Francesca, forgot everything except the sadness of what was to happen to them, and what they were about to lose. And realised she had given the whole problem no thought whatsoever for days. Well, it could wait just a little longer. It would have to. But a solution had to be found.

She hugged them both, told Mary to be a good girl, and that she'd be back soon, and turned her mind very firmly onto more immediate concerns.

As the car pulled out of the lane, she saw Colonel Philbeach's old Rover chugging down towards them; he pulled up alongside them, put his head out of the window.

'Good luck,' he said, 'with the nipper. She'll be fine, I'm sure. Very tough little things, babies. Send my good wishes to your daughter.'

'Thank you,' said Rachel, thinking what a very good thing it was Francesca was not in the car, and thinking at the same time what an extraordinarily good-looking man Colonel Philbeach was. She really hadn't noticed it before.

Bard sat on the Paris train. His plane left at four, five French time, he would have plenty of time. He hoped to God it was soon enough, that they wouldn't yet be moving into some kind of official action. Hopefully Philip would be stalling furiously. All he needed was – what? Five hours, five more hours, and then the plane would be in the air, on its way, and there wouldn't be anything else they could do. Or that he could do, come to that.

The ambulance seemed to be going quite slowly; Francesca had somehow thought they would race to London, with the bell ringing. The ambulance man laughed when she told him.

'No, my love. Not necessary. Maybe if we hit some traffic when we get there ... We're going fast enough. Anyway, she's fine. Don't you worry about her. Look at her sleeping like a baby.' He seemed to find this very funny.

He was very cheerful; kept telling her stories about past dramas. Francesca was finding it hard to be polite. And she was getting worried now, about Bard. She wanted to know where he was. Just so that she could tell him what was happening. No more than that. He was Kitty's father, and he ought to know.

After Reverend Mother had left them at Bideford, Rachel phoned the house.

'Sandie? This is Mrs Duncan-Brown. Would you give me the number of Mr and Mrs Channing's solicitor, please? It's very urgent.'

'Yes of course,' said Sandie. 'Just a moment. He's phoned this morning actually, left his number, here it is, yes, it's Mr Drew and he's on –'

She gave it to Rachel. Rachel dialled it; Drew answered at once.

'Mr Drew, this is Francesca Channing's mother. Did you phone her last night? At a convent in Devon.'

'No. No I didn't.' He sounded strained. 'You don't know where your son-in-law is, do you?'

'I haven't the faintest idea,' said Rachel, 'but I wish to God we could find him. And I'm beginning to think that might be rather difficult. What do you think, Mr Drew?'

'I'm beginning to think the same. Please phone, won't you, or get him to phone if you do find him.'

Philip Drew phoned the house again. Sandie answered the phone.

'Drew again here. Still no news?'

'No. But –'

'Yes?'

'There was one call last night. On the answering machine. But no message, they'd rung off. But I dialled one-four-seven-one – I thought it just might be Mr Channing.'

'Well done,' said Drew. His heart thudded uncomfortably. 'And –?'

'Well, it was an international number. That's all it said.'

'Oh yes, I see,' said Drew.

Yet again, and without much hope, he rang Bard's mobile. It was still switched off.

The train pulled in to the Gare du Nord. Bard got out, picked up his holdall, and walked carelessly, slowly but not too slowly, towards the ticket barrier. From now on, it might happen. And if it was going to, it could happen here. The ticket collector was talking to someone else, some official. Could be, could be. Steady, steady, don't rush it. He held out his ticket, looked at the man, met his eyes; the man looked back, blankly, took the ticket, carried on with his conversation.

First hurdle over. He bought a book of ten *carnets* and went to find the Metro station and the train out to Charles de Gaulle. He was surprised to find he was suddenly rather enjoyng himself.

They were just into the outskirts of London when Kitty was sick. 'Oops,' said the ambulance man, 'must be the motion. Never mind, darling, let's get you mopped up.'

She was fine really, but it had upset her, Francesca could tell. She started to cry; clung to her mother, and the crying made her cough. She coughed quite a lot; by the time they reached St Andrew's she was flushed, crying, very distressed. By the time they reached the room they had been given, Francesca was desperate.

A nurse had been allotted to them; she was very calm, very cool, rather well spoken. For some reason Francesca didn't like her; she wanted the rosy charm, the enthusiasm, the rich accents, of the Devon nurses again.

She looked at Kitty, quiet again now, lying in Francesca's arms, smiled a careful, slightly patronising smile. 'Mrs Channing, welcome. Do put Kitty down in the cot.'

'I can't put her down,' said Francesca shortly, 'she'll start screaming again. She's better where she is.'

'Of course.' The nurse gave her a look; it was a look she knew well, the sort of look Nanny often gave her. We know best and you don't, that look said, but we'll humour you for now. 'It must be so worrying for you. But of course she's in the best possible place now.'

'I hope so,' said Francesca.

'Ah, Mrs Channing.' It was Mr Moreton-Smith. 'How was your journey?'

God, she thought, what was this, a cocktail party? 'Fine. Thank you.'

'Well, you've done the right thing coming here.'

'I didn't have much choice,' said Francesca, 'actually.'

Moreton-Smith gave her the same look as the nurse; then smiled, a tight-lipped smile. 'Well, I'm glad you felt that. Now then, I haven't really had a chance to assess Kitty properly yet, but I'm going to make a full examination now, take a look at her X-rays and so on. Now you remember, of course, when I saw her in − what was it, May, yes, in May, the hole was very small and I thought it might heal of its own accord. What seems probable is that it has got larger, with her illness −'

'Or that you made a mistake,' said Francesca.

'I'm sorry?'

'I said perhaps you made a mistake. Perhaps it was bigger than you thought.'

'Oh I don't think so,' he said, and his eyes were suddenly very cold. 'No, I do assure you, that would not have happened.'

'Mr Moreton-Smith, don't you ever make mistakes, in your business? Most people do. It's not a crime.' For some reason challenging him, being rude to him, made her feel better. She was aware it was probably a mistake, but she didn't care.

'Well naturally, Mrs Channing, mistakes are made.' Mr Moreton-Smith's voice was very distant now. 'But in this case there was not a mistake, I do assure you. I can show you the original tracings, X-rays, if you like −'

Francesca caved in. And anyway, she didn't want to see them, didn't want to see the flaws, the damage in Kitty. While it was hidden from her, while all she could see was an apparently perfect baby, she could believe in one, believe she was all right, it was all a fuss about nothing, that she would be better in no time.

'No. No, don't bother. It doesn't matter. Thank you,' she added as a slight sop to his vanity. He nodded.

'Right: Well now, I think we should proceed. I would like to operate as soon as possible, probably tomorrow. There is very little point in waiting.'

'Well, unless,' she said, still clinging desperately to the hope, 'unless you decided it wasn't necessary.'

'Mrs Channing, it is necessary. There is absolutely no doubt in my mind. Your baby is not going to recover until this hole has been mended.'

'That's not what you said before.'

Mr Moreton-Smith sighed. 'Mrs Channing, I thought I had explained. Kitty's condition is worse. Much worse. The situation has changed. Surgery is essential. And what I'm going to do as soon as possible, today, is some further investigation. Now, do you want to hear about that?'

'Yes,' said Francesca wearily. 'Yes, I suppose I do.'

'What we will do is insert a cardiac catheter. We will go into one of her arteries, through her leg probably, and inject some dye into it, which will go right through into her heart, and then do some X-rays. That will show us exactly where the hole is, and how large.'

Francesca stared at him; it sounded brutal, horrrific. She looked at Kitty, asleep again, in her arms, so pale, so small, so trusting, and she felt she could not subject her to such a thing, to such an outrage. She felt an almost overpowering urge to run with her, to run out of the hospital, to take her home, where she would be safe, safe from these people with their dyes and catheters and drugs and knives, care for her herself, make her well, whole again, by herself, gently, carefully.

Mr Moreton-Smith talked on. 'Then tomorrow, when we do the operation, she'll be put on a heart-lung machine. That will take over the function of her own heart. We will cool her body right down, to slow her metabolism. And then we will go in, into her heart, and quite literally put in a patch over the hole.'

'And how long would – will it take?'

'Oh, between two and three hours. Afterwards we will probably put her onto a ventilator, keep her under sedation, delay bringing her round, possibly until the following day. She'll be under less strain that way.'

Francesca stared at him, taking all this in, trying to imagine it, trying to imagine Kitty enduring, surviving it.

'I don't know about all this,' she said finally.

'Mrs Channing,' said Mr Moreton-Smith, looking at her now with barely hidden disdain, 'Mrs Channing, you don't seem to understand. You really have very little choice. And afterwards, as I have said, Kitty will be absolutely fine.'

'Yes, so you say, but – well, I'm not sure if I –'

'Look,' said Mr Moreton-Smith, 'I have to go now, I'll be back to talk to you again later. With the results of the further tests. Incidentally, is Mr Channing around? I would very much like to see him as well.'

'No,' said Francesca, 'he doesn't seem to be, I'm afraid.'

She was afraid. Very afraid. And Liam Channing passed into total insignificance, and she wanted Bard more than she could ever remember wanting anything in her life.

'Mr Stainforth? This is Philip Drew. Look I'm sorry, but two won't be very convenient for Mr Channing. I've just heard from him. He's out of town.'

'I'm sorry to hear that, Mr Drew. When might he be back?'

'Well, I'm not quite sure, so –'

'I think the best thing would be if he called us himself, Mr Drew. As soon as possible.'

'Yes of course. Yes, I'll try and get hold of him again.'

'Thank you. I would like to speak to him myself, though … Shall we say within the hour?'

'Yes. Yes of course. I'll do my best.'

'Please do.'

Stainforth put the phone down, picked it up again and dialled Sloane. 'I don't feel very comfortable about Channing,' he said. 'He seems to have become a little elusive. What do you think?'

'Same as you. All Ports, I should think. Just in case.'

'Yes. I've said I want to hear from him within the hour. Drew certainly got the message. So if we don't –'

'Fine. Let's say we put it in motion at three, then, shall we?'

'Yup. Three it is.'

'Where is he?' said Francesca to her mother desperately, frantically, as she paced the small room, Kitty having been removed for her tests. 'What's he doing, where has he gone?'

Rachel looked at her; wondered if she could take any more, and decided she had to.

'I'm afraid,' she said carefully, 'well, that is, there is some view, that Bard has – left the country.'

'What do you mean? Left the country? Why should he –' There was a long, echoing silence. Then she said, 'Oh, my God.'

Philip Drew was not encouraging.

'I'm sorry, Mrs Channing. That's what it looks like. He obviously decided it was the only thing to do.'

'But he wouldn't have gone without – without –'

But he had tried to: hadn't he? He had phoned yesterday morning, and she had refused to speak to him. He had phoned again last night, almost certainly it had been him, and she hadn't been there. And so he had gone. She'd made him feel there was nothing for him here, no point hanging on, facing things, seeing them through, and had gone.

'Where – where do you think he might be?' she said finally.

'Well, obviously I have no real idea. He's taken his boat, as you know. And as far as we know he was out of the country last night. I suspect he'll be on his way to where there's no extradition agreement,

Brazil for instance, and he clearly can't sail there. Or northern Cyprus, he could just about make it there, I suppose. Long trip though, they'd catch him. The trouble is, they're very jumpy now, so even if he's just gone for a sail, which of course we must hope for, and which is still possible, I'm very much afraid they'll take his passport away when he comes home anyway.'

Well, it was her fault. As much hers as anyone's, at least. He had been desperate, quite, quite desperate and he had needed her, told her how much he needed her, had been prepared to forgive her, had humbled himself in a way she could never have imagined possible, and she had rejected him, over and over again, sent him away, for what had seemed like important reasons. And what were they, those important reasons? She could hardly remember now, so foolish, so unimportant did they seem, anger and disappointment and hurt, and hurt pride – and how much did any of that matter, now, when a small, tender life was at risk, when Bard had turned his back on his own life, the life he cared about? She had failed him, as surely and as harshly as he had failed her, and it was too late for either of them. Bard was gone.

Chapter Thirty-four

Bard stood at the Rio Airlines check-in desk; he was beginning to feel more confident. Everything seemed to be all right. There were no policemen at the airport, at the check-in. He looked at his watch: two-forty. Only just over an hour. Just as long as it wasn't delayed. He thought of sitting in the plane, on the runway, waiting to move, waiting to hear his name called over the plane's tannoy system, and felt sick.

He was next. He got out his passport, his ticket. The girl smiled at him. 'Good afternoon, Mr Channing,' she said, in thick, rolling English.

'Good afternoon,' he said. The name didn't seem to be making any kind of an impression on her; she hadn't reached for her buzzer, hadn't looked up at him.

'Just the one piece of luggage, is it?'

'Yes, that's all.'

'Business trip?'

'Yes.'

Just get on with it, for God's sake. Don't lose your temper, Channing, she's just being friendly, that's all.

'Smoking or non-smoking?'

'Non-smoking, please.'

A long wait while she tapped endlessly at her computer. A very long wait. He looked at his watch: two-fifty now. English time. God, flying was a bloody awful performance. Even if you weren't trying to skip the country.

'Ah,' she said finally. 'Ah, just a moment.'

Shit. Christ. This was it. He managed to smile. 'Problem?'

A long silence. Then, 'No, no problem. I've got one here. Window or aisle?'

'Aisle, please.'

'Fine. Right. Here is your boarding card, Mr Channing. Watch the screens for your gate. We board in about half of one hour. Have a good flight.'

A good flight. Well, maybe. Almost done it. Five to three.

Philip Drew decided to ring Bard just one last time. Just in case. You never knew ...

Peter Stainforth looked at his watch. Five to three. He decided enough was enough. There'd be hell to pay if he let this one get away. He decided to call Drew once more, give him the benefit of the doubt, then put a port stop in motion. He rather liked Drew; he was tough, talked straight.

He reached out for his phone and knocked his tea over. It trickled slowly, steadily across his desk, over a report he'd been reading, down towards him and his newly cleaned suit.

'Fuck,' said Peter Stainforth, and started rummaging frantically through his drawers for something to mop it up with.

'Please, please!' said Francesca Channing to the air, to the sky, to any power that might possibly be able to hear her, help her, as she paced the grounds of St Andrew's Hospital. 'Please, Bard, ring. *Please.*'

Micky Brett was very bored. The flight to California had been delayed twice, and he had totally exhausted what the airport had on offer: which wasn't in any case a great deal for a small boy of nine. He had already acquired a new transformer, a baseball cap that said Paris, and some popcorn; he had consumed two double burgers and fries and two strawberry milkshakes, and was now wandering about on a zigzagging course amongst the rows of weary, irritable people, half smiling at them, trailing his hand along the backs of the seats, occasionally bumping into their luggage, or even their feet. It was now his third circuit and people were beginning to recognise him, to grow wary, pulling their things towards them, looking at him crossly, looking rather pointedly for his parents; a couple of people even asked him where they were. Micky pointed vaguely towards the opposite end of the departure lounge from where they really were and continued on his course.

There was a man sitting on his own at the end of a row, reading a paper; a big man, not unlike Micky's own father. Not unlike Micky's father also, he was looking rather cross and edgy. He kept looking at his watch, then at the computer terminal; as Micky watched him, he suddenly disappeared in the direction of the toilets. His jacket was slung over the back of the seat next to him; as Micky passed, he brushed the jacket and it fell on the floor.

'Whoops,' he said, and bent to pick it up, glad the man wasn't there. Something heavy slithered onto the floor out of the pocket: a mobile phone.

It was just like Micky's father's phone, which was a constant presence in their lives, at every table, on every journey. His mother hated that phone, said she felt married to it. This one was switched off. That had to be a mistake. The whole point of having a mobile phone was that people could get you all the time, Micky's father had often explained that. You just didn't leave it off, something really urgent might be needing your attention. Micky switched this one on again: and it rang.

Micky looked over at the toilets; there was no sign of the man. He decided this was a moment to show initiative: his dad would never have ignored a call like this, you just couldn't. It might be urgent, might be business.

'Hallo,' he said.

'Bard?' said a voice. Crackly, distorted: obviously not in Paris. The Paris frequencies were very good, his father had said.

'No, this is Micky Brett.'

'Micky Brett? Is – is Bard Channing there?'

'Not just at this moment. He's –' Micky hesitated. His father had said never, ever say he was in the toilet. 'He's a bit tied up right now. Can I take a message?'

'Micky, where are you?'

'Oh, I'm at Charles de Gaulle. In Paris. Oh, hey, here he is now.' He held out the phone to the man. 'You Bard Channing? This is a call for you.'

Stainforth finished mopping up the tea, threw the unpleasant pile of tissues into his waste-paper basket, and reached for the phone to ring Philip Drew. The number was engaged.

Francesca walked back into the hospital room. Kitty was not there, she had been taken away from her, was somewhere else now, having needles stuck into her, having her arteries probed, strange substances pumped into her. She thought of her pain, her fear; thought of the greater pain and fear she would have to undergo the next day; wondered, still, if she was right to subject her to it; wondered, if she did not survive it, how she would possibly live with herself for the rest of her life. She felt absolutely and totally alone.

'Ah, Mrs Channing!' It was the well-spoken nurse. 'I have the consent form here. I need your signature here, look, and –'

'I don't think I can do it,' said Francesca helplessly. 'I'm sorry.' She looked at the form, just an ordinary piece of paper, with words in what she supposed was English written on it, but which seemed to her to be totally incomprehensible, just a white piece of paper, at the pen the nurse was holding out for her and wondered how anything so dangerous, so deadly, could appear so harmless. 'I'm sorry,' she said again, 'I really don't think I can.'

The nurse looked at her, and there was, briefly, an expression in her eyes of total contempt, dislike, removed almost at once, replaced by the bland cool of earlier.

'Oh, but you see, Mrs Channing, Mr Moreton-Smith can't proceed until we have your signature. It is only a formality, of course, but –'

'No,' said Francesca, 'no, it isn't only a formality. It's exactly as you said, he can't proceed until I sign. And I'm not absolutely certain, you see, that I want him to proceed.'

'But Mrs Channing, you don't understand –'

'Shut up,' said Francesca fiercely, 'just shut up. I understand perfectly. I'm just not sure what I want to do about it. You'll have to give me a bit more time. It's very important. She's my baby, and I don't want to be rushed. Now could you – could you please leave me alone. Just for a minute or two.'

'Yes. Yes, very well. But –'

'Please!' said Francesca. 'Just go.'

The nurse left the room. It was a very nice, quite large room, with a bed for her and a cot for Kitty, and a wardrobe and a chest of drawers and some nice curtains, and a radio and a television: not at all how most people would imagine a torture chamber. Francesca sat down on the bed, which was rather high and very hard, and looked down at her hands, and told herself she was being ridiculous, that these people had Kitty's best possible interests at heart, that she had to have this operation, that she would not get better without it; even managed to tell herself that babies were very tough; and still found herself quite unable to formally agree to her having it done.

Someone came into the room, a different nurse, and picked up the tray on which they had brought her lunch, the lunch she had not been able even to consider.

'You should have eaten something, Mrs Channing,' she said, sweetly concerned. 'Shall I get you some tea?'

'Oh – no. No thank you,' said Francesca. 'You're very kind, but –'

'Well, if you change your mind, just press the buzzer, there, look.' She smiled again, started to walk towards the door. Then: 'Is that a phone?' she said.

'A phone?' said Francesca, wondering what she could possibly be talking about.

'Yes, ringing, can I hear a phone ringing?'

'No, I don't think so.'

The girl was gone before she realised that it was indeed a phone ringing, her phone, and picked up her bag, started rather half-heartedly as first, then more desperately, because of who she thought, perhaps, it just might possibly, probably, almost certainly be, probing into its depths, its messy, disorganised depths, trying to find it; found it, pulled it out, attached to some damp tissues, a receipt for something, tried to press the button, failed at first, her hand was shaking so much, finally managed it.

'Hallo?' she said eventually. 'Hallo?'

But the phone was dead. Whoever it was had rung off. Whoever it was. And supposing it had been Bard, it could have been, calling just once more, trying just once more to talk to her, to make her listen; if it had been, then he had gone, really gone this time, he wouldn't try again, he would have given up, she had failed him again, she had lost him, Kitty had lost him, they had all lost him, and it was her fault, her own stupid, incompetent, wretched, arrogant fault. The phone lay in her hand, hopelessly silent. 'Bloody thing,' she shouted, throwing the phone across the room. 'Bloody, bloody thing.'

She sat down on the bed and burst into tears.

She heard the door open, looked up, saw Mr Moreton-Smith. He was looking rather stern, and as he came in, he tripped over her phone; he picked it up, handed it to her.

'Broken I should think,' he said, quite cheerfully. 'Never mind.'

'I do mind actually,' said Francesca, glaring at him, feeling for some reason rather better, 'and if you've come to ask me for that bloody form, I haven't signed it yet.'

'I haven't, no,' said Mr Moreton-Smith. 'I've come with a message from your husband, as a matter of fact.'

'Oh,' said Francesca. There didn't seem a lot else to say.

'He'd been trying to get through on your mobile. He says he'll be on the next plane from Paris and that there's no need to worry about meeting him, because as far as he can make out, the police will do it. I imagine that's a joke?'

'I'm afraid it's not,' said Francesca, and she knew now what people meant when they said they didn't know whether to laugh or cry, because she was at that moment doing both, quite hard, 'but never mind. Did he say anything else?'

'Yes, he did. He said to tell you he finds it hard to believe you can be so stupid and that he loves you very much. And that you are not under any circumstances to sign the consent form because he will obviously want to do that himself, after he's spoken to me. All right?'

'Yes, all right,' said Francesca, 'very, very much all right. Thank you. He really is quite impossibly arrogant,' she added, to nobody in particular.

Chapter Thirty-five

Francesca and Bard did not go home that night. Bard said that in any case the pavement outside the house was swarming with reporters and apart from the fact that Kitty needed them with her, it was a great deal easier for them to remain where they were.

He had not been joking, as Francesca had opined so correctly to Mr Moreton-Smith, about the police: they had indeed met him at Heathrow.

He had phoned Stainforth, as Philip Drew had said he must, and told him where he was, and Stainforth had said he had no option but to put out a port stop immediately.

'But they were very good, let me come straight here. I've become high-risk stuff, that's all. Won't be able to get away again. Not even to walk down the road, without reporting in. Huge bail, Philip Drew says.'

'Yes, he said that to me too.'

'But I had to come. Obviously.'

'Yes. Obviously.'

They were talking, very quietly, in Francesca's room at the hospital; Kitty slept in her cot in the corner, remarkably peacefully for a baby with so many traumas so recently behind her. She was, Mr Moreton-Smith had said, in surprisingly good shape, as ready as she could be for her operation the next day.

'I wouldn't have gone, you know,' Bard said, looking at her, his eyes very dark, moving over her face, 'if it hadn't been for you. What you said. I wasn't running away from it all. I was leaving a life without you. That's all. Perfectly simple. There didn't seem much point staying.'

'Bard –'

'Francesca,' he said suddenly, 'Francesca, I love you. I love you very much. Whatever's happened, whatever I've done, whatever you've done, you have to know that's true. Otherwise there's no point in any of it. Do you? Do you know that?'

'Yes,' she said, 'yes, I do know it. I know it now.'

'Good,' he said, and he sounded infinitely self-satisfied, sat back in the hospital chair. 'My mother was right.'

'Your mother?'

'Yes. She said I had to do something, to show you. She said saying wasn't enough, I must do something. Clever old stick, my mother.'

'Yes, she is. Very clever.'

'It isn't going to be easy, is it?' he said, his dark eyes heavy, sombre. 'Not going off into the sunset, not suddenly happy ever after?'

'No,' she said, 'not easy, not easy at all. I thought that, while I waited for you. But I also thought – well, we have damaged one another. We're both angry, both hurt. We can recover together. Hopefully.'

'It's a rather negative analysis,' he said, smiling at her, 'but, yes. Hopefully, yes.'

'What else did your mother say? Anything about me?'

'Yes,' he said shortly, 'yes she did. But I'm afraid she might have been less right about that.'

'What was it? I'll decide whether she was right or not.'

'Francesca, I don't think –'

'Tell me what she said.'

'No. I really don't think this is the time.'

Francesca stood up and picked up her jacket and her bag, walked towards the door. 'Goodbye Bard.'

'What? What the hell are you doing now?'

'I'm going. I'm leaving you.'

'Please don't joke. Not at a time like this.'

'I'm not joking,' she said, and looking at her, he could see she meant it, that it was true.

'Francesca, don't be so bloody stupid. Of course you're not leaving me. I've just risked arrest, being sent straight to jail, to come back, to be with you.'

'I know that. But you're doing it again already. You've been back less than two hours and you're already deciding what I shall and shan't know. I can't stand it, Bard, I'm sorry.'

'All right,' he said, throwing his hands into the air, 'all right, I'll tell you. I didn't think you were ready for it, that's all. What she said was,' he said, very tentatively, and there was no arrogance in him at all at that moment, 'she said you loved me too. But that you didn't know it, just at the moment. That's all.'

Francesca put down her things again, and went back across the room. She sat down on the bed, next to him, and put out her hand, touched his face very briefly, as so long ago he had once touched hers.

'She was right,' she said. 'And I do now.'

Next day, Mr Moreton-Smith came into the room where Bard and Francesca had been waiting for three and a half endless hours, and smiled at them. 'She'll be fine,' he said. 'Complete success, and I'm very, very satisfied with the whole thing. She's still on the respirator, but I'm probably going to be taking her off it in a couple of hours. Her condition is excellent. She'll be running around in days.'

'She can't run,' said Francesca, 'yet,' and went across to him and hugged him. 'Thank you, thank you so much, and I'm sorry I was so rude to you.'

'I'm not very used to it, I must say,' he said looking rather embarrassed. 'It was probably good for me.'

They went to look at Kitty in Intensive Care; she looked terrifyingly removed from them, naked apart from a nappy, a gash of scar on her chest, wires and tubes coming from all over her small body, still unconscious. The nurse smiled.

'Don't be alarmed,' she said, 'it looks much worse than it is. She's fine, honestly. Fit as a very small fiddle. She'll be smiling at you tomorrow. I promise.'

Later she was taken off the respirator; they went to see her again and stood, enraptured, watched the wonderfully satisfying, regular heartbeat on the monitor.

'I could stay here all night,' said Francesca, 'just looking at it.'

'Let's,' said Bard. 'We've got nothing better to do. Nothing better in the world.'

The nurse was right; next day, Kitty lay in her small cot and smiled up at them both. It was a slightly uncertain smile, but it was still a smile.

Rachel brought Jack in later that day. 'I wish I could have an operation,' he said, gazing at Kitty's drips and monitors. 'It's not fair, I like all this. Could I, Mum?'

'Perhaps not just yet,' said Francesca.

Rachel insisted on taking Francesca out for tea. 'It'll do you good, get you away from the hospital. And I have something I really want to talk to you about.'

'Well, what is it?' said Francesca, when they were settled in the slightly over-chintzed lounge of the Selfridges Hotel.

'I – just wondered if you were serious about the house.'

'What house?'

'The house in Devon. High House, Colonel Philbeach's house.'

'Oh God – I'd forgotten about it. God Mummy, I don't know. Why?'

'Well, because I want it,' said Rachel.

'You want it!'

'Yes, it seemed so obvious suddenly. I can move down there, you see, sell my flat, that would pay for it easily, terrible though it seems, and well, of course I shall miss London, but I can go up fairly often, I expect, and you can all come and stay, and it is so beautiful, and Mary can live with me there and won't have to be disrupted, she'll be near the convent and Richard and –'

'Oh Mummy!' said Francesca. 'At last! I thought you'd never get there.'

'What?'

'Well, obviously that's what I thought all along. From the very beginning. Only I knew if I suggested it, you'd never agree.'

'Oh,' said Rachel. 'Oh, I see.' She looked at Francesca and smiled.

'So you don't think it's such a stupid idea? You think I'll settle all right down there?'

'Of course not. I mean, of course I don't think it's stupid, I think it's a wonderful idea. I think you'll be as happy as anything, sorting out the village. And besides,' she added, 'the Curdle is awfully good looking.'

'Yes,' said Rachel, 'yes, you're quite right, he is. Lonely too,' she added.

'Oh really? And how do you know that?'

'He told me so,' said Rachel.

Kirsten came to see them, with Oliver. They brought Kitty an enormous toy panda, much bigger than she was, and some flowers for Francesca; Kirsten looked rather pale, but oddly happy.

'We had to come,' she said, 'to see you all. And to tell you something.'

'Yes?' said Francesca. 'What was that?'

'Well, everything is all right now. Quite all right. You know.'

'Yes,' said Francesca again, 'yes, I think so. Good.'

'And Oliver and I are – well, we're going out together.'

'You and Oliver!' said Francesca. 'But –'

'No, don't say it,' said Kirsten, 'don't say anything. That's what's happening. Isn't it, Oliver?'

'Yes,' he said, 'that's what's happening.' He smiled at her, and then at Francesca. 'Is – is Mr Channing about?'

'I'm afraid not,' said Francesca cheerfully, 'he's had to go to the police station. Why?'

'Well, we wanted to tell him too,' said Kirsten. 'We thought he might quite like it.'

'I think he would, Kirsten. I'll tell him.'

'Could you?' said Kirsten. 'And give him my love?'

'Yes, I will. He'll like that too, I know. Very much. It'll cheer him up, he's got a very difficult time ahead. Well, we all have,' she added with a heavy sigh, but still looking remarkably cheerful. 'Especially me.'

Epilogue

Bard Channing's trial was heard in September 1995; he was found guilty and sentenced to three years' imprisonment by a judge who was determined to make an example of him.

The trial had lasted eight weeks; Francesca and Jess had sat together through every day of it in the court at Chichester Rents, that part of the Old Bailey reserved specifically for fraud trials, with its large screens on which documents could easily be shown for examination by the court at any stage during the trial. They sat there impassively, both of them, hearing him charged, hearing him sentenced, hearing his life and his business picked painstakingly apart, hearing every detail of every manoeuvre carefully explained and expounded upon, every defence skilfully demolished.

He was indicted on five counts: of making a false presentation of company assets to his bankers; of illegally supporting his own share price; of converting company monies into his own personal bank accounts; of illegally disposing of his own shares; and of bribing council officials. However, Mr George Spackman, QC (defending) persuaded the judge in the legal arguments before the trial that it would be an abuse of the legal process to pursue this last charge as the events had taken place so many years previously, and the trial had proceeded on four charges only.

The trial attracted a great deal of press attention and was reported fully each day in the broadsheets, and its more sensational aspects in the tabloids. The new financial editor of the *News on Sunday* covered it particularly fully. The one-time financial editor of that paper, one Graydon Townsend, found the time from running his new restaurant, Lunch in the City, to attend it occasionally, and invariably took Bard Channing for a drink at the end of each of those days.

The verdict was a blow, but could not possibly have been described as a surprise; the evidence was highly conclusive and the jury was unanimous. The judge said he hoped that the sentence would serve as a warning to other men in Mr Channing's position.

George Spackman, who had taken the verdict hard, went to see Bard in the cells before he was taken off to Wandsworth, 'just for a few weeks, and then almost certainly to Ford. And of course, you will get remission, you should be home again in a couple of years.'

'Yes,' said Bard, 'two very long years.'

'I'm sorry, Bard. Very sorry. But I really don't think we could have done more.'

'No, of course you couldn't.'

'It couldn't possibly have turned out any differently, I don't believe. Unless of course –' He sighed, looked at Bard very directly. 'Unless of course your wife had after all been able to – well, you know, been able to recall exactly where you were that day. The day of the phone call. As you intimated she might, right at the very beginning. That might have made a difference.'

'Oh no,' said Bard, and he looked against the odds slightly more cheerful, almost complacent, 'that would have been out of the question, I discovered. Completely out of the question.'